Chocolate Pudding

&

Wicked Queens

Chanté A Campbell

ISBN:

Paperback: 978-1-969327-00-1

Hardback: 978-1-7353764-8-6

eBook: 978-1-7353764-7-9

Published by Fearless Lit

Interior design Chanté A. Campbell

Cover design by JV Arts / Title Art by sosoraso.studio

*To the **BITCHES** who won't bow
And the **DRAGONS** who doubt their strength.
I hope this book reminds you how **<u>powerful</u>** you are.*

And to the people who thought the first book in the series was 'too inclusive'...

<u>THE DRAGONS ARE QUEER, TOO.</u>

CONTENT NOTE

If you have ever uttered the words, 'Reading shouldn't be political', I need you to set this book down and walk away slowly. All books are political, but this one is LOUD about it. It's meant to be a middle finger to capitalism, classism, ableism, colonialism and the patriarchy. This book is about a found family of queer, disabled characters trying to fix a world that looks suspiciously like our own and trying to make it as kind and an equitable world as possible (and facing great adversity on the way).

That means, of course, that this book talks about and shows things that might make many of us uncomfortable right now. Please, protect your peace. If you need a book right now where queer and disabled characters can exist without fear of bigotry, this book is not for you (that's okay). If you need a book full of rage against these systems, then this series is for you. My promise to you is that, in my books, the marginalized will always eventually vanquish their oppressors and find joy along the way (if it looks like they haven't, trust that the story isn't over yet). You remember what happened to Marcellus, right?

That being said, this book is not for all people. Please see the list of content disclosure below. Be aware that content notes and trigger warnings do contain mild spoilers, but they are available here if you choose to use them.

<u>**This book contains multiple explicit scenes of sexual nature**</u>, including penetration, power play, bondage, orgasm denial, food play, asphyxiation and breath play, biting, anal, knife play, sensory deprivation and oral stimulation. A LOT of oral stimulation. Ayc is a baker, and he likes to *eat*.

Other content warnings that some may find triggering: Christian-esque type religion, ableism (including internalized ableism), bullying, classism, queerphobia, transphobia; denial of care and resources; racism (fae vs fae; fae vs human), sexism and misogyny; memory loss; refugee experiences; mentions of slavery and trafficking; classism; brief mentions of sexual assault and rape (no on-page depiction); forced arranged marriage; child abuse; emotional abuse and neglect; neglectful and manipulative mother; absentee father; cannabis use; alcohol use and misuse; brief discussions of [past] suicidal ideation; brief mention of the death of child; imprisonment, including unjust; kidnapping; blood and gore; body horror; animal death; animal cruelty; character death; physical injuries; mention of death of parent and spouse; grief and loss depiction; depiction of depression, panic attacks, and autistic meltdowns; knife, sword and axe violence; discussion of torture; discussion of colonialism; military scenes and depictions of armies; war themes and battle scenes; vomiting; animal illness and injury.

If you're still with me, welcome. I'm so glad you're here. It's going to be a hell of a dragon ride.

ALUINA
Tourmaline Mountains
Hearth
Northwest Province
Central Province
Northeast Province
Southwest Province
Southeast Province
Creed
Bellum Sea
EVERADYN
BROMALIS
Orchis
The Pink Elk
WYNTRA
Forest of Elodie
LUX AESTER
Ever River
Tarleps
Harenae Bay
AUDORI
TOTUS
Heimat
Silvae
OMNI
Splendor
Garrison
LYCENDI
Somnia Ignis
The Stella Rune Mountains
Pax
Duell
NOXUMBRA
Delphin
Somnia Vera
Adamant
Merinae Swamp
SAL MARIS
Southernmost Sea

Northenmost
Sea
DRAKR
The Untamed
Mountains
Morkt
Hemma
LAUD
Meditasis
Sea
Anaea
TENEBRA

CHAPTER
ONE

LORA

"All hail, Loraphne, the wicked queen," the Drakr says. "May your reign be short."

It's a threat. And Lora wants to kill him for it.

Yesterday, she wouldn't have hesitated. Yesterday, she'd have driven the dagger she holds where it would hurt the most and twisted until his last breath was one of agony. But this is *today*.

Today, she is Sovereign.

Today, she wears a black crown, the weight of it a reminder that every choice she makes has profound consequences. Her next words could be an act of war. With a single breath, the dragon towering behind the Drakr could incinerate Ayc and Irving and the hundreds of others in this castle and city.

So Lora sheathes her dagger and forces a smile. "Hello, Lord Lahlis."

The red in the Drakr's eyes fades. Lahlis sweeps down his hood. A wide smile stretches across his pale face, displaying teeth that are flat, human-appearing, instead of the pointed and jagged teeth of the Drakr. Somehow, he still looks malicious.

Beside her, Ayc tenses. Even now, she's painfully aware of her Fifth's every movement. He presses against her side, clutching his sword, ready to defend her...even though he must know it'll be certain death.

"Sheathe your weapon, Ayc," Lora says.

She casts him a glance and finds his wide gaze already boring into her. *Trust me,* she wants to plead, but she doesn't dare speak. The knob in his throat bobs up and down. He doesn't sheathe his weapon.

The red dragon swivels its massive head, its long serpentine neck curling over Lahlis's head until its snout looms before Ayc. Its head is nearly as large as Ayc is tall and twice as wide. Heat billows off the dragon, but Lora still feels cold. Icy fingers of fear creep across her skin. She wants to fling herself between Ayc and the dragon, but she fears any movement might trigger the dragon to attack.

"Easy, beautiful thing," Ayc coos gently.

The dragon's red eyes narrow. It snorts, and smoke coils from each nostril. Lahlis's smile twists wider. His teeth sharpen, one by one.

When Lahlis appeared during the Trials, Lora pretended she didn't know him, because she doesn't like her enemies to know they're already in her head. But of course she knows him. Lahlis is a name taught in Adamant. One must always be aware of the army commanders of other nations, especially a nation that was Everadyn's enemy for centuries before Yris changed the treaties. But Lora first heard his name long before Adamant. Lahlis's name was whispered between Yris and her Five before and after Creed. She even met him once when she was a child; she remembers him only as a shadowed figure that Yris once introduced to Lora. Even then, he made Lora's blood run cold.

Lord Lahlis is a dangerous, powerful man. A man she'd made her enemy the moment she told him no. She imagines it's not a word with which he's well acquainted.

The sound of wings once again rumbles against the sky like distant thunder. Surely, it's gryphon riders. Lora isn't certain how Lahlis landed in Wyntra without being intercepted by gryphon riders, but they must be coming to her aid now. If they see Ayc with a sword, they'll assume Lahlis means harm and will attack without hesitation. Lahlis is desperately outnumbered, but how many lives will be lost before he and his dragon fall?

At least *Ayc's* life.

The thought steals her breath.

"Ayc," Lora repeats, her voice steadier than she feels, "your sword."

Metal sighs against metal as Ayc slides his blade back into its sheath. He pastes on a friendly smile. The dragon lifts its head, towering high above them. Its heat still lingers on her skin.

Lahlis clucks his tongue. "Such an obedient human."

Lora's fingers twitch, aching for her dagger. Yesterday, she'd have gutted him for that, too. "What caused you to come all this way? It must have been a long flight."

Past the dragon, Irving and the two other royal guards steal forward carefully. She shakes her head, and Irving freezes. She knows him well enough that she can read the worry etched between his eyebrows, even from this distance.

The pounding of the wings grows closer. Perhaps, closer to their deaths.

She can't call off the riders, but Irving can. Each of the royal guards wears a stone in their ear. Enchantment connects them to one another. If Irving speaks, all the guards can hear him. Another guard will be able to signal one of the riders, who can communicate with their gryphons.

"It's fine, Irving!" Lora calls. "Everything is fine. Call off the gryphons."

"Fuck, Lora," Ayc says. "Those aren't gryphons."

Lora throws her head back to look at the sky, just as the shadows fall over her. Three massive pairs of wings block out the sun. One violet and one sapphire dragon lead the way. The sunlight sparks through their wings like twin jewels. The third lags slightly behind. Black streaks its deep orange scales—a rare color pattern, according to the dragon books Lora has studied. Awe and terror vibrate through her. They are gorgeous creatures. Terrifying, but beautiful.

Their riders aren't visible from here, but Lora knows they will be almost as powerful and dangerous as the dragons themselves.

Lahlis has not come to play a game. He has come to *win* it.

"I bring a message from Queen Volkna," Lahlish says, as though on cue.

Lora blinks. The queen of the Drakr has a message for *her*?

"A message?" Ayc says. "Four dragons seem a bit much for a message. You could have just sent a pigeon."

He uses that same silly, sarcastic tone she's heard him use many times, snapping back at the bullies who tormented him. Just as she did then, she wants to slap her hand over his mouth because it has never, not once, ended well for him.

Lahlis ignores him, but his dragon's lips curl back, baring rows of sharp, glistening teeth, a few of which bear the bloody remnants of its last meal. It roars. The ground quakes beneath Lora's feet.

"Easy, Sarck," Lahlis says, and the dragon falls silent.

A gust of wind drives at their backs as the three dragons dive toward the beach below the cliffs. Lora digs in her heels, but Ayc stumbles forward. Lora catches his forearm.

Lahlis's cloak bellows around him, but he's immovable as a statue. "Can't keep your feet under you, human? It's amazing that you survived my men at—" Lahlis cuts off and sniffs the air like the wind stirred up something new. He wrinkles his nose. "Seriously, what *is* he?"

Fear flashes on Ayc's face, but he swiftly hides it and draws himself up straighter. It's not the first time Lahlis has said those words. He asked the same question the first time he met Ayc, during the Trials.

What is he?

"He smells human, but not human," Lahlis spits in disgust.

Because Ayc isn't only human. He's Drakr, too, and with the Drakr's keen sense of smell—an ability the Everadyn fae don't share—Lahlis should recognize that. Something has disguised Ayc's scent, though.

Ayc brushes the thumb of his opposite hand over the leather

bracelet he wears on the arm Lora still holds. Lora locks onto the bracelet. *A little piece of tungsten certainly couldn't be responsible for this.* As Bronwen said, it would take magic—complex, powerful magic—to hide Ayc's Drakr abilities and identity while allowing him to keep the healing abilities he's demonstrated. They thought Ayc's baker mother couldn't have had the means to obtain bracelets that powerful, but perhaps they dismissed the possibility too soon. Perhaps his mother went through great lengths to ensure her half-Drakr child would never be found.

"It's confusing…and annoying." Lahlis grinds his teeth together. "I should have killed you myself."

Lora's hand flies to her blade, and her canine teeth elongate into points. Ayc seizes her other hand, the one still on his arm. It's the only thing that stops her from heaving her dagger into Lahlis's throat.

Easy, easy, she tells herself, unwinding her fingers from her blade.

"Be careful, Lahlis," she warns. "We won't get along with each other well if you threaten my people."

"Oh, I disagree." Lahlis's fingers flex at his side. "I think we're going to get along *splendidly*."

"Lora!" Irving calls. He stabs a finger toward the cliff to Lora's right. A black form crawls over the edge and slinks across the grass toward them like a sea of fog. It takes a moment for Lora to realize what she's seeing.

Shadow.

Power surges off Lahlis. Bronwen's magic feels like static, and sometimes, like a warm summer breeze, but Lahlis's feels cold. The bite of a glacier wind. This is his shadow affinity.

It's one thing to study shadow affinity in a classroom. It's entirely another to see it. The shadow weaves around her and Ayc's feet. Lora's instincts scream at her to run, but before she can take a step, the shadow bites down on her and Ayc's ankles, as strong as a rope. The shadow coils higher on Ayc, circling his legs. He jerks back, but he's held fast, like he's being buried in stone.

"Let's be very clear," Lahlis practically purrs. "The Everadyn and the Drakr are going to remain very good friends. If we get any inkling that you mean to break our treaty, we'll bring down war like you have never seen before."

The shadow continues to rise around Ayc, reaching his waist, his chest. He grunts. It's hurting him.

"Stop it!" Lora snarls. She reaches for her dagger, but a rope of shadow shoots upward and latches around her wrist, snapping down like a shackle.

How do you fight shadow? Shadow is everywhere, attached to everything. Even Adamant didn't have good answers on how to fight against truly powerful shadow wielders. The professors merely laughed nervously and offered two suggestions.

1. Hope that the person standing next to you has an affinity for a stronger magic.

But Bronwen isn't here.

2. Pray to the divine as you prepare to meet your end.

Irving rushes forward, but Sarck swings its head around and snaps the air before him. Irving peddles backward, his face contorting in frustration.

Lahlis continues, "And to prove you will remain *our* ally, Queen Volkna wants you to accept an invitation to visit her at Morkt Hemma during your Tour."

Lora forgot completely about the Tour. The one that every Sovereign takes in their first year, spending months visiting every clan in Everadyn. But a Sovereign has never used the Tour to visit a foreign nation.

Despite the treaty Drakr and Everadyn made after Aluina's fall, Yris has never openly and publicly embraced the Drakr. She conducted business in private, but she never invited the Drakr into her court, and the Drakr never invited Yris into theirs. If Lora accepts, she won't just be venturing into an enemy's land where she'll be vulnerable. She'll be sending a message that her loyalty belongs with the Drakr. Not with Aluina. And that thought makes her sick.

"Don't, Lora," Ayc says. "It's a trap."

The shadows rip Ayc's legs from under him. He slams onto the ground. His breath leaves him in a gasp, followed by a groan of pain. The shadows yank him upright just as quickly.

"Fuck you," he growls at Lahlis. Shadow clamps down on his mouth. Only his wide blue eyes remain visible.

"Stop it!" Lora yells again. She wrestles against the shadow, but it holds her fast, its touch as cold as ice.

A gryphon's cry shrieks through the sky. To the west, the direction of the gryphon pastures, a black dot soars across the sky. Somehow, Lora knows it's Tempest, recognizes instinctively the cry of the gryphon who has looked out for Lora since she was a toddler. Behind Tempest, other gryphons take to the sky. The barracks and rows of homes where the aerial army lives are a distance from this cliff, but she can finally see a scattering of figures rushing about.

Help is coming. But will it be enough?

Ayc makes a sound, muffled through the shadow, but it sounds like her name. He nods his head backward. Lora turns.

Three cloaked figures rise from the shadows as though they are formed from it. Their eyes burn red within the cloaks. These are the dragon riders, perhaps with their own shadow affinity. All three are certainly as lethal as the curved red blades they wear at their hips.

Lahlis takes a step closer. He's as tall as Ayc, and though Lora is far from slight, she has to tilt her head back to keep her gaze fixed on his face. Her skin itches at the eye contact. She's never enjoyed staring into a stranger's eyes, but she learned it's one of the most important parts of playing the theatre of life. Never look away.

"Cities are a funny thing, don't you think?" he asks. "They take years, even decades, to build. And yet a single dragon can reduce the place to ash in a day. As you can see, I have *four*...and Everadyn has none."

The three dragons below them roar, bellowing all at once. The cliff quakes once more. Her choice is clear. Solidify her allegiance with the Drakr or start a war here, now, today.

"What do you say, Lora?" Lahlis grins viciously. The shadow releases her wrist. He has her trapped now, anyway. "Will you be joining us at Morkt Hemma?"

She wants to tell him no. She wants to fight. She wants to see Lahlis drown in his own blood, or she wants to die trying. But she looks at Irving, at the barracks, at the approaching gryphons, at Wyntra castle where so many innocent people have gathered to celebrate the start of her reign. She's grateful, at least, that her grandmother, Hellevi, left as soon as she saw Lora crowned, needing to get back to care for Ohen—the boy she and Ayc helped escape Lux Aester. But there are others she could not bear to lose within those walls.

Yes, she welcomes war with the Darkr if that is what she must do to ensure Aluina's liberation. But to declare it now when they've had no time to prepare might spell certain doom. To declare it now might mean she goes down in history as the Everadyn Sovereign who died the day she was crowned. Even if she survives, Ayc will certainly die.

And put that way, she doesn't really have a choice at all.

Lora lifts her chin and says, "Tell Queen Volkna I accept her invitation."

AYC

"What the fuck just happened?" Peregrin roars as soon as Lora and Ayc enter the courtyard, both surrounded by Irving, the two other royal guards, and a small host of unmounted gryphon riders. Tempest trots behind the group. She ruffles her feathers and snaps her beak as soon as she sees Peregrin. By the glow of silver in Peregrin's eyes, Tempest is telling them everything.

After Lora gave her agreement, Lahlis and the other cloaked dragon riders all climbed back on their dragons and disappeared back across the sea. The gryphon riders who finally, *finally*, reached their Sovereign made a show of ensuring Lora's safety. She brushed them off, telling them she was fine, her entire being strong and steady. But Ayc noticed the way her hands fluttered before she tightened them into fists.

No one asked Ayc if he was all right, which was just fine, because he might have exploded at anyone who asked.

Lora was in danger. She was in fucking danger, and Ayc was *powerless* to do anything about it. He's not all right.

He's fucking furious.

Peregrin marches toward them, their cane stabbing into the

gravel with every step. Bronwen matches their pace. Her power billows from her, crackling in the air like little fireworks. When the gryphon riders don't immediately scramble from her and Peregrin's path, Bronwen moves them herself, a surge of power pressing against their chests until their feet slide through the gravel. They let out notes of surprise but don't dare protest as Bronwen and Peregrin stop before Lora.

"Are you all right?" Bronwen demands.

Lora doesn't look at her First. Instead, she searches the surrounding courtyard, inspecting every shadow and even the turquoise water of the fountain beside them like she expects a Drakr to be hiding within. She pauses on Tavish, who is approaching more slowly, guided by Saga and his cane, and on Xylie, who lingers near the entrance to the castle, her hands clamped over her ears. A small crowd has gathered, scattered in the corners of the courtyard and looking through the doors and windows of the castle. They murmur to one another like they're watching an interesting play. Ayc recognizes Dedryk and Harlowe, the regents of Noxumbra and Audori, among the crowd. Lora stares at them, too, until Bronwen touches two fingers to the back of Lora's elbow. Only then does Lora focus on Bronwen.

"I'm fine," Lora says. "Lahlis didn't harm me. But Ayc..." She jerks her head toward him and studies him as hard as she was studying the entire courtyard.

"I'm fine," Ayc says quickly.

It's a lie. Agony coils through every muscle of his back and legs. Every fiber *fucking* hurts. This is more than the way the shadow drove him to the ground. That action has only enraged the pain that has been lurking since Ayc touched the Severing stone, turning it from a whisper into a scream that echoes through his head. Hope died the moment his body struck the earth, and pain surged through his body. He might be free of the Bond, but he's not free of the pain. It's been with him for eight years, and it's still here.

Why the fuck is it still here?

Lora narrows her eyes, disbelieving.

Ayc puts on his shield of a smile. "I promise, I'm fine."

"Tempest says there were four dragons in Wyntra and that the gryphon army made no attempt to stop them," Peregrin says. "Is that true?"

They direct the question to the nearest gryphon rider. The gryphon rider's eyes flare wide.

"Is it true?" Peregrin snarls.

Ayc has never seen Peregrin this angry. As harsh and blunt as Peregrin can be, this is a new level. Their eyes glow a steady silver, and the normally green veins that weave up their neck—a reminder of the poisoned blade they took in the leg decades before—have darkened to an ominous black. This is Commander Peregrin, the one who led armies, including some of the warriors who stand before them. The riders all stare back, their stony faces beginning to crack with a touch of fear.

"It's true," Irving says. "The dragons came out of nowhere. No gryphon rider tried to stop them."

"Where were the patrols?" Peregrin's snarl turns to a roar. Tempest circles the group, flapping her wings and letting out low growls that emphasize her rider's words. "The gryphon riders shouldn't have let a dragon land in Wyntra unless they first painted the seas red with their blood, failing to stop them."

And Ayc feels the same rage burning through his veins. The army's inaction is either the worst type of negligence...or maliciousness. Either way, it means that Lora isn't safe in Wyntra.

And if Lora isn't safe in Wyntra, where is she safe?

Nowhere.

Ayc's heart lurches to a stop.

"Where is Commander Urbain?" Peregrin demands. "I want to speak with him."

The gryphon riders say nothing.

"Fucking useless. I'll find him myself."

Peregrin storms in the direction of the barracks. They only make it two steps before Lora speaks.

"Wait, Peregrin, stay. The rest of you can go." She waves her hand like shooing an insect. "Everyone but my Five, find somewhere else to be."

The gryphon riders follow the Sovereign's command, marching back toward the barracks, giving Bronwen and Peregrin wide berths as they pass.

"One of you, find Commander Urbain," Lora calls after them, "and tell him his Sovereign desires to speak with him. Immediately."

They chime a chorus of 'yes, my lady'. So apparently, they are actually capable of speech.

The crowd of spectators retreats into the building, some more slowly than others. But the royal guards don't budge.

"I said *everyone* but my Five," Lora says.

"But," protests one of the royal guards, "you must have a guard—"

"Irving can stay. No one else."

The two guards exchange a glance, but they, too, turn back toward the castle entrance. They pass Xylie as they go. She approaches at a trot, her hands already moving.

"Were there really four dragons? What did they look like?"

Of course Xylie would want to know everything about the dragons. Ayc gives her a small smile and signs back, *"I'll tell you later."*

And he would with pleasure. He especially wants to tell Xylie about the one striped like a tiger. Ayc didn't know they came in that color.

When the crowd is gone, Lora lets out a long breath.

"What did the Drakr want?" Peregrin asks. Their eyes fade from the bright silver of a full moon back to the soft gray of a hazy, morning sky.

Lora glances around once more. The massive courtyard seems empty. The only sound is their own breathing, Saga's soft pants, and the fountain that bubbles beside them. Still, Bronwen raises her hand. An orb forms in her palm and then explodes outward. Ayc jumps as the vibration of power passes through him and the fountain. It forms a dome around them, clear except for the shimmering spiderweb blue lines that weave through it.

"There," Bronwen says. "That should stop anyone from eavesdropping on us."

Outside the field, Tempest growls. Ayc supposes the field only keeps the sound in, because he can hear her protest.

Without being asked, Irving reaches up and takes out the amber stone fitted to his ear, silencing the communication between him and the other guards. Lora nods gratefully before beginning.

"I've been invited to the Drakr's palace by Queen Volkna herself."

Bronwen's lips part in surprise. "Queen Volkna?"

Ayc has heard the name before, whispered between Yris and her Five during desserts when they forgot Ayc even existed, as he lingered in the corner to serve them more if asked. Tales say the Drakr queen lives in a palace made of silver. Morkt Hemma supposedly gleams in the moonlight until it can be seen from Drakr's every coast.

"Queen Volkna," Lora confirms.

"It's a trap," Peregrin says.

"I'm certain it is. But Lahlis didn't give me the luxury of saying no." She runs a hand over her wrist where the rope of shadow clung. "I have studied shadow affinity, but I have never seen it to that degree. It's..." She stops as though she can't find the words.

Neither can Ayc. In all the nightmarish stories children whispered to one another in Aluina, he had never heard of shadow becoming a physical force. Nothing has been as unnerving as the way darkness came to life, coiled around him, crushed his chest, stole his air... Ayc draws a breath through his teeth just to remind himself he can.

"Shadow affinity can be quite unsettling," Peregrin agrees. "And Lahlis is one of the most powerful."

"He threatened war if I refused him," Lora says.

"Why would he do that?" Tavish asks. He now sits cross-legged on the ground. Saga lies before him, and Tavish's hand steadily caresses the guide dog's brown and white fur.

"Because Lora didn't say yes to the Drakr like Yris did," Bronwen says. "And now they fear they are losing their control."

"He wants me to publicly demonstrate that the Everadyn and the Drakr will remain allies by visiting them on my Tour," Lora adds.

"What exactly is this Tour?" Ayc asks. He sits down on the rim of the fountain. His muscles feel like they are slowly ripping from his spine, sinew by sinew. He leans back on his palms, trying to make it look relaxed and not like he's trying to stretch out his back. It offers little relief.

"Traditionally, the Sovereign and her Five spend their first several months traveling to the different clans," Lora explains, "so they can meet their new leader, and the Sovereign can learn their people. It usually only includes visits within Everadyn, so if we visit Drakr, it'll send the message that, during my reign, I intend to openly embrace our friendship, not hiding it in the shadows in shame. That is the *last* message I want to send."

She looks at Ayc once again. There's something within her eyes, in the way the brown of her irises edge with blue, that seems like she's pleading with him. Like she needs him, in particular, to understand. "I had no choice but to agree."

"I know," Ayc says. If she said anything else, Lahlis would have crushed the life from him. His dragon would have torched this city.

Lora drags her gaze away and fixes it on the far wall of the courtyard. "Perhaps I shouldn't go. Perhaps I should sever the treaty and go to war. I want to see Aluina free. I know we all do."

Everyone around their circle nods. Even Irving. Emotion claws up Ayc's throat to see it.

"But their liberation and independence won't come without war," Lora adds.

Ayc releases a breath. He is not naïve. He may have never seen war, but he knows its cost. The struggle for freedom will be long and bathed in blood. Destruction and death will be the reality of life for Everadyn, Aluina, and Drakr. There won't be a single person in either country who doesn't feel the impact. It makes his very soul tremble that Lora and everyone around him are willing to pay that cost for his people.

Peregrin drums their fingers on their cane. "As eager as I am to see Aluina free once more, if we rush to war, we are certain to fail. The Drakr are formidable. We've seen just a small percentage of their strength today. We must be strategic. Besides, breaking an existing treaty requires a majority vote from the regents. We would have to get them to agree."

"They didn't agree when Yris broke her treaty with Aluina," Ayc says, acid creeping into his voice.

"That treaty was made with the Creeds," Lora explains. "After the royal line was ended…"

"The treaty was ended, too," Ayc finishes for her, willing himself not to remember that day. That memory is more painful than his back. Than any physical pain he's ever experienced. "And Yris was free to form a new treaty. Fucking convenient."

"So why have the regents not called for a vote to break the treaty?" Bronwen says.

"Tradition states that the Sovereign must allow a vote to occur," Lora replies. "And as far as I know, she's never let the treaty be questioned."

"That seems like a bit too much power in one person's hand," Tavish murmurs.

"Perhaps it is. But it's *my* power now." Lora focuses on Peregrin. "What if I didn't follow the rules? What if I commanded the armies to go to war without their vote?"

"Then it would be an unlawful order. The commanders should—according to the oaths they took—refuse to heed it. Though some may care more about their position than their honor. They would know you could choose to strip them of their power and replace them with someone who'll do your bidding without question. That's what your mother would do."

"No." The word is a grunt. She lifts her fingers to her temple, and Ayc tenses at the way her face contorts like she's in pain. But she drops her hand and recovers quickly. "I don't wish to be my mother. I won't rule as a tyrant, no matter how just my causes."

Peregrin nods, expressionless. "Then we convince the regents."

Lora glances toward Ayc once more. Patient. He has to be patient. He knows if the people in this circle had their way, they would snap their fingers, and Aluina would be free. At least having Lora as Sovereign means Aluina is in an infinitely better position today than they were yesterday. It's not enough, but it's progress.

"Do you think the regents will agree?" Xylie signs, and Ayc translates the question for Peregrin and Tavish.

"Certainly not Lux Aester," Bronwen says, the static of her magic popping off her skin as the name of her clan passes her lips. "Amos despises the humans. But if we convince the majority of the others, that won't matter. I suppose the Tour will be the perfect time to assess who will and won't be on our side. With any luck, we can convince them before the date of Queen Volkna's invitation and not have to go."

"And if we do have to go?" Tavish wonders aloud. "How do we not send the message that we're visiting the Drakr out of friendliness?"

"What if you traveled to *all* the continents?" Ayc suggests. "Tenebra, Laud, the Stella Runes dwarves, or the ones beneath the Untamed Mountains. If you made a point of visiting every country, you would send the message that you are simply working toward building relationships with all. You wanted to try to repair the relationship with the giants, anyway."

Lora cocks her head, considering it.

Bronwen smiles. "You'd certainly be starting your reign by separating yourself from your mother."

"That's actually a really good idea," Lora says at last. "It would be *very* expensive, but—"

"You have the royal treasury at your disposal," Bronwen reminds her.

Peregrin and Irving exchange a look that contains entire

paragraphs. Perhaps they're considering how long they'll both be gone, how long they'll be separated from Zinnia and Ember. But neither says anything, both too bound by their duty.

Lora marks the exchange before shifting her attention. "Tavish, Xylie, what do you think?"

Xylie runs her finger down the bridge of her nose. Ayc imagines there will be many crowds on the Tour, and he wonders how she'll cope. But that seems to be the farthest thing from her mind because a smile teases her lips.

"Can we see the winged horses in Tenebra?" she asks.

Lora's lips twitch. The almost-smile unhitches something in Ayc's chest. "Yes, Xylie, I think we can see the winged horses."

"You'll love them," Tavish says. "And I'll be able to see it too, now." He runs a finger over the leash of the Kindred collar that is wrapped around the handle of Saga's harness but doesn't fully grab it. Ayc knows Tavish only utilizes the leash when he must, that the return of sight the Kindred collar allows can be jarring and overstimulating.

Lora nods with finality. "It's settled then. A world tour."

"We will have to prepare the party that travels with you carefully," Irving says. "We may need a small army to protect you in Drak—"

Gravel crunches near the entrance to the barracks. Irving falls silent as the fae approaches. Commander Urbain towers taller than most Everadyn fae, taller even than Ayc. Blond hair sweeps down his pale cheeks and ends at the spiked pads of armor on his shoulders. A deep red cloak, embroidered with the flame of Audori, drapes over one shoulder.

"About time," Peregrin snarls.

Lora snaps to attention. The subtle ways she's relaxed with only her Five disappear in an instant. She draws herself upright and squares her shoulders. The edge of blue in her eyes disappears, replaced by just a hint of silver. This is Sovereign Loraphne, the fearsome queen.

She is glorious.

Urbain pauses before Bronwen's dome. The sorcerer snaps her

fingers, and it falls. He takes one more step before halting a few feet away. He stands at attention, hands folded behind his back.

"You requested to see me, my lady?" he says. "And let me offer congratulations on your splendid victory. I think you will make the most excellent—"

"Save your flattery." Lora storms across the distance between them. Her voice doesn't raise. It goes deeper, colder. "I'm going to give you exactly thirty seconds to explain why you failed so spectacularly today before I render you an immediate resignation and install someone who can do the job properly. Why did the patrol not intercept the dragons?"

"Because I told them to stand down."

"You *what?*" Peregrin flings themself forward a step, but Irving seizes their arm to hold them in place.

Urbain cocks his head. "Were you not aware? The Sovereign sent word this morning to expect their arrival. Lord Lahlis has been a guest here in the past, though this is the first time he's arrived aboard a dragon."

"What are you talking about?" Lora demands. "*I* did not send any word."

"No, but *you* weren't Sovereign *this morning*."

It takes a moment for Ayc to understand what the commander means. Then rage rumbles through him.

Fucking Yris.

Ayc watches it dawn on Lora's face, too. The little cracks in her polished mask are subtle, there and gone in an instant. "I see," she says.

Peregrin shakes Irving's hand from their arm and steps forward. They are more composed now, but fury still lines their voice with a hard edge and their eyes with silver. "And you didn't think that perhaps the orders were no longer in effect, considering Yris was no longer Sovereign when the Drakr arrived?"

Urbain doesn't look in Peregrin's direction, but his nose wrinkles. Ayc senses there's history between the two, but he doesn't know what. Granted, Urbain took Peregrin's job, one that would still be theirs if Yris gave Peregrin a chance to prove themself after they were injured in battle, but Ayc suspects it's more than that.

Tempest drags her curved talons through the gravel, the stone screeching like a frightened scream. Lora's voice is just as chilling as she hisses, "Answer them."

"No, I didn't," Urbain says. "I assumed Yris told you."

Lora's lips curl in disgust. "And you're who is supposed to be leading my aerial army? You seem to lack even the most basic common sense."

Urbain's expressionless face doesn't waver, but silver weaves through the green of their eyes. Irving steps to Lora's other side, his hand falling on his sword's hilt. Ayc shoves to his feet. The wind shifts, filled with a static that raises the hair on Ayc's arms. More of Bronwen's power.

Urbain blinks, and the silver vanishes. "You have my sincerest apologies, my lady. I didn't believe your mother would ever jeopardize your life. I seem to have misunderstood. You have my word such an error won't happen again."

"And why should I even give you another chance?" Lora hisses.

A bead of sweat drips down Urbain's brow. "My lady—"

"Go!" she commands. "Get out of my sight!"

Urbain spins on his heel.

"And Urbain?"

He turns back. "Yes, my lady?"

"Peregrin may be your predecessor, but I want to remind you, they are my Third now. As such, they're an extension of the Sovereign. I trust you'll recall that next time they speak to you and that you'll remind your riders of it, too. The next time my Third asks them a question, they are to answer immediately, or you will have them disciplined for their disrespect. Do I make myself clear?"

Peregrin jerks their head toward Lora, as though surprised. Ayc isn't. Lora saw one of her people be disrespected, and she's handling it in her own way. A way that is both vicious and profoundly beautiful.

Urbain's throat works for a moment before he gets the words out. "Exceptionally so."

"Good. Now *go!*"

Urbain slinks away. Tempest snaps at his cloak as he passes, and he narrowly dodges, then quickens his pace. Lora glares at Urbain's back until he exits the courtyard and disappears down the road. Only then does she turn back to face the others.

"Fuck!" Bronwen flings her hand upward, and the dome reappears. "How did *he* get to be commander of the aerial armies?"

"By licking Yris' boots," Peregrin replies, not bothering to hide their disgust. "And proving himself to be her obedient little puppet."

"Then we can't trust him," Lora says flatly.

"No, we can't," Peregrin says, "and as much as I would like to see many other, more deserving gryphon riders replace him, I don't advise stripping someone of power on day one of being Sovereign. Some riders might decide to dissent."

"They'd be more loyal to their commander than their Sovereign?" Bronwen asks.

"If they were forced to choose between someone they've ridden into battle with and someone who's basically a stranger?" Peregrin rephrases. "Perhaps."

"Then I'll have to earn their loyalty," Lora says. "Until then, can you keep a close eye on Urbain?"

Peregrin nods. "I always do."

"Good. That's settled. Now, I need to deal with my mother." Lora spits the last word, her canine teeth sharpening. "Tavish, where is she? Something tells me she didn't pack up and leave as she was supposed to."

Tavish's hand stills on Saga's head. He bows his head, concentrating. His hand rises and points behind him at the turret at the northeast corner of the castle. Ayc knows the path well, remembers the way his knees used to tremble as he climbed up the stairs. He always knew what awaited him in that small tower.

The Sovereign's office.

"Very well." Lora starts toward the castle.

Ayc rushes to follow her. His back shrieks in protest at his careless speed, but he grits his teeth. The gravel crunches as Bronwen, Irving, and Peregrin follow as well. Tavish hurries to his feet. Xylie's hands flap at her sides, but she, too, steps forward.

Lora halts and twists back around. "No. I'm going on my own."

"Absolutely fucking not," Ayc snaps.

Lora arches an eyebrow. There's something alive in Ayc, something that has always been there but awoke with a mighty roar when he realized the danger that Lora was in when Lahlis slid off that dragon.

Mine.

Something primal snarls deep within him, demanding that he protect her, demanding he take her hand and drag her somewhere she'll be safe.

Somewhere like his bed.

It's a childish thought. Lora is far better equipped to protect herself than Ayc is, and hiding beneath his covers won't keep her safe. Besides, Lora in his bed is *not* helping that primal feeling. Not when the very idea of her body on his mattress makes heat and blood race to a place in his body where it has no business being.

Mine.

He needs to get his emotions under control, or what he feels for Lora is going to burn him alive. Yes, she's Sovereign, but she isn't *his*. She made that perfectly clear when she lied about kissing him. He has to ground himself in reality and calm down.

He draws a long breath through his teeth. "It's not safe to go alone."

"There are things I need to say to her that I don't want an audience for," Lora says.

"At least take a guard with you," says Peregrin.

Lora's hands fist at her side. "I don't need my every movement shadowed."

"Lora," Bronwen says gently, "you're Sovereign now. You need to be protected. It's part of it. You don't have to take one of us, but you need to take *someone*."

"The royal guards were Yris's first. How do I trust that they and *their* commander's loyalty rests with me now? After all, I don't see Captain Neric anywhere, which I find deeply concerning, considering I was just attacked."

Does everyone in this damn castle have gryphon shit where their brain should be? Ayc wonders.

"He—" Irving begins, then hesitates, looking like he's choosing his words carefully. He gestures toward his ear, where the communication device should be. "He told us over the agate that we were overreacting, which just added to the confusion. I suppose he was warned by Yris, too." A tiny speck of silver flicks in his brown eyes, but he seals his mouth shut.

Lora weighs Irving carefully. "Do you think I'm overreacting?"

"Lahlis threatened you," Irving says like it should be obvious. "He handled your body without your consent. If I removed his head from his shoulders, it wouldn't have been overreacting."

Good, Ayc thinks. Those are his feelings exactly.

"Peregrin," Lora says, "will the royal guards riot if I replace Neric?"

Peregrin's eyes crinkle, like they're holding back a smile. "On the contrary. It's tradition for the new Sovereign to choose their own captain of the royal guard."

"Fantastic." Lora faces Irving once more. "Irving, are you interested in the position?"

Irving's composure slips in his surprise. He pushes his thumb into his own chest. "Me?"

"Yes, you," Ayc says. Of course it should be Irving. He was born in Noxumbra, trained at Adamant, and served in elite forces in the armies before becoming a royal guard. But more than that, he's good, and he's noble, and he's kind, which isn't something

Ayc can say about many of Yris's guards. He would be exceptional at the job.

Irving and Peregrin lock gazes for a heartbeat, but it's enough to write stories about the affection between them. Irving arches an eyebrow, and Peregrin smiles. A question asked and answered.

"Of course, you should talk to both your partners," Lora adds. "Ask Zinnia her opinion. If you all agree, you and Peregrin can work together to assemble a team. If you trust them, I'll trust them."

"We'll have to hire a few new ones," Irving says.

There's a gleam in Irving's expression, and Ayc is certain he'll end up taking the job. If Ayc's friend is charged with Lora's protection, perhaps Ayc's roaring need to protect Lora will settle to something more manageable than the chaos currently within him.

Perhaps.

Not likely.

"I'll send out a notice tonight," Lora agrees, already turning on her heel. Irving follows, and this time, she doesn't protest.

"Go back to the party," she says to the others over her shoulder. "Or don't. Do whatever you would like. Just don't follow me. I'll see you all at dawn in the Sovereign's Garden for our first meeting."

She sweeps into the castle, past the two guards who try to follow before she casts them a deadly glance. And then she's gone. Ayc's heart is lodged in his throat. He tries to tell himself that Yris won't harm her, but he'll never trust Yris.

Bronwen blows a strand of hair out of her face, the exhale breaking the silence between them. "I'm going back to the party. People will think something is wrong if they don't see any of the Five."

"I'll go with you," Tavish says, grabbing Saga's guide handle.

Peregrin nods.

"Are you coming?" Bronwen asks Ayc.

"I'm going to stop at my kitchen first," Ayc says. "I'll join you shortly."

"Are you all right?" Xylie signs, her brow furrowing.

"Fine. I just need to be alone for a moment. Catch my breath."

Her hands hover in the air for a moment, then she drops them to her side and simply nods.

Ayc parts ways with the others in the castle's hallway, going in the opposite direction. Pain shoots down his legs with every step, but he shoves it down, refusing to acknowledge it. Only when he locks his kitchen door behind him does he let himself feel it. He sags against the door, biting down on the heel of his hand to hide his gasp. He heaves himself across the room to the shelves where Xylie stores her potions, hoping there are still a couple pain tonics that he missed when packing for the Trials. He searches through the shelves twice, growing more desperate with each pass, before he finds one behind a jar of pickled pig's feet.

He throws the tonic back, and his stomach tosses as it lands. He braces his hands against the counter at the center of his kitchen. The low heat of the oven, where the dragon egg is being kept, warms his back. He breathes through his nose and out through his mouth until the effects of the potion kick in. The tide of pain recedes until he's no longer drowning in it, but it's still present, ebbing and flowing.

"Fuck." He doesn't know what is happening, why the pain didn't disappear with his Bond. He could ask Bronwen, but then Bronwen might tell Lora, and Lora has more than enough to concern herself with other than him. She's the Sovereign, and he's her Fifth. It is *his* job to protect *her.*

But he doesn't know how he's meant to do that when his body feels old. Ancient. Like it belongs to someone half a century older than him. Even aside from his pain, Lahlis's power proved how utterly useless Ayc is. He might be able to go invisible, but what good would that have been? It didn't stop him from trying, though. When he was locked in Lahlis's shadow, he reached for his power, but it felt as distant as Everadyn's southern shores.

He looks at the bracelets of worn leather on his wrist. How did his mother come to possess such expensive magical objects? Why was she so desperate to ensure Ayc remained hidden from the

Drakr? He doesn't have answers for that, but he understands clearly now that the bracelets have been hiding his power—even from himself.

What will happen if he takes them off?

What will happen if he looks deep inside himself and finds out exactly what he's capable of?

His fingers find the clasp of the bracelet.

Crack!

A sound like splitting stone comes from the oven. Ayc swivels toward it, his heart lunging through his chest. The heavy oven doors remain closed.

Crack!

The sound repeats, louder this time. Ayc approaches the oven and swings the door open. The dragon egg sits on the oven rack, utterly still, but a fracture has formed along one side of its dark green shell. It vibrates and shudders on top of the metal rack and then—*crack!* The fracture widens and lengthens, and Ayc realizes in horror what is happening.

"Holy fucking shit!"

The dragon egg is hatching.

AYC

"Ten years of incubating, and you couldn't wait a couple more months before making your appearance, you little shit," Ayc grumbles into the oven.

In defiance, the egg issues another crack. A second fissure races down the opposite side of the egg.

"A few more days?" Ayc pleads. "Tomorrow, even."

Just not today. He can't have a baby dragon born on the same day Lora became Sovereign.

Baby dragon? Ayc gulps. It's one thing to care for an immobile egg. Caring for a living, breathing baby dragon is quite another. How is he supposed to keep it hidden from everyone, especially Lora, when he's living in this castle, let alone when they leave to go on this Tour?

I'm fucked, Ayc thinks. *Completely and totally fucked.*

The dragon's egg rattles again. This time, a dozen little cracks form along the edges of the fractures. He's running out of time, and he has no idea what to do.

Xylie! He needs Xylie.

He slams the oven door closed and locks it into place. Moving as fast as his aching back allows, he rushes out of his kitchen and toward the great hall. He finds Xylie where he suspected she'd be, nestled in the hallway of the servant entrance. She sits cross-legged on the ground with her back against the stone wall. Tavish and Saga sit with her in the place Ayc has often sat. Tavish is telling what Ayc imagines is another fable he learned at sea, while Xylie smiles softly and feeds Saga cheese and bread off a plate on her lap. They both look up as Ayc's feet slap against the stone.

"Oh, hi, Tavish, Xylie."

"Come to join so quickly?" Tavish asks with his kind, soft smile.

"Actually, I need to borrow Xylie for a second." Ayc tries to keep his voice calm, even as he signs frantic words he knows Tavish can't see. *"Egg. Hatch. Now."*

Xylie's brow furrows together.

His hands form a gaping jaw, his fingers curled like chomping teeth. *"Dragon."*

She lets out a squeak that makes Tavish jump. *"Right now?"* Her hands demand.

"Yes, right now!"

Xylie jumps to her feet. The plate clatters to the ground. Saga turns his head to follow a small roll of cheese that somersaults across the stone but doesn't move toward it, standing faithfully by Tavish.

"Is everything all right?" Tavish asks with a frown. He reaches out for the leash of the Kindred collar.

"Everything is fine!" Ayc promises quickly, but his voice is starting to crack from this panic. It's anything but convincing.

Yes, Tavish knows about the dragon egg, but he's terrible at keeping secrets from Bronwen...and possibly from Lora. Ayc isn't about to tell him yet and give him the burden of trying to hide it from them. The stress alone might cause him to go comatose.

Ayc grasps his best friend's arm and pulls her down the hallway. They say nothing on the way back. Ayc locks his kitchen door behind them. Xylie sprints for the oven and jerks it open.

"Oh, my divine!" she cries, a hand sailing to her lips.

Ayc races to her side and peers into the darkness of the oven.

Peeking out of a crack in the egg are two glowing, red eyes.

LORA

It's a door. Just a fucking door.

The sight of it shouldn't have the power to twist Lora's gut like a hand has reached inward and seized a hold. But as she stands there, balancing on the top step of the long spiral staircase, she feels like she's a child once more. She used to stand here for as long as she dared, taking deep gulping breaths until she was sure she could be calm and emotionless, until she was certain her hands wouldn't flutter. She knew whatever punishment her mother summoned her for, it'd be worse if she wasn't perfectly collected when she stepped inside.

But she's not a little girl anymore. She's Sovereign. She is the one who wears the crown, and this office is *hers*. Yris is simply a trespasser Lora means to throw out on her ass.

"I'll be right outside," Irving says from just behind her. "You may already know, but there's a spell over the room to avoid eavesdropping. I won't be able to hear anything unless you say the word that temporarily disengages the spell."

"What word?" Lora asks. She knows of the spell, but of course, her mother never told her the word.

"Pomegranate."

"Pomegranate?"

The dimple in Irving's cheek flashes. "The word doesn't often come up naturally in conversation." More seriously, he adds, "Say it if you need me. If I hear anything, I'll be inside in an instant."

Lora nods. She hates knowing her every step will be watched now, but if she must have someone, at least it's Irving.

Lora closes her eyes against the ache forming behind them

and draws another breath before seizing the doorknob. The door swings open, and she sweeps into the room.

Yris sits at the large desk in the heart of the office. The scratch of her quill against paper sounds harsh in the quiet. Lora can't imagine what or who she's writing to now that she's no longer Sovereign. Most likely, it's just a prop meant to make Lora feel less important than whatever is on that paper. It's why Yris doesn't look up, even when Lora slams the door shut.

"What game are you fucking playing?" Lora growls.

Yris dips her quill into the inkpot, eyes still fixed on the paper. "Is that how you talk to your mother?"

"I am not speaking to you as your *daughter*. I am speaking to you as your *Sovereign*. Answer me."

"Let's not give in to hysterics."

Hysterics. *Hysterics.* The word grinds against Lora's skin like sandpaper. Every emotion Lora ever expressed was labeled as hysterics. Yris has made the word a weapon, and so Lora draws her own.

The sound of metal sighing against metal finally earns Yris's attention. Lora holds her dagger loosely, letting it sway in her fingertips. Casual, to show Yris that she has no power over her anymore.

"I'm still waiting for an answer," Lora says.

"I would gladly give you one if you'd tell me what you're talking about."

"Of all the things I think you are, Yris, you're not a fool. And you didn't raise one either."

Lora gestures toward the only window in the room. Its shutters are open. From this height, Lora can easily see past the barracks to the cliffs where Lahlis's dragon landed, as well as the skies above where the three other dragons circled.

"Did you enjoy your show?" Lora asks.

Yris folds her paper and says nothing.

"You knew Lahlis was coming, didn't you?" Lora presses.

"Finally, a direct question," Yris huffs. "Yes, I did."

"And you told Urbain to stand down?"

"Yes."

"And what was the point of your little exercise?" Lora demands instead. "You let Lahlis come here and ensured I'd be caught off-guard. I'm sure you knew what he wanted to say to me, so I ask you again. What game are you playing?"

"I assure you this isn't a game." Yris strolls around the desk. She still wears her dress from the coronation, the dark color making her skin look nearly translucent. But she doesn't wear a blade, at least not where Lora can see. It doesn't matter. Yris herself is a weapon, just like Lora is, sharpened and honed since birth. "I only want to ensure that you don't ruin everything I have built, nor put Everadyn in jeopardy because Josias filled your head with some nonsense."

Lora's canines sharpen against her bottom lip as Yris utters her father's name. She paces across the floor to do something with the surge of rage, so she doesn't aim the dagger at Yris's mouth.

"I wanted to remind you of everything at stake," Yris continues. "The alliance with Drakr must remain. They provide an abundance of resources."

"Resources taken from the people of Aluina." Lora points her dagger at a map of the continents on the wall, directing the tip at the abundant forests within Aluina. It's a sharp contrast to the flat, barren regions of Drakr on the other side of the Untamed Mountains. The lumber from Aluina's forest feeds the forges for Everadyn's weapons; the mines in Aluina's Tourmaline Mountains supply the minerals used in many forms of alchemy, particularly in the type that powers the lights in this castle. Everadyn can't survive without either. "We once had the same agreement with the humans."

"The people of Aluina were a drain. We gave them far more than they gave us, and for what? What did we really get out of it? My father would have broken the treaties, too, if that sentimental Totus Omni fae, Siabhon, hadn't interceded on Aluina's behalf."

"*Queen* Siabhon," Lora corrects. "If you're going to give a history lesson, at least call the figures by their proper titles."

After all, Siabhon was queen of Aluina.

It's a romantic story frequently retold by bards at Totus Omni festivals. A simple painter from Totus Omni met, fell in love with, and married the human king. And when he died of old age, she lay down beside him and her heart simply stopped, so she could go with her beloved. They shared more love in a single lifetime than some do in an eternal existence. At least, that's how all the ballads go. It was Siabhon's child—King Cypress Creed— who Yris personally pierced to the throne, and Siabhon's grandchild—the crown prince—who died by Fennix's hand.

"It's wrong," Lora says. "What we did to Aluina. The Drakr had no right to seize control of their land. And we had no right to serve it to them on a silver platter."

We. It takes Lora's breath away because she carried a sword into Creed that day, too. She stood by and followed orders. She never offered a protest as they destroyed every remnant of the Creed bloodline so that the magical boundaries that once shielded Aluina would fall. The Drakr couldn't enter Aluina to do it, so Yris handled it herself. Aluina is in Drakr hands because of her actions.

Lora shakes off the self-loathing—it will not serve her now—and continues, "It is still Aluina's land and labor the Drakr are profiting from. The humans starve and work themselves to death under cruel conditions for meager wages while the Drakr grow richer and richer." She hasn't been to Aluina, not since Creed, but she knows the stories her father told her.

"By the divine," Yris groans. "This is exactly what I mean. Do you think the regents will support you going to war against the Drakr to liberate Aluina? Oh, many of them talk nobly about how much of a villain I am and spew hate at the Drakr. But when it comes down to it, they like the privileges and riches it has granted them. And I do mean *all* of them, Loraphne. Grey would let every human in Aluina die before they'd risk losing a single tree in the Forest of Elodie."

No, Lora refuses to believe it. She's sat with Grey, the regent of Aluina, in her grandmother's house. She has heard them discuss with Hellevi how much they wish Aluina could be restored to what it once was. Yris is only trying to isolate Lora, to make her feel as though she is utterly alone.

"The regents will never agree to go to war, and you can't go without them," Yris says. "Audori controls our weapons, Noxumbra the majority of our soldiers, and Lux Aester our food. If they decide to cut off those things, you won't be able to feed yourself, let alone the armies that you'll need for any attempt to get Drakr out of Aluina's land."

Lora glares hard at the dagger in her hand. Yris isn't wrong. It's the very same conversation she had with her Five in the courtyard. If she doesn't convince the regents to break the treaty, her road to helping Aluina will grow so much harder. But *she* will convince them.

"I wish you would look at me when I'm talking to you, Loraphne."

Another phrase Yris has turned into a weapon. Lora has always hated forced eye contact. She's taught herself how to use it, fighting to find a balance between too little and too much. She's forced herself to do it even as her skin crawls, driven by Yris's constant nagging of *look at me, look at me, look at me.*

But now, Lora searches the room to focus on anything but her mother. The wind coming from the open window stirs the loose papers stuffed into bookshelves. Beneath the window is a small table set with the chessboard, the one that Yris made Lora sit at for hours, playing round after round and snarling at Lora whenever she lost. And next to the map, there's a plain stretch of wall covered by a board. She can see the marks on the wood where Ayc once stood while Lora fired a knife she hoped would miss him. She wanted to cry at the sight of his blood, but she didn't dare let it show.

Since this is *Lora's* office now, maybe she can simply light a match and burn it all. Start anew. That might bring her some satisfaction, if it didn't mean important documents and priceless, historical books would go up with it.

"So, you let Lahlis come here in an attempt to force me to be the kind of Sovereign you want me to be," Lora says, still not looking at Yris.

"To remind you of the Sovereign you *must be* if Everadyn is to continue to prosper."

"I see." At least now Lora understands Yris's motivation. Perhaps she doesn't want Lora dead after all. She just wants to play with the little power she still has.

The ache in Lora's eyes intensifies. It's been a long time since she's had a headache this severe. Every one of Yris's words has seemed to make it worse.

No more. She's done.

"Do anything like it again, and I will see you arrested for treason and conspiracy against your Sovereign," Lora says before stabbing her dagger toward the door. "Now, get out of this castle, or I'll have you thrown out."

Yris crosses her arms over her chest and plants her feet. "Are we still on this tantrum? I'm not leaving. Tradition states the previous Sovereign and their Five will remain in Wyntra to ensure a peaceful and smooth transition of power."

"Fuck tradition." Lora lets her eyes flash with silver and curls back her lip to show her teeth. "Leave. *Now*."

Yris releases a long breath. "Loraphne, I'm sorry."

"You're *what*?"

Yris approaches slowly, and Lora watches her hands. Her nails are weapons all their own, sharpened and painted with a red that contains poison. She's never scarred Lora, but others are not so lucky. Some of Yris's own Five bear marks where others can't see. Ayc wears them on his neck. The reminder makes Lora flex her own fingers, the ones painted with the same poison in a subtle, nude shade.

"I'm sorry that you don't trust me." Yris's tone is soft, like she's trying to be soothing, but it sounds strange coming from her. She's never been gentle. "I'm not trying to jeopardize your reign. I'm trying to save it. Save *you*. From the moment you were born, I wanted to see a crown on your head. It's been your destiny. And yes, it happened far sooner than either of us would have liked. I have not prepared you enough for this. You are young. Inexperienced. You will need my help.”

“I don’t need your help. I don’t want it.”

“Who will run Everadyn while you are away on Tour? You leave from Bromalis in two weeks, and the way you won the Trials did not sit well with many of our people. You need to devote yourself entirely to gaining and earning their trust, not divided in running the country. This is a reason for the tradition of the previous Sovereign staying behind.”

“I’ll manage.” Fuck, she’ll give up sleeping if she must. “Now, leave.”

Yris scoffs and storms in the opposite direction of the door. “Well, if you won’t listen to reason, let me give you two other reasons. Let me stay. Let me *help* you for just a year, and I’ll tell you where your father is.”

Lora’s breath catches in her throat. Only Yris knows the destination of the ship she put her father on when she exiled him. Only she would have any idea where he went from there. Hellevi has searched, but her efforts have been fruitless. And Lora can pardon Josias all she wants now, but it does little good if Lora can’t get a message to him. She has resources now that Hellevi never did, but she might spend months scouring the continents for him and still not find him. Or she can play Yris’s sick game and find him sooner.

“I know you want to pardon him,” Yris says. “I suppose I can’t blame you, but I do hope you’ll keep it quiet if you do. The Drakr won’t handle it well if they know.”

Lora turns her back on Yris, using the excuse of pacing to shield her face from showing Yris that she hit her mark perfectly. “You said there were two reasons. What is the second?”

“The first is a bribe.” The corners of Yris’s lips coil in a smile. “The second is a threat.”

Lora scoffs, even as her hold tightens on her dagger. “Fine. Let’s hear it.”

That smile still plays on Yris’s face as she casually strolls back toward her desk. “If you don’t allow me to stay, perhaps I’ll decide to come clean with the Drakr after all these years. Perhaps, I'll tell them I let Ayc Waylonder, a boy in Creed, live. And perhaps they'll correct my mistake."

Lora's dagger slams into the wall, a mere inch from Yris's nose. Lora's vision is painted in silver, making her more focused, more lethal.

"I will cut out your tongue first, bitch."

Yris chuckles under her breath. "We both know that you don't have the stomach for it. I've tried to teach you, and you could never do anything but watch."

Lora blocks out the memories that threaten to come. Memories of screams that ended in blood and her locked in a dungeon cell, punishment for her weakness.

Yris pulls the dagger from the wall and tosses it from hand to hand. "I told you not to let yourself care about that boy. Kindness is weakness. So is love."

Lora's hands nearly flutter, but she pulls them into tight fists. The word echoes.

Love, love, love.

It isn't true. She doesn't love Ayc. She *can't* love him. It's just a myth Yris has made up in her head. It *cannot* be true.

I can't, I can't, I can't.

"It's a pity you didn't listen to me. If you had heeded my warnings about keeping your affection for him in check, perhaps you'd be rid of me." Yris slips behind the desk and sits down in the chair. She reclines in it as though it's a throne. "You know you can't be with him, don't you? If I can use him against you so easily, what do you think your enemies will do? You will be a puppet, and he will be your strings. And a Sovereign can't be perceived as weak."

Lora hates her mother for that. Not because it's untrue, but because it is. It doesn't make it land any less like a blow across her cheek, and it stings that Lora has never had a mother capable of a gentle touch. Who handles her daughter's heart not with care but with shame, like it's something to be squashed and broken apart.

Yris flips the dagger around, catches it carefully by the blade to avoid cutting herself, and holds it out to Lora. "Can I remain in the Sovereign quarters, or would you like me to move into a guest room?"

It's checkmate.

Lora reads it on the smile on Yris's face. The victory of this round goes to her. Lora only has two options. She can accept Yris's terms and spend a year dealing with Yris, or she can take the knife back and split Yris's throat. When Lora reaches for the dagger, she isn't quite sure which one she'll choose. Then she shoves the blade back in its scabbard.

Her head is killing her, but she forces fierceness into her tone. "Get out of my fucking chair."

She doesn't expect Yris to yield, but she does. She stands and steps to the other side of the desk. Lora takes her place and sits down pointedly. It's fucking uncomfortable. The edges dig into her thighs. Her mother always preferred appearance to comfort. She's going to burn it and replace it with something more comfortable.

"One year, Yris," Lora relents. "And only you. Your Five must be elsewhere."

"You won't let them educate your Five? Besides Peregrin, none of them has ever held a leadership position. They know little of law."

Lora shakes her head. Yes, she and her Five have much to learn, but they won't learn well from Yris's Five. They would terrify Tavish and Xylie and infuriate Ayc and Peregrin. "I'll hire professors from Splendor. I think they might actually understand the law better than your Five, considering how often they broke it."

Yris sighs. "Very well."

"You can remain in Wyntra, but I want you out of the Sovereign's quarters." Lora has no intention of moving out of the room that's been hers since childhood, but she doesn't want Yris in the esteemed chambers. "You can take whatever room is the furthest from me. When the year is up, you'll tell me where my father is, and then I never want to see you again."

Yris flicks her wrist. "Yes, yes, Loraphne, I get the point."

"My lady," Lora corrects.

"What?"

"I am your Sovereign. You will refer to me as my lady."

Yris's green eyes darken, but she smiles. "Yes, of course, my lady."

AYC

The dragon crawls from the shattered eggshell on trembling legs too long for its slender body. Its wings drag at its side as it moves onto the counter, where Xylie and Ayc carefully moved the oven rack, worried that with all the rumbling and vibrating, the egg would roll from the oven. Whatever fluid was within the egg coats the dragon's scales, obscuring its true color beneath a shimmering brown. Long wet marks stain the counter where its long tail trails behind it. The dragon succeeds in only a few wobbly steps before it flops down on the counter, its sides heaving.

The hatching process took time and effort. The dragon clawed and bit and tore its way from the stone-like shell, piece by piece. Ayc and Xylie debated whether to assist it. Xylie, for once, didn't have an answer. To her knowledge, this was the first time in history any Everadyn fae had ever witnessed a dragon birth. All that the Everadyn learned and then recorded about dragons was what Everadyn fae could learn from a distance, and dragons allowed no one close to their nests. But Xylie knew gryphon hatchings were supposed to be unassisted. The process of hatching is supposed to assist in building critical muscles and strength, but helping can inadvertently cause harm.

So, in the end, Xylie and Ayc merely watched the long, tedious process. Xylie scratched notes on a blank page of her hand-bound alchemy book, bouncing from one foot to the other, while Ayc paced anxiously like an expectant father in the hallway outside a birthing room.

The baby dragon's serpentine neck twists left and right, blinking its great red eyes around the room. It trembles, great spasms wracking its body like perhaps it's shivering. Ayc has already cranked up the oven. The kitchen is sweltering and humid. Fog steams up his window, and sweat drips down his spine. He might even have been grateful Lahlis's dragon clawed open the back of his shirt and vest if it wasn't his favorite outfit.

Ayc grabs a hand towel hanging from a cabinet door but hesitates. "Should I dry it off?"

Xylie looks up from her notes. "I don't know, but I don't think it could hurt anything." She scratches the feathered end of the quill along her nose. "Except, maybe you, if it senses you as a threat."

Ayc weighs the risk. "Well, it's only the size of a house cat. How much damage could it do?"

"Only a finger or two."

"Thanks for that, Xy. Next time, lie to me."

She shrugs and sets down the quill. "You dry it off. I'm going to the kitchen to find it some food. Raw chicken, maybe? Or perhaps lamb would be better? Dragons do like sheep." Her muttering quiets as soon as she slips into the hallway. She ducks her head back in a moment later. "Unless you want to offer up a finger or two."

Ayc gives her a finger. His middle one. She giggles as she shuts the door behind her.

Ayc draws in a breath and takes a step toward the counter. The dragon jerks its head in Ayc's direction and locks its eyes on him. Ayc's heart soars from his throat to somewhere in the rafters. The narrow pupils at the very center of its red eyes reflect Ayc back in their deep pools of black. Something deep within him lurches, like somehow that stare has pierced him through and is rearranging his very soul.

Ayc shakes his head to rid himself of the unsettling feeling and steps closer to the counter.

"Easy there, lovely," Ayc coos as he reaches forward with the towel.

The dragon cocks its head to the side but otherwise doesn't move as Ayc dries it. The brown wipes away to reveal white. In the sunlight pouring through the window, the dragon's scales gleam an iridescent rainbow, like they are made entirely of flattened pearls. Hard, dull protrusions trail down its spine and tail. Ayc imagines that one day they will be spikes, like those that lined the dragon's mother's back. The start of a spade tips its tail, and four, longer horns—hued in a dull gold—crown its little head. It's already gorgeous.

As Ayc works to clean it, the dragon leans into his touch and makes a low rumble in its chest, almost like a purr, like a cat being pet. The comparison doesn't seem right. The red eyes watching Ayc seem far more intelligent than any cat he's ever known.

The door creaks open, and Xylie steps in, carrying a covered pot in her hands.

"I see you have all your fin—" Xylie begins, before cutting herself off. She gasps and races to Ayc's side. The dragon jumps to its feet and scrambles closer to the edge of the counter, closer to Ayc. Ayc shushes, a soft sound meant to comfort the dragon and warn Xylie.

She lowers her voice, even as she tugs on his sleeve excitedly. "It's white. It's a white dragon!'

"Yes. And?"

"They're not supposed to exist. There are fables, oral histories passed down for generations, about white dragons, but there's never been one documented. At least, not by the Everadyn fae. Maybe the Drakr know more, but they'd never tell us." She gulps a breath before continuing, "There's a theory that a dragon's color isn't decided by hereditary traits. Instead, it's determined by the conditions in which the dragon incubated, which is why some colors and patterns are far more rare than others. Maybe that's why Tavish sensed this egg. I always wondered why, on an island that must be full of dragon nests, he sensed *this* egg as a great treasure."

The dragon's shaking has stopped. Ayc drops the towel but can't resist reaching toward the dragon again. He strokes his knuckle down the dragon's neck. It curls into his touch.

Xylie, too, reaches a tentative hand toward the dragon. It startles once more and leaps into the air. Its wings give one small flap before they collapse uselessly at its side, and the dragon collides with Ayc's chest. He yelps as talons sink past his shirt into his flesh. He throws his arms around it to keep it from falling and tearing all the way to his abdomen. Blood drips down his sternum, but it's unlikely to be deep enough that Ayc won't heal quickly. The tonic in his system is already easing his pain, and he forgets it completely when the dragon curls up in his arms like a cat. It shoves its head beneath Ayc's armpit.

Ayc releases a shuddering breath. That peculiar feeling shakes his chest again. He feels like lightning has gone off within him. There must be something wrong with him because he's being utterly ridiculous.

Xylie pulls her hand back and blinks. "I guess he likes you. Or she. I don't know, but it doesn't feel right to use it."

Xylie's right. *It* doesn't feel right for the dragon at all. "How do we tell if it's male or female?" Ayc asks.

"That's another thing the Everadyn don't know. You can't exactly walk up to a dragon and check, so they've labeled dragons only after seeing what role they play in procreation. The females bear the egg and then guard it."

"Well, I'm not about to lift its tail and go looking."

"Probably wise. I guess we'll just use *they* to be safe."

Ayc nods.

"Let's see if they're hungry." Xylie sets the pot on the counter and opens the lid. Trimmed pieces of raw chicken sit within.

The dragon pops their head out of Ayc's armpit and sniffs the air. Xylie wrinkles her nose as she gingerly picks up a chicken leg between two fingers, like she's trying hard not to touch it. She offers it to the dragon.

"Are you hun—*ahh!*" Xylie shrieks and drops the chicken as the dragon vaults from Ayc's arms and sinks their teeth into the chicken leg. They fall back onto the counter, pinning the raw meat between their two front feet. They tear off a chunk of flesh, flashing viciously sharp teeth. They make a small grumble of satisfaction as they swallow it down and then tuck their head for another bite.

"Fuck," Ayc says. "Imagine that being your face."

Xylie shakes her head. "No. No, thank you. I really don't want to."

The dragon devours the leg, bone and all. They then dive into the pot of chicken to continue with the rest of the meat, disappearing from view. The cracking of bone sends shivers down Ayc's spine.

Fuck. How's he supposed to pull this off? How's he supposed to keep this dragon fed and hidden? It's easy now, when they're the size of a house cat, but he can't exactly hide a dragon the size of a house in Wyntra...or anywhere, really. And how can they possibly control it? Sure, the dragon is docile now, but whatever it seems, Ayc isn't foolish enough to believe it will ever be a pet. Their wild nature will persevere, and they might begin seeing Ayc and Xylie as threats...or, perhaps, food.

He hadn't thought any of this through when he took the dragon's egg from the cave. He only wanted it to survive.

"What are we going to do with it, Xy?" Ayc asks.

Xylie gnaws on her bottom lip. "Perhaps we can send a letter to Splendor. The university could certainly figure out the resources to house a dragon. They could finally document dragon growth and development."

"House them in what? A cage?" The very idea makes Ayc's stomach twist.

Xylie looks at him sharply. "They couldn't. They *wouldn't.*"

Ayc arches an eyebrow skeptically. He's never been to

Splendor, but he's heard of their museum and the specimens, both living and dead.

Xylie presses her eyes closed and sighs. "But of course they would. We can't tell them." Her shoulders slump. "I don't know. We'll think of something. Take it one day at a time. The most important thing is we keep the dragon safe, and I suppose that means keeping them a secret. At least for now. No one can know. Especially not Lora."

Lora. In the excitement of the dragon being born, Lora grew distant in Ayc's mind. He wonders how the conversation with her mother went, if she's all right. And he wonders what Lora would do if she found out about the dragon. She was willing to leave the egg in the cave, but she also tried to save the dragon's mother. Ayc doesn't know if she'll view this rare white dragon as a treasure...or a nuisance.

"Do you think she would have them killed?"

"I think she would do whatever she thought was best for Everadyn," Xylie replies. "And I don't want to put her in the position of having to make that choice."

More crunching bone comes from the pot, paired with little growls and grumbles. Ayc's back has grown stiff with all the standing, and he tries to arch his spine subtly, seeking relief. Instead, he throws his muscles into a spasm that makes him gasp.

"Are you all right?" Xylie asks.

He gives her a reassuring smile. "I'm fine. Lahlis just banged me up a bit. That's all."

"Maybe you should see the healer."

"I'm *fine*."

She narrows her eyes. "Are you being honest with me?"

His smile wobbles, but he's well-practiced at holding it in place. "Of course. I'm always honest with you."

"No, you're not," she mutters under her breath. She presses her fingers to her lips like she didn't mean to speak. Still, the words hover in the air, the meaning behind them crushing Ayc's chest.

"That isn't fair," he protests. "I couldn't tell you about the Binding stone. Yris commanded me to tell no one."

Xylie pries her fingers from her lips. "You could have told me about being Drakr." Her voice isn't angry. Only sad. And that's worse.

Ayc turns away from her watery eyes and grasps the edge of the counter. "You want us to be honest with each other?"

"Yes, of course."

"Then tell me what deal you made with the Supreme sorcerer."

Xylie faced her anxieties, flew across the sea, and sacrificed gods know what else to the Supreme sorcerer at Velphin. And he's still in pain. Before he breaks that truth to her, he wants to understand exactly what she gave up.

"It doesn't matter!" she snaps.

The pot rattles. The dragon's head pops up over the rim, the chicken's rib cage dangling from between their teeth. They cock their head at Xylie and Ayc.

Ayc lowers his voice. "If it *didn't* matter, you would simply tell me."

She presses her lips into a firm line and shakes her head. The dragon tucks their head back into the pot. Crunching bone echoes once more.

Ayc huffs out a breath. "Now who's keeping secrets?"

Bang!

The pot tips sideways and lands on the counter. The dragon saunters out, their legs steadier now. Their wings tuck against their side instead of hanging limply. Their forked tongue drags along their teeth and lips. They tip up their nose and sniff the air, walking around the counter like they're seeking food. They pause halfway along the counter and point their body toward the back wall of the kitchen, where the oven and ice box sit. It crouches low on all four legs and shakes their tail so vigorously that even their rump sways side to side.

Ayc frowns. "What's it do—"

The dragon leaps.

They spread their wings wide, flapping once, twice, and then the wings buckle. They plummet. Ayc races around the counter, but it's too late. They shriek as they spiral through the air and slam into a large bag of flour leaning against the wall. Flour erupts in the air like ash, exploding into his face.

Ayc coughs, flour puffing off his lips and nose. Xylie shakes her arms, but it doesn't help. A fine layer of white cloaks her hair, clothes, and skin. Just as it coats Ayc's... and everything in his kitchen. The dragon's tail sticks out of the overturned bag of flour.

Ayc brushes flour from his hair. It releases a cloud, and he laughs. "You're a mess, Xy."

"Still a right sight compared to you!" she fires back, but the fierceness is broken by her own laughter.

The return of the familiar banter is a relief. He hates not knowing what deal Xylie made, but in the end, she has to decide when she's ready to tell. Ayc can't challenge that without being a hypocrite. Whatever it is, he'll find a way to protect her. He'll find a way to be better. Stronger.

He glances at the bracelets on his wrist.

The dragon retreats from the bag of flour. They shake, releasing another cloud, and then pad toward Ayc, leaving clawed prints in the layer of white on the ground. They sit down on their hindquarters and tilt their head quite like a cat. Flour dims the shine of its white scales.

"Look what you did," Ayc teases, laughing once more.

And he swears the dragon smiles, their lips curling apart to reveal their rows of teeth. Ayc crouches down and offers his hand. The dragon rubs his head against it.

"You're a silly little Muffin, aren't you?" Ayc coos.

"No!" Xylie snaps her fingers. "We are *not* naming the dragon Muffin!"

"You never let me do anything fun!"

FIVE

LORA

A knock sounds at the door of the office. Lora looks up from the pile of papers strewn across her mother's—no, *her*—desk. The daylight faded an hour ago; the office's window is now shuttered to shield against the chill of the night. The desk's lamp offers a dim, amber glow, the only light in the space. Anything brighter, and Lora's head might fully split open, as it's threatened to do over the last several hours.

"Pomegranate," Lora mutters and then raises her voice. "Yes?"

Irving creaks the door open and sticks his head in. The poor man has stood out there for hours, but no weariness shows on his face as he offers his kind, dimpled smile. "Feel up to a visitor?"

"Who is it?"

"Me!" Bronwen calls from behind Irving, still hidden from view. "And I bring food, so you're obligated to let me in."

Despite her weariness, Lora's lips pull at the edges. "Come in."

Bronwen slides around Irving. She still wears the burgundy dress from earlier, but she's thrown her sorcerer cloak over it and pulled her hair into a messy knot on top of her head, signs that she's done with today. Lora, herself, returned to her rooms briefly, trailed by Irving, to exchange her dress and armor for a silver, oversized tunic she found in a shop in Silvae years ago. It's only grown softer with time, and its touch is a comfort. She hung the leviathan's tooth on a hook on the wall of her bedroom. She's even dared remove her crown, but she isn't certain what she's meant to do with the priceless artifact that still doesn't quite feel like hers. So now it sits on a stack of books on the corner of the desk, the dark leaf-shaped jewels blinking in the lamplight.

Bronwen carries a silver serving platter layered with at least three types of desserts, fruit, and small sandwiches. Lora gestures to the one corner of the desk not littered with papers, and Bronwen sets the tray down. There's already an empty tray on the floor, bearing the remnants of roast chicken that Zinnia brought from the party. She came to bring Irving food and was kind enough to notice that Lora hadn't returned to the party to eat, either. Lora barely touched it. She was too nauseated from the pain in her head.

Zinnia and Irving must have spoken during that time because Irving officially accepted the position as captain. Lora happily composed a letter to Neric and delivered it by a page, stating he was immediately fired with two months' severance pay. She knows he'll easily find a position on any city or village guard in Everadyn, but Lora is grateful to be away from him. Neric was an ass who whined to Lora's mother whenever she so much as toed a line she wasn't supposed to cross and grinned gleefully whenever she was punished.

"Let me know if you two need anything," Irving says as he begins to close the door.

"Irving," Lora says.

He pauses.

"You should take a break. Go rest."

His smile disappears. "My lady—"

"*Lora* is fine. It's just us here. And Bronwen and I can protect ourselves."

His hand tightens on the doorknob. Lora sighs. A thud hammers through her head at the very idea of arguing.

"I'll cast a protective spell," Bronwen assures him. "No one will be able to get in." She flicks her wrist. Her power surges in the room like a lightning strike before fading down to a quiet hum.

Irving reaches into the room and jerks back with a grunt like something shocked him. His brown furrows. "Promise me you won't leave this room until I get back."

"I promise," Lora says.

"I'm going to go speak with a few of the guards, the ones I trust. I'll be back within a half hour."

When the door finally shuts, Bronwen smiles, her eyes glinting like she's about to do something naughty. "I brought something else." She lifts up her arm to show the velvet bag tied around her elbow by its drawstring.

Lora sits up straighter in the chair. She recognizes the velvet's deep purple hue and the golden leaves embroidered along its edge. "Is that what I think it is?"

Bronwen smiles. "Reselda came to see your coronation."

"That was kind of her."

Reselda has been the healer in Avia, the Totus Omni village where Lora's grandmother lives, since Lora was a young child. Her renown goes beyond their small village. She's earned respect for blending her formal teaching at Splendor, her Bromalis mother's skill with flowers and herbs, and secrets of nature she learned from her faun father. When Ayc was ill, Reselda didn't hesitate to answer Lora's summons and came to Lux Aester to give her opinion.

Lora winces at the memory. She owes Reselda an apology. Lora certainly didn't have kind things to say to her.

"She adores you," Bronwen says. "I doubt she would have missed it. And luckily, she had some of her infamous plant with her. I saw you rubbing your temples in the courtyard earlier, and I thought maybe you were having one of your headaches."

As always, Bronwen has the uncanny ability to see right through her. "This is the first I've had in a long time."

"Well, it's been a *loooong* few days."

An under exaggeration, really. The Trials took only a handful of days, and yet, they felt like the longest year of Lora's life.

"What do you say?" Bronwen opens the bag and draws out a small black pipe. "Want to take a break?"

Lora glances at the letters she's been writing. She should go back to work, but Reselda's herb offers more than just relief from the invisible knife embedded behind her eyes. It also grants a sense of well-being and ease, and if enough is consumed, the same soft intoxication that comes from drinking fae wine. And that certainly would help her complete the letters she's writing.

Writing the condolence letters has been a cruel form of torture. Writing condolence letters to Mienna's and Hason's families was difficult enough, considering Lora and her Five were the ones to deliver the killing blows. Lora doesn't know what to write to Marcellus's widow and children, and she's only stumbled through a few words in the letter to Dedryk. It'll be a delicate task to express her sympathy to the Noxumbra regent, whose oldest son failed to claim the crown and whose youngest son died in the attempt.

Fuck.

Lora hasn't yet told Bronwen what happened to Ryker, and she should have long ago. Perhaps lighting the pipe is a good idea for both of them. Maybe it'll blunt the blow Lora has to deliver.

When Lora nods, Bronwen grins and flops down on a chair on the other side of Yris's desk.

My *desk, for fuck's sake,* Lora corrects herself.

Bronwen uses the edge of her cloak to wipe down the pipe. "You'll never guess who else I saw at the party." She pauses for effect as she pinches a bit of the crushed leaves from the bag into the pipe. "Fennix. He was quite disgruntled that he's being kicked out of Wyntra. Apparently, you told Yris that she can stay, but her Five have to leave. Which bwas quite a surprise because I thought you came here to tell her to fuck off."

"I did," Lora says with a grunt, massaging her temple with the pads of her first two fingers.

"And?"

"And, as per usual, my mother is one step ahead of me." Lora explains Yris's deal regarding her father's location, though she doesn't mention the threat to Ayc's life. She's not sure why.

"Bitch," Bronwen snarls. The pipe in her hand burns briefly red, like it's become a living coal. Smoke coils up from the mouth. The smell, both sweet and sour, tingles Lora's nose as Bronwen passes her the pipe over the desk. "Is that why you've barricaded yourself away in here all evening instead of returning to your own party?"

Lora sticks the pipe between her teeth and pulls the smoke deep into her lungs. It'll take at least a quarter of an hour for the medicinal qualities to kick in. But the very act of inhaling the smoke deeply, holding it in, and exhaling it slowly eases Lora's rattling nerves. Reselda must have infused the leaves with berries because Lora tastes it on her tongue as the smoke passes her lips. "I had things I needed to do."

It isn't a lie. Lora has filled multiple pages of her notebook with things she must do now that she's Sovereign. It's frustrating how many are silly little things that will now consume her time. She wants to make preparations for Aluina. She wants to figure out a plan for Lux Aester, but that will have to wait until the morning when she meets with her Five.

But it's not the entire truth. Lora loathes parties, hates the mental effort of trying to figure out exactly what each person in the crowd expects from her. That says nothing of the constant noise that sets her skin on edge or the press of bodies that makes her want to eject from her skeleton.

Bronwen stares steadily at her. Lora passes back the pipe before she can ask any more questions. Bronwen tosses her legs over the cushioned armrest and inhales deeply. A hacking cough interrupts her exhale. Her eyes water.

Lora can't help but snicker. "Remember the first time you smoked? You coughed so hard you nearly pissed yourself."

Bronwen lifts her middle finger high, a retort that is weakened by two more coughs. "You ought to be nice to me, or I'll tell the tailor to dress you only in fleece for the entirety of the tour."

Lora shudders at the very thought. Fleece feels like barbed wire against her skin. "You wouldn't."

Bronwen cocks her head. A lock of nearly-white hair falls over her nose. "Probably not," she concedes, offering Lora the pipe. "But, according to Fennix, his responsibility of planning the Tour has now become my responsibility." She reaches into the pocket of her cloak and draws out a scroll. "He wrote down everything he previously arranged. I might need to ask the librarian to translate it for me. He either wrote it in an ancient language I don't recognize, or he has the handwriting of a fucking chicken."

"He has the handwriting of a chicken," Lora says. "And I can handle the arrangements." She reaches across the desk for the scroll, but Bronwen whips it out of her reach.

"No, *I* will handle it."

"I don't want to trouble you."

"It's not trouble." She shoves the scroll back into her pocket. "It's my new *job*. When I signed up to be your First, I knew very well it would include everything from vanquishing your enemies to managing your schedule. Besides, you hate parties. You certainly shouldn't be planning months' worth."

Fuck. Months' worth of parties. Lora shudders and takes another drag from the pipe. Careful. She needs to moderate herself, lest she be overly intoxicated by the time the smoke kicks in.

"I can ask Xylie to help with logistics. She has a great mind for it." Bronwen plucks a fruit tart into her mouth and inspects it before nibbling the crust.

"Very well," Lora relents, selecting a sprig of grapes. "But speaking of Xylie, I would like us to return to Wyntra at the beginning of summer, so Xylie can do her Final Testing."

"Do you think she still wants to do that, now that she's your Second?"

"She's dreamed of going to Splendor for alchemy, just like her father before her, since she was a little girl. She might need to put it off for a year until after the Tour, but we'll work together to ensure her dream comes true." Lora is determined that none of her Five will sacrifice every aspect of their lives for her. She wants Xylie to go to Splendor, Peregrin to prioritize their family, and Ayc to bake his wedding cakes if that's what he still would like to do. They won't abandon their happiness for her.

"She's certainly talented. Further training will only benefit all of Everadyn." Bronwen picks up another fruit tart and gnaws on it thoughtfully. "You should have one of these. They're not as good as Ayc's, though. Do you remember when your grandmother used to send us boxes of his sweets after those festivals? We used to devour them all in one night."

Lora certainly remembers how expensive the shipping fees she paid were. It was worth it. No other baker has ever compared to Ayc.

Bronwen giggles. Perhaps Reselda's plant is already getting to her. "Remember when I asked you why you hadn't married him because if the baker looked half as good as he baked, *I'd* marry him tomorrow? And as it turns out, he looks, well..." She twirls her wrist.

"Every bit as delicious?" Lora supplies, adding a roll of her eyes.

Bronwen's grin grows wolfish. "I was going to say he's *tolerable*. But thank you for your candor. It's good to know how you actually feel for once."

Lora's mouth falls open. A protest forms at the back of her throat.

Bronwen cuts her off. "Do you remember what your answer was? To why you hadn't married him?"

Lora does, in fact, remember, but she really wishes she didn't. "I'm afraid I smoked far too much of Reselda's plant at the time to remember."

"You said you wouldn't marry him because, unfortunately, he's human. And you feared the heartbreak of watching him die of old age while you stayed young. It was a terribly vulnerable moment. I think you regretted it immediately."

The silence that falls between them feels heavy and thick and sticky, like being dropped into a vat of molasses. Lora's jaw tightens so much she can feel it in her head, intensifying the pain there. She senses where this is going, and she doesn't like it.

"What's your point, Bronwen?" Lora demands.

Bronwen puts her feet on the ground and reaches across to snag the pipe from Lora's hand. "No point. I just think it's ironic. Considering Ayc is, in fact, fae. He will live for centuries." She shrugs and puts the pipe between her teeth.

A hand wraps around Lora's throat. Her mother's warnings still linger in the air. She can't even consider it. Whatever feelings she has for Ayc, it doesn't matter. Her duty must be to Everadyn now. She can't afford a single weakness.

I don't love him.

I can't. I can't. I can't.

Lora's mind grinds out the words like a boot digging into a wound.

"Would you like me to finish that letter to Dedryk?" Bronwen nods her chin at the paper before Lora. "You only have one sentence, so it doesn't seem to be going very smoothly for you, and I…" Her voice trembles, breaks, and Lora's heart plummets with it. "I knew Ryker better than you."

Lora closes her eyes, not wanting to read the utter heartbreak written clearly in Bronwen's eyes. "Fuck, you already know."

"Wylder told me."

Lora forces herself to open her eyes. Bronwen is once again poised, controlled.

"I should have told you sooner," Lora says.

Bronwen shrugs. "Like I said, it's been a long few days."

It isn't a good enough reason, but Lora asks instead, "Are you well?"

"Of course." Bronwen offers a wide smile, flashing teeth, but the light in her eyes is dim. "Why wouldn't I be?"

"Because Ryker was…" Lora stops because she doesn't know exactly what Ryker was to Bronwen. They weren't together, and they weren't *not* together. They found their way into each other's beds nearly as often as Lora found herself in Wylder's bed. Except it was different with them. It wasn't an expectation. It was real.

Whatever was between them was akin to the first warm day of spring. It was possibility and hope and a promise of beautiful things to come. Anyone who spent more than a few moments with them noticed it. And yet, Bronwen denied it. Whenever anyone asked, she always said the same thing. *We're friends. Nothing more.*

"Well, he was—"

Bronwen holds up a hand. "Let's make an agreement. I won't ask you about Ayc again if you don't ask me about Ryker."

"That's different," Lora protests.

"It's not, and you know it."

Before Lora can argue further, Bronwen stands and hands the pipe back. "Please eat, Lora, and try to get some sleep. It's late. There's nothing on your list that can't be dealt with tomorrow. My protective spell will last after I'm gone, but if you would prefer, you can walk with me back to your room."

"I'll stay here for a while longer."

Lora lets her best friend leave. She doesn't protest, even though she knows she should. She takes a few more breaths of smoke from the pipe until the haziness sets in, the ache in her head fading behind it.

In the stillness, she swears she hears the sound of a knife cutting through air and thudding into wood. Hears her mother hissing, "Checkmate."

She sways as she rises onto her feet, and she presses her palms into the desk to steady herself. She doesn't have a plan for where she's going, only that she wants out. Right now. She pauses only long enough to put on her belt, which she hung on the back of the chairs. The familiar weight of her twin blades is comforting. Her hands hover briefly over where her crown lies on the stack of books, but in the end, she leaves it there, safe behind Bronwen's spell, when she slams the door behind her.

Fortunately, Irving isn't standing in the hallway. He'll be furious when he finds Lora gone, but she just needs ten minutes of someone not looking at her. She didn't suddenly become incapable because she's the Sovereign now. She can protect herself... even if the room is a little blurry.

It's quiet in the castle now. No more music comes from the direction of the great hall, and the torches have all been lit. The flames elongate and swirl like ribbons crawling up the stone, but no, that's probably just the leaves playing with her vision. Everything feels dreamlike. The tension in her shoulders has faded. Her stomach rumbles, this time not with nausea. She imagines the tray of food now abandoned on her desk in the office. She's not about to go back. Her feet, almost on their own, have set a course toward the main kitchen. But to reach it, she passes the familiar door to another kitchen, and it snags her attention.

Her feet, almost of their own accord, stop. She hesitates before the door, remembering how she snuck in just last night. A shiver caresses down her spine as she remembers. The sweetness of the hot chocolate. The way Ayc's thumb grazed over her lips and his eyes burned into hers.

Maybe we both dreamed it.

She lied to him for a reason. She needs to keep walking. But her foolish, rebellious feet take a step toward the door.

Everything logical within her drums: *I can't. I can't. I can't.*

But something argues back. *I want, I want, I want.*

She reaches for the door handle.

"Lora!"

She knows Ayc's voice instantly, like it's another caress down her spine. She turns to see him trotting down the hallway from the direction of the kitchen. A metal pail sways in his hand, its contents covered by a cloth.

Fantastic. He's just caught her standing at his door like some kind of assassin. She moves down the hallway to intercept him. He's traded his shirt and vest for a plain, white linen shirt. Reddish splotches of cinnamon sprinkle across the cuff, and deep brown from chocolate marks the edge of the collar that dips down his neck. She follows that line, catching just a peek of his collarbone. Why is that hard line so deeply attractive? Why does it make her mouth ache to bite?

"It's late," he says, as he stops before her a few yards from his door. "What are you doing here?"

He wears a promise of a smile upon his lips, but he's rocking his weight onto his heels like he's nervous. But this is just Ayc. He's never still.

"I was hungry," Lora says.

"Unfortunately, my ice box is just as empty as it was last night."

"I know. I was on my way to the other kitchen when I got sidetracked."

He searches around them, and his smile wanes. "Where's your guard?"

"He's beneath his cloak," she lies. "Invisible."

Ayc arcs an eyebrow. "Is that right?" He raises his voice. "Irving!"

Lora slaps her hand over his lips. "Shut up! You'll wake...um..."

Her brain is soft and fuzzy, like unspun wool, and she can't remember what she was saying, not with Ayc's warm lips brushing against her palm.

Ayc gently grasps her wrist and pulls her hand down. "Wake who? There's no one in this hallway except me."

"I—" she starts, but absolutely nothing follows because the only thing in her head is the delicate piece of her skin where Ayc's thumb rests. "Um..."

"Are you all right? You're being... peculiar."

"I'm not." She pulls away from him and plants her hands on her hips. "*You're* peculiar."

"Undoubtedly." He shakes his head, bemused. "But that's scarcely a surprise. You, on the other hand—"

He cuts off as the door to his kitchen squeaks behind her. Lora stiffens. If Ayc is here, who's in his room? The spun-wool feeling in Lora's head blows away with the suddenness of a typhoon. Who followed Ayc back from her coronation party? The question makes her insides feel like war. She can't name the emotion, but it's violent and wretched.

Ayc stares over Lora's shoulder and shakes his head. The door creaks again, and his eyes fling so wide, the whites of them shine in the dim light. She begins to turn.

"Lora, wait!"

He drops the bucket, seizes her arm, and whips her around. It catches her off-guard, and she stumbles and lands against Ayc's chest. His arms come around her, but he's still staring over her shoulder like he doesn't realize what he's done, the way he's erased the distance between them. But she does. She's far too aware of him, and only him. Her senses saturate with the feeling of her hands on his firm chest. She remembers acutely how he felt beneath her hand when she kissed him in the hospital bed, soft and hard and alive. And just the memory is enough to make her hands ache, make her long to drag the clothes from his body, from her body. She knows that as good as his flesh felt against her fingertips, it'll feel even better pressed against her bare breasts, her thighs, every secret part of her.

Fuck, what is she thinking? What is she even doing?

She shouldn't be trusted to walk around after she's smoked. She certainly shouldn't be allowed near Ayc. She should be very, very far away from him.

But when he finally looks down upon her, she's doomed. Utterly transfixed on how the blue of his eyes seems far too bright in the dimness of this hallway, and she knows, if she lets herself, she'll lose herself in them. And she knows she *can't.*

I can't. I can't. I can't.

But she doesn't move.

The longing pools deep in her stomach until she aches. Until it tints her vision with silver.

"Ayc? she barely manages. "What are you doing?"

AYC

Ayc isn't sure how he got here, with Lora in his arms, but he's certain it's Xylie's fault. After all, she's the one who opened the kitchen door and peeked out in the hallway, likely drawn by their voices. He tried to shake his head, to get her to go back inside, but before she could shut the door, a streak of white burst between her feet.

So, now, there, directly behind Lora, is a baby dragon.

When Lora nearly turned, Ayc reacted without thinking. He grabbed her. So here he is, with Lora in his arms and a baby dragon in the hallway, watching him with their glowing red eyes. There's a strong chance Lora's about to eviscerate him for daring to touch her, but he needs to keep her attention on him, or she's going to turn and see Muffin.

He glances down to ensure she's looking only at him. The sight of her lands a punch squarely in his stomach. He's never going to get used to the impact of her. Never. It's a force nearly intolerable that he pierces into the very depths of his soul. Especially in that tunic.

Its soft, silver fabric flows off the abundant flesh of her curves, pulling taut on her chest and belly. It stops at her thighs, and after that, it's only bare, golden brown skin and honed muscles. Every inch of her thick, powerful body is on display, adorned in silver. And for fuck's sake, she can't go around looking like this. It will be the end of him.

With her hands on his sternum, she surely feels how his heart pounds in a rhythm that only she can create. But her eyes give nothing away as they meet his own. Her pupils are a rich, earthy brown that is perhaps Ayc's favorite of her eye colors, reminding him of the glorious Forest of Elodie she calls her home. But at the very edge, a ring of blue, just like a cloudless sky, forms.

And then it turns to silver.

He almost steps back, driven by an innate survival instinct that recognizes the threat, but he stills. She doesn't look angry. Her breath comes unsteadily past her lips as she presses her hands more firmly against his chest. He's seen her angry many times, and this is not anger.

This is *desire*.

"Ayc..." she says.

The way she says his name, breathless and airy, does something to him. It's like nails scraping down his spine. Every muscle in his body responds, growing taut, burning hotter.

"What are you doing?"

That's the question, isn't it? What is Ayc doing? He hasn't a fucking clue. He doesn't know what he's doing, and more importantly, he doesn't know what she is doing. She lied to him. She kissed him and then told him it never happened. So he slammed shut the possibility that she would ever feel the same. But here she is, not pulling away, with silver in her eyes.

His brain chases itself in a circle, even as he tries to keep his head on his shoulders. Xylie has crept carefully out the door and reached Muffin, where they sit in the middle of the hallway. She hesitates with her arms outstretched.

Please, Muffin, Ayc begs. *Go quietly.*

The dragon cocks their head just as Xylie seizes them. She clamps one arm around their body and the other around their snout. Still, they flap their wings in protest.

Lora twists toward the sound, and Ayc panics. He grasps her chin and pulls it back toward him. She gasps, and he expects her to stab him this time. But the silver in her eyes spreads. She shuts her eyes against it. And he's certain now. She wouldn't try to hide her anger.

She wants him.

Perhaps she doesn't *want* to want him. But she does. And fuck, he knows exactly how that feels.

It gives him hope.

It's just a glimmer, like the last dying star in a fractured night sky, but it's glorious.

"What are you doing?" she asks again, sounding almost pained. Her fingers curl against his shirt. He's not sure if she's pushing away or clinging to him.

Muffin's wings flap again, and Ayc hides the sound with his voice, blurting the first words he can think of. "I'm doing what I love best."

"And what's that?" She still doesn't open her eyes, her eyelashes fanning over her round cheeks. Still hiding.

When he says the next words, he stoops his head and angles his mouth toward her ear. To hide the sound of the door closing with Xylie and Muffin safely behind it. And to bring himself just a little closer to her.

"Getting under your skin."

She shivers but shakes her head. "Nothing gets under my skin." But her hands slip up his chest and then down again. The friction of the stiff cloth against his skin launches a bolt of pleasure through his abdomen, pleasure that only lurches to new heights as she fists her hands in his collar.

"Are you certain about that?" he asks.

She's still tilting her face toward his so that their noses touch. So that he can feel her every breath on his lips. And he remembers exactly what they tasted like. Kissing her was a glorious contradiction. Paradise and torment. Mercy and wickedness. And he wants it again—more than he wants to draw his next breath.

"I think you're lying," Ayc presses, pushing his luck. "I think I'm under your skin."

Her fists, still in his shirt, tighten. She inhales slowly, and he revels in her every breath. Whatever she'll do to him, he'll let it happen. He is powerless against her, and he doesn't mind. He is a wretched fool, but he knows he would gladly worship at her feet if she wanted him to. He would do unspeakable things for her if she only asked.

Then she growls. "Never."

She releases him with a shove. He stumbles to catch his balance as she storms away. He's left reeling with a strange mixture of disappointment and delight. Is this to be a new game between them, with her coming close only to leave him wanting? So be it. He loves a good game…at least when he's playing against her.

"Ah, pity," he calls. "Maybe next time."

She turns around and blinks, looking slightly dazed. Then she whirls on her heel to march in the direction she came. "Good night, Ayc."

"The kitchen is the other way!"

She doesn't pause. "I'm no longer hungry."

She's almost disappeared into the shadows when Ayc recalls that there's no guard with her.

"Wait!" He trots down the hallway even though it jostles his back, reminding him of the pain he'd almost forgotten. "Let me walk with you."

"Really not necessary," she says.

"There you are!" Irving calls as he marches down the hallway from behind Ayc and Lora. "I thought you were going to stay in the office."

Lora scowls and continues walking.

Irving gives Ayc one of his dimpled smiles before he trails behind Lora.

"You should rest," Lora scolds, her voice floating around the corner. "You can't be awake all night."

"I made arrangements with another guard," Irving replies. "She'll come relieve me in an hour."

"So you're just going to wait outside my door as I sleep?"

"Yes."

When their footsteps fade, Ayc smiles and grabs the pail that he carried from the kitchen from where he dropped it. It's filled with yet another raw chicken for Muffin. He hurries inside before Xylie can come looking for him again.

Xylie stands in the center of the kitchen, in the middle of a puddle of flour. White streaks down the black skin on her arms. Odd. When Ayc left for the kitchen, they'd managed to clean the flour off the floor and themselves. Muffin must have attempted to fly again.

"Do you think Lora saw them?" Xylie asks.

"No." Ayc surveys the kitchen. Other than the flour, it doesn't look in utter ruins like he feared it might. The only harm is a pile of strewn cloth on the floor.

"What happened to my oven mitt?" Ayc asks.

"I think they thought it was prey because they sort of pounced on it."

"And where's Muffin now?"

"We're not calling them—" She cuts off and spins in a full circle. The dragon is nowhere in sight. She stoops to glance under the kitchen counter and the oven.

A crash sounds from the direction of Ayc's bedroom, where the door is very much open.

"*Shit*! Sorry!" Xylie yells as she darts for the bedroom.

Ayc sighs and follows her. It's going to be a long night.

LORA

Lora awakes in her bed to find her headache gone, but the red, hot shame of last night lingering. The memory of her interaction with Ayc slaps her across the face the moment she opens her eyes.

"Fuck," she growls, planting her palms over her face. She was so close to losing control once again. She grasped a hold of commonsense just in the knick of time, before she shoved him against the wall and devoured him the way she craves.

She has to get it together. She can't afford to slip. She *must* keep him at a distance and deny herself this. Whatever *this* is that's between them. Attraction. Desire. Need.

More.

No, it can't be. She can't allow it to be.

Her duty as Sovereign must come first.

She takes a deep breath and then drops her hands from her face. A thin line of light peeks through her window shutters. She told her Five that their first meeting would be at dawn. She's going to be late to her own meeting. She should get up, get dressed, put on the crown she retrieved from the office before retiring last night. But the bed feels too comfortable, and there's a weariness in her bones that sleep can't touch.

Five more minutes.

She curls onto her side, pulling her thick feather quilt up to her chin. A sprig of flowers lies on the empty pillow beside her. The deep violet of petals is a glorious hue, outmatched only by its leaves, which are such a dark green, they are nearly black. She picks it up carefully, pinching the delicate stem in her fingers, and brings it closer to her face.

How did it get here? She certainly didn't put the flowers there.

Which means that someone else did.

She bolts upright.

Fuck.

She rips the dagger out from under her pillow and springs from the bed. She turns a slow circle, eying every shadow of her dim room, not knowing who could be hiding within. She dives toward the lamp on the bedside table and flicks it on. Its glow vanishes most of the shadows, but Lora doesn't trust the ones that remain. She refuses to turn her back to them as she retreats toward the door. Her heart slams against her sternum, but she reminds herself that Irving is on the other side of the door. He'll be here if she so much as screams.

The doorknob digs into her back. She throws open the door, leaps from the room, and collides with the guard on the other side of her door.

"My lady?" It's not Irving who looks down on Lora, whose hands steady her, but a tall, femme-appearing fae with slitted pupils and a shimmering of green, iridescent scales working up one side of her neck and face, contrasting with her otherwise white skin. There's mermaid somewhere in her lineage.

Shae.

Of all of Yris's royal guards, Shae ranks among the few who Lora knows and trusts. She was frequently assigned to watch Lora when she was younger. Shae used to trail after Lora as she ventured through Wyntra's streets and never reported anything negative to Yris's ears. She's a protector, not a spy.

"Someone was in my room." Lora holds up the flower. "They left this on my pillow."

Shae draws her sword and charges into the room. Lora follows behind her, adjusting her hold on her dagger.

"Stay there," Shae demands, even as she kicks open the door to Lora's closet. She tosses back Lora's quilt and stoops to peer under the bed. She turns on more lights as she goes until every corner is illuminated.

Lora does stay, but only because it's clear that whoever came is no longer here. What would be the point of lingering? If the person who put the flower on her pillow wanted her dead, she'd be dead. How long did they stand over her while she slept, far deeper than usual, thanks to the leaves she smoked?

She shivers.

"How did they get in?" Lora asks.

"Perhaps through the window." Shae throws open the shutters. Light bursts in as Shae leans out and peers down. This side of Wyntra castle is built on the western-most side of the city, and a sheer cliff is the only thing outside of Lora's window on the third floor. A near-impossible feat unless the intruder is a sorcerer.

Shae straightens. "Unless...they came through the door."

"You or Irving would have stopped them."

Shae lets her sword dangle loosely in her hands, glaring hard at the door before she finally speaks. "I didn't see Irving when I came to the door last night."

Lora's heart bobs—like it's a ship threatening to sink. "What do you mean? He was there when I went to sleep."

"He wasn't there when I arrived."

"Irving would *never* abandon his post!"

"No, he didn't. I called him on the agate." She points to the stone in her slanted ear. "He said he heard something and went to investigate, but it turned out to be nothing. He said to check on you and stay at my location. I checked on you, and I did. You were asleep, and no one was here. I told him, and he said good night. It's not like him to not follow protocol, which would be to switch off duty at the location of the Sovereign, but I assumed he was simply tired."

"Call out on the agate," Lora demands. "See if any of the other guards have seen him."

Shae does. She listens closely. Shadows fall over her eyes until the color, normally that of seaglass, turns into a stormy sea. Lora sees reflected there the same fear that is creeping inside of her like a cold, desolate fog.

"No one has seen him," Shae says. Then she swears.

Irving would never have failed to meet protocol, certainly not now, as the new captain of Lora's guard. Shae heard his voice, but mimicking is one of the simplest types of magic. Even those with weak affinity can manage it. Whoever Shae spoke with last night, it wasn't Irving.

Which can only mean that, when the intruder left Lora the flower, they took Irving with them.

Not caring whether or not Shae follows, Lora turns and runs.

SEVEN

AYC

"What time is it?" mumbles a sleepy voice.

The bed rustles beside Ayc, dragging him reluctantly from sleep. He groans but refuses to open his eyes. Surely, he only just shut them a few minutes ago. Surely, it can't be morning already. His back aches, like his muscles have coiled into a tight vice. He tries to shift, to find relief, but a heavy weight presses down on his chest.

The bed rustles again, slowly, and then quakes as someone vaults out of it. "Shit," Xylie curses. "Ayc, wake up! We're late!"

Ayc pries his eyes open. A dragon's head looms before him. He shrieks before remembering it's just the white baby dragon, who, after a night of chaos, passed out of Ayc's chest like an overly clingy house cat. Muffin looks calm, content, and not like the living embodiment of terror and destruction they truly are.

Last night is a blur of *"Don't do that!"*, *"Would you just stop?"* and *"Oh fuck, that was my favorite ring they just swallowed. Do you think they'll be able to digest it? Nevermind, they just puked it up. Can you get a towel?"*.

Eventually, Ayc and Xylie slumped on the bed as Muffin

chewed on a corner of the wardrobe, both too tired to scold them anymore.

That was in the wee hours of the morning. Now, only the faintest light seeps through the window. Xylie whirls toward him. "We have to go."

"Go where?" Ayc asks, keeping his voice soft.

"Lora said she wanted to meet us in the Sovereign's Garden at dawn."

That's right. The first meeting of Lora and her Five. "Fuck, I was supposed to make breakfast," Ayc says, remembering the promise he made before Lahlis arrived.

"No time for that now." Xylie smooths her hands over her shirt, rumpled from sleep. The coat she wears over it still has some smudges of flour despite their best efforts to shake it off.

"What are we going to do with the dragon?" Ayc asks.

"We have to leave them here. We don't really have a choice."

Ayc doesn't like the sound of it. He's likely to come home to his bed turned into nothing but feathers, but Xylie is right. They don't exactly have a better option.

Ayc tries to slide his body toward the edge of the bed, but Muffin has him completely pinned. "A little help here."

Xylie slips her hands beneath Muffin, lifts them enough that Ayc can roll free, and then lowers them back on the bed. Ayc holds his breath as he creeps away, fighting against the stiffness in his back. Muffin remains asleep.

Thank fuck.

Ayc pats himself over, ensuring his tan shirt and pants bear no claw marks, that his earrings are still in his ear, and that his bracelets remain on his wrist. There's no time to shave the stubble on his face, but he grabs a ribbon from a drawer of his wardrobe to tie back his hair. He wishes he could make himself look more presentable to show Lora that he's taking his new position as her Fifth seriously, but this is the best he can do in the time they have.

He glances at the dragon once more. Their nostrils flare with their deep breaths. "Please be good, Muffin," he pleads.

"We are *not* calling the dragon Muffin," Xylie says again, adding an irritable growl at the end.

"Do you have another suggestion?"

She opens her mouth, but only an indignant "Uh" comes out.

"See, you don't."

"Well," she huffs. "Not at this moment, but anything is better than Muffin."

"Little Shit it is then." Ayc slides past her and marches through his kitchen. "I certainly called them that enough last night. They might already think it's their name."

She rushes after him. "I can consult a few books to find a better name."

"*You* consult a few books. Until then, *I'm* calling them Muffin."

Ayc locks the door of the kitchen. He prays to gods he doesn't believe in that he won't return to everything being scorched inside. Just because the kitchen itself has been charmed to be fire-resistant doesn't mean everything within has been. He isn't sure when dragons develop the ability to breathe fire, but he hopes it's not anytime soon.

Xylie leads him toward the Sovereign's Garden, a place he's never been despite his years in the castle. Ayc has spent little time in the western wing, only venturing there when attempting to find Xylie in her room. It's full of guest rooms and the private quarters of the Sovereign and some of her Five. And Lora's a few floors up. It's still for this hour, though Ayc suspects important guests from yesterday's coronation have stayed the night in these rooms. Their feet echo against the stone as they quicken their pace down the hall.

"We're here," Xylie says, stopping at the end of a long hallway at a door Ayc is certain he's never seen before. Deep red wood frames a stained glass portrait of a garden. The sunlight behind glows through the vibrant shades of green and red and purple. Xylie turns the crystal handle and pushes the door open.

Grass billows out before him like a lush, green carpet. Flowers grow along the edges, their closed buds offering dots of color against the gray stone of the wall behind. The castle wall curves around the garden in a half-moon, completely enclosing it. A small bubbling fountain cascades down rocks and forms a stream that weaves from one side of the garden to the other. A single mighty tree grows taller than the walls, casting its sparsely covered branches wide.

Beneath the branches sits a round metal table and six chairs. Tavish, Bronwen, and Peregrin have already found their chairs. But Lora is nowhere to be found. That's a relief. Ayc can't be considered late if the main guest has not yet arrived.

"It's about time you showed up," Peregrin grumbles.

Damn. No such luck.

"Sorry. Overslept." Ayc flops down in the chair closest to Tavish. He reaches to pet Saga, who sits at Tavish's feet. The dog sniffs Ayc's fingertips, and his ears pin backward. Ayc swiftly pulls his hands back and tucks them into his pockets. Just in case he smells like a dragon. "Luckily, Xylie dragged me out of bed."

Xylie sends him a grateful look as she sits on Ayc's other side, drawing her feet beneath her.

"Late night?" Bronwen asks. She props her elbow on her crossed legs and balances her chin on her palm. A teasing smile graces the lips she's painted a fiery red, a burst of color that offsets her gray wool dress. "You never did return to the party. Did you have a distraction that kept you away?"

Ayc forces an easy chuckle. Let her think what she likes. Better than her knowing he was wrangling a mischievous little shit of a baby dragon. "Something like that."

Bronwen's smile drops like she doesn't like that answer. Tavish frowns and tilts his head. Ayc realizes his misstep; Tavish saw him leave the party with Xylie. Tavish's lips part, and Ayc wonders if there's a way to stuff a sock in his mouth without anyone else seeing.

The door slams open, and he breathes a sigh of relief that swiftly turns to ice on his lips. Lora races across the grass in bare feet, still dressed in only the silver tunic, holding a dagger in her hand. Ayc jumps to his feet, his heart clanging hard against his sternum like a warning bell.

Something is wrong.

Bronwen, too, leaps upward and moves to intercept Lora. "Is everything all right?"

Lora shakes her head and side-steps Bronwen to continue toward the circle of chairs. Someone dressed in the silver cloak of the guards marches behind Lora. Shae, Ayc thinks the guard's name is. Lora only pauses when she stands close to Peregrin, who has also risen, leaning heavily against their cane.

"Peregrin, did Irving return home last night?"

Peregrin goes still. Unnaturally still. Even their breaths are so shallow they scarcely look like they're breathing.

Ayc's own lungs grow taut, too. *Not Irving. Please.*

"No," Peregrin says, their voice more steady than even Ayc feels. "Irving was with *you* last night."

"Fuck," Lora swears. She presses the hand that holds her dagger against her forehead.

"Lora," Peregrin snaps, "what the fuck is happening? Where is Irving?"

"I—" Lora drops her hand back to her side. Moisture shines in her eyes, but then she blinks, and her face returns to its mask of stone. "I don't know. Someone was in my room last night. They left this on my pillow."

She lifts her other hand and opens her palm, revealing the sprig of purple flowers and dark leaves.

Ayc springs forward. "Fuck, Lora. That's midnight."

He uses his sleeve to knock the flower from her hand before he grasps her wrist and tugs her toward the stream. "Wash it off. If the oil gets on your skin and you touch your mouth, it'll be enough to make you sick." He doesn't wait for her to follow his directions but pulls her down with him as he kneels beside the stream. He thrusts both their hands into the water, ignoring the icy bite.

She stares at him. "It's poisonous?"

"Deadly." Ayc scrubs his thumb over Lora's palm, wanting to

ensure not a single particle of oil remains. "A single flower is all it takes to kill."

Bronwen swears. The air grows static with her power, with her anger. Ayc's blood is water beginning to boil, turning from a simmer to a broiling rage. Someone was in Lora's room. Someone stood over her while she slept and left poison on her pillow. They were so close. They could have hurt her. Could have killed her.

That primal feeling from yesterday returns, the overwhelming need to protect. Ayc's leather bracelets grow damp in the water, rubbing against his wrists. With each passing second, they feel like they're tightening. They have never been so restrictive, and he wants to rip them off, delve deep into the icy pool of his power, and see exactly what he's capable of.

Lora clasps his hand in hers, stilling his frantic movements. With her other hand, she makes a small gesture, a sign meant to reassure. *"I'm all right."*

He searches her over, drawing in every detail of her to prove she's being honest. And then he sees it. There, tangled within her curls, is a single purple flower.

"Hold still," Ayc says.

Lora stiffens as he reaches toward her. He pulls his sleeve forward to protect his fingers as he carefully disentangles it from the curls. As he pulls it free, his vision goes red with rage.

They put a flower in her *fucking* hair.

They wanted to make the message abundantly clear.

Her life is mine. I'll take it if I want it.

"I'm going to fucking kill them," Ayc growls.

Her eyes widen. Ayc flings the petal into the stream and lets it wash away.

"How did this happen?" Peregrin demands as Lora and Ayc stand. "Irving would *never* have let someone in your room. Not unless he..."The gray in Peregrin's face darkens. "No." The word comes through their teeth like it's meant to be a roar, but it's little more than a groan.

"Tavish," Lora says, twisting toward him, "can you use your gift? Tell me where to look for him.".

Tavish rolls the pearl that rests in the hollow of his throat, the one his mother gave him as a boy, between his two fingers. "I've been trying since you said you didn't know where he was, but I'm getting nothing."

"Nothing?" Peregrin repeats. "Like he's d—" They stop, choking on the word.

"No!" Tavish blurts. "It means nothing. It's like when I tried to sense Marcellus back at the hospital. I just can't sense anything."

"Magic might be shielding him," Bronwen says. "If someone knew about Tavish's gift."

Ayc is certain most people in this castle know about Tavish's gift. Gossip travels easily, as though the walls themselves whisper it. Xylie signs something similar, but Lora is the only one to glance her way.

"Keep trying, Tavish," Bronwen says. "Magic to conceal someone from you would need to be applied nearly constantly. They might lapse if the sorcerer isn't careful."

Peregrin marches toward the door, their cane stabbing deep in the earth with every stride.

"Where are you going?" Bronwen calls.

"To get Tempest. I'll find him the old-fashioned way."

Lora, too, draws herself upright. The commands drum from her tongue. "Tavish, keep trying. Bronwen, is there some spell you can use to search for clues to whoever entered my room?"

Bronwen nods.

"Good. Then go. Take Ayc and Xylie with you."

As Xylie springs to her feet, Lora sweeps away, hurrying to catch up with Peregrin, who has almost reached the entrance of the garden. Ayc fists his hands to deny the desire to reach out and grasp ahold of her. He doesn't want to let her out of his sight. She pauses by her royal guard.

"Shae, we need to notify the other guards and the captain of Wyntra's guard. I want this castle and this city locked down. No one leaves until we find him."

"Think carefully if you want to do that, my lady," says a voice from the doorway, a voice that wraps itself around Ayc's spine and yanks. It's a thrum of pain, a spear of dread, and a burst of rage all at once.

Yris.

She stands in the now open doorway, blocking Peregrin's path. Something seems off about her. It's not her dark velvet dress or her usual severe updo. Ayc glares at her for a long moment before he realizes what has changed.

She's not wearing her crown.

Ah, yes, she has no power. Not anymore. Not over him and not over anyone else.

Peregrin levels a glare upon her. "What are you doing here?"

"I saw our new Sovereign racing through the hallways like all of Eternal Damnation had been unleashed," Yris says. "Barefoot and indecently dressed, no less. I was quite concerned."

"I mean, what are you still doing in this *castle*?"

Yris cocks her head. "Did my daughter not tell you?"

Ayc looks sharply at Lora, but she crosses her arms over her chest, careful with the blade she still holds. "I'll explain later."

Yris smiles like she's played a perfect move in a chess game. And Ayc suspects she has. "Can you not guess? I know the Sovereign and most of her Five are drastically younger than any in history, but I thought you would at least bring some knowledge and wisdom to the group. Including tradition and decorum that goes with the change of power."

"I don't have time for you, Yris," Peregrin snarls. "Get out of my way."

Yris steps into the garden and out of the doorway. Peregrin rushes past her, and the three-beat gait of their footsteps and cane picks up on the stone hallway, fading rapidly. Lora moves to follow, but Yris steps into her path.

"Someone got into your room, Loraphne," Yris says. "I'm not sure that's something you want people to have knowledge of. It might reveal vulnerability to people who might use it to their advantage."

"I'll tell the guards to be discreet," Lora says. "No one needs to know why we're closing the city down."

Yris snorts. "Foolish to think they won't find out anyway. This castle has ears and very loose tongues."

"I don't know." Ayc barely conceals his fury behind a feigned smile. "You managed to keep the truth about me a secret for a decade, *Yris*." Her name is a rebellion on his tongue, a reminder to them both that she is nothing.

Yris flaps her hand in the air like he's an insect to be swatted. "Tongues are better behaved once you've cut a few out. And as I reminded you last night, Loraphne, you don't have the stomach for it."

The icy cold anger in Ayc is rising. He's never let himself feel it before. Never had the luxury of letting himself feel it. Now, it crashes over him, wave after wave. This is the woman who slaughtered everyone he knew. This is the woman who used to lock Lora in the dungeon for misbehaving and nearly let her drown. This is the woman who's responsible for why his back still feels like it wants to break in half under his own weight.

And she won't fucking talk about Lora that way.

He fiddles with the latch on his bracelet; he is about to undo the buckle when Lora speaks. "Consider yourself fortunate because, as we also established last night, if I was going to cut out tongues, I would start with yours. Now, get out of my way."

Yris narrows her eyes. Ayc's bracelet comes free, but Yris steps to the side. Lora and her royal guard storm through the doorway.

Yris turns her cold gaze at the four who remain in the garden, her nose crinkling more. Xylie grasps Ayc's back more tightly and steps closer, like she's trying to hide behind him.

"I hope you are all prepared," she says. "If Lora's going to survive as Sovereign, you must find a way not to be so useless. That goes double true for you, niece."

Another burst of rage ricochets through him. Ayc reaches for his other bracelet, but Xylie clutches his shirt more tightly. She drags her free hand down his back, a sign normally done on the sternum, but he recognizes it all the same. *Please.*

So, Ayc forces a smile. "Fuck all the way off, Yris. And when you get there, fuck off some more."

Yris blinks at him, her face blank. Bored.

"Let's go," Bronwen says, marching forward, her hands flexing at her side. "Before I curse this bitch to shit pinecones for days."

Yris jumps back as Bronwen comes close, her energy coming off her in waves. Xylie darts after her. Ayc waits only long enough for Tavish and Saga to join him before they all leave together, abandoning Yris in the Sovereign's Garden she no longer belongs in.

Later, Ayc thinks, grinding his teeth together. Later, he can demand why Lora would let Yris stay and hopes that it's a fucking good reason. For now, finding Irving matters more.

"Anything?" Ayc asks Tavish as they follow Bronwen down the hall.

"Nothing." A bead of sweat drips down Tavish's temple. "I lied to Peregrin. I don't know why I can't get a sense of Irving's direction. It could be magic, or he could be—"

"He's not," Ayc cuts him off. He refuses to think for even a moment that Peregrin will lose a piece of themself. That Zinnia will lose the partner she's been with for several decades. Or that Ember will feel the pain of losing a parent.

That Ayc will once again lose someone he loves.

"He's alive," he says again, forcing himself to believe it.

Tavish nods. "You're right. No sense losing hope until hope has actually been lost."

"There's nothing here," Bronwen growls in frustration as she halts before the ajar door of Lora's bedroom. She's been pacing the hall before the door for several minutes, scanning the stone beneath her feet, muttering under her breath.

Ayc straightens from where he's been resting his shoulder against the wall. "Nothing?"

"No blood. No footprints to track. No strange energies I can pick up on. Absolutely nothing."

Blood.

Ayc forces himself to pretend they are talking about a stranger. He locks his emotions back behind his mental wall, with his physical pain, and lets it be little more than an insistent nag at the back of his mind. He won't be useful if he lets himself feel the fear and despair.

"That still tells us something," Xylie signs. *"If there's no blood, there wasn't a struggle."*

"Precisely," Bronwen agrees.

"But Irving would have fought back against an intruder," Ayc says.

"It could have been a skilled sorcerer. Or someone he recognized and was able to get close."

Ayc tries to think of who Irving wouldn't have been suspicious of, creeping around the new Sovereign's bedroom in the middle of the night. The list is short, and most of the people on it are with him now. "What about Yris?"

"Irving doesn't trust Yris," Xylie signs.

"Why would Yris threaten Lora? She already has enough things to hold over her head."

"What does that mean?" Ayc demands. "What does Yris have over her?"

Bronwen pauses, as though considering whether she should say more, and then exhales. "Her father."

"What about her father?"

"Only Yris knows where he went after he was exiled. Yris exchanged that information for Lora, allowing her to stay for a year."

A year? A flare rises in Ayc but then recedes. At least, Lora has a good reason to allow her to stay, but the idea of Yris remaining anywhere close to him during that time makes him want to rage. He doesn't trust her. He never will. But he also can't deny Lora a chance to find her father.

He releases a breath. "The frigid, ass-faced crow."

Xylie bumps her elbow against his arm in solidarity. Her fingers spell a much more vulgar insult, and Ayc almost smiles.

"I think that's putting it mildly," Bronwen says, nodding to

Xylie. "However horrible she might be, I don't believe Yris has reason to harm Lora."

"Unless she wanted her crown back," Ayc says, the thought flushing him with cold.

"It's not that simple. If Lora is dead, the crown goes to me, at least until another Sovereignty Trial can be held. All of us would have to be dead before the throne would revert back to the previous Sovereign." She shudders. "That's a terrible thought. Let's check in the room."

She hesitates and glances to where Tavish sits on the floor, his legs drawn up and his forehead pressed against his knees. He's been like that since he came, straining himself to use his power. Saga obediently rests at his side, occasionally nudging Tavish's hand gently.

"Are you well, Tavish?" Bronwen asks.

"Shh." The sharp hiss is his only reply.

The door to Lora's room has been left ajar. Bronwen pushes it open and steps inside. It appears just as Ayc saw it yesterday morning before the coronation. The only thing undisturbed is the bed, the blankets flung halfway to the floor. Bronwen moves about the room and repeats the muttering again. Unable to stand still, Ayc himself paces around the room. Xylie tags along at his side, and he watches her hands out of the corner of his eye.

"I don't understand. Why didn't they simply kill Lora?"

Ayc flexes his hands, open and closed, before he uses them to speak, *"Because they don't want her dead. They want her to obey. And they want her to know the consequences if she doesn't."*

He knows the game that villains play. He knows how nails sinking into the skin of his throat, leaving scars, is far more effective than slitting a throat.

Fear is a leash that few are brave enough to tug upon.

But they chose the wrong woman to play this game with. Lora won't be so easily scared. She isn't prey; she is a predator. She is wildfire and fury unbound. She cannot be tethered. She'll fight back, no matter the danger.

And he'll do anything to protect her.

Anything.

"I found something," Bronwen calls. She kneels beside the bed, reaching beneath. She draws out something made of bright blue fabric. A stream of curses rips from her mouth. "Amos."

Ayc starts toward her. The air pops around her, releasing visible blue sparks. Ayc freezes. "Are you well? Your magic."

She draws a deep breath through her nose. When she exhales, the static eases. "Yes. I'm sorry. I'm generally better controlled than this, but my emotions have been getting the better of me. Affinities are very sensitive to emotion."

She offers the fabric to Ayc. The small drawstring pouch is stitched along the edges with the sun, the yellow standing out boldly against the bright sky blue. The symbol of Lux Aester. Ayc peers inside. A few deep purple petals remain inside.

"Foolish of them to leave it," Xylie signs.

"Or *intentional*," Bronwen suggests. "Perhaps after Lora's threat yesterday, Amos wanted to strike back. He wants her to know what will happen if she follows through."

Ayc's hand fists around the bag. "So do we call the guards to arrest him?"

"Only Lora can give an order to have a regent arrested," Bronwen says. "Or a high court judge."

Saga barks in the hallway. Ayc bolts toward the sound, Xylie and Bronwen rushing after him. Tavish reaches the door first, holding tight to Saga's leash. Sweat still shines on his cheeks, making the blue tinge on his otherwise onyx skin glisten.

"I found him!" he calls, a smile breaking through his furrowed brow. "I found Irving!"

Ayc races through the courtyard and out of the castle grounds into the streets that surround the barracks. He knows this path well, but he's never run it this quickly. He ignores the screech of his thighs and his back and focuses only on getting to Irving.

As soon as Tavish told them where he sensed Irving, they all flew in different directions. Bronwen is sprinting to signal Peregrin, who's likely already searching the skies, while Xylie and Tavish are racing to find Lora. And Ayc is taking the directest route to the home that Irving, Peregrin, and Zinnia all share.

He doesn't slow as he reaches the door but flings himself upon it. It's locked, and so he hammers his fist against it. "Irving!"

The door flies open, but it's Zinnia who stands on the other side. She isn't dressed in her usual maid uniform, but in a simple floral frock she prefers on her rare days off. Her bright green eyes are wide, but her skin, usually warm and glowing, looks nearly as gray as Peregrin. "Ayc, what in the divine is happening?"

"Is Irving here?"

She steps aside. Irving sits on the couch in the heart of the first room, his head resting in his hands. But he's breathing steadily, and there are no wounds that Ayc can see. Ayc lets out a breath that comes from somewhere deep in his soul.

"He just arrived," Zinnia says. She drops her voice to a whisper, so Irving can't hear. "He's...he's not well. He said he woke up on the beach and has no idea how he got there. He's not making much sense. Ayc, I need you to explain to me what's happening."

Her hand trembles in the air, and Ayc catches and squeezes it. "I will. I promise. But I need to talk to Irving first."

She nods, and Ayc moves past her toward Irving. He steps over scattered toys of gryphons and dragons, but Ember isn't in sight. "Is Ember at school?"

"Yes."

Good. At least Ember isn't around to be frightened.

Ayc crouches down before Irving. Sand dusts his leather guard armor, an imperfection he normally wouldn't tolerate in himself.

Irving drops his hands. He blinks at Ayc, and his brow furrows. No bruises or cuts mar his face, but he looks dazed. Lost, almost.

"Are you well?" Ayc asks.

Irving glances at Zinnia. She closes the door, comes to his side, and sits beside him. She rests a hand on his knee.

"Physically, yes," he says. "I'm just uncertain what happened. The last I remember, I was guarding the Sovereign's chamber, and then I woke up on the beach."

Magic That must be it. Some kind of magic rendered him unconscious until the sorcerer left him on the beach. But why had they kept Irving hidden for so long? Why not kill him?

He shudders.

"What happened?" Zinnia asks.

"Someone got into the Sovereign's room last night," Ayc explains. "They must have taken you."

Irving springs to his feet with a curse. "Is Yris all right?"

Ayc frowns, straightening to his full height. "Yris?"

Irving reaches for his belt. His scabbard hangs empty, and his fists clasp over air twice before he glances down and realizes its absence. "Does she think I abandoned my post?"

Zinnia presses a hand over her heart. What the fuck did they do to him? Ayc wonders. Perhaps they gave him a solid blow to the head, and now he doesn't remember the last few days. Except a blow like that would have left a mark.

"I need to straighten this out." Irving steps toward the door, but Zinnia catches his hand. He tries to shake her free, but she clings on. "If Yris thinks—"

"Yris isn't Sovereign," Ayc says.

"What?" he barks. "What are you talking about? Zinnia, who even is this?"

The question embeds hooks deep into Ayc's stomach and yanks.

"My love." Zinnia's hands shake as she reaches for Irving. She frames his face between her palms. "This is Ayc."

"Ayc who?" Irving asks.

"Fuck," Ayc swears.

Ten years. That's how long Ayc has known Irving, and Irving has forgotten him. What did they do they do to him? What torture did they submit him to that Irving has forgotten ten entire years?

The door flies open, slamming against the wall where Zinnia's apron hangs. Peregrin stands in the doorway. Their knees nearly buckle when they see Irving, but they grasp the door to keep them upright. "Irving." His name is the closest thing to a sob Ayc has ever heard come for Peregrin. "Oh, thank fuck."

Zinnia, too, sags in relief, dropping her hands from Irving's face. "Peregrin, thank the divine you're here."

Peregrin surges across the room toward Irving, scarcely using their cane and half-falling in their rush. Ayc waits for it. The look he's seen come across Irving's face whenever he's seen Peregrin before, at least within these walls, where letting emotions show is safe. The illumination in Irving's eyes, the quick flash of a dimple in his cheek, the tension fading from his shoulders as his beloved is close.

But it doesn't come. Irving just blinks in confusion as he did with Ayc. For the second time, Ayc's insides are ripped apart.

Perhaps Peregrin sees it, too, feels the dread of an oncoming, wretched storm, because they freeze. "Irving?"

Zinnia's voice trembles. "Irving, please tell me you know who they are?"

"Of course. This is Peregrin. The sword instructor."

"Sword instructor?" Peregrin repeats like it's an insult.

"But what are you doing here?" Irving asks.

Peregrin stiffens. "Why wouldn't I be here?"

A single tear streaks down Zinnia's cheek. "Irving, Peregrin is our partner."

"Our partner?" Irving looks between Zinnia and Peregrin. "I'm really sorry." Something in his voice breaks, as though he realizes that he's lost something irreplaceable. "But I don't remember. I don't remember us at all."

EIGHT

LORA

Lora's heart pounds to the same rhythm as her feet as she rushes to Peregrin's home. She left Xylie and Tavish behind several streets ago. They found her in the Wyntra's guards' public office, speaking with the captain. Tavish no sooner got the words out of his mouth than Lora began running. Her lungs burn from racing across most of Wyntra, but she pushes her feet faster. Shae keeps stride with Lora. Another guard, a newer face whose name Lora can't remember, has joined them as well.

She turns the final corner and screeches to a halt. Her pounding heart leaps into her throat at the sight before her. Ayc, Bronwen, and Peregrin all sit on the front stoop of the house. Tempest curls beside them in the small garden, apparently not minding that they are crushing the first buds of Zinnia's carefully planted blooms. Tempest's mighty head rests in Peregrin's lap, too large to fully fit. Her rider absently strokes their hand down their neck, even as they stare blankly ahead. The grimness in their faces sucks all the air from Lora's lungs.

Lora's next step crunches on the grave leading to the house. Ayc and Bronwen look up, but Peregrin doesn't even flinch.

"Is he…" She can't bring herself to say it.

"No." Ayc springs to his feet and rushes toward her. "No, he's alive…"

There's a heaviness at the end of the sentence, a 'but' he can't quite bring himself to say.

"I want to see him." Lora steps toward the door.

"Wait." Ayc's hand glides down her arm before he drops his hand. Goosebumps are left in his wake. "Just…wait."

"Why?" Lora demands. "What aren't you saying?"

"He doesn't remember you," Peregrin says, their voice flat and lifeless.

"What do you mean?"

"They did something to him." Ayc's voice holds a gentleness that feels like a disinfecting ointment. It helps in the long term, but in the moment, it fucking stings. "Altered his memories. He doesn't remember you. He doesn't remember Yris ever had a daughter."

Every muscle in her body stiffens. Her fingers flex toward where her dagger is tucked into the belt Wyntra's captain gave her. Fight or flight. That's the body's response to a threat, and she has always been more fight. But now, there's no clear enemy, no neck to break to make herself feel safer.

Ayc glares down at his feet, his hair falling forward to hide his face from view. "He doesn't remember me either. Or Peregrin. Well, he remembers who Peregrin is, but not who they are to him."

"What?" she says. It's all she can manage.

"He doesn't remember their relationship at all."

Behind her, Shae sharply inhales.

Peregrin doesn't move. They are a ghost. Here but not here. Dead but alive. And how can Lora blame them? If Irving's memories are truly gone, all they were to one another is also gone. To lose someone you love is one thing. To lose them while they are yet alive is another agony altogether.

What if one day, she looked at Ayc, and he did not know her?

It's not the same, she tells herself, shaking her head.

"How is that possible?" Lora asks.

"I don't know," Ayc admits. "The aerial army's head healer is with him now."

Lora stands in silence. How is she supposed to respond to this? What is she supposed to say? Her life often feels like theatre, but she has no script for this.

"It doesn't make any sense." Peregrin scrubs a hand over their face, and a fraction of life reappears in their eyes. It's a flicker of fire, a spark of rage, but at least it's something. "He doesn't remember our relationships, but he remembers this house is his home. This house that was given to me when I was forced to retire. The house he and Zinnia moved into with *me*."

Tempest raises her head and nudges against their shoulder. Peregrin closes their eyes and takes several calming breaths, the way they taught all their students. In through the nose, out through the mouth. Lora has never seen them so close to losing control.

Lora looks to Ayc. He's better at this. Kinder than her. Sweeter than her. Surely, he knows what to do. But Ayc only stares at Peregrin, looking every bit as lost and as heartbroken as Lora feels. Her fingers twitch with the desire to reach out to take his hand. She thinks of how he washed her hand earlier and how, when her hand was in his, the shaky world felt a little more steady. She knows if she takes his hand now, she'll feel that again, but she can't allow herself the luxury.

When Peregrin speaks again, their voice is level once more. "At least Irving seems to remember Ember. Small mercies, I suppose."

"It's magic," Bronwen says. "It's the only thing that makes any sense. It's like certain memories were carefully selected and plucked from him. But magic like that…" She shivers and drags her hands up and down her arms. "To alter someone's head like that. That is one of the darkest forms of magic. To delve into such things can mar your soul."

"Can it be undone?" Lora asks. It feels like the most pressing question.

Peregrin stiffens and tilts their head, waiting for the answer.

Bronwen gnaws on her bottom lip before responding. "Maybe. If we found the person who took the memories, they could restore them. I would have to do more research, send inquiries to more knowledgeable sorcerers, but it's possible."

Lora knows her friend well enough to understand what has been left unsaid. Possible. Not likely. But so long as there's a fraction of hope that they can restore what was taken from Irving and Peregrin, Lora will fight for that hope.

"And who would be willing to do such a thing?" Ayc asks. "If it's so dark,"

"There are sorcerers very willing to mar their souls for the right price," Bronwen says.

"The question is who hired them?" Lora says. "And why?"

Bronwen stands and reaches into her pocket to withdraw a bright blue fabric. She hands it to Lora. "Perhaps you should ask Amos. We found this under your bed."

Lora drags a thumb over one of the embroidered suns. Silver flashes through her eyes, and as it fades, clarity and focus set in. She latches on to the direction her rage has given her. She may not be good at comforting her friend, but she knows how to respond to *this*.

Whoever threatened her meant to scare her, to cow her into submission, but they have only harmed her friend, tried her patience, and awoken her fury. She was born the Sovereign's daughter and raised as an Adamant warrior. She was made and crafted to be a nightmare to her enemies.

"Where are the regents now?" Lora asks, shifting her gaze toward her guards. They are the royal guards; they are supposed to be kept informed of the movements of any guests within the castle. "Were they departing this morning?"

"Probably at breakfast now," Shae replies. "I believe they are departing later this afternoon."

"Good. Let's pay them a visit, shall we?"

Peregrin picks up their cane and uses it to climb to their feet.

"You don't have to come," Lora says quickly. "You can stay with Irving."

"Why?" they snap. "I can't do a fucking thing here. I'm coming, whether you like it or not."

"Very well," Lora relents.

Footsteps sound behind her. Xylie and Tavish step onto Peregrin's streets, questions written on their furrowed brows. She'll have to explain in a minute because Peregrin speaks: "I suggest we tread carefully." They nod at the bag in her hand. "That evidence could mean nothing. Anyone who saw your interaction with Amos yesterday might have left it to mislead you. Or it could be exactly as it looks. Either way, it's likely someone who knows us. This was…deeply personal."

Lora has thought the same. The sorcerer could have killed Irving; it would have been simpler. But they must want Lora to understand how powerful they are. More importantly, they want her to know they won't just come for her. They will come for all of her Five and the people they love. Who knows who they might come for next?

Rage burns through her blood. Her canines grow sharp against her bottom lip.

"If we can't trust any of them," Lora says, "then we'll send the message to *all* the regents. They need to know they failed to intimidate me and be reminded of who I am. Who *we* are."

"And who are we?" Ayc asks.

"We're in *fucking* charge."

AYC

A quarter of an hour is all Ayc has to prepare himself to look like one of the six most powerful people in all of Everadyn before meeting Lora and the rest of the Five back at the great hall. A page was sent to tell the regents to remain at breakfast because their Sovereign wants to meet with them.

A quarter of an hour isn't nearly long enough when there's a baby dragon who's been left alone for far too long.

Ayc unlocks the door to his kitchen. He holds his breath as he steps inside, but his kitchen looks just as he left it. A soft snore echoes from his bedroom, and he finds Muffin still sleeping on Ayc's bed, just as he left him.

Well, not just...

Ayc frowns and cocks his head. Is the dragon bigger? They seem to take up far more of the bed than they did this morning, like somehow, they've jumped from the size of a house cat to that of a medium dog in the space of a few hours. Surely, that isn't possible. Perhaps it's just exhaustion messing with Ayc's vision. Either way, he doesn't have time to sort it out now.

Ayc pulls on the leather armor he left discarded in the corner after the Trials and fastens his belt with the sword around his hips. He places his golden rings—trinkets he accepted for payment of his desserts at festivals—on his fingers and lines his eyes with black. Each thing he does is armor in its own way, transforming him from the silly, young baker to what he needs to be.

The Sovereign's Fifth.

He starts for the door before hesitating. He stares at his bracelets for a long moment before he takes them off and slips them into his pocket. He closes his eyes and focuses within himself. His power hisses like ice exposed to the sun, rising through his veins. He flings his eyes open. The desire to put the bracelets back on is almost overwhelming, but he forces himself to march from his room. He swallows down a pain tonic before exiting and relocking the kitchen.

He finds his way back to the main entrance of the great hall. All but Lora are waiting.

Bronwen has put on her Adamant armor beneath her sorcerer cloak and braided her hair back, her colorful staff in her hand.

Peregrin wears their gray flight armor and a stony expression. Both Tavish and Xylie have put their leather armor back on, but Tavish still wears his pearl necklace, and Xylie wears her ear cuffs and her multi-colored coat. They all look themselves, and yet, they are ready to show that they are so much more.

Boots sound on stone. Lora marches down the hall toward them like she's the goddess of death and life once more. Gone is the silver nightgown that tormented Ayc, but this is no easier to bear, even though it's how he's seen her so many times. Her Adamant armor gleams darkly in the light, and the cape bearing the Totus Omni tree snaps behind her. She keeps her chin lifted, as she always has, but the crown she wears is not imagined now. Its onyx gems, shaped like leaves, seem to absorb all light and reflect it back like stars blinking in the night sky. The broken leviathan tooth swings around her neck, a reminder of who she is and what she is capable of.

She looks fearsome. And glorious.

As always.

Ayc can no longer see the royal guards, but a slight shimmer in the air, unnoticeable if he didn't know to look for it, tells Ayc that they're still there. They hide under their invisibility cloaks to give the illusion that Lora needs no protection other than her own power.

Lora pauses before her Five. "Are you ready?"

"What's the plan?" Peregrin asks.

"Just keep your heads high and follow my lead."

I'd follow you into Eternal damnation, Ayc thinks, but it's too much, too heavy, too laden with the rebellious emotions clogging up his chest. So instead, he creaks out a smile, trying to ease the grim air around them.

"That's it? Fuck around and hope for the best?"

Lora shoots him a glare. He throws up his hands.

"No, no, on the contrary. I love it. It's a brilliant plan. That always works exceptionally well for me."

"Any further objections?" Lora asks, even as she arches a brow at Ayc that clearly spells out, 'Don't you fucking try.'

"No," Bronwen says. "We're ready."

Tavish nods and wraps his hand around Saga's Kindred leash. Xylie fiddles with her ear cuffs before signing her assent. Her hands flutter, and she stuffs them into her pockets, so Ayc puts himself beside her.

"Stay by my side," he signs. *"I've got you."*

She gives him what he thinks is meant to be an appreciative smile but is only a grimace. This is hard for her, more so than it is for any of them, and yet, he's so proud of her for facing her fears. He's going to have to tell her one day just how much he admires her courage.

Lora squares up with the double door, and her Five line up behind her. Ayc watches as she draws in a breath slowly, and then, on the exhale, she flings the doors open. The hinges whine, loud as a cannon's boom. The seven regents drop their conversation and twist to look. They're still gathered around three separate tables scattered with the remnants of breakfast.

Lora takes the room by storm. She grants no one a single glance as she and her Five march past the regents. When she reaches her throne, she pivots to face the hall. Her Five gather around her throne.

Ayc watches Lora just as the regents do, utterly transfixed. Power and authority radiate from her, the same way Bronwen's magic hovers around her. Static. Tangible. A bit terrifying.

"Did you have a good breakfast?" she asks with a twitch of her lips that almost looks wicked.

A few of the regents glance at one another. Amos sinks deeper into his chair, like the fucking worm he is. Only Busara, the regent of Lycendi, nods.

"Good."

Lora moves so swiftly, Ayc almost misses it. She tosses something in her hand upward, then seizes the dagger at her belt and launches it. The regents duck as it soars above their heads and embeds itself in the pillar right behind them. Pinned by the blade is what Lora tossed: the bright blue sack that once contained midnight.

Only then does Lora sit upon her throne and, oh so calmly, cross her legs over one another. "Now that I have your attention, let's talk about which one of you was foolish enough to threaten me."

CHAPTER
NINE

LORA

Lora studies the regent's faces carefully, seeking a flinch, a bead of sweat, a bob of their throat. The sunlight pours through the stained glass windows above, offering more than enough light to illuminate every detail.

She knows their faces well. Most of them have been elected and reelected to serve as the regent for their clan for the last two or three decades. Her childhood was full of entertaining them at Wyntra or being hosted at their own homes. Before each visit, her mother would always counsel her: *"Watch their faces carefully. Memorize their every nuance, every tik. Learn to read them like those books you like so well."*

So Lora did.

Only Qadira, the amber-skinned Sal Maris regent, is a newer face to Lora, having only been elected as regent two years ago. She blinks coolly back at Lora, casually adjusting her tiered, white skirt with arms covered in jingling bracelets. Beside her, Busara appears utterly serene. Even the lines of her deep brown face, which reveal how truly ancient she is, don't deepen. The Bromalis regent, Briar, takes off the lopsided crown of lilies he's worn on his curly head of hair and lays it down on the table before him, wiping his frequent smile from his sun-tanned face.

Dedryk and Harlowe, the Audori regent, move toward her dagger, now embedded in the pillar's wood. Dedryk reaches it first and yanks it free. The blue pouch remains impaled on the blade. Both Dedryk and Harlowe glance sharply at Amos. He slides further down his chair, then catches himself and bolts upright, stacking his spine like a tower.

"Why don't you explain what has happened, Lor—my lady?" Grey catches themself and corrects. They fold their hands over the table and grant her the same expression they often wear on their face when they are listening to the concerns brought to them by one of their Totus Omni constituents, a look that expresses both empathy and the reassurance that they will, in fact, help them.

Lora explains, "It seems that someone—a powerful sorcerer most likely—was hired to come into my room and left midnight on my pillow. They also harmed my guard. And I'm prepared to take that *very* personally."

From the corner of her eye, Lora sees Peregrin's fingers spasm on their cane, even as their gaze never wavers from the regents. She swiftly snaps her gaze forward before she lets herself feel the way her heart twists.

"That bag was left in my room," Lora continues. "And I would like to find out who left it."

"It seems obvious," Briar says. "I can see the Lux Aester symbol from here. And he's the one who didn't want to bow yesterday."

"Amos is perhaps not the greatest mind among us," Qadira says with a roll of her brown eyes. "But surely, he's not foolish enough to hire someone so reckless they would leave such an obvious clue."

"I assure you," Amos spits, "I played no part in it."

"Bullshit," Bronwen mutters beneath her breath. Blue magic spins between her fingertips.

Amos narrows his eyes upon Bronwen, and Lora can read the disgust so clearly that her hand aches to reach for one of the many knives she's hidden on her body. The one in her boot would fit perfectly into his eye socket.

"Why are you so certain it's one of us?" Harlowe's hands clench, crinkling the leather gloves he always wears. They hide the burns he earned during an accident in the Audori's forges, where he used to be a renowned swordsmith. "It could be so many people."

"Like who?" Grey asks.

Dedryk throws up his hand. "The Drakr were here just yesterday aboard dragons. Perhaps we should ask them."

"I think four dragons fully expressed their point. Why waste time leaving a poisonous flower?" Briar says.

"And you would know all about poisoned flowers," Amos snaps.

Lora leans back, letting them talk, watching them carefully.

Briar doesn't growl when he's angry. He smiles. But it's a dangerous-looking thing. It belongs on a cat devouring a mouse. "I don't like what you're suggesting, Amos."

"Well, you certainly implied it was me quickly enough. And I—"

"Again, it might not be any of us or anyone within Everadyn," Dedryk leaps in again, his booming voice overpowering Amos. He always needs to feel as though he's in charge. "We need to consider outside our borders. Or within. Perhaps the dwarves sent a message."

Harlowe snorts. "The dwarves? Really? They have never wanted anything to do with anyone outside of their mountains."

Dedryk's ears turn red at the edges. It's the same color change that Lora has seen countless times in Wylder's ears whenever he's enraged. It's why he wears his hair longer, to hide the tell. In contrast, Dedryk wears his dark hair short, but his beard long and braided. It quivers as he snarls, "I'm aware. But we have to at least consider—"

"Perhaps we are asking the wrong question," Busara interjects softly, breaking up what Lora knows might quickly turn to blows between the two regents. It certainly wouldn't be the first time.

The ancient fae folds her hands over her deep blue robes, trimmed in stars. "Perhaps we should be asking not who, but why? If we understand the motivation, it might lead us to the culprit."

Lora straightens. "I think the message was clear. If you don't lead as we want, I will kill you. Would you like to hear my response?"

Seven heads slowly nod.

"Fuck you," she says through her teeth. "You can take whatever bloated foolhardiness made you think I would ever be so easily cowed, and you can shove it up your ass."

A soft cough sounds to Lora's right. She tilts her head to where Ayc stands just behind her throne. His lips straighten into a flat line, even as his eyes gleam with the smile he's withholding. He's trying not to laugh, not in a way that mocks her, but in delight. It might have made Lora smile, too, if she wasn't so deep into the role she's meant to play.

The fierceness of the role comes easily, but she knows she must now pluck up the fortitude for something else. To soften her voice, to let her shoulders drop, to choose her next words carefully. She doesn't know if the words she's choosing will be the right ones. But she knows that even though she can trust almost none of those before her—with the exception of Grey—she also needs all of them if she wants to fulfill any goal.

"I am Sovereign now. And I know that most of you wish I wasn't. You all had your own victors you wanted to see upon this throne. You all lost something in the Trials. Some more than others."

Dedryk refuses to look at Lora. Instead, he digs the tip of her dagger into the table before him. Bronwen's magic swirls around her fingertips more swiftly.

Lora continues anyway, each word feeling more delicate than the last. "I don't have the right words to express my regret to anyone who mourns, other than to say this. I will reign in the way I believe is best for Everadyn. I will work every day to make Everadyn better than it was yesterday, to a place where everyone is free to prosper. I want all of you to be part of that. I want you to bring the unique needs of your clan to me. I want us all to work together. But I can't do that if I think that you, or someone in your clan, left poison in my bed."

The silence lingers. Perhaps the words she chose were the wrong ones. She's not sure. Her fingers shudder, and she folds them around the arms of the throne, the ones shaped like a gryphon's front feet.

At last, Dedryk and Harlowe exchange glances. Busara nods. Qadira blinks, emotionless and unreadable. Amos glares, and Briar's smile grows more genuine.

Grey speaks, "What do you need us to do?"

"Prove to me where your loyalties lie. In two weeks' time, I will begin my journey into your homes and your towns. In the meantime, I hope you will do your due diligence to ensure that, within your borders, there is no one plotting against my life or meaning to do me harm. Investigate. Send me weekly reports on your progress. I'm certain I will find them sufficient."

"And if you do not?" Harlowe asks.

"Then I will assume you are conspiring to harm the reigning Sovereign, and I will charge you with treason."

It's a death threat, and they know it.

There's another prolonged silence. Lora's heartbeat slams against her eardrums.

Qadira throws up her hand. Her bracelets rattle on her wrists. "Sea and fucking stars. You all are acting like she's asking you to sail into the mouth of a leviathan. Doing our part to investigate who threatened our Sovereign is the *least* we can do."

Lora resists the urge to smile at her. She can't show preference, but she thinks she might like Qadira.

"I will put investigators to work as soon as I arrive back on the mountains," Busara promises. "And I look forward to seeing you there."

Everyone else murmurs their assent. Amos can't hide the frustration in his voice. She doesn't know if he's responsible for the midnight or if someone is merely making it look like he is, but she's certain he means to be her enemy. Even if he's not attempting to threaten her, he's still the bastard who harms his people and strips them of their rights. A bastard she intends to deal with soon.

Dedryk pulls her dagger from the table and holds the hilt toward her as an offering. "May I approach?"

She's not quite sure what he intends, but she nods. She feels the air shift around her, Bronwen and Ayc growing more tense as Dedryk approaches the dais and hands her the dagger. She lets it rest on the arm of the throne, the bag still speared to it. She nods in a silent thanks, but he doesn't retreat.

"I think you are ignoring a rather large problem that might have led to this. I've been meaning to bring it up. And since we're all here, perhaps now is the time."

Somehow, Lora gets the feeling that whatever he's about to say is going to piss her off. But she inclines her head anyway. "And what is that?"

"I mean no offense—"

Peregrin interrupts. "I find that those who begin a sentence in such a manner do, in fact, mean offense."

The red reappears in Dedryk's pointed ears and creeps toward his cheeks. "It needs to be said."

"Then be bold enough to state it bluntly," Peregrin says.

Dedryk hesitates.

"I agree," Lora says. "Spit it out, Dedryk."

So he blurts it, "Some of your chosen Five make you seem weak, and they will be the death of you."

And Lora found she was wrong. What he has to say doesn't piss her off.

It makes her want to kill him.

AYC

Dedryk's words are an explosion that reverberates around the room. He's certain everyone feels it. Tavish, who presses his knuckles over his lips, and Bronwen, whose magic crackles. Xylie slinks even further behind Lora's throne. Qadira presses fingertips to her temple, and Busara lets out a long, tired sigh. But Harlowe and Amos stare on without flinching.

And Ayc certainly feels the percussion of the question, like an icy cold burn on his cheeks and deep in his gut.

He means me.

Thick silence lingers. It's broken by the hiss as Lora's dagger scrapes against the throne as she picks it up. Her softness has been replaced with a lethal stillness that Ayc has seen before, like when she stormed through the temple to rescue Ayc. He shivers.

Dedryk doesn't know the fury he's just unleashed.

"Is that right?" she asks.

"I can't be the only one thinking it," Dedryk says. He searches the other regents over, but no one speaks, and he rushes to fill the silence. "At best, they make you look vulnerable. I should have said something before your coronation, but it's custom that the Five who competed in the Trials with you also swear in at the coronation. But there's precedence of the members of the Five being replaced afterward when it becomes clear that they weren't the best to help lead. Perhaps you should reconsider a few of your choices."

Rage rises in Ayc's blood, cold and consuming. With every heartbeat, ice forms in his veins. His blood crystalizes. Dedryk looks so much like his eldest son, the boy who tormented Ayc for sport. The boy who fucked Lora and then betrayed her like he wasn't the fucking luckiest person alive to have the privilege of touching her skin. Of course Dedryk would be an asshole, too, if he raised a child like that.

"Don't mince words, Dedryk," Lora presses. "Say what you mean. Which of my Five do you think I should replace?"

A bit of silver highlights her eyes. The confidence in Dedryk's voice cracks. "I was only suggesting you consider it a factor. I wouldn't—

"No," Lora says firmly. "I want to know. Surely, if you're bold enough to make a suggestion, you're bold enough to be explicitly clear. Which of my Five do you think I should replace?"

She points her dagger toward Bronwen. "Are you speaking of my First, who is a graduate of both Velphin and Adamant? Look at how powerful her magic is. She has to fight even to keep it contained. She could turn you inside out without breaking a sweat." She directs the blade toward her other side. "Or perhaps my Third, who's one of the most decorated aerial riders of their time. I assure you, their aim is as lethal as ever. I'm certain that if I asked them, they'd put a knife exactly where I directed. Perhaps between your legs. It might be a small target, but I'm sure they'll get it on the first try."

Despite his rage, a smile curves on Ayc's face.

"Of course not," Dedryk sputters. "They are wise choices. And Busara says that your cousin is the most promising young alchemist she's seen in two generations, so I can understand that choice. But, my lady, you chose a blind man."

Tavish tenses. Ayc's vision darkens, the room becoming dimmer as his focus narrows on the fucker who just insulted his friend.

Bronwen's magic glows along her arms, and Dedryk rushes to add, "I understand he has certain talents that came in useful for solving quests, but as to protecting you from your enemies, well—"

"Hush!" Lora snaps, cutting him off. She twists her head toward her navigator. "Tavish, where is Dedryk's wife right now?"

"Excuse me?" Dedryk snaps.

Tavish reaches into the pocket of his trousers and pulls out a folded piece of paper. A map, Ayc assumes. Bronwen flicks her wrist, and the map snaps open before Tavish, hovering like it's laid upon an invisible table. Tavish releases Saga's leash, but the dog remains obediently at his feet. He smooths a hand over the map before tapping it.

"Duell," Bronwen reads for him.

"That's easy deduction." Dedryk's nostrils flare, proof he

doesn't like this game. "Almost everyone knows the regent's house generally resides within the port city."

"Enter through the western gate." Tavish's voice rings clear and precise. "Take the third right and then the second left. When the street reaches a fork, turn right. At the end of the street, there's a house. Enter through the back door. She's there."

"In the kitchen?" Lora says. "Ah, yes, it's the sixth day of the week. Tell me, Dedryk. Does Evadne still like brewing her oils on the sixth day of the week? She'll be at it all day. Peregrin, how long will it take you to ride there?"

Peregrin trails a finger down one of their knives on their chest. "On Tempest, I could be there by midafternoon. Quicker than he could get a warning to her. And I'll take Tavish with me, just in case he manages somehow."

"And you could try to find a sorcerer willing to hide her," Tavish adds, with a confident smile, "but as I've found today, that magic eventually fades. Slacks. Even the smallest slip, and I will find her."

"You wouldn't dare," Dedryk growls.

"Oh, I mean your wife absolutely no harm," Lora says. "Evadne was always kind to me when I was a guest in your home. But you feel that fear in your heart? The one that says you need to flee from danger. That is what my enemies are going to feel when they realize that there is not a single place on this earth where I can't find them."

"Well, damn," Briar says beneath his breath.

Lora's lips tip upward in a hint of a smile. "Do you know something about disabled people? Those that you foolishly look down upon? They have learned how to exist in a world never meant for them. They thrive with illnesses and struggles you could never withstand for a single day. They know how to *survive*. Do all of you?"

The knot in Dedryk's throat bobs.

"Even without his gift," Lora continues. "I would still choose Tavish. He understands the needs of those who, like him, have had to work twice as hard to overcome what the world has dealt them. In many parts of Everadyn, those with disabilities have been ignored for far too long. He has wonderful ideas on how to fix that. We will work together to ensure they come to pass. The disabled will no longer be invisible. Not as long as I am Sovereign."

Ayc tucks those words away in his heart. Later, he'll marvel at them, grow excited at Lora's vision for Everadyn, but for now, he can't feel it. He can only see the darkness creeping over Dedryk's face. He looks uncowed, enraged, dangerous. Like he means to be a threat.

"Are we done here?" Amos demands, standing.

Lora starts to rise from her throne, but Dedryk, apparently, is foolish enough to keep pushing his luck.

"And what about your baker?"

Ayc's vision flashes with red. "What about me?"

Dedryk rolls his eyes. "Your red eyes don't scare me, boy. You forget that I know you. Most of us have known you since you were a scrawny boy. Yris used to lament that your invisibility would be so useful if you weren't so utterly untrainable. You could barely lift a sword without harming yourself."

Ayc should laugh it off as he's done so many times. But he can't. He knows why he made Yris think him useless. He'd rather look pathetic than be made into her monster. He's never cared what anyone thought. Until now. Not if his perceived weakness makes Lora seem vulnerable.

But before he can defend himself, Lora rises slowly from her throne. The dagger in her hand points to the ground, but her hold has shifted from casual to deadly. A snake about to strike. "I would be careful not to mistake his kindness for weakness," she growls through her teeth.

"There you are again," Dedryk says. "Defending him, just as you've always done. My son told me how you used to threaten him and his friends to be nice to the human. If he's such a strong Drakr, why did you need to protect him, hm? Why couldn't he stand up to a few bullies?"

His words propel Ayc backward in time until he feels as

though his head is being shoved deep into a fountain. His lungs ache like they might burst. Then he's on the ground, pinned beneath some asshole kid whose name he doesn't know, a fist pummeling into his gut over and over. And Ayc is taking it. He's letting it happen, never even considering removing the bracelets from his wrists. He never dared fight back because he feared the monster inside him.

But Ayc no longer fears it. No bracelets ensnare his wrist now, and the icy sting of his power hissing through his vein feels so fucking good. Finally, he lets himself feel it. He basks in the rage and the power. It feels good to feel it after all this time.

"Careful," Busara warns. "He certainly demonstrated himself two days ago against Marcellus's men."

Dedryk snorts. "Yesterday was a fluke. He caught the fae off-guard. We didn't know what he was. No one is going to make that mistake again. We're prepared to deal with his invisibility."

"Is it getting darker in here?" Qadira asks, squinting up at the windows above their heads.

"Yes," Grey says with a bit of a smile. "I believe it is."

"Fuck me," Briar whispers. "Look at the shadows." He lifts a trembling finger and points toward Ayc. No, not toward him. Behind him.

Ayc twists. A wave of shadows stretches from the fall wall. They ebb toward Ayc and then flow back out, like the tide, almost timed to the pounding of his raging heart. It looks so much like Lahlis's did yesterday that it takes Ayc a moment to realize what is happening.

It's his. His shadow affinity. He has no idea how he's doing it, but his icy power sings out within him, and the shadow is answering its call.

Fuck. He was right. He's capable of more than just invisibility. So much more.

CHAPTER
TEN

AYC

Ayc feels Lora's gaze like fire nipping against his frozen skin. He shifts his focus from the shadow to her and finds her eyes wide. But she blinks, and the expression of shock disappears. She squares her shoulder and glares at Dedryk. Behind her, Bronwen does the same. Ayc takes the hint; they should play this like he's known of this power all along. But to do so, he has to control the shadow. Intentionally.

He imagines tugging the shadow toward him with an invisible hand. A lightning clap of pain slams through his head, strong enough that he sways. But he knows how to withstand pain. So he remains standing, but whatever power he summoned disappears. His skin warms, the room lightens, and the wave of shadows vanishes.

He pastes a smile on his face as he turns to take in the regents, all of them wearing various degrees of shock. His heart feels like it's conducting a race through his ribcage, but he keeps his voice light. "What? You thought cinnamon rolls were my best talent? Trust me. I'm full of surprises."

This time, when Ayc lets his eyes flash red, Dedryk takes a step back.

"Are we good now?" Ayc adds with a bit of a laugh. "Perhaps you want Xylie to exhibit her talents, too." Out of the corner of his eye, he sees Xylie shake her head, but he continues anyway. "She's quite gifted in explosives. I'm sure she has one in her pocket now."

In one jump, Briar leaves his chair and lands a full yard away. He holds up both his hands. "No, no, we're good. We're good." He lowers his voice into a command. "Aren't we, Dedryk?"

Dedryk's nostrils flare.

"Leave," Lora hisses, and silver fully overtakes her eyes. "And never question my Five again."

Dedryk spins on his heels and marches away. Amos, Harlowe, and Briar are quick to follow him toward the door.

"Except for you, Amos," Lora calls.

Amos freezes, his back ramrod straight. He doesn't turn around.

"I wish to speak to you in private. Wait outside. A guard will escort you to my office."

Amos slips out the doors, and Ayc hopes the little fuck doesn't attempt to run. Busara and Grey bow deeply before Grey offers their arm to escort her out.

Qadira is last. She stretches her arms above her head as she stands from her chair. "Pity. I wanted to see an explosion. You all are an entertaining bunch. I look forward to seeing you in Sal Maris."

Then she, too, is gone.

As soon as the doors boom shut behind her, Ayc feels all eyes turn to him. Even Saga's, with Tavish once again holding his leash. Every friendly face bears the same shock that he's sure is reflected in his own expression.

"Ayc," Peregrin says, "what the fuck was that?"

"I have absolutely no idea. I didn't..." Ayc shakes his head, rubbing his hand over his wrist. His bare wrist. "I didn't mean to. I was just...angry."

Xylie rushes forward and takes both his hands in hers, turning them over and peering down upon his bare arms.

Bronwen notices what he's staring at. "You're not wearing your bracelets."

"Yes, I took them off. I don't think I've ever gone this long without wearing them."

"I guess I was wrong about them," Bronwen says. "They were suppressing your power. Somehow. I need to look at them more closely. Do you have them with you?"

Ayc digs them from his pocket, and she takes them carefully. She holds them gingerly in her hands as though she understands how precious they are to him. Or how powerful they might be.

"Give me a minute." She retreats to an empty corner of the room, already muttering and running her fingers over the bracelets.

Lora's gaze upon Ayc is heavier than the rest, a soft caress against his chest. The deep brown is edged in light blue once more, slowly moving toward the center like a rising dawn, and his chest tightens.

"That was amazing, Ayc," she says, a little breathless. And the words steal whatever air he had in his lungs.

Ayc recalls what Dedryk said, the threats she gave Wylder. Has she really protected him against the bullies all these times? Or at least tried, as much as she was able, without her mother suspecting she was being too kind?

Of course she did. Of course.

He tucks the information away inside him, where it soothes against wounds he often pretends do not exist.

They wait in silence for Bronwen to return. Ayc feels naked without the bracelets for this long. His power churns like an unexplored ocean deep within his soul. When Bronwen returns and hands the bracelets back, he swiftly puts them back on. Until he learns how to control it, it's best if he wears them. He doesn't want to inadvertently harm someone.

"Still nothing," Bronwen says. The lines that curve beneath her eyes are darker now, like she just used a tremendous amount of power. "We could try another sorcerer…"

"Like who?" Lora asks. "Onanna?"

"No," Ayc says quickly. The sorcerer who was Yris's Second is powerful, but she's as cruel as Yris. He's been near her enough for one lifetime. "If Onanna recognized what those bracelets were, she would have stripped them from me long ago."

"Good point," Lora says. "What about the Supreme sorcerer?"

"No!" Bronwen snaps a bit too loudly. "Dealing with her comes with costs no one should pay."

Ayc glances at Xylie. She stares at her toes, curling them in and out in her slippers.

"But if I wrote her a letter, she would come," Lora says.

"Lora." Bronwen's sharpness carries with it a hint of desperation now. "I'm begging you to trust me on this."

Lora rolls the cord of the leviathan's tooth around her fingertips. "It's up to you, Ayc."

"Me?"

"It's your power. Your past. I can write to the Supreme, and she might be able to tell us something about the bracelets. If we can find who made them, we can perhaps understand how your mother obtained them and why she wanted to ensure that your power was contained. It might give us a clue about your father's identity. But that's up to you."

Ayc feels a cool shiver down his spine. Since he realized that his father was a Drakr, he's never wanted to know who he is. He's spent most of his life trying to run from and bury his Drakr side. Now, there's some small flicker of curiosity. His mother must have sacrificed greatly to obtain these bracelets for him; she must have good reason. But Bronwen's eyes are wide, shaking her head in a silent plea. Xylie lifts her hands to sign, *"Please don't."*

Perhaps some things are best left buried. Once they are dug up, they become so much harder to silence again.

"No," Ayc says. "I don't care to know the bastard who sired me. And finding out who made the bracelets doesn't change anything. We know now that it was suppressing my power. That's what matters."

"All right," Lora agrees.

Bronwen releases a breath of relief.

"I need to learn how to control it," Ayc asks her. "Can you teach me how to wield it?"

Bronwen frowns. "Do you mean me?"

"Yes."

Bronwen's mouth drops. "I'm not a shadow wielder, Ayc."

"But you have a magic affinity. Maybe it's similar. We don't exactly know a Drakr who could teach me."

"A pity," Peregrin murmurs.

"Please, Bronwen," Ayc pleads. "Don't make me beg."

A little noise of protest starts, but Lora says, "Can you try? Please."

Bronwen crosses her arms over her chest and sighs. "We can try. No promises."

"Thank you," Ayc says.

"Oh." Bronwen lets out a little laugh, one that betrays that she doesn't think it's funny at all. "If it's anything like learning sorcery, trust me, you won't be thanking me later."

Well, that sounds... ominous.

Peregrin clears their throat. "Are we done here?"

Lora nods.

"Good." They toss up their cane to grasp a better hold. "Then, if you don't mind, I'm going to question the herbalist shops in town to see which one of them has sold midnight recently."

They march toward the front doors. Ayc follows.

Lora calls out, halting them both. "Peregrin, wait! You should be with your family right now."

Peregrin swings back around, grinding their cane into the floor. "A crime against the Sovereign should be investigated by the captain of the royal guard. Seeing as he is unable to do so, someone needs to be in charge of it."

Lora protests, "I can assign—"

Peregrin bears their teeth, flashing their sharpened canines. "Lora, I don't need to sit around and grieve. I need to find the fucking bastard who hurt the man I love."

Lora releases a breath. "All right. But I can come. Amos can wait. It'll be good for him to sweat."

"No!" Multiple voices echo it at once—Ayc's, Peregrin's, Bronwen's, and even Shae's, the guard appearing from beneath the cloak.

"My lady," Shae says, "there are festivals going on in Wyntra today celebrating your coronation. There are many, many strangers in this city, and there was just a threat to your life. We can protect you if you insist, but it'll be putting yourself at an unnecessary risk."

"Besides, no one who thinks they might have broken a law is going to talk to the Sovereign," Tavish points out.

Lora pinches the bridge of her nose, and Ayc fears she might continue to argue. Even more, he fears that primal thing within him and what it wants to do if she insists on leaving this castle. Like lock her in his room. He would never take away her free will, but fuck, this thing within him is violent with its need to protect her.

"Fine," she relents. "I'll deal with Amos."

Peregrin grunts and continues toward the door. Ayc rushes after them. "I'm coming with you."

"Of course you are, boy," they say like it should be obvious, never slowing their pace.

"I'm coming, too," Tavish says, stepping carefully off the dais. "Perhaps my talents will be of use."

Ayc glances over his shoulder to catch Xylie's eye. He hates leaving Muffin behind, but he has to do this. He needs to help figure out who's responsible for the midnight on Lora's pillow. And ensure they can never hurt her again.

Xylie signs back, *"I know. Go."*

"Keep up, boy," Peregrin calls, already pushing open the door to the great hall. Ayc hurries after them.

Wyntra's main streets are alive with celebration. The Totus Omni flags—a tree on its blanket of emerald green—still line the eaves of the shops. They flap in the strong breeze that carries with it the smell of salt, but also the cacophony of smells the vendors and their stalls have brought with them. Cheese and freshly baked bread and flowers newly cut from the gardens of Bromalis. Crowds press shoulder to shoulder, their voices a steady murmur like the Ever River as it flows by. The only thing that overwhelms it is the playing of several instruments scattered throughout the crowd, each performer playing their own tune.

"Do you sense anything?" Ayc asks Tavish.

"No," Tavish says, rubbing the heel of his hand into his temple. "I've never tried to use my gift to find someone whose identity I don't know. And if I try to navigate toward just clues in general, the sense comes from so many directions it makes my head spin."

"Let's start with the local shops then," Peregrin says. "Then we can move on to vendors."

If the crowd notices them as they weave through, no one says anything. A few stop to gape or point them out to a friend, realizing that their new Five are amongst them. But most seem like they're already a glass of fae wine in, too filled with their own enjoyment to notice.

The first herbalist shop is stuffed full of patrons. The shop's owner and their employees look harrowed as they seek to help multiple customers at once. Ayc grits his teeth in frustration. He doesn't want to risk being overheard by so many customers. As much as Ayc hates to admit it, Yris was right. Announcing that someone got into the Sovereign's bedchambers last night is unwise. If the wrong person found out, they might try to harm her. They need to figure out a way to get the employees alone.

Peregrin pounds their cane on the door. Voices snuff out, and silence falls as everyone turns to look.

"We're here on the official business of the Sovereign." Peregrin's voice booms through the store. "If you're not the owners or employees of this establishment, get out."

The customers rush out the door, leaving only the people behind the counter. Well, Ayc supposes that's one way to do it.

The owner and their employees are noticeably anxious when

Peregrin begins asking questions about midnight. But the more they talk, the more Ayc suspects it's just Peregrin that's made them anxious, not any hidden guilt. It's through their fumbled explanation that Ayc learns that Everadyn law greatly monitors the growing, harvesting, and selling of midnight. It requires a permit, one that they've never gotten.

Ayc didn't know that, but then, he knows quite little about law, particularly for someone who is Fifth to the Sovereign. He's going to have to find a way to learn. Read books, or maybe convince Xylie to read to him. He's always been able to focus better when listening to a story, as opposed to reading words on a page.

Ayc wonders how Wren got ahold of midnight, the ones she gave him in the hopes that he'd unknowingly kill Lora. Did she have a permit? Or did she obtain it through nefarious means? Both sound equally likely of the bitch.

It's the first time he's thought of her since the Trials, and he would much prefer to never think of her again. Ayc scrubs all thoughts of Wren from his head as Peregrin presses a coin into the palms of each of the employees. "For your discretion," they say before they turn on their heel. Ayc and Tavish follow Peregrin out.

The second shop in Wyntra tells the same story. They do not have a permit to harvest, grow, or sell midnight. They could be lying, but Ayc doesn't think so. They return to the main street.

"Let's split up and talk to the vendors," Peregrin says. "Tavish—"

"I'm going to wander," Tavish interrupts. "See if my senses take me anywhere."

"Good idea," Ayc says. "Peregrin, I'll take the next street over."

Ayc crosses through a narrow alleyway between shops. The next street over isn't as crowded as the main street. Fewer booths have been set up here. He spots a stall selling flowers and dried herbs at the far end and makes his way down. When he passes a small tent made up of draped, brightly-colored blankets, an arm shoots out and beckons him.

"Handsome stranger," a voice calls from within. Black tattoos cover the entirety of the hand and arm in dark, swirling shapes that contrast against the white skin beneath. "Come, let me tell you secrets about your future."

A fortune teller, huh? There's always a few at festivals. Some are actors putting on a good show for money, leading people willingly into self-fulfilling prophecies. Others are divina, who have a gift for looking into the future. Ayc doesn't know which one this person is, but he wants to avoid them, regardless. Nothing good can come from knowing your fate.

"No, thank you." Ayc pauses long enough to send a friendly smile in the direction of the tent. Through the slit of the opening, he catches sight of a masculine face: strong cheekbones, long chin, a prominent forehead. But their lips are painted a brilliant blue, and their eyelids glisten like a sky of stars, all framed in long, curly hair. The blend of masculine and feminine is alluring, and if Ayc wasn't here for Lora, he might have let it distract him. Instead, he says, "Very busy, I'm afraid."

The fortune teller steps outside. Their eyelids glisten in the sunlight, but they wear only a simple gray tunic and leggings. "You'll want to know this, as it pertains not to your future but your present."

They crook a finger at him, and something about the intensity in their expression makes Ayc step closer.

"You are being followed," they whisper, so only Ayc can hear. "The one in the purple cloak. I saw them step out behind you in the alleyway you came through."

With the smallest movement of their chin, they gesture to the left. Ayc pretends to inspect the fortune teller's sign more closely and glances discreetly from the corner of his eye. A figure cloaked in amethyst stands at the next stall, their hood pulled up. They pretend to inspect a dagger the merchant is selling, but their head is shifted just enough to be watching Ayc. When they see Ayc's head move, they duck their head. But it's too late.

Ayc has caught a glimpse beneath the cloak's hood.

Fuck.

"Thank you," Ayc says to the fortune teller. "I'm afraid I don't have any coin on me. I'll come pay you tomorrow if you're still here."

"No need. Bears need to stick together." They tuck their curls behind their ear. Their very curved ear.

Bears, just like the ones on his bracelets. This person is from Aluina. Ayc wants to stay even more now, to learn the story of how they ended up in Wyntra, but for now, he has to deal with his stalker.

"Good day to you," he says and continues in the direction he was headed. His mind spins, quickly formulating a plan. A subtle glimpse over his shoulder confirms he's being followed. He keeps his wrists in front of him so the person won't see him undoing his bracelets and sliding them into his pocket. At the last second, he diverts his path and darts into the alley between two buildings. And he vanishes into the shadows.

He waits, holding his breath, not making a sound. She steps into the alleyway, the hood of her cloak still pulled up. She searches the darkness, her fingers playing with the dagger on her belt. Her eyes pass over him before she continues onward, never seeing him. She takes another step, close enough now, and he springs.

He slams into her with enough force to send her against the opposite wall of the alley. He clamps one hand over her mouth to muffle her scream and uses his other to drag her dagger from her belt. He angles it against her ribs, so if he applies even the slightest pressure, he can impale her corrupt fucking heart.

Her face has changed since he last saw her. Three long, red scars slice from her forehead and down to the opposite cheek. But it's still her.

"Five words," he growls. "When I move my hand, you have five words to convince me not to kill you, Wren."

CHAPTER
ELEVEN

AYC

"**Y**ou won't kill me, Ayc," Wren says when he moves his hand.

It's the wrong fucking thing to say.

"Bullshit!" He clamps his hand over her throat, not enough to cut off the gasp in her throat but enough to cause it. "This morning, Lora woke up to midnight on her pillow, and not three hours later, I find you stalking me through Wyntra. I'm about angry enough to start stabbing first and asking questions later."

He never thought he'd be here with his hand wrapped around someone's throat, but he's barely restraining himself from strangling the life out of her. He's shaking with rage, with the primal need to protect Lora, and right now, Wren is a threat. His vision sharpens and tints with red.

She gasps again and strains backward, away from his hand. He doesn't release his grip but loosens it enough that she can speak. "Midnight? What? I don't know anything about that. I'm—"

He peels his hand off her throat and slams it back over her mouth. "Then what the fuck are you doing here? Five words, Wren. Don't fuck it up this time."

She nods, and he lifts his hand just enough for her to speak.

"The Aluina rebellion lives," she whispers.

His hand spasms, and he nearly drops the dagger. He tightens his hold just in time and keeps it directed at her heart.

She lifts her shoulders in a delicate shrug. "Well, that's four words, but still."

"What the fuck are you talking about?" Ayc demands.

She glances toward the end of the alley, where a group of giggling fae pass by without glancing into the alley. "Not here. I can't risk talking about it here. If the wrong person were to overhear, it would spell doom. I'm staying at an inn nearby." She slips sideways, away from Ayc's dagger, and he allows her to go. "Follow me there."

Ayc knows better than to trust her. The last time he followed her anywhere, he literally died and nearly lost Lora her sovereignty. But if Wren is telling the truth, and the rebellion lives… If she knows how to reach them…

Then he can help his people.

"Fuck," he mutters to himself, knowing his decision is a foolish one and making it anyway.

She smiles in victory and cocks her head in the other direction. "This way."

He slips the dagger into his own belt but keeps his bracelets off as he follows after her. He knows nothing about controlling his power affinity, but the icy feel of it deep in the recesses of his soul is comforting, a reminder that he is not the same foolish boy he was two weeks ago. He's the Fifth. A Drakr. A shadow wielder.

He's Ayc fucking Waylonder, and he won't be taken advantage of. Not again.

When she reaches the inn, she leads him up a flight of stairs on the outside into a balcony that runs the length of the building. She stops before one of the outside doors and pulls a key from the pocket of her robe. She opens the door wide for them.

"After you," Ayc says because he sure as fuck is not turning his back on her.

She shrugs and steps inside. Ayc steels himself before entering and shuts the door behind him. She flicks on a light, and an amber hue fills the small room. Still, shadows remain untouched in the corners. Enough for him to get lost in.

Trunks and bags linger on nearly every surface of the room, far too many for the day's ride to Orchis, the port city in Bromalis.

"Going on a long trip?" Ayc asks.

"My presence isn't welcome in Orchis right now. There aren't many who don't know that I destroyed the golden root. Since I did it as part of the Trials, I can't be arrested for it. Still, many would like to see me prosecuted and even beheaded for it." She folds her arms over her chest, a subtle note of vulnerability. Ayc feels no sympathy. She's been dealt the fruit of the rotten seeds she planted. "The people of Orchis made it quite clear upon my return to the city that it was best if I moved my business elsewhere."

So here she is, with the contents of her botany shop in trunks. Ayc's suspicion still clings to his skin, sticky and hot, refusing to let go. "Do you have a permit to sell midnight?"

"Yes," she snaps. "Is this about the midnight in the Sovereign's bed? I told you. I know nothing about that."

He narrows his eyes at her, searching her face for any small flicker of deception. But then again, she's a very good liar. She pretended to want him, even care about him, and he never believed she didn't until the moment she put midnight in his hand and tried to use him as her puppet.

She sighs. "You don't believe me, do you?"

"I wonder why," he says with a roll of his eyes. "You've always been *so* trustworthy."

She throws up her hands. "Very well." She marches toward a small leather bag and flips it open to reveal rows of jars carefully tucked within. She searches through, the glass clinking against one another, before holding up one for him to see. "You seem to be surprisingly knowledgeable about plants for a baker, so I'm sure you recognize it."

The plant within looks just like a weed one could see in a

garden, but it's labeled truth weed. He holds out his hand. "Let me smell it. It could be common foxtail."

She presses it into his hand. He unscrews the lid and holds it to his nose. It smells like honey and dill, a contrast of flavors he remembers on his tongue. He hands it back to her. She places a pinch of the weed on her tongue, chews, and swallows. Ayc knows from experience that it works quickly, but it works better the longer it lingers in the system. He also knows that words can be chosen carefully so that they're not a lie, but they aren't fully the truth either.

"I have not stepped foot in Wyntra Castle since the Trials began," Wren states. "I have not sold midnight for weeks, and I'm very careful who I sell to. People I know personally who use it to kill vermin in their gardens. But I did not put midnight on Loraphne's pillow, nor do I know who did. I didn't even know of it until you mentioned it. I came to this city to find you, and I did so at great personal risk. There are many people who might be ready to kill me if they saw me. Particularly, the new Sovereign."

He listens to each one of her words carefully, weighing them to see if they could be vague enough to be a lie. But he doesn't see how.

"Satisfied?" she asks, arching an eyebrow.

He hesitates, then nods.

"Good, now that's settled." She crosses her arms and surveys him, her gaze trailing over him as though she's truly looking at him for the first time. A spark fills her eyes, like perhaps she likes what she sees. He hates himself a little; a few weeks ago, he would have rejoiced just to be gifted that small fragment of her attention.

"You look good," she says. "Power suits you, Ayc."

He *also* hates the way she says his name, like she's holding it on her tongue longer just to savor it. She has no right to say his name like that.

"You look—" Ayc searches for the right word. The scars on her face are rare. The fae heal so quickly that few things scar them unless additional elements are added to the weapon. The ones that decorate his jaw are due to the poison Yris coats her fingernails in. Whoever scarred Wren did so on purpose. "You look like you pissed off the wrong person."

"Oh, this?" Wren runs a finger down one of the raised pink lines. "The new Sovereign did this."

Ayc stiffens. "Lora?"

She nods.

"When?"

"After..." She winces like the words hurt to admit. "After I betrayed you to Marcellus."

Damn. Lora must have been furious. The strike across the face was calculated. Lora knew the scar she'd leave behind, knew that, for the rest of Wren's long life, she would look in the mirror and remember exactly what she did. Perhaps something changed in Ayc during the Trials because he knows his heart should twist in sympathy. He should want to condemn Lora's violence. Instead, he struggles to quell the smile that pulls at his lips.

He might not be as deeply under Lora's skin as she is under his, but clearly, she cares, or she wouldn't have done this.

"I am grateful she didn't kill me," Wren adds, her tone softening. "I would have deserved it."

"Yes, you would have," Ayc says coolly.

She flinches again. "I'm sure it means little, but I deeply regret what—"

"Stop," Ayc snaps. "Did you lure me in here to make some ploy at gaining my forgiveness?"

She hesitates, and that one beat of silence has him twisting on his heel. "Fuck off," he growls. To use Aluina and rebellion like some cheese in a mousetrap...

"I wasn't lying!" she calls swiftly. "The fae rebellion seeking to liberate Aluina still lives."

Ayc turns back around.

"Do you remember what I told you about my mother and how she was beheaded because Yris thought she was the leader of the rebellion?"

Ayc nods.

"She was not the leader. Yris exiled many of the members, and the Drakr killed many more when they attacked the seven villages. But the rebellion survived."

Ayc winces. So that was why the Drakrs attacked the villages. It wasn't just mindless revenge; it was a targeted attack against the rebels fighting against them. Xylie's village was among them. She survived out of luck and a quick spell by her mother.

"We had to be quiet for a time," Wren says, "but the rebellion continues. It's growing stronger. We call it Asbjorn."

Ayc's heart pounds in his throat. Asbjorn. It's not an Everadyn word, but Aluinic in original. Asbjorn is the name of the Aluina patron god, a god of home, hearth, and the forest. They are a genderless being who lore states often takes the shape of a bear. It's the reason the symbol of Aluina, found on their flag and on Ayc's blankets, is a bear.

Asbjorn.

Ayc tries to grapple with the new information. When Wren told him of the rebellion before, it never crossed his mind to ask if it survived because even if it had, what could he have offered them? He was a baker who lived every breath in pain bound with magic to serve the Sovereign of Everadyn. Now, if he can harness his power, he could be incredibly useful to a rebellion. He can help his people *now* without waiting for Lora to sort through the politics of it all.

"You said *we*," Ayc says. "Are you part of the rebellion?"

She swallows. "I *was* a part of it. They have not spoken to me since the Trials. I fear they no longer trust my judgment."

"How would I find them? If I wanted to help."

"It's not that simple. New recruits must be invited." Wren rifles through another bag on the bed. She withdraws a small velvet box and opens it. Inside, there are six golden coins. Aluina coins bearing the symbol of the bear. Except traditionally, the bear carved upon this is calm, like the ones on Ayc's bracelets. This one is roaring and bearing all its teeth. Wren flips them over one by one. Five of the coins have her name scratched upon them.

The sixth coin bears Ayc's name.

"I was hoping I would get the chance to give this to you. The members of Asbjorn are only given one spare coin at a time, and I suspect I'll never be granted another. I could think of no one better to have it than you."

She holds it out, and Ayc opens his palm to allow her to drop it inside. He folds his fingers over it, pressing it deep in his palm. It feels heavier than a mere coin. It feels like possibility.

No, it feels like vengeance.

"You will still need four more," Wren says. "In order to be accepted into Asbjorn by the leader, you must earn five coins from five existing members. They will only give them to you if they believe you are worthy."

Ayc's heart sinks. "How is that possible? Am I supposed to wander around Everadyn and hope I stumble upon them?"

"We are allowed to offer clues on where to find them and who they might be."

Ayc tucks the coin into his coat pocket next to his bracelets. "What about Sterling? I'm assuming they are a part of Asbjorn as well. Are they in Orchis?"

"Sterling has no intention of returning to Orchis. They left Wyntra yesterday to begin traveling."

"Traveling where?"

Moisture lines her lower lash at the question, and she blinks hard. "I don't know. Away from me is the only destination they stated in their letter. I hoped to catch them here, but they were already gone."

The emotion in her eyes, the softness in her face, remind Ayc of the person he thought she was when they first met, the person who rested her head on his chest and confessed about her mother's death.

Apparently, Ayc can muster some fragment of sympathy because it singes his chest. He doesn't like it, wishes that soft part of him would die a swift death. This is just her reckoning, the consequences of her actions, just like the scars on her face.

"What's my clue then?" Ayc presses.

She clears her throat. "Look for dawn that arises in pink."

Ayc blinks. That isn't a clue. That's a riddle. And he fucking hates riddles.

"That's it?" he demands.

Wren places her box back in her bag. "I'm certain you'll figure it out. You'll leave on the Tour soon, and I'm confident you'll end up where you need to be."

"You can't just tell me?"

"I like being alive. The oaths I made are abundantly clear, as are the consequences of breaking them. The Asbjorn did not survive so many years because we allowed those who might betray us to live." She takes two steps closer, and in the small room, that's too close. She's an arm's distance away now, and he has nowhere to retreat, his back too close to the door. "And I have to emphasize you can't tell anyone either. If I put my faith in you and you tell someone not in the group, *both* our lives will be forfeit. Or at least the leader may refuse you entry to the group. You can tell no one. That includes your Sovereign."

"*Our* Sovereign," Ayc corrects.

She frowns.

"She is your Sovereign, too."

She presses her lips into a hard line. "Perhaps."

A retort rises up his throat like bile, but he swallows it back down. He's had enough. It's time to go. He's been gone much too long. Peregrin and Tavish might have noticed his absence and be looking for him. Tavish would easily lead them here. He won't exactly have a good reason to give anyone who noticed why he's in a room at an inn with the woman who betrayed him.

"Thank you for the information," Ayc says. "And the coin."

He turns to go.

She reaches out and snags his wrist. "Ayc, wait."

He jerks away and fists his hands, barely restraining the instinct to lash out.

"Ayc, I'm sorry. I truly am. You were never supposed to get hurt."

"Don't," he warns from between his teeth.

"Just listen to me, please. I know you probably think

everything between us was fake. It wasn't. I did have feelings for you." Her lips tremble. "I still do."

"Is that supposed to make it better?" Ayc snarls. His power jolts within him, like a dog on a leash demanding to be set free. He doesn't know how to restrain it without the bracelets. The shadows in the corner creep toward Wren's feet. His bones begin to ache, but he almost doesn't notice. He's used to pain. "If you cared about me and were still willing to harm me, then it makes it so much fucking worse."

"You weren't supposed to get hurt," she repeats.

"I don't care." Ayc's voice deepens until it reverberates in a growl. His vision tints with red, just at the edges at first, but narrowing as he speaks. "I don't care what you meant. I don't care that you have feelings for me. And I don't care about *you*. I won't forgive you, but I'll certainly *forget* you. When I walk out the door, I will *never* think of you again."

At last, his eyes burn completely red. Wren gasps and takes a step back. His shadow parts around her, but she must feel its icy touch because she jerks and looks down. She shudders at the sight, and it feels good to be the one with power now, if just a bit frightening because he has no control of it.

"I almost didn't believe Sterling when they told me," she murmurs quietly. "Or my own eyes when I saw it in the alley. But you are Drakr, aren't you?"

It still comes as a shock to hear himself called a Drakr, even if that's what he is. Perhaps it's the little note of disgust and hate that tinges the word. Cruelty. Rage. Desecration. Those are words associated with the Drakr. The long history of the Drakr attempting to take the lands that do not belong to them still exists within some fae memories. He doesn't blame them, but he doesn't want to be associated with it, either.

He draws a breath through his nose, and as he regains control of his emotions, his power also calms. The red fades, his shadows retreat, and he takes a step backward. "Goodbye, Wren," he says, spinning toward the door.

She doesn't attempt to stop him. He slams the door behind

him. Back in the street, he returns his bracelets to his wrists and then finds his way back to speak to the vendor. He finds Peregrin and Tavish already there.

"There you are," Peregrin calls. "Did you find anything?"

For a moment, Ayc considers telling Peregrin. But Wren's warning comes back to him. He can't afford to gather all the coins only to be turned away by the leader because he dared talk.

"No," Ayc says, slipping his hand into his pocket to reassure himself of the coin's presence. "Nothing at all."

TWELVE

LORA

Lora swings open the door to the Sovereign's office to find Amos sitting in *her* fucking chair, and that tells her exactly how Amos has chosen to play this game. Good. It's been a shitty couple of days, and Lora's in the mood for a fight. If she makes the fucker bleed a little, she might feel a little better.

She mutters *'Pomegranate'* beneath her breath to ensure that Shae can hear whatever happens once the door closes. Bronwen slips in behind Lora and lets her magic slam the door shut. Amos jumps but tries to hide it with a smile as he curls his hands around the arms of the chair. Lora searches him over. The guard who escorted him to this room should have removed any weapons from him, but she's not willing to take any chances. She sees nothing, but she lets her thumb caress the swords at her side, reminding herself she's far from unarmed.

"You seem to be sitting on the wrong side of the desk, Amos," Lora says, keeping her voice calm and her chin lifted.

Amos's normally sour face twists up even further. "By rights, it should be Marcellus's d—"

The chair flies out from beneath him, and he lands on his ass on the floor, disappearing from sight behind the desk. An oomph sounds out. Lora swallows down her laugh, but she sends Bronwen a small, grateful smile. She winks.

"I see you watch your ass about as well as Marcellus watched his throat," Bronwen says, a laugh echoing beneath her words.

Amos's palms slap down at the desk as he shoves himself upward. His mouth is already open, but Lora speaks first.

"Let's be abundantly clear, Amos. That is *my* chair in *my* office in *my* castle. This is my crown on my merciful head, and you would do well to remember that I am, indeed, *merciful*." She slowly rounds the desk, and Amos retreats, like the coward he is, keeping the solid wood object between them until she's reversed their positions with him on the other side of her desk—just as she intended. "With the bag that I found beneath my bed, I don't think a single regent would have objected to me throwing you into prison. I am refraining from doing so until after a thorough investigation, and you should be grateful for my sense of fairness."

"I didn't put midnight in your bed," he spits. His pale face grows redder by the moment.

"Sit down, Amos," Lora says levelly, gesturing to one of the chairs on the other side of the desk. He obeys, though he lets out an indignant huff.

Bronwen perches on the corner of Lora's desk, crossing her legs at the ankle. She summons a little thread of magical energy and weaves it through her fingers, casual and threatening all at once.

Amos casts her a glance, and it's not nearly as weary and respectful as it should be. The narrow, pointed tip of his nose wrinkles. Lora resists the urge to break it.

"I didn't put midnight in your bed," he repeats.

"Do you know who did?" Lora demands.

"No."

She has to hand it to Amos. If he's lying, he's good at it. He stares directly at her, an uncomfortable bit of eye contact that she has to force herself not to look away from. Even though it makes her skin feel as though it's separating from her muscles in discomfort. She ignores the urge to shake her hands, or itch, or rock her body in an attempt to ease the feeling. Instead, she rolls the cord of her necklace between her fingers, drawing Amos's eyes to the tooth she drove into his friend's neck.

"And why should we believe you?" Bronwen asks, giving that smile of hers that might seem sweet to anyone else, but Lora knows the danger. She's seen the aftermath of what follows that smile.

Amos doesn't turn his head to acknowledge Bronwen. He only continues to stare at Lora.

"Why aren't you answering Lady Bronwen?" Lora asks.

"Lady—" He begins, and then he snaps his teeth shut. She can just imagine what's pinging around in that hateful skull of his.

"Please continue," she says calmly. She leans forward, pressing her hands on the desk. Amos studies her painted, poisoned nails. Perhaps he's wondering if there's any attribute of her mother she decided to keep. "Give me a reason to kill you. It would thrill me greatly and save me many future headaches, I'm certain."

He squares his shoulders. "I'm getting weary of your threats. After your little fit yesterday, I sent a letter to the head of Lux Aester's Council of Elders. As you know, he would replace me in case of an untimely demise until a special election could be held. I've instructed him that if you kill me, he is to stop all future shipments of produce and livestock out of Lux Aester's borders."

Lora refuses to let her stone mask even waver at the threat, even if it ripples fear through her stomach. It's what her mother warned about. Lux Aester, as the largest clan, holds the source of most of Everadyn's food. Everadyn has other resources, certainly. There are farms in nearly every clan, but the loss of Lux Aester would be harmful. Supply would not equal demand. Costs would grow immensely. The wealthiest of families would likely be unaffected. But many would suffer while she plays the game of politics.

But this is theatre, so Lora shrugs. "Wyntra has deep stores and an even deeper treasury. My belly will remain full. And you?

You'll be dead. There's little sweetness in vengeance if worms are eating your flesh."

He cocks up his chin. "Death doesn't scare me. I'll be welcomed into eternal paradise."

Bronwen snorts.

"Don't fear death, hm?" Lora repeats. "The sweat on your upper lip says differently."

His lip curls, but that only makes the moisture gleam more. His fingers latch around the arms of the chair to hide the way they tremble. He's afraid of her. Lora's never wanted to rule through fear. She craves respect, loyalty, maybe even love. But those are things she'll never have from him, so she supposes she'll have to lean into what her mother taught her and play into his fear.

Lora drums her fingers on the desk. "I meant what I said yesterday. I expect that you'll be making changes within your clan to ensure that everyone has the same freedoms that you enjoy."

"You don't get a say in what happens in *my* clan," he snaps. "There's a separation of powers for a reason. To prevent anyone from being a tyrant."

"The law that governs greater Everadyn supports the freedoms of all people to live in their authentic identities and to love whomever they love. Everadyn would not be the great nation it is without its diversity. That is a rule that you are in vagrant disregard of."

He bares his teeth. His canines sharpen as he growls. "I have not disregarded that law."

A blur of movement shifts in the corner of Lora's eyes, but when she glances in that direction, it's gone. There's a guard in here, hidden beneath their cloak. They are moving closer in case Amos strikes. She's armed well enough she could handle it herself. Perhaps that would be best. If she could goad him into acting irrationally and going for her throat, no one would blame her for ending him. But who would take his place? The head of the council seems like he would be every bit as much a pain in her ass. And then, who would the Lux Aester elect? The conditions and beliefs that led to Amos being elected again and again still exist. Is the enemy she knows better than the enemy she doesn't?

"You're a liar," Bronwen says. Her voice is steady, but the blue energy weaves more swiftly around her arms. "You've continued to marry the young off to the highest bidders without their consent. You've—"

"Lies!" Amos barks, jumping to his feet. "It's a father's right to help his daughter find a strategic match. They always consent."

Bronwen slowly rises. The thread of her magic disappears, but silver glows slowly in her eyes. She's become more focused, more lethal, and Amos stiffens. Lora remains in her chair. Her best friend can handle herself, and with all the history with her clan, she deserves to be the one to put Amos back in his place. Still, Lora loosens her dagger from its sheath. The air stirs subtly as the guard creeps closer.

"Consent is only consent if you feel your choice matters," Bronwen says. "That says nothing of your other infractions. You've rejected licenses to healers unless they refuse to prescribe gender-affirming herbs so that those who need them can't access them. Your priests refuse to perform marriages except between a man and a woman. You've encouraged a culture that makes it unsafe for anyone to live authentically and failed to prosecute hate crimes against them. None of this ensures the freedom of your people."

"This is why it's utter foolishness that someone so young has taken the throne. Your memories are short, and you know nothing of history. The Lux Aester have been this way for centuries. We are merely preserving our ways from the disgusting, unholy culture so pervasive in other clans. The last time our practices were challenged, Sovereign Ellanher affirmed that we were acting in our rights to be independent as a clan."

"I am not my grandfather," Lora says. "And I'm sure you'll find that when that appeal reaches my ear again, I'll rule differently."

His face burns a hue of red only fitting for a hot coal in a forge. "This is ridiculous," he sputters. "I will not stand for this. I'll—"

Lora holds up a hand. "For divine's sake, there's no reason to get so emotional, Amos."

A boy made the mistake of telling her that once during her school internship at the Sal Maris school. The professor had to restrain her from clawing at his eyes after he shoved her into the ocean. Never mind that she had already explained to him that she had nearly drowned in the Ever River the year before and didn't want to go in the water.

There's no reason to get so emotional.

Since then, she's found that it works exceptionally well... against pathetic men. Amos is no exception. He releases a growl of frustration. Men like him are used to making light of women, stating they are too emotional to be trusted, to hold power, which is ironic because she's never seen emotion ruin someone so completely as it ruins a man.

"Sit down so we can keep talking like two reasonable adults," Lora says. "Unless you feel unable, in which case you can feel free to take a break and come back."

He blinks his wide eyes. He's not used to this. Yris used to coddle his arrogance and stroke his ego, because doing so became the strings that allowed her to play him like a lute without him even noticing. She tried to teach Lora to do the same, but she has absolutely no patience for it. So, instead, she'll treat him like the petulant child he is.

"Which will it be, Amos? Are you going to sit, or do you need to take a walk to calm your delicate nerves?"

He perches reluctantly on the very edge of his chair. Lora stands and rounds around the desk so that Bronwen towers on his right and she on his left. Two powerful women putting him in his place. Lora hopes it fucking burns.

"You have a choice to make," Lora explains coolly. "You can either bend, or you can break. You can bend to my reasonable requests and make changes to the issues that Bronwen has mentioned. If you do, you can keep your position and some semblance of power. Or I can *break* you."

"Death does not—"

"You're a fool if you think death is the only way to break someone," Lora interrupts. She gives him the smallest of smiles, like she has a plan laid out he knows nothing about. Just an act. In truth, she has no idea what her next move should be if he doesn't bow to her intimidation; she only has certainty that she will win. One way or another, she won't rest until all of her people are free.

"I'm done here." Amos shoves the chair backward when he stands, allowing enough room for him to slip past Lora without brushing against her. He draws himself up, tugging at his tunic to straighten it as he marches toward the door.

"I'll expect your report of the changes you and your Council are implementing by the time I arrive on my Tour," Lora says.

His only answer is to slam the door behind him.

The guard in the room takes off his hood. His gaze is fixed on the door with a hard glare. "Would you like me to drag him back? It would thrill me greatly."

Lora only vaguely recognizes the guard. He was hired after Lora left for Adamant, so he's not among the many who used to guard her as well. He's short in height, only reaching Lora's shoulder, but broad in stature. A thick, brown beard is the only hair on their face. Their skull has been left bald, save for a single braid down the back of their head.

"No, thank you," Lora says. "I'm quite sick of his face."

He nods. "As you wish, my lady."

"What is your name? I know that we've met before, but I apologize, I don't recall."

"No need to be sorry. My name is Davos."

"Davos, do you mind stepping outside? I would like to speak to my First in private."

He steps outside and pulls the door shut behind him. Lora reminds herself to ask Irving his thoughts on Davos. Anyone who looks at Amos with such contempt is someone she would like on her team if Irving thinks they are trustworthy.

The thought tugs at her stomach. Irving does not remember her. Perhaps, he doesn't remember Davos either. The thought of having to give someone else the position of captain makes her want to scream. But she pushes it from her mind. Only time will tell, and she can only deal with one issue at a time.

"Pomegranate," Lora mutters to restore the privacy spell.

"He's not going to yield," Bronwen says.

"I know," Lora replies with a sigh. Which means she has less than a couple of months to put into motion whatever she must do to strip him of power. "Do you think the Lux Aester would do it? Cut off the food supply if I cut off Amos's head?"

"Yes. They scarcely care about the needs of the poor in their own clan. Why would they care about the needs of those in others?"

Whatever decision Lora makes, innocent lives will pay the cost. She can ride to Aluina's aid tomorrow, but the last time anyone stood up to the Drakr, seven villages burned. Xylie nearly burned with it. Whatever choice she makes, people could suffer. But if she does nothing, people will suffer as well.

This is the weight of the crown.

"What should we do, Bronwen?" Lora asks. "You know them best."

"We should call a meeting of your Five, and we should all decide together. Tomorrow evening. Give Peregrin the day."

Lora swallows and nods. The quiet of the room seeps under her skin. In it, she can hear the lamps above her head making the buzzing sound that she's been told no one else can hear, but that makes her molars grind. She hates leaving matters unresolved, but Bronwen's right. She needs the rest of the Five before they decide how to handle it. Fortunately, she still has a very long list of things to do.

She strides to the door.

"Where are you going?" Bronwen asks.

"To work."

Bronwen, without hesitation, follows after her.

CHAPTER
THIRTEEN

AYC

Ayc swings his sword at the wooden mannequin once again, but this time a spasm racks down his spine. He barely manages to hold onto the blade. The metal strikes wood far lower than he intended, bouncing off the hip instead of the neck.

Fuck. Ayc grinds his teeth and gasps for breath. He glances around, but the courtyard is quiet. No one has witnessed his humiliation. A sweat has broken across his forehead, not from the effort but from pushing past the pain. Granted, he's been at this for thirty minutes when he hasn't trained with a sword for over a year, but the pain radiating through his body is far greater than what it should be for the small amount of exertion.

There were no more tonics in Xylie's store this morning, and he didn't dare ask Xylie for more, not wanting to deal with her suspicions. He's young, and he's free. His body shouldn't hurt this fucking much, and he can't begin to explain it. He doesn't want Lora and the rest of the Five to think that the pain might stop him, might slow them down, or prevent him from fulfilling his duty. He managed during the Trials, and he'll find a way to manage now.

Perhaps that's why he picked up the sword. That, and the boredom from waiting for Bronwen. She was meant to be here an hour ago for their first training session, and after thirty minutes of waiting, he decided to pick up the sword.

He just needs to be stronger. Tougher. Better trained. If he can do that, perhaps the pain will be better. Perhaps he won't notice it as much, or it won't ever get the better of him. It's foolish logic, but he must try something. Lora—and the Aluina rebellion—need him to be stronger.

Again. He needs to try again.

He tightens his grip on the broadsword, holding it with both hands as he lifts it upward.

"Your grip is off."

He nearly drops the sword again. Lora stands on the outside of the practice ring, her arms crossed over her chest. She's wearing her armor, as black as the heavy expression on her face. He swears she wasn't there moments before. Two guards linger twenty paces away, near the courtyard's fountain, so at least she hasn't snuck away from them again. She's been much more cautious since yesterday. Peregrin has insisted she have two guards with her, instead of one, at all times, and she hasn't argued.

"You should slide your hands apart," Lora adds. "They shouldn't overlap."

"Or perhaps I should hold it in my ass cheeks," Ayc suggests. "I'm certain that would disarm my opponent."

She rolls her eyes and then swings gracefully over the fence. "Here, let me show you."

She reaches toward his hands, and Ayc slides a step back out of instinct. She can't go casually touching his skin because the brush of her fingers feels anything but casual to his rebellious body. He sticks the point of the sword into the grass beneath his feet and leans against it. "I'm sure there's something else you should be doing other than trying to help with my sword grip."

"For your information, there is, but I saw you, and I thought I would render some aid."

"Uh-huh." Ayc arches both of his eyebrows. "*And?*"

Her forehead scrunches together. "*And* I'm hiding from the tailors. They've held me hostage all morning."

"What for?"

"Apparently, it's tradition that, during the tour, I wear fashion that matches clan customs, so I'm having seven different dresses made. There's a whole team of tailors from each of the clans. The Bromalis tailors are particularly chaotic with stress. "It's very…" Her hands shudder as she reaches toward her temple. It reminds him of Xylie when she's overstimulated and needs to calm herself, and Ayc resists the desire to erase the distance between them. "I don't really like the fuss of it all."

"If you don't like it, don't do it," Ayc says sincerely.

She presses her eyes closed and sighs, pinching the bridge of her nose between her fingertips. "It's what the clans will expect."

"Well, fuck that. Fuck expectations if it costs your own comfort."

She drops her hand from her face, and her mouth parts in surprise. She stares at him for a long moment before she clears her throat. "I think I've pissed them off enough in my reign already. And just wait—the tailors are coming for you, too."

"What do you mean? I can't afford seven outfits."

She waves a hand. "It's coming out of the royal budget. And besides, you *can* afford it now. Did you not get the letter from the treasury regarding your salary? I sent it with a page last night."

Ayc completely forgot about the letter. When the page knocked at his door, Muffin was once again attempting to fly. Ayc opened the door a crack, just enough to snag the letter before slamming the door. "*From the Sovereign,*" the page called through the door, but Ayc scarcely heard over the sound of Muffin tumbling into his sink and shattering his dinner plate. Ayc tossed the letter on the counter to go help and forgot it even existed until Muffin shredded it.

The little shit is thankfully sleeping once again, though Xylie has stationed herself in the kitchen so someone is present when they wake up again.

"I didn't have time to read it last night," Ayc says. "And I couldn't find it this morning. I'm terrible at misplacing things."

She shrugs. "I guess it can't hurt to just tell you."

She mentions the number, and Ayc stumbles. The sword finally tumbles from his grasp and crashes to the ground. "I'm fucking sorry. I think you added a figure to that."

The corner of her mouth ticks up slightly. "I did not."

It's more money than he's ever dreamed about. When he took this position, he never truly thought about the salary that might come with it. He assumed, like before, he'd be given enough to pay for his basic needs and little more. That he could save up and scrounge for the trinkets he wanted, but anything else was beyond his reach.

"It's actually quite a bit less than what Yris's Five made," she adds. "They will all be retiring absolutely dripping in wealth, while most of the staff in this castle, you included, have been woefully underpaid. At least according to the treasury reports I reviewed. I've used the difference between her Five and mine to adjust the guard and the staff salaries as well."

She watches him carefully, as though she expects him to protest. On the contrary, he bends to pick up his sword because he's afraid that if he looks at her right now, she's going to see wonder written in every line of his face.

She continues, "My mother's philosophy has always been that hungry and desperate people won't bite the hand that feeds them. My grandmother taught me that loyalty grows when you keep people well-fed and happy. I think I'm going to lean a little more on that wisdom."

"You will be twice the Sovereign Yris ever was," he says, keeping his eyes fixed on his sword.

The air parts with her sharp intake of breath. The exhale rushes right after, carrying a quick change in subject.

"You don't have to continue staying in your kitchen if you don't wish," she offers. "You can take up one of the Five's previous chambers. They are massive. Or we could find you property in the town. Maybe a place with a storefront at the bottom. You can open up a baking shop."

Ayc frowns. "Do you plan to fire me?"

"What? No, of course not."

"I'm uncertain how I can manage a shop and be your Fifth."

"Ayc," she snaps. "Do you still love baking?"

"Yes." If things were simple, he would want to spend his days baking sweet things that are as delicious as they are beautiful. He would live off the joy of his patrons taking their first bite or seeing the cakes he crafted for them. But nothing is simple—not with being Fifth or with Muffin or Asbjorn, all the little secrets he's keeping from Lora that twist him up with guilt.

"Then we'll find a way for you to keep baking," Lora says, like it is, in fact, simple. "You can hire help, divide your days between this castle and your shop. Whatever it is you decide to do. Don't surrender your dreams so easily."

The earth itself seems to shudder at the passion for his own dreams he sees in her eyes. Fuck. She can't keep doing this. She's clawing her way deeper within his skin with every word, making it impossible not to love her.

Dreams?

If he dared to dream, then he would dream of her. A world where he dared to love her openly, and she loved him in return.

Reckless, impossible dreams.

"And what are your dreams, Lora?" he asks, to deflect from himself.

Her face contorts, pained, and she looks away, toward the entrance to the barracks on the opposite side of the courtyard.

"Have you seen Peregrin today?" she asks, like she didn't hear the question, even though Ayc knows she did.

Ayc lets it go. "Briefly, this morning. They've been keeping themself busy with the investigation."

Peregrin has tasked royal guards with interviewing people within the castle, the town, and the barracks to uncover if anyone noticed anything suspicious. It'll be a long process, and Ayc fears there are too many people staying in the castle and town for the coronation. Too many strangers who were supposed to be there for any single one to stand out.

"I should go see them and check on Irving," Lora says.

Anyone who didn't know her would see nothing more than the fearsome new Sovereign. But he sees it—the line between her eyebrows, the shoulders that tilt slightly downward. She looks as though the weight of the world is pressing down upon her, and yet she's strong enough that her shoulders barely give. He wants to take the weight from her, put it on his own back. Gods know, he knows how to carry pain, but he can't. And he certainly can't follow his desire to pull her into his arms and shelter her from all her worries. Or better yet, drag her into his bed and kiss every inch of her until everything and everyone outside of his bedroom ceases to exist.

No, he definitely can't do any of that. But he can offer a distraction.

"Well," he says, wrapping his hands around the hilt of his sword once more, overlapping them even more than they were before. "First, show me what I'm doing wrong."

The line between her brows eases as she steps toward him. "Like this."

She sets her hands over his and glides them just a little more apart. And just as he knew it would, the impact goes straight to his heart like an arrow.

She taps one of his feet with a boot. "Feet further apart. Broaden your stance."

He knows this already, from all the years Peregrin taught him, but he's grown lazy without practice, so he lets her correct him. She circles to his back and taps a finger between his shoulder blades, a touch that sends shivers racing down the length of his spine.

"Now, shoulders back."

He pulls his shoulder blades together and grits his teeth as the muscles stretch like a taut band. He refuses to wince, to let her see his discomfort. She steps in front of him and surveys him. The intensity of her expression as she looks over his body makes his skin grow taut and hot with longing. He knows only one method of coping with these feelings when they get this strong. And that's to piss Lora off.

"All right, draw your swords, then." He jolts his chin toward the blade on her belt. "You and me. Right now."

She lifts a single brow. "You can't be serious?"

"Why not? Are you afraid I might kick your ass?"

She scoffs. "Please. You won't last ten seconds."

"Promises, promises, villainess."

The hiss of the 's' turns into an *'oomph'* as his feet fly out from under him, and he slams upon the ground. Shockwaves surge through his back, but agony halts as weight—Lora's weight—falls onto his stomach, pressing him into the earth. The razor-sharpness of her blade hovers over the delicate skin of his throat.

And fuck, the pain is far, far away now because all that exists in the world is her. The weight of her body, the fullness of her thighs as they curve around his sides, the way her curls free-fall around her face, the deep violet of her eyes. It instantly transforms him from a man into a hopeless mess of want. He fists his hand in the grass to keep from touching her and prays she doesn't slide back any further, or else she'll know exactly how she's impacting him, how hard she's made him just by existing.

"I warned you." She presses her sword just a little closer to his throat, and that only reminds him of the dream that tormented him when he was ill: the way she held her knife to his throat when she fucked him.

He clamps his teeth shut to withhold the moan. It still rattles deep in his chest, anyway.

She searches him over, a flutter of concern softening her face. "Did I hurt you?"

He forces a smile. "I'll live."

She shakes her head and stabs the blade into the earth, next to his head. "You've really got to learn to keep your feet under you."

Don't say it, Ayc pleads with himself. *For fuck's sake, don't say what you want to say.*

But he's an incorrigibly reckless fool, and if he can't touch her, he must try to impact her somehow. Try to level the ground between them, even if it's destined to always be a treacherous incline tilted in her direction.

So he lets his grin grow wider. "Or maybe I have you right where I want you."

"*You're* pinned beneath *me*."

"Precisely. I quite like being the bottom."

She frowns down upon him, a crease reforming between her eyebrows. She doesn't get it. And then she does. She growls in frustration, throws back her head, and closes her eyes, an image that torments him to his core.

But she doesn't get off of him. "Let me guess. You're still trying to get under my skin."

"Always."

"Why are you so intent on this game?" She opens her eyes. The violet is yielding to a lighter blue. "Do you like to see me flustered?"

"Yes."

"Hm." She cocks her head, and two springs of hair tumble over her nose.

His fingers ache, longing to brush them from her forehead, and he tightens them into fists even harder. *Every* part of him aches for her, an ache that only grows when she sets her hands on his chest. Her fingers play with the deep collar of his shirt.

What the fuck is she doing?

Whatever it is, he hopes she doesn't stop.

She trails her fingers higher still, and he doesn't dare move, afraid if he does, he might wake from whatever dream he's fallen into, where she is touching him. His breath freezes as her palm rests at the hollow of his throat and the pads of her fingers trace the curve of his neck. They pause, resting over the place where his pulse thrums. She doesn't squeeze, but still, she must feel how fast his heart pounds for her.

"Do you remember in Elodie?" she asks, her voice thick and languid. "When you stole my book?"

He barely manages to nod. Of course he remembers. He remembers every time she's ever touched him.

"Did you mean what you said?" She lowers her head so he can feel the heat of her next words against his lips. "Do you really like it harder?"

She applies the slightest pressure against his pulse.

And just like that, he's done for. Heat blazes from every inch of his skin. Want—a deep, endless well of it—twists his body so hard it hurts. He might break apart if he cannot have her, if he doesn't feel her hand tighten around his throat as she lowers herself upon him.

"Yes," he growls.

She presses just a little harder, and then, just as swiftly, she releases, leans back, and grins wickedly. "And as you can see, two can play this game."

His vision is filled with only her wicked grin. He can't breathe, can't think. He can only want. He can only imagine sinking into her heat as her hand cuts off his air.

Fuck.

"Divine's sake," a voice calls, "let the poor man up!"

FOURTEEN

AYC

The stranger's voice comes from the edge of the arena.

Lora's cheeks deepen in color. Perhaps she, too, has forgotten that anything existed except their two bodies. She jerks her head in that direction, but Ayc drags his gaze away to take in the handsome, familiar-looking fae who leans against the fence post. He grins broadly, a shock of turquoise hair falling into his laughing eyes. A Wyntra guard, identifiable through the uniform, stands beside him.

"Veni!" Lora says. She grabs her sword from the earth and leaps to her feet.

The absence of her is both torture and relief. Ayc can finally breathe, and yet it feels as though something vital has been ripped from his lung. He can still feel her fingers around his throat, and fuck, that was cruel.

And he fucking loved it.

He pushes himself to his feet, watching as Lora stops before Veni. Ayc recognizes him, the guard from Avia, Lora's home village in the Totus Omni territory. Mr. *Shoot first, and never ask any questions.* His crossbow is strapped to his back, matching the three daggers and broad sword on his belt. The lethality is a sharp contrast to the bright colors he wears: a tunic made of vibrant and plentiful shades of green.

Veni gestures with his thumb to the Wyntra guard beside him. "Can you tell this kind gentleman that you know me so he can go back to the exciting work of staring at nothing?"

The Wyntra guard grunts.

Lora looks him up and down, her lips pulled into a serious line. "I've never seen him before in my life."

The Wyntra guard surges toward Veni. Veni yelps and jumps back. Lora thrusts up a hand.

"I'm joking. I'm joking. I obviously know him. You can go back to your post."

The Wyntra guard turns a shade Ayc has only seen on a beet. He pivots on his heel and storms away.

"For fuck's sake," Veni mutters.

The smile that curls on Lora's face is playfully vicious, and Ayc saves the image in his head because he wants to keep it forever. "That's for the time you put the snake in my bed," she says.

Veni scoffs. "We were nine. And as I recall, you befriended it and named it Lady Slithers of Danger Rope."

Ayc barks out a laugh.

Lora's smile disappears. "I did no such thing."

Veni leans both arms back onto the fence. "Are you going to introduce me to your friend, Lora? Or is it 'my lady' now?"

"Lora is fine." Lora lifts a hand to beckon to Ayc. He joins them. "You've already met. This is Ayc."

Veni snaps his fingers. "Ah, yes, you're Nobody." He stretches out his hand, and Ayc takes it. Ayc doesn't miss how Veni holds on just a little longer than necessary or the way his thumb strokes across Ayc's wrist. "Absolute pleasure to meet you again, handsome."

Ayc smiles back, though it lacks the warmth it might normally have. If Ayc's nerves weren't still in shock from the aftermath of having Lora so close, he knows he would absolutely flirt back. He would have admired Veni's toothy smile, glistening blue eyes, and strong collarbones peeking out of his shirt. But it all pales next to Lora. The entire sun and stars pale in comparison to Lora.

"Must you flirt with everyone, Veni?" Lora demands. Her smile is gone, replaced by a deep scowl.

"Not *everyone*," Veni says. "But I'm contractually obligated by the universe to flirt with *every* cute man. Lightning will strike me down if I ever stop."

"What are you even doing here?" Lora asks.

"A notice came that you're hiring a few new royal guards, and as soon as they hung it up in Avia, my mother told me to get my ass here."

"Did she? You made great timing getting here. I'm surprised my notice even made it to Avia already."

Veni shrugs. "What can I say? I'm an overachiever. It seems I've arrived a few days early for the interviews and qualification trials, but I'm hoping that might win me some affection from the new Sovereign."

A bit of brightness breaks through her sour expression. "Truly? You want to be a guard?"

"If you'll have me."

"So long as you qualify, I'd be thrilled. Though the interview may need to be postponed until the captain can participate."

Veni's smile dims. "What happened to the captain?"

Lora swallows. "Injured in the line of duty."

Veni's face darkens completely. "Is he all right?"

Lora hesitates, glancing at Ayc as though she's silently asking what she should say.

"He will be," Ayc says.

Gravel crunches behind Veni as Bronwen rushes forward. Finally. Her nearly white hair flies behind her, loose and tangled. She squints in the little sunlight the cloudy day offers.

"I'm sorry I'm late," she says when she stops before Ayc. "Hello, Veni."

Veni lifts his hand in a flourished wave. "Hi, Bronwen."

"Come on," Lora says, gesturing to Veni. "I'll show you to a guest room."

"Lora," Bronwen says, her voice edging on scolding, "you can delegate that. That's what the pages are for."

Lora ignores her as she vaults over the fence. "I'll see you both later at the meeting."

"What meeting?" Ayc asks.

"The meeting I mentioned in that letter you misplaced, for all the Five. Dinner in the great hall."

"I'll be there!" Ayc calls, but Lora and Veni are already halfway across the courtyard, headed in the direction of the castle. The royal guards follow at a distance. Veni casts one last glance at Ayc over his shoulder, and Ayc considers winking back, but he can't make himself do it. Instead, he shifts his attention to Bronwen.

She still wears the same gray dress from yesterday. She rubs both her palms into her temples. The air around her isn't static as it has been, but it feels heavy and appears darker, like she's an abyss that light is being sucked into.

"Fuck, what happened to you?"

He immediately regrets his tone when she shoots him a glare. He is, actually, concerned. Being this late doesn't seem like her at all.

"I overslept," she explains. "Lora had me up late going over plans for the Tour and doing a thousand other little tasks that someone else could do if she learned to delegate. And then... Well, I may have drunk an entire bottle of wine. Or two."

"You want to talk about it?" he says more gently.

"No!" she snaps.

"Clearly, something is bothering—"

"I'd much rather talk about what I saw when I first entered the courtyard," she interrupts. "How Lora was momentarily using you as her personal chair. Are you ready to begin your lesson, or do you need to take a cold plunge in the ocean first?"

It's Ayc's turn to glare at her. Point absolutely taken. "I'm ready."

"That's what I thought. Come on. Let's go to the dungeon. It's too bright out here."

Ayc has never been in the dungeon of Wyntra castle before, despite threats Yris heaved his way over the years. He imagined it as the most terrible place on earth, dark and terrifying and rank with the smell of decaying corpses. He finds it's dark, yes, but otherwise, it's nothing more than a windowless room with three distinct but empty cells. It bears the must and damp of a cellar, but the stone walls and floor are clean, even of cobwebs. He supposes he should have known it would be the case. They don't house convicted people here. The cells are only used temporarily to house Everadyn fae who have appealed their cases all the way to the Sovereign's ears. Or those awaiting trial for treason.

Still, there's something unnerving about the bars, about the chains still hanging on the walls. He can't imagine Lora being put down here and left. Did Yris at least leave her with a lantern, like the one Bronwen grabbed before descending the stairs, or did Yris leave her daughter utterly alone in the dark?

Bronwen sets the lantern on the ground. It creates a halo of light that they stand in the center of. Beyond it is darkness.

No, shadow.

Ayc removes his bracelets and slips them into his pocket. The icy power rises with a vibrating hiss within him. Perhaps he's imagining it, but the shadows almost seem darker. "What do I do?"

Bronwen crosses her arms and drums her fingers against her biceps. "What was it like for you yesterday?"

"Completely unintentional. I just got angry. I didn't realize I was doing it until the regent pointed it out."

"And then what did you do? Did you try to control it? Stop it?"

"I tried to will it closer, but I got this pain. Right here." He taps his forehead.

"That's expected." Bronwen gives him a sympathetic look. "We may be born with affinities, but they still come with a price.

Do you remember when I held the force field on the Island of Nightmares?"

"Yes." He remembers the drip of blood down her nose and the way she shook, but then he's seen her cast magic effortlessly. "So it hurts every time?"

"At first, yes. Simpler manipulation of magics hurts less, and once you build up strength, you will no longer notice the cost. Long, sustained, or massive tasks cause more."

"But when I go invisible, it takes no effort. It's as easy as breathing."

Bronwen shrugs. "I'm sorry. I don't know why. Shadow affinity is not sorcery. People don't even know or understand all there is to know about magic. People like Onanna or Serene, the Supreme Sorcerer, study all their lives and are still left wanting. If I had to theorize, there's a couple of different possibilities." She holds up a finger. "One: there's the law of like recognizing like. That theory states that magic is drawn to a sorcerer, but it also lives inside of a sorcerer. I've heard of fire elementists who can walk through fire without being burned. Maybe shadow is like that. Maybe it's drawn to you, but inside of you, too, so disappearing inside of it takes no effort because it's already *you*."

Ayc blinks at her.

"Does that make sense?"

"No."

Bronwen chuckles good-naturedly. "Think of it this way. Magic is like air. It's out here." She waves her hand above her head and then presses it to her chest, over her heart. "But it's also in here. It gives to us, and we keep it inside us." When Ayc looks no less confused, she tosses her hand up. "That's just one theory. There's whole books written on it, and I'm probably not summarizing it well."

"You said you had two theories. What's the other?"

"That shadow is *meant* to hide and conceal. So by disappearing within it, you're only asking the shadow to do what it does inherently. But wielding it—to ask it move into the light, to contort into new shapes, to obey you—that's forcing shadow to do something that goes against its nature."

That, at least, makes a little sense to Ayc. "But why didn't it hurt when my emotions controlled it?"

"If it's anything like magic, it's because certain forces can make magic stronger."

"I remember you saying that," Ayc cuts in. "Blood, love, death, sacrifice."

"Good memory," Bronwen says. "Though I was mainly talking to Xylie."

Ayc frowns. "Why?"

Bronwen's eyebrows shoot upward. "Hm?"

"Why just to Xylie?

"Oh, no, particular reason," she says in a way that makes him think it was, in fact, for a very particular reason. But she rushes onward before he can press. "It's theorized that these things—blood, death, sacrifice, love—can all be substituted for personal energy and pain, making it easier to sustain magic or to perform larger tasks than you would be able to do yourself. Emotion is like that, too, but it's volatile and unpredictable and absolutely difficult to get the magic to respond to emotion in the way that you want. The first task for most promising sorcerers is to build up a mental wall to separate their affinity from their own emotions, or else they'll never be able to wield it predictably. You'll hurt someone or kill yourself, even. Luckily, you have your bracelets because it can take years to learn just that. And even skilled sorcerers sometimes have their emotions get the better of them."

"Like you recently?" Ayc asked. "I've noticed your—"

She narrows her eyes in a look so sharp he fumbles with his words and rushes to choose a description. "Your magical farts."

"My *what?!*" Bronwen gasps, and he realizes it was absolutely the wrong thing to say.

"Your little bursts of magic," he swiftly amends, miming small explosions with his fingers. "You've been losing control this last week." Ayc thinks back to what might have happened before the coronation that resulted in her loss of control. And it hits him square in the gut. All his mirth flees to the dark. Fuck. "Are you certain you don't want to talk about Ryker?"

She jerks so hard she nearly kicks over the lantern, as though the name alone nearly makes her soul leave her skin behind. "No," she growls, her hands curling like she's squeezing an invisible neck. "I have it under control."

The magic that appears and crackles like a ball of lightning between her palms says otherwise.

Ayc retreats back a step. "All right. All right. Of course you do. I'm just...concerned."

Bronwen clenches her fists, and the magic disappears. She presses them to her forehead and takes several long breaths to calm herself. Ayc resists the urge to pull her into a hug...or perhaps to run back upstairs and bake something. Hugs and desserts are the only two things he knows how to offer, but neither of them is about to fix the deep grief that has taken root in Bronwen's heart.

"I'm fine," she says, dropping her hands. "Or I will be."

The single tear that escapes down her cheek betrays her lie. Ayc knows he should pretend that he doesn't see it, but his desire to respect her privacy drowns beneath his concern. "Bronwen—"

"Ayc." His name is a heavy sigh, a weight he didn't mean to make her carry. "Everyone has the monsters they fight. This darkness in my head—" She taps her forehead. "It's mine. I've fought it before, many times, and I've always won. I'll defeat it again."

He knows that darkness she speaks of. It's a sinister one. It starts dim, and then quietly pulls draperies closed and blows out every lantern until you find yourself lost in darkness, not quite sure when you last caught a glimpse of the light. When he was a boy, trapped in a kitchen downstairs like it was its own dungeon, he thought he might never see light again. His chest aches thinking of Bronwen in such a prison. "Can I help you fight it?"

Her lips tremble like they mean to smile, but don't make it into a curved bow. "You have your own monster to fight."

He swallows. She's not wrong; this power within him is its own kind of monster. It's why he's hidden from it for so long. "It doesn't mean you have to fight alone."

"I promise I'm fine," she insists. "And I'll ask for help if I need it."

He weighs her carefully. She juts out her chin. He fears that if he presses, he will only deepen the void she's keeping between herself and everyone else. So he changes the subject back to their training. "Well, now that you've thoroughly made my head numb with theory, how do I get started controlling shadow?"

She grants him a weak smile of gratitude. "I want you to try to move the shadow into the light. The goal is to extinguish the lantern."

Ayc squares up his shoulders and bounces from foot to foot like he's about to enter a sparring match. Her smile grows a little wider at his silliness. "So do I need to say something? Mutter a spell?"

"No, but you can speak your goal if it helps. The incantation of spells is simply to provide mental focus on the spell or the task you want to accomplish. Sorcerers use an ancient language that has long been forgotten, which the magical forces seem to respond to best. But you can manipulate magic without any words. So can the elementists, though I've also seen them speak words to guide intentions. That's all it is, shaping your own intentions to help your focus and make the action more clear."

He stops bouncing. "So if I want the shadow to move, I should just tell it to move."

She nods.

"That doesn't sound nearly as cool as you do when you mutter spells," he grumbles.

"We can't all be as glorious as me. Now focus and give it a try."

Ayc takes a breath and shuts his eyes. He tries to focus inward, at the hissing, icy power. He can picture it within, a swirling mass of darkness, cool to the mental touch. He imagines it as it did yesterday, filling up his veins, crystallizing his blood, burning his skin with its frozen touch. When it's there, he opens his eyes and sets them on the shadow once more. He inhales and pictures reaching out a mental hand, tugging on the shadows just as he did yesterday.

"Come," he commands.

The searing pain slams into his forehead once more. He grits his teeth against it, refusing to let it shake his focus. He can do this. He's done so much while being in pain. He's lived an entire life in pain. He can do this.

A bit of the darkness breaks off from the rest, stretching forward like a single finger.

The pain spreads from his head down his jaw, like his face might be splitting open. The shadow retreats as his focus wanes, distracted by the crack forming on his skull. He shakes his head to reorient himself.

He imagines that mental wall, the one he built inside him to survive the days when even breathing felt like too much. Just like Peregrin taught him. He constructs it back, brick by brick, and puts this pain behind it. And then he pulls the shadow closer until a whole hand is creeping forward. Each inch sends a new wave of pain that he forces another brick before, even as sweat breaks out along his forehead.

"If it's too much, let it go," Bronwen coaches. "It's like a muscle. It takes time to develop."

But they don't have time. Lora's life is in danger now. He must protect her, must find a way to control this power so she can survive. He pulls on the shadow harder, and it speeds up, rushing toward his feet, eating up the light as it goes.

A note of concern bites into Bronwen's tone. "Don't overdo it."

He doesn't look away from the shadow. The hand has become another wave of darkness, sweeping over their feet and toward the lantern. "I've got it."

"Overdoing it can kill you," she snaps.

"I can do this."

He wills the shadow to cover the lantern, even as his body trembles with the effort. The flame within the lantern flickers.

The cracking, tearing pain has made it to his chest now, like claws are attempting to pry open his ribcage. But he grits his teeth.

I can do this.

I've survived worse than this.

He adds another wall to separate him from the pain, building it as high as he can. If he must make his mind a fortress against the pain, that is what he'll do.

I am stronger than my pain.

If that must become his mantra, he will make it a battle cry.

"Lights out," he commands.

And the candle goes dark.

Everything goes dark.

FIFTEEN

AYC

He did it.

He fucking did it.

A smile tugs on his lips as he revels in the darkness he's created. But Bronwen seizes his arm, her fingernails digging in. "Release it, Ayc!"

He releases his hold on the power. The pain eases. Warmth returns to his body. It's utterly dark, but Ayc can see well enough anyway. His vision has always been sharp in the dark when he takes the bracelet off, another trait he's certain he earned from his Drakr father. He can easily read the fear in the width of Bronwen's eyes and the gaping of her mouth.

"Shit! Are you well?"

Ayc nods, but a wave of dizziness slams into him. He swiftly sits on the ground so he doesn't fall. Bronwen lowers herself to her knees before him, even as she tosses a hand above her head. A ball of light flings upward and hovers, filling the room with its sapphire glow like a chandelier of blue flame.

"I'm fine, I'm fine," Aye reassures. The dizziness is already fading. In its place is an intense and sudden fatigue, heavy enough that he lies flat on the stone. He feels like he could curl up and sleep right here, dungeon or not. "I'm just tired."

"Tired?" Bronwen repeats incredulously. "Just tired?"

"You didn't actually think I could do it, did you?"

"Ayc, I thought it would take you months to do what you just did. When I started at Velphin, it took me a month to overcome the pain just to form magic into a single ball of energy, and then I passed out. How are you still conscious?"

Ayc shrugs. "Perhaps it's just because I'm accustomed to pain. I withstand it every day."

Bronwen's mouth drops open. "Every day. What do you mean every day?"

Fuck, he shouldn't have said that.

"Your pain didn't go away after the Severing stone, did it?" When Ayc's jaw locks, she adds a bite to her tone, "And don't fucking lie to me!"

"No," Ayc says through ground teeth. "Don't tell Lora."

"Fuck! That's your concern? Have you seen a healer?"

"No. What is a healer going to do?"

"Determine why you're still in pain. If it's not the stone, there has to be something causing it. Maybe she can fix it. Come on." Bronwen stands and offers her hand. "I'm taking you now."

"Where? To the castle's healer? No, thanks." He thinks of the healer's tough hands as she pulled the stitches through his ear. Or how she told him to get out of her sight when he was so delirious with fever, he thought he was going to die, like his mother, begging for water. Zinnia ended up fetching a healer from Wyntra town and nursing him back to health herself. "She's got the bedside manner of a cranky opossum. No, actually, I would prefer the opossum. A cranky opossum would be a fucking delight in comparison—and would probably have warmer hands."

"Yes, I've heard she's wretched and unskilled. That's why Lora fired her and hired a new healer."

"When did she have time to do that?"

"Yesterday. She barely stopped moving after our meeting with Amos. I had to chase after her all day. She's got a list that nearly fills up the whole book of things she wants to do before we leave on Tour, and she refuses to let any of us or the staff do it. She's going to burn herself out if she's not careful." Bronwen huffs. "But...one crisis at a time." She wiggles her fingers. "You'll like the new healer, I promise. And I'm not taking no for an answer."

"Can't I just take a nap instead? This stone floor seems awfully comfortable right now."

"No! Gets your ass up, Ayc."

"Fine, fine!"

The new healer is flitting around the infirmary like she, herself, is comprised of an entire hive of working bees. She seems to be simultaneously tightening bed sheets and sorting through supplies on the carts beside the bed. Just as quickly, she turns and marches to the other side of the room, her hooves that stick out of her flowing linen pants clomping on the ground. A matching beige tunic hangs almost to her knees, an apron tied around her ample hips. She stops by the healer's desk along the opposite wall, picks up a quill, and jots something down on paper there. She hums quietly to herself, tilting her head of short, brown curls this way and that. Long, leaf-shaped earrings dangle from her ears, reminding Ayc of a dream he once had, though he can't quite remember it.

Bronwen clears her throat from where she and Ayc stand at the doorway. "Getting settled in all right, Reselda?"

The healer jumps and spins around, pressing a hand to her heart. "Oh, you startled me, darling. I'm sorry. I was in my own world." Her smile curls up her freckled, alabaster cheeks, making her brown eyes shine from behind large, round spectacles. From this angle, Ayc can make out the short-curved horns peeking through her curls. "I'm very well, Bronwen. I need to return to Avia tomorrow to ensure that my apprentice is ready to take over the practice. It's unexpected, and the timeline is short, but she's ready."

If there's an audible equivalent to the smell of freshly baked bread, it's her voice. Soft, soothing, and with the simple power to make one feel immediately at ease. It's familiar, too, just like her earrings.

Reselda continues, "Lora requested a list of supplies before I leave. I wanted to poke around in here before I left. I'm afraid I'm finding more dust than I'm finding useful medical supplies. Whatever did the previous healer do here anyway?"

"Drink fae wine mostly," Ayc says.

Reselda's eyes widen until they are nearly as round as her glasses. "Oh, that explains all the bottles in the tonic cabinet."

"Thank you, Reselda," Bronwen says. "And please give me the list when you're done. I'll see it gets to the castle supplier. If you give it to Lora, she'll try to do it all on her own."

"Still thinking it's her responsibility to run the world all on her own?"

"Now, more than ever."

It seems, for the second time today, Ayc is meeting someone whose history with Lora goes deeper even than his own. It should come as no surprise, as Reselda is from Avia, a place where he suspects Lora was always far more free than she's ever been allowed to be in this castle. He's grateful, then, that these walls are being filled with people from that village. Perhaps it will make the cold stone seem more like a home.

"Enough of my jabbering," Reselda says, wiping her dusty hands on her apron. "How can I help you both?"

Bronwen folds her arms over her chest and looks pointedly at Ayc.

"I..." No other words follow. He's spent so much of his life hiding his pain from sight, never acknowledging it even to himself. He doesn't know the words that fit the shape and size of his pain, how to summarize entire years into a few sentences.

"He needs your help," Bronwen says impatiently. "He's just too stubborn to ask for it."

"Bit hypocritical, don't you think?" Ayc mutters.

"I'm going to summon your balls through your throat," Bronwen mutters back.

Reselda folds her hands together and gives a deeply kind smile, like she has all day for their foolishness. "Bronwen, why don't you give us some privacy?"

"Because I'm afraid he might bolt as soon as I leave."

"If he does, he does. You can't force anyone to accept help. The choice is up to him. But I'm going to make some tea, and I hope he joins me." She turns on her hoof and walks back toward the hearth at the back of the infirmary, where, for the first time in Ayc's memory, a fire is actually blazing. She takes a black kettle from the mantle and moves to the sink nearby to wash away the years of dust and cobwebs.

Bronwen gives Ayc one more glance, one full of threats of bodily violence if he dares leave this place without talking to Reselda. Magic bursts in a static cloud from her palm to punctuate the point.

Ayc sticks out his tongue. "Fart along, Bronwen."

She snarls something unintelligible and thrusts a crude gesture at him as she storms toward the door, a single blue spark firing from her middle finger—which really, just proves his point.

Reselda hangs the newly cleaned kettle above the fire and turns around to face him. "You can sit wherever you like. Or stand. Whatever makes you comfortable."

The fatigue from using his magic affinity rests deep in his bones, even though he's put his bracelets back on. He chooses one of the beds and sits on the edge. He's grateful that the sheets, for once, are clean. He's less grateful at the way his entire body winces at the contact of the soft surfaces, as though his back has been waiting for this moment to tell him just how much it fucking hurts.

He's tempted to lie down, to grant his muscles some relief from his own weight, but he's certain if he does, he'll be asleep in an instant.

When he looks up, he finds Reselda has been carefully

watching him through her gold-rimmed glasses. "It's good to see you looking so well, Ayc."

"You know me?"

"I saw you in the hospital in Lux Aester."

Ah. The leaf earrings. The familiar voice. Ayc should have known. "I'm sorry I don't remember you. I wasn't exactly at my best."

"On the contrary. You were fighting to survive. And look, you succeeded!"

He smiles at her optimism. The kettle whistles, and she uses a towel to remove it and carry it back to the counter.

"Do you fare well with lavender and vanilla?" she asks.

"Yes."

Her broad frame blocks her movements from view, but he can hear the water pouring and the clink of the spoon against the porcelain. She talks as she works.

"How do you think I should decorate this place? It's a little grim. Places of healing should be comforting."

"I think you've already made a huge improvement," Ayc says. She's opened up the curtains, flooding the room with more light than he's ever seen. A few she's even cracked open, so the air doesn't feel stuffy and lets in a bit of the salty breeze.

"Hm," she says. She carries the two teacups over to the bed. She hands him one. "Let it steep a little longer."

"Thank you." He cradles it in his palms, enjoying the warmth. The smell of lavender soothes his nerves, tempting him even closer to sleep.

She ignores the wooden stool that the previous healer generally preferred and instead sits on the next bed. She crosses her legs beneath her and balances her tea on one knee. With her freckled face and big glasses, she looks young, though Ayc suspects she has at least several decades on him because her eyes look much older and wiser. She studies, like she's assessing everything about him, cataloguing every symptom he might be letting show despite his attempt to hide it.

Ayc stares down into the cup of tea, at the bag bobbing on the surface, turning the water into an ever-deepening gray. "I suppose I have to talk to you now."

"Only if you want to. And we can discuss whatever you want. We can talk about the weather." She twirls her wrist toward the window. "Or we can drink our tea in silence. It's up to you."

Ayc taps the side of the cup. "Will you tell Lora?"

"And betray your trust in me as a healer? Never. I take the privacy of every person I see very personally."

He nods, grateful. He blows on the tea, but it still nearly burns his lips when he lifts it to his mouth. He lowers it back down again and searches around the room once more as though perhaps the right words or the will to speak them might be written on the stone.

"Can I ask you why you don't want her to know?" Reselda asks.

It takes Ayc a long moment to answer. He has to root out the truth deep in his stomach first. "I don't want her, or anyone, to think me weak. Or a burden."

Reselda cocks her head. "That certainly doesn't sound like the Lora I know. Do you believe she'd truly think that?"

"I don't know," Ayc says honestly. Something within him screams that she would. But he thinks that thing is called fear, and he knows better than to trust its logic.

She picks up her teacup and adjusts a little closer to the edge of the bed. "My blood runs thinner than most. A single cut might bleed for hours before it stops. I have bruises all over my skin, hidden beneath my clothes from the smallest of bumps. With a single fall, I could turn from healer to a patient. Do you think that makes me less of a healer?"

He shakes his head. "No, of course not."

"And what of your friends? Tavish and Xylie and Peregrin. Do you find them weak? Or a burden?"

"No!" he says, more intensely than he means. "They're the strongest people I know. I'm *honored* to know them."

She leans forward and lowers her voice into a gentle whisper.

"Then why are you so quick to hold yourself to a standard you wouldn't enforce upon anyone else?"

Ayc's mouth hangs open. Because he has no answer to that question. None. But he finally finds the words he's been seeking since he entered the infirmary. No, words he's been failing to speak for years. "I'm in pain. I'm in pain *every day*. And I've been in pain every day for over eight years."

Her gaze softens, and she sets the cup of tea down beside her to give him her full attention. "Tell me more," she says. Not like she's a healer with a job. Like a friend who cares.

So, he tells her. He tells her about the Binding stone and about the lie he told that left him in agony. He tells her about surviving through gryphon feathers and Xylie's pain tonics and the love of baking and music. When emotions threaten to choke him, he pauses to sip the soothing tea, and she waits patiently, silently, until he moves on. And then he tells her about the Severing stone, about the way Lora and Xylie saved him, about how the pain never went away but seemed better for a time.

"But now it's not better," he says. "And I don't know why."

She stands. "Can I assess you further?"

He nods and stands with her. Her fingers trace the bones of his neck, his back, and his hips, and then she moves to his muscles. When she finds a place where he winces, a place particularly tender, she pulls a book from her apron and makes a note. She steps away to retrieve a bag from the corner and pulls a clear rod, rounded on one side. She runs it over the same places where her hands have just scanned. She has him bend and twist, noting when the pain limits him or when it stops him altogether. She has him lie on his back and then lifts his legs in ways that nearly make his back arch off the bed. Finally, she steps away, giving him a sheepish smile.

"I'm done torturing you now."

Ayc sits up and tries to study her face as she studies the notes in her book. "So what's wrong with me?"

"I'm not certain." She snaps the book closed. "I do have a theory. We need to do further testing to confirm it. I don't have the equipment I need here to do so. We will have to wait for supplies to come in.”

“What’s your theory?”

“Perhaps we should wait until after the testing so I know for sure.”

“It’s that bad, huh?” he teases, laughing a little.

She says nothing.

His laughter dies in his throat. “Fuck, it’s that bad, isn’t it?”

“I don’t believe that there’s a malformation of your bones or another identifiable, specific physical ailment, such as a tear in the muscle. This Surveyor”—she pulls the glass contraption from where she stashed it in her apron—“is enchanted to turn red at the presence of a physical abnormality, and it demonstrated nothing.”

“Nothing?” The word tastes like cow dung on Ayc’s tongue, and he can’t make himself swallow. “So there’s nothing wrong with me? My pain is just in my head. It isn’t real.”

Because it feels pretty fucking real.

“No!” Reselda says emphatically. “I would never say such a thing. Of course, your pain is real. You *feel* it. That’s the only qualification for pain to be real.”

He finally manages to swallow, but it still feels like something is choking him. “Then what’s wrong with me?”

Reselda sighs and presses her glasses back up the bridge of her nose. “I’ve seen this before. People who have pain without having something that can be specifically pointed at to address the *why*. They all have one thing in common: they have survived more than anyone should have to. Physically, emotionally, mentally. They’ve endured trauma, and when the body has to endure that much trauma, there’s evidence to support that it fundamentally changes a body and how it responds to its environment and the sensations it’s exposed to. What caused the pain has ended, but that doesn’t mean that your body doesn’t remember. Or that it will *ever* forget.”

There’s something in the way she stresses the last line, the way she accents it with a look of profound empathy that tells Ayc something he truly doesn't want to know. But he ignores it. He's not ready yet.

"I had golden root. Why wasn't that enough to fix this?"

"I don't truly know. I'm sorry, but I don't. Golden root is powerful, but it has its limits. It can't completely change how our bodies are created or how they adapt."

"So is there anything that can be done?" he asks.

"Of course there is. I can give you exercises to help you. Massage can also be both comforting and healing. I will be traveling with you on the Tour and can provide those treatments. Of course, pain tonics and even some muscle salve would also be useful. I have a special herb that you could smoke, but I tend to save that for when other remedies aren't sufficient."

"But it'll never go away." The words slam into his chest, even as he says it. Something burns at the back of his eyes, and he clenches his hands over his knees to keep it at bay.

"If my suspicions are correct, then no, Ayc." Her voice is every bit as soothing as it was before, but it doesn't remind him of freshly baked bread anymore. It reminds him of cinnamon rolls with blood sprayed across the top instead of icing, a moment when his life changed. It feels like that, like the earth is opening beneath him and the walls are closing in. "We can't go back and blot out the things that happened to us. I wish we could. The only thing we can do is to move forward and find the tools we need to prosper in the life we've been given."

Ayc shoves to his feet. He desperately needs out of this room. Pressure is rising within him, something he cannot name. He might explode with it, and if he does, he doesn't want to hurt anyone but himself. "Thank you for your time. I appreciate it." He turns and half-bolts toward the door.

"Wait. I have a few panic tonics," she calls after him, "if you want to take them with you."

"I already have some." It's a lie, but he can't wait while she retrieves them.

"It's all right if you're sad," she says urgently, like she needs him to hear it. "It's normal to grieve the life and the health we might have had if things were different."

He forces himself to turn around, to give her a smile. "I'm not sad. I'm fine. It's good to have answers."

It's a truth and two lies.

He's not sad. That's not the right name for the pressure that's rising in him. But no, he's *not* fine, and it's *not* good to have answers. At least, not *these* answers.

He flings the door open with a force that makes the hinges groan and then rushes down the stairs that lead out of the tower where the infirmary resides. He's not certain where he's going, only that he must go, as though somehow he might be able to outrun the pain in his back, the truth of the healer's words.

Gods damn Bronwen! This—*this!*—is why he didn't want to fucking come to see a healer.

At least when his pain was caused by the Binding stone, it had a reason, something he could point to and blame. And he had hope. A fool's hope, but hope, nonetheless. A cure existed out there somewhere, and maybe one day, luck would smile upon him, and he would be free.

But now he is free of the stone, but not of the agony it wrought on his body for eight years.

Now, he has to face the truth. He is almost twenty-three years old, and his body is broken in a way that can never be fixed. And that means whether he lives for a year, or a decade, or three centuries, he will never see a day when he does not know pain.

As soon as Ayc slips into his kitchen, he's greeted by soft growls. Muffin stands on the center counter, Ayc's remaining oven mitt pinned beneath their front feet, their jaw clamped around the thumb. They shake their head back and forth, and the last valiant thread gives way.

"Well, I think you've killed it," Ayc says with a long, tired sigh. "I really liked those, you know."

Muffin spits out the thumb. They plop down on their rump and even curl their lips back, flashing teeth as though they are smiling, the picture of perfect innocence. They're too cute for Ayc to get mad at. Not that Ayc even has it in him to still feel angry. The rage he felt when he left the infirmary has faded to only the pain and the weariness, a fatigue that digs down into his very marrow. He wants nothing more than to sink into his bed and sleep for the rest of the day. Maybe, if possible, for the rest of the week.

But seeing as Xylie is missing and there's a dragon that needs babysitting, that doesn't seem like a possibility.

"Where's Xylie, anyway?" he asks like he expects the dragon to answer.

They turn their head to the left, toward the cabinet by the oven. There, a note is pinned to the wood. Surely just a coincidence on the dragon's part. Ayc pulls it from the wood.

> Meeting with Tavish.
> ~~Muffin~~ The dragon is asleep on the bed.
> Be back soon.

He might have felt a little victorious to see the scratched-out name, but now Ayc feels nothing. He wants to keep feeling nothing.

Since his bed isn't an option, he sinks down on his stool instead. He folds his arms on the counter and leans heavily upon them. "How are you, Muffin? You'll never believe the day I've had."

Muffin cocks their head and blinks their big red eyes, like perhaps they are listening. Or maybe Ayc is simply imagining things.

Ayc lets his head fall into his arms. It all feels too heavy. The emotions of the day entangle in his chest, fighting to be the one felt the hardest and the strongest. His back shudders beneath the load.

Ayc isn't sure how he's supposed to live like this every day. Not for decades. Certainly, not for centuries. Maybe he's not strong enough for this.

Something nudges his hand. Ayc lifts his head. Muffin nuzzles their nose against Ayc's fingers once more.

"You're a sweet thing," he murmurs as he strokes his fingers down the pearly white scales. Muffin leans into Ayc's touch and snuggles closer to his body until Ayc encircles his arms around the dragon. They let out a low, happy growl in their chest, almost like a cat purring.

Ayc wonders if they know somehow. If Muffin sensed Ayc's emotions and wanted to provide comfort, or if Muffin solely wanted to seek it. Either way, Ayc tightens his hold, cuddling him closer, and lets his face fall into Muffin's neck. Despite the hardness of dragon scale, they are silky to the touch, like a snake's skin.

Muffin nudges Ayc's fingertips. Their breath is somehow both warm and cold. The dragon sniffs, dragging air in as though scenting something new.

"What is it— *FUCK!*"

The curse blares from his lips as the dragon sinks their teeth into Ayc's hand. They release just as quickly and spring back to their feet, startled by Ayc's roar. A cold burn surges through his arm. Ayc jumps backward, knocking over the stool in his haste to scramble to his feet. He inspects his hand, expecting to find it mangled, bloody, torn to shreds, but the puncture marks are already healing, faster than even his fae blood should allow.

The icy throb still pulses, spreading through his veins and up his arm. White, pearly lines mark the back of his hand and disappear up his sleeve. He yanks his sleeve back to watch the lines weave across the circumference of his arm and up onto his bicep. The cold surges up his shoulder before it fades just as quickly as it began.

Ayc races to his bedroom, hauls his shirt over his head, and tosses it aside. He surveys himself in the mirror of his wardrobe. White marks blossom from where Muffin bit him--the bite mark already completely gone—and up to his shoulder. The lines mimic patterns of his veins until it looks like a bolt of lightning. It glistens in light from the window and simmers like a rainbow. No, like a mother of pearl. Just like Muffin's scales. Ayc licks his thumb and rubs at it like it's ink from a quill or chocolate he has spilled, but it doesn't budge.

"What the fuck?" He isn't sure whether to feel horror or awe. Both, actually. He's probably feeling both.

The dragon pads into the room, their lips curled back, almost smiling like they're proud.

"What did you just do to me?" Ayc asks, glancing back at the mirror. He twists, trying to look at his arm from a different angle.

A response comes in a deep, purring voice.

"Ayc."

Ayc freezes in place, then, slowly, ever so slowly, turns to face the white dragon. They smile at him. He's certain of it.

Muffin's lips and mouth do not move when they speak, but Ayc hears them all the same. *"Ayc,"* the dragon says again.

And then:

"Mine."

CHAPTER
SIXTEEN

LORA

"Xylie, where is Ayc?" Lora asks, stabbing her spoon in the bowl of stew until the carrot dies a torturous death in a thousand orange pieces. She imagines, briefly, that it's Ayc's head. They've been waiting for Ayc for fifteen minutes. The stew the kitchen staff prepared is growing cold, thickening into a gelatinous brown blob. Lora won't be able to eat it now. The film that settles over it makes her shudder.

"I don't know," Xylie signs, her signs growing bigger and exaggerated to demonstrate her frustration. *"I'm not his babysitter."*

"You kind of are," Bronwen points out, from where she rests her head on her arms on the table, where she's kept it the entire meal. She over-indulged in wine last night and has a horrific headache. Xylie gave her a freshly brewed pain tonic when she first arrived, but it doesn't seem to be doing the trick.

Xylie bats one of her braids out of her face before signing. *"All right. I am. But I haven't seen him."*

Bronwen groans, pressing her eyes shut like the candlelight hurts.

A familiar warning bell chimes deep within Lora's gut. She's seen Bronwen hungover many times. Her First has never been a stranger to a bit of over-indulging, of letting alcohol buzz through her veins until the world's harshness softens and laughter flows more easily. Bronwen possesses a carefreeness that Lora sometimes envies. It's equal only to the sadness that lurks within her, an insidious monster meant to devour, a deep, all-consuming sadness that sometimes appears for no reason at all.

The first time Lora witnessed Bronwen get lost in the sorrow, in their second year at Adamant, she didn't recognize the signs— the drinking not to thrive, but to forget; the lesser control of her magic—until Bronwen just... ceased. Ceased to get up for class, ceased to bathe, ceased to exist in any way other than breathing. Lora wrote Reselda, afraid that if she took her to Adamant's healers, she'd be kicked out. Reselda prescribed a daily tonic, and Lora forced Bronwen to swallow it every morning. Eventually, Bronwen returned to her bright self, until she stopped taking the medication, thinking herself cured. It always came back, the insidious little enemy it is.

Bronwen has been off the medication for six months now. She's been fine. But after Ryker, it makes sense that the sadness might be rising once more. Is that what's happening now? Is this normal grief? Or is the monster returning once more?

"Don't look at me like that," Bronwen whispers, peeking a single eye open. "I'm fine."

"Are you?" Lora asks quietly.

"Yes."

Lora hesitates. She must tread carefully. Sometimes, a push is just what Bronwen needs, and sometimes, it makes her retreat deeper within herself. She weighs her decision, but Peregrin speaks.

"Wasn't Ayc training with you this afternoon?" Their bowl of stew is already empty, as it was within minutes of being served. Peregrin has always treated eating like a mission to be completed as quickly as possible. Since then, they've been spinning a knife around on the table. The whirl, whirl, whirl of it against the table sounds like a little shriek in Lora's ears.

Bronwen lifts her head only slightly. "Yes, but I haven't seen him since he went to—" She stops and starts again abruptly. "Uh... the dungeons. Where we were training."

"Nice save," Tavish remarks. "Very believable. Where was he really?"

Bronwen casts him a glare so fierce that, though Tavish can't see it, he certainly feels it. "Nevermind," he says swiftly and fills his mouth with a chunk of potato.

Bronwen lets her head fall back on her arms with a groan.

Lora is about to press Bronwen when the side door flies open with a bang. Ayc rushes in like a whirlwind. His hair hangs loose about his face. The ties of his collar have pulled taut, bunching up the cloth. She remembers the way, just hours ago, she played with that same collar.

Heat burns her cheeks even now. She must have temporarily lost all common sense. Why else had she pressed the heel of her hand to the base of her throat? Why else did she revel in the way his pulse skipped into an entirely different rhythm as her fingers poised over the artery in his neck?

For fuck's sake! They were in the courtyard. Anyone could have come across them. Her guards saw! Veni, too, most certainly saw.

But with Ayc's body beneath her, she forgot everything but the shape of his waist between her thighs. She grew consumed with this game between them. The play of power, the give and take, the push and shove. It's always been like this between them, and she can't make herself surrender now. She certainly can't let him know that she's already lost.

He's trying to get under her skin, and she can never admit, even for a moment, that he already lives there. And that's how she ended up with her hand around his throat, asking him if he liked it harder. And he said yes.

Fuck.

She's not sure how she's supposed to live with that answer. Now, she can scarcely look at him and the damn curve of his neck without imagining how hard he might feel within her as she closed her fingers around his neck. How he might gasp for her, moan for her, beg for her.

I can't, I can't, I can't.

I want, I want, I want.

Bronwen clears her throat, and Lora jerks her gaze away. Fuck, she was staring. Just the sight of him, and she's completely lost her focus. She has to get it together.

"Sorry I'm late," he says as he pulls the chair away from the table.

Right, she's meant to be irritated with him.

"There better have been a fire," Lora snips.

Ayc cringes. "Not exactly." He tugs on the edge of his glove, carefully folding his sleeve over it. "Just a small, inconsequential problem that no one else needs to be concerned with."

"That sounds very reassuring," Peregrin murmurs, spinning their knife once more.

Xylie catches Ayc's eye and raises both of her eyebrows. He shakes his head. The two have always had an uncanny way of speaking to one another without using sign language, probably arising from the time when they were first friends before Ayc learned to sign.

"Oh, you're being odd, too," Tavish observes.

"I'm not—"

"Can we just get the meeting started?" Lora interrupts Ayc's protest. She's got enough on her list of problems without adding whatever it is Ayc is dealing with.

Bronwen groans again but finally sits upright. "Yes, please."

"Not feeling any better?" Ayc asks.

"No. Worse, actually."

Ayc pushes a tray laid out with star-shaped cookies toward Bronwen. "Have a cookie. I recognize Zinnia's handiwork. She makes the best anise cookies." He winks. "She got the recipe from me."

Bronwen eyes it skeptically. "Will it help?"

"Of course," Ayc says. "Dessert always helps. It may not fix your shitty situation, but at least then you're in a shitty situation *eating dessert.* Which is much preferable."

Bronwen shrugs like he has a point. She snatches a cookie from the tray and stuffs it into her mouth. It's been glazed and rolled in colored sugar, and when it crumbles between her teeth, it leaves a dusting on her upper lip. She swallows it down so quickly, Lora isn't sure she's actually tasted it. "I just don't understand why the tonic Xylie gave me didn't work like the one in Somnia Ignis. That one was the best potion I've ever had. It worked immediately and lasted for so long. This is nothing like that."

Xylie clasps her arms over her chest and sinks down in her chair.

"I don't mean any offense," Bronwen adds. "I'm just confused, that's all. Did you not imbue these with magic?"

Lora frowns. What the fuck is she talking about?

Xylie's eyes narrow, and her hands snap in a way that makes it clear she's yelling without even making a sound. *"I don't have affinity."*

Bronwen releases a humorless laugh, like Xylie has told a joke, and she doesn't understand the punchline. "Of course you do. Doesn't she, Lora?"

"No," Lora says flatly. She just wants to start the fucking meeting. "She's just remarkably gifted in alchemy."

"*No one* is that gifted in alchemy. Her potions are better than others because she imbues them with magic." She gestures to Ayc. "Ayc, tell them."

Ayc's brow furrows. "No. If Xylie had affinity, I would know."

Xylie tucks her head toward her chest.

"Dammit, I know magic when I see it." Bronwen whips her head down the table to where Peregrin sits, still spinning their knife in a casual circle. "Peregrin, you would have assisted in her testing. Tell them I'm right. Xylie has affinity."

Peregrins slaps their hand down on their knife, arresting the spin. "Perhaps, Bronwen, you should consider that it isn't any of your fucking business."

Bronwen recoils at Peregrin's sharpness. Regret climbs over her face. "You're right. I'm sorry, Xylie. We should start this meeting before I say more things that make me look like an ass." She grabs another cookie and stuffs half of it into her mouth.

Lora studies Xylie. Her cousin rocks side to side in the chair. When they were young, it pained Lora to see her movements. She used to wrap an arm around her, thinking it would ease her distress. But Lora was wrong. Xylie's stims distressed others because they pressed against their ideas of what normal is, but they comforted Xylie. Lora learned that the best thing that she could do was create a safe space for Xylie to utilize her coping mechanisms, without judgment or feeling the pressure to hide. The way Lora felt like she always needed to hide it when she wanted to do the exact same thing.

"Let's begin," Xylie signs, even as she continues to rock.

The Five look toward Lora at the head of the table. Lora pulls her book from her pocket, where she's written a list for the agenda. It's long. "Where should we begin?"

"Perhaps it's best to discuss what's most likely to lead us into war," Peregrin says. They tuck their knife back into the belt that crosses over their chest. "Lux Aester and Aluina being the two most notable."

Lora told Peregrin in the letter that they did not have to come to the meeting if they wished to remain with their family. She wasn't surprised when they were seated at the table before she even arrived. She's selfishly grateful they came. Their advice is invaluable.

"How was the meeting with Amos?" Tavish asks.

"I'm sure it was as delightful as swimming in a river of piss," Ayc offers.

Lora shudders. "Thank you, Ayc. That was—" She hesitates, then admits, "Quite an accurate description, actually."

A delighted but slightly surprised smile crosses Ayc's face. He hides it by taking too large a bite of the stew, but crosses his eyes as he does so. She finds herself simultaneously wanting to laugh and to heave her spoon at his head. She's trying to be serious, dammit.

"Behave," she hisses.

He holds up his hands in surrender.

Lora refuses to look at him again while she explains about the meeting with Amos, about her ultimatums, and his threats to cut off aid.

"It's just one reason that—unless we find further evidence that he's conspiring against you—we can't have him arrested," Peregrin says. "I also recommend you leave the actual arresting to the high courts. Then no one can accuse you of bias."

"I've been thinking the same," Lora says. As Sovereign, she has the authority to arrest and punish whoever she likes. She can operate as judge and jury. That's certainly how her mother operated, how she kept fear in the hearts of her people. But the high courts handled cases of national importance, including treason, and allowing them to issue a warrant would set her apart from her mother. But... "They'll require significant evidence before they indict a sitting regent. Do you have anything more to report?"

"No," Peregrin says. "But I'm still searching."

"And what should we do in the meantime?" Lora asks. "How do we help the people of Lux Aester? I can't continue to do nothing."

"I wouldn't call helping Ohen doing nothing," Ayc says. "You and Bronwen set up an entire organization to help. There's no reason that has to stop."

"The organization was only meant to be a bandage on a gaping wound until we could do something more. All the organization can do is get people out of Lux Aester."

"That is still an important task," Peregrin states.

"But people should not have to flee the only home they know in order to be safe to be themselves and love who they love."

The light in Ayc's smile dims. "I know."

"A bandage on a gaping wound is better than no bandage at all," Xylie signs.

"But I was the one who funded it," Lora says, "and I can't continue to do so."

"Why not? Last I checked, we are sitting in a castle." Ayc gestures with his spoon above his head and then directs it toward her. "That you own. You have access to that royal treasury your mother always ensured was packed to the rafters. No one is going to notice if those funds go elsewhere."

Lora stops. She's very grateful that she had the guards wait outside and had Bronwen cast a silencing spell on the room, similar to what is on the Sovereign's office. "That would be... incredibly illegal."

"The organization has always been illegal," Tavish says. "It's never stopped us before. What could they do? Arrest you."

It's a fair point, and one that feels like a heavy weight. As Sovereign, she could do anything. She could behead someone in front of a crowd of hundreds, and no one would have any recourse to do anything against her. Perhaps, that's more power than anyone should ever have.

And it is hers. Whether she wants it or not.

Her scalp itches where the crown presses, and she ignores the desire to dig at her skin to make the sensation stop.

"It would be a far better use of the funds than your mother ever used them for," Peregrin says.

"We'd have to hire a treasurer that we're certain we can trust," Bronwen says. "But also one who is willing to look the other direction in case the numbers don't add up."

Lora scoffs. "So a trustworthy crook."

"I, uh," Tavish begins, "I may have a recommendation."

"A pirate?" Xylie signs. Ayc translates for her.

"He's a former pirate, yes. Lovelace is what we called him. He's a human from Aluina. He used to be a merchant, but he escaped with his family to Everadyn after the Drakr, well—" Tavish trails off, cocking his head toward where Ayc sits across the table.

Ayc only reaches for an anise cookie and crams it into his mouth.

"They settled in Sal Maris," Tavish continues, "but he has five kids, and there weren't a lot of well-paying jobs available to him, so he signed up for a pirate crew. He mostly kept track of the books and handled buying and selling of stolen goods, so we weren't caught. As long as he was paid well, he did his job. But when Zephen decided to dabble in slavery, he couldn't stomach it. He waited until we made land and fled the crew. He told me he planned to take his family to Silvae since he heard Totus Omni are friendly to immigrants. After you rescued me, I wrote a letter to Silvae, hoping to find him. He was always kind to me, looked after me when I was younger. And to my surprise, he wrote back. He and his family are doing all right. Getting by. But I don't think he would say no if the new Sovereign needed a head treasurer. I can also help double-check his work. I'm good with numbers if someone is willing to read them to me, or the librarians can engrave them."

Well, if anyone is going to fit the role, it would be someone like him. Tavish has always been an impeccable judge of character. His social anxiety gives him little other choice.

"Send him a letter and tell him I would like to interview him. As soon as possible." Lora flips to an open page at the back of the book and quickly scrawls a message. She tears it out and passes the note to Tavish. "You can give this to the existing treasurer. The amount he gives you in return should cover passage from Silvae for him and his entire family."

Tavish tucks it into the pocket of his vest and smiles. "Thank you for giving a chance to a pirate."

"I'm willing to support anyone who's willing to go through such great lengths to support his family, so long as they stop that line at slavery."

"I can write to Vidar," Bronwen says, referring to the innkeeper who owns the Pink Elk, a tavern in Bromalis territory, who has been involved in the organization since the early days. "Ask if he's willing to take more of a leadership role since none of us are going to be able to devote as much attention to it as we should."

Lora nods. They're a good choice. There are others, too, deeper within Lux Aester who might be options as well. Identities that only she and Bronwen know, and she wants to keep it that way.

"It doesn't have to be just helping those who wish to escape," Peregrin says. "With additional funds, we could encourage those within Lux Aester to become a little braver. Protest. Begin to create change from the inside."

"Lux Aester has a history of not treating those people with any sense of kindness and justice," Bronwen says, her voice scarcely a whisper. A reminder that this is more than just theory to her. She's lost friends, both by their own hands because of their suffering, and because Lux Aester charged them with petty crimes and threw them away in prisons with unjustly long sentences.

"And the last two Sovereign refused to hear the appeals," Peregrin points out. "That is not the case anymore. If they suspect they have a Sovereign sensitive to their cause, they might be more willing to fight. If Lux Aester is going to have any lasting change, it must come from within. They are allowed to rule as they see fit, and the people are allowed to elect those who lead them, and those rulers rule as they see fit. Without internal change, they will continue to vote as they always have."

"Fools, the lot of them," Bronwen mutters.

Peregrin nods. "People rarely know what is best for them. They're much more comfortable with familiarity, even if what is familiar is the weight of invisible chains."

Peregrin almost has sympathy in their tone, and she doesn't understand. She doesn't think people who choose to remain ignorant and harm others with their careless decisions deserve much empathy. But then, Amos and those beneath him have certainly done their part in aiding that ignorance. The education system in Lux Aester is horrendous, and perhaps that's intentional.

Xylie snaps her fingers, and Lora translates as Xylie signs, "In the meantime, we could begin stocking away supplies. That way, in case we have to take dramatic actions and Lux Aester cuts off the food supplies, we can help those impacted."

"We should begin doing so for Aluina, too," Peregrin says.

The subject shifts with that. There's much more to be discussed in terms of Lux Aester, but there will be daily meetings after today. They will discuss Lux Aester every day until the people within are all safe and free.

Lora and her Five discuss Aluina. They are all in agreement that the best course of action is to attempt to get the regents to support them, even though Lora knows that may take time. Even Ayc nods along in agreement. Peregrin and Lora discuss who they think will most likely be the most difficult to convince. Grey will certainly side with Lora, but she's uncertain about the rest. Briar has a good heart, but they are too unserious to be prepared for war. Busara is wise but old enough to remember the last great war with the Drakr centuries ago, when they attempted to take Everadyn land. She may not want to relive it. Amos will certainly side with the Drakr. Lora wishes she knew how the others might react, but she isn't certain.

She needs three of them to side with her on breaking the treaty. Four votes. In the event of a tie, her Five can break it, and they are all in agreement on which way it should go.

In the meantime, they'll prepare. Quietly. They'll store up weapons; they will grow more food; they'll hire and train more recruits for the armies. By midsummer, there should be gryphon fledglings ready for the bonding ceremony, where only soldiers recommended by their commanding officers can meet them and have a chance to be chosen by one of the gryphons. They need time. If necessary, Lora can go to Drakr on Queen Volkna's invitation. She hopes it won't be necessary, but the date Lahlis gave her is only a handful of months away. There will be very little time to avoid it.

"Speaking of the Drakr," Lora says. She squints down at her book, at the new line item she needs to address. "I wish to discuss the matter of pardoning the fae who were exiled for attempting to aid Aluina."

Peregrin stiffens, and Ayc snaps up straighter in his chair. "Do you mean your father?"

"All of them. If I pardon him but not the others, it wouldn't be just."

"I understand you wanting to pardon him," Xylie signs, with Ayc translating, *"and I think we should. But..."* She drops her hands.

"Go on," Lora encourages.

"Won't that infuriate the Drakr if you pardon their enemies?"

Just as Yris warned. It feels surreal to see Xylie and Yris agreeing on anything. Perhaps it's advice she should heed, but every hour that she's Sovereign without fixing that injustice—one she could fix with the stroke of a pen and her signature—grates on her skin like a hot iron.

It's been seven years since her father's exile. She wants him home. Fuck, she just wants to hug him.

"What if I was discreet?" Lora suggests. "If, on the Tour, I met with the families and told them to get a message to their loved ones that it's safe to come home, so long as they do so quietly. I could strike their name from the list of people exiled. There would be no announcement, no declaration."

"It's not without risks," Peregrin acknowledges. "But I think it's one worth taking. Do you truly believe Yris knows where your father is?"

Lora sits straighter in her chair. She hadn't explained to them why she let her mother stay. But clearly, Bronwen did because as she glances around the table, no one seems surprised, so they must be aware.

"I think so," Lora says.

"You think?" Ayc repeats. "Should we really let your mother stay just for a possibility?"

She should tell them all about the second threat, the threat on Ayc's life that truly made her yield. But Ayc is a weakness she wants no one to know of. Not even her Five, and especially not Ayc himself.

"It's a year," Lora says. "It's worth the chance."

Ayc grabs a cookie and shoves the entire thing in his mouth, like he needs to fill his mouth with something before something besides cookie crumbs spills out of it. He's angry that her mother is still in this castle—that she can still pull at puppet strings they all want severed--and he has every right to be. She's angry too.

"Just," Peregin says, "keep her on a short leash."

"I plan on it."

Lora looks down at her list, taking her time scratching out other marks until only one remains.

The Tour.

She reaches for a stack of parchment on the corner of the table and passes them out. Tavish's is much thicker, the words engraved upon it so he can feel the curve of the letters with his fingers. A librarian in the Archives created it for her. "This is the schedule of the Tour as Bronwen and I have currently arranged it. Please review it, and let me know if you want to suggest any changes."

She gives them all a moment to look over it, resisting the urge to sway in the chair. She reaches forward to grasp a cookie and nibbles on it.

"There's a question mark by Laud, Tenebra, the Stella Rune dwarves, and Lux Aester," Tavish says, tracing over it with a finger.

"I sent gryphon riders yesterday to the giants, the fae, and the dwarves with the requests to add them to my Tour. There hasn't been enough time for them to return."

Xylie taps Ayc on the arm, and he looks up from the schedule to watch her movements, before he speaks what Lora already knows. "She wants to know why we are returning to Wyntra for so long at the beginning of summer."

"For your Final Testing," Lora says.

"*I'm not testing,*" Xylie replies.

Lora's eyebrows shoot upward. "What do you mean you're not testing?"

"*I'm your Second. What does it matter what my Final Testing reveals?*"

"It matters because you can't get into Splendor without it."

"*I don't want to go to Splendor.*"

Lora's fingers spasm. The cookie falls from her grasp and breaks apart as it strikes the table.

"What?" Ayc sounds every bit as perplexed as Lora feels, as though the sun has decided to rise in the west. "You've wanted to go to Splendor for as long as I've known you."

"Not anymore."

Lora searches Xylie over, trying to find something in her face that will reveal who this strange creature is. It certainly isn't her cousin, who's wanted to go into alchemy since she was a toddler playing with a toy cauldron.

"If this is due to fears about forsaking your duty as Second," Lora says, "you won't be. There is precedent for this sort of thing. I looked it up before I ever asked you to be my Second. My grandfather chose his younger sister to be his Fifth, and she was still in Adamant at the time. When they won, they had a surrogate while she was away at school. It was in duties only, not in title. I would still seek your counsel. But you can't squander your talent. You are the most promising alchemist in this generation. Your schooling is eight years out of a hundred, but the value it'll provide for the rest of my reign is immeasurable." She pauses, then adds, "And more importantly, I won't let you forsake your dream for me."

Xylie stares down at the schedule for a moment that passes like wax dripping down a candle. Then, finally, she lifts her hands. Each sign is meticulous and over-emphasized to drive in the point: *"I am not Testing."*

Bronwen opens her mouth and snaps it shut, but she shakes her head. Lora suddenly understands the feeling that possessed her to push so hard, to accuse Xylie of hiding something. Because Xylie *is* hiding something. It's the only explanation for the radical shift in her desires.

What deal did she make with the Supreme? Why will she still not tell them?

The pit forming in Lora's stomach demands to be filled with answers, but she bites his tongue. Demanding answers from Xylie will only shut her down more. Still, she can't help the way her nostrils flare. "We'll discuss this later."

Xylie forms a protest with her hand, but Lora cuts her off with her own passionate signs, *"We will discuss it later."*

Lora doesn't give her another chance to argue. "Peregrin, do you have any thoughts on the schedule?"

They do, though not many. Most of theirs has to do with the logistics of moving her party—which will be filled with guards—from place to place. Airships or on foot. They would know, having moved armies from place to place. It changes the timeline slightly, but not much. She still returns to Wyntra frequently, which is good because she doesn't want to leave Yris alone here for long.

"What about you, Ayc?" Lora asks. "Any suggestions?"

"No," Ayc says. "I trust all of your judgments, and I'm thrilled to be going."

"That makes one of us," Lora murmurs. She didn't mean to say it, but she can't unsay it. She leans back in her chair with a sigh.

"Are you well?" Xylie signs.

"Yes," Lora says swiftly. "It just feels so fucking wasteful, doesn't it? This Tour. We're supposed to spend all this time partying while we could be doing so much more."

"Building relationships with the regents and their clans is not a waste," Peregrin says, but even they release a sigh. "But doing it in such an extravagant way does feel that way. The money alone could fund a war. It's a performance, Lora. Everyone is watching their new Sovereign to see if she will succeed."

She knows that. The greatest bit of theater she'll ever have. "I feel like we're preparing to take part in the Sovereignty Trials once more."

"Perhaps we are."

Bronwen picks up a cookie and passes it to Lora. "Have a cookie. It helps."

Lora ignores her.

Tavish tentatively raises his hand.

"You don't have to raise your hand, Tavish," Lora says, tempering the exasperation in her tone with a heavy dose of fondness. "Please speak."

"I was wondering if I could look through the treasury reports. I want to find funds—without increasing taxes—to pay for more resources in the schooling system. I know many students with disabilities do not attend the internships at clan schools, because those schools aren't equipped to deal with their needs. But all they need is the right sources, and I think I can find a way—if you'll allow me."

"Fuck yes!" Lora blurts.

Ayc chuckles under his breath. She tempers her voice. "That's a wonderful idea, Tavish."

Tavish tucks his head to hide his bashful smile. "It's just my dream that *every* child has the same opportunities."

"Yes, and that's exactly what I want all of us to do. I want us to *dream*. Dream for yourselves"—she looks pointedly at Xylie, who looks away—"dream for others, dream for Aluina and Everadyn. My father used to say that dreams are hopes you dare to create for yourself."

"Your father was a wise man," Peregrin says.

She means to look at Peregrin, but her gaze snags on Ayc. He's looking at her in the unguarded way again. The way she's caught him looking at her too much lately, like she is the sun and he's foolish enough to stare directly at her. Wonder and bewilderment — and fuck, he has to stop looking at her like that. She can't breathe when he looks at her like that.

What do you dream about? he asked her earlier. She couldn't answer him. She couldn't even think. She could only stare at him, knowing that what she dreams about is right in front of her.

And she can't.

She has wars and rebellions to plan, an entire country to run. She has to get a hold of all these silly emotions. She can't afford to hope. Whatever talk she gives to her Five, she doesn't have the luxury to dream. She is Sovereign, and her mother instilled a deep skepticism of dreams within her. One her father couldn't break, no matter how hard he tried.

Because when he told her about dreams all those years ago, Lora scoffed at him.

"Dreaming?" Lora snorted, sounding far too much like her mother. "What good does dreaming do?"

He only chuckled fondly and tucked the blankets around her. "It does a lot, sweet pea. In fact, it's one of the bravest things you can do. It takes courage to dream when everything feels impossible."

But looking at Ayc, she knows she's a fucking coward. Because he will always be impossible, and she's not brave enough to dream. Her duty will always come first.

Lora snags a cookie from the tray and bites into it.

It doesn't help.

CHAPTER

SEVENTEEN

AYC

"**X**ylie." Ayc drags an inhale through his nose so that he doesn't lose his temper. The smell of warm cinnamon from the cake loaf cooling on the counter doesn't help like it normally does. "At what point were you going to tell me we are really and truly fucked?"

"When was I supposed to mention it? Hm?" Xylie asks, from where she perches on the center counter, swinging her heels. A massive book sprawls on her lap, and she's been carefully studying the rows of numbers written on the pages. "I thought you had enough stress just with finding out that you're a powerful shadow wielder and trying to figure out whatever this is."

She gestures to his right arm, where he has his sleeve carefully pulled down to hide the majority of Muffin's bite. Despite it being a week since it happened, the marks caused by Muffin's bite have not faded. He doesn't know how he made it through the meeting with Lora and the Five immediately after he was bitten while acting mostly calm and collected. But he supposes his lifetime of lying has finally proved useful.

They still haven't sorted out what the mark even is. Xylie has

181

read almost every single book in the Archives of this castle and at the public library in Wyntra town, and when Ayc showed her the mark, she immediately ran to scour those same books over again. And yet, she has absolutely no idea what caused it.

Supposedly, there is one book she hasn't read that she hopes might have the answer. *Dragons and Drakr*. But unfortunately, she states it was borrowed by Ember months ago and never returned. Which is part of the reason Ayc is now baking a cinnamon loaf.

Muffin hasn't bitten Ayc again. They actually haven't done much other than be a little reckless shit, sleep, and of course, grow. Which is the problem.

"I don't know, Xylie. Anytime sounds like a good time to mention that it's suspected that dragons grow to their full adult size in the first year. The first *year*! Go look at them." Ayc stabs his spatula toward his room, where rumbling snores echo from the slumbering dragon. Xylie leans back on the counter to avoid a spray of cream that fires past her nose. "They were the size of a cat a week ago, and now they're the size of Saga. They take up half my bed, and they do *not* share well. How are we supposed to keep them hidden?"

Xylie lets out a deep sigh. "We have to tell Lora."

Ayc swallows, and he wants desperately to argue with her. But he knows she's right. Dammit.

He turns back to the stove, carefully stirring the soft custard he's making to serve with the loaf. He's tired, and his body aches. He didn't realize how dull and benign his life was before, with little more than baking to occupy his time. His new schedule is full of meetings with the Five every morning, classes by the law professors visiting from Splendor, practicing his shadow magic, and caring for Muffin. Other than the morning meetings, he's scarcely spoken to Lora since she wrapped her hand around his throat.

Lora is always so busy, the way Yris was busy, always managing a thousand little things that utterly consume her time. Tavish and Xylie have been going through the treasury reports. Peregrin has mostly been spending time at home or investigating what occurred with the midnight. That leaves Bronwen as the one chasing after Lora, disgruntled sparks of magic following her like blue, sparkling farts. Calling them that still annoys Bronwen, so he's taken to referring to them as such whenever possible.

The only time Bronwen is away from Ayc is during their daily sessions to practice his affinity. After that initial big push of power, he hasn't managed anything quite as great. He can still manage to move shadow, though not as far or as greatly, but he hasn't been able to grab or bind or shape it into a weapon as Lahlis did. He tried too hard once and woke up on the floor of his kitchen, with Muffin licking his face with their forked tongue, leaving a thick glob of mucus on his cheek.

Ayc keeps thinking that if he can just push himself harder and conquer his afinity, it'll make the pain better somehow. Perhaps, not that it'll make the pain disappear, but that he'll be stronger. Better. More in control. So far, he's only managed to make his entire back feel like it's been tied in at least thirteen complicated knots. But he refused to go to see Reselda, who's now permanently at Wyntra.

He hasn't even shared with Xylie or Bronwen what Reselda told him. Still, Xylie must guess because a new batch of pain tonics has been placed in his cabinet, and he's noticed her counting them, noting how many he's using... which is more than before. Bronwen was right. Something is different about these tonics. The relief they provide isn't as immediate or as long-lasting. But then, perhaps, his pain is getting worse, aggravated by the time he's spent paying the price of using his power.

Ayc removes the pot from the stove and sets it on a bath towel. It's all he has, thanks to Muffin's relentless and successful hunt to destroy every oven mitt or hot pad in sight. "Yes, we have to tell Lora. But what happens after?"

The idea of Lora sending Muffin away, perhaps to release them back to Somnia Ignis to fend for themself or to Splendor to be poked and studied up close, makes Ayc feel physically ill. The idea that someone might harm Muffin makes him feel a rage that borders on violence, that makes the marks on his arm burn like he's touching ice with a bare hand.

Muffin's voice still echoes within his head. *Mine.* He hasn't heard the dragon talk again, and so perhaps he imagined it.

"I don't know," Xylie says. "But *we'll* tell her. Together. And we'll work together to figure out a solution that is best for Muffin."

"Hey!" Ayc claps his hands together, a ray of delight piercing through his dark gloom. "You just called them Muffin."

Xylie shakes her head. "No, I didn't."

"You *did*!"

She sends him a sign that tells him to do very inappropriate things to himself but doesn't argue anymore. She looks down at the book, dragging her fingers over the paper. She taps on a number. "That's odd," she mutters.

"What's odd?"

She jumps to her feet. "I need to talk to Tavish."

"Talk to Tavish?" Ayc repeats. He knows she can't mean signing because Tavish doesn't sign. "You talk to Tavish?"

Since the day her village was massacred, she's only ever talked out loud to Ayc and Lora.

Xylie shrugs. "I don't know. I was just with him the other day, and I needed to ask him something, and it just came out. I think he's more anxious than I am, and...I don't know. That makes him easier to talk to."

Ayc smiles. "I'm proud of you, Xylie."

She flicks her wrist. "I want to talk to Bronwen and Peregrin, too. I don't know why I can't."

"You know you don't have to force yourself to do anything that makes you uncomfortable."

She smiles back. "I know. But I do have to go."

She's nearly to the door when Ayc remembers. "Wait! I thought you were going to watch Muffin so I could take the cinnamon loaf cake to Irving and ask Ember about the book?"

"Sorry!" she calls over her shoulder. "But this is important. Muffin—dammit! Uh, the dragon should be fine until I get back.

They generally sleep for almost a day at a time. Oh!" She stops and spins around on her heel. "I think you should tell Peregrin about the dragon. And about the mark."

"Are you serious?" Ayc plants his hands on the counter. "It'll be Peregrin's last straw, and they'll finally murder my foolish ass."

"Don't be silly. Peregrin would never kill you. Bodily harm, however..." Xylie fiddles with the doorknob behind her. The door creaks open.

"Xylie!"

She shuts it once more. "They know dragons, Ayc. They've fought dragons. And Drakr. They might know something about the mark on your arm. And we can trust them."

For the second time, Ayc swallows down his arguments because he knows Xylie is right.

"Be back soon." She darts out, and Ayc grumbles to himself all the way to lock the door from the inside.

Once the soft custard has cooled, he pours it into a jar and then seals it. He wraps the loaf in cloth and tucks it into the basket next to the jar. He adds a few raw salmon and apple muffins he made for Tempest, but not before wrapping them twice in two separate cloths so their smell doesn't ruin everything else. Before leaving, he checks on Muffin, ensuring the dragon still slumbers on Ayc's bed. The blanket that covers the dragon floats upward with every sonorous snore.

Ayc pulls on a pair of gloves before he goes, fully hiding the dragon mark. He locks the door from the outside on the way out and walks as quickly as his sore muscles will allow out of the castle and toward the barracks. As he traces the familiar streets to Peregrin's home, a weight presses into his chest. Irving was given paid leave, and as far as Ayc knows, he has been at home with Zinnia, Peregrin, and Ember, trying to sort through everything. This will be the first time that Ayc will have seen him since his memory was taken. He's not sure how he'll navigate that.

When he turns onto Peregrin's street, Tempest is already trotting toward him. Ayc fishes one of the muffins from the basket.

"Looking for this?" he asks.

Tempest snaps her beak, and Ayc tosses the muffin. She grabs it from the air and swallows it down in a single bite. She leans toward Ayc, and her sides heave with two deep inhales, like she's sniffing. The air pulls through her beak.

"Do you want the other—"

Tempest shrieks a cry, a deep bellow that explodes hot in Ayc's face, before she bolts into the air with a slap of mighty wings. She flies away quickly, still calling angrily as she goes.

Fuck. What got into her?

The door to Peregrin's house swings open. Peregrin sticks their head out, frowning into the sky after the rapidly shrinking dot of their gryphon. Ayc waves to grab their attention and rushes the rest of the way to the door.

"You look like shit," Peregrin says by way of greeting.

Ayc chuckles. "Did Tempest tell you to say that?"

"No, I personally think so."

You're one to talk, Ayc almost fires back, but he bites his tongue. The visible veins that work up Peregrin's neck have deepened from green to black, and their cheeks look hollowed. With their pale gray skin, they look closer to a grave than to life. The pain and poison are winning the struggle at the moment, but who can blame Peregrin?

"What's wrong, boy?" Peregrin asks, their brow furrowed.

"Nothing."

Peregrin drops their voice lower. "Then why the fuck did Tempest—"

"Don't interrogate him," Zinnia calls from within the house. "Let him inside."

Peregrin swings the door wider to reveal Zinnia dressed in her simple brown dress and an apron. Half moons of exhaustion have risen below her green eyes. Still, she greets Ayc with a smile. "It's wonderful to see you, Ayc. If I'd known you were coming, I'd have put the kettle on."

Ayc brushes a kiss to her cheek. "Don't trouble yourself. I just wanted to bring you some cake."

"Thank you. That's too kind." She takes the offered basket and lifts the cover. "Cinnamon loaf?"

"Yes," Ayc says. "It's Irving's favorite."

Zinnia's smile disappears, and Ayc winces.

"I mean, it was. I don't know if…"

Peregrin shuts the door a little harder than necessary, cutting Ayc off. Ayc rubs at the back of his neck, at the muscles that feel even tighter thanks to his absolute fuckery of a mouth.

A heaviness lingers in the air, one that doesn't feel like it belongs here. Not in this home of love and family.

"How are you?" Ayc asks to break the silence.

"Fine," Zinnia says, though she glances toward Peregrin, and the word ends in a note that almost sounds like a question.

"Come on," Peregrin says, tapping Ayc's ankle with his cane. "Ember is finishing lunch. He'll be happy to see you."

Ayc falls behind Peregrin and Zinnia on the way to the kitchen. He hears the laughter before he gets there and recognizes Ember's high-trilling one and Irving's deeper baritone. Some tension eases in Ayc's spine. He knows it's not perfect anymore, that something has happened that will never be undone, but he's so relieved to still hear laughter here.

Where there is laughter, there is hope.

Irving and Ember sit at the end of the table, mostly full bowls of soup and a half dozen toy soldiers between them. They move the figures around, chattering in excitement, playing out some elaborate story. Ayc feels grateful that whatever sorcerer went into Irving's head didn't take Ember, too.

Ember looks up, and a wide smile splits across his face. "Ayc!" He jumps up from the chair and runs to him. Ayc catches him, and his little arms practically choke Ayc. Damn, he's missed this kid.

"Where have you been?" Ember asks, squeezing Ayc's face in his hands the way he often does. "It's been ages."

Ayc opens his mouth to agree, but Ember slaps a hand over his lips. He tilts his head back and sniffs the air like he's a hound dog.

His eyes go wide. "Did you bring cake?"

Ayc can't help but laugh. "I did! But it looks like you haven't eaten all of your lunch. Better scoot and fix that before your mother sees.”

Ember slides down and flings himself back into his chair, where he begins rapidly shoveling the soup into his mouth.

Zinnia hums in appreciation as she makes her way to the dish cabinet. She pauses with four plates in her hand. “Will you be joining us?”

“I’m afraid I have to get back.” Before Muffin wakes up.

“No!” Ember moans with his mouth still full of soup. It dribbles down his chin. “No fair. I wanted to go fossil hunting.”

“Soon,” Ayc promises. He wonders what Ember would do if he told him there’s an infant dragon in his room. Probably demand to see it. Irving, who has a deep love for creatures both current and extinct, would likely be thrilled as well, though he would temper it for the sake of being cautious.

But then, Ayc doesn’t know if that Irving is still here anymore, what all the sorcerer reached in and scraped from his mind.

Irving has been watching Ayc the entire time, his arm dangling over the back of his chair. He finally stands and offers Ayc his hand and a warm smile that flashes his dimples. “Hello, I’m Irving.”

It lands, for the second time, like a punch in Ayc’s throat. But he forces a smile and takes Irving’s hand. “Yeah, I-I know.”

Zinnia’s knife clinks on the kitchen counter a little too hard as she cuts up the cake. Peregrin leans on the door frame with a grunt.

Irving’s smile grows strained as he pulls his hand back. “Of course you do. Because you’re Ayc.” His dimple reappears in the depths of his brown cheeks as he recovers. “Zinnia and Ember have told me a lot about you. I seem to have a lot of catching up to do. I’m sorry for that.”

Ayc shakes his head. “Oh, no. You have nothing to be sorry for.”

Irving nods. He looks at Ayc with friendliness but absolutely no recognition. Because what Zinnia and Peregrin are telling him about Ayc are merely facts to Irving. Not memories. Not coated with the emotions of the moment.

Ayc rocks his weight from heel to toe, unsure what to say or what to do.

Peregrin rescues him. "I'll see you out, Ayc."

Ayc snaps his fingers. "Actually, one more thing. Xylie wanted me to ask Ember if they still have a book they borrowed from Wyntra's library. *Dragons and Drakr* is the title."

"Do you have that book, Ember?" Zinnia asks.

Ember shakes his head. "Nope."

"I'll look around for it," Zinnia promises.

Peregrin nods toward the front door. Ayc bids farewell, pretending not to hear Ember's protests, which might convince Ayc to stay when he really can't. Zinnia quickly ends the soft whine by laying a piece of cake, served with the custard, down before him. It turns into a cry of delight, followed by, "Look, Dad. It's your favorite."

When they reach the door, Peregrin opens it, but to Ayc's surprise, they follow him out onto their stoop and shut the door behind them. Peregrin folds their arms over their chest and draws in a deep breath.

"How are you really?" Ayc asks, not really expecting them to answer honestly.

Peregrin exhales a quick breath. "We're getting to know each other again."

Ayc winces. "I can't imagine how complicated this all is."

"It's not complicated. It's simple. I love him. With all my soul. But he has no obligation to love me in return. It matters little. I will love him still."

Ayc finds himself suddenly winded, like the words have slammed him square in the chest. And they have. Because fuck, he knows exactly how that feels. "Still fucking feels like there's a gaping hole in your chest where your heart should be."

Peregrin presses their eyes closed. "Aye, it does." Peregrin inhales, exhales once more, and then opens their eyes and fixes Ayc with a hard look. "But I don't want to talk about it." They drop their voice into a whisper. "I want to talk about why Tempest told me you reek like a dragon."

Ayc's mouth goes fully dry. "Come again?" he blurts.

Peregrin searches the street before them again. Still empty. They step closer. "The egg hatched, didn't it?"

Ayc weighs his options. All of which are shit. Then he nods.

"For fuck's s—" they begin, but their voice has crept too loud. They stop and lower it once more, this time talking through their teeth. "Ayc, you can't keep a dragon like it's a pet. It's going to hurt someone."

"It won't," Ayc reassures, his own voice a whisper. "Muffin isn't like that." It sounds ridiculous, especially because Ayc once had the same fear as Peregrin. But now he's certain that Muffin would never harm a person unless they felt threatened.

"Muffin?" Peregrin repeats. "You fucking named the dragon *Muffin?*"

"Yes."

"Divine damn you, Ayc!" Ayc starts to peddle backward to escape, but Peregrin seizes his collar like he's a foolish young boy once more. "This isn't a game."

"I know! Just calm down, all right. I have a pl—"

"What the fuck is that?" Peregrin cuts him off. Their wide eyes fix upon Ayc's collarbone, where a few pearly lines are visible. Peregrin drags the collar down further, so they see where the marks extend down his arm.

Peregrin releases him and jumps back, their eyes surging ever wider. "Holy fuck!" They slap a hand over their lips and eye the door behind them. They pry their fingers away from their lips and drop their voice. "The dragon claimed you."

Ayc blinks. "The dragon did what *now?*"

"The dragon marked you. Claimed you. *Bonded* with you."

"A bond?" Ayc repeats. "Like you have with Tempest?"

Peregrin loosens the tie on their tunic's collar and parts it. Beneath the deep green veins that curve down their neck and chest, another mark, dark as onyx, tattoos Peregrin's skin. Four claw marks across their collarbone. "Tempest left this when she claimed me. There aren't a lot of similarities between gryphons and dragons, but how they bond with a person? That is more similar than different. I've seen marks on Drakr dragon riders very similar to yours."

Claimed.

Drakr.

Dragon rider.

Those are words Ayc knows, and yet his brain can't make sense of them. It's not possible. Not him. This isn't happening to him.

As though reading the doubt, Peregrin asks, "Can you hear the dragon talk?"

Ayc hesitates before admitting the truth. "Maybe. Possibly. I might have."

"Then it bonded with you," Peregrin insists.

"Don't all dragons talk? The mother dragon in Somnia Ignis talked."

Peregrin arches an eyebrow. "No, Ayc. It didn't. At least, *I* didn't hear it. If it spoke, I assure you, it spoke only to you. I suspect because of your Drakr blood."

Ayc shakes his head. It can't be possible. He's a baker. A foolish, ridiculous baker who didn't even know he could wield shadow until a week ago. Who can barely wield a sword without his body screaming in pain.

Surely, a dragon wouldn't have chosen him.

Peregrin searches him up and down. "Shadow wielder and dragon rider often go together. But to see it in *you?*" They shake their head, the disbelief clear.

"Sorry to disappoint," Ayc says with a heavy breath. Yes, those were Ayc's thoughts exactly, but it hurts to have Peregrin confirm his unworthiness.

Peregrin's brow furrows. "I didn't mean—"

A horn blares, a deep, bellowing alarm that's so loud it makes the ground beneath Ayc's feet tremble. It's the alarm horn, the one at the center of the barracks used to alert the soldiers. Ayc has only heard it for drills, but the timing for that is wrong, and so is the rhythm. Instead of one long blast, it comes in brief spurts, quickly followed by another. Each one sends a chill down Ayc's spine.

Peregrin counts them beneath their breath. "One, two, three, four."

The horn bleats, pauses, then begins again.

One, two, three, four.

"What is that?" Ayc asks.

Behind Peregrin, the door flings open. Irving stands in the doorway, throwing on their guard cloak. His sword belt is already fastened on his hips.

Peregrin reaches around Irving to grab their belt of knives and fastens it around their chest. "That's what's supposed to happen when dragons are approaching Wyntra."

EIGHTEEN

LORA

"My lady, please don't slouch." The tailor's voice is scarcely a whisper, but it's loud enough to startle Lora. Her eyes snap open, and she blinks in the light. Fuck, she was actually falling asleep still standing up, while the tailor who's creating her dress for the Noxumbra court kneels at her feet, pinning hems.

She stares with aching eyes into her bedroom mirror before her. The rich, black velvet of the dress hugs taut to her skin from the thin straps on her shoulders, over her full breasts and stomach, and down her hips, where it loosens as it cascades to the floor. Deep slits rise up the front of both her legs. Rows of glistening metal chains pull the cloth together over her thighs, but still offer a view of plenty of flesh. Artistically twisted metal, sprinkled with clear jewels, decorates the center of the bodice. The tailor is adding a second skirt, a structured piece that bows out from her hips in gauzy, nearly sheer fabric. Altogether, it's much fancier and more revealing than what she would have chosen, and she hasn't decided if she likes it or not.

When the herd of seven tailors and their teams, summoned from each of the clans, showed up to make her gowns, they came with plans and designs already made. This one gown would give them enough publicity to last for years of business, so they were offering their most extravagant work. They all stated they were open to feedback, but Lora didn't know what to suggest. If it were up to her, she'd simply have shown up in her armor, or perhaps her knit sweaters and tunics. There wasn't enough time to do all the research she would have needed to conduct to design a single gown she'd have loved, let alone seven. So, she gave them only one qualification for the design: she had to easily reach a dagger strapped to her thigh. This dress, which bears most of her thigh, will certainly be able to do that.

"Did you not sleep well last night?" Bronwen asks from where she sits upon Lora's bed, just out of Lora's field of vision.

For the last week, Bronwen has fit into her role of First extraordinarily well. She scarcely leaves Lora's side, just like Fennix scarcely ever left Yris's. Only late in the evening does she slink away before returning the next morning with dark lines beneath her eyes. Perhaps she's scarcely sleeping either.

"Not well," Lora admits. Though she doesn't want to share the particular reason.

"Maybe you should rest after this," Bronwen suggests.

"I can't," Lora says. "I need to finalize the names of those I wish to hire to be royal guards by the end of the day." And, of course, the current guards she wishes to replace. She's been staring at the list for days.

"Just let Peregrin handle it," Bronwen says. "Or Irving. He's captain, and he was at the qualification trials. I saw him."

Lora resists the urge to shift her weight on the narrow tailor's block. "Irving shouldn't have been there." She saw him there, too, sitting next to Peregrin, watching every applicant carefully. She should have been brave enough to speak to him, but she couldn't. "He hasn't officially returned to duty. And Peregrin needs to focus on the investigation. And their family."

A snap fills the air. Lora twists, ignoring the cluck of the tailor's tongue. Bronwen lays Lora's book back on the pillow. *A Measure of Perfection.* Her favorite. She dragged it from her bookshelf last night, thinking she might read it, but she fell asleep before managing a word.

"Fine." Bronwen jumps to her feet, a little spark shooting from her fingertips. She paces over the rug in Lora's room to come stand at her side. "You can use that excuse for Peregrin. But what of all the other things you should be delegating but aren't?"

Lora sighs. She doesn't want to have this conversation. Again.

"You spent three hours today trying to figure out rations and provisions for the Tour, Lora. Three hours for something that the people you have hired to go on this journey should be figuring out. If you don't trust them, put Ayc on it. He's run his own kitchen for years, served hundreds of people at festivals, and I've been told he is good friends with the kitchen staff. He would be happy to handle it."

Oh yes, Lora knows well what the kitchen staff thinks of Ayc, particularly the new and young ones. She's heard them whispering as she passes in the hall or the times she's snuck into the kitchen to eat leftovers because she failed to show up on time for the dinner they prepared for her. They say he's sweet and funny and oh, so handsome—compliments that have gotten no less intense now that all of Wyntra castle knows he's a Drakr.

Just last night, she heard one of them whispering. *"Do you think his eyes go red when he...you know?"*

The comment left Lora feeling hot. Sticky. Empty. It completely rid her few hours of sleep of any actual rest. Instead, she dreamed of shadows and red eyes and skin that tasted like chocolate pudding. She woke to his voice, a deep growl of "villainess," only to find herself drenched and very, *very* pissed that she was the only one tangled up in her sheets.

She took the coldest of showers, hammering her mantra into her head.

I can't, I can't, I can't.

"Lora, are you falling asleep again?" Bronwen snaps her fingers in front of Lora's face. "Did you hear me?"

"Yes, I heard you," Lora snaps. "And I don't understand the

problem. There's no harm in ensuring everything is completely taken care of."

"And the only way to do that is to do it yourself? You're Sovereign, Lora. Learn to delegate."

"I *am* delegating."

"Not enough."

"She's right, you know," comes a voice from the door.

Lora didn't even hear it open, and yet, when she glances over her shoulder, she finds Yris peeking her head in the door.

Shae, who has been standing inside the room, glares at the guard outside of it, who has let Yris enter. Lora will certainly consider that when making final decisions on the guards.

Lora presses her eyes closed and drags a deep breath through her nose. She doesn't have the strength to deal with her mother right now. The lack of sleep, the attention of the tailors, already has the pressure building up inside her like she's a kettle on the stove. Her mother is not a safe person to be around when she already feels like she might explode.

"Should I escort her out?" Shae asks.

Lora's about to say yes, when Yris quickly presses, "I've only come to ask how I can help you."

"Help?" Lora repeats like it's a foreign word. It is, on her mother's tongue.

"Yes." Yris steps a little closer. Shae copies the step, but Lora shakes her head, and Shae resumes her post at the door. Lora doesn't look away as her mother comes to stand at her side, and the tailor huffs at her twisted posture. "The things that you're busying yourself over are things that I should be doing as the previous Sovereign. Yet you've failed to call on me even once. Every time I attempt a task, I'm told you've already completed it. And I'm told you're returning to Wyntra every two to three weeks. What exactly do you mean for me to do while you're gone?"

"I don't know," Lora says. "Perhaps take up the organ. It's a fabulous instrument." Bronwen snorts, and Lora continues, "All I want you to do while I'm gone is make sure the castle doesn't burn to the ground. Assemble reports for me and my Five to deal with when I get back.”

Lora expects her to argue, but instead, she lets out a sigh. That sigh. The one she always gave Lora when she expressed even a mild emotion that she found inconvenient, one that betrays just how ridiculous she feels Lora is being.

“If that’s what you wish, that’s what I’ll do,” Yris says. “But you’re wasting me as a resource. You’re going to burn yourself out. Your focus needs to be on winning over the regents and gaining their support.”

“You’ve said it before. You forget that I know the regents, and I’m prepared to win their favor. After all, you raised me to be Sovereign, didn’t you, Mother?”

“I certainly did my best. But I also thought I’d be here to help you. I never thought you’d be so foolish as to push me aside, to not heed my counsel.” She pauses and looks pointedly at the tailor. “Leave,” she commands him.

Before Lora can protest, the tailor rushes to their feet and hurries for the door. The fear Yris instilled as Sovereign was felt throughout all of Everadyn, and it won’t have faded, even though she no longer wears a crown.

Shae shuts the door behind the tailor, but despite their relative solitude, Yris still lowers her voice. “I fear you’re going to do something rather foolish on this Tour. I’m warning you one more time, Loraphne. Do not bring up the matter of Aluina to the regents.”

Lora’s canines ache as they sharpen. She curls back her top lip so her mother can see their points. “What I do is none of your concern.”

“You’re my daughter. What you do is always my concern.”

Perhaps the words are meant to be loving, but they feel suffocating. *My daughter* has never indicated affection, only ownership.

“Do you know something I don’t?” Lora growls. Bronwen presses two fingers on Lora’s elbow, and Lora draws a breath to speak more levelly. "Do you know anything about the threat on my life?"

Lora knows Yris has been questioned. Peregrin made sure of it themself. But though Peregrin found no evidence to doubt her testimony, Yris certainly has not given them reason to trust her either.

Yris stacks her spine straighter, and her eyes narrow until only a flash of silver remains. Her voice is a hiss when she speaks again. "If I knew someone had tried to harm you, I would have killed them where they stand. You are still my daughter. And now my Sovereign. My suspicion is it was orchestrated by Amos, but I have no proof to offer you. So be careful, Loraphne. Do not make enemies out of people you need to be your allies."

"Thank you for your advice," Lora says, letting her sarcasm shine through. "Now, can I trust you not to let the castle burn to the ground, or not?"

"Of course. I love Everadyn," Yris assures. "Wyntra and its Sovereign are this land's heart and soul. I won't allow any of it to come to harm."

Lora believes Yris means it, but it offers no comfort. They have very different ideas about what protecting Everadyn means. Before she can decide the best way to respond, a horn blares.

It comes in through the open window, carried by the wind. Bronwen and Yris jerk their attention there as well, both of them stiffening as they recognize the call, just as Lora does.

The horn blares again and again and again. Four times.

Lora's heart stills.

Dragons are coming. The Drakr have returned.

Her heart springs alive again, slamming against the cage of her ribs. She whirls to fully face her mother.

"Did you know about this?"

"No!" The subtle wideness in Yris's eyes suggests she isn't lying.

Still, Lora shows her teeth once more. "If this is another one of your lessons—"

"It's not! I don't know why the Drakr would return so soon."

Lora jumps off the pedestal. There isn't time to interrogate Yris. There isn't even time to dress. Her army, her people, need her.

Bronwen has already summoned Lora's armor from the stand it rests upon, undoing straps, and Lora shoves the secondary skirt down her hips. Pins scatter across the floor. The tailor might combust when he sees it, but that isn't his concern.

"Loraphne, we need to—" Yris begins, and then she catches herself. "What do you need me to do?"

At any other moment, Lora might have been amazed at the correction, at the sudden pivot from commander to helper. Yris looks briefly pained, so perhaps it's authentic. But right now, Lora doesn't have time to consider it.

"We need to get the civilians out of the barracks and into this castle," Lora says. "In case the Drakr have come to attack."

Lora reaches for her armor in Bronwen's hands, and together, she and her First fit the armor over her dress. Adamant frequently had drills in the middle of the night. The students were meant to be dressed in full armor and reporting for duty within five minutes of an alarm awakening them from sleep. If any of the class failed, they did it again and again...until they got it right. They learned that the only way to be successful in such a short time is to help one another. The skill comes in handy now.

"I'll summon the city guard and start the process," Yris says. She starts toward the door and then pauses. "I have faith in you. You've been prepared for this. You are my daughter, after all."

Then she's gone. She leaves the compliment clinging to Lora's skin, and she isn't sure if it should feel like a balm or a sting. She shakes her head and snaps the last buckle into place. Without the underlayer she normally wears, her arms remain more exposed than she would like them to be, but they are able to cross the enchanted leather over her chest and abdomen, the twisting of decorative metal—armor in its own right—visible beneath. Lora's thighs will simply have to be exposed.

When she turns toward the bookshelf where she's left the

swords, she finds that Shae has already grabbed them. The guard holds them out to her.

Lora quickly fastens them into their rightful place on her hips. "You aren't going to tell me to stay inside, are you?"

"If you hid, you would not be the person I know you to be," she says. "I'll follow you into the dragon's fire, my lady."

Lora nods. Good. She's definitely keeping Shae. "Then keep up."

She turns, and Bronwen and Shae run with her toward the door. When they fling it open, they don't pause to speak to the royal guard—the one who let Yris in without question. They fall in behind, anyway. The four of them race through the hallway. A staff soars around the corner ahead of them.

"Watch out," Bronwen yells, and Lora and Shae barely fling themselves out of the way as her staff flies through the hallway toward Bronwen's outstretched hand. She catches it without slowing, and Lora and Shae fall into pace once more.

It feels like an eternity before they reach the doors to the courtyard. They are already open, a stream of people being directed in by the guards. Lora spots Yris among them, barking orders, but Lora doesn't miss a pace.

In the courtyard, Lora attempts to get a sense of her surroundings. The horn is no longer sounding, but the skies above are filling steadily with gryphons and their riders, their wings blocking out the sun as they circle into formation. A crowd has gathered on the battlement that surrounds the courtyard. Lora recognizes the back of Urbain's blond head and takes the stairs two at a time onto the wall. The soldiers who surround Urbain part before her and Bronwen. Her guards fall behind, but only by a few feet, granting her space to speak to the commander of the army.

Her army.

Urbain lowers his spyglass and passes it to Lora. "Three dragons approach. A blue, a purple, and a striped orange."

Lora puts the glass to her eye. The dragons are still far enough away that their color is all she can determine. She can't see their riders, but she recognizes the beasts from a week ago.

"Did we have any notification that they were coming?" Lora demands, handing Urbain his spyglass back, even though she already knows the answer.

"No, my lady." He tucks the glass in a pouch that he wears on his side. He, too, is dressed in armor. His is a sky-gray, like the other gryphon riders wear. "Do we engage?"

The weight of the question lands upon her back like an anvil. Her decision to make. Her consequences to bear.

She glances up at the aerial army and their glorious gryphons. "What is the anticipated loss of life if we engage?"

Urbain clears his throat. "My riders are well-trained. They—"

"Anywhere from twelve to fifteen," Peregrin says as they ascend the stairs. The tension in Lora's shoulders eases if only a little. Bronwen and Shae step aside to let Peregrin join her. They ignore Urbain's glare. "If the Drakr have no shadow affinity."

"And if we assume they do have affinity?" Bronwen demands.

"Closer to twenty or thirty."

Peregrin delivers the information bluntly, and that's how Lora makes herself take it. Like a glancing blow against her armor. Not like real and breathing people.

"And if we risk letting the dragons make it to land in the chance they come in peace?" Lora asks.

Peregrin's level tone does not change. "Then we risk having to engage them directly over the castle and the town. Much of the city could burn to the ground before we stop them."

Lora looks sharply back at the castle, with its turrets and towers. Xylie is in there. Tavish and Zinnia and Ember and, perhaps, Irving. Dozens of her staff and the families of gryphon riders. And Ayc.

She could lose them all.

As though summoned by the thought, Ayc rises up the stairs. Just behind him is Irving. She knows the moment Ayc truly sees her because he freezes so quickly, Irving nearly collides with him. His blue eyes sweep over her, and she's suddenly reminded of the inappropriateness of what she's wearing. But the way he's looking at her, his eyes darkening as he takes her in, doesn't make her feel embarrassed.

It makes her feel like she's on fucking fire.

She turns her head, though she watches him approach from the corner of her eye. He joins the close cluster, nearly brushing her back, and the inferno builds.

She pulls in a small gasp of air. Now is not the fucking time.

"Zinnia and Ember are in the castle," Irving whispers to Peregrin, who visibly swallows before nodding and wiping any trace of emotion from their face.

"We don't have much time, my lady," Urbain presses. "What is your decision?"

Lora swallows, but her mind is made up. "There's a third option. *I* ride out to meet them. If Tempest is willing," she adds to Peregrin.

"She's willing," Peregrin says after only a brief pause.

"I'm not certain that's wise, my lady," Urbain protests. "Let my men—"

"Your Sovereign has spoken," growls a voice from behind them. It takes Lora a moment to realize it's Ayc who has spoken. His voice is so fierce, so utterly different, that she only recognizes it by the shiver that trails down her back and coils into a knot at the base of her spine.

Urbain nods. "Of course. I'll send five of my best riders with you."

"Two," Lora says. "We will meet with equivalent numbers."

Urbain nods. He taps two of the fae near him. They snap to attention and step toward the stairs.

Bronwen grabs one by the shoulder. "I'm riding with you."

Urbain raises an eyebrow, and Lora nods her assent. *'Take the powerful sorcerer with you'* is always a solid battle plan. The two riders continue on their way, and Bronwen hurries after them.

"Tempest is coming," Peregrin says. "She'll meet you down below."

Lora moves toward the stairs. Shae, Irving, Ayc, and Peregrin all follow her. By the time they reach the bottom step, Tempest slams into the ground of the courtyard, sending gravel flying.

Lora marches toward her, but a hand brushes by her wrist as she passes. Even though it doesn't make contact, it grabs hold of her all the same. She turns toward Ayc.

"Be fucking careful," he whispers so no one else will hear. "If anything happens to you, I'll..."

She lets out a shaky breath, trying to make it sound like a disbelieving laugh. "You'll what?"

He grins wickedly. "I'll hire a dark sorcerer to resurrect your soul, put it in my favorite baking dish, and tell you all of my worst jokes while I use you to make only raisin-filled desserts."

Lora shudders. "I hate raisins."

"I know."

"That's a very convincing reason to stay."

"Good."

It feels like prying off a bit of her own skin to turn away from him and march toward Tempest. Tempest flutters her wings and snaps her beak. "Are you ready, pretty girl?" Lora asks.

Tempest bows their front legs in response. Lora is grateful because this fucking dress doesn't make it easy to mount. She manages, though she's certain it looks less than graceful. She barely has a moment to catch a fistful of feathers before Tempest rockets into the air. The other gryphon riders fall into formation with Tempest, Bronwen holding tight to the shoulders of the rider to Lora's left. She can see the dragons clearly now, three spots above the sea, and she holds tight as the gryphons rush to meet them.

NINETEEN

LORA

She clings to Tempest's feathers and bends low over the gryphon's neck, attempting to hide from the wind that scrapes against her cheeks like icy fingernails. Despite the force, the crown on her head doesn't even wobble, whatever magic it holds keeping it in place. The two other gryphons keep pace right behind her, eating up sky with every fierce clap of their wings.

The dragons before them are quickly nearing. One of them is nearly as big as all three of the gryphons. The scales of the two jewel-toned dragons gleam in the sunlight. The orange with the dark stripes has a duller tone but is no less breathtaking.

As they near, the three cloaked riders come into view. Lora holds her breath. They are close enough now that one breath of fire could incinerate them. Bronwen can only shield against dragon fire for so long. But none of the dragons part their mouths. Instead, the blue dragon breaks away from the other two. The rider's hefty frame is completely cloaked from view. They lift their gloved hands, showing them empty.

"The queen herself rides out to meet us." Despite the roar of the wind, the Drakr's voice is strong, demanding, and carries a higher tone that suggests they might be a woman. "What an honor!"

"If you come on friendly terms," Lora calls back, "I wanted to be the first to greet my guests. If you don't, then I will lead my people to defend Everadyn. I won't hide in stone as they burn."

A laugh sounds from the rider. Neither flying creature can stop moving and remain in the air, so the blue dragon and Tempest circle in the air, Tempest hovering just over the dragon's right wing. The muscles in Tempest's lion body are tense, but she flies calmly and coolly. Down below them, the other dragons and gryphons do the same large pirouettes around each other. The purple dragon flies smoothly, but the orange occasionally darts toward one of the gryphons before the rider yanks them back into place with what appears like large reins. The leather straps are connected to a large collar fixed at the base of the dragon's long neck. Inside the circle are blood-stained spikes that dig against the dragon's already damaged scales.

Lora grinds her teeth. The purple and blue dragons wear no such contraption. The first two must be bonded willingly to the riders, but the orange is captive and controlled. Only cruelty can keep such a powerful creature obedient. It's barbaric, a damn tragedy, but she forces her voice to be calm.

"So which is it, dragon rider? Should I offer a welcome or a sword blade?"

"We've come on friendly terms. We've been sent to deliver another message. From Lord Lahlis!"

Lora bites the inside of her cheek to keep from saying what she wishes—that Lahlis can stick his head up his own ass for all she cares. She's not one whose attention he can demand whenever he wants. But antagonizing them will do no good. Besides, if Lahlis is up to something, it's best she knows it.

"And?" she fires back.

"Can we have this conversation on the ground?" the Drakr asks. "It's quite hard to keep yelling!" Lora hesitates, and the Drakr adds, "I swear to you, I've only come to talk."

"And why should I trust your word?"

They do a full circle before the Drakr responds. "I probably wouldn't if I were you. But you're also smart enough to know that if we wanted you dead, you would have been in the ground a week ago."

Lora hates that she has a point.

Down below, the gryphons and dragons still circle one another. The orange snaps toward a gryphon's wing in irritation before being jerked by the reins. It roars a sound that is half fury, half pain, and blood pours down its chest and rains into the sea below.

She can't trust the Drakr, but if they do have some ulterior motive, then the best strategy is to separate the dragons from their riders. They are both dangerous on their own, but together, they are the force that Lora was taught to fear the most while at Adamant.

"Very well," Lora says. "But if you try me, you'll find that the only way I'm going to a grave is if I'm putting *you* in it."

The Drakr throws back their head and laughs. "Oh, you're so much more fun than Yris."

The gryphons land upon the shore in a spray of sand and pebbles, but it's nothing compared to the impact of the dragons. They slam into the earth, one after another, and disappear behind a cloud of soot. The ground shudders with each landing, the cliffs quaking until a few loose stones tumble from their homes and drop down below.

Lora swings off Tempest. A small crowd has gathered her to watch the events in the sky. Urbain and his highest-ranking lieutenant sit upon golden-brown gryphons, that nearly double Tempest in size, a subbreed of gryphons that sacrifice speed for sheer size. Her royal guards, Shae and Irving, and a few others whose names she hasn't learned hurry toward her. Peregrin and Ayc wait closest to the sea. As her feet hit the ground, Ayc takes a few sprinting steps toward her, and her feet nearly rebel and step toward him.

She catches herself in time and lifts her chin higher as she marches toward where the dragons have landed. The three riders stride from the cloud of sand. Lora feels the crowd gather behind her back—Bronwen and Ayc and Peregrin, her guards, and the gryphon riders. Somehow, it doesn't feel like enough when nearing three dragons and their well-trained shadow wielder riders.

Lora stops and holds up her hand, halting their group two dozen feet from the dragons. Any closer, and they won't be out of range of the dragon's fire. The purple and the blue dragons flop down on their bellies into the sand, looking quite calm and almost bored. The orange dragon, however, paces through the sand, kicking up more clouds and growling low in their chest. Lora can't blame them. With each movement, the spikes from their collar grind upon their scales.

"What the fuck is that?" Ayc murmurs under his breath.

He's right behind her. She can feel the heat of his body as he towers above her, and she can't resist the urge to turn. His attention fixes on the dragon, at the streams of blood that work down the dragon's chest. Lora reads rage in the way his jaw locks, but something else is written on his face too, in the bob of the knot in his throat. She can't afford to analyze it. If she thinks too hard on what Ayc might be feeling, seeing such a magnificent creature enslaved, she'll be forced to let herself feel it, too. And she's not sure what emotions she feels looking at the dragon. She's only certain they make her want to both cry and tear the Drakr apart.

The dragon hisses again and swings its tail. The spiked ball slams into the cliff wall. Stone sprays and tumbles from above. When a boulder lands just to the dragon's left, it reels toward it. It parts its mouth and roars, loud enough that it feels like talons dragging down her eardrum, and Lora clamps her hands over her ears. Instead of glowing red fire, something green shoots from between its teeth. It lands upon the cliffside in thick, sticky sludge that bubbles as though boiling. The stone beneath it melts away, and when it's gone, a great divot has formed in the cliff's side—an entire section has simply disappeared.

"Shit," Ayc whispers. "I didn't know dragons could do that."

"It's rare," Irving whispers from behind him. "Truly rare, but some dragons do breathe things other than fire."

Lora drops her hands from her ears and tightens them into fists at her side, trying to look more controlled. It's difficult, with her nerves shaking in the wake of the dragon's roar. The dragon's *acid*.

"Pay Kivka no mind," says the Drakr on the right as the trio finally stops before Lora. Their voice is deep, haughty, like they're restraining a laugh. Even though, whatever the joke is, it's deeply unfunny. "She's a testy bitch."

"I would be too if you put a collar on me, Caius," says the Drakr in the center, and Lora recognizes the voice as the one she spoke to in the sky. Unmounted, they stand a head shorter than either of the other two, and their large, feminine frame spills out of the cloak, dressed in the black Drakr armor, the one that shimmers red wherever the light touches.

"You don't need a collar, *sister*," Caius snaps back. "You need a muzzle."

Caius's shadow rears up from the sand before them and slams its shadowed fist into Caius's hood. Caius stumbles backward, his hood spilling from his face. His eyes blaze red, and every one of his teeth elongates and grows sharp. Metal hisses from behind Lora as members of her party draw their blades. Lora holds up her hand to halt them.

She suspects that Caius is every bit as temperamental as the dragon they ride, but where Kivka has a profoundly relatable reason, what is Caius's excuse? She suspects because he's the sort of boy who thinks the world should kneel before his feet and gets personally offended when it fails to do so. She knows the type. Adamant was full of them.

Pathetic, whiny bitches, the lot of them.

Which is why she's entirely unsurprised when his sister

makes him heel with only a look, a burning of her own red eyes from within the darkness of her hood. Caius drags a breath through his pointed teeth. His red eyes fade to blue.

Behind them, a similar scene is unfolding. The orange dragon, Kivka, continues to pace until the blue rises and steps into its path. Kivka hisses, baring all its teeth, and the blue only stands, patient, unflinching, utterly in charge, until the orange slowly lowers themself onto their belly in the sand. The purple nudges Kivka gently with their nose.

Only then does Caius's shadow return to lay at his feet.

"Excuse my brother," says the Drakr in the middle, turning back to Lora. "He's devoid of any manners. We should introduce ourselves."

She lifts a gloved hand to her hood and pulls it down. The similarity between her and her brother is clear. Both have brown hair, white skin, and eyes the color of the sky. Where her brother wears his hair cut just below his ears, hers spills down her shoulders. Her lips are painted a bright red, and they curl up her round face. Something about the two strikes Lora as familiar, but she's certain she's never met them before.

"I'm Damara of the Dom Vari."

Dom Vari.

The name makes Lora's spine tighten. Five distinct houses exist within Drakr. But the Dom Vari is the very highest, the house of the queen. Which would make Damara—and her brother Caius —Drakr royalty. But then, the houses are massive. Though they are not nearly as diverse as Everadyn's clan, they aren't limited to a single, direct bloodline. Damara could be second in line to the throne, or she could be three hundredth in line to the throne, and no one in Everadyn would know. The Drakr have carefully hidden knowledge of Queen Volkna and her children. Even the generals and commanders, like Peregrin, who fought directly against the Drakr, are not quite sure how that family tree is constructed.

"This here," Damara continues, gesturing to the Drakr on her other side, the one who has yet to speak, "is my youngest brother, Brekken. He is also, historically, low on manners."

Brekken says nothing in response. Caius only quietly seethes.

Damara stretches out her hand toward Lora. "My pleasure to meet you, Queen Loraphne."

Lora takes her hand without hesitation because she doesn't want Damara to think, even for a moment, that she is disarmed by them. "*Sovereign* Loraphne," she corrects. "And you should join us for dinner."

Ayc inhales sharply, but she has a plan. A simple one. She wants them to talk. About themselves. About Lahlis. About Drakr. About anything and everything she can get them to talk about.

It's far past time she gets to know her enemies. Ignorance gets people killed. Truth, however, is a powerful weapon.

Damara drops her hand. "Are you certain you wouldn't rather us deliver our message now?"

"I think if you're going to make it a point to fly to see me so frequently, I should get to know you better."

Damara's red lips tip farther upward. "Well, I *am* starving."

Lora forces a matching smile. "Fantastic." She twists partly toward her crowd behind her but keeps the three riders fixed in her peripheral vision. "Irving, Shae, and Bronwen, please escort our guests into the castle. Find a page to help them get settled into a guest quarter so they can rest and clean up for dinner. I'll inform the kitchen staff we will have three extra for dinner."

Bronwen studies Lora carefully with concern in her eyes. But it has to be Bronwen. She's the only one in this castle who stands a chance at subduing shadow wielders.

"You're my First, and they're important guests," Lora says, hoping Bronwen will get the message weaved within the words. "Stay close to them in case they need anything."

Bronwen must understand because she feigns a smile. "I'll attend to their every need."

"Good," Lora says. "I need to speak with Commander Urbain. I'll join you at dinner shortly."

It's an excuse, but it doesn't appear Damara recognizes it because she practically purrs, "Looking forward to it."

"Follow me," Bronwen says and then leads the three dragon

riders away. Irving and Shae follow in their footsteps, their hands on the blades.

Lora remains fixated on their backs until they begin the climb up to the barracks. Only then does she release a breath. She feels as though she's run several dozen miles without taking a single breath. "Fuck," she swears.

Ayc, Peregrin, and her gryphon riders watch her as though waiting for orders.

"Commander Urbain—"

"Not here," Peregrin cuts her off. "Not in front of their dragons." They point their cane to where three pairs of giant red eyes stare down the length of the beach. Very, very intelligent eyes. Lora has to stop treating them like they're horses and more like they're gryphons who are mentally linked to their riders.

"Then let's get off this beach," Lora says.

"We'll walk with you," Urbain says, sliding off his gryphon.

Lora nods.

No one says anything as they leave the dragons behind. Tempest, too, stays, prancing up and down the beach like she intends to hold the line against invading dragons all on her own. Lora brushes her hand across the gryphon's neck as she passes and mumbles another word of thanks. A few of the other gryphons remain as well, steadily watching their mortal enemies.

When they must fall single file up the path, Urbain and one of the lieutenants takes the lead, a common guard tactic. She finds herself in the center with Ayc right at her back as she works her way up the steep path that leads up the cliff. She clutches at her skirt to avoid tripping over the hems. The tailor might just have to be admitted to the infirmary to convalesce when he sees the sand ground into the velvet.

"Hey, *Loorrraaa.*"

His voice is a whisper so that none of the gryphon riders can hear, but Lora knows that note all too well. The one he taunts her with right before he tells a joke that will certainly make her want to shove him off this cliff. A retort to silence him is right on her tongue, a familiar habit, but she stops because, perhaps, she does actually want to hear the stupid joke.

Not that she'll ever admit it.

"It better be good," she says instead.

"They're never good," Peregrin mutters from further behind her.

"This one is," Ayc says. "What do you call a dragon that can juggle?"

Lora is so busy trying to imagine how a dragon could possibly juggle—would they use their front legs? Or perhaps their wings?—that she nearly misses the punchline.

"*Talon*-ted."

"What?" Lora asks, pausing so she can glare at him over her shoulder.

"*Talon*-ted. Get it. Because they have *talons*."

She looks past Ayc at Peregrin. "Let's go back. I'm going to feed him to the dragons."

Ayc grins that ridiculous smile that absolutely makes her want to kiss h—No! Shove him off the cliff. She absolutely wants to shove him off the cliff.

She spins back around and hurries the rest of the way up the slope. And perhaps it's just coincidence, but her steps don't feel quite as heavy.

When they have all reached the top of the cliff, Lora turns toward the group. "Commander Urbain?"

He snaps to attention.

"Ensure your riders stay on high alert. No one should breathe a sigh of relief until we see the dragons' retreating form."

"We will be at the ready."

"Peregrin and Ayc," Lora says, turning toward them, "have you received the new armor for the Tour?"

Both Peregrin and Ayc nod.

"Good. Wear it. Find Tavish and Xylie and tell them to wear it too."

Ayc laughs, but it sounds thin. Fake. "Are we going to dinner or battle?"

"This is politics, boy," Peregrin says. "It's always both."

CHAPTER
TWENTY

AYC

Ayc can hear someone calling his name. It's faint, at first, like someone is whispering to him from the shadows. He pauses on the street through the barracks and glances around. Gryphon riders jog up and down the street, a gryphon occasionally stalking behind them. But no one is even looking at him. Peregrin parted ways to return to their home to dress for dinner, and Lora lingered behind to speak more with Urbain about plans. Surely, Ayc's brain is playing tricks with him.

But the closer he moves to the castle, the louder it gets. When he steps from the barracks into the courtyard, his name bursts like an explosion, like someone is screaming it directly into his ear.

"Ayc! Ayc! Ayc!"

Ayc swings around in a full circle. The voice sounds like an excited toddler, but only a handful of adults linger in the courtyard.

"Ayc! Ayc! Ayc!"

Ayc freezes, facing the castle, staring at a window. His kitchen window. From behind the glass, a dragon looks back at him.

Shit, shit, shit. He didn't think to close the shutters.

"Ayc! Ayc! Ayc! Ayc!" Muffin's white head bobs up and down.

Only Ayc hears it, through whatever mental bond Muffin forged when he bit Ayc. But that doesn't mean that anyone couldn't turn, right at this moment, and see a fucking dragon in Ayc's window.

Ayc bolts as fast as his legs will carry him back into the castle and down the hallway. He ignores the looks staff throw his direction as he rushes past them. He unlocks the door to his kitchen and slams it shut behind him.

"Get away from the window!" he hisses.

Muffin plops their front feet on the ground and whirls around to face him. *"Ayc! Ayc! Ayc! Dragons, Ayc! Dragons!"*

Ayc shoves past them and throws open the window so he can reach the shutters. He grabs their ropes and pulls them shut. He yanks the curtain closed, too, just for good measure.

"Dragons! Out there!"

The impact of the voice makes Ayc's head spin. It takes a moment to grasp what Muffin means. "Dragons? Yes, there are dragons out there."

"Go see!"

Ayc recoils at that thought. Don't dragons eat the babies of other dragons? Or is that crocodiles? "No."

Muffin flicks their tail in irritation; the golden knub he was born with has grown into a spade. It nearly takes off the legs of the table before the window. *"Go. See. Now!"*

"They'll swallow you whole, Muffin. You wouldn't even be a decent snack."

Muffin narrows their red eyes and snaps in the air, the statement as clear as curse words.

"Mind your manners," Ayc says.

He almost laughs at how absurd this is. He's having an argument with a dragon. A creature that, though vastly intelligent considering they were only born a week ago, now seems to have the temperament of a toddler who hasn't taken a nap.

Muffin growls, deep and low. *"Hungry."*

Ayc sighs. "Fair enough. I'll get you something to eat."

"No. Hunt."

Fuck. Of course, a baby dragon needs to learn to hunt. It's the very nature of them. Another problem for him to solve.

"I promise I'll figure out a way for you to hunt later. Right now, I'll have to get you something from the kitchen. Just be good, all right?"

Muffin whips their tail once more.

"Muffin?" Ayc presses.

"Muffin be good."

Ayc will take that as a *yes*. "Just give me a minute to get dressed, and I'll go."

Ayc hurries into his bedroom and opens his wardrobe. Within is the armor that arrived from Lora just yesterday. Dozens of armorers must have been working to get this done so swiftly. The note from Lora stated it was the expected uniform of her Five, to be worn on official business. Yris's Five also had outfits, theirs practical and pitch-black armor and cloaks.

At first glance, Ayc thought Lora's selection was also black. Instead, the leather is the darkest of greens, like that on the leaves of midnight, a green so dark that it only looks green when the light shines on it just right. Ayc shrugs into the skintight long-sleeved shirt and the leggings given to him by the armorer. They are smooth against his skin, but the thick fabric makes him believe it has some ability to protect all its own. Then he shrugs into the breast piece, the one that falls like a tunic to his knees. Gold accents curl across the chest, giving the vague illusion of a tree.

The armorer showed him multiple times how to do the buckles at his side and neck to ensure the parts of the leather overlap, but it still takes him far longer than he wishes to do it up. He can hear Muffin pacing, their sharp claws scraping against the stone floor. Occasionally, they curl their long neck into the room and inspect his progress. No words come across their mental link, only a series of grumbling noises and a feeling of general displeasure. So, Ayc supposes he can also sense the dragon's emotions, too.

Ayc secures his sword belt around his center, trading the

sword he borrowed from Irving to his Audori-made one. He ignores his wrist guards because he can't wear them over his leather bracelets. He doesn't like the separation of his power, but his control of it is unpredictable, and he's not ready for the Drakr to know he's something other than human. But Ayc does trade his brown gloves for the matching dark leather, to hide the dragon's mark.

He slides into his new boots before slipping into the final piece: the leather coat. It echoes the design of the armor but also that of Lora's cloak, the one that the Totus Omni stitched her before the Trials. The gold thread fully forms a tree in the back, with leaves of gold, burgundy, reds, and emerald greens. Down the sleeves are golden symbols of each of the clans of Everadyn.

He slips on his rings and adjusts the tie in his hair before studying himself in the mirror on the back of the wardrobe's door. He's surprised at just how striking of a figure he creates. He looks strong. Powerful. No longer just a baker but a warrior.

He adjusts the collar of his coat. A flash of gold on the inside of the collar reflects back at him. He steps closer to the mirror and flips the collar up. There, stitched in the same gold as the emblems of the Everadyn clan, is a bear.

A bear for Aluina.

Emotion clogs Ayc's throat, but he barely has time to consider it before Muffin roars across their mental link, *"HUNGRY!"*

"All right, all right!" Ayc presses his rings onto his hand, grateful he recently touched up the nail polish on his hands. He has no time to line his eyes in black. He rushes through his kitchen and out the door, calling after himself. "I'll be right back." He stops only long enough to lock the door.

He passes a page on the way to the kitchen and passes on Lora's message to Tavish and Xylie. It feels strange. The staff in this castle used to be his peers, and now, he's giving them directions. It feels even stranger when the page nods and says, "Right away, sir."

He's never been a sir before.

Ayc finds the kitchen in organized chaos. The staff is racing around, prepping to make a dinner that is likely far more extravagant than the one they initially planned, with very little notice. The first course, a stunning salad covered in the brightest of the seasonal fruits, is being prepped on the central counter. A slab of meat roasts over a fire in the kitchen's corner. Ayc spots Zinnia over the large stove, with pots bubbling on each of the four burners. Ember sits on a stool nearby, his nose pressed inside a book with a wyvern fossil sketched on the cover.

Ayc could slip off his bracelets and fade into the shadow, but who knows how keen Drakr senses are? So he keeps close to the wall, hoping no one will notice him on the way to the icebox. The one in this kitchen is the size of an entire room, and he shivers as he steps in. He grabs the nearest slab of raw meat he can find and tosses it into the pot he snagged on his way through the kitchen. He slides back out and nearly collides with Zinnia.

"Are you the one who's been stealing all the chickens?" she demands, folding her arms over her chest.

"Uh…" is the only thing Ayc can manage to say.

She taps her foot, something he's seen only when Ember is truly testing her patience.

"Yes," he says. "But I have a good reason. I promise."

"Well?" She makes a 'come' gesture with her hand. "Let's hear it."

"Now?" Ayc glances over at Ember, who peeks over his book. Peregrin will surely tell Zinnia the truth, anyway. But he doesn't have time to explain now. "I really don't have the time. I'm sorry."

Zinnia huffs. "Fine. Just take it. But you better have a really good reason. Someone was about to get fired."

Ayc winces. Shit. He never considered someone else might be impacted by his stupid choice. Foolish of him. He'll have to set it right quickly, but that means telling Lora, and fuck, she has enough going on today. "Thank you. I'll explain when I can."

He darts out of the kitchen, racing back down the hallway to his own smaller kitchen. He freezes when he rounds the corner, and his heart soars straight out of his chest and collides with the floor.

Fuck.

The door is open. Teeth marks dig a hole into the door where the handle once was. Ayc flings himself into the kitchen. *Please be in there, Muffin. Please. Please.* He pulls the door closed behind him and searches through his kitchen.

"Muffin!" he calls mentally, trying to holler it down the connection he can feel between them.

There's no reply.

His heart must have reentered his chest because it slams against his ribcage as he runs into his bedroom. But Muffin isn't there either.

"Fuck, fuck, fuck. Muffin, where are you?"

Ayc frantically looks beneath his blankets, in the wardrobe, in all the cabinets, even the ones he knows Muffin can't reach. Out of sheer desperation, he even looks in the oven and inside of his teapot resting on the stove.

But Muffin is gone.

LORA

Lora sits down at the head of the long table that now sits at the center of the great hall and wonders where the fuck the rest of her Five are. The staff has done a tremendous job turning what should have been a routine, modest affair into a formal setting. A tablecloth lays over the table, and a dozen golden candleholders are set down its length, each holding a single lit candle. The candelabras have been moved closer so that they create a rich aesthetic, a circle of light against the darkness.

Perhaps if the food and wine and atmosphere are good enough, the Drakr won't notice that the entirety of the royal guard line the parameter of the room. The darkness certainly won't hide it from them. Not with their Drakr vision.

Peregrin sits two seats to Lora's left, just past Damara. The armor Lora selected fits them well. The leather chest piece and coat are shorter than what she selected for Ayc and Tavish. She made the selections based on Peregrin's flight armor to make sure they would be able to fly as comfortably as possible.

Bronwen's is different, too. Knowing her friend, Lora selected a more feminine cut. The pieces gather at her hips before bowing out and sweeping down to her ankles. She's draped her green sorcerer cloak over it. She sits directly on Lora's right, as she should be as Lora's First. Next to Bronwen is the youngest Drakr, Brekken. His coloring is nearly identical to that of his siblings, but he wears his own brown hair shaved close to his head on one side. On the other side, it sweeps down to his shoulder, concealing half of his face. Caius sits at the very end, frowning down at the empty crystal goblet.

But Ayc, Tavish, and Xylie are missing.

Lora locks eyes with Bronwen and subtly signs, *"Where are they?"*

Bronwen shakes her head.

"What is that you're doing?" Caius demands. "Waving your hands? Some kind of enchantment?"

Damara snorts. "It's sign language. The fact you don't know that is concerning, Caius."

"Sign language? She's not deaf. She was communicating with us just fine," Caius snaps.

Lora reaches down to where her knife is strapped to her thigh. She has to hand it to the tailor. He designed a dress that bares so much skin it gives the illusion that she can't possibly be hiding anything, and yet, it falls just perfectly to hide the knife. It's the reason she remains in the dress she was being fitted with earlier, with the armor still over it. She's added her cape, the one the Totus Omni people made her, but she was too busy conspiring to do little else.

She instructed the royal guards to make sure that no one carried weapons into the great hall, including her Five. She even left her own swords in the cabinet outside the door. She wants to limit the number of weapons in the room and lower the chances that someone will get stabbed before the dinner is over. Still, there are plenty of weapons remaining. Forks and candlesticks and dinner knives. Even a spoon can be dangerous if aimed at the sensitive flesh of an eyeball.

Not to mention their shadow power.

"What did you say?" Caius demands.

"Nothing of any importance," Lora replies. "There's no need to get so emotional."

Caius's eyes flare red. That line never fails with little bitch boys like him.

His hand coils around his fork.

"Behave," Brekken warns. His voice is deeper than Caius's. It reverberates through the room.

"We should have left him at home," Damara says with a deep sigh.

Brekken grunts as though in agreement.

Caius tosses down the fork. It clatters on his plate. Petulant child. Next to him, Damara and Brekken seem friendly and safe in comparison. Perhaps that's their plan.

"Well, are we going to eat or not?" Caius demands.

"The first course will be served any moment," Lora assures, though she isn't actually certain why the staff hasn't arrived already. "With wine. I've told our steward to select the very best."

And with any luck, the Drakr will drink it, and maybe Lora will get a few answers out of them.

"I hope you will not consider us rude for not drinking it," Damara says. "Flying and fae wine doesn't mix well. I don't want to drag either of my brothers from the ocean because they indulged too much."

Lora forces a smile. "No. Of course not."

Fuck. There goes that plan.

The side door of the great hall flies open and slams against the wall. A shock of turquoise hair appears past the dimness. A guard moves to intercept Veni, but Lora swiftly waves them aside. He springs a few steps, then catches himself and slows. Lora bites her tongue to keep from demanding what he's doing there. She hasn't officially hired him as a guard yet. Of course she will. He scored brilliantly on his qualifying tests over the last week, but she hasn't wanted to tell him until she finalizes the list of new guards.

Still, he strides toward her like he's already a guard. Veni lifts his hands to sign, just like Xylie, a skill he's learned from his mother. She is the sweetest of souls, another person in Avia who Lora considers a dear friend, but she's been profoundly ill for the last several years, an illness that struck her hearing from her.

"We have a huge problem," Veni says. *"You need to come with me."*

When Lora hesitates, he insists, *"Right now."*

Lora fixes a smile on her face as she turns back to the Drakr. "There seems to be a hold-up in the kitchen. I'll be back swiftly."

She rises and forces herself to be calm as she follows Veni back out of the hall. Irving and Shae fall in behind her. Irving isn't supposed to be back from leave yet, but he insisted on staying. He pulls the door shut behind them.

Veni blurts, "There's a dragon in your kitchen."

CHAPTER

TWENTY-ONE

"What do you mean there's a dragon in my kitchen?" Lora demands. She feels like this is the start of some joke that Ayc might tell, and the punchline will be some absurd pun that will scarcely make any sense. Perhaps that's why she responds with logic, "A dragon wouldn't fit in this castle, Veni."

"This one does. It's white and this tall." Veni drops his arms and gestures just about mid-thigh. "I think I locked it in there, but I don't know if the door will hold. Is it fireproof?"

"Why don't you start at the beginning?" Irving says calmly.

"Of course, but can we walk and talk?" He gestures with two thumbs over his shoulder. "Before it completely destroys any hope you have of making a good dinner for the Drakr guests?"

"Let's go," Lora says, pushing past him and down the hall toward the kitchen. Veni falls into step beside her. The two kitchens are close to this side entrance. She can't hear anything from the main one, but that's the enchantment at work. Her mother had the kitchen spelled to hide the clanging of pots and the sound of work. Divine forbid, staff dare to be seen or heard.

Veni talks in a rush, his words fumbling over each other. "So I was standing in the hallway near the kitchen, flirting with this really handsome page who I just happened to pass by. We were talking about the dragons and the Drakr—"

"Is this relevant, Veni?" Lora says.

"Yes! Don't interrupt."

"Watch your tone when you speak to your Sovereign," Irving warns, his voice laced with a threat.

Lora swallows. It sounds exactly like the Irving she's always known, like he's known her for two decades and not two hours.

"Sorry. Don't interrupt, *my lady*," Veni corrects. "We were standing there when, all of a sudden, the door to the kitchen flew open, and the staff came running out, screaming that there was a dragon. And so I went to help. And sure enough, there's this little white dragon with what I assume was a pig they were roasting for dinner in its mouth. And this one maid had her kid there. The kid is going, 'Mama, a dragon,' and the mom started banging on a pot with a spoon. And the dragon dropped the pig and started screaming, too!"

Lora frowns. "You mean roaring?"

"No. This was definitely a scream. It was almost as though it was scared. It started running in a circle, trying to get away from the maid. I grabbed the kid and hauled him out, even though he was whining about wanting to pet the dragon. Cute kid. No survival instincts."

"Did everyone else get out unharmed?" Irving demands from behind Lora.

It clicks then. A maid with her kid. Zinnia and Ember.

Lora picks up her pace.

"Yes," Veni says. "No one was hurt. The maid and I made sure everyone got out and then barred the door from the outside. I told the staff to go to the second floor in case the dragon gets out."

Irving lets out a breath.

When they arrive, the kitchen door is barred and quiet, but it's unclear if that's enchantment or reality. Lora draws her dagger and creeps forward. She slides the bar out of the way and opens it slowly, so it doesn't make a sound.

The kitchen is in ruins. Spatters of green lettuce cling to the walls and the floor. The roasted pig lays abandoned with gouges out of its side. Pots and pans roll about. And the dragon is pacing. It flutters its wings and flaps its tail, and Veni is right. It's incredibly small. And beautiful. The light of the cooking fire gleams off its white scales like flattened pearls.

She can feel Irving peek above her head, trying to catch a glimpse. He inhales sharply in awe. The sound draws the dragon's attention. It snaps its head in Lora's direction, its red eyes focusing on her. Despite its small size, her heart reacts with an innate fear. It darts toward the door, and Lora slams the door shut. She throws the bar back in place. The door shakes. It makes no sound, but it quivers like a force has hit the other side.

"All right." Lora drags a breath through her teeth. "There's a dragon in my kitchen." She looks at Irving. "What do we do with it?"

"I don't know," Irving says. "I think it's young. Very young. Dragons grow fast, so if it's that small, it can't have hatched very long ago."

The door shakes again.

"Could it have come with the Drakr?" Shae asks.

"No," Irving says. "I don't know if it can fly yet, but it certainly couldn't make the journey all the way from Drakr."

Lora presses the heel of her palm to her aching forehead. She can't leave it in there, ruining dinner for her Drakr guests. And she doesn't want the Drakr to find out. They might try to capture it and enslave it like they did the orange dragon. The idea makes Lora feel ill.

"We have to trap it and move it somewhere else," Lora says.

"What?" Veni says. "You're not going to just..." He feigns swinging an imaginary sword. "Slay it?"

The door shudders once more, and Veni gestures at it like it's some irrefutable evidence.

"It's a baby," Lora says. "You said yourself it just seems scared. It hasn't hurt anyone. It seems wrong to kill it."

She's already responsible for the death of one baby dragon.

She still thinks about that egg they left in that cave on Somnia Ignis after the mother dragon died. She abandoned it to certain death. Xylie might have kept it if Lora hadn't insisted on leaving it behind. She's regretted that decision ever since.

"What are you going to do with it after that?" Shae asks.

"I don't know. One step at a time." She tucks her dagger back into its sheath. "Rope. I need rope."

"I'll be right back." Irving races down the hallway, and he returns swiftly, a coil of rope in his hand. Lora takes it from him and lets one end of it drop at her feet. The other end, she uses to tie a slip knot, leaving a large loop on the end. She grasps one side of the circle.

"Veni, hold the other side. Irving, you open the door. With all luck, the dragon will run straight into the loop, and we'll get it onto its neck. Shae, please go make sure that the Drakr do not leave... no matter what they hear." She could call another guard on the agate, but she doesn't want to risk them creating a scene. She trusts Shae to handle it well.

Shae murmurs something under her breath that sounds quite like a prayer but hurries back to the great hall.

Lora tightens her hold on the rope and coils some slack in her other hand. "Ready?"

"Absolutely not," Veni replies, also tightening his hold.

"Now, Irving."

Irving reaches around them, unlocks the door, and flings it open before springing back. The dragon is sprinting toward the door as though intending to fling itself against it once more. Its red eyes widen as the door opens, but it only picks up speed. As it bolts through the door, the rope slides over the head, the horns, and down its neck. Lora yanks the slack tight. It snaps down on the dragon's neck.

The dragon lets out a sound that does, in fact, sound like a scream. But it doesn't slow. The full weight of the dragon slams against the rope, ripping it from Lora's hands.

"Fuck!"

Irving and Veni dive for the coil of rope. It unfurls rapidly as the dragon charges down the hallway, and they scramble for purchase only to have it yanked from their hands. The dragon is far stronger than the small size makes seem possible. Lora dives for the rope once more but misses it.

"Fuck!" she swears, watching the dragon flee down the hallway.

Something bites into her ankle and rips her legs out from under her.

She slams onto the stone and has no time to catch her breath before she's sliding across the floor. Chandeliers fly past. She kicks at whatever has a hold of her, only to realize that it's the rope connected to the dragon. It's coiled around her ankle as the dragon yanks her down the stone hallway. Her hands scrape uselessly against the stone. Her skirt is being pushed above her head, and she's quite certain she's flashing her guards her underwear.

Irving and Veni call out to her as they race after. The dragon slows so it can turn a corner, and Lora uses the chance to draw her dagger. Veni leaps and grabs hold of her, stalling her just long enough that she's able to sever the rope. The dragon bolts free.

"Shit!" She kicks the rope off her ankle and jumps to her feet just in time to see the dragon dart through the open door...of Ayc's kitchen.

Perfect—it'll be trapped in there.

She finds the dragon pacing within the kitchen, its mouth open wide, its head searching around. It sounds...almost like a baby wailing. It's terrified. The kitchen is otherwise empty, so wherever Ayc is, he isn't here.

"It's all right," Lora says, trying to keep her voice soothing, though she knows she's quite far from a soothing person. "I won't hurt you."

It freezes and quiets a little like perhaps it understands. It cocks its head at Lora, and there's something so intelligent about its eyes. Intelligent and good.

Don't be foolish, Lora. It's a dragon. It can still hurt you.

Still, she lowers herself onto her knees, hoping that by making herself seem smaller, she might not be as frightening.

"My lady," Irving says, her title a note of caution.

"It's all right," Lora says. To Irving. To the dragon. "It's all right." To herself, this time, trying to convince her pounding heart to believe it.

She lifts her free hand toward the dragon, and it stretches its neck out. It sniffs at her fingertips, cocking its head once more, and she's all too aware that its sharp teeth are within inches of her fragile skin. But still, it's such a beautiful thing.

"Lora," Veni murmurs again, in awe.

Lora dares. She stretches her fingers to brush down the dragon's snout, and it allows it. Allows her to trail her fingers down its snout and then across its cheekbones to its neck. It stiffens, and Lora freezes.

"It's all right," she coos again.

It blinks its big red eyes at her, and she slowly, so slowly, drops her hand to the rope, still wrapped around his neck. And seizes hold.

The dragon reels back its head and lets out another little shriek.

"It's all right! It's all right!" Lora yells, but it continues to shriek. She refuses to let go of the rope, and with her hand so close to its neck, it doesn't have enough force to truly yank out of her grasp.

"Stop!"

Ayc shoves past Irving and Veni and into the room. Just behind him are Xylie, Tavish, and Saga.

"Stop!" Ayc repeats. "Please don't hurt them." He grabs the rope from Lora's hand, and Lora is so shocked she lets him take it. He positions himself between Lora and the dragon. The dragon presses itself against the back of Ayc's legs, shaking like a puppy left out in the rain.

Ayc holds his hands out in a calming gesture. "I'm sorry. I can explain."

Lora's mind slowly presses the pieces together. Ayc's

disappearance from the dinner. A baby dragon in the kitchen, who ran immediately back to these quarters as though it knew the way.

She climbs to her feet and narrows her eyes upon Ayc. He looks far too gorgeous in the dark armor and coat she gave him. Which is good because she has a feeling it's going to be the *only* thing keeping her from murdering him.

"I can explain," he repeats.

"You had fucking better," she growls through her teeth.

TWENTY-TWO

AYC

Ayc pries his lips apart and hopes that something intelligent comes out of his mouth.

"Um…"

Fuck.

"So…"

Nope, still not enough.

He tries again, but this time, only a cough works up his throat. Lora arches an eyebrow, and damn, the slant of that one brow speaks so loud it might as well be screaming. As if he can't already read the fury in the stiffness in her jaw or the way her fingers work on the hilt of her blade.

At least, when she stabs him, it'll be a lovely last sight. Lora's taut curls are tangled in the peaks of her crown, and the strap of her dress has worked its way down her shoulder. And that dress? Fuck. It's magnificent. Earlier today, when he first saw her, his heart nearly exploded from his chest. The expanse of her thick thighs, the accent of armor, the way it boldly reveals every curve of her wide, powerful body. Even in chaos, she looks divine.

"Well?" she demands, even though her eyebrow says it just fine.

Ayc glances past Lora at the five other sets of eyes staring at him. Xylie's hands remain still at her side, her teeth grinding on her lower lip. Irving's expression is carefully guarded, but Veni leans against the door frame and grins like he's enjoying the show. Tavish presses his fist to his lips, and the only one whose eyes are bigger than his is Saga. The dog stares at the dragon behind Ayc's leg with eyes completely rimmed in white.

Granted, Tavish has only known about the hatching of the dragon for merely an hour and a half. When Ayc realized that Muffin was truly gone, he ran to find Xylie and Tavish both. It was a lot to blurt at Tavish all at once, but to his credit, he immediately jumped in to help Ayc and Xylie locate the dragon.

Ayc wasn't sure if Muffin was purposefully trying to take them on a wild chase or simply exploring, but Tavish's senses led them through a confusing series of turns. They darted through random halls, ran into a dead end, peeked between the shelves of the Archives with no success. Whenever Ayc thought he might have seen something, he looked again, and it turned out to be merely a glint of light.

The three drew suspicious looks from the staff who passed by, but Ayc didn't bother to ask them. He figured if anyone had seen Muffin, there'd be a lot more screaming.

Tavish lost any sense of where the dragon might be when they circled back to the doors that lead to the courtyard. Remembering Muffin's interest in the adult dragons, Ayc raced to the beach as fast as his aching legs would carry him. Xylie, Tavish, and Saga rushed after him. He feared he would find nothing but a few drops of blood, but the adult dragons looked absolutely calm, and most importantly, so did the gryphons and their riders who were posted on the cliffside. Again, the considerable lack of yelling gave Ayc a clue that Muffin was never there.

And then Ayc heard the scream. It pierced between his eyes like an arrow. But not pain. A voice.

"Ayc! Help! Ayc!"

And somehow, perhaps because Muffin wasn't blocking him

out anymore, Ayc's feet knew exactly where to find them. And he ran once more.

So, here he is now, standing before his dragon like the reckless, brainless ass he is. With Lora getting angrier with each waning second.

Ayc clears his throat and tries again. "This, uh... This is Muffin." He gestures down to the little shit who presses their nose into the back of Ayc's knee.

"You named the dragon Muffin?" Veni asks from the doorway.

"*Of course* he named the dragon Muffin," Lora snaps back at him. "That is literally the *least* surprising thing about this entire situation." She grinds her teeth together. "But I didn't ask for the dragon's name, Ayc. I asked why the *fuck* there is a *fucking* dragon in my *fucking* castle."

"I kept the egg," Ayc finally blurts.

"The egg?" Lora repeats.

"The one in Somnia Ignis."

"*That* egg? You've had *that* egg this whole time?"

"Yes."

"This whole *fucking* time?" Lora's voice pitches to an octave Ayc has never heard before, one that reveals she's trying desperately to keep calm. And failing.

Ayc swallows. "Yes, Lora. The whole fucking time."

"And then it hatched?" she demands.

"Obviously," Veni mutters.

Lora spins around, stabs her dagger in his direction, and snarls, "Veni, keep your divine-forsaken mouth shut before I find a new use for my embroidery needles."

Veni mimes locking his lips shut and tossing away the key.

"And you two." Lora gestures to Tavish and Xylie. "Did you both know about this?"

"I... Well..." Tavish stutters. "Perhaps...slightly. A little bit."

But Xylie's hands are steady when she signs, "*When I put the egg back, I knew Ayc would never leave it in that cave.*"

"Don't get mad at them," Ayc says. "The only one you should be mad at is me."

Lora's back stiffens, and she turns her head just enough that he can see her eyes when they flash silver. "So be it," she growls.

Ayc tries to swallow again, but there's no more moisture left in his mouth. *Muffin, we're so fucked.*

Fucked? Muffin tips their nose upward to look at Ayc. *What fucked mean?*

Ayc doesn't know how to explain the concept of being fucked to a baby dragon, and he hardly has the time. Lora is already issuing commands as a prelude to his imminent murder.

"All of you get out. Everyone except Ayc."

Veni peels himself off the wall and casts Ayc a sympathetic look. "Divine be with you, friend."

Friend. It's certainly an exaggeration. Ayc and Veni have had one brief, friendly conversation. Veni seemed like he might like to talk longer, and Ayc wanted to—or at least, he wanted to *want* to. But when he tried to flirt back, he instead found himself making an excuse and hurrying away. It has nothing to do with the handsome guard and everything to do with Ayc's recent inability to want anyone but Lora.

Lora ignores him. "Tavish, go to the great hall and explain that a small fire broke out in the kitchen. Dinner is delayed, and I'm seeing to it. I'll be there shortly. Xylie, go with him if you feel able."

Fuck me.

For a moment, Ayc forgot about the Drakr. He's supposed to be helping Lora with whatever she has planned, not nearly ruining it with his poor life decisions.

"Fuck, I'm such an asshole," he groans.

He doesn't realize he's said it aloud until Lora mutters, "You won't hear me arguing."

While the others shuffle out, Ayc stoops to remove the rope from Muffin's neck. Muffin blinks at him with their red eyes, looking sad. *Muffin sorry. Muffin little shit.*

A laugh jumps up his throat. He silences it with a snort because now is really not the time. He runs a hand down the dragon's neck and marvels at the intelligence. A week old and already managing an apology better than Ayc can.

It's all right. This is my responsibility. I'll handle it.

The door clicks behind him, and Ayc climbs to his feet. Lora stands only two feet away, still holding her dagger. Every muscle in her body looks tense, coiled with anger.

"I'm sorry," Ayc says quickly before she can begin.

She scoffs. "Are you really?"

"Yes. I'm sorry Muffin got out of this room at the worst possible time. I'm sorry that I didn't have the courage to tell you I was taking the egg. But I couldn't leave it there."

"Of course you couldn't," she says, rolling her eyes toward the ceiling. "Your goodness never ceases to cause me trouble. How long ago did it hatch?"

"On your coronation."

She paces away from him and presses her free hand against his counter. She glares down at the wood, perhaps noting all the new gouges in the surface that were not there a week ago— placed by Muffin's talons.

"Why didn't you tell me?" Her voice is now as cold and steady as a glacier mountain. And somehow, that feels worse than the heat of her anger.

Ayc searches his mind for a rationale that feels gentler than the truth, but after all his lies of omission, he should be honest. "I thought you'd have Muffin killed."

Her fingernails scrape against the counter as she curls her hand into a fist. "Do you truly think me so cruel?"

"I think you're *practical.* I think you'll do whatever you think is best for Everadyn. Weren't you intending to kill them right before I came in?"

Muffin squeaks, a sound Ayc hears with his mind but not with his ears, an echo of their previous scream.

"No!" She tosses the dagger onto the counter. The clatter echoes through the kitchen. "I was just trying to get the dragon out of the main kitchen and someplace safe where I could keep it until I could figure something else to do with it. But I didn't intend to kill it."

"Oh." It's all Ayc can say.

She picks the dagger back up, and the ice of her tone crackles. "And what exactly was *your* plan, hm?"

"I was going to tell you."

"When? How long were you going to continue to jeopardize everyone in this castle?"

"Muffin wouldn't hurt anyone."

"It's a fucking dragon, Ayc. It's not a pet!" She points the knife toward his face in a way that almost says she's forgotten she's holding it rather than any true intent for harm.

Still, Muffin curls back their lips and lets out a low growl, creeping around Ayc's legs. *"She hurt Ayc? Muffin bite."*

Ayc shifts to keep Muffin behind him. "No, Muffin! No bite!"

"Just a little."

"No! You've caused enough problems. Sit!"

Muffin huffs in protest but plants their rump on the ground and tucks their wings around them.

When he looks back at Lora, the knife is still frozen where she's pointed it at his face. A deep furrow digs into her brow as she glances between Ayc and the dragon at his feet. She looks like she might be failing to solve a complex puzzle... or maybe, perhaps, she's concerned she might need to fetch Ayc a healer who specializes in mental wellbeing.

Fuck. I was talking out loud.

He really needs to get used to this mental link.

"Can you put away the knife?" Ayc asks gently. "Muffin thinks you're going to stab me. Unless, of course, you *are* going to stab me because in that case, can we just get it over with?"

"How do you know that?" Lora asks. "How do you know what the dragon thinks?"

Ayc draws in a breath. "Because I can hear them talk."

"Dragons don't talk."

"And neither do gryphons, but Peregrin hears Tempest just fine."

"That's because of their…" Ayc can see the puzzle pieces connecting behind her eyes.

"Their bond," Ayc finishes for her. He pulls the glove off his hand and holds it out before her.

She lets out a soft breath, a tell that she, like Peregrin, knows the significance of what she's seeing. She drifts forward and reaches toward it, but her fingers hover over his hand, not quite touching. Still, her nearness makes him shiver. She traces over the pattern of lines, never letting her finger fully touch him. The moment stretches onward as his focus boils down to the space between their flesh.

Until he can't take it anymore.

"Say something, please."

And she does. "Holy fucking shit."

A burst of laughter escapes from his lips. He certainly wasn't expecting that.

She meets his gaze, her pupils once more rimmed with just a hint of blue while the rest remains steadfastly brown. He's uncertain what has caused this new combination of eye colors to appear so frequently, but he likes it.

"Ayc, you're a dragon rider," she breathes.

Ayc's brain has been in chaos since Peregrin told him the meaning of the mark. He has the evidence before him: the lines that match Muffin's color, the mental connection, this feeling in his chest like his soul no longer belongs only to him. And yet, he hasn't had time to fully accept it, some part of him fighting against the clear truth.

But something about the words on her lips and the awe painted across her face makes it settle.

He's going to be a dragon rider.

A year from now, when Muffin is fully grown, he'll be aboard their back, soaring through the sky. The thought burns at the back of his eyes. He never imagined such a thing.

Not him, a simple, foolhardy baker.

Not him, who has only just stopped running from his power.

Not him, whose body even now aches in a reminder that it's broken and will always be broken.

"Mine," Muffin says softly, nudging the back of his knee once more. Like the dragon can sense his thoughts. Of course they can.

"I think you chose the wrong person," Ayc replies.

Muffin's only response is a low growl.

"I'm not riding anything right now," Ayc speaks aloud. "They're not even the size of a pony."

"Well, they will be soon enough," Lora says. "They're going to be too big to fit in this castle. Fuck, the cost alone to feed them. I'll have to ask the agricultural steward if Everadyn's current livestock breeding can support a grown dragon. Surely, it can't be that much more difficult than feeding a few grown gryphons."

Both of Ayc's eyebrows shoot toward his hairline. How did she go from looking like she wants to eviscerate him to now trying to make a food budget? He feels like he's tipped sideways into a different universe.

She takes a step back and squares her shoulders. "But that's a problem for tomorrow." She reaches above her head to fiddle with her hair, blindly trying to disentangle it from her crown. "Right now, we have three Drakr who are expecting a dinner, and I have nothing to serve them."

"Why not?" he asks.

She stops fiddling and gives him a pointed look. "I'll give you one guess."

Ayc sighs. "Dammit, Muffin."

Muffin scurries out from behind him and darts into Ayc's bedroom. They hit that door with their tail, and it slams shut behind them.

"Will they stay in there?" Lora asks.

"Muffin stay," they call.

"I think so, but they chewed through my door, so I can't lock them in."

"I'll ask Veni to stand outside and keep an eye on them." She tugs on another curl and winces when it snags.

"Allow me." Ayc reaches forward but awaits her nod of assent before he takes another step forward and gingerly takes the curl between his fingers. Her hair is soft as a good dream, and fuck, it still smells like anise. He tries not to think of it as he focuses on unraveling the hair from the metal. But being this close to her is entirely too distracting. He has too close a view of the way that the dress cuts down in front, the way her full breasts fill it up perfectly.

He takes a shuddering breath.

Lora starts to tilt her head back.

"Don't move," he warns, as the movement threatens to tug her hair. "I don't want to hurt you."

She stills. "Are you well? Your breath is off."

"I'm fine." It's a lie. He's not fine. That dress is killing him. With that skirt, she's so accessible. It would be all too easy to brush it to the side, hook her knee over his shoulder, and feast upon her. Fuck, he already knows she'd be the sweetest thing he's ever tasted in this kitchen.

"Are you certain?" she presses.

And his mouth, the foolish thing it is, spills the truth. "It's just that dress. It's..."

He clamps his mouth shut. They've been teasing each other at times, but that could be passed off as a game. What he's thinking is too real, too intense. And they are in the middle of avoiding war. Now is not the time to spill his emotions at the feet of the new Sovereign.

She sighs. "It's horrific. I know."

He shakes his head. "That wasn't what I was going to say. Quite the opposite, in fact. But if you don't like it, then wear something else. Or nothing. That will certainly bring your enemies to their knees."

The air thickens between them, the way it has so often lately, like a storm is gathering. There is lightning here—he hopes he gets struck by it.

She releases her own stuttering breath but recovers swiftly.

"Be careful," she warns. "I may change my mind and stab you."

He reluctantly drops his hands from her hair, ignoring the way his hands ache when he's not touching her. He forces a smile. "If I'm dead, I can't fix your dinner problem."

"You have an idea?"

"Yes. Send some kitchen staff to the Roaring Gryphon tavern in town," Ayc suggests. "The owner owes me a favor after I made his daughter a cake for her wedding, and they're always busy. They prepare dinner for dozens. They can certainly spare enough for nine. In the meantime, we can serve them dessert first. I have chocolate pudding in the icebox. I made it last night. I was going to give it to you later."

She cocks her head. "Chocolate pudding?" she murmurs almost to herself. "That might work better than wine."

"Hm?"

She starts toward the door. "Wait here. We need to add an ingredient to the pudding. I have to retrieve it."

"What ingredient? My chocolate pudding is perfect as it is, and you know it."

She pauses at the door. "Good. That means they'll never taste it."

CHAPTER
TWENTY-THREE

AYC

Ayc enters the great hall with a flourish, like he often did before he performed before a crowd. And of course, he is. This, after all, is politics, as Peregrin said. He's watched this game play out in this great hall many times, but he never thought that he'd one day be a player. He especially didn't think that he'd be using the tray of desserts he carries above his head to scheme in such games.

"I have good news and bad news," he calls out like it's the beginning of a punchline. "The bad news is dinner still isn't here."

Caius grumbles in a language that sounds like the rumbling of stones before an earthquake, rough and crackling. Drakr, no doubt. Ayc doesn't know what he's saying, but he's been cursed out enough times to know a swear word when he hears one, whatever the language.

Ayc lifts his voice and practically sings out the next line to drown him out. "The good news is that means we're having dessert first."

Lora and Irving enter behind him. Lora strides around Ayc and takes her place at the head of the table. She sits like it might be her throne, chin lifted, back straight. Powerful and glorious.

Bronwen pointedly raises an eyebrow at Lora, but she doesn't glance her way.

"What the fuck took so long?" Caius demands.

"What my brother means to say is I hope everything is well," Damara corrects.

"Yes," Lora replies. "As I'm sure Tavish explained, a small fire broke out in the kitchen."

Tavish nods from where he and Xylie sit near Peregrin. The only chair left available sits between Brekken and Caius. So Ayc will soon be sitting there. Fantastic.

Lora continues, "I apologize for the inconvenience, but please enjoy some chocolate pudding. My Fifth is an extraordinary baker."

Ayc sweeps to Lora's side to serve her first, a habit from his years serving Yris. He carefully selects one of the crystal bowls, identifying it by the tiny drip of pudding he's allowed to remain on the rim of the bowl, an error in the presentation he normally wouldn't allow. He's complemented the pudding with deep red berries, chocolate shavings, and a crown of whipped cream. It looks absolutely marvelous.

As he stoops to set it before her, he whispers into her ear, "You think I'm extraordinary?"

Her eyes become daggers as they dart toward him. Her face transforms from her congenial mask to a vicious scowl that threatens bodily harm. He shivers. He wishes he didn't like it, that his instinct of seeing a flicker of rage in her eyes wasn't to dig in and make it worse. His survival instincts are wretched.

She schools her expression quickly and looks away.

"Your Fifth is a baker?" Damara asks. "As a pastime or a profession?"

"A profession." Ayc straightens and sets a bowl before Damara, this one without the drip on the side.

Damara picks up her spoon and pokes at the pudding, a demure smile still marking her ruby-red lips. "How does one go from being a baker to one of the most powerful people in all of Everadyn? A human, no less?"

"Perhaps the goddess of good fortune and mischief smiled upon me," Ayc says, serving Peregrin, Xylie, and Tavish bowls with a drip of pudding on the rim.

"Perhaps," Damara muses. "I'm certain it's an interesting story. I would love to hear it."

Ayc rounds the far end of the table, meant to hold twenty and not just nine. As he comes around the other end, he finds Lora watching him carefully. She tilts her chin side to side—the smallest shake of her head. The smallest of warnings. Ayc doesn't know why he's drawn Damara's interest, but he knows, even without Lora's warning, that he would be foolish to assume it's innocent conversation.

Nothing is innocent conversation in politics.

"It's actually rather boring." He fakes a laugh as he stoops between Brekken and Caius to slide pristinely clean bowls before each of them.

"I doubt that," says Damara.

Brekken tilts his head in Ayc's direction, his nostrils flaring as he sniffs the air. Ayc tenses and curls his gloved hand so he can feel the bracelets still upon his wrist, still disguising his identity. Brekken's long hair shifts, revealing the side of his face previously covered. Purple lines curve like veins across his cheek and forehead, originating from beneath the high collar of his armor. It's the same pattern that runs up Ayc's arm, except Brekken's is purple. Just like his dragon. Perhaps it bit him, too, somewhere on the shoulder, and it tattooed upon his face. He wonders if Damara has a mark somewhere hidden beneath her armor. If maybe Lahlis does, too. Caius certainly doesn't. His dragon doesn't obey him willingly.

A clink of a bowl sounds from across the table. Ayc looks up to see Xylie staring at Brekken—at the mark on his face. The wideness of her eyes tells him she's connecting the dots. The beaming smile that she quickly hides by tucking her head tells him exactly how she feels about it. Later. They will have to talk about it later.

Caius sniffs, too, loudly and makes a sound of disgust. "Lahlis was right about him. He doesn't smell right."

Ayc ignores him and backs away to lay the second-to-last bowl before Bronwen. All that remains on the tray is his own.

"Really?" Damara says with a soft smirk. "All I smell is cinnamon."

"That's your deficiency, sister. Not mine."

Brekken sighs but says nothing.

Damara merely rolls her eyes. "Be grateful you have no siblings, your highness," she says to Lora. "They are a constant thorn in my ass."

"Perhaps we should eat." Lora leans closer to Damara and lowers her voice to the perfect feigned whisper. "At the very least, it'll distract his mouth."

Damara laughs. "I like the way you think."

Ayc smiles as he takes his own bowl off the tray. He lays the now-empty serving dish at the far end of the table before returning to his seat. Sitting down between the two Drakr brothers feels like sitting between two ravenous wolves. The hair on his arms stands upward, and a deep instinct wants him to rip off his bracelet, remove the barrier between him and his power. But he knows better.

He isn't certain how long he can keep his identity hidden from the Drakr, but he knows his mother went to great lengths to ensure he was a secret. He's hesitant to surrender all her hard work now.

Spoons scrape on bowls as those around the table begin to eat. But the Drakr are not among them. Caius glares down at the pudding.

"What's wrong?" Ayc dares to ask. "I thought you were hungry."

Caius turns the hot gaze upon him. Pinpoints in his blue irises burn red like a hot coal is within. "How do I know you haven't poisoned it?"

"Poisoning is a coward's way," Lora says from the head of the table. "Not to mention, forbidden among international guidelines of ethics that have governed us for centuries."

Caius snorts. "From what I've heard, you cheated to win your throne. Why should I trust that guidelines and honor mean anything to you?"

"Doubt my honor if you wish," Lora says calmly. "But don't insult my intelligence. Do you think I would risk war with Drakr just to see the death of a few inconsequential dragon riders?"

"Inconsequential?" Caius barks. "We're—"

He cuts off as Ayc picks up his spoon, dips it into Caius's bowl, and sticks a bit of pudding into his own mouth. He swallows it down pointedly and gives Caius a chocolatey smile. "See, no poison."

Though Ayc *is* tremendously happy to find that the dill-like taste of truth weed isn't detectable at all.

"Well, that settles that," says Bronwen. She gestures to Brekken with her spoon. "Unless, of course, you'd like me to taste yours."

"That's unnecessary," Brekken says. He takes a bite. Caius shoves a spoonful of pudding into his mouth, glaring the entire time. Damara plucks out a single berry and places it on her tongue. The little stain of chocolate mars the perfect red.

Ayc resists the temptation to look at Lora. She'll be the only one to realize what he's done. The risk he's taken. But Ayc has experienced the impacts of truth weed before. He saw Wren skirt around the truth. He can do it, too. He's a master of lies.

"So tell me about your dragons," Ayc says, leaning forward. He wants to buy time: more time for them to eat more. More time for the truth weed to loosen their tongues. "I *adore* dragons. I have a strong preference for gorgeous, fearsome creatures."

Damara takes a bite of pudding before responding. "I would tell Stjarna you said so, but I fear it would go to his head."

"Stjarna?" Bronwen repeats. Ayc doesn't know if Lora clued her into the plan or if it's just her intuition telling her to join in. "That's a beautiful name. Is there a reason you chose it? A special meaning, perhaps?"

"Oh, a dragon names themself. I called him Blazi, the Drakr word for blue, before he told me his true name."

Hm, Ayc muses to himself. Interesting. Perhaps Muffin has a true name, too.

Ayc glances at Xylie, who sits directly across from him. She, too, wears leather armor, similar to Bronwen's, but she's kept the multi-colored coat Lora stitched her all those years ago. Only now, the very edge of the sleeves have been embroidered with symbols for each of the clans.

Xylie lifts her hands from where they've been tucked beneath the table. Her fingers tremble, and she has to pause and start again before Ayc understands what she's said.

"Xylie also loves dragons," Ayc says. "She's probably read every book Everadyn has published on the matter. But there's a lot we don't know. She wants to know how to tell the difference between male and female dragons."

"We aren't supposed to give away our knowledge about our dragons," Damara says.

Damn. Apparently, she's either not had enough of the truth weed, or it hasn't given her the same impulse to blurt out the truth Ayc feels.

Then she continues, "But I suppose there's little harm in speaking on their biology." She leans forward so she can peer down the table at Xylie. "All dragons are born with both male and female reproductive parts. I refer to Stjarna as a he only because that's what he prefers."

Xylie's hands fly. Her movements are steadier now, her excitement soothing her anxiety.

"How does that work for mating?" Ayc translates.

Damara shrugs. "I'm certain they just do whatever they prefer and feels good to them. I've never asked. It feels like quite an invasion of privacy."

Ayc clamps a hand over his mouth to stop the bark of laughter that nearly launches from his chest. His shoulders shake, and Lora narrows her eyes upon him, a look that clearly reads, *Don't you dare.*

It only makes him want to laugh more.

Damara frowns at him a moment before she realizes. "Oh, fuck." She drops her spoon in the bowl. "You meant for *reproductive* purposes."

Bronwen snorts loudly. Her shoulders, too, tremble. She's holding in her laughter so hard her eyes and lips pinch together. It almost looks painful.

"Are you quite all right, my lady?" Brekken asks.

It breaks her. The laugh bursts from Bronwen, and Ayc presses his hand tighter to his mouth, almost losing control.

"I'm sorry. I'm sorry," Bronwen says, waving her hand before her face. "I'm just— I can't wait to tell the Lux Aester priests when we visit there on Tour. They love to say that *I'm* going against nature and that gender is fixed and finite. But their divine created *dragons*. Can you imagine their faces?"

Ayc can no longer help it. The laughter breaks from him, too. Caius and Brekken swivel their heads toward him with wide eyes.

"Whatever feels good to them," he repeats Damara's words. "Oh gods, I never thought I'd have so much in common with dragons."

"Me neither!" Bronwen laughs harder, slapping her palm down on the table.

Peregrin rubs a hand over their forehead. Tavish bites his lip to hide a smile. Lora inspects her spoon like she's considering how well it might scoop out both of their intestines.

Xylie snaps her fingers. *"She hasn't answered my question."*

Ayc sucks in a breath, calming his laughter. Bronwen, too, grabs a hold of her composure. But before he can ask again, Damara must sense what Xylie wants because she answers the question properly this time.

"When they decide to procreate, they decide which will bear the egg based on which partner is strongest and best suited for it in temperament."

"Practical," Peregrin says. "Child-rearing is not for the faint of heart. Not when done correctly, at least."

Damara nods. "Sometimes the one who doesn't bear the egg

will also attend the nest, but only when the two share a mate bond."

"A what?" It's Tavish who asks this time. He can't see Xylie already asking herself, but surely he knows. Surely, he hears her excited hands dancing in the air.

Damara opens her mouth, but Caius hisses, "That's enough secret sharing." His bowl is completely scraped clean now, but though the truth weed has clearly loosened Damara's tongue, it's done nothing to improve his temper. "Can we stop playing around and do what Father has sent us to do?"

Lora cocks her head. "You said you were sent by Lord Lahlis. Is he your father?"

"Yes," Caius snaps.

Ayc curses himself. It should have been obvious. The coloring between the siblings is similar, and it struck him as familiar when he first saw them on the beach. Because he's seen it before. Dark-haired, blue-eyed dragon riders. Just like Lahlis.

"I wasn't aware that Lahlis had a child," Peregrin says. "Let alone three."

Damara's gaze shifts toward them. "He's had far more than that. He's quite prolific, my father."

"How many more?" Lora asks. "I'd like to know how many other children he intends to send my way without a moment's notice."

Damara scoffs. "Unless someone is practicing necromancy, you have nothing to fear. We are all that's left. That we know of at least."

Thick silence permeates the air. Saga's breaths from beneath the table sound like little explosions.

"I suppose I should offer you my sympathy," Lora says.

Damara flicks her wrist dismissively. "Don't bother. Such is the way of the Dom Vari line. Only the strongest survive. Can't risk a weakling ever ascending to the throne."

"And yet you're still here," Caius mutters.

"Caius, if you could kill me, you would have done so already. You've tried. Many times. But we both know, if *I* wanted *you* dead, you would be." She parts her lips in a wider smile, one that lacks any joy but clearly shows the point of every one of her teeth. "So be quiet. I've grown wary of you."

The side door to the great hall opens, and two staff push a cart laden with food inside. When they enter the light around the table, Ayc recognizes Zinnia as one of them. Peregrin straightens their already ramrod spine at the sight of their partner, but she only briefly glances their way as she and the other kitchen maid work to unload the food from the cart onto the table.

The tavern owner has certainly repaid Ayc. The platters are full of roasted sausage and potatoes and carrots in portions that are enough to feed thirty, let alone the nine of them.

"It's about time," Caius says, stabbing a sausage with a fork. He must have gotten over his fear of poisoning because he bites down savagely.

Zinnia disappears with the cart as quickly as they've come, Zinnia sweeping her finger across Peregrin's shoulder as she goes. Silverware scrapes across platters for a moment as they serve up their dishes.

"Now that dinner is here, I suppose we should finally get down to business," Lora says, looking to Damara. "Let's you and I talk."

Damara tucks her hair behind her ear, dragging her smallest finger over the shell of her ear. The *round* shell of her ear.

Ayc nearly drops his fork. Her ears aren't pointed like the fae. They are rounded, just like his.

She's part human, too.

"Yes," Damara says. "Let's."

LORA

"Tell me why you've come all this way," Lora says. She keeps her focus on Damara. The dynamic between the siblings has made it abundantly clear she's the leader of sorts, and besides, Damara seems the most reasonable. Caius is a loaded catapult pulled taut and ready to fire. Lora could easily rile him, and he'd spill the truth, but not without causing harm to someone at this table. Brekken is stony and silent. It's hard to believe Lahlis sired all of them.

Damara saws at the sausage on her plate, dividing it into perfectly even sections. "Lord Lahlis realizes—"

Glass clatters down the table. Ayc rights his goblet. "Sorry," he murmurs as he sponges at the table with his napkin. "Continue."

Damara's smile quirks up her face. "As I was saying," she continues, moving on to section her large potato and carrots with the same amount of precision. "Lord Lahlis has realized that our last interaction likely did not leave the best impression upon you. And because of this, I was made an envoy between our two countries."

"I thought Lahlis was the ambassador to Everadyn," Bronwen says.

"He's prioritizing his focus elsewhere. He's quite busy."

In the talk of dragons, Damara didn't eat much pudding, though she did eat all the berries that bore the pudding upon their red skin. Enough that Lora can trust she's telling the truth, but it's also vague. Vague truths are so useless they might as well be lies. But Damara certainly isn't going to blurt out information. Not unless Lora applies pressure.

"You flew all this way *just* to inform me of the changes?"

Damara's lips part but only to welcome a carefully curated fork of even portions of sausage, potato, and carrot. She nods as she bites down.

"Do Drakr's have an allergy to ink?" Ayc asks. "Or does your family have a predisposition for making meetings for what could have been letters?"

"Unfortunately, life is full of meetings that should have been letters," Damara says. "But, actually, that is but the first matter I desire to discuss."

"Oh." Lora picks up her goblet, filled with grape juice as

requested, and swirls it before her lips. It's a trick she learned from her mother. A well-positioned goblet can give off an air of nonchalance while hiding any involuntary movement of the lips that might give emotion away.

"I hoped you'd allow me to accompany you on the Tour."

Lora is grateful she hasn't started sipping her wine yet because she would have choked on it.

Absolutely fucking not.

That's what she wants to say. But she digs her free hand into her thigh to restrain the urge. Lora glances past Damara to Peregrin. She suspects them to be shaking their head, trying to send some signal. They only stare stoically back. It doesn't matter. Lora isn't foolish enough to invite a spy right into her midst.

"I'm afraid I'm keeping my party small," Lora says, "My Five, my guards, my healer, and a few attendants. Nothing more."

"Then one more shouldn't be too much of a bother." Damara sets down her fork and picks up a pale napkin, dabbing it against her lips. The pale cloth comes back free of her lip color. Her lipstick is strong enough to withstand eating and a dragon ride across an ocean. If she were anyone else, Lora might have asked where she buys it. "Stjarna would remain close by, of course. But he mostly fends for himself."

"We won't win any favor if your dragon is eating Everadyn's cattle," Bronwen says.

"Don't worry," Damara says. "I'll tell him to hunt deer instead. I hear they're a real nuisance to crops in many regions within Everadyn."

There's a good thought. Lora tucks it away for later. It'll be useful for Muffin.

"Why do you really want to come?" Lora presses. "What's your true motivation?"

"Traveling with you would give us abundant time to build a relationship between Everadyn and Drakr. As well as send a statement to the rest of Everadyn that our allyship is strong."

"Is that not why I accepted Queen Volkna's invitation to Morkt Hemma?" Lora sets down her goblet but keeps her hand fisted around it. "To prove our alliance is strong. Is that demonstration no longer enough for Lahlis?"

Damara barks out a laugh. One that is cold and bitter as an icicle driven through skin. "*Nothing* is enough for Lahlis."

Her eyes widen, and she presses her fingers to her lips. She didn't mean to say that. Caius glares down the table at her, and Brekken arches a single eyebrow.

"As much as I value peace between our two nations," Lora says swiftly, wanting to distract her before she gets too suspicious, "We are still, indeed, two separate nations. An ambassador, I will accept. A spy, I will not. You may not go with us."

"Reconsider," Caius says through his teeth.

Lora rolls her eyes at him, exaggerating the movement so he can see how utterly bored she is with him. "No."

His bared teeth turn into a vicious smile. He looks *exactly* like his father. "Or don't. Lord Lahlis gave us orders on what to do if you refuse, and I'd really like to see what happens to you."

The threat is lightning. One crack, and it electrifies the air, making her hair stand on end. She isn't the only one. Peregrin drops their fork and slides a hand beneath the table. Lora's certain they, too, have hidden a blade somewhere. Lora hears the crinkle of leather armor and the tap of hands clasping swords as, in the shadows, her guards shift closer. Damara and Brekken both stare past the candles, and Lora knows their sharp eyes are tracking the movement.

"Please, let's hear it," Lora says, with a roll of her eyes. "What's Lahlis's threat this time? Will your dragons raze this castle to the ground? Will you begin a war? You realize that the more you threaten the Sovereign of this nation, the less patience Everadyn fae will have with our alliance. It is new and fragile, and we are a stubborn, prideful folk with memories of the times we used to be enemies. Eventually, if someone keeps threatening a fight, we will stop avoiding it and start welcoming it."

"Tell her, Damara," Caius presses, a note of mocking infused in her name. "Oh, fearless big sister."

"Let's remain calm," Damara says in his direction before twisting in her chair to face Lora. "I implore you to reconsider. There are many ways to strip someone of power other than outright war."

Lora glances past Damara. Xylie clutches hard onto the side of the table while sweat beads on Tavish's brow. She should not have asked them to come to this meeting. Across from them, Ayc appears calm. He plays with the edge of his coat's sleeve, his fingers sneaking in slowly. Toward his bracelets. Lora shakes her head, and he freezes. She doesn't want him discovered.

"Spit it out, Damara," Lora says. "I grow tired of the theatrics. What does Lahlis intend to do?"

She shrugs and leans back in her chair. "We will tell the truth. As you said, any alliance between Everadyn and Drakr is new… and it was quite unexpected. I might look like the picture of youth, but I *also* have a long memory of how, well, sudden everything seemed when Everadyn failed to come to Aluina's aid and instead gave the treaties to Drakr."

"A glorious day that was," Caius says, lifting his goblet in a cheer.

Ayc wraps his fists around the dinner knife, a darkness taking over his eyes. It used to be that Lora feared Ayc would be the victim of a justified stabbing because he pushed someone too far. This is the first time she's feared Ayc might *be* pushed too far. He's not the same baker he was before he left for the Sovereignty Trials, and she's sorry about that. She never meant for so much blood to fall upon his hands.

"I didn't ask for a history lesson," Lora says quickly. "I asked for your point."

Damara continues, "I'm certain most Everadyn fae would be eager to discover why Yris's policy about the Drakr was so different during her reign. They would be greatly interested in the deal she made."

Lora blinks. "That's it. You want to reveal my mother's dirty secrets? Go right ahead."

Damara leans forward and lowers her voice. "Don't you know

that you can't reveal the parents' secrets without getting their offspring dirty, too? If your mother took a deal to win her throne, people could easily think that her daughter did, too."

The lightning strikes once more. Lora's hand slides to the dagger on her belt. "That's a lie. Lahlis offered. I told him no. I won only on my own merit."

"But will your people believe that?" Damara asks. "Or will they use it as another reason to imply you are a wicked queen unworthy of her throne? From what we hear from informants, many already think so. After all, both the Noxumbra and the Lycendi victors were eliminated by Drakr. *Someone* made a deal with the Drakr."

Caius laughs, a staccato, humorless noise. "Ah, yes, I remember that. The Noxumbra victor's brother squealed so sweetly when I gutted him."

Lora has no time to brace before the blue wall of energy slams into her and propels her backward. She collides with the floor a few feet from her chair, her head slamming against the stone. The symphony of thuds and shattering glass tells Lora she isn't the only one impacted. A whine sounds through her ears, but all she can hear is the wretched scream coming from her best friend's mouth.

"You fucking bastard!"

TWENTY-FOUR

LORA

"Bronwen!" Lora calls as she scrambles upward. She doesn't make it far before a body slams into her, pressing her back to the ground.

"Stay down, my lady."

Irving. A green glow arches over Lora as he casts a shield around her. Streaks of blue screech across the force field, chased by dark fingers of shadow. Pinned by Irving, Lora can't see what's happening, but she can hear it. Bronwen's continued shriek, the familiar sound of something hard meeting flesh, Peregrin's booming cry of "Stop!"

Saga barks.

Someone whimpers.

"Let me up, Irving!" Lora demands.

"That's not a—"

Lora slams her elbow backward, and it connects somewhere. His jaw, perhaps, judging by the bony quality and the way it has the intended effect. The shield fades for just a second, and Lora leaps to her feet.

But it's already calmer. Whatever fight of magic and shadow exploded through the room has ended in a stalemate. Broken shards of glass and bits of sausage roll across the floor. The candelabras are tipped to the side, most of their candles extinguished. The greatest light comes from Bronwen's magic, its blue, translucent glow pinning Caius to a pillar. His neck careens backward as he gasps for breath. Blood weeps from his nose. He kicks, but Bronwen's magic holds him tightly. But she is bound, too. Shadow wraps around her arms and legs as she strains against it. Brekken stands between the two, his hand outstretched toward Bronwen.

"Release him," Brekken commands.

"Fuck you!" Bronwen spits. Caius's head careens further backward. His gasps stop, and he turns a deeper shade of purple. "He doesn't deserve to live."

"Undoubtedly," Brekken agrees. "But I can't let you do it."

Lora marks where the rest of her Five are: Xylie and Tavish, who have ducked beneath the table, looking unharmed. Ayc lingers close to Bronwen's side. His lip is split, but otherwise, he, too, looks unharmed. Peregrin holds a dagger between their fingers, poised to throw it at any moment. The guards linger a few steps away. Perhaps because they fear what will happen if they move any closer, or perhaps because they realize what Lora does. Brekken restrains Bronwen with his shadow, but he isn't hurting her. His shadows aren't forming ropes like Lahlis's did to Ayc. Instead, it drapes like a blanket swaddled tightly around a kicking infant.

Damara, too, doesn't intervene. She stands with her arms folded over her chest, watching.

"Bronwen," Ayc says gently, softly, "I know you're angry. You have every right to be. But think this through. Will killing him ease your pain?"

"I'm willing to find out," Bronwen snarls. Her eyes burn silver so bright, it shines like the full moon. Caius's own eyes roll back in his head.

"Bronwen!" Lora calls. "Wait. Let him breathe for a moment."

Bronwen bares her teeth, her canines sharpened. But she

must shift her magic because Caius gasps for a breath, some of the color returning to his face.

"If she releases him, can you control Caius?" Lora asks Damara. "I won't tolerate any harm coming to her."

Damara nods. "I won't allow him to harm a hair on her head. Neither will my brother. Right, Brekken?"

"Not a hair," Brekken agrees.

And neither of them can lie.

"Release her," Lora demands, closing the distance to her best friend.

And to her surprise, Brekken does. The shadows disappear from around Bronwen. She stumbles a step. Ayc lunges toward her, but Brekken gets there first, steadying her with a hand on her shoulder.

"I'm sorry for your pain, my lady,"

She jerks away from him. "Were you there, too?"

"No. I'm not my father's assassi—" But the word turns into a choke. He coughs, and his brow furrows.

The truth weed, once again.

"Don't be ridiculous, Brekken," Caius hisses. Even pinned to the pillar, he refuses to shut up. "Assassin. Butcher. You've been whatever father wanted you to be since the moment you came out of that Dom Eldi whore."

The word ends in a choke as Bronwen's magic slams down on Caius's neck once more. "You do not speak of women like that," she roars. "You do not shame them for what they do with their own bodies."

Brekken's eyes flash between red and blue as he shifts his focus between his brother and Bronwen. He makes no move to stop her. The cold air wafts from him, his power rising silently in his rage, shadow twisting at his feet. Lora wonders which words angered him: 'whore' or 'Dom Eldi'. The Dom Eldi are considered the lowest of classes among Drakr society. The class whose labor is exploited to prop up those of richer, wealthier classes above them, while struggling to feed themselves. Being a laborer should not be an insult, and yet, Caius uses it as such. Likely, Brekken sees it as such, too.

Lora steps to Bronwen's side, pressing two fingers to the back of her elbow. *I'm here.* She wants her to know. *I'm with you.*

"Are you going to stop me?" Bronwen growls. She loosens his grasp on his neck, just enough for Caius to drag in a breath, but not enough for him to speak.

"We both know that I don't have the power to stop you," Lora says. "But I want you to think about the consequences of this. There will be many."

"Blood for blood is the Drakr way," Damara says. "You can take his heart, and it'll be justice. But I promise you, it won't stop there. Our father is quite attached to him, or I'd have killed him myself long ago."

Bronwen stares at Lora.

"The choice is yours," Lora says, pressing her palm over her sternum, over her heart. She has faith that Bronwen will make the right decision.

Bronwen turns her head. The silver in Bronwen's gaze grows less bright, but it lingers. "What would you do?"

Her eyes shift past Lora, and Lora doesn't have to follow the line of vision to know where Bronwen looks.

To Ayc.

I won't ask you about Ayc, Bronwen said a week ago, *if you don't ask me at Ryker.*

But here she is, asking. And Lora knows exactly what she would do.

If Caius had hurt Ayc, Lora wouldn't hesitate. She would kill him. Slowly. Painfully. She would make him beg for death before she allowed him to meet the darkness. Even if it meant Everadyn would go to war. And that's the problem.

"You are not me, Bronwen. Let him go."

Bronwen draws a breath through her nose and exhales. With the breath, Caius falls to the earth. The blue light fades. A single stubborn candelabra is all that gives off light. Lora grabs hold of the dagger on her thigh as Caius's eyes glow red. He leaps upright and takes a step toward Bronwen.

Damara slaps her hands down on the table. Caius freezes.

"I will pin you there myself if you even think about it," she growls. "Brekken, take him back to the shore. Wait for me there. I'll join you shortly."

Brekken pivots, seizes Caius by the arm, and drags him toward the door. Shae and another guard shadow behind them. The doors close with an echo that booms through the darkness.

Xylie and Tavish crawl from beneath the table. Ayc rushes to their sides to ensure they're all right. Bronwen cringes.

"I'm sorry," she whispers. "I should not have lost control."

"Do not apologize," Lora says. "Are you all right?"

"Yes," Bronwen says quickly. But her head droops low, her hair flared around her face. Tears have dragged salty paths down her strong cheekbones, deepening the purple moons beneath her eyes. She's exhausted from the output of power, but those lines were there before this dinner ever began.

She isn't all right.

And it's Lora's fault.

By refusing to delegate, by wanting to keep all the burden upon herself, she has unwittingly thrown far too much on her best friend's shoulders. She's run herself ragged in just a short week, all while trying to piece together a fractured heart. She's falling apart so drastically, she can scarcely control her magic.

It has to stop.

"I implore you to reconsider, Your Highness," Damara says.

Lora drags her attention back to the lone Drakr. Damara still presses her hands against the table, leaning her full frame halfway over it.

"Let's come to an agreement. Let's negotiate."

Lora slowly closes the distance between them. "Why should I? It's quite clear that the Drakr are scared of me. Otherwise, you wouldn't have come all the way to Everadyn to threaten me twice in one week."

Lora stops at the other side of the table, close enough to reach.

Close enough to remind Damara that no matter what just happened, Lora is not afraid of her.

A muscle in Damara's jaw quivers, but she forces out a scoff a second later. "Afraid of you, no. I think Lahlis is just disappointed. He expected to get Marcellus, the fool too arrogant to protect his own neck. Instead, we got you. The bitch who refused to bow."

"Watch it," Ayc snarls.

"It's all right," Lora says calmly. "I'm quite proud to be known as the bitch who won't bow."

Damara's lips twitch. "As a fellow bitch, let me be honest with you. I promise you would much rather deal with me than deal with Lahlis."

"Why?" Lora demands.

"Why what?"

"Why would I rather deal with *you* than with *Lahlis*? Will you not report everything you see and learn back to his ears? You'll be just an extension of him, so why should I trust that you're any better?"

"Because I'm—" She slaps a hand over her own mouth, and the words spilling from her tongue become a muffled, unintelligible growl. Her brow furrows, and she searches around her as though seeking a threat, but she locks onto the shattered remains of a crystal bowl still stained with pudding.

"Truth weed," she hisses, whirling back on Lora. "The pudding had truth weed in it."

Lora refuses to even flinch. "I don't know what you're talking about."

"Bullshit," Damara growls. "You put truth weed in the pudding."

"What?" Peregrin demands.

Lora doesn't look at them. She can hear the judgment in their voice just fine. Peregrin would call this dishonorable, a violation of their international guidelines. Yris would call it using every resource available. Lora thinks it's both all at once.

You!" Damara stabs a finger toward Ayc. Lora slips her hand between the slit in her skirt to grab her dagger as Ayc steps in front of Xylie and Tavish. "You tasted Caius's bowl. Did you put truth weed in the pudding?"

Ayc locks his jaw and says nothing at all.

And that says everything.

"Your silence is loud as fuck." Damara leans back on her heels, shaking her head as she looks Lora up and down. "All that talk of guidelines, huh? I suppose you really are a wicked queen."

Lora lets the words glide off her skin. "Perhaps if I could trust my allies, I wouldn't need it."

"You're foolish if you think you can trust anyone. Even your Five could betray you if you aren't careful."

Lora mocks a laugh, not because it's funny but because she wants Damara to know her words have not sunk in. That's the thing with truth. It's relative to the person speaking. Damara might think that Lora's Five could betray her. After all, she has at least one brother who she's admitted has repeatedly tried to kill her. But Damara does not know Lora's Five. Ayc's dragon-hiding and troublemaking tendencies aside, they would never betray her.

"Laugh all you wish," Damara says. "But everyone has their secrets. Don't they—"

Peregrin cuts her off. "Isn't this a bit counterproductive to your goal? The more you run your mouth, the less likely the Sovereign will ever be persuaded to reach an agreement."

Lora frowns, twisting to look over her shoulder at her Third. Does Peregrin want Lora to work with the envoy? She would have thought they would be one of the first to burn the Drakr ally ship back to ash and ruin.

Damara only rolls their eyes and finishes what she was going to say, "Don't they, Ayc?"

"What?" Ayc asks.

"Whatever I said about cinnamon, you do smell...odd. You smell like secrets. Like you're hiding something."

Leather creaks as Ayc's hands flex into fists.

"Leave him alone," Lora warns, but Damara ignores her.

She paces down the table length so she's parallel to Ayc

instead of Lora. "Your silence once again is loud." She squares up with him.

Ayc steps closer to her.

Lora sweeps around the closer end of the table, so no wood will separate her from Damara now. Damara's hand wraps around a fork that has miraculously remained on the table. Lora pauses a few feet away, not because she fears for herself, but because Damara is within stabbing distance of Ayc's throat.

Rage simmers deep in her gut. It's probably been there this entire time, but seeing Damara so close to Ayc, a threat in her eyes, makes Lora feel it. She counts how many steps it will take. One. Two. Three.

Three steps, and Lora could be slitting her throat.

But Ayc smiles, that same smile he's given her every time she's held a knife to his throat. It's a shield. No, a weapon. "You're really acing this performance. You have the role of big, intimidating woman down, but I fear the dialogue is a little rambling and vague. Do you want to go away and rehearse a little, or are you going to get to the point?"

Damara nose wrinkles a moment before she presses the fierce, intimating mask back into place. "Are you human?" she demands.

"Yes," Ayc replies without hesitation. "And so are you."

"I saw you noticing my ears," Damara says. She releases the fork to sweep her hair back behind her ear, and Lora sees it now. The curve. "But I'm not *only* human. Are you?"

Ayc's throat works, like he's trying to swallow down his truth. It comes out anyway. "No."

Damara smiles at the victory. "Then what are you?"

Lora tells herself it doesn't matter if Damara knows the truth. Too many people witnessed Ayc on the last day of the Trials. It's only a matter of time before all of Everadyn knows, until the wrong person with the right connections spills it to the Drakr. So at first, Lora doesn't react until Ayc's smile drops from his face.

And then she surges forward. At her lunge, Damara spins around to face her and retreats back a few steps. And that's exactly what Lora wanted, to see Damara retreat before Ayc.

"Leave him be," Lora warns, "or I will cut out your tongue, and let you choke on the blood."

Damara cocks her head. Her blue eyes flick between Lora and Ayc and back again a half a dozen times. She lets out a low whistle. "Well, I'll be damned. *You* don't need truth weed to spill your secrets. And it certainly answers the question of how a baker became sixth in line to the throne. You two are fucking."

No!

Lora bites her tongue to keep from crying it out in horror. No one can assume that. Least of all the Drakr. They'll use him as their pawn.

But then Lora realizes she's been silent too long, and she doesn't know how to break it. Does she deny it, snarl at her to mind her own business, say nothing at all? What is the right move, the right words?

Her silence is no better.

"Oh shit," Tavish whispers.

"I'm right, aren't I?" Damara asks.

"No," Ayc says, every trace of his smile gone. "We're not."

"Not that it's any of your business," Bronwen snarls, stepping closer to Ayc. "You're overstaying your welcome."

Damara ignores her. "Really?" she asks Ayc, appearing truly baffled. But then she shrugs. "It scarcely matters. Everyone is going to assume it anyway."

"I want you out of my castle," Lora demands.

Damara finally looks away from Ayc. "Fine." And to Lora's surprise, she starts toward the door, but she calls over her shoulder, "But I'll be back tomorrow. And the next day. And the next day. I am quite persistent."

"I could have you shot from the sky!" Lora threatens.

"Would you risk war so freely?" She turns around but continues to walk backward. She presses a finger to her soft cheek, putting on a mock expression of thoughtfulness. "How will Queen Volkna react if something were to happen to her favorite grandchild?"

"Grandchild?" Bronwen repeats. "You're *all* her grandchildren?"

"One of many originally," Damara says, "and one of few yet living. It's the Dom Vari way. A way to better your odds of rising to the throne."

Lora swallows. Damara grins viciously as she continues to retreat, the steps jaunting. Victorious. That was well-played, Lora admits. She might even be impressed with Damara if she didn't hate her so fucking much.

Lora can't kill her, and Lora can't be rid of her. So, there's only one option.

"Once a month," Lora offers. A compromise. That's hardly more than what she'd be willing to do for any ambassador. "I can meet with you once a month."

Damara pivots on her heel, still wearing the smile. "Once a week."

"Every fortnight."

"Deal."

"Good." Lora bares her teeth, letting her sharpened canines show. "Now leave."

"I'll see you in two weeks, Queen Loraphne." Damara practically skips toward the door. But once she reaches it, she pauses and turns. It's Ayc she seeks. She studies him with an intensity that makes Lora want to aim a knife at her throat.

"Ayc?" she says.

He arches an eyebrow and presses his smile back on. "Is the show not over?"

She smirks right back. "You kind of look like him, you know."

Then she slams the door as she goes.

And the silence she leaves behind is loud as fuck.

CHAPTER
TWENTY-FIVE

AYC

Look like him. *Look like him. Look like him.*

The words pulse in Ayc's ears. He glares at the place where Damara just stood, willing himself not to have heard those words. Because he doesn't want to think about them, doesn't want to feel them rubbing against his brain like a pebble stuck in his shoe.

"What did she mean by that?" Ayc asks. "That I look like him?"

He searches around the room, looking at his friends. He desperately needs one of them, any of them, to offer an alternative to his suspicion. Surely, she can't be implying what he thinks she is.

But Lahlis certainly produces blue-eyed, brown-haired dragon riders, doesn't he?

"She's just trying to get in your head, Ayc," Bronwen says.

Ayc scrapes his hair back from his face. It fell loose when he was flung across the room by Bronwen's explosion of magic. The impact tore through his neck and upper back, the muscle fibers feeling like they were pulling apart. He desperately needs a pain reliever, but it's nothing compared to the torment in his stomach.

It twists and contorts at the very idea that Lahlis might be his father.

"Do I…" He swallows and tries again. "Do I look like Lahlis?"

For a long moment, no one says anything. He feels every single second of their silence like a knife scraping against his skin. Xylie studies him like she's seeing him for the first time, and Lora stares hard at the wall, the floor, anything but him.

Finally, Peregrin speaks. "Yes, you bear some resemblance to Lahlis, but it's not an uncommon coloring amongst the Drakr, so it's a resemblance you share with many."

"I didn't admit to her I was Drakr," Ayc says.

"Then Bronwen's right. She suspects you are and said what she did solely to mark your reaction." Peregrin scrubs a hand across their face, fatigue written in their expression. "There's no use stressing over a mere possibility."

"And it doesn't matter," Lora says, finally focusing upon him. "It doesn't matter who your father is. It doesn't change who *you* are."

Her face holds no disgust; only the same protective fury that crossed her face when Damara got too close. The sickness in Ayc's stomach eases. He draws a breath through his teeth. He's not… whoever his father is. It doesn't matter.

"Now, if you'll excuse me, I need a drink." She strides toward the side of the room. "You all are welcome to join me. I'll be in the Sovereign's Garden." She opens the side door and steps into the hallway.

Ayc follows Lora. A drink is an absolutely wonderful idea. And he isn't the only one. Irving is the first to slip out of the great hall after her, but every single one of her Five follows her. Hearing the footsteps, Lora glances back. "Oh, and Ayc, bring your dragon. It'll be good for them to touch some grass."

"Dragon?" Bronwen squeaks. She looks around at the others, and when no one shares her same expression of shock, she throws up her hands. "By the divine, what the fuck am I missing this time?"

Muffin hesitates at the door of the garden and stares at the grass like it's something they've never seen before, which, of course, is true. *"What this?"*

"It's grass," Ayc replies. *"This is outside."*

"Outside?" Muffin repeats, like it sounds suspicious.

"You'll like it. Come on."

Ayc squeezes around the dragon and strides a few feet across the grass. Night has embraced the garden, bringing with it a comforting coolness. A campfire built within the circle of chairs fights against the blackness with its warm orange glow. There, he sees the shadowed form of Lora, the rest of the Five, and Irving. Shae stands at the door to the garden, her return signaling that the three dragons and their riders have left. Otherwise, he might not have felt safe enough to bring Muffin.

Ayc glances over his shoulder. *"You coming? Or is the great and powerful dragon scared of some dirt?"*

Muffin narrows their eyes until they are little more than ruby slits before lifting a single foot. They touch the grass with a single talon, jerk it back, and then lay all five of their fingers down. They take a tentative step and then another until all their feet are on grass and dirt.

"See," Ayc says aloud. "Not so bad."

Muffin bursts forward in a sprint. Ayc scarcely leaps out of the way before they tear past with a speed that kicks up patches of dirt with his claws. Just past him, Muffin jumps into the air and flares their wings wide. They remain suspended in the air for longer than Ayc has ever seen, their talons glazing over the tops of the long blades of grass. Ayc holds their breath as they start to descend and give their wings a single flap... and collapse. They collide with the ground and tumble through the dirt until they land on their back, legs sticking toward the sky.

Ayc bites his tongue to keep from laughing, though some in the circle don't share the same consideration. He picks up the soft, musical sound of Lora's laugh. He's heard it so rarely, but he knows it's her instantly. Gods, her laugh. If he could learn how to bottle it and keep it with him always, it might work better than any pain tonic.

And there he goes, waxing poetry in his head like the saccharine fool he is.

Muffin rolls onto their feet. They shake out their wings, like a dog shaking off water, and sneeze. A cloud of dirt bursts from their nose.

This time, Ayc laughs.

Muffin snorts again before trotting off for a second attempt. Certain there's no way his dragon can make it over the tall wall, Ayc jogs over to the glow of the fire. While he retrieved his dragon, it seems the others have raided Wyntra's wine storage. Half a dozen unopened bottles scatter on the ground around the circle. Lora and Bronwen pass an open bottle back and forth from where they sit on the ground beside the flames, a blanket drawn over their laps. Xylie pours a bottle into wooden cups held by Peregrin and Tavish's hands. Irving sits in a chair pushed back from the rest as though he's trying to keep himself separate.

Bronwen thrusts the bottle toward Ayc when he comes. "Ayc, your dragon is *be-u-ti-ful!*" Her words slur. "How did you manage to hide them for so long?"

Ayc takes the bottle from her. He sloshes it around, finding it almost empty. "Have you had a whole bottle already?

"Not a whole bottle," Bronwen says. "Don't be silly. Lora had half of it."

Lora shakes her head and signs, *"I've had three sips."*

"I saw that." Bronwen thrusts up a hand, holding up a finger far too close to her nose. Lora bites at it playfully, and Bronwen jerks it away with a screech that would never have left her mouth if she wasn't already horrendously wasted.

"You all right?" Ayc asks.

She snorts, and Ayc expects her to lie. But apparently, alcohol makes her honest. "No. Grief's a bitch."

Ayc can only nod. "That it is."

"Want to talk about it?" Tavish asks over the rim of his cup.

Bronwen screws up her nose. "No, I *want* to get *drunk*."

"Goal accomplished," Ayc teases, clutching the wine bottle closer. "Let's maybe slow down."

"Give it back!"

Bronwen lunges toward him, and he backpedals away. She lands on her knees, too unsteady to make it all the way to her feet. She claws at him, and he continues to backpedal even as he puts the bottle to his lips and gulps down the remaining wine. The deep red wine is drier than he normally prefers, but the hint of chocolate eases its bitterness as it warms his throat.

"Careful," Peregrin warns. "Truth weed *and* fae wine? You are likely to spill all your secrets."

I have no secrets, Ayc tries to say, but the words lock on his tongue. Because, of course, that isn't true. There's the secrets of the pain that still lives within his muscles like an ever-demanding monster. There are his feelings for Lora locked behind his sternum. Both secrets he's confessed only to Bronwen.

He avoids looking at Lora, afraid that even one glance at her might give him away.

"The secret of Muffin is already out," Ayc says instead. He gestures to Muffin as they attempt to soar again. This time, they manage a single flap of their wings, glide a little farther, and then land on their ass. Progress, Ayc supposes.

Saga whines from where he sits beside Tavish, who has also chosen the ground over the chairs in the circle. Muffin spins toward the sound and hunches low, like a lioness disappearing behind tall grass.

"*Food?*" Muffin asks.

"*No!*" Ayc snaps back. "*Saga is not food. Dogs are friends.*"

Muffin snorts out more dust but doesn't argue. They swing around and trot off. Saga whimpers again, and Tavish shushes him with a hand on his head. Xylie snaps her fingers, and Ayc turns to where she's curled into one of the large chairs, her feet tucked beneath her. She holds two wooden cups and holds one out to him.

He takes it from her and hesitates. Should he take a chair or sit on the ground? His back would certainly prefer the chair, and yet, the soft earth at Lora's side beckons him. He gulped down a pain tonic when he retrieved Muffin, but he'll certainly feel the decision tomorrow. Still, he ultimately lowers himself there, his own thigh inches from brushing the blanket that covers Lora's. Far away enough to be unsuspicious, close enough that he knows he'll be aware of her every movement. He loves to taunt himself, doesn't he? Putting himself through torture just to be near her.

She grants him the smallest smile. He treasures it like a gift.

"Tavish!" Bronwen claps her hands. "Did you bring your lute?"

Tavish chuckles. "The one you demanded I retrieve from my room?" He reaches behind him to where an instrument is attached to a strap around him. He swings it to the front and fits his hand around it. "Yes."

"Play for us!" she demands.

He strums the strings in a playful series of cords that he moves through deftly. "All right. Would you like something sad? Or something happy?"

"Happy," Bronwen, Peregrin, and Lora chime in unison.

"For fucks sake," Bronwen adds, "play something happy."

Tavish smiles. The music he plays is jaunting and merry, a rhythm Ayc instantly likes but doesn't recognize. And after a few chords, Tavish's voice joins. It's rich as chocolate, smooth as silk.

"Damn," Ayc whispers to Lora. "I didn't know Tavish could sing."

Lora's lips tip upward. "He's a man of many talents. Speaking of, how goes the shadow wielding? Bronwen says you're doing better than can be expected of a beginner."

Bronwen doesn't even glance Lora's way at the mention of her name. She sways to the time of Tavish's song even as she summons a new bottle of wine to her. She pops the cork with a spark of magic and brings it to her lips. Ayc suspects she's going to regret her overindulgence in the morning, but he understands the desire to numb emotions with wine and substance. At least, she's doing it here amongst friends where she's safe. He can carry her to bed if he must.

Ayc sets down his cup of wine in the dirt. His mind is already feeling the soft fuzz of the few swallows he took, and he doesn't want much more if he has a dragon *and* a drunk sorcerer to look after. "Want to see?" he asks Lora.

She nods.

He removes his gloves and tucks them into the pocket of his coat. He then reaches into his sleeves to remove his bracelets and tucks those next to his gloves. The feeling of his power rising within him reminds him of those first few gulps of wine. Heady and intoxicating. He focuses on the shadow at the corner of the fire. A single tendril breaks off it and creeps toward the empty bottle of wine. He means to tip the bottle over, but it only curls around it, not even making it sway. Since that first day with the candle, he's never managed to impact anything physically. It's not much of a weapon until he can do that.

"Impressive," Lora says.

She reaches over to Bronwen and plucks the bottle of wine out of her First's hand. She's too busy dancing in place to notice.

Ayc releases the shadow, and it returns to where it was previously. "Not really. Nothing compared to what Brekken and Damara did."

"I suspect they've known about their power for more than a week."

She brings the bottle to her mouth, and Ayc knows he absolutely should not be staring at the shape her lips form around the glass. Should not be thinking utterly indecent thoughts about how her mouth would look wrapped around other things. He shifts as his body goes hot and hard, and he's incredibly grateful for the layers of protection his leather armor offers him.

When she lowers the bottle, a single deep red drop crawls down her chin. He wants to lick it away. She wipes it away with the back of her hand and catches him looking. He should glance away, but he can't bring himself to. Not when she stares back. Not when her eyes fall to trace the lines of his lips.

The air is alive between them. He's certain he's not the only one who can feel it. He's certain that, at this moment, he's not the only one remembering how she kissed him, what it felt like when their bodies pressed together. After all, *she* kissed him. She teased him with her hand on his throat. She's played this game of teasing, of torment and bliss.

He can't be the only one only *pretending* he feels nothing.

Can he?

"Keep practicing," Peregrin says.

Ayc jumps. He nearly forgot that anyone else existed besides Lora, let alone that Peregrin was just behind his right shoulder, observing Ayc's little display with shadow.

"It will come," Peregrin says, cradling their wooden cup in both their hands. "Don't underestimate yourself."

Ayc remembers the words Peregrin uttered earlier. The shock and disbelief that he was a dragon rider. "I don't know if that's possible."

"Don't speak so harshly about yourself," Lora snaps.

Ayc blinks, surprised by the aggression in her voice. "Why not?"

"I thought I made it abundantly clear that no *one* is disrespectful to my Five."

"What are you going to do?" Ayc chuckles. "Stab me?"

"Don't tempt me."

"Forgive me, Ayc," Peregrin says, pulling Ayc's attention back once more. "I think you misunderstood me earlier when I learned of your dragon mark. I meant only that I'm quite used to fate placing power in the hands of those who don't deserve it. Seeing power fall into the hands of two people"—they nod to Lora—"who actually deserve it within the space of a week is not something I was prepared for." They glance toward Irving, lift their cup to their lips, and take a large swallow. "Sometimes fate is kind. Not often. But sometimes."

"Shh," Bronwen snaps, as Tavish's song picks up its cadence. "This is the best part."

LORA

The Sal Maris are known for their songs, ones that are not just a melody but an epic story. Tavish's songs stretch for minutes and lead them on journeys across the sea to places yet undiscovered. It's woven with jokes and innuendos that leave Bronwen and Ayc bursting with laughter and even Xylie giggling behind her hand. The sound of laughter and music fills Lora's chest with a lightness she has not felt since a crown was placed upon her head.

She knows there is a pile of tasks awaiting her on the Sovereign's desk, but she chooses to forget that here and now. That is a problem for beyond these walls. Right now, she only wants to soak in the music, the stars above, and the silly antics of Muffin as the dragon tumbles around the garden. She wants to keep letting her knee brush against Ayc's ever so often, ignoring that she's breaking her own internal rule.

She's loved this place since she was a little girl. It's meant to be a place for the Sovereign and their Five, but Yris never possessed much interest in nature and growing things. So, she scarcely used it. Perhaps she forgot it existed until she had a toddler and wished that she didn't. Lora's nannies would bring her here so she could run and explore safely within these walls. Her mother never once visited her here. It became a place of solitude even as she aged.

Because of the memories, she thought she might use it as intended, for business meetings with her Five. But right now, she's decided that she's going to keep this garden for moments like this. To escape, to sing, to rest, and pretend, even for a moment, that they are an unlikely group of friends and that the fate of Everadyn doesn't rest on their shoulders.

Here, they can just *be*.

Lora snags the bottle from Bronwen and finds that it's already nearly empty. She's likely had no more than a glass of it.

Bronwen's eyes are glossy with drink, and perhaps with something else. Bronwen swiftly glances away and wipes at her cheeks, but Lora has already seen.

Enough. Lora has let this go for too long.

She touches two fingers to the back of Bronwen's elbow. Bronwen doesn't turn, so Lora leans close and whispers in her ear. "Tomorrow, you and I are going to talk to Reselda."

Bronwen stares down at her hands. Blue sparks pop from her fingertips, and she curls them into fists. "The medicine won't stop me from missing him," she says, her voice so low it's barely audible.

"No," Lora agrees. "But it'll keep me from losing you, too."

Lora has been close to losing her before. She remembers it too well, sitting on the edge of a tower in Adamant, the night air cool on their faces, convincing Bronwen to stay. They stayed up all night before Lora coaxed her off the edge. That's what Lora is doing now—pulling Bronwen from the edge. She'll stay up all night now, too. Fuck, she'll never sleep again if it means she can make her friend see just how much this world needs her. How much Lora needs her.

She's silent for the longest moment before she nods her head. Lora presses her palm against her breastbone, above her heart, the way Bronwen did so many times in the Trials. Whatever darkness Bronwen fights, she doesn't fight it alone. Bronwen blinks her watery eyes and presses her hand over her heart as well.

She can sense Ayc watching them, his gaze like a hand resting on her shoulder.

"Tomorrow," Bronwen agrees, lifting a bottle to her lips and turning her attention back to Tavish.

Lora glances away from Bronwen and toward where Peregrin has moved to a chair closer to Irving. The two talk softly to one another. Her old teacher wears a warrior's mask well, but Lora can occasionally glimpse sadness in their eyes.

These are her Five. Her friends. Her family. It is her job to protect them, help them, in whatever way she can. Bronwen has been handled, at least until morning, so now it's Peregrin and Irving's turn.

Lora leans backward to grab a new bottle and a cup abandoned in the grass behind her. She slips between the blanket and the slit of her skirt to draw her blade. She should have changed out of her dress before coming, but she thought that if she returned to her chambers to change, she would collapse upon her bed and never come out. She digs at the cork with the tip of her blade but has barely poked it when the cork shoots free with a loud pop. She nearly drops the bottle.

Lora glares at Bronwen before pouring the wine into the cup. "A little warning next time, friend."

Bronwen shrugs.

Lora climbs to her feet and carries the bottle and cup around the fire to where Peregrin and Irving sit. "Here." She offers the cup to Irving.

Irving holds up a hand. "I'm on duty."

"You haven't even officially returned to duty," Lora says. "Besides, change of guard was a quarter of an hour ago." She nods to near the door, where Shae has been replaced by a guard whose name she doesn't know.

Irving hesitates and then takes the cup. "Very well, but I would like to return to duty if you'll allow me. The healer doesn't see a reason I can't return."

"You should discuss it with your family," Lora says.

"Oh, please take him back," Peregrin says with a flick of their wrist. "He's getting restless. We've already relived all our same debates about leviathans and dragons and wyverns." They pause and drain the last drop of wine in their cup. "Not that you remember we've had them."

"It gives you an unfair advantage," Irving says with a sheepish smile. "Seeing as you know all my counterarguments."

"Doesn't make much difference. They were shitty arguments before, and they're shitty now."

Peregrin gives them a smile that Lora has seen them give no one else. Even for Zinnia, Peregrin has a different smile, but this one belongs only to Irving. A bit wolfish, transforming their face into something far more youthful. Normally, Irving returns it with a playful smile of his own, but now, he ducks his head as though bashful. Still, his dimple flashes.

They'll find their way back to each other. Lora is certain. They fell in love once, and they fell in love every day for over twenty years. Irving will fall for them once more. She's certain because she's seen their love. She is a cynical person, molded that way by a mother who has nothing but disdain for affection. But she can't deny what her own eyes have seen in Peregrin and their partners.

Love exists because it exists in them.

She turns her head, instinctively seeking out Ayc. She catches him already looking at her back, but he jerks his attention away like a child caught doing something he shouldn't. She draws a deep breath through her nose to steady the emotions weaving through her.

It's been a long day.

"Very well," Lora says to Irving. "I'm sure the guards will be grateful to have their captain back."

"I understand if you want to give the position of captain to someone else," Irving says. "Seeing as I don't…" He taps his temple.

"I didn't hire you because you're my friend. I hired you because you're the best man for the job and someone I can trust to have my back. You proved that today over again." She pauses, then adds. "I should warn you that I'm nothing like my mother."

"Oh, I know," Irving says with a smile. "Your mother never struck me in the jaw to run directly into danger in order to help a friend."

Lora inspects his jaw, but it looks untouched. "I would apologize, but I'm not sorry."

"Good," Irving says. "I have a feeling that protecting you is going to mean protecting you from yourself, at times."

Peregrin snorts and then silences it behind their cup. Lora is mature enough she doesn't argue.

"What do you say?" she asks. "Are you still interested in the position?"

"It would be my honor," Irving says.

"Good. I have a list of candidates for you to review. I want Veni. Otherwise, do what you and Peregrin think is best."

Irving arches his eyebrow. "Veni? The young fae who was with us. They're a bit... immature."

"He's known me since we were young children. It's honestly refreshing that he treats me no differently. He'll rein himself in formal situations, I'm certain. I'm sure you'll find his qualifying scores satisfactory."

Irving nods. "Very well. He was particularly accurate with his crossbow. Etiquette is something that can be taught, and he'll be loyal, which is important."

"Also, the first round of reports on investigations within the clans should be coming from the regents in the morning. If you two could look through those and report back to me, I would appreciate it."

"Sounds like we have quite a bit of work to do, Peregrin," Irving says as he rises to his feet. "In that case, I'll take this"—he wiggles the cup in his hand—"to go. Thank you, my lady."

He sweeps a bow, and Lora waves him off. "Lora is fine."

"Very well. But only in private," Irving says. "Peregrin, would you walk with me, or would you like to stay a little longer?"

Peregrin grabs their cane and pushes to their feet, wincing as they rise. "I'll go with you. Before Zinnia sends out a search party. We will have a report for you tomorrow. Call a meeting of the Five so we can all go over it together. But perhaps make it to the evening." Peregrin nods behind Lora. "Bronwen's going to need to sleep this off."

Ayc has shifted into Lora's spot, and Bronwen's head rests upon his lap. When he catches Lora looking, he shrugs. "She was about to fall over."

Ayc. Forever the caregiver.

"That was quicker than I thought," Lora says.

Peregrin and Irving leave side by side, and Lora returns to the other side of the fire. She unbuckles her cape from her back and spreads it over her legs as she sits beside Ayc—that way, she can sit however the fuck she wants, not like a lady.

Tavish ends a song with a long, low note. "Another?" he asks.

Xylie reaches over to tap her knuckles on his shoulder, and somehow, he recognizes this as a yes because Tavish begins again. He doesn't sing this time. It's a slower tune but sweet and romantic, like a love ballad without lyrics. Saga has finally relaxed and rests his head on his paws, though his two-colored eyes are still shifting, watching Muffin's every motion. The dragon's efforts are growing wearier. They are slower to get up and pause longer between attempts.

"Should we carry her to bed?" Ayc asks, gesturing to the slumbering Bronwen.

"No," Lora says. "Let her sleep there for a bit."

Ayc nods and tucks the blanket around Bronwen's shoulders. A pang goes through her chest. It's not jealousy, she tells herself. Ayc's movements speak of nothing but respect and friendship. But yet, it's exactly jealousy. Because Lora longs to have the freedom for her head to rest in his lap, to have him tuck a blanket around her as she sleeps, to be someone who can be so close to his skin without fearing the consequence of what would happen if someone else knew.

But Damara's comments tonight remind her of exactly why it can never be.

Even if Lora finds herself longing for him more day after day. Even as she can't help the way her gaze traces the shadow that has risen on his chin. How she can't help but imagine what that scruff would feel like as it trailed across her thighs.

Lora takes a swig from the bottle in her hand. It won't help. There's no degree of drunkenness that will make her stop wanting him.

Bronwen groans in her sleep, something that sounds like, "Fucking red eyes. Still an asshole."

Lora frowns. "Perhaps we *should* get her to bed."

Tavish silences his song by clapping his hand down on the

strings, stopping their vibrations. He tucks the instrument behind his back. "I can help."

"I've got it," Ayc offers.

Xylie signs, *"You have to carry Muffin."*

She points behind them to where Muffin lies in the grass like they have just fallen from a flying attempt, their wings sprawled out beneath them, their talons sticking straight to the sky. But their eyes are closed, and their breaths rise and fall slowly. It's like they fell asleep right where they fell. A small laugh sneaks past Lora's lips, and Ayc stares at her.

"What?" she demands. "Do I have wine on my face?"

"No."

Ayc and Lora manage to wake Bronwen enough that they get her to her feet and walking. Xylie and Tavish brace her between them, Tavish grabbing the Kindred leash with his other hand.

"We've got her," Tavish says. "You two can stay a little longer if you want."

Lora frowns. She nearly demands what he means by that *and* with the smile he swiftly hides behind puffed cheeks. Ayc, too, narrows his eyes. But neither of them moves as Xylie and Tavish head towards the door. Even the guard is standing outside the garden, the door creaked.

Alone with Ayc is a very terrible idea, and yet, she doesn't budge, and neither does Ayc as the three walk away. Only the snores of his dragon fill the air. Ayc studies her, his eyes taking on that look—the one that makes her feel like the starry sky above. Like she's something he's seen a million times but hasn't lost the wonder of looking at.

"Do you want to go?" Ayc asks, his voice scarcely above a whisper.

She should. She should absolutely turn around and go. She hasn't drunk enough that she's not aware of all the risks of staying. She's absolutely in her right mind.

But perhaps it's made her care just a little less.

"No," Lora says. "Do you?"

"No," he says quickly. There's still truth weed in his system.

And she shivers at the reminder. She's not sure she wants the truth behind why he's looking at her like that.

They stare at each other for a long moment, her heart hammering. There's a stalemate here, and she's not quite sure what to do.

Ayc breaks it first. He moves back toward their blankets on the ground and grabs one of the unopened bottles of wine. "Then let's sit."

LORA

She sits beside him in the grass, pulling her cape back over her knees. She has inadvertently sat closer than is wise, but it would seem strange to move away now. Their knees press together, and with each area of skin that contacts his trousers, shocks pour through her. She wants to run away from the sensation, and she wants to press into it, wants to crawl into his lap and feel him skin-to-skin.

Fuck. What is she doing? Will it be too obvious if she bolts for the door?

Ayc breaks the quiet between them. "I've been meaning to tell you thank you," Ayc says, his voice low, husky. She's watched him drink only a few sips of wine, so she knows he's not drunk.

"For what?" Lora asks.

"For this." He grabs the lapel of his coat and turns the collar inside out to show her the golden bear there. "You had a tailor stitch this."

He lowers his hand again, placing it beside the blanket he's pulled over his lap, right next to her own hand that rests on the ground. She's momentarily distracted by it. Fuck, she likes his hands, the width and breadth of them, the strong cords of them, the way he decorates them with rings and nail polish. It makes it difficult not to imagine what he could do with those hands, to prevent her mind from wandering into dangerous places.

"Lora?" he prompts.

She swallows. "No."

"No, what?"

She grabs hold of her wandering thoughts. "I stitched it there myself."

Something gleams within his eyes, sparking in the moonlight. His pinky brushes against the delicate skin of her own. She fights back a shiver. One brush and she feels like her very soul is trembling. "I don't know that I can express how deeply it means to me that you would put Aluina on my collar."

"Just on your collar? I did it for *all* of us." She adjusts the cape on her lap to show him. She had a group of Totus Omni tailors add the symbols of the Everadyn clan at the bottom hem of the cloak. But she turns it inside out. And there, on the inner lining, is the bear on all four legs. The symbol of Aluina.

His throat bobs once, twice, before he speaks. "You put Aluina on your cape."

On the ground between them, his hand shifts just a little closer. His pinky hooks over hers, and fire surges up her arm and into her chest. Her heart nearly explodes through her chest. She has to swallow multiple times before she can speak.

"I put Aluina on *all* six of our uniforms." She had to forfeit a tremendous amount of sleep, but it was worth it. "I wanted us to never forget. Aluina was once under the protection of the Sovereign of Everadyn and their Five. One day, before the end of my reign, I swear it will be again."

Ayc clears his throat and looks pointedly up at the sky. But Lora can see the emotion shining in his blue eyes, anyway, turning them into a shade she's certain she's never seen before.

With that look on that face, she wants to swear to him that Aluina will not be forced to wait much longer for her to correct her mother's mistake. With the warmth of the wine in her blood, she wants to tell him the truth. She would raise armies for him, would fight wars for him, would risk it all... for him.

He lowers his head and dares to lean closer. His voice is scarcely louder than a hum that she feels deep within her own chest. "Do you have any idea how extraordinary you are?"

He slips his hand to cover hers fully. He keeps the weight light. She could slip away so easily, but she doesn't. Almost of its own accord, her wrist rotates so their palms meet, and she slips her fingers through his.

Her heart nearly flies from her chest once more.

By the divine... It shouldn't feel like this. She's never been one who grew giddy with little things like holding hands, but she feels... She struggles to describe it. She feels like Bronwen's magic feels—like static, like every particle of air is alive with potential. And she feels happy, so happy that her eyes burn with the absurdity of it.

It shouldn't be like this. Holding hands should not be this powerful. But that is what her feelings are. Powerful.

He lifts his other hand and pauses with his fingers so close to her chin she can feel their warmth. He searches her over, and she realizes what he's seeking. Consent to touch her.

She bobs her head in a little nod. Like a fucking fool.

He trails his thumb across her jaw. She shivers like she's afraid. And she is. She feels like she's standing ankle-deep in the Ever River. She knows it can't harm her, and yet, she's terrified all the same. That's what this is: she's terrified. Terrified of *him*. Of this feeling inside of her. It feels too big to contain. It feels like peeling back her ribcage and exposing her heart.

But unlike the water where she wants to run, here, she wants to leap. So she doesn't pull away, even as his fingers tease over the curve of her neck.

Her voice trembles when she speaks. "What are we doing, Ayc?" She's asked the question before, the last time he was this close.

His blue eyes gleam like faded embers. She wonders if they

would be blazing red if he weren't wearing his bracelets. "We're pretending."

She can't place the tone of his voice. It's both teasing and utterly serious. She doesn't know how to respond, so she only repeats. "Pretending?"

"Yes, isn't that what you and I do now?" His thumb ghosts over her bottom lip, so light it could be a butterfly wing. But she feels it fucking everywhere. In her lips, in her heart, in the pulse awakening between her thighs. "*You're* pretending that you didn't kiss me. And *I'm* pretending that I wouldn't sell my soul to some malevolent god in order to kiss you again."

Fuck.

She shudders at the words, both because of their impact and because this is a moment she's been dreading— him bringing up their kiss, making her face it.

"I thought you thought it was a dream," she says, buying time.

"Perhaps, at first, but only because I had other dreams." He drops his thumb from her lips but keeps his fingers traveling across her neck, her shoulder. He follows the movement with his eyes, his look of wonder growing ever stronger. "When I slept, in that space between death and life, I dreamed of only you. Would you like to know what I dreamed about?"

No, she thinks. But it's a lie. She absolutely wants to know.

When she says nothing, his lips curl into something wicked. She revels in the way it transforms his face; the way it makes something hot and wanton rise within her.

"It involved that knife of yours."

He leaves the rest to her imagination. At first, she's too stunned—that he might have had a dream about something like that. But then she can imagine it, and fuck. *Fuck.* She can see it so clearly. His body splayed out beneath her, his hands tied to the posts of her bed, her knife at his throat as she hovers over his face. She'd utter commands, and he'd obey like a good fucking boy. Would he want that? *She* does. She wants it so bad she can feel it between her legs, hot and wet with want, and he's barely even touching her yet.

There's an emptiness inside of her. A deep and endless cavern. A chasm of want that she fears that only his hands, his lips, and his cock will be able to fill.

Fuck, she wants him. More than she's ever wanted anyone. She's clinging to the last of her logic, and it's slipping through her fingers like sand.

She is Sovereign, dammit. She's Sovereign. And love makes you vulnerable. It's the truth her mother has drilled into her, along with the surety that if she lets herself care for this man, he'll die, and it will be her fault.

She stiffens, her shoulders tensing toward her ears, and just like that, he pulls his hand away.

"I should not have kissed you," she blurts.

The light in his eyes dims into confusion. "Why not?"

Lora shoves to her feet, dropping his hand. "I just should not have."

He stands just as swiftly. "That is not an answer."

"We should go." She adds a snap to the voice, the firmness of slamming a door shut.

He opens his mouth as though he means to pound against it, but then he presses it shut. He shakes his head, his loose hair flowing around his face. "Very well."

He turns and marches over to where his dragon still slumbers. He carefully picks the up and cradles them over his shoulder like one might a slumbering toddler. Muffin's wings drape down, and their long neck curls over his shoulder. Lora's chest aches at the tender sight. Or perhaps it just hurts to watch him walk away, a wound of her own making.

She can't bear to keep looking at him. She's going to do something foolish, more foolish than staying in the first place.

"Good night," she says. She turns. Her hands tremble, and even putting them into fists does not stop it.

"Lora?" Her name is a gentle caress in his mouth.

She stops, but she can't bring herself to turn back around.

"When you're ready to stop pretending," he says softly, "just let me know. Then we should talk."

She starts walking without a word because she doesn't know what to say. They *should* talk. It's what a grown, reasonable adult would do, but she doesn't know what to say.

I want you.

You want me.

And it doesn't matter. Everadyn must come first.

Those are not truths she's ready to speak into existence. So, she slams the door shut behind her.

Lora is on fire.

It's the only explanation for how her skin boils. She's tossed all her blankets off her bed, and yet, sweat still lingers on her skin. It's been nearly an hour since she was with Ayc in the garden. An hour since she played and lost a dangerous game of staying alone with him when she knows she should not.

His words still echo in her ear, spin in her mind, boil in her blood.

I would make a deal with a malevolent god just to kiss you again.

It involved that knife of yours.

Those words are a match, and she is only kindling. Yes, she managed to walk away, but she carried the fire with her out of that garden. She felt it as soon as she crawled into her bed, and the more she thought about Ayc, the more it grew.

And now, she's hot.

So fucking hot.

She sits up and yanks off the tunic she wore to bed. She tosses it onto the floor next to where she abandoned the dress. The brush of the sheets against her bare skin only taunts her more. The want has taken over her entire body.

She wants. And she wants. And she wants.

She wants to get out of this bed and return to Ayc. She wants him to tell her more about his dreams, and she wants to make them a reality. She wants to wrap her hand around his throat and see his eyes burn red as she tightens her fingers.

She knows how wrong she is, and yet, lying there, she knows she's one slip in willpower from leaving this bed and pounding on Ayc's door. It certainly felt like he was giving her an invitation in the garden.

When you're ready to stop pretending...

Fuck, she might even beg him to fuck her if it would bring her some release.

I can't, her head reasons.

I want, her body argues.

She presses her hand against her sternum, finding her heart pounding there. She shuts her eyes, sinks deep into the mattress, and caresses her skin again. But this time, she pretends it's Ayc's finger sweeping over the delicate skin. That it's his hand that covers her breast. When she swirls her fingertip around the peaked nipple, she imagines it's his tongue. When she plucks, it's his teeth.

He doesn't rush. He takes his sweet, diligent time as he works his fingers and lips over her body. He finds that spot just below her navel that makes her nerves sing and her center throb with need. He works her like he works his dough, with sure hands, both firm and tender. And fuck, it's torture.

And it's paradise.

Lora crooks up her knees and glides her nails down both her thighs. She traces down, down, down, imagine that it's him teasing her. First with his breath, then with his lips, growing ever closer, but never being quite where she needs him.

Finally, she can take it no more, and she sinks her finger inside of her, imagining it's *his* touch parting her. She groans at her wetness, her hips bucking, as she imagines the way he would thrust in and out of her. How he would add a second finger. How she would rock against his hand, desperate for release.

She traces up her seam, but it's *his* tongue gliding upward, covering her aching clit. Her hips rock, and she dreams of it. The way he would moan when he tasted her. The warmth of his mouth, the glaze of his teeth, the feel of his long hair between her fingers as she holds him in place. The way he would look up at her like he's a starving man and devour her.

With the fantasy burning bright in her head, she doesn't last long. She arches from the bed as release overtakes her. She bites down on the palm of her hand to muffle her moan, lest her guards hear her.

She drops back to the mattress and finds she is utterly unsatisfied. The well of want remains bottomless. She's not certain how she will survive it, but she has no other choice.

TWENTY-SEVEN

AYC

"**G**et down!" Ayc yells across the courtyard. He jumps from the wagon sitting just outside the stables, leaving behind the stacks of supplies he's been checking on one last time. He marches toward the wall of the courtyard.

From where they stand on the parapet, Muffin hesitates with one foot dangling over the edge of the wall. "*You don't have to yell, you know?*" they say in that obnoxiously matter-of-fact voice they've possessed since their most recent growth spurt.

"Maybe if I didn't have to say it five times," Ayc says, still out loud, "I wouldn't have to yell."

"*Oh.*" Muffin inspects their talons before setting their foot back on the stone. "*I wasn't listening.*"

"Yeah, no shit."

Ayc hears laughter from behind him, and he glares back at where Xylie and Tavish stand near the carriage. Tavish holds the Kindred collar's leash, Saga laying patiently at his feet. They both grin at him and wave.

The courtyard is filled today with a carriage and a wagon and a dozen horses swiftly being readied by harrowed-looking stable hands. Lora's personal royal guard, a few attendants, a cook, and the healer, Reselda, are what Lora and her Five are taking with them. They are leaving for Bromalis in less than an hour.

The day of the Tour has officially arrived, and he's dealing with a grouchy dragon. Earlier in the week, Muffin fell into a sleep that lasted for three days. Each morning Ayc woke, he had less and less space on the bed as Muffin underwent rapid growth, until Ayc was sleeping on the floor in a mound of blankets.

Now the dragon takes up nearly the entire width of the castle wall, double the size of Saga. It's become impossible to hide them. If the kitchen staff hadn't been such unbelievable gossips and had already told everyone in Wyntra, everyone would know by now anyway. The people of Wyntra have mostly gotten used to the dragon by now. Muffin's presence only startles them and makes them scream occasionally now instead of almost all the time. Though, to be fair to the fae, Muffin might actually be trying to do it on purpose. Ayc thinks he heard the dragon call 'boo!' across their link right before a kitchen maid popped around a corner.

And with the size change has come other changes. Like the ability to form full sentences and an attitude as large as a fully adult dragon.

Ayc waves up at Muffin. "Come down."

Muffin snorts. *"I was going to fly."*

"I know what you were doing," Ayc says. "And I've already told you no. You can practice taking off from the ground, but no more leaping off of things. Remember what happened last time?"

Muffin sends him a feeling equivalent to rolling their eyes, but Ayc plants his hands on his hips and presses on. "You plummeted straight to the earth."

"I was unharmed."

Ayc snaps his teeth shut. *"The poor student you fell on was not."*

Muffin snorts.

"They required stitches. On their eyebrow and chin."

"It was an improvement upon their face."

"Muffin, come down *now!*" Ayc snaps, lifting his voice once more.

"Fine, fine." The feeling of annoyance intensifies as Muffin retreats from the edge. They've reentered a phase where their legs do not quite match their body size, and they nearly tumble over the battlement before carefully righting themself and sauntering toward the stairs. *"Do not call me Muffin."*

Ayc sighs. "I will stop as soon as you decide on another name I should call you. Have you decided?"

The dragon shakes their head, their neck weaving back and forth. *"No."*

This is another new thing since the growth spurt. They no longer want to be called Muffin, but they don't know what they *do* want to be called. Xylie has tried to assist by reading lists of names she finds in books. None of them has appealed to Muffin.

They seem more certain about their pronouns. When Ayc asked them if they identified as male or female, they clearly said, *"Not male. Not female. Dragon."*

"Well, let me know," Ayc says, "and I'll call you whatever you like. And stay off the wall."

Muffin harrumphs, even as they pick their way carefully down the stairs. Ayc turns and returns to the wagons. He picks up the list and quill he's dropped and studies the supplies once more. He peeks toward Muffin once more, just to ensure the dragon has, in fact, finished coming down the stairs.

"This is why gryphons are a year old and fully grown before we allow the Fledgling ceremony," Peregrin says, from where they lean against the wagon. They pull their eyes away from where they've been watching Irving talk to the new recruits. "Can you imagine Tempest as emotional as that?"

Tempest lets out a call of protest from where she circles in the sky way above their heads.

"Is she ever going to forgive me for bringing the dragon back here?" Ayc asks. Tempest has been as testy and moody as Muffin has been, but it's clear that for her, it's personal.

"She said she sensed the rider in you from the time you were a boy. She just supposed you would eventually bond with a gryphon."

Ayc drags his eyes away from the list. "She thought I would be a rider all those years ago."

Peregrin shrugs. "I suppose so. She did not tell me until now. Aw, there's Lora."

They nod their head toward the doors of the courtyard. Ayc hears the glide of the hinges and hears boots crunching against the gravel toward them in a fast, cutting rhythm he recognizes. Fuck, he recognizes even the sound of her footsteps. She's dressed in armor, the same armor with the golden accents she wore over her coronation dress. But now, she's placed it over tight, black leather that hugs her legs and peeks through the breastplate. The cape catches the wind behind her, the cape that bears her people and his.

He tries to draw another breath, but he fears there isn't any air left in his lungs. Every day since the night in the garden, it feels like it's harder to breathe around her. Even harder is the struggle to keep his reckless mouth in check.

Since then, he's only seen her at meetings, after which she quickly retreats. The message is clear. Whatever desire she feels toward him, she's denying it, and she doesn't want to talk about it any further.

He desperately wants to know why, to understand what hinders her, but he doesn't feel like he has the right to press. If she were anyone else, perhaps he would. But she's Sovereign, and she only just stepped into her new role. She's trying to navigate politics, run a rebellion, prepare for war, make Everadyn a better place, and investigate a threat on her life. To add to the stress, Laud has refused Lora's request to visit on her Tour, though both the Stella Rune dwarves and the Tenebra court have said yes. But the Tenebra fae suggested a new date that puts it after the Drakr visit, which was not what they had planned ideally.

In the scope of that, his feelings seem a little trivial. Forcing her to slow down and speak with him, when she clearly doesn't want to, feels quite like a dick thing to do.

So he's just... waiting, attempting to keep his mind off it. He, at least, has toddler dragons and shadow affinity and his new role as Fifth to keep him distracted.

Lora passes by him, and he keeps focusing pointedly on his list to resist the urge to stare at her any further.

"Are we ready?" Lora asks when she comes to a stop at a midnight-colored horse whose withers are taller than even she.

A chorus of agreement rings out through the party. Ayc gestures to Muffin, who is pawing against the gravel.

"In the wagon."

Muffin snorts. *"I can walk."*

"You're going to get tired two minutes down the road."

"No, I won't," they snap, pawing at the gravel again.

Ayc rolls his eyes. He's not having this fight. If they want to walk, they can walk. They hopefully won't startle the horses. He's brought Muffin to the stables multiple times to desensitize the horses to Muffin's presence, progress that was almost ruined when Ayc caught Muffin about to take a bite from a poor unsuspecting goat.

"Have it your way. But you're getting into the wagon before we get to Orchis."

Lora wrote to the regents to inform them that they would have a dragon with them. She assured them it was well controlled and bonded and would not harm a fae. Still, Ayc doesn't want Muffin to become some kind of sideshow attraction. Both because Muffin deserves more respect, and because Muffin is unpredictable. He fully trusts Muffin won't harm someone on purpose, but they are still figuring out what they are capable of. They haven't learned to fly or breathe fire, and Ayc shudders to think what might happen if that latter ability starts suddenly presenting itself.

Tempest lands a few feet from Muffin with a spray of gravel. Muffin darts away as Tempest sets a single silver eye on them. Tempest flutters her wings as though in satisfaction.

"Toddlers," Peregrin mutters.

Tempest snaps her beak in protest but still bows down to let Peregrin mount. They wave to Zinnia, who stands near the entrance of the courtyard, holding tight to Ember's arm. They've come to see Irving and Peregrin off—or at least Zinnia has. Ayc suspects the Ember is mostly there to watch Muffin, hence Zinnia's fierce grip on his arm, to keep him from running up to the dragon.

"I'll fly ahead," Peregrin says to Irving, "and warn you if I see any trouble."

Irving nods, and Tempest launches upward with Peregrin clinging to her feathers. A jealous whine hums across Muffin's mental link, and Ayc's stomach twists in sympathy. Dragons are meant to fly, and it must be frustrating not to achieve it.

Ayc approaches the carriage and pulls the door open. Tavish, Xylie, and Saga are already situated on one bench.

"Room for one more?" Ayc asks.

"Of course," Reselda says as she leans forward from the other bench, into his view.

Fuck. It's going to be much more difficult to disguise his pain, riding next to a healer. He fears she'll see straight through him.

"Are you not riding?" Tavish asks.

"I don't much care for riding horses," Ayc says. It's a lie. He's only had a handful of opportunities to ride, but he's loved it. What Ayc doesn't like is the way that riding causes his back and thighs to ache. His back has been giving him enough fits already.

"The dragon rider doesn't like riding," Tavish teases.

"Aye, I hear the irony," Ayc says.

Another reason it's foolish is that he hasn't spoken to Reselda. Xylie's pain tonics are not enough, and there have been days this last week when the pain is enough that he hasn't wanted to eat, has barely been able to sleep. If he doesn't figure out his pain soon, he's not sure how he'll ever ride aboard Muffin.

Better. Stronger. He has no other choice.

"Ready?"

Lora's voice is so close that Ayc jumps. He whirls around. His heart rate picks up. She's standing far too close to him for his body to safely handle, and she's still out of arm's reach.

"Yes," he says quickly.

"Is your dragon?" she asks, tipping her head in a pointed gesture.

Muffin has returned to the wall, flaring out first one wing and then the other.

"Fuck," Ayc says through his teeth. He sprints toward the stairs. "For fuck's sake, *get down!*"

"*I fly!*" is their only response before they vault off the parapet. They flap their wings, but immediately begin to fall. Ayc throws his arms over his head, though it'll matter little when the dragon crashes onto him. He feels the talons right above his hands, and then the air cracks with Muffin's wings. Ayc peeks up in time to see Muffin fly higher, lifting toward the sky for one, two strokes of their wings. Pure glee bursts across their link, and Ayc isn't certain if it's Muffin's emotion or his own.

"Holy shit!" Ayc calls, jumping up and pumping his fists with excitement. "You're flying, Muffin! You're flying!"

Even Bronwen claps, and Tavish cheers from within the carriage, Saga and Xylie both peeking out their heads to watch. Lora tracks the dragon with a small smile that feels far too large for Ayc's heart to contain, as Muffin flies over her head. The horses neigh and skitter and have to be calmed by the stable hands.

Muffin begins to lose altitude, and Ayc might have thought it was intentional if panic didn't come across the link. Muffin is headed straight toward the wall beside the stables, at the other side of the courtyard. And they don't know how to turn.

Fuck.

Ayc runs, but he won't make it in time. Muffin twists their wings and manages to drop closer to the ground. Their talons scrape across the gravel, but they land too quickly. Their momentum carries them forward, and they tumble—tail over head, ass over horns—forward.

Fortunately, they come to rest in a soft landing.

Unfortunately, the soft landing is a pile of manure.

They slam into it, disappearing into the mound. A moment

later, Muffin's head pops out, their neck smeared with green and black muck.

Ayc sighs, coming to a stop beside Lora. "Actually, I need ten minutes," he says. "And a lot of buckets."

Xylie climbs out of the carriage to help. The stable hands provide them with buckets and sponges. Muffin hangs their head as Ayc and Xylie approach them, and Ayc can't help but offer encouragement.

"Congratulations, Muffin, you flew. Now, um, let's just work on your landing."

The main gates of Orchis open to reveal that the main square has been decorated in the color of the sunset, the same color as the sky above when the new Sovereign and her party arrive. Ayc peeks out of the carriage as it comes to a halt, taking in the banners of pink and orange that dangle above their heads. The shops around the square are pressed together and painted the same shades— one orange, one pink, one yellow, until the square is alive with color.

Booths are set up around the circumference of the square, laden with beautiful wares: fresh flowers and herbs, cosmetics, bottles of tonic. The smell of baked goods and fried things lingers in the air. As though on cue, music begins, horns and string instruments scattered throughout the area picking up a shared tune.

Ayc smiles. He loves a good festival.

"Welcome!" booms a voice, and Ayc glances out the other side of the carriage to look out the other window.

Briar stands on the rim of the fountain in the middle of the square, his voice carried over the music by an amplifier shaped into a rose. He's wearing a vibrant pink tunic and a crown of flowers on his head.

"Welcome to Bromalis's sunset city, my lady!" he says again, sweeping a bow as Lora dismounts at the front of their party.

Attendants dressed in Bromalis colors sweep forward to open Ayc's door. He climbs out, his back sighing in relief to be able to move. Riding in the carriage was definitely preferable to riding on horseback, but he grew stiff and began to feel every bump in the road. He glances toward the wagon at the very back. They've closed the doors so that Muffin isn't visible, and when Ayc reaches across their link, he hears nothing but soft breathing and a wispy image of flying through the clouds. Muffin is asleep... and dreaming.

Just as Ayc predicted, Muffin didn't keep up with the horses. They were too busy racing through the long grass of the plains outside Wyntra. Ayc frequently barked at them to keep moving forward, to not eat the dandelions, and for fuck's sake, leave the butterflies alone. Their lives are so brief that they don't deserve to spend their few days chased by a giant, winged lizard.

Eventually, Ayc managed to convince the dragon to lie down in the wagon, and they fell asleep soon after.

Satisfied Muffin is in a safe place, Ayc turns and offers his arm to his friends in the carriage. Tavish ignores it and utilizes Saga's handle and the Kindred collar. Saga's head wags from side to side and up and down, drinking everything in for the sake of his owner. Xylie, however, grasps Ayc's arm tightly as she comes out. Her ear cuffs, which are spelled to dampen sound, are firmly in place, and yet a shudder works through her body.

Ayc leans forward to whisper. "What do you need?"

She only stares at the colors with wide eyes.

"Do you want me to let you go?"

She clings to his arm tighter and shakes her head.

"Very well." He tucks her closer to his side. "You and me together, as always."

Her lips tip slightly upward as he steers her toward where Lora and her Five are lining up before Briar. Bronwen stands at Lora's right, and Peregrin a few paces to her left. Normally, as second, Xylie would be immediately on her left, but Ayc simply steps into line. Fuck such silly tradition if it makes his best friend uncomfortable.

The regent jumps down from the rim of the fountain and gestures to a child standing in the gathered crowd. They carry a basket of various colored roses. Briar selects a green rose and offers it to Lora. A Bromalis custom.

"For you, my lady. Grown in my own personal greenhouse. Green to celebrate the new beginning we have with you as Sovereign."

Lora takes it with a gracious smile. Ayc has now seen enough of her genuine smiles to recognize this as the theater it is. She nods at Bronwen, who holds up a hand. A yellow rose rises from where it was tucked into the saddlebag of Lora's steed and floats toward her hand. Lora grasps it from the air and passes it to the regent.

"Yellow, to represent the friendship I hope we will cultivate."

A nice, elegant display of power, just like they all planned.

Briar grins and tucks the stem between two buttons in his shirt. "And to your mighty Five." One by one, he passes green roses to the rest of the Five. The thorns have been carefully removed, and the stem is short enough, so Ayc places it behind his ear. Someone snorts behind him. Veni stands nearby, dressed in the royal guard garb, staring straight ahead with his arms neatly folded at his side. But when he sees Ayc glancing, he breaks seriousness just enough to wink.

Without thinking, Ayc winks back.

When he focuses again, Ayc catches Lora glaring at him. Fuck, he needs to be careful. All eyes are on them. He can't embarrass her.

Briar hands a flower to Tavish, then grasps another. "Might I present one to Saga as well?" he asks Tavish, waiting for a nod of assent before he stoops and tucks it into the leather vest Saga wears. The crowd murmurs in delight, but Saga never relaxes or reacts. Ever the bestest boy on duty.

"Once more, I welcome you," Briar says as he returns to Lora's side. He offers her his arm. Ayc sees her back stiffen, but she quickly recovers and lays her hand in the crook of his elbow.

Briar pulls Lora toward the nearest stall and beckons over his shoulder at the rest of the Five. "Come along, come see all that Bromalis has to offer."

Ayc hesitates, glancing back at the wagon. As though reading his mind, Irving steps from the guards. As he passes to follow Lora, he whispers, "I've assigned guards to stand with the wagon. No one will come close, and they'll alert me if your dragon gets restless."

Ayc nods and follows after the Five. Soon, they are being lost in the crowd, beckoned to come to this stall or that stall. Xylie clings to Ayc as the noise rises. The instruments play, and people murmur. The Bromalis people shout their congratulations and press flowers into their hands, which they're forced to then drop on the street because they already hold too many. Performers rush forward to show them their talents. They juggle balls and play their instrument. One, who must practice the sleight of hand that Ayc himself is well practiced at, pretends to find a rose in Xylie's ear. She jumps at the nearness of his hand, and the hand not holding Ayc flaps close as though shielding herself from a fly. Stimming, but she doesn't calm. She shudders. Ayc looks quickly for some type of exit. But they are surrounded by bodies.

Bronwen sweeps in behind them and takes Xylie's other arm.

"I desperately need a privy, don't you?" Bronwen says, loud enough that the crowd around them hears and parts. A few point down a mostly empty street, and Bronwen and Xylie hurry that direction.

Ayc glances around him. Lora is being fawned over by a person selling lotions. The fae opens bottle after bottle to allow her to smell each, as she smiles politely. Her hand is pressed tightly against her thigh, and her fingers tap one by one, over and over again. Ayc cocks his head at the repetitive movement, before she curls her hand into a fist. Making herself stop.

Irving and Veni remain between her and the rest of the pressing crowd, granting her at least a little space. Ayc debates going to her, but perhaps he's the last person she needs after the awkwardness between them.

Tavish has found a stall selling wine and cheeses and is sampling them. His social anxiety seems to be faring well, at least for now. Peregrin remains close to him and Saga, their eyes always trailing the crowd diligently. They never stop being the commander, not for a moment.

Ayc moves through the crowd. He stops to listen to a lute player who has composed some lyrics about Lora's win of the Sovereignty Trials. Or some fictionalized version of it. It vaguely mentions 'surviving nightmares untold on an island of bone and soot', but that's the only part that rings true. It mentions nothing of Marcellus or the fossil tooth that hangs around her neck. Perhaps that's for the best.

He looks in the store windows that line the street. He passes a display of books and wonders if Lora has read any of them. A wedding cake sits in one, and he spends too long studying every little detail, marveling at the decorator's skill. He steps before the next store and draws up short.

In the midst of color and gaiety on the street, the building's long shadow casts an ugly bruise. Dark cloth covers its windows; splashes of red streak down the once yellow walls. A sign dangles above the door, clinging to a single chain. No words, only a picture of a tiny bird with a sprig of lavender in its beak.

Not just any bird. A wren.

Wren wasn't exaggerating when she said her presence was no longer welcome. She may be free from justice of the law, but the civilians are not so forgiving. Did this happen after she left? Or was she forced to leave in a hurry? Did she leave anything in her wake that could be a clue to Asbjorn?

Ayc surveys the crowd around him. He can't be caught lurking around an abandoned store. But it's rapidly getting dark. He walks a bit further, into the dimness cast between a storefront and a tent in the street. He loosens his bracelets as he goes and tucks them into his pocket. When he's hidden from the street behind a booth, he disappears into the shadows.

He pauses, waiting to hear any gasps at his sudden vanishing.

When the crowd goes on its merry way, Ayc turns back to Wren's shop. A splash of sunlight breaks the space between the buildings. He has a choice: become momentarily visible or take the shadow with him. He reaches for his power, letting the coolness settle over his skin. He focuses on the shadow before Wren's shop. With a curl of his fingers, he beckons it to him. The pain between his eyes is but a momentary distraction, before he tucks it behind the wall in his head. The shadow stretches, like the sun is shifting, until it forms the thinnest of bridges. It's all he needs to remain hidden as he walks between.

Ayc peeks into the window on Wren's front door. The glass is cracked, but intact, and he has to squint to see past the spider-webbed fissures. Papers scatter across the floor. Shards of shattered jars sparkle in the little sunlight that breaks through the windows on the side of the building, the wood floor beneath stained by whatever was in the jars before. More red paint stains the walls within.

Ayc tries the doorknob, but finds it locked. A glance from a slightly different angle shows the skeleton key is still within the inside lock. If he could just make his shadow turn it...

Getting the shadow to the lock doesn't take long, but trying to bend the shadow around the lock, to make the shadow into a living thing that can turn the key, proves to be impossible. He focuses hard, but within a few minutes, he surrenders. His head throbs from the effort. He rests his forehead on the door, trying to catch his breath.

He doesn't have enough time to keep trying. He has to find another way in. The ache lingering behind his eyes, he peeks behind each of the curtains that have been hung over the windows. The ones on the front only have a few holes, like rocks were thrown through, but one on the side has been completely shattered. Ayc carefully picks his way through the shop windows, grateful for his armor and gloves to keep his hands from being cut.

Once inside, he's not certain where to begin searching or even what he hopes to find. His heartbeat feels like a clock, ticking away the little time he has. He sifts through papers on the floor. Most appear to be invoices. Books dumped behind the front counter are filled only with recipes and sketched maps of flowers. Tucked behind a tapestry, he finds a set of stairs and follows them to a door. He tries the handle and finds it locked. He has no strength and no time for another attempt at shadow locksmith, so he descends the stairs once more. His boot lands on a piece of paper abandoned on the bottom step. A broken seal clings to either side of the paper. A letter.

Ayc picks it up and turns it over.

YOUR REQUEST FOR A RESERVATION HAS BEEN DENIED. YOU ARE NOT WELCOME HERE.

- V

Ayc refolds the letter and fits the embossed stamp back together. The pink wax bears the image of an elk head, with strings of beads woven through its antlers. He's seen that symbol before.

The Pink Elk.

V for Vidar, the tavern's owner. The inn is only five miles from here.

The dawn rises in pink, Wren said.

Perhaps there's a connection there. Ayc isn't certain what the dawn part means, but the tavern is certainly pink. And he knows Vidar is already involved in one secret organization. Would it be all that peculiar if he were involved in another, let alone one that was focused on aiding his homeland?

They will be going to the Pink Elk on the last day of their Tour in Bromalis. He'll need to confirm his suspicions before he can risk showing Vidar his own coin, but it's at least a start.

He drops the letter and hurries back to the window, aware that he's been out of sight for far too long. If Lora or Irving or any of the Five notice he's gone, they'll send out a search party. He slips out the window and wanders back up the street. He drags the shadow with him, patching sunlight as he goes. When he's several stores away from Wren's shop, he releases his power and steps back into the sunlight.

TWENTY-EIGHT

LORA

Bromalis's Grand Gardens are a glorious piece of art during the day. At night, they look as though stepping into a dream—or into one of Lora's favorite novels. Lanterns line cobblestone paths surrounded by carefully trimmed hedges, blossoming rose bushes, and hundreds of flowers of various colors and species. Enchanted strings of white light dangle like willow branches from trees that tower above. It grants a magical glow over the gardens that stretches as far as Lora's eyes can see, taking up over fifteen acres at the very heart of Orchis.

Bronwen releases an appreciative gasp. "It's straight from a fairytale."

"It is," Lora agrees.

Bronwen has never been here before, but Lora has explored the gardens dozens of times when her mother visited the regent whose mansion borders this garden. She longs to take her best friend to all the best places: the maze made of rose bushes as tall as a castle wall, or the gazebo that glows down upon them from the highest point in the garden, or—Lora's favorite—the waterfall in the far corner whose crystal-clear water flows into a deep, reflective pool. It's the most private area because few know it's there. With the towering trees, someone could walk right by it and not know.

Lora knows she won't have time to revisit such places. Dozens of party-goers dressed in bright clothes dart through the pathways or cluster on the benches. A ribbon is tied around each of their wrist, holding a wooden placard that contains a list of tonight's activities. According to the invitations, each activity must be completed to obtain tonight's party favor. What exactly that is, not even Lora knows, but Briar promised it would be well worth it.

Most of the activities seem reasonable, like *Skip a stone in the Lily Fountain's pool* or *Solve the Rose Maze.* But the very first one on the list makes Lora's already harrowed nerves stretch thinner.

Bow and give best wishes to our new Sovereign.

There won't be a single person at this party who won't say hello to her, and hundreds have been invited. She'll have to feign enthusiasm for every single one, or worry that someone will feel slighted. She's already exhausted from the crowd and constant noise of the earlier festival.

She draws in a deep breath—or tries. The corset of the dress, constructed by the Bromalis tailors, digs into her rib and cuts off the expanse of her chest. The dress is a walking piece of art. Embroidery of vines and flowers overlays fabric that blends vibrant turquoises and pale pinks. The corset gathers in at her waist, allowing the bell-shaped skirt and her hips to look fuller, but it strangles her ribs. Lora curses herself for not saying something about the corset when she tried it on last week, but she knew there wasn't enough time for extensive alterations. And they did honor her request. A single deep slit ends near her hip, allowing her to reach the dagger that is fastened to her thigh.

At least, she looks divine in it. Lora's attendant ensured it fit her well enough that it emphasizes her already impressive breasts and highlights the feminine curve of her waist without being so restrictive that it disguises her larger shape. She's never been thin, and she's never wished to appear that way. Her body is large, but it's powerful, and the dress accentuates that.

She wishes she could forget the feel of the dress and just enjoy the beauty, but her brain has always had that fault, ever hyper-aware of how things feel against her skin.

"Are you ready?" Bronwen asks. The pale green dress she chose from the tailor's pre-made options looks extraordinary on her. With the pink and white rose appliques dotting the tulle skirt, Bronwen looks like she belongs in this garden, a stunning vision of femininity, complemented by the bright oranges and pink she's applied to the lid of her eyes.

Lora has rubbed cream into her skin to give the brown a warm, translucent glow. She bathed her lips in clear balm to make them glisten, but the only cosmetic she allowed her attendant to apply was the gold eyeliner that comes to a fierce point past the corner of her eyes.

Xylie—who stands on Lora's other side—has not a touch of cream or cosmetics, but before she left Wyntra, she traded the turquoise woven into her dozens of braids for white. It makes her look older than her eighteen years, which is fair because she's already wiser. She's chosen her outfit well: loose green trousers and a matching shirt and cardigan that flows as long as a cloak. Tiny roses are stitched across her scalloped collar.

"Are *you* both ready?" Lora asks.

"Of course," Bronwen says, wrapping her arm through Lora's. "We're going to have fun."

Xylie adjusts the noise-dampening ear cuffs over her slanted ears and nods her head. Lora offers her other arm, and Xylie takes it. With her First and Second by her side, Lora steps into the garden. Her guards on duty, Shae and Davos, follow a few feet behind her. Irving said he'd be here, too. He's assigned guards to watch Muffin in the wagon and notify Ayc or Xylie if the dragon wakes. Others will also be scattered throughout the party, watching for anything suspicious. The rest of her guards are back at their assigned rooms within the regent's mansion, resting before they change shifts.

Lora, Bronwen, and Xylie have made it three steps down the main cobblestone path when the first party-goers rush up to them. They bow deeply and gush, "We wish you prosperity in your reign, my lady."

She dips her head in return, and they mark off the cards on their wrists before continuing on their way, giggling. It happens three more times in the space of twenty feet. No one stays to say anything more, and perhaps if they did, it would be more tolerable. If they had questions, demands, favors, even challenges for their new Sovereign, she would have felt like a ruler and not like entertainment.

"My lady!" Briar booms, approaching from a different side pathway. "You look magnificent. As do you two ladies." He bows to both Bronwen and Xylie in turn, flaring out the tail of his pink coat. White flowers embroider the sleeves and hem, and he has donned a brand new crown of pink roses.

"And you look dashing," Lora says. "But then, you've always been the regent with the most impeccable style."

She knows well that Briar is butter in the right hands, and he will utterly melt from flattery.

His grin is wide, speaking of her victory. "Can I escort you to the main courtyard? That is where most of the entertainment and food reside."

Lora reluctantly releases Bronwen and Xylie to take Briar's arm instead. He pulls her down the pathway he's just come from toward a tall wall of hedges with an iron gate between them. Bronwen and Xylie clasp arms and follow closely after. Bronwen's step holds a little skip while Xylie's expression suggests she's being escorted to the gallows.

Briar leads them through the metal gates and into the heart of the ball he has prepared. Small lanterns hang from strings above their heads, so numerous that it's nearly as bright as daylight. Dancers swing below them, swaying in time to the music played by the musicians on the lifted stage. Food-laden tables are assembled along the edges. People gather around them to load up their plates while stopping to watch entertainers who have positioned themselves throughout the crowd. Tavish is among them. He's holding the Kindred leash as Saga watches a pair of elementists. The fire elementist forms shapes with their flames, while a water elementist summons the water from nearby vases. It fountains into an arch before connecting with the flames. Steam stamps the air in the lingering shape of the heart. They continue to work in unison, an artistic display of fire, water, and steam.

Another pair of entertainers stands a half dozen yards away. One juggles flaming torches while their companion swallows a sword, and Lora quickly looks away, hiding a cringe. Her focus locks onto another performer, one who stands on a stone bench so that the dozen people who have gathered around him can see him. Purple sparks ignite in his hand, and a flower appears in his palm. It's a simple trick, one Lora has seen dozens of times. She knows now it's simply sleight of hand and not some weak magic. Either way, in a world of magic, it's unimpressive, simple entertainment, and yet, the crowd is transfixed.

But it's not the trick.

It's him.

"Why didn't the dragon eat the jester?" Ayc says, offering the rose to one of the crowd. "Because he tasted funny."

The crowd laughs.

"I certainly don't remember hiring him," Briar says good-naturedly, "but my, he's splendid."

Lora feels as though someone has yanked her corset tighter. She can't breathe because he is that splendid. And she's unsure whether she should give the tailors who created his outfit more money or have them imprisoned for making her lungs do such traitorous things.

The corseted vest harkens to Ayc's style before, the old brown vest he wore when he performed, but this cuts closer to his body, the ties pulled taut down his spine. It hugs his frame like a second skin, even over the shirt with puffed sleeves he wears beneath it. Its fabric complements her own dress, bringing in the same shimmering blues and pinks and embroidery. The collar cuts low on his chest, as does the shirt, revealing the hollow of his throat, the valleys of his collarbones, and the beginnings of his dragon mark that gleams like pearls in the lantern light. His blue eyes gleam in the lantern light, rimmed with exquisitely applied black that makes his eyes look hauntingly beautiful.

For the first time today, she feels hungry, but not for food. She wants to feast upon the column of his throat, wants to drag her lips through that hollow of his collarbone, wants to trace every line of his body with her tongue. She's had a taste of him only once, in that hospital room, and it has ruined her because she's desperate for more.

She's desperate for him. Everything has felt tenuous between them since the night in the Sovereign's Garden. He's so...careful with her. So respectful. He doesn't tease, doesn't torment her, doesn't try to burrow deeper within her skin. And she hates it. It's selfish and ridiculous of her because she knows she can't have it both ways. She can't keep him distant and also wants him close.

But she does.

Lora watches as Ayc cracks yet another terrible joke and simultaneously produces another rose in his hand. He offers it to another fae, and it takes a moment for her to realize she knows that fae, too.

Veni.

He's changed from the guard uniform into a forest green tunic, and he wears a grin she knows well to be flirtatious. He has every right to be here, enjoying himself off duty. He has every right to flirt with whomever he wants. She has no claim on Ayc, and yet her canine teeth grow to points in her mouth.

She wishes that she had thrown that snake—the one Veni left in her bed all those years ago—straight into his face. She only hadn't at the time because she feared it would have been unfair to the *snake*. She regrets that mercy now.

"Careful," Briar warns, with a shake of his head. "All of Everadyn is going to fall in love with him."

"Quite right to," she says. "My Five are magnificent."

She keeps her voice good-natured so he can't hear the bitterness that could so easily infect her tone.

Jealousy is a poisonous bitch, and her blood runs thick with it.

Mine, something within her snarls.

But he isn't. He cannot be.

Lora fears that somehow Ayc has some special sense that alerts him whenever she is looking at him. Because he turns, and their eyes connect. The tension is there in an instant. The smile tips from his lips, and perhaps it's the shadow playing tricks, but his eyes look like they darken. He's yards away, and yet she feels the heat of him as though he's as close to her as he was in that garden, nearly pressed against her, his breath hot on her ear.

"Are you hungry?" Briar asks

"Ravenous," she says.

Fuck. What the fuck did she just say?

Lora jerks her gaze away from Ayc and forces herself to focus. "The food looks fantastic. I'm ravenous for it."

Fortunately, Briar only notices the flattery and not her slip. He pulls her toward the nearest table and loads up her plate with an eclectic mixture of foods—all bathed in flowers and fragrant herbs.

She tries to take another breath. A corset's boning digs deeper into her ribs.

The string music picks up a new tune, one that is faster and somehow louder. The dancers cheer and break into a new jig, complete with stomping feet and clapping hands. People laugh. It all blends together and forms knives in her head until she feels every painful sound like a stab in her skull.

But she pushes it down, down, down.

She's always loathed parties—with the close bodies and the noise and the restrictive clothes. But she's been raised for this. She's been molded to have the best manners, the finest conversation skills, and the ability to hide the discomfort that builds and builds. No one can see it, see her, so she puts on a mask for the world to see instead.

Xylie swiftly disappears to find some quiet corner to hide in.

Bronwen sweeps off to charm guests. After all, that's the point of this party: to make everyone fall in love with Lora and her Five. Bronwen and Ayc are the ones most suited to earning the affection of a crowd, but it's Lora who knows she must do the best job.

So, she paints on a smile like it's makeup. She samples the food and pretends she likes everything, even though she nearly gags on the slimy texture of the stuffed mushrooms. She greets every single person who bows and wishes her well with the demure and grace expected of the Sovereign. She shakes hands with members of the Council of Elders and tells them she is so looking forward to meeting with them over the next week. She exchanges pleasantries with the wealthiest merchants, carefully asking questions and stashing away information she knows will be useful in the future. Wars and rebellion, after all, take money.

And, most importantly, she absolutely does not allow herself to stare at Ayc, even when she hears a laugh above the others and knows it's his. She doesn't scowl at him when she catches him dancing with multiple people. Yes, she told her Five to have fun and make people fall in love with them, but for fuck's sake, why does he have to do it so well?

She tolerates it all. Perhaps she even looks like she's tolerating it well. But within fifteen minutes in, she wishes she could loosen her corset. By thirty minutes, the sound of her own falsely cheerful voice is grating on her nerves. By two hours, her very nerves feel tender to the touch, every noise hurting like an electric impulse. Her hands want to shake to release the tension, but instead, she fists them into her skirt. She tries to breathe, but the fucking corset is too tight. She feels like she's coming undone, and if she keeps it up, someone is going to notice.

She steps away into a corner, grabbing a glass of water from a nearby tray. She gulps it down, hoping it'll help.

"Can I have the honor of this dance?" Briar asks.

She nearly chokes on the water at the suddenness he appears with but recovers quickly. She passes the cup to Shae.

"Of course," Lora agrees, even though she really fucking hates dancing. At least this type of dancing, where she is on display. But it would be bad diplomacy to say no.

She takes his hand and lets him pull her into a dance. At least it's a slow one, a simple waltz so that her feet can easily remember the steps. She was forced to take dancing lessons as a child, but she's always been more graceful when holding her swords than she is without them.

"You've gone to great lengths to start my Tour off splendidly," Lora says, to distract herself from the music and the movement and his hands on her side. He's nothing but respectful, keeping her at arm's length. "I can't thank you enough."

Briar spins them around, and Lora catches sight of Ayc, dancing with one of the handsome merchants she spoke with earlier. Whatever Ayc whispers into his ear makes him laugh, and Lora burns with jealousy once more.

She catches the hem of her dress and stumbles. Briar tightens his hold and helps her get back on balance. "Are you well?"

"Yes," Lora says swiftly. "I'm sorry. What were you saying?"

"I was saying that my husband and I look forward to having you and your Five at breakfast tomorrow."

"I do as well. I look forward to being able to discuss the needs and desires of your people with you more intimately. What is most near and dear to your heart." She hesitates, considers carefully, and then adds, "And what is near and dear to mine."

"And what is that?"

"Ensuring prosperity for all Everadyn fae, no matter what class or privilege they come from."

He smiles and nods.

"Ensuring Lux Aester deals more fairly with *all* their people."

"Oh, most certainly. It's about time someone did something about that."

Good. She guessed Briar—and his husband—would have sympathy for that. That leaves only Aluina.

He lifts his arm for her to spin beneath it, and she takes that opportunity to say it most casually: "And, of course, restoring our old allegiances."

He stiffens. It lasts only a moment before his smile is back in place, but she's certain she didn't imagine it.

Fuck.

"What allegiances do you mean?" he asks.

"Aluina, of course." She can't help the bluntness that creeps into her voice. "Are you in favor of the treaty with the Drakr?"

"No," Briar says. "It broke my heart when your mother signed that treaty. I look forward to it being ended."

A tiny spark of hope lights. If Briar is on their side, then she will only need to convince one more regent to agree. She's certain she already has Grey's vote.

Then he adds, "I'm grateful that you will be our Sovereign when it ends in ninety years so that it will not be renewed."

The words are a knife between her rib cage. She bites back a gasp at the impact. Ninety years is lifetimes for humans. The people who are alive now will be mostly dead and gone. Their grandchildren might be free, but they would not. It's unacceptable.

But Lora can't press him because the song ends, and he steps away. Briar sweeps a bow. "Thank you, my lady. Let me know if you have need of anything." Then he sweeps away so grandly, it *almost* looks as though he's not running away from their conversation.

Fuck.

Fucking selfish coward. How can anyone know of that injustice and want to do nothing?

Lora's hands shake. Something is building up inside of her. Rage or panic or overstimulation. Perhaps all three. The next song picks up, and its tempo clangs in her head. Someone laughs, and it feels like nails embedding in her forehead.

She needs a break, just a few moments, to sew herself back together. She locates Bronwen close by and grasps her elbow, pulling her away from the merchant who's staring at her like he might already be wrapped with a bow around Bronwen's little finger. Bronwen calls an excuse over her shoulder, then turns her focus on Lora.

"I need five minutes," Lora says. "Possibly ten."

Her First asks no questions, only nods. "Take as long as you need. I'll cover for you."

As Lora turns and cuts a direct path toward the exit of the courtyard, she signals for Shae to step closer.

"What do you need?" Shae asks softly.

"Privacy. There's a pool in the corner of the garden that's mostly hidden. Can you clear the area and then give me some distance?"

"If we can secure it, yes, my lady."

The noise lowers the farther she goes. Occasionally, when they pass the Rose Maze or the gazebo, voices and laughter pick up again, but they fade once more. The light that illuminated the party dims as they go, and Lora has to pause twice at crossroads to get her bearings in the dark. At last, she reaches the familiar grouping of closely clustered trees and thick bushes.

Lora nods, and Davos sweeps into the narrow, easily missed path while Shae remains at Lora's side. The willow branches rustle as he passes through him, but as he disappears, the sound disappears with him. Some enchantment that rests over the glade, ensuring privacy to whoever enters there.

Lora paces as she waits, unable to sit still, listening to every movement. She hears feet on the grass nearby, but when she turns toward the sound, she sees no one, only the darkness. She freezes, her fingers slipping into the slit of the dress, toward her dagger.

Shae tracks the noise, too. She reaches for her sword. "Who goes there?" the guard demands.

"Easy," Ayc says, appearing just as he steps on the path. "It's just me."

But that doesn't make Lora's heart beat any slower. Not as he prowls toward her like a gorgeous creature of the night.

It's ridiculous that she's never felt more in danger.

It's even more ridiculous that she likes it.

"Perhaps I should have Shae stab you anyway," Lora says.

"Not anywhere vital, only where it'll hurt. For sneaking up on me."

"I didn't intend to sneak up on you. I noticed you were gone, and I worried. I had no idea where you went, though, and I didn't want people to see me, so I took off my bracelets. I didn't mean to startle you." He searches her over, kind concern in his eyes. "Are you all right?"

He noticed her absence. And he came after her. She tries not to feel it, tries to swallow down whatever emotion is quickly rising. She fails.

"I'm fine," she manages. "I just needed a moment to catch my breath. This damn corset." She hooks a finger on the side and pulls it away. It feels like it's digging even harder now, or perhaps she just can't ignore it anymore. "Can you breathe in yours?"

"Of course." He cocks his head. "Can you *not* breathe in yours?"

"I think the point of a woman's corset is to be as uncomfortable as possible."

"Why wear it if it isn't comfortable?"

Lora rolls her eyes. "I suppose women do it because it makes their breasts look fantastic, but at what cost?"

Ayc chokes on nothing but air and jerks his eyes toward the sky. Lora immediately regrets her candor because it's now abundantly clear that he's attempting to look anywhere but at her breasts. The foolish part of Lora, the part that clearly hasn't grasped the reality of their situation, wishes he *would* look. She wants to watch his black-rimmed eyes burn for her. She wants the power of knowing she made that look come upon his face.

He clears his throat, still not looking at her. "I want it to be stated clearly that I am choosing to *not* say what I'm thinking at this moment."

"I appreciate your restraint," she says, though for once, she'd quite like to know whatever indecent joke is fluttering through his head.

He continues to gaze up at the sky for a moment that feels like it stretches forever. She continues to gaze at him, at the angle of his waist in that corset. It makes it far too easy to imagine what the line of his body would look like bare. They stand in silence for so long that Davos returns.

"All clear, my lady."

"What's all clear?" Ayc asks, finally dropping his gaze.

"There's a waterfall back there," Lora says. "I wanted to go in alone. For privacy."

"Aw," he says. The line between his brow deepens as he searches her over. "Can you truly not breathe easily in your corset?"

"Not easily, no."

He closes the distance between them so quickly she has to plant her heels to deny the urge to retreat. That feeling—the one that isn't quite fear but isn't not fear either—makes her heart pound behind her sternum. It quickens further when he carefully wraps his hand over hers. "Come with me."

He tugs her arm, and she follows him, though she's certain that she probably shouldn't—particularly since he's pulling her toward the thin break in the willow trees, the path that leads to the pool. "Why?"

"So I can loosen your corset in privacy. If it hurts you, it's too tight. You don't need to suffer to look beautiful. You're always fucking exquisite."

Divine be damned, he has to stop saying stuff like that to her. It makes her feel like all her will is unraveling.

"Should we follow, my lady?" Shae asks. "I could adjust your corset."

"It's fine," Lora says, even though she knows it's a mistake to, once again, let herself be alone with Ayc. She's reeling too much from the contact of his hand, from his blunt but sweet words.

She lets him pull her down the path, ducking beneath the fanned branches of the evergreens that lie beyond the willows. The sound of flowing water greets her. The dark waters reflect the tops of the towering trees and the silver speckles of the stars that shine beyond. Its stillness breaks only beneath the cascade of water tumbling down the dark rocks that form a wall on one side of the pool.

Romantic. This place is too romantic.

She coils her fists tighter until her fingernails grind into her skin without breaking them. Ayc stops them beside the pool and gently turns her around. She can do this. He's simply assisting her with loosening her corset, something she knows she should have had someone do long ago.

"Is this all right?" he asks, his breath teasing the back of her neck.

She shivers. "Yes."

His fingers brush the hair at the nape of her neck. His touch is ginger, careful, almost reverent of her curls in a way she's unused to. He sweeps her hair carefully over one shoulder, so he can reach her corset.

"Why did you come here?" he asks.

She opens her mouth to respond, but at the same moment, she feels the tug as he pulls out the bow Lora's attendant tied. Her mind goes blank. It refuses to form a coherent thought. How can it when it's completely consumed with the confident but gentle way he's pulling at her strings.

His hands still. "Lora?"

Right. The question.

"I just needed a few minutes to be alone," she says.

"I understand that. It's part of the reason I took off my bracelets. I wanted to have a moment where people were not looking at me." He's midway down her back already. She draws a deeper breath than she has in hours. At least until he reaches for the next tie, and his knuckle brushes against the bare skin of her spine.

Fuck, there's something wrong with her because that tiny brush is all it takes to make her feel as though she's melting. Desire coils deep in her stomach as her mind fills with impossibilities. Ayc loosening the corset enough that he can reach inside and cup her breasts in his palms. Ayc's mouth sweeping over the arch of shoulder as he kneads her tender flesh.

She sucks in air through her nose and tries to distract herself. "You wanted to hide? I thought you enjoyed these parties."

"I do. Very much." Another tie. Another brush of Ayc's skin. Another coil of desire deep in her stomach. It aches; it empties; it demands to be filled. "But sometimes I need a moment of quiet to appreciate it without feeling...overwhelmed."

With the way he's always been able to work a crowd so effortlessly, it's a surprise he ever feels overwhelmed. It's a relief to know she isn't alone.

"You've never liked parties much, have you?" he asks. "It's why you've always hid in a corner, trying to avoid being seen."

Lora nods.

"Only now you're the center of attention. There's no avoiding it." He hums a soft note of sympathy.

"Such is being Sovereign."

"Is that why you wore your corset too tight? Because you thought it was expected of you as Sovereign."

"It was fine."

His voice hardens. "I can see the line in your back where it was digging in. It was *not* fine."

Lora shivers. There's intimacy in that, a vulnerability that he's close enough to see that line on her back. She shivers once again, harder this time, as he runs a single finger across that line. It's the softest of touches, like he means to soothe the tortured skin, but her stomach tightens and her knees quake.

Divine help her.

She has to grit her teeth to get out the next words, to pretend he's not impacting her. "I want to make the best impression. And I didn't want to inconvenience the tailors who made the dress."

His hands still, his finger hooked within the very top of her corset. That hardness in his voice deepens even further. "Your comfort is *not* an inconvenience."

"Just because I'm Sovereign doesn't mean—"

"Not because you're Sovereign. *No one's* comfort should ever be treated like an inconvenience."

"There you go again, cinnamon roll," she teases. "Being far kinder than anyone deserves."

It's an old impulse, and she hates the words as they leave her tongue. They sound too similar to her mother's *'Kindness is weakness,'* and she knows she isn't right. Kindness has always been a strength in Ayc. But she wants things to feel like they did before the Trials. She wants him to taunt her back, to call her villainess and snap back at her with a wide grin and a wink.

But he says nothing as he works the corset strings a second time, speeding through them skillfully.

She takes a deep breath and chooses her words carefully, hesitantly, like pushing a finger against a bruise to see if it's still tender. "Is everything well between us?"

"Why would they not be?"

She tilts her head to the side so she can see him from the corner of her eye, but from this angle, in the darkness, he's scarcely more than a shadow behind her. "Things have been... distant between us since the garden."

He ties the excess string back into a bow and tucks it behind the ties. His hands drop from the corset, hovering behind her hips. "Have you not wanted them to be distant?"

"No," she says. But that's a lie. "I mean... Yes, but..."

He cuts her off. "I'm trying so hard to be respectful of you." When he repeats it, it's growled through his teeth. "So fucking hard." His hand spasms, fisting in the fabric of her skirt.

She's transfixed by the sight of his hand twisted around the layers of her skirt. His broad fingers are tipped with a deep purple that complements the pinks and blues. With his body nearly pressed to her back, it makes it far too easy to imagine him raking her skirt up to her hips, bending her over, working himself within her. Her pussy clenches at the thought. She clamps her thighs together, trying to create friction to relieve the building ache, lest she do something foolish and beg him to touch her.

He continues, his voice deepening, growing huskier. He angles his lips close to her ear. "I've kept my distance because whenever I'm near you, I find it increasingly difficult not to tease you, not to touch you, not to—" He cuts off with a growl of frustration. "Fuck, Lora, I need you to tell me to walk away."

In defiance, she feels her feet plant deeper into the earth. "Why?"

When he doesn't answer immediately, she twists her head to look at him over her shoulder. She tries to suck in a deep breath. It will not come, and she can't blame her corset for it this time. But she can blame his eyes.

They are burning red.

"Because if you don't, I'm going to kiss you."

CHAPTER
TWENTY-NINE

AYC

Ayc is losing it.

His control. His common sense. The little sense of self-preservation he possesses. Loosening her corset was a foolish idea. He should have known the impact it would have on him. He should have known that once he touched her, he would never want to stop. Well, he did know, but he couldn't stand the idea of her discomfort.

And now he has to beg her to end this because he can't.

"Tell me to walk away."

She doesn't speak.

He pries his hand from his skirt and flings himself back a couple of steps. It's all he can manage before she turns fully around, and the sight of her floors him again. She was right. Her breasts do look fucking fantastic in that corset, their ample flesh nearly spilling out. The way the bright colors look against the brown of her skin tone. The peek of her leg through the slit of her skirt. She's more exquisite than the waterfall that trails down the rocks behind her.

She stares at him. Her eyes, which were a deep gray before, flash silver.

Fuck.

She can't do this to him. She can't look at him like that and expect him to walk away again.

"Lora," he says her name like a warning, and it seems to snap some sense into her.

She shakes her head, and the silver dims but doesn't fade, flickering just like the stars play off the pool beside him.

"Maybe we should go," she says.

"Then go," Ayc replies.

But she doesn't leave.

Why the fuck isn't she leaving?

Her breath passes her lips unsteadily, but she doesn't retreat. She takes a step toward him, then another, until her chest nearly brushes his.

"This is a mistake," she murmurs, but it doesn't sound like she's talking to him. It sounds like she's mostly talking to herself. "We have to be careful. People will think…" She trails off and then starts again. "It's what Damara said. People will assume that we're f—"

The silver in her eyes grows brighter.

"Fucking?" Perhaps he's a fucking idiot, or perhaps he's just fucking done pretending, but he can't make the words stop. He maneuvers his mouth to her ear once more, and the truth growls from his chest. "I wouldn't fuck you, villainess. I would *worship* you. I would memorize your body with my tongue. I would lavish you with pleasure until you came on my hand and then on my mouth. Over and over. And once I've learned all the places that make you squirm, then… Well, maybe then I would fuck you."

Those will be the last words he ever says.

He's certain of it.

There's no universe where she doesn't draw that dagger strapped to her thigh and end him…or at the very least, banish him to some unknown country far, far from here. He waits for the impact, but she doesn't move. Her breaths come in rapid succession, the air scraping past his chin like a physical, torturous touch. When he dares tilt his head back just enough to look down on her face, her teeth grind against her lower lip. Her eyes still burn silver.

It emboldens him. He dares to reach for her face again. His fingers tremble just before impact. He's ached to touch her again like he did in the garden, and it's a relief when his thumb trails across her jaw once again. He searches her over, waiting for her muscles to tense, for her eyes to shift away from his like they did before. If she gives him the smallest sign that she doesn't want this, he'll stop. It might kill him to do so, but he'll stop.

Her breath comes even faster. Her hand lands on his chest once more, but it doesn't push him away. Instead, it coils into the front of his vest.

So he pushes his luck once again. He bends down until his lips press against her temple when he speaks, "Would you like that, my lady? Because the fact that your dagger isn't at my throat right now makes me think you would like it."

"Ayc."

Perhaps she means it to be a roar, but it comes out as a whine. A keening. And it damn near breaks him.

"Tell me if I'm wrong," he murmurs, his other hand rising to cup the back of her neck. "I'm holding on by a thread, Lora. Tell me you don't want me before I lose my last fiber of restraint."

Nothing.

She says nothing.

Ayc grinds his teeth together. It takes all his will to pry his hands from her skin, but he manages it even as his very soul cries out in protest. He starts to step back, but she seizes his vest in both her hands.

"Damn your mouth," she snarls. "You're going to be my ruin."

She drags him back to her with a force that leaves them both stumbling, fumbling backward for support. His hands don't wait for sturdiness. They seek the nape of her neck, seek enough control to haul her mouth to his.

And then, thank holy fuck, he's kissing her at last.

Her lips are hot and eager, parting for him at the moment of impact. So when they meet, they meet like a rock against flint stone. First their mouths, and then their tongues, and then their bodies as Lora's back slams against the rock wall beside the waterfall. He barely manages to brace his hand behind her head to slow the impact so it does not hurt her. The spray of the waterfall mists against their skin, but all Ayc can feel is her body as it presses firmly against his. Even through their clothes, it feels better than any fantasy could conjure. She is all muscles honed to fight and soft rolls of flesh meant to be adored, and he wants to learn every inch of her.

A deep growl forms in his chest, but releasing it would mean breaking away from her lips, and there is no chance in fuck he is doing that. He remembers kissing her before, but this is sharper, harsher, more desperate. Lora kisses fiercely, filled with that viciousness he's come to adore. Her fingers rake into his long hair, her teeth yank at his bottom lip, demanding more. And fuck, he loves it. This mixture of pleasure and pain. And he wants to give back to her. Wants to give her everything he is.

Never breaking the kiss, his hands trail downward. He roams across her sides, her shoulders, her collarbones, hovering just above the swell of her breast. He rejoices at every newfound millimeter of her skin. It's as though he's always been meant to touch her, and not doing so has been his eternal agony. And now, his very soul is sighing with relief, even as he growls harder, his cock straining against the restraints of his trousers.

She pulls away to gasp for the air Ayc has forgotten they both need, and his lips ache from her absence. He satisfies them with her jaw and then her neck. He languishes kisses down her chest, and she tightens her fingers at the back of his head, tangling into his hair as she presses him closer to where her breast spills from the corset. He trails a tongue across the beginning of the slope. And fuck, he feels like the luckiest man who has ever lived because if he's not lucky, how does he have the privilege of tasting her skin?

He slides his hand lower, slipping between the slit in her skirt to grasp the thick flesh of her thigh. He knows for as long as he lives and breathes, the weight of it will forever be branded into his palm.

"Ayc," she moans.

"Yes, my lady?" he asks, smiling as he hikes her leg up to his waist. He knows there's no way Lora doesn't notice how desperately he wants her as he steps between her legs. As he fits their hips together, she arches back her neck and scrapes her nails down the back of his corset, tugging at the strings.

"Fuck," he groans, grinding his teeth together. He could come apart like this, knowing only bits of fabric separate her sweet cunt from him, but he wants this to last. He's waited so long, there's no way this is ending before he watches her scream his name. And this time, it won't be a dream.

Right?

"Fuck, tell me I'm not dreaming," he says. "Tell me this is real."

"Must you always talk so much?" Lora growls from behind her teeth. "There's so many better uses for your mouth."

His eyes flare with red, and she must see it because her eyes widen. He's never not worn his bracelets during sex, and for a moment, he feels vulnerable, afraid that the sight of the red eyes might startle her away. But the fear is erased as her hand urgently claws against the back of his vest once more, clumsily seeking the tie.

He grasps her hand to still it. "You're *so* impatient," he teases.

"And you're so infuriating." She tugs her hand free only to seize his hair once more and guide him back to her lips.

He works the hand on her thigh lower, trying to form a path to the place between them, but his hand hits against her dagger. He fumbles with the buckles for a moment, but he's too distracted, his hands too clumsy. He drops to his knees and flings her leg over his shoulder to get a better angle. But still, it takes him several attempts to undo the two simple buckles. He's too distracted by the weight of her leg on his shoulder, the crease of her thigh where her underthings begin, and the way she looks staring down upon him. He wants to soak it in, memorize it.

Finally, he tosses the dagger aside. He places a kiss where the buckle once was, and her fingers tighten in his hair, pressing him closer to her center. He surges back to his feet before he can give in to the demand of her hands.

"Ayc!" she protests as he resumes their previous position, her leg on his hip.

"First my hand, and then my mouth," he reminds her, taking back her lips. His hand returns to where it paused on her thigh. He presses into the flesh unhindered and continues his descent, down the back of her thigh, and then curving around. Toward the center, between their bodies, to that perfect crease where the last barrier between them resides.

Laughter and voices sound on the path outside the trees. Ayc is so lost in her that he might not have noticed, but she tenses. Her hands drop from his hair to his shoulders, pressing away instead of pulling closer. He freezes, searching her face that is now furrowed in an expression of pain.

"Stop," she pleads. "We have to stop."

Ayc stumbles backward, dragging his hands away from her. It feels like torture, the worst pain he's ever known, to release her, but he does. Shadows scatter away from his feet, going back to wherever his emotions summoned them from when he wasn't aware he was doing so.

Lora twists away from him and uses her reflection in the pool to set herself straight. Trembling fingers smooth the wrinkles he's created in her skirt, and his heart sinks lower in his chest because he feels like she's attempting to erase him.

She presses her fingers to her lips, the ones that are puffy and swollen from his attention. He feels some satisfaction that there's nothing anyone can do to hide that evidence. His own lips feel the same, hot from her passion, aching from her teeth. He wonders if anyone could see her tooth marks if they look close enough. He hopes so. He wants to be marked by her, for all the world to know he's hers.

Perhaps for that reason, he's reluctant to run his fingers through his own hair, but he does. After all, he can't return to the party with hair that looks like he was fucked beside a waterfall. Even if he wants to.

Finally, she swings toward him. She's replaced her expression with one that is carefully guarded, and fuck. Fuck. He knows whatever she's about to say to him, it's going to break his fucking heart.

Oh, well.

It's hers to break, anyway.

"That was a mistake," she says. "It can't happen again."

"Why not?" he demands.

"I need to get back to the party."

She's running away from him again. Emotionally and literally. And he's tired of it, so when she tries to storm around him, he steps into her path. The look that cracks her stony mask is fierce enough that Ayc should be a little afraid. He isn't, though. It only makes him dig into the earth harder.

"Lora, you cannot keep kissing me and then tell me it was a mistake. Not without telling me why. I deserve an answer."

She huffs out a breath and fixes her gaze past him. "For many reasons."

"Then let's hear them."

She takes several long breaths before she speaks. "I just... I need to get through the Tour without people thinking I'm fucking my Fifth."

He cringes as logic breaks back through his haze of desire. If she let him, he was going to fuck her against that stone in this public garden where there's a party being held in her honor. He needs to be more responsible with her. No matter how eager she seemed, he should have had the common sense to wait until they were in private.

"You're right. I'm sorry," he says. "This was reckless. We should be more discreet—"

She shakes her head. "People would inevitably find out."

His heart slips even lower, down to where his gut is twisting into knots. He forces himself to keep his voice calm. "You're concerned what people might think if they found out you were fucking me? Why?"

She only shakes her head.

"No one actually cares who is in your bed," Ayc says.

She scoffs. "You are *not* a woman. No one cares who *you* fuck. But me? A woman, and a woman in *power. Everyone* will care."

He doesn't argue because he's never experienced life as a woman. He would be an ass to refuse to accept her own lived experience as anything but fact. Instead, he reasons, "People might think we are together anyway. Damara thought so, even when it wasn't true."

"Because I let too much show," she snaps, a hard edge soldering into her tone. Ayc doesn't know what she means by that, but she continues before he can ask. "I have to stop. I can't give anyone any more evidence. I can't allow anyone to doubt that my loyalty and duty are to Everadyn first. Nor can I afford anyone thinking that I have a weakness. If they think you're more than my Fifth, my enemies could try to use you to control me, like Marcellus tried to do during the Trials. I am trying to protect you."

Ayc grits his teeth at the reminder. "I am not weak."

"I did not say *you* were," she says quickly. "I do not think you are." The silence hangs heavy, broken only by the soft crash of water upon water. She folds her arms over her chest, rubbing her hands over her biceps like she's cold. "But love is vulnerability, and a Sovereign cannot be vulnerable."

"Love is vulnerability?" Ayc repeats. He's heard those words before, but they weren't said by Lora. "I didn't think you actually listened to your mother's opinions."

Lora's hands tighten on her biceps, so hard the flesh pales around her fingers. "The source doesn't make it less true."

Ayc scrubs his hands over his face, growling a note of frustration into his palms. "Lora, for fuck's sake..."

He drops his hands, prepared to argue, to fight, to do something to not have it end like this, but she holds up a hand. A flicker of that same look of pain passes over her face, and it halts him.

"Can we please just forget this ever happened and go back to what we were before I kissed you?"

"And what was that?" Ayc asks, because he doesn't know. There's never been a moment that he can recall when he has not been in love with her. There was just before—when he was foolish enough to pretend he hated her—and now—when he can't continue to lie.

"I don't know." She's still not looking at him. Her throat works as she swallows hard. "Before. When you did not want me."

Ayc lets out a long, tired sigh. "Lora, that isn't possible. I have wanted you since I knew what it is to want."

She makes a sound deep in her throat, like his words are a punch. She presses her eyes closed, but not before he sees the way they suddenly glisten like stars. "Do not say that. Please. This is hard enough already. Are you not hearing me?"

"I'm hearing you. I hear all the reasons why you're too afraid to risk being together."

She snaps her eyes back open, and the glisten has changed to a glare. "I am not afraid."

"Bullshit," he snaps, daring to take a step closer to her so she has to tilt her chin back, so she has no choice but to actually look at him. "Because in all your excuses, there is one reason I have not heard."

Her nostrils flare. "And what is that?"

"You haven't said that you do not want me."

She retreats a step. Like the words are a threat that has caught her off guard.

"That's all you have to say." He needs to hear it. It's the only way he's going to be able to walk away from her and let this thing between them rest. If she can't do that, then this desire to fight, to resist, to dig in isn't going to fade.

"Ayc..."

"Lora, just tell me you don't want me."

She's silent for so long, Ayc thinks he might actually hear the creaking of his own soul beginning to break.

"I don't want you," she says at last, her voice scarcely more than a whisper.

It's a lie. He knows it's a lie. She would not have kissed him—twice—the way she's kissed him if she didn't want him. But the honesty of her statement is relative to its impact.

She doesn't want him *enough*. Not enough to risk the consequences that might come with it. Not enough to fight the fear that her mother has implanted in her head. Not enough to even consider putting her crown at risk.

And who can blame her? This isn't a fairytale or one of her books. This is not a game. The fate of both their countries rests upon her shoulders. Of course she has to choose that.

He swallows hard, forces down his pride and his emotions and the bleeding of his heart. "Very well, Lora. Very well. Forgive me. I've taken up enough of your time. I'll make sure I'm not seen leaving. I don't want anyone to get the wrong idea."

She nods, but she's already twisting away from him, like she can't bear to look at him anymore.

He steps backward and disappears into the safety of the shadow.

LORA

Lora waits until she's certain that he's gone before she releases it. The scream that's been building inside of her.

She bites down on her hand to muffle the sound, hard enough she tastes blood. It's a scream of rage and overstimulation and, most importantly, pain.

The crown on her head is tugging on her hair. She pulls it off her head and nearly hurls it into the pool at her feet. She catches herself just in time and fists her hand around it, the onyx stones and peaks digging into her palm.

"My lady," Shae says softly from the entrance. "Is everything all right?"

Lora quickly returns the crown to her head. She drags the back of her hands over her cheeks, banishing the moisture that has dared to fall. "I'm fine, Shae."

There it is.

Yet, another lie.

She wants to scream again, but she turns and walks away from the pool.

THIRTY

AYC

"Vidar!" Ayc exclaims as he explodes through the door of the Pink Elk, the first of the party to enter the inn. The rest of the tour party is still collecting in the yard outside, but he wanted to be the first to speak to the innkeeper. "How are you? I love the gown."

Vidar glowers at Ayc from behind the front counter, his eyes disappearing behind his red, bushy eyebrows. His dress is darling, a loose linen smock with bell-shaped sleeves. It's, of course, the same eye-watering pink that decorates his inn and the nails of the falcon that rests on the human's shoulder. The pupils of the bird's amber eyes are blown wide as they let out a little screech, one that seems to say, *Not this asshole again.*

"Who is your tailor?" Ayc asks, sauntering across the room and perching his elbows casually on the counter. He gives Vidar his very best grin. "Are they local? I may have them make me something for the next Tour. Get rid of this ol' thing." He points toward the pink and blue corset on his chest.

Throughout the last week, as they have traveled across Bromalis territory, he's interchanged the corset vest with his black armor and coat, depending on where they were visiting.

They've gone to military out-postings, been entertained at mansions, toured the richest vineyards and plant nurseries, and gone into some of the smallest villages and farmsteads. The latter is apparently something Lora insisted upon, though it wasn't usual for new Sovereigns to visit the working poor, to bring them baskets of food, and to hold town halls and listen to their concerns. But Lora and her Five have.

The village meetings have all started the same, with scarcely a few villagers there, wearing their clothes still dusted with soil from their long days tending to the gardens, orchards, and fields. At first, they come with hesitant, even skeptical looks, but as Lora talks to them, questions them on their wants and needs, and then, most importantly, *listens* to them, they begin to blossom just like their fields. She never flinched when they sometimes lost their temper at the tax laws or at the cost of lumber and livestock. She expressed sympathy with a grace Ayc knows she must have learned from Hellevi; she certainly didn't learn it from Yris. And by the end, the hall was filled wall to wall. When they left, the villagers' eyes shone with something new.

Hope.

Now, it's the very last night of the Bromalis leg of the Tour, and after a day of meetings at nearby villages and estates, the crew has arrived at the Pink Elk for a night of relaxation before returning to Wyntra. Ayc is eager for a warm, soft bed, and that's why he's here, trying to charm the innkeeper.

"What do you say, Vidar? Help me out with the name of the tailor."

Unfortunately, Ayc doesn't think he has the figure to pull off Vidar's gown. *But...* a little bit of flattering goes a long way.

And also, unfortunately, Vidar is on to him. His glower doesn't soften. He folds his burly arms over his chest, the sleeve of his dress riding up just enough to reveal thick, red arm hair and the dark lines of the start of a tattoo. "If this is about your dragon, I told our lady that your dragon has to sleep in the stable."

Fuck. Ayc sags more of his weight onto the counter, hoping it will relieve the way his spine feels like it might buckle under his weight. The wagon and the stable are where Muffin has been regulated for most nights of the Tour because most people have understandably been anxious about a dragon sleeping within their walls. It's why Ayc's entire body aches. He can't bring himself to let Muffin sleep in the stable alone, so Ayc has slept with them. Between the long hours in the carriage and the even longer nights on an unforgiving cot, every single muscle in his body feels like it's taken a blow. He's nearly out of pain tonics, and it's barely touching the pain today. He was so hoping for an actual bed tonight.

Besides, he was hoping to spend more time in the inn. It would better his chances of confirming his suspicions that Vidar is a part of Asbjorn.

"But Muffin will be so well-behaved," Ayc protests. And it's mostly true. Sort of. Muffin is simply a toddler. They don't mean to do bad things. They just haven't really learned what bad is and don't have the attention span to learn, so they generally just wreak havoc and chaos wherever they go.

"In the stable." Vidar's falcon lets out another screech as though to back him up. "And if they eat any of my goats, my lady has assured me I can take my repayment out of your ass. Those goats are like children to me. Especially Snowflake."

Ayc sighs. "I promise you no harm will come to any of your goats." He massages a hand into a particularly tender area of his shoulder. "But just in case, which one is Snowflake?"

Vidar gives him a glare that could curdle fresh milk. Ayc throws up his hands and backs toward the door of the inn.

He nearly collides with Xylie, Tavish, and Saga, who enter without him noticing.

"Any luck?" Tavish asks.

Ayc shakes his head. He has found it increasingly difficult to hide his pain from the two. Xylie sees every time Ayc shifts in the carriage, trying to find some position that doesn't stress his back or where he won't feel every jolt of the wagon wheels. And Tavish *hears* the constant shifting. Ayc has tried to pass it off as just regular aches and pain, but how can they believe him? They are scarcely younger than him, and they are not nearly as uncomfortable as he is.

He needs to talk to Reselda. She's seen his struggle all week and asked multiple times if there's anything she can do, ensuring that she only does so when they have some privacy. He's always lied and said he's fine. He's not sure why. Her job is to ensure the health of the party, and she's discreet. She's passed medicine so subtly that Ayc wouldn't have noticed if he didn't know. She slips Peregrin tonics for their pain like they're handshakes and adds Bronwen's medicine for her depression into her tea like she's simply adding milk. He knows she's treated Lora's headaches and possibly other members of the attendants, but he doesn't know when or how because she's always so careful. If he wanted people to continue not to know, they wouldn't know. At least, not from Reselda.

But he can't bring himself to ask.

"I can sleep in the stable tonight with Muffin if you like," Xylie signs.

"No, it's—" He begins to sign, but then Lora steps through the doorway behind them. Her hair is windswept, tangled in her crown. At the sight of her, he temporarily forgets what he was saying, what he was thinking, what he's even doing in this moment of existence.

Ever since they kissed, being near her is a tender mixture of torture and wonder. Every time they stand even in the same room, he finds it impossible not to remember the fleeting moment in time where no distance separated them.

He knows where things stand between them. He accepts it. But it doesn't mean it's easy. He needs distance. Lots of distance. But distance is impossible on the Tour. At least, while sleeping in the stables, he's not sharing Lora's same air. It's a pity the air has to smell like horse shit.

Xylie clears her throat, and Ayc jerks back into movement, like a music box that had been stuck before beginning to play again. *"It's fine,"* he signs. *"I'm going to get Muffin settled. We can switch off for supper."*

He slips around Lora with a respectful nod of his head, scraping his back against the door frame to prevent his body from brushing up against hers. She keeps her gaze fixed directly before her.

Out in the yard, the wagon, carriage, and half a dozen horses cluster between the inn and the long thatched-roofed stable. Tempest towers over the horses, even though she is currently bending her head to accept the snack Peregrin offers—one of the apple and carrot muffins Ayc baked her this morning. There's no hired groom at the Pink Elk, so the pages scramble against the dying daylight to unhitch and untack the horses, rub them down, and turn them out in Vidar's pasture. The back of the wagon, however, remains shut.

No one but Ayc or Xylie has had the nerve to approach Muffin. Even the experienced guards who are used to being around gryphons seem to be wary of the dragon, though they tolerate, even respect, Muffin's presence. Perhaps because the guards know what it means for Everadyn to have a dragon rider. Even Lora, Peregrin, Tavish, and Bronwen keep their distance, though that isn't out of fear but respect.

Ayc swings the door at the end of the wagon open. Muffin lifts their head, their red eyes glowing in the dimness. Ayc swears they've grown again. As they've used the supplies in the wagon, Muffin's long, awkward body has filled the space they've cleared. Muffin needs to master flying soon, or Ayc isn't certain what they will do.

"Bed?" Muffin asks hopefully, climbing to their feet.

"Sorry. I tried. We're in the stable again."

Muffin snorts out a breath. *"Fuck."*

"Well, look at that. You've learned the proper connotation of fuck. I'm so proud."

Muffin slaps Ayc's head with his tail as they jump from the wagon. They're careful to not use the spikes. Still, it hurts.

"That was uncalled for, Muffin," Ayc scolds before quickly correcting himself. *"I'm sorry. I know you don't like being called Muffin."*

Muffin stretches out their wings. The membranes catch the last rays of dusk and shimmer, turning the white into an iridescent rainbow before they tuck them back to their sides. *"Muffin is fine. You can call me that. But it's not...not really my name."*

Ayc grabs his personal pack and the cot from the wagon. He follows the dejected-looking dragon toward the stable, careful not to trip on the tail they are dragging through the earth behind them. *"Have you figured out what you would like to be called?"*

"No."

"Well, Muffin can be your nickname until you sort it out. Ayc isn't my full name either, you know? It's Ayciah. My mother named me after her younger brother, who died in childhood. She only ever called me Ayc, though."

"Your mother named you after a dead boy?" Muffin cocks their head and surveys Ayc out of the corner of their eye. *"She didn't like you very much, did she?"*

Ayc rolls his eyes. *"Well, we could always call you Little Shit. I think that suits you well."*

"Some days, I really wonder why I haven't eaten you yet."

They choose a clean, spacious stall, relieved to find it laid with a heavy layer of fresh straw. Ayc sets up the cot while Muffin flops into the straw. They stare through the slats in the wood into the next stall over, where the goats are bleating at the smell of a predator in their midst.

"Food?" Muffin asks, with hope in their voice.

"No," Ayc says, *"not food."*

"We ate goat last night."

"Yes, but we can't eat these *goats."*

"Why?"

"Because the owner is very attached to them."

Muffin peeks through the opening once more, then gives Ayc an accusatory look. *"The owner is not joined to this goat."*

"I mean emotionally."

Muffin blinks. *"So you two-legged creatures decide what animals are food based solely on emotions?"*

Ayc shrugs and unrolls his blanket over the cot. *"Yeah, basically."*

The dragon snorts. *"Ridiculous."*

Ayc collapses on the cot. A groan escapes him as his back meets the unforgiving surface.

Muffin's head appears in Ayc's field of vision. *"Are you wounded?"*

"I'm fine."

Muffin cocks their head. *"What does one call someone who tells untrue things?"*

Ayc frowns. *"A liar."*

"Why are you a liar?" This time, Muffin is close enough that Ayc feels their snort, an icy breath of wind breezing past Ayc's cheek.

"I'm not lying," Ayc lies.

"Do you forget I can sense what you're feeling?"

Yes, perhaps Ayc did forget about that. He's not used to having someone constantly in his head. A horrible notion occurs to him. He sits up and swings his legs over the side of the cot. *"Do you sense everything I'm feeling?"*

"Everything," Muffin says, planting their rump on the ground but keeping their long neck stretched so they are still at eye level with Ayc.

"Everything everything?" Ayc repeats, something like panic swelling in his throat. *"Like when I look at Lora, what do you sense?"*

"It depends. Sometimes, you're sad. And sometimes, you get…" Muffin pauses, confusion fluttering across their connection. *"You get all…growly. Not angry, just kind of growly. It's very odd. What emotion is that?"*

Ayc clamps a hand over his forehead. Fuck. This dragon can sense him being *aroused*. He has to talk to Peregrin about how to shut off their mental link. Muffin did it once before when they escaped the kitchen. Certainly, Ayc can do it, too.

He's suddenly quite grateful that he never accepted any of the invitations that have been passed his way this week. A young, innocent dragon being in his head is not something he wants to contend with while he's fucking someone. But it hasn't been a dragon in his head that's kept him from falling into bed with someone else.

It's Lora.

Three nights ago, he made it to a handsome merchant's door, some stranger whose name Ayc didn't know. It would have been so good to patch the aching wound within him with some gorgeous man grinding into him. But as soon as the fae's lips touched his, Ayc froze. He felt nothing—not even arousal. All he could think of was the way Lora kissed him, her teeth sinking into his bottom lip as though she was claiming him. As though she meant to ruin him for anyone else.

There was once a time when he could hide his desires in the beds of other people. Not anymore.

"I sense it again," Muffin says. *"Are you wounded?"*

"No," Ayc says. *"Not exactly."*

"Then why did you make that noise?"

"My body is just…" He shakes his head, unable to come up with the right words to explain his everyday reality. *"It just hurts."*

"Always?"

"Yes. Some days are worse than others, but yes. Always."

They push themself to all four legs and let out a low growl. *"Unacceptable. I must fix it."* They pace toward the stall door before swinging back around. *"How do I fix it?"*

Ayc smiles faintly. *"It can't be fixed."*

Muffin shakes their head side to side. *"Why do you not speak to the woman? The one who helps the others when they are wounded?"*

"Reselda?"

"If that is her name."

"Yes. She's a healer."

"Good. Go see her."

Ayc pushes himself to his feet. *"I'm fine."* He stretches his arms above his head to prove a point, fighting the wince as it pulls on the stiff muscles around his spine. *"See, I'm just f—"*

Muffin lets out a snarl so fierce, Ayc jumps. It's the loudest roar he's heard from the dragon, a reminder that they are not actually a child. They are a fierce and awesome creature. *"Stop lying!"*

Ayc swallows. *"She can't fix this, Muffin. She already told me so. She can't make the pain go away."*

"Can she make it better?"

Ayc shrugs. *"I don't know."*

"Then go. See."

Ayc sinks down on the cot again and lets out a long breath. *"I don't want to."*

"Why?"

Ayc lifts his hands. *"I don't know."*

It's not a lie. He doesn't fully know why he doesn't seek help. He knows he needs it. He knows, objectively, that he won't be less if he asks for that help. If anyone he loved was experiencing what he is experiencing, he would drag them to a healer himself, like Bronwen did for him. So why can't he bring himself to go?

He doesn't know, only thinks that perhaps he'll have to stop running from this, to stop pretending that one morning he's going to wake up and find his pain gone. Once he admits he needs help, he'll have to accept that his body is forever broken, and then he'll have to do the hard work: facing the pain and figuring out a way to live with it.

Muffin's voice grows softer. *"What is that word you humans use when you really want someone to do something?"*

"I don't know what you mean."

"Yes, you do. The one that sounds like begging".

"Oh. I think you mean 'please'."

Muffin rests their chin on Ayc's knee and gazes up at them with their large red eyes. *"Please. See the healer, Ayc. Please."*

And how the fuck can Ayc say no to that?

Ayc eats his dinner outside the Pink Elk at a table tucked into the corner of the flower garden that surrounds the inn. Even so, he thinks the people inside might still be able to smell him.

When Ayc knocked on Reselda's private room on the upper floor of the inn, she didn't demand answers for why he'd avoided her for so long. She simply smiled and helped him. The salve she massaged into his back and shoulders was strangely warm as she applied it, a heat that eased his muscles, followed by a coolness that quieted his rattling nerves. Along with an extra-strong pain tonic, it has eased the pain from a scream to a whisper. But the salve also reeks so strongly of mint and cayenne pepper, it makes his eyes water. It's not a bad smell; it's simply overpowering.

Hence, he's decided to eat outside. He would have returned to the stable, but Xylie is there, keeping an eye on Muffin, and he knows as soon as Xylie smells him, she's going to know. Fuck, she probably already knows and is just waiting for him to confess it, the same way he's waiting for her to confess whatever deal she made with the Supreme. Neither one of them wants to press. Fools, the both of them.

So he takes his time eating the roasted chicken and vegetables, all drizzled in a delightful lemon and thyme sauce, hoping that by the time he finishes, he'll stink less. Maybe then, he'll dare to explore the inn to confirm his suspicions about Vidar.

Torches hang from poles around the yard, creating a soft hue of orange that holds the night at bay. He studies the shadows lingering around the edges of light. Now that his pain is better under control, it might be a good time to practice. He sets down his fork, removes his bracelets, and sets them carefully on the table.

The more time he spends without the bracelets on, the more different he feels. His senses sharpen as his Drakr side becomes unleashed. The night air feels crisper on his skin, the stars seem brighter, and the voices around the corner of the inn, scarcely whispers before, become audible.

"—the reports Briar gave me seem thorough. No evidence points to the culprit being in Bromalis."

There's a grunt, and Ayc recognizes that sound. Peregrin. It must be Irving who's talking.

"You think Briar is hiding something?" Irving asks.

Ayc vanishes into the shadows and slips around the corner to where Peregrin and Irving sit at a table, one lit up by a nearby window that looks directly into the main room of the Pink Elk. From where the two sit, they both have a clear view inside the inn —a direct line of vision to where Lora sits at a table in the lobby. The sight of her nearly snags his attention like a hand on his throat, but Ayc forces himself to remain focused on Peregrin and Irving.

"Do I think Briar put midnight in Lora's bed or arranged for it to happen? No," Peregrin says. "Do I think he knows more than what he's saying? Perhaps."

They pick up one of the papers that are scattered over the table, next to their half-eaten plates of food. Most likely, it's Briar's most recent report regarding his investigation into who put midnight in Lora's bed. Briar went over it in his meeting with Lora and her Five days ago. Ultimately, the report's only value was to show that their investigation is continuing, but they've found nothing.

"You don't trust the regents," Irving states. It's not a question.

"Trust them to do what? Put their people before their own wants and desires? No. Be loyal to Lora? Only if they think it profits them to do so, and after this week, she's making it very clear that her sole interest is no longer just the rich and the powerful."

Irving turns his head toward the window. "She has surprised me."

"Lora is not Yris's daughter." Peregrin picks up his spoon and uses it to poke at a potato on his plate. "She's Josias's, through and through."

Irving's eyes widen. "Josias? She's *Josias's* daughter?"

Peregrin nods.

"Fuck, what else did they rob from my brain?" Irving scrubs a hand over his forehead. "Josias and Yris? How did that happen?"

Ayc shifts another step closer.

Peregrin gives a wolfish smile. "I hope I don't have to explain the mechanics to you, darling. Surely, they didn't take *that* from your brain."

Irving shoves Peregrin in their shoulder, but a dimple flashes briefly in his cheek. "You know what I mean. The Josias I knew would never have touched Yris."

Peregrin's smile falls, replaced with something more solemn. "Do you truly not remember?"

Irving rubs his hand over his forehead. "I remember... something, I think. Just not Lora. The more I realize what I do and don't remember, the more strange it seems. I read a book once on dark magic that had a chapter on the ability to search and steal memories. It's a messy and chaotic magic. I remember the advice that, if one was at the mercy of a person attempting to search their memories, they should try to focus on selective, safe memories and avoid thinking of what you do not want them to see. I wonder if I did that. If I resisted. And that's why I remember *some* things about you and not others."

"Shhh," Peregrin says. They pick up an abandoned potato on their plate and throw it in Ayc's direction. It strikes him right between his eyes.

"Fuck," Ayc says. He lets himself reappear, standing beside the table.

"Ayc," Peregrin says levelly, "if you're going to sneak around in the shadows, you probably shouldn't reek of divine-damned muscle salve. Why *do* you smell like muscle salve?"

Ayc rubs away a bit of marinade the potato left on his brow. "I tweaked my back sleeping in the stables. That cot is abysmal."

"Liar!" Muffin snarls across their mental link.

Ayc jumps and looks around him, surprised he doesn't find the dragon next to him. Fuck. He's uncertain he'll ever get used to their connection. Speaking of.

"Can you shut the mental link you share with Tempest?" Ayc asks. He pushes his hands into the pockets of his trousers and rocks back onto his heels. Trying to look casual and not like he's, you know, wanting to prevent a dragon from knowing that he can't look at Lora without wondering what it'd be like to have her legs wrapped around his shoulders.

"Yes," Peregrin replies. "Of course. It can be hard to have no privacy, even in your own mind."

"Can you teach me?"

"Of course, boy. You need only to ask. In exchange, perhaps you could practice signing with me, so I can communicate with Xylie better. I've been learning signs from books, but it would help to have someone to converse with. It doesn't seem fair to ask Xylie to do it. Especially when I should have devoted more time to learning her preferred method of speech long ago."

"Yes, of course," Ayc agrees quickly.

Ayc glances into the inn, watching Vidar as they lay another platter of food on the table, and then heads back toward the kitchen. It occurs to him the opportunity he has before him. Peregrin knows far more than they ever reveal. "Peregrin, do you know how Vidar got involved in Lora's organization?"

"Yes," Peregrin says. "I recommended him."

"Oh." Ayc arches an eyebrow. "And how did you get to be friendly with an innkeeper in Bromalis?"

"Zinnia has family in the area. We've stayed here when we were visiting."

Ah. Ayc forgot Zinnia grew up not too far from here. They visit her family frequently. Perhaps they stayed at the Pink Elk while traveling to see them. It's strange that Ayc knows more about Zinnia's family than he does about Peregrin. He's uncertain he even knows what clan Peregrin hails from; they rarely ever speak of themself and their past.

"Vidar's a good soul," Irving adds. "That damn bird of his is a menace, though. Dawn has as big a temperament as Tempest wrapped into her little body."

Dawn. Dawn. Dawn.

The name echoes in his head. It's just what Wren said. *The dawn rises in pink.*

A falcon called Dawn, whose talons have been painted a glorious pink. In an inn also gloriously pink.

Ayc grins. *Found you.*

THIRTY-ONE

AYC

Vidar isn't behind the desk when Ayc enters the inn, so Ayc does something that, as a baker, he knows he shouldn't do.

He walks into someone else's kitchen uninvited.

Vidar stands over the counter, slicing a large carrot. The soft chop, chop, chop is interrupted by a rush of air and a shrill cry too close to Ayc's ear. He flings himself into a crouch moments before Vidar's falcon soars where his head just was. The bird snips angrily as it circles around to land on a pot rack that dangles from the ceiling.

Ayc straightens. "Fuck. That bird doesn't like me."

Vidar smiles as he continues to chop the carrot. "Dawn doesn't like many people, but if you're just going to barge in here, the least you can do is make yourself useful." Vidar nods to the pile of vegetables and apples on the counter next to him. "There's a cutting board in that cupboard." He lifts his knife to point. "Unless it's beneath the Fifth."

"Happy to help." Ayc washes his hands at the sink, then gives Dawn the Falcon a wide berth when approaching the cabinet. He snags a wooden cutting board from beneath a haphazard pile of bowls and grabs a knife from the holder on the counter. "What are we making?"

"Porridge."

Ayc frowns at the onion and potatoes in the pile of vegetables but bites his tongue and selects an apple. No sense risking angering Vidar by questioning his cooking skills, though Ayc may want to find and hide the salt if any of them have any hope of eating breakfast come morning. "Diced then?"

Vidar nods.

Ayc sets to work on the apple. He has to tread carefully. Vidar will only give him the coin if he thinks Ayc worthy of it, so he bides his time. "How long have you owned the inn?"

Vidar grabs another carrot. "For nearly ten years now. I ended up in Bromalis about a year after the Creed massacre."

Ayc's hand stills. He swallows hard and grounds his feet into the wood floor of the kitchen to remind him he isn't standing on the blood-soaked floor of Creed castle. He resumes digging out a bruise in the apple's flesh.

Vidar goes on, "After the new treaty was signed between Everadyn and Drakr, me and my wife knew we needed to get out. We took the chance to reach here. Thought it better than staying in Aluina and working ourselves to an early grave so the human dukes and their Drakr overlords could live in prosperity." He pauses. "You can leave the bruise. No one will notice when it's cooked down."

"Lora will notice. She always does." Even in apple desserts, Ayc noticed that Lora would never eat more than a couple of bites if he didn't remove the bruises. When he did, she would eat the whole dish. He picked up on it in the first few years of being Yris's baker, and it became habit to always remove the bruises, even when Lora was in Totus Omni or Adamant and wasn't there to eat the dessert.

Vidar pauses, giving Ayc a long look before he nods. "Go ahead then."

Ayc traces the edges of the bruise carefully with the knife.

"You said your wife." Ayc lets the statement linger in the air, asking no questions and letting Vidar explain if he wants.

"She didn't make it out of Aluina. The Drakr guard the borders. Many try to leave. I'm one of the lucky few who made it, and I'm grateful for the people who helped me, or I would not have. It was always my Sigrid's dream to own an inn, and pink was our favorite color." He sniffs and mutters, "Damn onions," though he's only cutting a potato.

Ayc pretends not to see the way his eyes rim with red. "I'm sorry for your loss."

Vidar nods. "I tell myself that I'm lucky to have had a love that was so deep I still feel it like a knife wound after all these years. Doesn't make it hurt any fucking less."

"No, it doesn't."

Neither speak for a long moment. Ayc does not disturb the respectful silence. He lets the air fill with nothing but the knives hitting wood, the ruffle of Dawn's feathers, and a quiet sniff.

"How long has it been since you stepped foot in Aluina?" Vidar asks.

"Ten years," Ayc says. "I was a boy when I left, and I know almost nothing about what it's like now. No one ever talks about Aluina, even the other humans I've met."

"Well, they wouldn't speak to someone in Yris's court, would they? Even another human. It would break the oath."

Ayc frowns. "What oath?"

"The settlers' oath." Vidar must read the confusion on Ayc's face because he continues. "It's an oath Yris made us all take when we settled here. To not speak of Aluina and be completely loyal to Everadyn. I'm not even supposed to display the goddess I have on the mantle. Some ass might report me, but fortunately, I find most fae in Bromalis don't seem eager to enforce it."

Another thing Ayc has been foolishly unaware of, but now that he's Fifth, he has the power to change it. He makes a note to bring it up to Lora as soon as possible. Surely, if it's a law Yris made, the new Sovereign can override it. Everyone, no matter where they now live, should have the freedom to remember, celebrate, and love the place they came from.

"Did you not take the same oath when you came here?" Vidar asks.

Ayc hesitates, unsure how to answer. Then he remembers that he's no longer bound from telling the truth. "I didn't come here willingly. Yris took me."

Vidar sets the knife down and presses his palms into the kitchen counter. "Took you from where?"

There's heft in the question, and Ayc weighs it carefully. Do members of Asbjorn know what really happened in Creed? Wren didn't seem to know, didn't seem to put the pieces together of where Ayc truly came from. But then, Wren was lying and playing games with him from the start. Maybe she knew exactly where he came from.

"From Creed," Ayc says at last. "I was the sole survivor, the only person she let live."

Vidar curses. "Why are you telling me that? Yris might not be Sovereign, but that doesn't mean she won't still try to take your tongue."

"She's kept the truth in the shadows long enough." Ayc sets down the knife and reaches into his pocket for the coin. "And speaking of truth." He sets the coin down between them.

Vidar's eyes disappear behind his eyebrows as he glares down at the coin. He turns on his heel and marches to the kitchen door. He slides the bolt closed and locks it down before turning back to Ayc, his arms crossed over his chest. "Who gave you that?"

"Wren of Bromalis."

Vidar shakes his head as he returns to the counter and picks his knife back up. "Bold of her to think we'll still trust her judgment."

"If I have to prove myself worthy of someone else for the leader to accept me, I'm willing to do it."

Vidar gestures at him with the point of the knife. "You're half Drakr."

Ayc flinches. That news seems to have spread across Everadyn by now, along with whispers of Ayc's dragon. But the way Vidar says it makes it clear that Vidar sees it as a flaw. "I'm Aluinic first."

"There are many in Asbjorn who won't be so convinced." He strums his fingers through his beard. "Yris didn't know you were Drakr, did she? If she had, you would have been her assassin and not her baker. How'd you keep it hidden for so long?"

"With great personal sacrifice." One he still feels now. Why he stinks of muscle salve. "I wasn't going to let her make me a monster."

Vidar chops an entire potato, and Ayc dices three apples in perfectly even cubes before Vidar speaks again. Ayc feels every one of those moments like an itch beneath his skin.

"I met Ohen," Vidar says. "He stayed with me for a bit. He told me you were the one who went into that Lux Aester camp to get him. Used your Drakr abilities to do it. Why did you help him?"

It's not just a question. It's a test. Ayc doesn't know what answer Vidar wants, but he decides honesty—the painful, ugly truth—is the best path forward.

"Because I was once a boy who needed rescuing, and no one came for me."

They tried. Ayc knows they did. Peregrin, Irving, and Zinnia all protected Ayc but couldn't pry him out of Yris's talons. Lora shielded him all she could, and when she knew about the stone, she chose to free him. And Xylie. Even as a scrawny, traumatized kid, she gave him a reason to stay on the worst of the days, when the thoughts that ensnarled his brain grew dangerously dark. When his existence seemed too much, and death beckoned like a reprieve. Then Xylie flew across the ocean and made a deal that she still will not speak of. That certainly didn't mean nothing. All those kindnesses are why he survived.

"Ohen was a kid who needed help," Ayc goes on, "and I had the power to help him. I have the power to help Aluina. Please, let me help my people."

Vidar stares at him for a long, long moment, and Ayc isn't sure what he sees. He just hopes it is enough.

"All right," Vidar says at last.

He goes to a tall cabinet, whose contents Ayc can't see from his angle. There's the banging of pans and a rustling of jars and a few swears from Vidar. When he returns, he holds a coin in his hand. He picks up the knife and scrawls Ayc's name across the back. He lays it beside the one Wren gave him.

Ayc scoops them up and tucks them back in his pocket, swallowing down a tangle of emotion. Two down, three to go. "Thank you. For your faith in me."

"Don't thank me yet. You've got a long road ahead of you." Vidar shifts his hand on the knife and lifts it, directing the point toward Ayc's face. The way he holds doesn't resemble a cook. It resembles someone who uses it to carve things other than chicken. "And you can't tell our lady. I'd cut your tongue out now if I thought you'd say anything."

Ayc laughs, a bit nervously. "Is that something you have experience in? Cutting out tongues?"

"Makes good soup." He shrugs and returns to chopping.

Ayc cringes. He's never eating anything Vidar cooks again. Ever. "Do I get a clue on whom to get the next coin from?"

"Seek the queen who walks on water but never on land."

Great. Clear as mud. Ayc puffs out a breath. "What is it with Asbjorn and riddles?"

"It's not a riddle," Vidar says flatly. "If you can earn her trust, I think you'll be able to convince *anyone* in Asbjorn. She fucking hates Drakr. She's more likely to show you your intestines than engrave your name on a coin."

Ayc blinks at Vidar. He grins and reaches across the counter to slap Ayc on the shoulder hard enough it hurts. "Good luck. You're going to need it."

THIRTY-TWO

LORA

"What is this?" Yris demands.

Lora drags hard on the pipe she holds between her teeth. Judging by the look on her mother's face, she's going to need the aid of Reselda's herb even more now, or the migraine that has settled like a hoof pick behind her right eye is never going to surrender its hold. It's lingered since she returned to Wyntra five days ago, and she's desperate to be rid of it before they head to Audori in two days.

Veni hesitates at the door to the Sovereign's office as though he senses Lora might regret her decision to allow Yris in. He drags his thumb across his throat as he signs. *"Do you want me to kill her?"*

Normally, Lora might have kept her expression schooled, but she's held the smoke in her lungs too long. She coughs. Yris jerks her head around, and Veni wipes his expression into something more solemn before slamming the door behind him.

Lora sets the pipe down and unfolds her legs from beneath her. She places her feet squarely on the floor. She was so enjoying sitting curled in the chair—a wide plush one she exchanged her mother's with—smoking her pipe for the last ten minutes, but she doesn't want to deal with the lecture about poise and grace befitting of a Sovereign that Yris always loves to give. "What can I do for you, Mother? By the look on your face, I suspect it's not just a new agricultural report."

To Lora's abundant surprise, her mother listened to Lora's instructions while she was gone. She kept Wyntra from burning down and left anything that was not urgent for Lora to deal with when she came back. She did leave little notes, suggestions for how Lora should handle the situation in the margins of reports, but Lora would have expected nothing less.

Yris lifts a paper. She holds it so tightly, it crunches in protest. "What is this?"

Lora has to squint at it to read it properly. She makes out the first line. Whoever copied it did a wonderful job capturing Lora's flourished handwriting.

By royal decree of Loraphne, Sovereign of Everadyn, and her Five...

"Are you having trouble reading in your older age?" Lora asks. "Because I would think it would be self-explanatory."

Shit. Perhaps the herb is impacting her. It doesn't sound like something she would normally say. It sounds like Ayc. Perhaps he's rubbing off on her, but she can count on one hand the number of hours she's seen him since returning to Wyntra. Most of his time is spent with Muffin, attempting to teach the dragon to fly, or with Peregrin, learning how to close the mental link with the dragon, or in the dungeon with Bronwen, practicing his shadow affinity. She hears that neither the flying nor the affinity is going well, but her reports are from Bronwen or Xylie. Lora has not dared to ask Peregrin, knowing their response will only be, "Go ask Ayc yourself." Which Lora would do if she could trust herself to be alone with him for any length of time. She can't even listen to him speak without wanting his mouth back on her body.

It's torture to be near him, and it's even worse to be apart. She misses him. It's the only word for the ache behind her sternum whenever she thinks of him. It seems ridiculous to miss someone she sees every day, but she does.

"This is exactly what I'm trying to warn you about." Yris crumples the paper into a ball and tosses it onto Lora's desk. "Do you understand how this looks? The first decree you make, and it's for the benefit of *Aluina* citizens."

"No, it concerns Aluina immigrants, who are now Everadyn *citizens*. And I would not have had to do it if your law was not a *bad* law."

A law that Ayc had to point out to Lora because, somehow, she didn't know that those who fled here from Aluina were forbidden to speak of their former country. Perhaps it made sense she didn't know. Humans she met would either have assumed she already knew or thought it too dangerous to speak to her of it.

"Their loyalty to Everadyn is a small request in exchange for safety," Yris says.

Lora speaks slowly, like she's talking to a petulant child. "If it's a matter of loyalty, why isn't the same law applied to any other home country? Neither fae nor humans from Tenebra are subjected to the same requirement. Nor are the dwarves."

Yris folds her arms over her chest. "You're distracting from the point."

"Which is?"

"That the first decree you made as Sovereign was not in the interest of the Everadyn people."

Lora presses the pad of her thumb into the place just beneath her eyebrow where her headache pounds. With every word Yris utters, the pain is getting worse. "Again, the immigrants *are* Everadyn. The decree freeing them from the oath benefits them and harms no one else. Besides, it was not the only decree. We also sent a notice at the same time, which stated that we will be making further funds available to provide resources so *all* children can have accommodations in order to attend internships at clan schools."

Lora reaches across to tap the lower half of the paper, which has the second part of the decree right above her signature and those of her Five. It also gives contact information for the head of education, so parents and caregivers can send letters for further information or specific requests. Xylie and Tavish, with the help of Lovelace—her new accountant—found plenty of funds to pay for the further resources.

Lovelace also found multiple discrepancies in funds, places where the sum of the treasury increased without there being any clear record of where the money came from. Sometimes, it was noted as 'weapon forgery assets.' But it made no sense why that money was coming in and not going back out. Lora was certain it was her mother doing something illegal, but when she asked Yris about it, she simply said the numbers must be in error.

"Don't be obtuse," Yris says. "No one will notice that. It affects so few. I taught you how people are. If something doesn't directly benefit them, they believe it harms them. They believe if someone gained something, they must have lost something."

"People should not be so selfish. They've lost nothing."

Yris screws up her nose. "It doesn't matter if they *should* be. People are *exactly* that selfish. Are you not aware of Lux Aester's opinion on immigration? What about Audori and Noxumbra? The regents of those clans will not react kindly to this decree. It doesn't reflect their position on the matter."

"Well, it reflects *mine*." Lora shoves up from the desk, ready to escort Yris to the door.

But Yris chooses that moment to seat herself in one of the tall-backed chairs before the desk and folds her hands into her lap. "You need to take my advice. Politics is chess." She gestures to the space where her chess table once was. The chessboard is gone; Lora had it removed, but the ghosts of all the long lessons there still linger. "You must understand each piece in play and the unique way they move. Only then can you properly orchestrate a successful campaign."

Lora rubs her temple, the ache growing.

"Do you want my advice?"

"No."

Yris continues without hesitation, "You need to follow this

decree with something widely popular. Work with the regents to pass something more popular. Get them on board, get them to vote, and then announce it in a decree. Most people will be none the wiser and will give you all the credit. Tax cuts are always well-received."

"As long as the richest always get the largest cut, right?" Lora snaps back.

Yris lifts her hand in a delicate shrug. "Gold talks."

"Only if people listen."

"Never forget that your power is precarious, Lora. Our legacy—"

"*My* legacy," Lora corrects, and there's more snarl to her voice than she means. Lora is *trying*. She's aware of the delicate scale she treads upon in order to push fae—some of whom lived through the entirety of her grandfather's reign—into a new era that she and her Five dream of. Is it not enough that she didn't demand it in one day? Is it not enough that she is denying herself the things she wants to be the Sovereign she must be? Is Ayc not enough of a sacrifice to prove her devotion?

The thoughts are illogical, and she draws a breath through her teeth. The smoke is settling into her bones and blood, easing her rattling nerves and her lightning mood.

Her next words are steadier. "You've had your reign, Mother. This is mine. If you truly want to help me, you can focus on helping me achieve that."

Yris's back stiffens, and Lora waits for her to either stand and leave or remain sitting and argue. She does neither. She merely sighs once more. "Very well."

Lora isn't certain she means it. Before she can press her on it, something catches in the corner of her eye. She spins toward the window. Three silhouettes have appeared in the sky over the sea: three gryphons and the dragon they are escorting to land. No alarms are sounding, so it must be Damara.

But she's a day earlier than she said she would be. There's already a knock on the door, probably Irving having received a message of Damara's arrival from the gryphon riders and awaiting Lora's commands. And Lora is foolishly intoxicated with smoke, the effects making her mind foggier by the moment.

This Drakr bitch is officially starting to piss Lora off.

AYC

"Dragon!"

Muffin yells the word as they jerk out of a dead sleep on Ayc's bed, nearly startling Ayc from his skin. His kitchen stool tilts beneath him, and he seizes the counter. His shadow affinity snaps out of his control with a suddenness that makes the cost, the pain, rattle through his nerves like an explosion. The shadow he was controlling evaporates like smoke. The spoon in the center of the table has not budged at all.

"Dragon!" Muffin roars again as they scurry from the bedroom and into the kitchen; even with their wings tucked to their sides, they can barely make it through the doorway. *"A dragon is here!"*

Ayc hurries to his window. A flurry of activity unfolds in the courtyard, castle guards scurrying onto the parapet to stand at the ready. Something is happening, but Ayc didn't think Damara was supposed to come until tomorrow. Ayc rushes past Muffin into his bedroom to swiftly change into his leather armor and coat. He's become much more efficient in getting it on quickly. Soon, he's hopping on one foot back to the kitchen, pulling on his boots as he goes. He stops by the counter to grab his leather bracelets and fasten them into place.

Muffin peers out the window. They are tall enough to not have to put their front feet on the window anymore. It's difficult to believe that they are scarcely a month old.

"Stay here," Ayc says.

"Why can't I see the dragon?" they demand.

"Because they can't know I'm a dragon rider. If they do, they might kill you—or both of us—to eliminate us as a threat."

Muffin blinks, and Ayc is certain they'll argue. But the dragon is stubborn and pigheaded. They aren't a fool. "*All right.*"

Their head hangs, and a wave of emotion pours across their link. It makes Ayc's chest ache. It's an emotion he knows well because he's felt it many times.

Loneliness.

Ayc swallows. Later. He will have to figure out a solution for that later.

He heads for the door and nearly collides with the person standing just on the other side. He stops short, avoiding contact, but his heart doesn't seem to know the difference. It pounds against his sternum in a rhythm that almost matches some of his favorite songs. Fast and too loud and far too familiar.

Lora.

"I need your help," she blurts before he can quite get his bearings.

"What do you need, my lady?"

She seems to flinch at the formal greeting he's been using lately. But he's not using it as a term to create seperation. It's using it as a term of affection, a recognition of the power she has over him, one that goes far beyond her being his Sovereign. She's the only one he's called 'my lady' without begrudging it.

"I'm—" Lora hesitates. She glances at Veni and Magdon, a newer guard who has told Ayc that xir brown skin harkens from xir fae father, but xir shortness and stoutness speak of xir dwarven mother. The two guards take the silent cue and retreat down the hallway to give them space.

Lora lowers her voice. "Damara has come a day early, and I've... partaken of an herb that Reselda gives me for my migraines."

Ayc remembers Reselda mentioning a particular plant she had, though she's yet to offer Ayc any. So far, she's been giving twice-weekly massages and daily exercises to strengthen the muscles of his core, both of which have been helping. She's encouraged him to return to swimming in the ocean. She believes both the frigid cold of the water and the exercise to be therapeutic, and he's been doing it. It's hard work, caring for himself. It helps that Muffin threatens to bite his ass if he tries to slack.

"It's the only thing that really helps," Lora continues to explain, "but it clouds my thinking and my judgment."

Realization dons, and Ayc lowers his voice. "Are you talking about—"

She cuts him off. "Yes, *that* herb."

He knows the one. He remembers the smile on Evander's face when he lit up a pipe of it one day, saying it held lots of medicinal purposes. It could be used for nausea, headaches, pain, and even refined into an oil to help control seizures. But when Evander lit it, he gave Ayc a wink. *"But I'm not using it for any of those reasons. You can try when you're older."*

And now, Ayc notes how Lora's now-lilac eyes have a glassy, far-away look.

"Lora." A smirk crawls over his face as he leans against his door frame. He can't help it. "Are you high right now?

The color deepens in Lora's face. "No, not really. But I'm not fully sober either. And I want to be clear that I use it for *strictly* medicinal purposes."

He shrugs. "I don't care why you use it. You deserve to feel good."

I would make you feel so good if you let me.

He bites down on his tongue hard to keep hold of the thought, but he must make a face because Lora frowns.

"What?"

"Absolutely nothing." But his smirk grows wider.

"Shut up!" she snaps, her color deepening further.

"I didn't say anything."

"Your face said it for you."

"I can't help it. I only have the one face, my lady," he says with a laugh.

She bites down on her bottom lip. She almost looks, for a moment, like she's trying to hold back her own laugh. She shakes her head like she's shaking it away. "The effects don't last long, and I didn't take much. I should be clear-headed in an hour. I just need you to entertain Damara for that long. Tell her I'm in a meeting or something."

"Done." Ayc straightens from the doorway and steps into the hallway. He carefully closes the door behind him. It's been repaired since Muffin chewed through it, but he doesn't lock it. He's certain that Muffin could charge through the door now if they really wanted, but he hopes they won't.

"Thank you," Lora says. "Take Tavish and Peregrin with you. Xylie, too, but only if she wants."

"Why not Bronwen?"

"I last saw her an hour ago when she came to take some of the herb. I don't trust that she'll be able to control her emotions—or her powers—around the Drakr right now."

Ayc nods. "I'll handle it. See you soon, Your Royal *High*ness."

He laughs at his own joke, ignoring the crude gesture Lora heaves at his back as he strides down the hallway.

"Dragon!"

Xylie's excited fingers flutter through the air as she sees Stjarna for the first time. The great blue dragon is already settled on his belly, his tail curled around his body like a gigantic cat. Its red eyes gleam in the last dying embers of sunlight.

"He's beautiful," Xylie signs. *"I wish I could talk to him the way you talk to Muffin."*

Ayc swallows. He still can't shake the feeling that Muffin made a mistake. If Muffin was going to bond with anyone, they should have bonded with Xylie. Ayc can only think that it must be his Drakr blood that led Muffin to make their choice.

Damara leans casually against Stjarna's shoulder, cleaning her fingernails with the tip of her knife. She straightens as she sees the welcome party. Peregrin takes a slight lead from the others while Ayc, Xylie, and Tavish remain in a line. Tavish left Saga behind in the castle, afraid of the dragon and dog interaction. His cane sweeps through the sand before him. A selection of royal guards follows after them. Gryphons and their riders pace on the cliffs above, ready to watch over the dragon in their midst.

"All this welcome party, just for me?" Damara says as she approaches them. "You shouldn't have."

She's dressed in dark, red-hued armor. Her hair is tangled, and her cheeks are flushed from the flight. Her face twists into a smile as she nears. It's a bit mischievous, maybe even a little wicked, and it strikes a chord because it's deeply familiar. His stomach twists.

Fuck.

She does, in fact, look a little like him when she smiles.

"What I want to know," Damara says, stopping before them, "is where have you all been hiding the dragon?"

THIRTY-THREE

AYC

"**D**ragon?"

This time, it's Ayc who blurts the one word. He blinks, hoping the look on his face comes off as bewilderment and not panic.

"Oh, aren't you adorable?" Damara coos. "Trying to play the fool, I see. Not the best move, considering Stjarna can *smell* them. All our dragons were worked up when we left last time because they knew there was a dragon here."

Of course. If Muffin sensed Stjarna, Stjarna must be able to sense Muffin. Ayc didn't truly think he would keep his dragon hidden for long, but still, a boiling mixture of rage and protectiveness blaze up his throat. He fears that if he tries to swallow it down, he might choke on it.

"Are they young?" Damara presses when no one speaks. "You certainly couldn't hide a larger dragon anywhere in this castle, so they must be small. Only a few weeks old, I'd guess."

Xylie glances at Ayc and shifts uneasily, but Tavish and Peregrin remain utterly still. No one answers her question, as though they are waiting for Ayc to speak. But he doesn't know what he can say that will fix this. Lying will do no good, but she can't be trusted with the truth.

Damara searches them over, then shrugs and turns back around. "Nevermind. I'm sure Stjarna won't take too long to find them once I give him permission. Not the best option because dragons aren't too picky about eating their young."

"Stay the fuck away from my dragon!"

The words erupt from Ayc's throat, a volcano of molten rage. He knows it's not the right move, the diplomatic one, but he can't help it. It's all he can do to grind his heels into the sand and not launch himself foolhardily at her, the threat to *his* dragon.

She swings back toward him, her wicked smile now victorious. "I should have known it would be you. I knew you were Drakr." She laughs. "Damn, I love it when I'm right."

Ayc instinctively reaches down for his magic, his power, but he's wearing his bracelets, and he can feel nothing there. Still, foolishly, the threat rises to his tongue. "If you go near Muffin—"

"You're going to what?" she cuts him off, her tone still amused. "Do you mean to tell me you have shadow affinity, as well as being a dragon rider? I doubt it, or at least, I doubt you'd stand a chance against me. You're doing us a favor by doing whatever it is you're doing to hide your scent. So long as you're routinely blocking, concealing, and hiding your Drakr side, you're creating blocks between you and your affinity. I suspect you're far from mastering it."

Damara's eyes shift to Peregrin, but Peregrin, uncharacteristically, doesn't intervene or say anything. Ayc hardly notices; he barely even comprehends what Damara is saying. He can only feel his boiling rage.

Damara holds up a hand. "Easy there, baker. You look like you're two seconds away from going for my throat. I didn't mean my threat. I'm here to *prevent* us from going to war. I'm not going to jeopardize that by harming Everadyn's only dragon. I just knew it would get a rise out of you. That bond *chafes* sometimes, doesn't it? Especially when it's new. And wait." She blinks as though just now realizing what he said. "Did you really name the dragon Muffin?"

"Yes," Tavish says with a nervous laugh. "It, uh, suits them." He keeps going, fumbling with his words but keeping up a smile, clearly trying to diffuse the situation. "Though I think personally Pearl would have been a better choice." He feigns a laugh.

"Pearl?" Damara repeats, her eyebrows sailing upward. "As in *white*? Is your dragon white?"

Ayc wants to snarl again, but he grabs hold of his emotions. He's supposed to be diplomatic, and now that it's clear Damara knows of the existence of the dragon, there's no harm in answering the question.

"Yes," Ayc says. "Why?"

"It's rare," Damara explains. "Extremely. Perhaps only black dragons are more rare. A black dragon hasn't, to our knowledge, been born since Queen Volkna bonded with her dragon three centuries ago."

"Three centuries?" Xylie's hands move quickly through the air. *"Dragons live that long?"*

Damara inclines her head. "What did she say?" The question is soft, curious, not at all annoyed.

Ayc repeats the question.

"They do," Damara replies, to Ayc's surprise. She seems much more willing to speak now that her brothers aren't here. "At least, they do when they're bonded. It's uncertain if they live that long in the wild. They so frequently die of unnatural causes. Killed by other dragons or by fae while hunting. Dying of starvation when food is scarce. Sickness." She shrugs. "Such is nature. Beautiful, but merciless."

Xylie's hands are already forming another question, but Peregrin clears their throat. "Perhaps we should walk and talk. It's getting dark."

"Ah, yes," Damara says. "On that matter, where is your Sovereign?" She looks over them again as though just now realizing Lora's absence.

"She got held up in another meeting," Ayc lies smoothly. "She will be along as quickly as she can, but she was expecting you tomorrow."

"Something came up, and I needed to come early. I didn't have time to send a message. Let's walk then."

Damara starts forward, following their footprints in the sand. Ayc follows just behind her, and the other three join. The guards take up the rear so they can watch Damara's every move.

Xylie signs another question, and Ayc hesitates. But Damara seems quite knowledgeable about dragons, and it would be wise to gather all the information they can—at least, for Muffin's sake.

"How long does it generally take a dragon to learn how to fly?" Ayc translates.

"They learn pretty quickly. From the younglings I've personally observed, it takes about two weeks. Why? Is yours not flying yet?"

Ayc doesn't admit it. Doing so might put Muffin in jeopardy. Instead, he asks another question, "What about fire?"

"Ah, that one generally takes a while. A few months or even up to a year. And you can't be certain your dragon will breathe fire. The dragons who have more rare coloring tend to have more unique abilities. Kivka, for example. Her pattern is very rare, and she can spit acid. Black dragons exuded this thick, near-toxic smog, legend says."

"Legends?" Tavish repeats. "Do you not know for sure? Have you not seen your grandmother's dragon?"

She stills but then proceeds to walk quickly once more, a missed step that reveals more than Ayc thinks she meant. "I try to avoid being at that end of a dragon I'm not bonded with. Teeth, smog, fire, it makes no difference. I try not to piss a dragon off, so I've never personally seen Nottirlyn's power. Interestingly enough, lore says that generations ago, black dragons also had the ability to disappear completely into shadow. Sound familiar?"

Ayc nods. "Very."

Damara pauses before the path that ascends the mountainside, gesturing to Ayc. "After you."

Ayc doesn't have any interest in putting his back to Damara, but he likes the idea of Xylie being closer to her even less. He steers Xylie to the front with a hand on her shoulder before he, too, steps onto the rocky path. When they are all climbing single file up the embankment, Ayc asks, "It's not a coincidence, is it? That black dragons may have had the same power as the Drakr."

"It's not. According to Drakr lore, the Drakr descended from dragons—specifically black dragons. Hence, why we have red eyes and sharp teeth, and why many of us have the power to hide in the shadows. You call it shadow affinity, and we refer to it as *drakinn ykur*. Translated as best I can to the Everadyn tongue, it means 'the dragon within us.' The stronger the power, supposedly, the more dragon blood that runs in our veins."

Ayc isn't certain he buys that myth any more than he gives any credit to the divine or the existence of gods, but it's fascinating. Xylie glances over her shoulder. She can't afford to speak for long, traversing the path, but she twists enough to toss a few signs Ayc's way. He recognizes the shorthand enough to put together her question.

"What does the lore say about Everadyn fae? Are they descended from gryphons, since they both have silver eyes?"

"She's sharp as a knife, that one," Damara says. "That's exactly what the lore says. The Tenebra fae are said to be descended from leviathans. Supposedly, leviathans had green eyes."

"And what do humans descend from?" Ayc asks, pausing to face her as they reach the top of the cliff, waiting for the others to join them.

She plants her hands on her hips and blows out a breath to chase away a strand of hair that fell over her nose. "I don't wish to repeat it."

Ayc grits his teeth. He can imagine it's something vile and cruel.

"Do you know what I think?" Damara asks.

"Hm?" Ayc muses.

She lowers her voice like it's their secret. "I think they descended from bears." There's a soft spark in her blue eyes, the shade of blue so like his own. "Have you ever seen the polar bears in the northern provinces of Aluina?"

"No," Ayc says. He's seen their hides, though, and heard the tales of hunters who stomped into his village of Hearth from over the mountains. They'd stop in his mother's bakery, trading some bear meat and a few stories for something sweet to eat. Ayc would stare wide-eyed, drinking in the tales.

"I have," Damara says. "I've watched one dive into a hole in the ice and drag a fully adult walrus out of the water. Fierce and frightening and glorious creatures. It's cruel to compare them to dragons and gryphons. They may not be able to fly, but that does not mean they aren't powerful in their own right."

The meaning of her words shivers across his skin like a ghostly touch. A reminder that they aren't so different after all. There's a connection there if Ayc lets it be forged. They are both half Drakr, both half human. Both dragon and bear, and it feels like she's trying to tell him that she doesn't find shame in either part of herself. But Ayc resists the pull. Whatever similarities they have, she is Lahlis's daughter. She serves her Queen, the wicked conqueror, willingly.

If she's trying to gain his trust, that means Ayc absolutely should not trust her.

"Was your mother from Aluina then?" Ayc asks to turn the questions away from himself.

Peregrin steps onto the cliff, the last to rise, leaning heavily on their cane. Damara's gaze flicks in their direction before refocusing on Ayc.

"Pay me no mind. I tend to talk too much after such a long flight. Let's go."

Silence wraps around the group as Ayc leads them back toward Wyntra. He keeps his pace slow down the path through the barracks, buying Lora more time. Damara falls into step beside him. If she notices the way the curtains stir in windows as she passes, she doesn't pay it any attention. She only saunters, like this is a leisurely stroll through a familiar path, and not her walking through an army that sees her as, if not an enemy, certainly a threat.

Ayc is almost to the courtyard when he realizes he might be missing a grand opportunity. If Damara is willing to trade information to gain his trust, perhaps he would be a fool not to use the circumstances to his benefit. To Muffin's benefit.

As they cross beneath the parapet, Ayc admits, "My dragon can't fly yet."

"Oh," she says like she already knew.

"Is there anything I can do to help them learn?"

She arches a brow. "Do *you* know how to fly?"

He shakes his head as he comes to a halt. He hears his name, a vibration across his mind, as though Muffin didn't say it so much as they thought it. Ayc glances toward the window to his kitchen. Muffin peeks out through the glass. Damara follows his line of vision, and Muffin swiftly ducks. Or at least, they try to. They forget to tuck their tail, so it can still be seen, the spade pointing toward the ceiling.

Ayc rubs his fingers over his forehead. This damn dragon...

Damara makes a noise, almost like a laugh she swallowed down before it could escape her throat. "Dragons weren't meant to learn to fly alone."

She tilts her head to her right. It might be just a stretch of her neck, or it might be a gesture. One that directs Ayc to Peregrin, who watches Damara with narrowed eyes. Ayc isn't certain if she did it on purpose, if she's truly helping him and his dragon. But the effect is the same.

He may not trust another dragon to come near Muffin. But he does know a gryphon.

"I'm sorry for making you wait!"

Lora's voice works its way across Ayc's skin like a shiver, making every nerve stand at attention. She strides across the courtyard toward them, Veni, Magdon, and Irving just behind her. Bronwen, however, is still missing, which is probably for the best. It hasn't quite been an hour, Ayc is certain, but Lora's eyes no longer have that glazed look to them. They are sharp and focused as they cut toward Damara.

"All is well," Damara says, inclining her head in a slight bow as Lora comes to a halt between them. "Your Fifth was delightful company. In fact, it's been so enlightening, I think I can end my visit there." She twists on her heel, back the way she came.

Lora blinks. "You're not staying? You just got here."

"And I'm expected back in the morning." Damara pauses and peeks back over her shoulder. "Unless you have something you would like me to report back to Lord Lahlis."

"No," Lora says. "There's nothing to report."

"I have nothing to report either. Fare thee well, my lady!"

She's already halfway through the courtyard before anyone shakes off the surprise enough to move. The royal guards follow after her.

"I'll call Tempest and follow her past our shores to ensure she's actually headed back to where she belongs," Peregrin says.

"Please do," Lora says. A deep line forms in her brow, one that only worries deeper as Peregrin presses their cane into the gravel with each step toward Damara. The Drakr must hear because she slows her gait to allow Peregrin and the guards to catch up.

Ayc stares after their retreating backs. He repeats the events over in his head—what she said, the questions she asked. All of that, and she's just gone. A heaviness settles on his chest, and he hauls a breath through his nose to steady himself as a realization sits in.

Perhaps they all know it, but it's Tavish who says it. "It's almost like she didn't come to see you at all, Lora."

"Maybe she didn't," Lora says. "What did she say to you, Ayc?"

"Nothing," Ayc insists. "We talked about Drakr lore and dragons and polar bears—" He stopped, realizing what that question about polar bears really attempted to establish. She was trying to gain understanding about Ayc's past, perhaps trying to locate where in Aluina he came from. Last time she was here, she asked him how he ended up in Wyntra. Was it casual conversation, or a plan devoted to digging up information? They certainly hadn't asked personal questions about any of the other Five.

Why the curiosity about *him*? Was it because Damara suspected he was Lahlis's child, as she insinuated, or because of something else? Were they making a connection to Creed?

The gravel scatters beneath Lora's feet as she turns around and marches back toward the door. "Ayc, come with me."

His feet follow her before he's fully aware he's moving. Xylie and Tavish do not follow as Lora leads him back into the castle and through the hallway.

"Where are we going?" he asks.

"To drag Bronwen from whatever stupor she's currently in. If we're going to protect you from whatever the Drakr are planning, then we need to find the information they're searching for before they do."

"Protect?" Ayc's hands curl into fists. "It's not your job to protect me."

"Yes, it is," she snaps.

He reaches for her arm, then remembers himself just in time. She jerks at the closeness of his touch, plants her feet on stone, and turns toward him.

"We're not fucking kids anymore, Lora!" he snaps.

Down the hallway, Ayc sees Irving hold up a hand to Veni and Magdon. They retreat backwards a few steps, but still, Ayc lowers his voice.

"I'm the one who's supposed to be protecting you now, remember?"

Lora's lips curl, and a little point of her tooth shows up against the full plane of her bottom lip. "Fuck that. Just because I became Sovereign doesn't mean I stop caring about you. I can't just snap my fingers and shut off all these years between us. If something were to happen to you—" She cuts off. Her eyes widen, her sharpened teeth retract, but she shakes her head, and whatever emotion fluttered across her face is gone. But it's enough to make him soften his voice.

"You would what?" he presses.

She shakes her head and walks away, but she only makes it three steps before she stops once more. She sighs, her shoulders sagging. "If you tell me you don't want me to dig deeper into your past, then I'll respect that. I don't think it's for the best, but it's your past."

A choice. She's offering him a choice, and Ayc's desire to resist fades that quickly. Perhaps that's the only thing he needed.

"What do you think Bronwen can do?" he asks.

"I don't know. Look at your bracelets again. Perhaps there's something she missed."

"There isn't."

Lora folds her arms over her chest. "Then perhaps it's time to summon a more powerful sorcerer." The line between her brow deepens. Ayc runs his thumbs over the tips of his fingers, trying to ease the itch that demands he touch her and soothe away the concern there.

"Do you mean the Supreme?" he asks.

"Yes. I know Bronwen said it isn't a good idea, but I don't know another option. If we want to figure out your past before the Drakr do, then maybe it's time for me to send the Supreme a letter."

Ayc remembers the fear in Bronwen's eyes the last time they discussed this. And if Bronwen's terrified, then they would be wise to be cautious. But Lora is also right. They need to know what the Drakr suspect, or it could endanger them all.

Ayc drags his thumb across the bracelets of his opposite hand, feeling the thick thread. Something Damara said comes back to him. Something about how, so long as he's blocking away his Drakr side, he'll never be able to control his magic? It seems strange that she would offer that advice. Foolish that she would mock him in a way to give him a clue of how to make his power stronger. Unless it's a trap. There's only one way to find out.

Perhaps it is time to take them off.

Perhaps it's time to face the truth of who he really is.

"It's up to you, Ayc," Lora says. "Should I send the letter?"

Ayc unfastens the buckle of his bracelet, knowing this time, he will leave them off for a long time. "Yes."

THIRTY-FOUR

LORA

Fortunately, Audori's welcoming party is much more subdued, a simple banquet compared to the Bromalis's extravagant ball. It's not nearly as loud, which Lora's nerves appreciate, but it's still theater. The banquet hall in Harlowe's mansion is decked in reds and golds and packed with more guests than it seems could fill the place. And she's seated at the head table on a lifted stage, dressed in a gown that matches the decor.

Fucking tailors.

The entire place reeks of the pan-seared halibut they are serving. The noxious smell of fish clings to her nostrils, and she has to bite back the wretch that lingers at the back of her throat. She shouldn't have been surprised. Forfyre, the main city in Audori territory, sits right on the Bellum Sea. The staple of their diets is whatever has been caught today by the fishers who patrol these coastlines. But Lora hates fish. The smell, the taste, the texture of the flesh.

Still, she keeps a smile pinned to her face. This is theater, and she is on display.

So she forces herself to ignore the smell and the crowd that stares at her. She pretends to be fascinated by stories Harlowe—who is seated on her right—tells, recreating how he used to make the most exquisite swords. She doesn't look at Ayc, seated on her left, because she knows if she does, she'll only stare at how good he looks in the gold-trimmed red corset vest he wears. She cuts her fish into tiny bite-sized pieces, buying time. When she can't procrastinate any longer, she stabs a piece with her fork and brings it to her lips, and then—when Harlowe leans to his other side to tell Bronwen the same story, Lora swiftly tucks the meat into the napkin on her lap.

It would be rude not to consume the food she's eating, but she fears if she puts it in her mouth, she might wretch. She tries a potato instead and presses her fingers to her lips to hide her gag. The vegetables have clearly been cooked in the pan with the fish because the briny flavor has seeped into the potatoes.

"Good?" Harlowe leans back to ask in Lora's ear.

She nearly chokes, but she swallows it. "It's fantastic. Thank you for going to such great lengths to prepare such an exquisite banquet for me. I—"

Her voice trails off, and from the corner of her eye, she catches a fork darting toward her plate, spearing a piece of fish, and retreating. Harlowe is too focused on her to have noticed, and she swiftly gathers herself to keep speaking.

"I'm quite looking forward to touring Forfyre's weaponry forge tomorrow," she says.

"Ah." Harlowe lifts his goblet and takes a drink. The fork once again steals a piece of Lora's fish. Lora shoots Ayc, who holds the fork in question, a quick glance before turning back to Harlowe by the time he lowers his cup. "I'm afraid that there won't be a tour tomorrow. There was a bit of a fire containment issue at the forge. Nothing major. Just enough it won't be safe for any extra people to be there."

"Oh. Perhaps I could tour another forge. I would like to speak to the workers."

The flat line of his mouth grows harder. "Perhaps." He turns away and leans across the table to speak with Tavish. "Tell me. How did you come to be Lora's Fourth?"

"That, uh, is quite a long story," Tavish says. "And involves pirates."

Lora can't shake the feeling of oddness that covers the exchange, but she can't quite figure out why it struck her as odd.

Ayc's fork goes for her plate a third time. She seizes his wrist. He's not wearing his bracelets; he hasn't for multiple days now. He said he feared it was causing a block in him mastering his magic. But now his skin contacts her palm. She releases him quickly, but the heat of him lingers like the sweet scent of perfume. Fuck, she hates him in that moment. Hates how glorious he looks with his hair falling loosely around his shoulders and the black once again lining his eyes. Hate how much her skin feels naked because he's not touching her.

She leans closer than she would normally dare, so only he can hear, and hisses, "What are you doing?"

"Eating your fish for you." He smiles and brings his fork to his mouth, placing the fish behind his teeth.

"Why?"

He swallows down the bite. "Because *you* hate fish."

She blinks. "How do you know that?"

"Because I know *you*." He rolls his eyes like it should be obvious. "I've known you forever. I noticed."

Well, he did serve her plenty of meals. He must have noticed how she wouldn't touch the fish on her plate, no matter how her mother yelled at her. No matter if she was made to sit there for hours. But then, Wylder, who was the closest thing she's had to a long-term partner, never noticed. Whenever Adamant served fish, he always told her to try it, no matter how many times she said she hated it.

Ayc glances around to ensure no one is looking directly at them before he takes another piece of fish from her plate.

"Someone will catch you," Lora warns.

Ayc shrugs. "Then we'll laugh like it's a funny joke. Better than someone finding it in your napkin."

Emotion coils up at the back of Lora's throat. He's being so unbelievably kind, and she doesn't deserve it.

She hurt him. He's done a good job of hiding it, but she knows she did. If he feels anything for her like she feels for him, then her choice hurts. And yet, here he is, tenderly caring for her as though it isn't a big deal at all.

She takes a trembling breath, afraid for a moment that she might actually cry.

And then the door to the banquet hall bangs open.

It's a gryphon rider. They are easy to identify by the gray armor and the pin of a gryphon's feather over their heart. They search around briefly before they locate Lora at the head table, and then they march straight for her.

If someone is sending a gryphon rider with a message, then it must be dire. Lora springs to her feet. The piles of red fabric, stenciled with elegant gold, are heavy, and she's forced to gather her skirts in her hands as she rushes around the table. Other chairs screech against the floor as people jump up to follow. A hush falls over the crowd as she sprints to meet the gryphon rider.

The rider bows deeply. "I have a message for you, my—"

"Outside," Lora says, nodding toward the door the rider has just come from.

They nod and pivot, and together, they march back through the door. She glances briefly behind her to find that Harlowe has followed right at her shoulder, as well as Peregrin and Ayc. Bronwen remains at the table, and when Lora glances back at her, she signs. *"Should I come?"*

Lora shakes her head. Bronwen, Tavish, and Xylie all remain at the table as though to assure the murmuring crowd that everything is fine.

In the hallway, Harlowe pushes the door closed. The hallway outside is narrow, forcing all of them to huddle together tightly. The gryphon rider ends up before Lora. Peregrin ends up on her right, Harlowe on her left, and Ayc between her and the wall behind her. She can feel his warmth, and she has to fight the instinct to lean toward him, like someone who's cold instinctively seeking the heat of a fire.

"Speak, soldier," Lora says.

A sheen of moisture covers their forehead. They smell of salt air and sweat. They've ridden hard and fast to get here.

"My name is Lieutenant Merciri. She/her. I was sent here from the Harenae Bay Garrison." Lora recognizes the name from the military maps she studied at Adamant. The post is just south of Forfyre, a couple hours' ride, and it is one of Everadyn's largest, though even the smallest of garrisons has at least two gryphon riders stationed at it to be able to deliver messages swiftly.

"We knew you were here," she continues, "and wanted to notify you as soon as possible that the navy warship, *Vanguard*, is missing."

"Missing?" Harlowe barks. "What do you mean it's—"

Lora holds up her hand directly in his face. "Let her finish her report." Perhaps she should simply dismiss him back into the hall, but if there is a warship missing off the coast of Audori, then Harlowe will be able to provide resources that she likely needs. So, she drops her hand and permits him to stay, so long as he's quiet.

He locks his jaw, but his lips seem to have lost a bit of their color.

Lora gestures at Merciri, and she goes on. "We expected the ship to arrive early this afternoon. It has not yet arrived. We've sent out gryphon riders to their last known location, but so far, we have found nothing. We knew you were here and wanted to be aware as soon as possible."

"You've found nothing," Lora says. "Not even a sign of wreckage?"

"Not even a single piece of driftwood," Merciri says. "The riders are extending the grid."

"How many souls are on board?" Lora asks.

"Three hundred and thirteen, my lady."

Ayc swears under his breath.

It's a relatively small crew for a warship. Some of their largest can carry up to eight hundred, but it's a number she can scarcely fathom, double the size of the people in the banquet hall. And they are all missing. It could have been a shipwreck, or it could be more nefarious. And if someone purposefully sank Everadyn's ship, the only way it can be interpreted is as an act of war. And this is not the first warship to go missing under mysterious circumstances. There was another at the end of last summer. She heard about it from reports in Adamant. They never found out what happened to the ship. There was only one survivor who washed up on shore, but the stories he told were muddled and confused. The healers feared the trauma was too much for his mind.

"Where was the ship coming from?" Peregrin asks.

"North," Merciri says.

Lora frowns. "From Wyntra?" That is the closest out-posting north, but their beaches are not generally meant to host warships. They can't dock but could anchor and take longboats ashore, but there certainly hadn't been a ship that size there when she left yesterday morning.

"I'm not certain where it was last docked," Merciri says. "Only what direction I was told to search."

"Do you know what the ship was carrying?" Peregrin asks.

"No, I'm sorry. I can fly back with your questions and ask Admiral Eira."

"That won't be necessary. I can ask her myself," Lora says. "Fly back and tell her I'm on my way. I will be there—" She does a careful calculation, considering how long it will take to mobilize her party of guards and attendants to move further south. They will have to travel through the night, and her party is already exhausted from the travel here. "As soon as I can. We'll leave immediately. I will bring my Fourth. If he can't find the ship, no one can."

Harlowe makes a choking sound in his throat. He hides it with a protest. "But the banquet—"

"I will not sit here and feast while over three hundred of my sailors are missing, and their loved ones fear for their safety!"

The ferocity in her tone is purposefully placed. Harlowe rubs at the red stubble on his face but doesn't argue again. "It would be quicker to go by the water. I have a personal vessel. It's small but fast. I'm not sure it will accommodate all of your party, but you're welcome to it."

"Thank you," Lora says.

Merciri still stands, not moving, her back stiff, her heels together. She reminds Lora of all the times she stood just like that, waiting for the professors and trainers at Adamant to dismiss her. And she realizes that's exactly what Merciri is doing.

"Thank you, soldier. You're dismissed."

"I'll give the admiral your message," she promises before sweeping a bow and turning on her heel. Her boots click along the hallway.

Lora faces Harlowe. She nearly brushes against Ayc's chest once more as she does so, making the knots in her stomach erupt in a fluttering of wings. "Is there a place I can meet with my Five in private?"

"My office, just up the stairs there. First door on the right." He pulls a key from his pocket and holds it out to her.

She folds it into her palm. The door to the banquet hall groans as it opens, and she realizes Ayc is already there. He sticks his head in and beckons. It's not long before the remaining three and Saga have joined them in the hallway. Harlowe attempts to follow them into the office, but Ayc pointedly closes the door in his face before he can enter.

Harlowe's irritated throat clearing can be heard through the door. "Let me know if you have need of anything, my lady." He curses under his breath, and then his feet carry him away.

Lora catches the other three up on the message. Bronwen's eyes grow wider by the moment, glowing in the light of the chandelier above them. Lora thinks Harlowe should talk to the alchemist or sorcerer who helped install the chandelier, which turns on at the flick of a switch. It's buzzing much louder than most lights do, a sound that feels like little pinpricks in her eardrums. At least she's escaped the smell of fish.

"It's eerily similar to the *Beholder*, the ship that went missing in the Southernmost sea last year, don't you think?" Bronwen asks. She's dressed in a red gown that hugs her frame like a second skin. The air around her seems calm tonight. The medicine that Reselda has been giving her takes time to work, but Bronwen says she already thinks it's helping. Lora knows it'll never take away from the darkness of grief, but she hopes it makes Bronwen feel less lost in it.

"I overheard Yris discussing it with Onanna," Ayc says from where he leans against the door. His arms cross casually against his chest. His puffed sleeves have been pushed up to reveal his forearms, revealing the iridescent lines of his dragon mark weaving up his arms. Lora drops her gaze to the floor at his feet. "Didn't the ship sink?"

"That's what we supposed," Lora replies. "But we weren't certain. We never found any signs of a wreckage. No bodies."

"Lack of bodies aren't too surprising in the Southernmost," Tavish says. He pulls at the straps of Saga's harness that hold the guide handle and pulls it from the dog. Saga shakes, now that he has the freedom to do so. "The sharks there like nothing more than when a ship goes down. Drowning was always the least of my fears in those waters."

Lora feels the heat drain from her face. Her phobia of the water seems far more realistic when she remembers what beasts lurk within the ocean.

"Lack of wreckage is peculiar, though," Peregrin says from where they sit in an armchair. "I know we sent our best gryphons and riders to search that region, and they found nothing."

"One survivor managed to get away in the rowboat," Bronwen recalls. "It was weeks later when he made it to shore, nearly dead from dehydration. The healers thought he drank the salt water because he was rambling and didn't make sense. Tragically, he died before he recovered. Blood poisoning from a shark bite."

Xylie signs, *"What did he say happened?"*

"Something about a pirate who walked on water," Lora replies.

Ayc stands up straighter. "What did you say?"

Lora frowns at the width of his eyes.

"Ah." Tavish pulls a ball from his pocket and tosses it for Saga. He chases after it. Without his harness, he's transformed from guide dog to puppy. "That's a common sailors' tale. It's not very old, though. I only recall hearing it in the last couple of years on Zephen's crew. They told a tale about a pirate queen—or some said a sea witch—that could walk upon the water from one ship to another and incapacitate an entire crew all on her own. But she would never dare step on land because if she did, it would destroy everything and everyone she touched."

As he speaks, his voice grows more distant. He stoops to pick up the ball that Saga dropped on his foot and squeezes it absently. He looks like he's a thousand miles away.

"Is there something you're not saying, Tavish?" Lora asks.

She waits for it. The telling way his cheeks puff up when he's trying not to say something. He's almost never been able to hide anything, not when asked about it directly, so she's comforted when his bright smile comes easily.

"No, I was just thinking about who first told me. Wasn't a great memory."

She doesn't press. He has many unkind memories from his time on Zephen's ship. He rolls the ball for Saga again, and the dog trots after it.

"That tale is exactly what the survivor said happened," Bronwen says. "The healers assumed it was simply his illness speaking."

"Is there—" Ayc begins. He grimaces and massages a hand into his shoulder. "Could there, uh, be any truth to the tale?"

"Maybe some grain of truth," Peregrin says. "That's what most superstitions in the military branches tend to be. One small grain of truth surrounded by dozens of salacious details to make it more interesting."

Ayc leans back against the door, but he's not nearly as relaxed as he was before. It's an unnerving tale, but she's certain Peregrin is right. No one can walk on water.

"I feel strongly that I need to be there to help with the

investigation," Lora says. "Tavish, I think you could especially be helpful. The question is should we all go by land? Or should we go by boat? It would be much faster, but not all our party can go. "

She looks around at them and waits patiently. She hopes they will say by land. She can handle being on a boat over water much better than she can handle swimming, but she loathes it. But she also recognizes the need for haste.

"If you get me out on the water," Tavish says, "I think I can find it much easier than trying to sense it from land."

"The sooner we get there, the more likely we are to find survivors," Bronwen says.

Well, that settles that.

Irving clears his throat, stepping forward from where he and Shae have been standing in silence near the bookshelves. "I want to be clear that this is a transportation to the garrison, not a search mission. If we are going by sea, we need to take you on the most direct path to the garrison and not deviate from the course."

"But if Tavish senses anything—" Lora protests.

"Then I can investigate on board Tempest," Peregrin interjects.

Lora nods in agreement. She's learned it's useless to argue with those two on anything when they agree, especially when it comes to matters of her safety. Mostly, because she knows they are probably right.

"What about Muffin?" Ayc asks. "If the ship is small, I'm uncertain they can be aboard it."

Lora nearly forgot about the dragon. They've grown once more, requiring an entire wagon by themself, and took up considerable room on the airship that flew them from Orchis to Forfyre. Certainly, they can't take Muffin on the trip, but she can't ask Ayc to leave them behind, either. It would be simpler if the dragon was flying, but though Tempest has been attempting to help them fly, Muffin is still only managing short distances. They wouldn't be able to make the flight down the coast over open water with nowhere to land.

"I suppose you can stay." She doesn't like the sound of that, and by the way his face contorts, he doesn't either.

"No. I go where you go."

She ignores the way her foolish heart attempts to grow wings and fly at that. She looks swiftly away from him toward Xylie.

"I can stay with Muffin," Xylie signs.

"You don't have to do that," Ayc says.

"Your eyes could be useful while we're sailing," Peregrin says. "As Drakr, I suspect you see far better than I do in the dark."

Ayc hesitates, staring at Xylie. There's a war going on within him. Lora can feel it in the way the room grows a little cooler, like on a sunny day when a cloud passes over the sun. The shadows seem a little more alive, like they're churning.

He releases a breath, and the room warms. "All right."

"Perhaps I should stay too," Bronwen says. "As your First, I can take part in the activities planned for you tomorrow. That way, people do not feel forgotten. That might soothe over any wounds your absence might cause."

It seems silly that people might not understand her absence, but then no one likes to feel less important than something else. Even if, objectively, a missing warship is far more important.

"I can extend your deepest regrets," Bronwen continues, "and assure them that you'll make an additional trip to visit them at the end of your scheduled Tour. Just, please, I beg you, don't do anything reckless between here and the garrison. Once there, you'll be surrounded by several sorcerers, I'm sure."

"We'll keep close to the shore," Irving says. "We'll take enough guards to ensure we can handle whatever we might come upon. Reselda and the attendants can stay."

Lora nods. A buzz of both excitement and anxiety vibrates through her palms. She fists them in the layers of her skirt. She longs to be back in her armor, with her swords at her sides. "It's settled, then. I'll tell Harlowe to ready his ship. Make whatever preparations you must. We leave in an hour."

AYC

"**V**idar, you have to be fucking kidding me," Ayc mutters as he stomps back to the stable where Muffin has been staying.

A queen who walks on water, but who never walks on land.

That's exactly what Vidar told him before saying it wasn't a riddle. It was a factual description. Now, Ayc finds out that there are tales describing exactly that, which have been going around for years. A pirate who can walk on water but never sets foot on land. And apparently, they're associated with entire warships going missing.

He'll have to return to Vidar and plead with him to let him meet with someone else, or he'll have to find other rebels on his own. There's no way he's going anywhere close to this pirate, certainly not if Lora is with him. He doesn't foresee an opportunity to search the seas on his own.

"When I learn to fly, we can seek the pirate together," Muffin's voice enters his head.

In his frustration, he's let the barrier slip against their mental link, the one Peregrin has helped Ayc construct. It hasn't been too difficult. Peregrin already taught the basics of the skill when they taught Ayc pain management techniques. Constructing a mental wall in his head to keep his pain behind is very similar to blocking out their link. Usually, he imagines closing the door on the long tunnel he senses between them. Sometimes, he has to imagine putting a chair in front of the door, too. Muffin can be a nosy little shit and can plow back in during the most awkward of moments. Like when Ayc was working his hand over his cock to thoughts of Lora bent over her throne. Luckily, Muffin slammed the door shut themself and didn't come back for hours.

"Better wait until you can breathe fire too for that one," Ayc responds as he enters the stable. But they have a point. The best option for finding this pirate is to go alone. But he can't see that happening for at least a year.

Fuck.

Down the stable, he can see Muffin's spiked spine and horns peeking over the stall door. They lift their head as Ayc nears. Blood drips from their teeth. They drag their forked tongue over their lips.

"You owe Harlowe one goat," they say without a hint of regret.

Ayc pinches the bridge of his nose and draws in a long breath. *"Gods damn you, Muffin."*

They duck their head below the stall gate. Ayc keeps his gaze fixed on the ceiling, but he still hears the sound of tearing flesh.

"Gods do not exist, so they can't damn me," Muffin says. *"Also, it was Tempest's idea."*

"Sure it was." He's grateful that Tempest agreed to teach the dragon how to fly. They have made considerable progress in the couple of days they've worked together. Tempest has succeeded in getting Muffin to take off and fly for straight distances. Turning and landing continue to be a hit-or-miss experience, leaving everyone at Wyntra ducking for cover.

Ayc shifts his weight from heel to heel, trying to decide the best way to broach the news. Muffin appears in his field of vision, towering over them. They narrow their great red eyes.

"What's wrong? You seem nervous?"

"Something has come up, and I have to go."

"Where are we going?"

"I can't... take you with me." Each of the words feels like a talon digging across his brain.

Muffin snorts. Two little clouds puff out of his nostrils. *"What do you mean?"*

Ayc explains the situation while they crunch loudly on the goat's femur. *"Xylie will stay with you."*

Muffin spits out the very end of the bone. It slams against the wall of the stables and bounces back to land in the straw. *"I like Xylie, but I am meant to be with you."*

"I'm sorry. I really am. I want you to come, but you can't. And I have to go."

Muffin lets out a long sigh, and their neck droops, dropping their head toward the ground. *"This would not be a problem if I could fly. I feel like I'm never going to be strong enough."*

The pain in Muffin's voice is a hand twisting around Ayc's heart. He knows that pain acutely. He feels it almost every day, whenever his magic refuses to obey or whenever the pain in his back holds him back, even if he's the only one who notices. And he hates that Muffin feels this way.

Ayc draws a deep breath and lays a hand on Muffin's nose. They lean into his palm. *"I don't have faith in many things, but I have faith in you. One day, you'll be the absolute terror of the sky."*

Muffin lifts their head. *"And then we'll fly together?"*

"And then we'll fly together," Ayc promises with a smile, imagining it. The wind coming from Muffin's wings. The land passing far beneath them. It'll be a dream.

"Don't die," Muffin warns when Ayc turns to leave. *"If you do, I'm going to eat your corpse. Would be a shame to let all that meat go to waste."*

The dark ocean water parts before the bow of the ship like ink before a quill pen. The heaviness of the darkness is only increased by clouds that have concealed the moon and stars. Even with his

Drakr-enhanced vision, Ayc can make out nothing but an endless and eerie dark. Even on the port side, the Audori shore can scarcely be seen now that they've put the city lights of Forfyre behind them.

He's always been able to see well in the dark when his bracelets are off. But it seems sharper now than before. Perhaps Damara was right. Now that he's spent so much time without his bracelets, his senses are stronger, and his magic within him feels deeper and larger somehow. He hasn't seen much change in manipulating the magic, but perhaps it will come in time. The trade is that he has to be diligent in keeping his feelings in check. The shadows respond to his emotion like a dog responds to a whistle.

The ship's small crew bustles around the guards who are scattered on deck. The ship moves quickly, just as Harlowe promised, sending up spray against his face. Ayc feels the growing distance in his chest, like someone is tugging something vital from him. It's Muffin, he knows. He can't feel them at this distance, and it feels like leaving behind a piece of his soul. He's not certain he'll ever get used to how deeply they are entwined.

Tavish, who stands behind him, smiles at the wind in his face, his taut springs of curls falling over his eyes. Even Saga, sitting behind him, looks a bit like he is smiling, or perhaps it's just the wind blowing against his muzzle.

"Sensing anything?" Ayc asks.

His smile dampens. "Something. But I'm not certain what or where it's coming from. It's this odd tug here." He taps his chest over the leather armor that looks quite like Ayc's. "But I can't quite locate what direction it's coming from."

Large wings flap overhead as Tempest, bearing Peregrin, circles overhead. They are doing long spiraling loops to watch for any ship that might approach, an extra caution for Lora's security. Peregrin wears one of the agate stones in their ear, connected to the rest of the guards. Only around half have come—Irving, Veni, Shae, Davos, and Magdon. Lora is in the small cabin below deck, saying she wanted to rest before she arrived at the garrison. But

Ayc knows it's mostly to do with not wanting to see the water. Out here, in the dark, Ayc can't blame her for being scared of the ocean. It feels rational to be afraid of this endless depth. Who knows what lurks ahead or below? In the night, the boat beneath their feet feels too flimsy to be the only thing separating them from eternal darkness.

He shivers. The air is quite chilly, but he's also thinking about her again—the pirate queen.

"Is there any truth to it, Tavish?" Ayc asks. "The story of the pirate who walks on water."

Tavish rolls his pearl between his thumb and finger, the way he does when he's nervous. Still, he smiles almost convincingly when he says, "It's just a silly story, as far as I'm aware."

Ayc doesn't know why he doesn't believe Tavish, but he doesn't. Because Vidar knows that this pirate is real. Perhaps others do, too. He lowers his voice. "Are you certain? It's import—"

"Shh!" Tavish flings a finger to his nose. He turns his head toward the starboard side of the ship, where the water disappears into a solid wall of darkness.

"There's something there." Tavish reaches down to pick up the leash of the Kindred collar, wrapping it around his hand. With his other hand, he gestures, and Saga swivels his head to the other side of the ship. "I feel it. The *Vanguard*'s close."

Ayc's stomach twists. Even in the darkness, a warship as large as the Vanguard is something they should be able to see. Surely, it would have at least some lights on. Unless, of course, it's in pieces at the bottom of the ocean.

"I'm certain of it, Ayc," Tavish says.

Fuck.

Ayc glances over his shoulder and calls to the guard closest to the stairs that lead below deck. "Veni, can you ask Lora to come here? Tavish senses something."

Veni nods and rushes down the steps to the cabin below. Irving leaves his post at the side of the ship and joins them.

"What direction?" Irving asks.

Tavish points directly at the starboard side. Irving presses two fingers to the stone in his ear. "Peregrin, Tavish believes the *Vanguard* is directly west of us. Can you fly over and see?"

A rush of wings sounds as Tempest flies over the ship, swallowing the little light that pokes through the clouds with a long shadow. Ayc makes out the shape of Peregrin on her back as she glides along, her wings outstretched in a slow downward decline. They are perhaps a hundred yards from the boat, still twenty feet from the ocean water, when Tempest releases a screech. It slams into Ayc's chest like a sharp blade, a warning that something is wrong. A warning that comes too late.

Peregrin tumbles from Tempest's back and slams into the water below.

"Peregrin!" Ayc screams, but it's nothing compared to the sound that Irving makes, a cry that sounds like a soul rending in two. Ayc bolts toward the railing, Irving right at his side, as though perhaps they can both reach out their arms to grab Peregrin. But they are still dozens of yards away, and they are aboard a boat rapidly traveling away from Peregrin.

"Stop the ship!" It's Lora's voice that bellows the command. When she calls it the second time, it's nearly shouted in Ayc's ear as she stops next to him. She's dressed in armor now, and her hands clamp down on the swords at her side.

It takes too much time for the sailors to yank up the sails, to slow their pace. But even when they do, the ship keeps moving, carried by a strong current. The captain careens on the wheel, fighting against it, but they can only turn so quickly without rolling the ship.

"I don't see them," Irving says through his teeth like he's biting back a scream.

"I do," Ayc says. He points at a white dot bobbing in the waves, a dot being pulled further away with each passing second. Something is wrong with Tempest. She's flying in a disordered circle, dropping and then gaining altitude, screeching out. She looks as though she's fighting someone, and yet there's no one there.

Peregrin is slipping away from them, and the boat is getting further away.

"Are they a strong swimmer?" Irving demands.

"No," Ayc says. All the years Peregrin encouraged Ayc to swim, they never once entered the water. *I was made for the skies, not for the water,* they would say.

A choice cements in Ayc's head. Peregrin might not be a strong swimmer, but he is.

"Irving, grab that rope." Ayc gestures toward a coil wrapped around the nearby railing. Irving doesn't hesitate. Ayc tugs off his coat and lets it fall to the ground.

"Ayc, wait—" Lora begins like she means to talk him out of it. She turns her gaze back out to sea, to Peregrin, who they are quickly losing. And then she's at Ayc's side, grasping at one of the buckles of his armor. "If you go into the water with this on, it's going to drag you down."

They work together to get the buckles undone and then drag it from his body. The underlayer comes with it, leaving his chest bare in the wind. He undoes his belt and lets the sword drop to the ground. There isn't enough time to unlace his boots. Irving has already prepped the rope. He slides around Ayc's waist and around his shoulders.

"Be careful," Tavish says, pressing his fist to his lower lip.

Ayc turns to the railing as Irving knots the other end of the rope around the railing.

"Come back to me," Lora hisses into Ayc's ear.

"No place I'd rather be," Ayc says.

And then he dives into the darkness of the water.

The depths pull at him like physical hands. He fights his way upward and breaks above the surface. The waves knock him left, then right. He forces himself to relax, not to fight them, until he gets his bearings. He locks his eyes upon the bobbing dot that is Peregrin and swims hard in that direction.

Normally, he's mindful when he swims to warm up, to let the pain in his body fade against the gentle movement. Now, he pushes it. After these weeks of training his body, his magic, and his mind, he's keenly aware of what his body is capable of, but he pushes it past that point. He reaches deep and relies on his nerve, his determination, and his need to reach Peregrin. He scarcely even feels the cold because he's used to it. He feels strong, good—

And then pain slams into him like a dagger has ripped across his spine. The suddenness nearly makes him scream. He feels as though his very blood is boiling. Like his muscles are being ripped apart, sinew by sinew. Like his head is being ripped open and his brain squashed beneath the impact. It's a pain that's all-encompassing, rattling through every fiber of his being. But it's not *his* pain. He knows his pain, the one he lives with daily. It's as familiar as breathing, but this is not that.

He sinks, his head disappearing beneath the waves. He nearly inhales water before he forces himself to clamp his mouth shut. He doesn't understand what's happening, but he knows if he doesn't control the feeling of agony, he will die here and now. He swiftly conjures up that mental wall inside his head. He imagines building four sides of it, bricking up this new pain with the old. It works slowly, enough to get his head back above the water, to gasp for breath, and then to look for Peregrin again.

They are only ten feet away. They have rolled onto their back, drifting in the waves instead of fighting against them. Or perhaps they're just not conscious. Ayc puts on one more burst of energy, a few more strokes, and he's grabbing hold of Peregrin, hauling them toward his chest.

"You fool of a boy," Peregrin snarls.

Not dead, then. Thank fuck.

"I love you too, Peregrin," Ayc says. He waves a hand above his head to signal the ship. "I've got them!" he calls, though he's not certain they can hear him over the wind.

"We have to get back to the fucking ship," Peregrin groans. They're pale, their lips a shade of blue that reminds Ayc of Damara's dragon. "Something is coming. Can't you feel it?"

"Feel what?" Ayc asks.

"The pain. The way the water moves."

They're right. There's something strange about how the water moves, as though it's pulling upward. The deep curtain of darkness has not budged the closer that Ayc has come to it, standing like an impenetrable wall only another hundred feet away, even as the ship comes closer, bringing light. Something is...wrong about it. It shifts, like when a guard wearing an invisibility cloak moves too quickly, and the air stirs, giving away the illusion. Above them, Tempest is frantic. She tries to fly toward Peregrin, screeches, and retreats once more.

Ayc wants out of this water. Right now.

The rope tugs around him, and he's being hauled back. It threatens to pull Ayc over, but he fights to keep both of their heads above as they move backward. A glance over his shoulder shows Lora and Irving hauling, working together to quickly bring them back. The ship is much closer now, but fuck, they can't come over here. They will slam into whatever barrier Ayc did. "Don't bring the boat over here! Don't come any closer."

"What?" Lora calls.

She can't hear him.

Ayc kicks harder, propelling them through the water. Peregrin kicks with him. Ayc passes the same wall of pain again, but this time, relief pours through his body. Moments later, they're at the boat. Hands reach downward, grab Peregrin from Ayc, and drag them over the side. The rope heaves one more time, pulling Ayc far enough from the water that he seizes the ship's railing. Hands grasp the ropes coiled around his body and haul him over.

He slams into the deck and gasps for breath. When he exhales, he manages, "Get away. Turn back. Something is wrong."

Lora's brow furrows, but she rushes toward the captain. The captain yanks on the wheel, trying to avert course. The sailors fight with ropes and sails, but it's already too late.

The pain surges through Ayc again once more...and everyone else. Sailors drop to their knees with a chorus of groans and gargled screams. Guards cling to the rails. Irving drops his head into his hands. Tavish collapses but reaches toward Saga, who whimpers loudly.

Ayc's bones feel like they are snapping, one by one. But, above Ayc's pain, his very soul seems to cry out. *Lora!*

Ayc is no stranger to pain. He's not known a day, a moment, that has not been tainted with its color. But the thought of his Lora experiencing this sends a wave of rage through him. He shoves the pain back, behind the wall he's so carefully constructed for so many years, and seizes onto something else— something stronger.

Lora, Lora, Lora.

On the other side of the ship, Lora clutches the wheel, fighting to keep it steady. The captain is retching a few feet away. Her head droops onto one of the spokes, her knees buckling, her knuckles turning white with the effort to keep herself upright.

Ayc uses the ship's rail to haul himself to his feet and stumbles past those crumpled on the deck. When the pain threatens to take his knees from beneath him, he fights against it and focuses only on Lora. Only once does the pain win, slamming him into the deck, but he shoves himself onto his hands and knees. He crawls toward Lora until he gathers up the strength to stand again.

"I'm here," he says when he makes it to Lora.

"Fuck, Ayc, I—" She's trembling like a leaf even as her hands yank at the wheel she doesn't have the strength to turn. "I feel like my blood is... Fuck, I'm being boiled alive."

"I know. Me, too."

"We have..." She gasps, then growls through her teeth. "To turn the ship."

Ayc covers her hands with his own and yanks. Together, they manage to heave it in the right direction, completing the turn that the captain began. Without the crew to adjust the sails, however, the retreat is slow. The groans are only growing stronger. More people are retching now.

Lora finally buckles, and Ayc catches her. Or at least tries. Her weight bears them both to the ground, but at least his body breaks her fall. She rolls off him, but they are both on the deck, gasping for air.

"Ayc, look."

She points a shaking finger through the slats of the railing, toward the port side where that thick wall of darkness has stood. Except it's breaking apart, rippling, like a curtain dropping at the end of the show. No, like a puddle of water breaking beneath a large stone. It rains down and slams into the ocean below. A wave stirs up in its wake, racing across the ocean to their ship and slamming against its side. The ship tilts. Ayc slides against the deck before it rocks back in place.

And then the curtain is simply gone. It was never darkness but an illusion of water, unnoticeable in the dark. Just behind it, three ships loom against the horizon, only a hundred yards away. One a smaller galleon with three large masts, and two that tower above even that. They are massive with rows of cannons peeking through the ports on the sides.

Warships.

Ayc can't read the large painted letters that climb down their mast, but he already knows what ships they are.

The *Vanguard* and the *Beholder*.

They've found their lost warships.

The smallest ship heads straight toward them. A massive flag waves from the foremast, large enough he can make out the symbol on the black field. An octopus wraps around a human skull, its tentacles sticking from the eye sockets.

Pirates are coming.

THIRTY-SIX

LORA

"**A**yc!" It's Irving's voice, bellowing out from where he's using the mast to pull himself to his feet. "Get Lora beneath deck. Hide her. Whatever happens, no one can know she's on this ship."

No. Lora rolls onto her knees and presses her hands against the damp wood of the deck. The air reeks of salt and vomit from the sailors and guards who can't get to their feet. She can't stand either. Whatever magic this is, it's more powerful than anything she's ever felt, and it's getting worse. As the pirate ship draws closer, it brings with it a new vibration of pain through Lora's nerves. She feels like her body is rubber being stretched too far; any moment and she will snap. Her guards groan louder. More people vomit.

She has to do *something,* not just run and hide. But the pain is crushing. Her nerves are screaming, her blood is boiling. She has to gasp to keep herself from vomiting.

A hand alights on her arm, and her body instantly recognizes it as Ayc's. "On your feet, soldier," he says with a groan.

Somehow, he's managed to get himself upright using the ship's wheel. She seizes his hand and, with his help, manages to sit on her heels. She grasps the wheel as well, and together, they get her on her feet.

He wraps an arm around her, and she clings to his shoulder as he half-drags her toward the door that leads below deck. She sucks a breath through her fanged teeth and manages to growl, "I'm not going to simply hide while everyone—"

"Yes the fuck you are," Ayc interrupts with his own growl. "If they find you here, they could hold all of Everadyn for ransom."

She sags against him. He's right, and she couldn't fight him even if she tried. The pain is sapping all her strength. She knows he's feeling the pain, too, by the sheen of sweat that covers his skin, and yet he's managing to move them along when everyone else is on the floor. Even Irving has fallen back to his knees. Peregrin is the only other person upright, their body stooped as they press their hands into the railing and stare out at the pirate ship.

The ship rocks again, rocking them both into the rail. Ayc grasps ahold of it so they don't tumble over.

"Fuck," he swears. "The water."

Water arches upward from the sea below, from their ship all the way to the pirate ship, until a bridge forms between the two ships. A figure steps from the deck of the pirate ship and onto the arching water. They walk forward like it's made of stone.

A pirate who walks on water, just like the survivor of the *Beholder* said.

Lora searches for Tavish on the deck. He's near the mast, clutching onto Saga, his face buried into the dog's fur. Lora tries to take a step toward him, but a surge of pain rips through her spine, making her feel like it might shatter. The pirate takes another step closer, and Lora feels it again—the thunderclap of pain. Ayc grunts. Peregrin rests their forehead on the railing. Someone screams again.

Ayc drags her toward the stairs once again. She doesn't fight him this time. She must conserve the little strength she has for whatever is about to come.

Ayc and Lora nearly fall down the steps. He turns so that

when they slam against the door below deck, his body hits first. He thrusts it open. The cabin is meant only as a leisure space for a handful of people. It holds a low table, a cabinet filled with bottles of liquor, a soft couch she was sitting on only a few minutes before, and a bed hung from the ceiling so it sways with the waves.

Ayc stops to blow out the lantern that hangs from above. Darkness descends. He pulls her into the corner and sags against the wall. She falls against him, clutching at his shoulders, her forehead pressed against his bare chest, which is still damp and cool from the ocean water.

His arms tighten around her, pressing on her lower back. Something other than his hands brushes against the back of her legs, rising upward swiftly. She twists just enough to see shadow, darker than the surrounding lack of light, climbing up her body. It's cold but comforting, like a cool cloth against a feverish forehead. Ayc continues to direct the shadow until it wraps around them both, floor to ceiling. Just like the ships were hidden by water, he's hiding her in a wall of shadow. She knows he could go fully invisible within the dark, but he remains with her.

She doesn't know how he's managing. She feels each footstep of the incoming pirate like a hammer at the back of her skull. It threatens to steal her focus, every one of her thoughts. She buries her face into his chest once more. Vaguely, she knows it's a bad idea to be this close, but she can't remember why, not when he's the only thing offering comfort. Not when he's the source of strength in a world being devoured by pain.

"It hurts," she murmurs.

He presses a hand to the back of her head, and it doesn't make the pain go away, but it's a soothing balm. A shelter against this vicious storm. She leans into it, wanting to disappear inside his strength.

"I know," he whispers against her hair.

She knows the moment the pirate steps onboard because her body quakes as the pain reaches a crescendo. Every nerve screams, and she bites her tongue to keep from screaming with it. Ayc tightens his hold, but he, too, shudders.

Feet pound above them. More than one person has arrived. Lora tilts her head upward toward a grate in the ceiling a few feet away. Reddish brown boots stomp down upon it. They are small and dainty, and tiny glass beads are woven through the laces. They seem out of place on a person who has wreaked so much havoc so easily.

"You're on the wrong ship." It's Peregrin's voice, low and slightly muffled, as though they're speaking through thick wool. But stronger than Lora could dream of managing.

"On the contrary, I think this is exactly the right ship." The woman's voice sends a shiver down her spine. It's bitter as acid, already hot as fire, as she snaps back.

Lora grinds her teeth against a scream of frustration. She hates this, being down here while her people are facing this above.

"There's nothing...nothing here of value," Irving reasons between grunts.

"Is it truth or lie, Candor?" she asks.

A second pair of boots thuds down on the grate, these ones large and black and laceless.

"Lie, Malady," Candor's deep baritone replies.

"Is this your entire party?" This is a third and new voice. It bears an accent, light and airy, that Lora recognizes as a Tenebra accent. Still, they speak the Everadyn tongue effortlessly.

"Yes," Irving replies.

"It's a lie, Morrow," says Candor.

"You are trying my patience," says the woman, Malady. "You see, my friend here—Candor, we call him—is divina. I know what you're thinking. *It's rare for a dwarf.* Save it! We've already heard it a million times. He can tell whether or not someone is lying. Quite a handy talent, for sure. So don't lie to us again."

"Stop," pleads a voice. It's Veni. Lora recognizes it immediately. His voice is broken by soft sounds, like he's sobbing, and Lora feels the noise clawing at her chest. "What...whatever

you're doing, stop. We can...we can negotiate better if we can...
Please just stop."

"Couldn't if I wanted to," Malady says. "Fortunately for me, I
don't want to."

"Is there someone down below?" Morrow demands.

No one answers. But the silence speaks for itself.

Malady stomps her boot against the grate. It rattles. Ayc
gathers more shadows around them, sealing the place where Lora
could see the grate. Her vision goes dark, but Malady's mocking
voice rings clear.

"Come out. Come out, little rat," she nearly sings. "Or I'll flush
you out."

"You're making a mistake," Peregrin snarls. "Leave. Now."

The grate rattles as though stomped once more. "Not until we
see your Sovereign, gryphon rider."

Lora flinches and closes her eyes. Fuck.

"Do you think I'm a fool? I don't think the new Third of
Everadyn would be that far from their new Sovereign, do you?"

Shit. It was foolish to think that Peregrin wouldn't be
recognized. The word of who her Five are, along with their
descriptions, would be published in every corner of Everadyn.
Any pirate who cared to know would know by now. Perhaps they
saw Tempest flying through their watery curtain, and they've
made a connection between the gryphon and the person before
them, bearing Peregrin's unique appearance.

"Get off this ship," Peregrin roars, at the same time as Veni
mumbles, "She's not here."

"Lie," Candor hisses.

The boots lunge forward a step. A scream rents the air. It
pierces Lora's ears. Her very heart.

Veni.

Rage breaks through the pain, and she propels herself away
from Ayc. He lets her go, and she makes it a handful of steps
before she collapses.

"You think it hurts with just my presence," Malady yells over
the sound of Veni's screams. "Touching hurts far, far worse."

Lora crawls toward the door. Ayc grabs her shoulder, but she bats his hands away.

"I have to go," she whispers.

"I know. Let me help you."

"No, stay here. You can disappear. They won't find you."

"Fuck that," he curses in her ear. "I go where you go, remember?"

No. She can't bear it if he's unsafe, but she can't think. Veni's screams are still continuing, drowning out everything else. Peregrin's orders. Irving's reasoning. And then a voice calls above the rest.

"Calliope! Stop! Please stop this!"

Malady's boots stumble backward, back onto the grate. The screams quiet, turning instead to whimpering and cursing.

"Please." It's Tavish's voice, soft and pleading. "I know it's you, Calli—"

"Who the fuck are you?" Malady storms forward once more, her boots pounding against the wood above Lora's head. Undoubtedly toward Tavish. He gasps with every one of her steps.

Lora shoves past her pain and scrambles on her hands and knees for the door.

"Tavish. I'm Tavish. Do you remember me?"

Nothing comes back but an eerie silence. Ayc seizes the back of Lora's armor and groans as he pulls her to her feet. They cling to each other once more as they make their way back to the door.

"I always wondered if it was you," Tavish continues. Lora has to strain to hear him. His voice is weak, thick with pain. "When I h-heard the stories...stories of a pirate queen who could cause pain by her very p-presence...I thought it might be you. But when I heard your voice again, I knew."

Lora seizes the doorknob and twists it open. They pause at the stairs.

"Tavish?" Morrow repeats. "The boy who saved you?"

"No," Malady finally speaks. Or perhaps her name is actually Calliope. "When I heard that a blind man named Tavish had become the Sovereign's Fourth, I didn't believe it. I thought, surely, there's a mistake. There must be another Tavish. It couldn't be you."

The stairs are harder to manage upward than they were down. Lora's vision is narrowing. She nearly falls twice, and Ayc—only Ayc—allows her to make it to the top while still on her feet. Bile burns at the back of her throat. A drop of blood drips from her nose.

"It's me," Tavish reassures. "Please, stop hurting us."

"I can't just turn it off," Calliope says. "It's not the way my gift works."

Lora and Ayc finally make it back to the deck. A male-presenting fae stands nearby. He must be the one they call Morrow, but she recognizes him immediately. It's been six years since she saw him, but she's certain.

He's always reminded Lora of a moonlit night, with skin the deep black of the sky above and silver hair that pours in dozens of taut braids to below his shoulder blades. He's traded the richly embroidered dress coats she last saw him in for a shirt unbuttoned to his naval, a long navy-blue coat, and a cutlass hanging on his belt. Recognition burns through his dark eyes as he looks upon her.

The other two pirates are unaware of her presence, their backs to Lora. Candor, a dwarf, stands only as tall as Lora's chest with long black hair artfully braided on the side and a short, manicured beard. His sleeveless shirt reveals dark ink that crawls in artful patterns up the tanned skin of his arms and over his collarbones.

Calliope stands only a little taller than Candor, but she cuts a sharp, impressive form where she stands above Tavish. She wears a dark, tricorn hat like a crown, untamed waves of light brown hair spilling out beneath. A few braids are randomly worked within, strung with brass beads. A dark coat snaps in the ocean wind. She looks like what the rumors call her—a pirate queen. She doesn't wear a cutlass on her belt, but then...she doesn't need one. She's a weapon all on her own.

"How could you, Tavish?" she says, even as she peddles away

from him, creating space. Perhaps relieving him of pain because as she comes closer to Lora, the agony worsens. "How can you serve that woman who would hide away like a coward while her people suffer?"

"I'm right here, bitch," Lora hisses through her teeth. She's not quite certain where she finds the strength, but she clings to it, dragging herself to her full height. Ayc keeps one hand upon her lower back, pressing into her like perhaps she can absorb his strength into her.

Calliope spins around, and Lora is struck by how young she looks. She's perhaps Tavish's age, just reaching her twenties. Lora knows she's not much older, but she wasn't expecting someone younger. Certainly not this scrawny thing with round hazel eyes and a galaxy of freckles scattered across her sun-tanned skin. The illusion of a queen temporarily fades, and Lora remembers.

She may be a queen in silly tales, but Lora is fucking Sovereign of Everadyn. It's not a hat on her head; it's a crown.

"You wanted to see me," Lora says, putting power behind her words. "Well, here the fuck I am."

Calliope's eyes narrow into a look of rage. Her eyes don't change color. Perhaps she's not fae, then. Lora can't see her ears. Candor turns around more slowly, and their expression is level, weighing Lora carefully.

Lora shifts her focus back to Morrow. "And what of you, Nkechi? Do the King and Queen of Tenebra know their youngest son is out playing pirate?"

His hands flex at his sides. "That's not any of your business, *Lora*."

Lora recoils. That's quite different from the painfully polite man she met six years ago when the royal Tenebra family visited Wyntra, the king, the queen, and their three sons. She was only sixteen, sullen from her father's banishment, and gave only the smallest effort to be kind in return. Still, he always referred to her as Lady Loraphne. She knew then he was a water elementist. He tried to amuse her with little tricks using the water from their goblets, but she had no idea he was this powerful. Powerful enough to hide three ships behind a curtain of water.

"It seems you've made it my business," Lora replies. "You're hurting my people."

She locates Veni, stretched on his back, color leached from his body. Unconscious but breathing. He's not the only one who has lost consciousness—most of the sailors have. Shae, Davos, and Magdon do not stir. How long before Malady's gift robs them of their lives? There are so many people on this ship, not to mention the two warships. How many of her soldiers are on those ships? And how is she supposed to save them? She doesn't know how long she'll be able to remain upright.

Calliope surges toward Lora. "If you can still talk, you're not hurting badly enough." She stretches out her hand, and Lora can already feel the pain rushing up inside of her with every step. She braces herself for the impact of Calliope's touch.

This is going to hurt like fuck.

A ball of darkness slams into Calliope with enough force, she flies. She collides with the wood and rolls head over heels until she stops a few feet away.

Lora whirls her head toward Ayc. His arm, bearing the dragon mark, is outstretched, his fist curled. Blood trails from both his nostrils, and his body trembles, but his eyes blaze red.

"Don't fucking touch her," he growls, fierce as a dragon.

Lora's awe disappears behind panic as blood drips at his feet. She's seen Bronwen's nosebleed when she uses power. It's nearly killed her. This is far too much power, far too soon. The cost will be too great. It'll cost him his life.

"You're going to regret that," Nkechi says.

He flicks his finger in Ayc's direction. A stream of water surges over the side of the deck and crashes directly into his chest, sending him flying. Water splatters Lora's hair and face, but she doesn't feel it. She feels only the scream that tears up her throat like dull knives as Ayc slams into the deck and rolls several feet away, near Tavish. He doesn't move again. Her knees buckle, her strength utterly lost at the sight of his limp body.

"Drakr!" Calliope roars as she shoves to her feet. She comes up with a knife—a small, serrated thing—and charges forward.

Lora claws at her leg as she storms past, but Calliope shoves her boot into Lora's shoulder. A shockwave of blistering pain explodes through all of her at the contact. The world spins. Her vision darkens. One of Lora's hands fights for purchase on the soaked wood, trying to pull herself toward Ayc's still unmoving body, even as she fumbles with the sword at her side.

"Calm yourself, Malady," Candor says, but she ignores him.

When Morrow reaches toward her, she darts around him.

She lifts the knife as she surges the last few steps. Peregrin fights to get around the bodies that separate them from Ayc. Lora drags herself one more foot forward, another scream wrestling up her throat, the world tipping left and right. It narrows down to a single pinpoint: the knife above Ayc as it catches the light of the lantern.

"Stop, Calli!" Tavish's voice is slurred as it meets Lora's ears. His body is blurred in her vision as he flings himself over Ayc. "My friend," he gasps. "He's my..." He can't finish. His body stoops, his forehead resting on the deck. Saga nudges his hand with his nose, whimpering.

The knife wobbles in Calliope's hand. A moment of hesitation. Water, little more than a cupful, races from the side of the boat and splashes in her face.

"Calli!" Morrow barks. "Control your anger. This is not the plan."

She shakes her head and glares at him, but she tucks the knife back where it came.

What is your plan? Lora means to ask, but she's losing consciousness fast, so she can only manage three words, "Tavish, is Ayc—"

"Breathing," Tavish manages before he collapses.

Alive. Ayc is alive.

It's Lora's last thought before she surrenders her war against the pain, and everything succumbs to darkness.

THIRTY-SEVEN

AYC

If there is an eternal torment, Ayc is there. He's certain of it. Pain ravages through every fiber of his muscles, tears through every screaming nerve, and ricochets around his head. Fuck. He thinks he can feel it tangled within his very soul. That's how deep the pain goes.

It will consume him if he lets it.

One thought sparks like a torch in the darkness. His parched lips move, but his dry throat feels like it's tearing open just to let him speak. "Lora," he croaks.

"She's here, boy." It's Peregrin's voice, summoning Ayc back to himself. "She's all right."

Ayc cracks his eyes open. The world whirls like the red and white top his mother gifted him as a young child, a treasure he cherished. The wood above his head is nowhere near as colorful, but it twirls so quickly, Ayc's stomach wrings with nausea. When the spinning finally stops, he doesn't dare try to sit up from the floor he's lying on. Instead, he turns his head to get his bearings.

Peregrin sits against the iron bars of some kind of prison cell. They've been stripped of the knives they wear on their chest. Their skin has taken on an eerie shade of green. Tavish lies on the floor next to him, still asleep, his arm wrapped around Saga. Ayc turns his head in the other direction, and there Lora is, draped on her back, her hair scattered on the straw that dusts the hardwood floor, tangled in her crown that somehow never budges. Her breath rises and falls evenly. He hopes she is truly as unharmed as she looks, because the thought of her feeling even an ounce of the havoc he feels makes him want to sob.

Distantly, Ayc can hear shouting of many different voices, rising as one. A lot of people are closeby. The swaying of the floor beneath him and the distant shush of water meeting a hull tell him they're still on a ship, just not the one they were on before.

"Where are we?" Ayc asks.

"In the *Beholder*'s brig," Peregrin replies.

"Where's Irving? The other guards?"

"I think they left them back on the ship, floating in the ocean." Peregrin's head falls backward on the bars. "Fuck. Irving will never forgive himself for letting Lora out of his sight."

There was nothing Irving could do. Nothing Ayc could have done. It comes back to him, those moments right before he lost consciousness. He nearly wrecked himself to summon that shadow that collided with the pirate. He doesn't even remember how he did it, only that rage poured through him and demanded he end the person attempting to harm his Lora. The shadow bent to his desires.

It seems Damara was right. He can't hide from this darkness, this power within him, and still expect it to obey him. But why the fuck would she have given him that piece of advice? Why would she want to make her enemy more powerful?

That's a question he doesn't currently have time or the mental capacity to analyze.

Lora moans, and that small sound is all it takes for Ayc to finally move. He rolls to his side. His muscles spasm in protest, but he bites back his own groan as Lora turns her head. The curls curtain her face, revealing only a flash of dark eyes behind them. He carefully brushes the curls from her face. She doesn't swat his hand away like he expects, only studies his face.

"Are you all right?"

They both ask at the same moment, and under different circumstances, Ayc might have laughed.

"Surviving," he replies. "You?"

She stretches her ankles and rolls her wrists. "The pain is gone. I'm still sore from whatever it was, but I don't feel it anymore. What changed?"

Peregrin holds up their wrist. A string of cord wraps around their wrist, bearing a single red bead. "They put these on us. Some kind of protection spell against Malady's gift. They must have a sorcerer on their crew."

Ayc lifts his own wrists and finds the bracelet there. There's one on Lora's and Tavish's wrists as well. They've even wrapped one around Saga's collar. The dog has opened his eyes, one blue and one brown, both focused on Ayc. He hasn't stirred, though, so as not to disturb Tavish.

Still, pain racks down Ayc's back. Ayc lets him focus on it briefly, just long enough that he recognizes it as his own. It's like running into someone you rather wouldn't see at the marketplace. *Ah, it's you. You ol' fucker.*

Lora sits up with a grunt. Ayc forces himself upright, too, and slides back to rest his back against the bars behind him. The metal digs into his tender muscles. Fuck. He really misses Reselda right now.

He searches around them, but there's not much to see—just wooden walls and metal bars and several chains latching the door of their cage shut. Across the room, there's an identical cage, this one empty. A small walkway between leads to a door that surely leads to the rest of the ship. Pale light coming from two portholes in the ship walls is the only thing that tells him it's morning.

When he looks back at Lora, she's already staring at him, her eyes roaming over his chest. His bare chest. His leather armor is still on that ship somewhere, where he dropped it before he dove into the water. Her gaze feels like fingertips crawling over his skin and across his hipbones. Fire sparks in his blood, and he pulls a breath through his nose to calm it. Now is not the time.

She drags her gaze away, focusing on Peregrin. "Where are the others?"

Peregrin explains again. Their voice finally disturbs Tavish because in that place between waking and sleep, he murmurs, "Calliope."

Saga licks him gently on his jaw. Tavish shoots upright and fumbles for the leash while calling, "Ayc! Lora!"

"We're here," Ayc says quickly. "Peregrin, too. The others are not, but they're safe."

Well, he hopes.

Tavish clamps his hand over the leash, looking through Saga's eyes. He draws in a breath and lets it out with a "Fuck" that seems to come from the very depths of his soul.

"Do you want to explain who Calliope is?" Lora asks. "Or do you want to lie to me again?" She doesn't sound angry. Just tired.

Tavish scrubs a hand down his face. "I'm sorry. I should have told you my suspicions, but I didn't know for sure, and—"

"Tavish," she says gently. "Just tell me who she is."

He clears his throat and folds his legs beneath him. "About five years ago, I led Zephen to a small boat near the southern border of Aluina. They had a handful of children, who were being sent by their parents to go work in Drakr factories."

Ayc's jaw tightens. Children should be children. They should not be forced to work, let alone in places as dangerous as he's certain factories are. "What kind of parent would do that?"

"Those who can't afford to feed any of their other children," Peregrin says softly. "One child becomes an indentured servant, so the others don't starve."

"It still isn't right," Ayc snaps back.

Peregrin doesn't even tense at his tone. "I did not say it was. I would sell myself before selling my child. But desperation rarely offers the luxury of many options."

Tavish continues, a far-off look in his eyes like he's travelling back in time. "It was pretty easy. It was two Drakr on a boat mostly crewed with humans, so Zephen's crew handled it well. There were about ten teenage girls there. Calli—well, Calliope

Redferne, her full name is—was one of them, and she... Divine, she was fire." A grin crawls onto his face, and fuck, Ayc knows that grin. A foolish one. One that says that, even after five years, Calliope still lives under Tavish's skin.

"She punched Zephen right in the face. I couldn't see it, but the sound was glorious. She mouthed off to everyone. She bit anyone who dared try to touch her. She was utterly fearless. I was immediately..." He searches for the right word. "Fascinated with her. And so, I did something I'd never done before. I let myself get to know her. At night, I would bribe the guard with a few coins so I could sneak the girls food. I knew if Zephen caught me, it wouldn't end well, but I couldn't seem to stay away. I would sit by the cage, and Calli and I would talk for hours. At first, we just talked. About her life in Aluina and my life at sea. I told her about my mom and Saga, and she told me about her siblings. And then, we started planning on how I could help them escape."

He sucks in a breath. "I've never been brave enough to try before, but I knew the plan was to sell them all at a brothel in Tenebra, and I just... I had to do something. I don't know why I found the courage to try when I never had before...or since."

"Yes, you do," Ayc says.

Tavish lifts his palm. It's a helpless gesture, and Ayc knows the feeling exactly. "Perhaps I do. It was a long time ago."

"So you helped her escape?" Lora prompts.

"I tried to help them all escape," Tavish replies. The look of wonder fades away as he reaches this part of the story. He fiddles with the bead on his wrist. "It didn't go according to plan. I was on kitchen duty, and I stole a couple of sleeping tonics from our healers' stores and put them into the food. But I think I underestimated how much I would need because no one stayed asleep for long, or they didn't fall asleep at all. And I didn't realize until it was too late. I'd already stolen the key and let the girls out. The plan was to get out on a rowboat. We were close enough to Tenebra that we thought we could make it. I was going to go with them."

The glow on his face returns just briefly. "When I let her out of the brig, she threw her arms around me...and she kissed me. I'd never been kissed before." Tavish stops, sputters. "Fuck. Sorry, that's not important to the story."

"Of course it is," Ayc says gently.

Lora makes a soft hum of agreement.

Tavish rubs the back of his neck. "Uh...anyway..." He clears his throat and sobers."The plan went wrong as soon as we got on deck. I don't know exactly what happened. Someone grabbed my arm. There was a lot of shouting, crying, screaming. I heard Zephen yell, *'I'll drown you myself,'* and then Calliope started screaming. That's when we felt it. When we all felt it. The unbearable pain. She told me she had a scar, just like mine. A divina mark, but she thought it was just a birthmark because she didn't have any extraordinary powers. At least, she hadn't had it yet. But it unleashed in that moment."

Ayc knows well that divina gifts sometimes only unleash under times of great stress. It's why Yris had him tormented and tortured when he first arrived at Wyntra. Her goal was to unlock whatever gift lurked inside him. Except he was never divina. He was only ever Drakr.

"She got away," Tavish says. "We couldn't do anything to stop her. We were all paralyzed and suffering, just like we all were last night. We didn't stop feeling it until her rowboat was too far to overtake. Even then, Zephen was smart enough not to follow."

"I'm surprised Zephen didn't kill you," Lora says.

"Me too." A shadow crosses his face, his brow furrowing even more, and Ayc knows that it cost Tavish something. But Tavish doesn't share that part of his trauma, and it isn't theirs to demand.

"So, a year later," Tavish says, "when I started hearing stories about a pirate who could bring pain by her very presence, who could walk on water but wouldn't come on land, I wondered if it was her. I think Zephen thought it was her, too, because he was far more cautious. He started dealing more in stolen goods than in people. At least until that last time, when he had a shipful of children as he pulled two other dangerous women from the sea." Tavish cocks his head in Lora's general direction.

And somehow, after Calliope rowed away from her captors, she found herself in the company of Tenebra royalty and a dwarf who is also a divina. She started a pirate crew—large enough, apparently, that they now have two warships. And somehow, in that time, she also got involved in Asbjorn, an Aluina rebellion. It's been a busy five years for her.

At the thought, Ayc's heart freezes in his chest. His hand flies to the pockets of his pants. The two Asbjorn coins he's kept there are gone. Fuck. Did they fall out when he jumped into the water after Peregrin? Or did the pirates take them?

Either way, they're gone now. He'll have to retrace his path back to Vidar and plead for another coin.

He can't worry about that now. He needs to get Lora off this ship and back to safety. It scarcely matters if Calliope was once a suffering girl Tavish fell in love with. She's a ruthless pirate now who's taken the Sovereign of Everadyn captive for unknown reasons. Now that they understand who they're dealing with, they need to plan an escape.

The door to the brig rattles. A key clicks. It swings open. Nkechi—or perhaps it's Morrow—enters, carrying a bag over his shoulder. He's trailed by a fae so short and slender, they seem to be drowning in their orange cloak trimmed with swirls of white. A sorcerer then. Their pinched face makes it look like they would much rather be anywhere else.

"Ah," the Tenebrae prince says. "You're all finally awake. Good. It's time we talk."

Lora shoves to her feet. "What do you want, Nkechi?" she demands.

"I prefer Morrow. And patience, Lora. We can go somewhere more comfortable to talk."

Ayc drags himself upward, using the bars to steady himself when his back protests. Morrow tracks his every move with eyes as dark and vitreous as the sea at night.

"But first, I want to make it clear what will happen if your

Drakr calls upon his shadow again," Morrow says. He snaps his fingers at the sorcerer.

They raise their hand. The tie on Lora's bracelet unravels itself. The protection slips from her wrist and flies through the air into the sorcerer's fist. She pulls a gasp of air through her teeth. Her hands tighten on the bars as her knees threaten to buckle. She's no longer protected from Calliope's gift.

He is hurting her. Morrow is fucking hurting the woman he loves.

Something dark and murderous rises deep in Ayc's gut. His world turns red, and shadows rise, curling like smoke at their feet. Through the haze of rage, he remembers his own bracelet. He can give her his protection. He tries to sweep it from his wrist, untie it, but it won't budge.

"It's spelled to remain on your wrist unless the sorcerer removes it," Morrow explains.

Ayc slams his fist against the bars. He scarcely feels the impact against his knuckles. "Give it back to her," he snarls.

His shadows creep higher. The sorcerer backs away. The smallest flash of fear darkens the shine of Morrow's eyes, but he keeps his voice flat.

"Calm yourself. Do we need to take the bracelets from the others as well?"

Ayc drags in a breath. He imagines pressing the power down within him. It resists, sparking with his anger the way fire sparks from the powder he uses for magic tricks. One breath, two, and the shadow goes back to merely being shadows.

"I'll behave," Ayc says through his teeth. "Give. It. Back."

Morrow nods at the sorcerer. The bracelet retraces its path and winds itself back around Lora's wrist. She sucks in a breath and shakes her head as though shaking off the residual pain. She raises her chin.

Morrow pulls a key from his pocket and unlocks the door. He pulls the bag from his shoulder and tosses it to Ayc. Inside is a bundle of deep green leather. His armor and coat.

"Get dressed," Morrow demands, "and follow me."

Once Ayc is dressed, Morrow leads them out of the brig and into the depths of the dock. The halls are busy, and the faces of those who rush around are eclectic. Fae and human pirates dressed in sun-bleached shirts and fae sailors dressed in pristine navy uniforms, all hard at work to keep the ship going.

It's a maze down here, and perhaps that's the point of the warship's design: to ensure that no one can escape. None of the four even dares step out of line. The sorcerer trails after them, their presence assuring that any misbehavior will result in pain. Ayc stays by Lora's side. Once, her hand drifts close to his and brushes the tip of her pinky down the back of his hand, like she wants to be certain he's there. His heart quakes at the brief touch. The urge to take her hand in his is powerful. He defuses it by sending her a cross-eyed smile, like everything is fine. Like he isn't halfway convinced they'll never make it off this ship.

It's promising that the pirates haven't killed anyone so far. Perhaps they know the Sovereign of Everadyn is more useful alive. Ayc doesn't know if that makes their situation better or worse.

Morrow stops at a door at the end of another long hallway. He shoves it open. Within the room is a long mahogany table, its rich wood shining in the light that pours through the portholes that line the walls. A bowl of fresh fruits gleams in the center.

Candor sits in a chair close to the middle of the table, digging a comically small spoon into a grapefruit halved and sprinkled with sugar. Calliope is at the end, where an Admiral might sit, glaring at them like a pirate queen on her throne. She's fiddling with something that flashes gold in the sunlight. Coins, Ayc realizes. He can't see his name engraved upon them from here, but when her narrowed eyes cut to him, he instinctively knows whose coins they are.

"Sit," Morrow says.

Lora slides around him and perches in the chair at the other head of the table, directly across from Calliope. Ayc bites back a smile at the clear strategic move and takes the seat next to her. Tavish and Peregrin sit on her other side while Morrow sweeps around to sit across from Candor. He leans back in the chair and props his ankle on his opposite knee, bearing the calm, composure of the confidence that comes when you are aware of just how beautiful you are. And he is gorgeous, undoubtedly. Ayc thought so the last time he saw him, years ago at Wyntra. At the time, Ayc thought that Morrow looked exactly like how the prince in a storybook should look. He looks no less so now, just because he's dressed as a pirate.

Morrow pushes the fruit bowl from the middle toward the end. "Eat. If that's not satisfactory, I believe there are still some more grits in the galley. We can have something brought up to you."

Clearly, someone who is gifted in preserving spells is on their crew, because the grapefruit, oranges, and bananas within the bowl are pristinely ripe, like they were just picked. The closest place they grow, in the Sal Maris territory, takes several days to get to, even by ship.

Ayc's stomach tosses. It's been a long time since the fish they had the night before. It feels strange to eat when he feels like he's about to negotiate for all their lives, yet he needs all the strength he can get. He selects an orange. "If you're trying to offer a last meal," he says, "I think I'd prefer something a little sweeter. Like cinnamon rolls. Cinnamon rolls would be the perfect last meal."

Lora casts him a glare before she selects an apple, testing its firmness carefully beneath her fingers before she chooses it. Peregrin and Tavish make their own decisions and slide the bowl back down the table.

"We are hopeful that this will not be your last meal," Morrow says. "We have only a few simple demands."

Lora's fangs flash as she bites down on the apple and breaks its flesh. She chews and swallows before she answers. "Let's hear them then. I'm very busy, and this little cruise I'm on was not on my itinerary. In fact, by now, the captain of my guard has likely made it to the garrison to report what's happened. It's really only a matter of time before an entire army of gryphon riders will know I'm missing and come find me."

"They won't be able to get close," Calliope says. "Peregrin's gryphon has been trying and can't get close without nearly tumbling from the sky. And your guards are in the *Vanguard*'s brig."

Peregrin flinches. "I thought you left them."

"We changed our minds," Morrow explains. "We thought it would give us more time before they realize their Sovereign is missing."

Fuck, Ayc curses to himself.

"Don't worry," Candor assures. "The first mate is under instructions to keep the ship far enough away that they don't feel the effects of Calliope's power. They're being well taken care of, so long as they don't cause problems."

Peregrin runs a hand over their face. "You do not know my partner. He will cause problems."

"Is there a way to send a message?" Lora asks, setting down the apple. "I don't want them inadvertently harmed because they believe I'm in need of rescuing."

The three pirates exchange glances. Candor presses the spoon back into their grapefruit and stands. "I'll fetch some paper and a quill. You can send a note. Don't talk until I'm back."

In his absence, a heavy silence falls over them. The coins rattle as Calliope lifts them and lets them drop back onto the table. Ayc debates saying something, but Tavish speaks before he can.

"How are you, Calliope?" Tavish asks, peeling his own grapefruit.

"Cursed," she says flatly, bitterly. She doesn't look down at him. The fiddling of the coins quiets. "And you?" She softens her voice. "I thought you were dead. I thought Zephen would have killed you."

Ayc sets down the orange to track the exchange. Lora gnaws on her apple, but in a slow, careful way so that she doesn't hide their words behind the crunch.

"Me, too," Tavish says. "But no, I was too valuable."

Calliope's eyebrows disappear behind the red strip of cloth. "Is that how you ended up as Fourth to the Everadyn throne? Because you were too valuable?"

Tavish's fingers pause before he resumes peeling a little more aggressively than before. "I ended up there because Lora is my friend."

"Some taste in friends you have," Calliope says. "A Drakr bastard and a heartless bitch."

Ayc's power lurches within him. The pain twists and turns, and he isn't sure if it hurts more to let the power out or keep it in. Both feel as though they're demanding a price, but it silences when Tavish slams a fist down on the table.

"Do not insult my friends!"

It's the first time, the only time, Ayc has ever seen Tavish's dark eyes turn silver. Calliope freezes, her eyes widening at the sight, and Ayc suspects that she, too, has only known the sweet, timid boy. But he's not timid, no matter what he may seem. He's faced pirates and dragons and wraiths and a whole world that has never been easy for him to exist in. He's stronger and fiercer than most people give him credit for.

"Lora saved my life," Tavish continues. "She saved me from Zephen when you simply rowed away and left me."

Calliope's mouth falls open. "That's not fair. I didn't know what was happening, what the power was, and I was afraid I would kill you if I didn't get away. And I was right. That's what this gift"—she spits the word, making it clear that she views it as she first described it: a curse—"can do to people. Anyone I'm close to who is not protected will die if they remain close to me for too long. I haven't set foot on land for five years, Tavish. *Five years.* I can never go home." Her voice creaks, nearly breaking. "Do you have any idea what that's like?"

Tavish's face contorts with sympathy, and Ayc feels the same in his chest.

"Yes, I do," he says. The reasons may be different, but he, too, knows what it's like to be taken from your homeland and be unable to return.

She glares at him, her face flushing with heat. She looks furious, and he wonders if she's mostly just angry at herself for letting them see her emotions. His suspicion is confirmed when

Morrow reaches a hand toward her shoulder, and she bats it away. "I wasn't asking you, you bast—"

"Enough!" Tavish snaps. "My heart breaks for you, but I will not tolerate you calling my friends names."

Calliope's mouth opens to protest, but Morrow holds up a hand. "Calliope, I know you carry enough anger to burn down the world, as you have every right to. But you promised you wouldn't antagonize people. If you're going to make this more difficult, I'm going to politely ask you to leave."

Calliope huffs and leans back in the chair. Lora subtly reaches out her hand and pushes two fingers into Tavish's elbow, a silent thanks.

The door reopens, and Candor stomps back in, paper and quill in hand. He looks about the room as though he can sense the heaviness that has fallen. "Uh, fuck, you let her talk, didn't you, Morrow?"

"It couldn't be helped," Morrow says, sounding regretful. "Calli does what she wants."

"Shut up," Calliope hisses.

The tension in Ayc's chest softens. Perhaps it's due to Calliope's confession, which twists how Ayc sees her, making her less of a villain and more of a child hurting others because she is hurt. Or perhaps it's the way the three are behaving like bickering siblings, a clear affection between them all that makes it difficult to believe they want to gut him like a fish. Calliope—and perhaps all of them—is a part of Asbjorn, the resistance set on saving Aluina. Perhaps, if they play this right—and they don't foolishly try to hurt Lora—they can leave here as allies.

He's an optimistic fool, he knows, but it's worth an arrow's bolt in the dark.

"Hey, why did nobody want to play cards with the pirate?" Ayc says.

"Ayc," Lora warns.

He ignores her. "Because they were standing on the deck."

Morrow blinks. Calliope glares. Peregrin presses a hand to

their forehead. Lora sends him a look that says, *"If you don't shut up right now, I'm going to cut you up and feed you to the sharks."*

That look is cute. He likes it.

Candor laughs as he sets the quill and ink next to Lora. It's a deep, one-note thing, but it's a laugh. "The Drakr has jokes."

"The person from Aluina," Ayc repeats with a smile, "has a name. And it's Ayc. Ayc *Waylonder*." He places emphasis on his last name, reminding Calliope *Redferne* of its significance. Fae have titles, clans, or houses, but they do not have surnames. "I hail from the Northwest province of Aluina in a sleepy little village called Hearth. My mother, who raised me, was a baker just like me. I do not know my Drakr father, nor do I wish to."

Calliope glances at Candor, who nods as he returns to his chair, a confirmation of the truth. She sweeps his coins into her hands and forms a fist around them. Well, so much for soothing the waters. "Enough with small talk."

"You said you had demands," Lora says. She's eaten the apple down to the core, and she sets it aside and picks up the quill. "What do pirates want from the Sovereign of Everadyn? Wealth, titles, land?"

Morrow snorts softly. "Hardly. I didn't get into piracy because I was interested in becoming rich. I'm rich enough on my own. We don't do it for the gold."

"Then why did you get into piracy?" Tavish asks.

"To wreak havoc and mayhem on people who would cause others harm," Morrow says.

"To fuck up the livelihoods of anyone who profits off of the exploitation of others," Calliope rephrases.

"And what exactly does that have to do with my warships?" Lora asks.

Morrow cocks his head. "Do you truly not know?"

"Know what?"

"That the *Vanguard* was taking people from Aluina to work as indentured servants in your weapon forges."

THIRTY-EIGHT

LORA

"What are you talking about?" Lora asks, her teeth tingling as her fangs grow out once more, but it isn't them she's angry with. "Everadyn doesn't enslave people. It's illegal."

"It's not legal in Tenebra either," Morrow says. "That doesn't stop it from happening. There's always loopholes in the laws or people who disregard them entirely. Even some of those charged with upholding the law."

"Don't try to play innocent," Calliope says. "You had to know what the *Vanguard* was doing. It's done it *many* times."

Lora considers the immature desire to throw her apple core at her head. She sympathizes that Tavish likely has some unresolved feelings for the woman, but she's acting young and immature, and Lora doesn't have the same patience that Morrow has with her.

"I assure you, I have no idea what you're talking about," Lora says.

"She's not lying," Candor says, digging into the grapefruit like he's only half paying attention.

"How do you not know?" Calliope demands. "They are your ships."

That's precisely what Lora would like to know. She's scarcely been Sovereign for a month, so whatever mission the *Vanguard* was on in Aluina was set into motion prior to her being crowned.

"Explain it to me," Lora says. "Every detail."

Morrow frowns. "The *Vanguard* has made several trips to Aluina. The humans there are offered contracts. Safe passage for them and their families to Everadyn in exchange for working in one of your forges. It seems a good deal for the desperate, and people in Aluina frequently are. But when they get there, they find that the contracts they've made are predatory in nature. All the minuscule wages they've been offered go to paying back the fee to the navy for the crossing, which winds up in your treasury."

Assets to the forges. That's what Lovelace noticed. A positive balance lining the treasury. Lovelace was right to think it suspicious. Harlowe must know of it, must know how she would feel about it. Why else did he suddenly want to keep her out of the forges?

Her stomach tightens in rage so fierce she feels sick with it. She tightens her fingers around the edge of the table, digging in her fingernails, because there's no one to direct the rage toward.

"And the owners of the forges get cheap labor," Morrow continues, and each word is a fire poker, stirring the embers of her rage, twisting her stomach up tighter. "They're given little more than a roof over their head in barracks and scarcely enough food to maintain their work. Even their children sometimes have to pitch in."

Children. Fucking children?

Working in the forges is dangerous work. With hot fires that are always burning, there are a variety of laws meant to protect the fae who work there, but she doubts that those laws are protecting strangers from a foreign land. Her mother and Harlowe invited desperate people here, offering them the promise of something better, and they exploited them when they should have been taken care of.

Ayc takes a hot breath, and she doesn't dare look at him. She fears if she sees her own fury reflected in his eyes, she might combust. She feels like she could run on water and race all the way back to land. Like she could storm into the factories and pull out the people there.

She sucks in a breath through her teeth, her canines sharp against her lower lip. "How do you know this?"

"We can't reveal our sources," Candor says. "But we've been able to confirm that it's been a regular practice since the treaty with the Drakr was signed."

"So we took your warship," Calliope explains. "And we offered the humans a place on a pirate ship instead. It might not be a safer life, but it'll at least be a free one."

"Good," Lora says. Her fingers spasm on the table. Action. She desperately needs action. Her brain is spinning, tumbling, faster than she knows how to act. She picks up the quill. She writes as she talks. "You can tell them all that they are free of their contracts. If they would like to keep a place on your crew, then they can do that. I can't promise that my navy crew will not try to hunt them if they break international laws as pirates, but they're well protected with you, Calliope. If they would like to settle in Everadyn, myself and my Five will personally ensure they are settled safely. Fuck, I'll put them up in Wyntra if I must."

Calliope's nose wrinkles, a look that is more confused than disgusted. "Are you serious?"

"I am utterly serious. We have more than enough room." She jots down a few more words on the paper. Morrow, Calliope, and Candor all exchange another shared glance that she catches out of the corner of her eye. Ayc leans closer in an attempt to read over her shoulder. She flicks him with the feathered end of her quill, and he sits back in the chair.

When she's done writing, she signs it with a flourish. She hands it to Ayc, sliding the quill and ink pot closer. He reads it over, and a smile winds up his face. Not his larger one, his teasing one. This one is genuine delight. It makes her heart flip over in her chest, and she fixes her eyes on the table. He picks up the quill and signs his name with a flourish, the letter A as large as his smile. He slides it across the table to Peregrin. They, too, read it.

"Harlowe isn't going to like it," Peregrin says, but they're already signing it, one side of their lip quirked higher than another.

"Fuck Harlowe. I am Sovereign, and I decide who is considered an Everadyn citizen. From now on, anyone who lives here and abides by our laws is Everadyn, and that affords them all the protections and rights of Everadyn citizens. Harlowe will be forced to ensure that all the workers within the factories are paid and cared for properly. Or I will prosecute him for violating workers' rights."

"Would you like me to read you the decree, Tavish?" Peregrin offers, sliding the paper before him and placing the quill in Tavish's hand.

Tavish shakes his head. "I think we should have someone who knows the law to read it to ensure the wording is perfect and make sure that no one can find some kind of loophole, but this will work for now." He places his signature—a single T. They would need to get Bronwen and Xylie's signatures, but Lora is certain they will agree.

"That's it?" Calliope asks. "Just like that?"

"Was this not what you wanted?" Lora asks.

"Yes, of course, but I thought..." She blinks rapidly.

Candor chuckles. "You two prepared such good threats."

"I'm sorry," Lora says dryly. "Would you like to get them out of your system? Please, be my guest."

Morrow leans forward and snags the decree she has written. Lora doesn't protest, only studies every wrinkle of his forehead as he reads it. "Just that simple? You do realize that the weapon forges and the royal treasury are heavily connected? The money from this has afforded you all the privileges."

Lora fists her hand around the leviathan necklace she wears, which she's grateful the pirates did not take away. She realizes that her actions have consequences. The production of the factories might slow, and the treasury might run thin, neither of which is a good place to be in when they are preparing to go to war against the Drakr. But she won't allow this to stand, knowing that she has personally benefited from this evil practice only feeds that desire, like fuel to the fire of her rage. It builds. She wants to set fire to the world with it. It's so bright it hurts, like her insides are scolding.

"I do not want privilege," she says. "I want equality. I won't let the labor of the many be exploited for the benefit of the few."

Morrow stares at her. She stares back.

"Candor?" he asks without looking away.

"She's not lying," Candor says. He spoons up a piece of his grapefruit.

Calliope's mouth parts, but no words come out.

"Anything you would add?" Lora asks, nodding toward the decree. "I'm willing to listen."

Morrow squints down at it. "It's very thorough. But you need to weigh the consequences carefully. Many people fear strangers in their land."

"Foolishness," Lora says. "Diversity only leads to prosperity."

"I agree, and I wish all shared our sentiments. But scared people can often be dangerous. Your mother has certainly worked to increase that fear with tireless stories and propaganda during her reign. My parents and her have had many disagreements on her messaging. If people who have bought into the lies see this as an open invitation for humans to flood their borders, they might react poorly. Even violently."

Lora's teeth sharpen at the very thought. "They will find that I feel very differently from my mother. After all, I have chosen an Aluinic human to sit at my side." She gestures to Ayc at her side and then lowers her voice to a growl. "And I will not tolerate hate to spread within my borders. If someone harms anyone because of who they are, I will have that person punished. Publicly and *violently*."

Candor whistles lowly. "Damn. Not a lie."

"You're ruthless, aren't you?" Calliope says, leaning back in her chair to survey Lora once more. She doesn't say the word like it's an insult.

"Yes, I am," Lora says. "My mother raised me to be a sword, but I get to decide where I direct it. And since you all seem well aware of what goes on in my lands—even things that it seems people are trying hard to hide from me—I hope that if you have further concerns, you will bring them to my attention. Without kidnapping me first, I prefer. I will handle them."

Morrow, Candor, and Calliope exchange a look. Candor smiles broadly.

"What about the *Beholder*?" Peregrin asks. Lora nearly forgot that there is a second ship involved in all this. "Was it also dealing in indentured servants?"

"No," Morrow says. "The *Beholder* was taking wheat and beef to Drakr, where it is used to feed the armies that keep people of Aluina oppressed."

"You were disrupting trade between Everadyn and Drakr?" Ayc asks.

"Armies who don't eat can't fight," Morrow says. "At least not well."

"I quite enjoy fucking with the Drakr whenever possible," Calliope says, visibly brightening at the very thought.

"Smart," Peregrin responds.

It is. Very smart.

A wild idea leaps into Lora's head. She's not quite sure if it's utter recklessness or genius, but she *is* quite sure she doesn't care which.

She leans forward. "What if I wanted to hire you to keep doing that— how did you put it? Fuck things up for those who hurt other people?"

"You want to hire us?" Calliope repeats. "What type of queen hires pirates?"

"A wicked one," Lora replies. If people are going to call her that, perhaps it's time she embraces it, at least a little. After all, no one around her is trying to play these games with any amount of decency.

"Why would you want to hire us?" Morrow asks.

"Because I'm going to start a war with the Drakr."

Tavish sucks in through his teeth. Lora understands she's taking a risk by telling them her plans. But who are they going to tell? They're pirates running from the law. Which perhaps makes them the perfect ally.

"Why?" Calliope demands.

"Because we want to see Aluina free," Ayc responds. Clearly, he understands where Lora is going with this. "We want to break the treaty with the Drakr, but it's… complicated."

"I need to convince the regents to be willing to break the treaty," Lora says. "And I need to ensure we are in the best position for the oncoming war once I do."

"Food, weapons, soldiers," Peregrin says. "It's what we need to fight a war. We've begun stockpiling them."

"What?" Calliope murmurs. She looks like she might fall out of her chair.

Peregrin only narrows their eyes. "It seems that perhaps our goals align closely, and a lot of pain and suffering could have been spared if you simply—" They draw a breath, their hand coiling into a fist on the table's edge. "If you stopped to simply have a conversation."

Calliope makes a sound of protest. "Well, maybe—"

"Calli," Candor says softly.

She audibly snaps her teeth shut and ducks her head swiftly, hiding her face behind the brim of her hat.

"And say we're interested?" Morrow asks, twisting his hands together. "What are you proposing we do?"

"I send you the names of ships that are carrying cargo to Drakr," Lora says, "and you ensure that delivery doesn't make it. As payment, you can keep forty percent of it. Sell it, use it to feed your crew, whatever. But sixty percent of it comes back to me. I can store it to ensure we have enough for the long road ahead." If not to feed armies, she will have a store to fall back on if Lux Aester ever follows through with its threat to boycott the other clans in response to her attempting to curb their power. "I'd prefer you not take our warships and soldiers every time, though. I will need them, and I don't want to see soldiers hurt." She stops, warmth draining from her cheeks. "What happened to the sailors on the *Beholder* and *Vanguard*?"

"Most survived," Morrow reassures. "A few did not withstand Calliope's power before we could equip them with the protective bracelets. Most chose to join our crew. Some were abandoned in Aluina and Drakr territory. Those who insisted on fighting back did not survive."

Lora's stomach clenches. If she implements this plan, there will be more sailors who do not survive when they are doing nothing more than their jobs. It's enough to make her second-guess. To doubt.

"War is messy," Peregrin says. "Not everyone survives, and not everyone who dies by our own hands deserves to."

Lora releases a breath, knowing they're right. She must find the strength to withstand the guilt of her decisions. "For this arrangement to work, do not harm them if it can be avoided. Incapacitate them long enough to empty their hulls and leave."

"Perhaps we should give back the *Vanguard*," Candor suggests. "If the people of Aluina decide to leave, we won't have enough crew to man both ships."

"Wait." Calliope throws up her hands. "We haven't even decided if we're going to help yet."

"Haven't you?" Tavish asks, cocking his head in her direction.

"Should we leave you be and let you discuss it?" Peregrin presses.

Calliope glares at Peregrin, then glances swiftly from Morrow to Candor. They both nod. Then Calliope bobs her head as well. Lora smiles, victorious.

"We can abandon the *Vanguard* to be found in a week or two from now," Morrow suggests. "When we figure out which of the sailors who are either too unintelligent to make a connection of your presence and our decision to leave it... or smart enough to know to keep their silence regarding their Sovereign's dealings."

"Send a bird when you do," Lora says. She pushes back her

chair. "Now, if you please, I have a decree that needs to be sent, a regent to speak to about how he's been treating some of his citizens, and wars to prepare for. I'm quite busy. And I'm not even sure how I'm going to explain why I've been missing."

"I have a better idea," Ayc says. "A bit more theatrical, and we'll have to move quickly. But if we play it right, Lora will come out of it looking like she negotiated the release of the *Vanguard* from pirates instead of being in league with them."

Morrow cocks his head. "Let's hear it."

AYC

Ayc wants his coins back, and time is running out.

They are leaving the *Beholder*'s deck soon. Both of the pirates' warships have dropped anchor, and the sorcerer aboard the *Beholder* has sent a message to the sorcerer on the *Vanguard*. Ayc's plan is a simple one. Lora will return—hours later than she was expected—but with the *Vanguard*, its crew, and the people of Aluina. The sailors are being told a simple but marvelous tale. Their Sovereign was taken prisoner, but through quick wits and powerful threats, she negotiated their release.

Harlowe's ship, manned by Morrow's sailors with protective bracelets, is crossing between them now. They must pick up Lora and the others from this ship before returning to the *Vanguard*. They want to spare the royal guards and the sailors the pain of being within a hundred yards of Calliope. They haven't been gifted the same bracelets as Ayc and the others yet.

Peregrin, Candor, Lora, and Morrow all watch the ship cut across the waves from where they wait near the stern, talking in low voices. Ayc leans against the head mast nearby, trying to ignore the spasms twisting through his back. Tavish stands at his side. Saga is at his feet. His hand wrapped in the Kindred leash, Tavish has given silent commands to the dog to look toward the starboard side, where Calliope leans against the railing of the warship. Calliope's hair casts in the breeze, and she uses the curtain to pretend like she isn't glancing at Tavish every few minutes, too.

It's painful to watch. Ayc hesitates, indecisive. They only have a few minutes before they disembark, and who knows when Ayc will get a chance to retrieve his coins? But also, who knows when Tavish will be able to speak to Calliope again? They both clearly want to, but something prevents them. Ayc shifts his weight, decides, and sighs.

He doubts Calliope will give him back the coins now, anyway. It'll take time to win her trust.

There's still time for Tavish, though.

Ayc elbows Tavish gently in the side. "You should go talk to her."

"I, uh…" Tavish rolls his pearl between his fingers. "I can't."

"Can't? Why not?"

"Because she's…" He heaves a sigh that sounds like it comes from the depths of his soul. "Well, she's different."

"All the more reason you should talk to her before you lose the opportunity."

"No, I mean, she's different. She's the *only* person I've ever kissed…and—and—and—" He stammers and then swallows audibly and says in a rush. "The only person I've ever felt more for. And I've never, well…you know." He makes a peculiar gesture with his hand, and it takes Ayc a second to understand what he means.

"Oh!" Ayc says, a bit too loudly. He curses himself silently and adds more softly, "Oh." He can't figure out what else to say, so he shuts his mouth and holds space in the silence, knowing Tavish is trusting him with his vulnerability.

Tavish lowers his voice further. "Zephen and the pirates used to bully me mercilessly for it. Used to say there was something wrong with me because I didn't want to go to bed with anyone and everyone who gave me an opportunity."

"Assholes," Ayc hisses. "There's nothing wrong with you."

"I know that. At least I know that now. When I was in Totus Omni, I started to think that maybe I was like Xylie is, and I just didn't feel desire like that. But I know that I felt...felt that longing for her. Only her. And I still feel it for her after all these years, so maybe I can only feel it when I have a deep connection with someone." He throws up a hand. "Maybe I shouldn't still feel those things for her. It makes no sense whatsoever. I barely know her now, but I can't...I can't make myself stop. Even when she was torturing us, I felt that longing for her. How ridiculous is that?"

Ayc lets out a long breath and forces himself not to look at Lora. "I think arguing with our hearts about what it wants is a foolish task. You should go talk to Calliope."

Tavish shakes his head so vigorously, the taut springs of his curls bounce. "No, I don't... It's not... I simply can't—"

Ayc straightens from the mast, biting back a groan, and wraps a gentle hand around Tavish's elbow. "Let's go, handsome."

The role of pining asshole is already filled by Ayc, anyway. If they have more than one in their little party, it's going to be insufferable.

Tavish continues to form protests as Ayc pulls him toward Calliope, but Saga wags his tail. Calliope turns at their noise, propping her hip against the rail. She narrows her eyes at Ayc.

"Tavish wants to talk to you," Ayc declares.

The crinkle around Calliope's eyes softens as she focuses on Tavish.

"I, um..." Tavish says, rubbing the back of his neck. "Hello."

Well, hello is at least something.

"Is this Saga?" Calliope says.

The mention of Tavish's beloved dog immediately eases the tension in his shoulders. "Yes."

"Can I pet him?" she asks.

Tavish nods and gives Saga a soft command, one that tells the dog he's off duty. Saga relaxes and sits down, their tongue lolling out. Calliope stoops down and allows Saga to smell her fingers. He licks them.

"*You're* a beautiful boy, aren't you, Saga?" she coos.

"You're beautiful!" Tavish blurts at a level that is much louder than necessary. A few nearby pirates stop the swabbing of the deck to stare at him. Tavish presses his knuckles over his lips, his cheeks inflating in embarrassment.

Color flushes Calliope's freckled cheeks. She ducks her head to hide behind her hat.

Ayc bites the inside of his lip to keep from laughing. "That's perfect, Tavish," he whispers. "Try again. Just lower the volume."

Tavish releases a breath and dares to try again. "You're even more beautiful than I imagined you would be."

Calliope peeks up. "You can see me?"

Ayc grins. As Tavish explains about the Kindred collar, Ayc peddles backward to give them space. He returns to the mast and turns his attention to the wispy clouds in the sky above. When he looks back a Tavish and Calliope, their hands rest on the railing of the ship beside one another. Close to touching, but not quite. Millimeters and miles.

Don't waste it, Tavish, Ayc silently begs, but the two still haven't touched when Harlowe's boat comes to a rest beside the warship.

A pirate lowers the ladder. Ayc comes to the rail to squint over the side. He gulps. He might as well be escaping from a third-floor window as tall as the ship is. Damn. That's going to be awful. His back will be screaming more than it already is. Peregrin glares down it, like they're thinking the same thing, but they tuck their cane behind their back, slipping it into the strap of their knife holster. The ladder swings, rocking with the strong waves. The sailors down below are struggling to keep the little boat from ramming into the side of the warship.

Lora waits until Peregrin is all the way on the ship before she steps onto the ladder. She nods to Morrow and Candor, then slides down it effortlessly and jumps from the last few rungs, landing squarely on the deck in a crouched position.

Fuck. Does she purposefully do things that are ridiculously sexy just to torment him, or is it just a happy coincidence?

"You and Saga next, Tavish," Ayc says, realizing that he has one brief opportunity to ask about his coins if he's the last one on the ship.

Just as they did in the fisherman's boat before going to Somnia Ignis, they wrap Saga carefully in ropes, and the pirates help Ayc and Tavish lower the dog down. Lora calls up to Saga. The words are lost in the sea and wind, but the soothing gentleness carries.

"He's safe," Ayc assures Tavish as soon as Lora and Peregrin free Saga from the ropes.

Tavish releases a breath, then twists in Calliope's direction. She positions herself fully in front of him, within reach, clearly waiting. Hoping.

"It was good seeing you again," Tavish says. "I, uh…"

Ayc wanders a few steps away and turns his back, giving them the space for a goodbye. Candor and Morrow do the same.

Candor snaps his fingers at a sailor who stops to stare. "Find somewhere else to be," he hisses.

"I'm afraid I'll hurt you," Calliope says, her voice so soft that Ayc would have missed it if the wind blew any other direction.

"What do you mean?" Tavish asks.

"If I touch you. Even with the bracelet, I'm afraid that I would hurt you."

"I'm not," he says swiftly. "Afraid, that is."

The wind whips in the sails. Saga barks from down below.

"Everything well?" Lora's voice finds a break in the wind.

"You should go," Calliope says.

"Yeah, all right. Goodbye, Calli."

Ayc rolls his eyes as he turns back around to find Tavish reaching for the ladder. *For fuck's sake…*

Then Calliope closes the distance and raises her hands to Tavish's face, her palms cupping around his cheeks. His lips part in surprise.

Calliope whispers words Ayc doesn't quite hear, but by the shape of them, he thinks she says, "Does it hurt?" Her thumbs tremble as they stroke across the deep blue on Tavish's cheekbones.

Tavish shakes his head, and then he kisses her.

Ayc snaps his head back around, biting back the desire to cheer. Candor smiles behind his beard. Morrow shoots a glare at someone else who tries to stop and gawk, his eyes glowing a frightening green.

It's several long moments later when Ayc hears voices again. "I'll find a way to write to you," Tavish promises. His expression twists, and he looks like a man being led to the gallows as he steps away from her and carefully climbs over the railing.

She presses her fingers to her lips, trying to hide her smile.

Ayc pauses beside her on the way to the ladder. A minute, maybe two—that's all he has to convince her. "Can I have my coins back?"

She drops her hand. The smile tumbles. The fierceness returns to her narrow eyes. "I'm not certain you deserve them."

He bites back the desire to fight with her. She's judging him unfairly, but she grew up in a world where Drakr could not be trusted. Where men she didn't know tried to sell her for their own gain. She has every right to be wary. He's not owed her trust just because he thinks he deserves it.

"All right," he says simply. "But the ones who gave me the coins did, and that's not your decision to make. Vidar trusts me, and he sent me to you. You can choose to trust me or not, but those two coins are mine."

She glares at him. Ayc stretches out his hand.

She reaches into her pocket and slaps the coins down in his palm. Only there are no longer only two. There are three. "I've only met one other Drakr worthy of trust, and I'm not certain of you yet. But Tavish is. So that's for him. I owe him everything. And besides, Asbjorn could use another shadow wielder."

Ayc tampers his desire to smile, afraid if he does, she may change her mind. She strikes him as volatile as the sea. "Are you going to give me a clue?"

"I already did." She crosses her arms over her chest. "Now get off my ship." She storms away.

Ayc doesn't have time to sort through what she said because Lora hollers, "Ayc, get your ass down here!"

Ayc braces himself for the pain. He has one of Reselda's pain relievers. It's tucked in his pack in the cabin on the ship below, put there when he started the journey. He just has to reach the bottom.

Each sway of the wind stresses his muscles as he fights to remain balanced. He grits his teeth against the pull and climbs down. He's only five feet up from the deck when someone yells, "Brace yourself!"

The gust of wind slams against the ladder and rips it from Ayc's hands. He slams down on the deck of Harlowe's ship.

THIRTY-NINE

AYC

His body screams. He can't breathe. Can't fucking think. For a blinding, disorienting second, everything is pain.

"Ayc!" Lora calls. Through his spinning vision, he sees her boots rushing toward him. "Are you all right?"

He gasps a breath and forces himself to move, to roll to his knees. He can't lift himself any farther, and his head sags onto the wood. "It wasn't…far," he says between pulls of breath.

It's true. It wasn't that far of a fall. On someone else's body, it wouldn't hurt like this. But in his body? The body that hurts on even good days, that survived Calliope's power, that withstood his pull of power, and now took this impact? That body feels as though it's going to combust with the pain, fall to ashes, and be blown away in the wind.

"Bullshit," Lora says. Her fingers brush against his hair, trying to push it away so she can see his face. The touch is torture, a different kind of pain. "Where are you hurting?"

"Everywhere," he says.

Maybe he's in too much pain to lie, or maybe he's just kept it hidden for too long, and he's so tired of it. So tired of pretending he's fine when he's not. It's foolish that this little fall should be what breaks his resolve, but perhaps he should have let it shatter long ago.

"What do you need?" Tavish asks.

"Pain tonic," Ayc says. "My bag. Below."

Lora races away. Peregrin—or perhaps it's Tavish—works to help him sit up. At first, they try to steer him to sit against the railing, but he grits his teeth and fights to get to his feet. "Downstairs," he says. He doesn't want to be seen by anyone else —not like this, not when he looks weak.

Peregrin offers their elbow. Ayc might be able to make it without support. He did it with Calliope's pain, but his body feels exhausted, simply done with bearing it. It demands rest in an unforgiving way. So he takes Peregrin's elbow.

"Breathe, Ayc," Peregrin encourages softly as they help Ayc down the stairs. "In through your nose, out through your mouth. Like I taught you."

Lora throws the door open before they reach it. Concern writes itself in every wrinkle of her brow, and Ayc wants to ease it away. He forces a smile, even as she moves out of the way. He collapses on the low couch, resting his back down upon it. Its softness offers immediate relief. Lora presses the alchemy bottle into his hand, and he swallows it down. It'll take a while for it to kick in, so he takes slow breaths, just as Peregrin taught him, and imagines that protective wall. The wave of pain recedes.

"Perhaps we should turn around. Perhaps, the *Beholder* has a healer on board," Lora says.

"No," Ayc says. His words come in between broken breaths. It hurts to even speak. "We can wait. Until we get back to Reselda. The fall didn't. Injure me. It's just flared. My pain. I just need a minute for the pain tonic to work."

"I don't understand," Lora snaps. "What do you mean it flared your pain?"

Ayc hesitates, dragging yet another breath through his teeth.

"Do you care to finally explain why you've stunk of muscle rub?" Peregrin presses. They settle onto the other couch, leaning back like they are determined to wait.

The line between Lora's brows deepens. "I thought it was a consequence of how hard you've been working to control your power. Is that not why?"

Something with Ayc surrenders. It's time. It's far past time, but he isn't prepared for the impact of the truth. It's heavy. But he unlocks the tightness in his jaw and, finally, lets the truth pour out. About how his pain never faded after the Severing stone. About Reselda's theory and the therapy she has provided. As he explains, Tavish sits beside Peregrin. At first, Lora stands, and then she paces, and then she finally sinks down on the couch next to his feet.

He watches the truth settle upon her like a storm overtaking the sky. She tries to hide it, but he sees it in the way the color of her eyes shifts from violet to the dark of a rain cloud. She cares about him. The truth would not impact her so greatly if she did not, and her empathy is a gift, a balm. It doesn't make him want to protect her from the weight of him any less.

When he finishes, all three of his friends are silent. They have only a little longer to be alone. The ship has been swaying this entire time, the water shushing on the hull, carrying them to the *Vanguard*.

"Why didn't you tell us?" Lora demands.

Ayc winces at the anger in her voice, but there's something deeper beneath the anger. Something that sounds like a warrior who has been mortally wounded.

"I just..." The pain tonic has finally begun to work—enough that he can sit up. He slides upward slowly until he's in a sitting position. He sags against the pillow resting on the arm of the sofa. "I just wasn't ready to face it yet. I didn't want everyone to see it."

Something sparks in Lora's eyes before she shutters them closed. Ayc's heart twists.

"I'm sorry," he says. And he is. He's sorry he wasn't strong enough to tell the truth. And he's still sorry that he's not nearly as strong as she needs him to be—her Fifth, her shadow wielder, her dragon rider. "I should have told you."

"I understand, boy," Peregrin says, their voice

uncharacteristically gentle. "It can be hard to find the right way to speak of your pain. Much of the world is not kind to people who suffer in invisible ways. If you mention your suffering, you're complaining. If you don't, it must not be that bad. It's hard to know what you're supposed to do. But I find the best thing to do is not to hide from the people who love you. We would have helped you. Tempest would have given you feathers willingly."

Emotion wells up in Ayc's throat, and not all of it is sad. It still makes swallowing hard. "I know."

Lora glares at him, her fingers fisting around the edge of the couch. "If you knew we would help you, then why did you not tell us?" The steel in her tone tells him that the vague answer he gave before will no longer work. Only the truth—the deep, painful truth that feels like scooping out his chest cavity to speak—will do.

"I am your Fifth. Your shadow wielder. I was chosen by Muffin to be Everadyn's dragon rider. And I did not want you to fear that Muffin made the wrong choice or that I will fail you."

Her mouth parts. He casts his gaze toward the cabinet of liquor that gently rocks in the sway of the ship.

"Fail me?" Lora repeats as though he's spoken in a foreign language. "Fail me?" She releases a series of curse words, and Ayc knows he's fucked up because he's never heard her use quite that many in a row. "Peregrin, Tavish, can you give us a minute?"

Aye, this time, he's a dead man.

He continues to stare hard at the liquor bottles as Peregrin and Tavish leave him behind to face Lora's wrath on his own. The door shuts.

"Ayc, look at me."

He glances her way, bracing himself for what's to come. She has every right to be angry with him for hiding it for so long, for lying to all of them, for jeopardizing them by not being honest about his limitations. But he doesn't find anger when he looks at her. He finds...well, he can't describe it. He only knows that it makes it more difficult to breathe.

"Firstly, I want to say I'm sorry you're in pain," she says. "I wish that I could go back in time and help you sooner. Perhaps then, you would not be." Sorrow appears in her eyes, so deep that he nearly goes to her. He wants to pull her into his arms to kiss her cheeks, and to beg her forgiveness for ever making her feel a fraction of that sorrow. And that's exactly why he stays on the couch—to avoid crossing the line she's laid between them.

But the sadness is gone as quickly as it came, and a little growl appears beneath her voice. "Secondly, if I hear you suggest again that you're not worthy of being my Fifth or Muffin's rider, I'm going to personally kick your ass. You will not fail."

"Lora—"

"Shut up," she snaps. "You will not fail." She returns to the sofa that Peregrin and Tavish abandoned and perches on the edge. She leans toward him as she presses sincerity into every word. "You will not fail, because I know you. I've known you for a decade, and never once have I ever thought you were weak. Foolish, yes. Too kind for your own good? Absolutely."

He parts his mouth to protest, and she shushes him with a slice of her hand. "I said shut the fuck up."

He snaps his mouth shut.

"You have always been one of the strongest people I have ever known. All that life has thrown at you, and you've survived it and never once let it steal your joy or goodness. Last night, I was rendered utterly useless. I couldn't even have walked if it wasn't for you. You withstood Calliope's power when no one else could except Peregrin. You've been able to do things with your power that Bronwen tells me should not be possible without years of building up endurance, all because of your ability to withstand pain. You've sought help from Reselda and dedicated yourself to doing the treatment, and that alone would be enough. All of that is the very opposite of weak. That's why I'm certain Muffin made the right choice. That's why I do not believe there is anyone more worthy than you. And more importantly, so long as you live and breathe, you can't fail me. As long as you keep existing, day after day, that is enough."

Ayc presses a fist to his lips and says nothing because he's quite concerned that if he speaks, he will cry. It feels as though she's reached inside his soul and knitted together cracks in the very foundation of his being. It isn't just what she's saying. It's the way she's looking at him. There's an emotion in his eyes he can't dare name because it would require hope, hope he has not entertained since he kissed her in the Bromalis Garden.

She reaches toward him, her hand almost resting on his knee, before she quickly pulls away. She clears her throat and replaces her stony mask, and just like that, the hope vanishes. Still, she cares deeply about him. She's offering friendship and concern, and all of those are things he will treasure, even if his foolish heart will never stop wishing for more.

"Are you feeling better?" she asks.

He nods.

She narrows her eyes at him skeptically. He's earned that. He's sure it'll be a while before he says he's fine, and she trusts him. "Promise me we're done lying to each other. Promise me you won't hide anything again."

The words slam into his stomach. There's three golden coins in his pocket that come with a host of knowledge she deserves to know. But he can't tell her that. So he lies, "I promise."

"Good." Lora stands. "I think the ship is slowing. Let's get Irving and get back."

"Worried about what the aerial army is going to do?" Ayc asks.

"No, I'm worried about what Bronwen is going to do if I'm not back soon. She's my best friend. The world should tremble in fear."

Xylie, Bronwen, and Muffin are all waiting on the dock at Forfyre when the sailors steer the ship into the marina. Ayc feels Muffin before he sees them because the link between him and Muffin snaps back into place. He feels it like his heart has been fitted back into his ribcage before he hears the roar in his head. *"Ayc!"*

They took the *Vanguard* to the garrison first, escorted by gryphon riders who located them only an hour after they separated from the pirates. Peregrin and Tempest rode ahead, the gryphon very relieved to be able to approach her rider once more. They prepared the Admiral for what was about to happen. Of course, Admiral Eira was already prepared for the people of Aluina. She was not prepared for Lora's demands that the navy house them for the time being, until she can make other arrangements for them. While they helped get the immigrants settled, a gryphon rider took a message to Bronwen and Xylie, who had just received news of Lora's lack of arrival at the garrison thirty minutes before. Not enough time for Bronwen to wreak havoc. At least, not too much.

After things were settled at the garrison, they got back aboard Harlowe's ship and headed back to Forfyre.

Ayc doesn't wait for the boat to be anchored in place before he steps on the dock. The wood trembles beneath his feet as Muffin races toward him. They try to pull up short, but they're moving too fast, and they slide into Ayc with a force that knocks him to the dock. Thank gods, he drank down one of Tempest's gryphon feathers at the garrison, or he might not have gotten back up again.

"Fucking shit, Muffin," Ayc groans.

Muffin stares down at him, his great white muzzle taking up most of Ayc's field of vision. *"Are you dead?"*

"Yes, Muffin, I'm dead. You've killed me."

Muffin sniffs over his face, the long drags through their nostrils pulling Ayc's hair upward. They snort out. *"You're not dead."*

"No thanks to you." He pushes Muffin's head to the side and sits up. Xylie is there, offering her hand, and Ayc takes it. Xylie throws her arms around him, and he's surprised to hear her whisper against his chest.

"I thought you were dead," Xylie says. "For only about five minutes, but still."

Ayc hugs her back. Soon, he's going to have to come clean

with her about his pain. He's going to have to make it clear that there will never be a day that he's not grateful for everything she did to set him free. He'll have to make sure she understands that there are some fates that are far worse than the lot he's been given. His life may be filled with pain, but it's all full of joy and friendship and love. And Xylie is no small part of that.

Over her head, he sees Bronwen embrace Lora. When she leans back, she presses a paper into Lora's hands. It's the decree that Lora sent with the rider, and Ayc is certain Bronwen and Xylie have already signed it. Lora whispers something to her, and Bronwen nods. Together, they turn and stride back up the dock, the two most powerful women in Everadyn walking toward a small crowd of people who have gathered.

Harlowe stands at the end of the docks, and there's a crowd with him. Ayc recognizes a few of the faces from the interrupted banquet. Council members and forge owners and investors and merchants. Rich people whose lives Lora is about to fuck up.

Good.

Ayc can tell by the look on his face that Harlowe will not be their ally after this day. Ayc has no regrets, not just because it aids the workers in the factories who have been taken advantage of, his Aluina community, but because it is exhausting to pretend to be something they are not. Today, Lora and her Five decided to pretend a little less, to let the truth of who they are shine over the games that politics force them to play.

For better or for worse, the truth shines clearer today, and the world feels brighter for it.

CHAPTER

FORTY

LORA

Home.

Lora is home.

The forest of Elodie stretches beneath the airship like a thick, deep green blanket that Lora wants desperately to wrap herself up in. She didn't realize how much she missed the trees until this moment, gazing down upon the forest of the Totus Omni people. It feels as though she's been breathing through smoke, and finally, she's able to have a breath of oxygen. A knot in her chest unhitches, and the anxiety that has grown as a heavy weight upon her sternum no longer seems so heavy.

She's home.

It's been a long few weeks since pirates abducted her, since Harlowe reacted like she was destroying the country by her decree. Dedryk also did not react kindly to the decree. It did not make the Tour through Noxumbra and Audori any easier. Her timeline was already thrown off with the entire pirate business, and it was hard to get it back on schedule. But visits to the towns and villages were full of conflict. Some were not excited about her new decrees. They saw newcomers as competition, not neighbors.

Some praised her for her kindness, but they did it in quiet voices, nowhere near the volume of the opposing side.

Kindness is not weakness, but it will always be seen as such if people respond to screams of hatred with murmured whispers.

Lora wished they would speak louder. She wished that *she* could speak louder. Sometimes, the injustice and the foolishness of it all built up until she wanted to scream with it. She has always felt like that, like every injustice she finds is sown into her very soul, and she has to bear it. It's a weight that grows heavier and heavier. It's enough to make her want to rage, to slam her fist into something, to turn into the volcano that could explode the world and put it back together.

She's having a harder time holding it all in. The parties are the hardest, with the hand-shaking and the touching and noise, noise, noise, noise. By the end, every sensation, even ones she normally finds comforting, made her want to scream when they brushed her skin. She locked her jaw, chomped her teeth, shifted her weight, played with the cord the leviathan tooth hung on, and once, even excused herself to find a quiet room where she bit down on her hand to scream again. Only once, though, because it startled Irving, who has been on edge since the pirates. The tooth marks also took forever to fade.

By the time she arrived back in Wyntra, several days late, she was desperate for rest. And *quiet*. It did not come. She was only home for hours when she received word that Morrow, Calliope, Candor, and their crew pillaged one of her ships. She spent the rest of the time at Wyntra meeting with navy officers, mirroring their concern that the sea witch they thought was just the ravings of a dying man was, in fact, real. There were plenty of survivors this time to confirm the tale.

At least, all the drama gave her a reason to cancel the visit with Damara. The Drakr sent only two words in response to her letter asking that they skip this visit due to unforeseen emergencies.

Very well.

Lora has already received a letter from Morrow, brought by an eagle, saying they deposited her part of the bounty where she expected. It also came with it a thick parchment: a letter from Calliope to Tavish. She embossed the letters into the parchment so he could read it with his fingertips. The smile on his face made Lora's heart twist in both delight and sickening jealousy. She fought not to look at Ayc.

There were so many other matters to attend to while at Wynra. Another round of reports for the clans arrived, but offered no viable leads for who put midnight in her bed. Laud is still declining Lora's invitation. Lux Aester wants to postpone their dates on the Tour again until it is past when they go to Drakr. She knows they are stalling, or perhaps they are busy with the nonviolent protests popping up in their cities or trying to suppress the court cases that are attempting to get an appeal to Lora's ear. Either way, she's tired of Amos's games.

All of it has accumulated. Exhaustion has settled into her bones like someone has sewn lead into them, weighing her down with every step. At least she's in the Forest of Elodie for a week, among the people and the clan who have always seemed to understand the importance of every soul. She'll finally get to speak with Grey and secure them as an ally. Perhaps, if she does that, she'll feel less like a volcano about to explode.

"Muffin, I know what you're thinking. If you think I had scraping your ass off the forest floor on this trip itinerary, guess the fuck again."

Lora drags her eyes away from the tops of evergreens to the opposite side of the airship's dock, where Ayc is marching toward Muffin. Their front feet are poised on the railing of the ship like they are considering leaping from it.

The ache that lives beneath Lora's sternum grows fiercer at the sight of him. He lives there, like a knife beneath her armor, the only one who's ever been able to slip beneath. If absence and distance are supposed to help, supposed to make her stop wanting him, it's done nothing to blunt the acuteness of *him*. He's there constantly, on the edge of her thoughts, on the border of her heart, haunting her like her own shadow. Making all of her valiant reasons to stay away from him feel thinner by the minute.

Muffin snorts, the breath making curls as it comes out of their nose. They drop their feet down to the ground but swish their tail. Whatever they are communicating, it makes the irritated look on Ayc's face grows more intense. The kohl that lines his eyes looks even darker when he's angry.

"Tempest is not mocking you," he says. He does that a lot. Forgets about the bond and speaks aloud to Muffin, especially when he's particularly irritated.

Tempest seems to take that as her cue to fling herself out of a cloud above them, tuck her paws beneath her, and pirouette into the next cloud. Such a showoff.

Muffin lets out a low growl of protest. Ayc huffs out a breath. "Very well, perhaps she's teasing you a little."

The dragon and gryphon have continued to work together, and Muffin has made exceptional progress. The two can be seen doing loops in the sky around their camp, but Muffin still doesn't have the endurance to make the flight from Orchis to Silvae. And Muffin's wings still spontaneously buckle. Lora has to have part of the Wyntra castle's stable rebuilt, thanks to that. Ayc offered to do the repairs, but she wouldn't hear of it.

It won't be like that for long. Soon, both Ayc and Muffin will dominate the sky. Lora is certain of it. She can already see it. Muffin, with their white scales gleaming like a rainbow in the sunlight, and Ayc upon their back, dressed in the uniform she gave him. It will be glorious.

And she'll watch, dreaming that she's the one he's flying home to, even as she knows they are a fool's dreams.

Fuck. She's too tired for this.

The ship drifts lower toward the massive clearing ahead, where she knows Silvae will be. The captain's voice booms, magically amplified, reminding everyone to go down to their cabin as they prepare to land. Ayc stays on deck with Muffin, but all the others in her party file downstairs to the common area. It's a mistake because they have not taken a private flight, and she's immediately cornered by a merchant who would also like to discuss an issue. He's made it only a couple of sentences when Bronwen sweeps in to rescue her, making some polite excuse about needing to speak with the Sovereign privately.

"Are you well?" Bronwen asks when she steers Lora back to their private cabin. "You seem tired."

"I am," Lora admits. "But I'll be fine. It'll be good to be home. How are you?"

It's a change in subject, but Lora does want to know. The medicine seems to be finally fully working, but being in Noxumbra, where they both had so many memories of Ryker, was hard on Bronwen. Lora is certain that's why Wylder stayed far away during her time in Noxumbra. His father made excuses—he took a position in a special division in the armies, and he was busy training. Maybe that was true. Or perhaps Wylder couldn't bear for the three of them to be together when it was so often four before.

"Better," Bronwen says. "I still miss Ryker every day."

"Oh," Lora says. It's the first time she's said his name since the night in her office after his coronation. She sits on the edge of her bed and pats the blanket next to her.

Bronwen sits down, her back stiff. "I want to say something to you, but I don't know...now might not be the right time. But I need to say it, and I want you to think about it, all right?"

"All right," Lora says, though she's not certain if she wants to hear what Bronwen has to say.

"I loved Ryker, Lora," Bronwen says. "I loved him, and he loved me, and everyone knew. But I was a fool who refused to admit it." Moisture gleams in her blue eyes, but she swiftly bats away the tears and takes a breath to steady her voice. Lora reaches over, offering her hand, and Bronwen takes it and holds it in both her own. "Growing up, being forced to be someone I wasn't, made some part of me believe no one would ever really see me. Ever really love *me*. So I made excuses rather than take a chance. I told Ryker we were too young. That he didn't really know what he wanted. And it was all such a ridiculous attempt to protect myself. I wanted to keep myself from getting hurt. And now he's dead. And do you know what I realized?"

Lora fights to swallow. Bronwen squeezes her hand.

"It still fucking *hurt*. I tried to protect myself, and it didn't matter. It hurt anyway. And I would tear my soul apart if it meant I could turn back time and cherish every single moment we could have had together if I hadn't been so fucking scared."

Lora can scarcely breathe. The words wrap around her heart and lungs like wool yarn that has come unraveled and tangled into an irredeemable mess. It pulls tighter with each attempt to draw in more air.

"I'm sorry," Lora finally manages.

Bronwen swipes at a stray tear. "I didn't tell you this for empathy. I told you it as a warning."

"A warning about what?"

"I think you know."

Lora shakes her head, but she does know. She can hear Ayc's accusation. *I'm hearing you. I hear all the reasons why you're too afraid to risk being together.*

It's logic. That's what she's been using this entire time. Her mother is not wrong. Love is vulnerability. It could risk her crown. It could risk her duty.

Excuses that have felt more and more like just that. Excuses.

How can Ayc be a weakness when, on that pirate ship, Ayc was the only thing that kept her upright? How can being with him be a weakness when he is the strongest thing she knows? Learning about his persistent pain, about all he survives daily, has only strengthened that feeling. And yet, she maintains her distance, even though staying away from him hurts like a wound she refuses to let heal.

Maybe Bronwen has a point. Maybe it has never been about protecting him.

Maybe Lora is simply afraid.

Cheers erupt, so loud they roar through the wood of the hull. The entire ship shudders as it settles down at its dock. Lora shoves to her feet. She pats her armor, her hair, the cord of the leviathan tooth around her neck, ensuring everything is in place. Perhaps if she reminds herself that she is perfectly together on the outside, she can feel as though she has it together inside, as well.

"Are you ready?" Lora asks.

"Forgive me," Bronwen says, pressing two fingers to the back of Lora's elbow. "I shouldn't have said anything now. I've been trying to find an opportunity."

"It's fine," Lora says. "Let's get on deck."

The cheers are even louder outside. A vast crowd has gathered to see her land. She lifts her hand as she approaches the side of the boat, and somehow, the cheers grow even louder. They're all calling one word, but it's not what other crowds have called, not Loraphne. Not Sovereign. It's *her* name.

Lora, Lora, Lora.

A genuine smile creaks onto her face, even as she shudders from the volume. She can feel the sounds inside her, vibrating her eardrums, rattling her bones. She spies Xylie coming from the cabin below. She clamps her hands over her ears, even though she's wearing the ear cuffs that quiet the sounds.

Lora wishes she could do the same. She did it once when she was a child. Her mother yanked her hands down and seethed, "Don't be rude."

Is it rude? To attempt to soften a world that has always been a bit too loud, a bit too bright, a bit too everything?

Lora presses her smile wider and keeps waving. She spots Grey at the front of the crowd. They blow her a kiss.

She reminds herself she's home.

Home.

It becomes a mantra as Grey leads Lora and her Five through Silvae, visiting the shops and sampling the food. She's been to Silvae many times, and it's familiar. Or it should be, but something feels strange. People she doesn't know want to hug her like she's a long-lost friend. Most here are at least polite enough to ask, but she doesn't feel as though she can say no, even when she grinds her teeth with every touch.

Shop owners speak to her pointedly about small business law when all she wanted was to ask if they had changed the formula of her favorite shampoo. The anise doesn't smell quite as strong. She's bought it from their shop many times.

When she visits Silvae's library, she doesn't go near the section she normally would like to. There are so many people watching in the aisle, even though they pretend they aren't, and she's not sure she wants everyone to know that she likes books where the major plot line is the main character getting fucked and getting fucked well.

Her favorite food stall asks her who will serve at her first Sovereign Day party and makes sure to give a card to each one of her Five. Lora thinks they've changed the recipe to their battered cheese because it doesn't taste the same.

Home. She reminds herself. She's home.

But it feels different. Whatever they cheer, she is not just Lora. Not just Hellevi's grandchild. She is the Sovereign. And they treat her like that.

She presses a fist over her gut, but it doesn't ease the ache there. She has come home, but it doesn't feel like home. What if it never feels like home again?

Every touch. Every sound. It still accumulates in her body. It doesn't bounce off. It gets stuck in her bone marrow. She breathes slowly. She rubs her fingers over her palm. She plays with the cord around her neck. She doesn't break. She won't break, even if she feels herself fracturing at the seam. She is stone, even if she feels like glass about to shatter.

She gets only a little reprieve when they return to their camp. Grey's home is far more modest than the rest of the regents, and they don't have room to house them. But they've set up a beautiful camp in a secluded area of Silvae's large public park. Vast tents of stunningly white fabric have been erected amongst the towering trees. Hers is at the very heart of the camp, and it appears that her grandmother has sent some things from her home to ensure she's comfortable. Among the large bed, fainting couch, and low table made up with bowls of fruits and sweets, Lora finds her favorite knit blanket, a large sweater she left at her grandmother's house last summer, a stack of books—some old, some new, but exactly the kind she likes. There's even a basket of yarn and knitting needles. Lora almost sobs when she sees it.

Home.

She buries her face in the knit blanket. It smells like her grandmother's house, a scent she can't describe. It's too many scents rolled into one, until it's become something entirely its own. Lora wants to wrap herself inside the blanket and stay curled up, read one of the books while working on her knitting. She's done none of those things since becoming Sovereign. Even during her busiest time at Adamant, she made time to weave and knit. It funded their organization, true. But it also helped steady her. The rhythmic movement of the knitting needles or the loom always centered her.

She did not realize how much she missed it until this moment. There is nothing she would not give for her people, for justice, for a better world. She just didn't realize she was losing herself in the process. Wearing the crown on her head demands it all.

She doesn't have the time. She needs to dress for the party. At least this dress does not require an attendant to assist her with it. It's a loose, forest green piece with long flowing sleeves. It's so sheer it looks like she's not wearing a dress at all—she is simply wrapped in the vines and leaves that embroider the fabric. She wears a slip beneath that matches her skin tone, and she studies herself in the mirror. She looks glorious, but the fabric rubs and itches on her skin. She doesn't remember the fabric itching when she tried it on before.

She tries to ignore it. She's just tired, and her skin is oversensitive when she's tired.

She puts on brown leather boots with an etching that mimics the dress and slides a knife inside of it. It's not as large as the one she straps to her thigh, but it was a compromise she was willing to make for the design of the dress. She pins her hair back on only one side with a pin that looks like a leaf and applies silver to her eyelids.

"Can I come in?" Bronwen says from the other side of the tent flap.

"Yes," Lora agrees.

Bronwen makes it only a few steps in when she pauses and gives Lora an appreciative gasp. "You look glorious, Lora."

"Thank you. As do you."

Bronwen gives a curtsy, grasping her deep brown skirt in her fingers. An embroidered pattern of orange and black works from the hem to the bodice, giving an illusion of monarch butterfly wings. When she straightens, Bronwen mutters a few words to herself. Lora has heard Bronwen do the spell enough times that she recognizes it as a silencing spell.

"Thank you," Lora breathes. The privacy the spell offers is a small gift, but it's a relief to know that she now has a place where she can fall apart in peace. Hopefully, she will not need it.

Night has fallen when Lora and Bronwen step outside. She finds all the others waiting, all looking exquisite in their tailored outfits. But her rebellious eyes lock onto Ayc. His green corset vest, stitched with a subtle leafed pattern, fits taut against the curve of his waist. Her palms ache. She wonders if her hands will ever stop aching from the desire to touch him.

Lora glances around the camp once more. She notes that Davos stands near Ayc's tent. A silhouette of a dragon remains inside. Good. Muffin has made it back. As soon as they landed, Muffin trotted off with Tempest to practice hunting. If the sound of crunching is any judge, it was successful. Maybe Ayc won't have to pay for any goats while here.

Lora squares her chin and focuses. She can feel overstimulated later. She must keep it together. She needs to find an opportunity to speak with Grey about Aluina. Perhaps, if she does, she can sneak out early to read a book.

Foolish dreams, but one she lets herself entertain as they all make their way across a bridge that stretches over the Ever River and through a thick line of trees. On the other side is a clearing where festivals are often held. The branches of the trees above them are so close that they interweave like a ceiling. They've been threaded with lanterns that hold lights of reds and blues and yellows, until it nearly looks like a dome stained glass. Blankets cover the ground below, people already stretched upon them. They laugh, pass around bottles of ruby red wine, and share food bought from one of the vendors who have set up on the edges of the clearing. In the very center, on an erected dais, a flutist plays a gentle tune, one of the first entertainers. They will have many: poets with their poetry, actors performing skits, and jesters telling jokes. Children race through the blankets, and in one area, have started a game of kicking a ball back and forth.

Normally, Lora would find herself on a blanket with a few close friends. She's attended events with Veni and other children from Avia and sometimes Hellevi. She even has memories of her father bringing her to one of these events. They abandoned the blanket to chase fireflies and put them in the jar. The memory makes her eyes burn. She wants to do that now. If she could eat and laugh and even smoke with her Five, she might have the best night of her life. But there are too many eyes upon her. The world is always watching.

Grey stands from a blanket nearby. They bow and offers their hand. "Come. Sit with us. There's so many of the Council who want to speak with you. Your Five are welcome to join as well."

Bronwen and Ayc join them, but they are on the corner of the blanket while Lora is pushed into the center of the Council. Peregrin wanders the perimeter of the party. Tavish and Xylie and Saga find a more distant blanket. Only a few minutes later, someone beckons to Bronwen. Lora recognizes them as a contact within the Lux Aester organization. Bronwen excuses herself, and they slip into the shadows together. Lora wants to go with them, but she would draw too much attention.

Lora scratches at her skin. She's itchy and hot, even though the late spring weather is mild. A choir comes out to sing, the loudness of it startling a bird. Someone is off-tune, and Lora wants to clamp her hands over her ears. The chatter of those around her turns into a hum. She can't focus.

"Lora, did you hear what I asked?" Grey repeats.

She stands. "I'm sorry. I need to get a drink." She ignores Grey's protest that someone can get it for her and rushes back toward the line of trees that separates her from the river and the camp. There are fewer people on this side of the clearing, so she tries to hide within the shadows. Shae, who is assigned to her side tonight, presses a cup into her hand. Lora isn't sure where her guard got it, but she forces herself to sip her drink. She draws in deep breaths and paces a small, tight path. A few people try to approach her, but Shae scares them away with a lift of her hand and a glare fiercer than any threat.

Shae studies Lora carefully. "My lady, are you—"

Ayc steps from the shadow, so close that Lora nearly collides with him. Startled, Shae swings, and Ayc darts to the side before he takes her fist in his face.

"For divine's sake," Shae snarls, "you have to stop doing that."

"Sorry," Ayc says. "I was trying to be subtle." He turns his attention to Lora. He searches her face, and she doesn't the way he seems to peer into her very soul. "Are you well?"

She nods because she's too focused on breathing in and out through her nose to speak.

He bends his head closer and drops his volume. "I don't believe you. Tell me what's wrong."

The kindness in his soft implore nearly shatters her, and she can't do that here. If she speaks, she's going to fall apart. She might fall apart anyway.

She has to go. Now. She pivots on her heel and escapes between two of the trees.

FORTY-ONE

LORA

The branches of the evergreen are so thick that they completely swallow the multi-colored lights of the party. She doesn't wait for her eyes to adjust to the darkness but pushes through. Feet crunch on the leaves behind her. Three pairs. Shae. Ayc. Maybe another guard she didn't realize was close.

She picks up her pace as though she might be able to run away from them, but she can't truly flee. If anyone saw her running from her own party, the entire realm would hear of it. She breaks from the line of trees, but she draws up short. She thought this direction would lead her back to the bridge over the Ever River and to the camp. She's too far upriver. The water extends before her, trapping her forward progress, blazing past the stones.

Ayc steps out of the trees just ahead of her, blocking the path between her and the bridge, though she doesn't think he intends to trap her. Shae steps out just beside him. They both move toward her at once, and Lora instinctively backpedals. She doesn't have anywhere to go. Back to the party or into the water—both feel like drowning.

"Are you all right?" Shae and Ayc both ask, their voices weaving onto each other.

Lora turns her back to them and drags a desperate breath through her nose.

"Go on, Shae," Ayc says, the implore soft as a lullaby. "I have her."

Shae protests. "But—"

"I *have* her," he insists. "Give her some space. Whatever is the greatest distance your duty lets you be, be that far away. We will shout if we need you."

I have her.

He's laced the words with such authority, such certainty, that Lora believes them. More than that, she feels them. The words are a warm blanket wrapped tightly around her shoulders, which isn't much against the war being fought within her, but it's something. It allows her to draw a breath.

She's fine. She *has* to be fine.

The last step Ayc takes toward her falls harder than the rest, and she can't help but think it's intentional to alert her of his nearness. It's unnecessary. Even in her state, she's as aware of his presence as she is of her own skin, the way it pricks with anticipation.

He asks the question softly, "What do you need?"

Lora sucks in a breath, ensures that her mask is back in place, and turns around. "Nothing. I'm—"

He cuts her off. "Lora, I've known you for half my life. Don't lie to me. I know you're not fine. I've been watching you ever since the Bromalis Gardens. You keep having to find times to escape. These parties are harming you in some way, and I wish you would tell me, so I can help you."

She swallows and shakes her head.

"Lora." Her name is a plea on his lips. "We swore we would not lie to one another. I told you of my pain. Please tell me of yours."

"It's different," she protests.

"It's not."

It doesn't seem fair to compare his physical pain to the way her skin reacts to everything, like she is a pincushion and all the world is dozens of needles pressed inside of her. But this *does* hurt, as real as any wound that has ever broken her skin. She looks fine, but then, so does he. Pain is no less real because someone can't see it.

When she says nothing, he crosses his arms over his chest, rocking back on his heels. Not in a way that suggests anger but instead whispers that he's fine waiting for as long as he needs. And it's strange that she wants to speak with him when she hasn't wanted to speak to anyone else. He's right. They've known each other for half their lives, bonded together since that day bathed in blood, tormented by the same woman, playing her same sick game, trying their best to survive. If anyone can understand why she's so done up in knots, it's him.

She's yet to decide when Grey emerges from the trees.

"Lora, are you well?"

Fuck! Not now!

Shae steps a little closer. The trees rustle, like another guard shifts closer, too, but does not reveal themself.

"Everything is well." Ayc pastes on a wide, seemingly easy smile. "Could you give us a minute?"

"It's fine, Ayc," Lora says.

She draws in a breath, and she shoves it all down. It feels akin to how she imagines a volcano feels—all that lava and brimstone pushed deep down within. She presses on her invisible mask, a calm but friendly expression as she turns full to face Grey. "I'm well. I apologize. I just needed a moment of quiet."

And she needs a distraction. Perhaps, now is not the time, but if she could speak to Grey, it might help with how she's feeling. It might help ease the explosion building from within her at all the injustice she has not yet corrected.

Anything, really, to get out of her own head. That's not a safe place to be right now.

"In fact," she says, "I've been meaning to speak with you all night."

Perhaps, it's a trick in the darkness, but Grey's easy smile wobbles before being pressed back into place. "Oh. Something you could not bring up earlier with the Council?"

"I would like to speak to you alone."

They rub their hands together as though they're trying to warm them, though the air is quite comfortable. Or hot. It certainly has felt hot. "Perhaps not tonight? We are at a party, after all."

"Right," Lora agrees quickly. This is not a conversation she wants to press on unwilling ears. "Tomorrow then."

They step closer. "Might I have a hint on what the conversation will entail?"

She forces her lips to tip upward and hopes they'll take the expression as a smile. "If you don't want to speak tonight, then let's leave it for tomorrow."

"I suppose I could render a guess. Lux Aester? Or perhaps Aluina? I know your heart is quite...tender on those topics."

Ayc presses closer to Lora's side. His smile is still easy, but his spine is stiff. He can sense something isn't right. She doesn't like that Grey continues to press, but this is Grey. She knows Grey. She's approaching a known ally.

"Yes," she agrees. "I know your heart is tender on those matters, too."

"Certainly." Grey paces toward the river's edge, where a bench has been constructed out of small boulders and a fallen log. "I feel deeply for the plight of the people in both places."

"Good. Then we can discuss next steps."

"Next steps?"

"On how to b—" She nearly says 'break the treaty' but pivots at the last moment, not sure why. "Best render aid."

"Ah, yes, I *do* look forward to discussing it with you." But their voice trails off, like their sentence ends in an ellipses, not a period.

"Why do I sense there's a 'but' in that?" Ayc presses.

"But..." Grey releases a breath so long, it's practically an entire novel. He sags onto the bench. "I think I should make it clear that

I will not support any action that might lead to Everadyn going to war, either civil or foreign."

A rock forms in Lora's throat. Fuck. She did not suspect that response.

She clears her throat of the emotion. "I would hope that we could find a way forward without war. But *something* must be done to stop the suffering of the people of Aluina and Lux Aester."

"Of course they should be helped." Grey flicks their wrist with a benignity that makes Lora's teeth ache the way they do before her canines sharpen. Grey has always been as calm and tranquil as an alpine lake. She's always admired that about them, but she doesn't appreciate it now. They sound like they are discussing the watering of trees, not people who have been oppressed for far too long.

Lora allows an edge to appear in her voice. "Then what would you have us do?"

"We could negotiate a better treaty with the Drakr."

"That's ninety years from now," Ayc says with a soft growl. "That's too long."

"We might be able to convince them back to the table early. Ninety years of an imperfect peace is better than ninety years of war." Grey offers a small smile that drips of pity like wounds drip of blood. "In the meantime, we can accept more refugees from Aluina. You've already prepared the way for that with your most recent decrees, which I applaud you for. As for those in Lux Aester, they can always leave. You know I will welcome them with open arms. If they chose to stay... Well, that's on them, isn't it?"

Ayc makes a sound like a growl, deep in his chest. The air around him grows cold. "Good to see your empathy dries up as soon as it jeopardizes your own comfort."

Grey's smile disappears. "*My* comfort? Without that treaty, what lumber would go to feed our forges or light our hearths or build our homes? Houses do not materialize on their own." They gesture above their heads, at the branches that arch between them and the night sky. "The Forest of Elodie is sacred. I won't see it harmed."

"Everadyn *had* a treaty for lumber," Lora reminds him. "With *Aluina*. With the royal family. One that went back for centuries."

They run a hand through their silver-touched hair, giving another of those long sighs. "And I grieve that Yris chose to break it in such a way. But undoing her action, mistake though it was, is not without significant cost."

"In such a way?" Ayc repeats through his teeth.

Lora hears it when Ayc repeats it. It rumbles through her like an earthquake. The heat of her feelings threatens to rise. She coils her hands into fists to keep them from shaking, to keep herself from completely erupting.

"Do you know what happened in Creed?" Ayc demands. "What *really* happened?"

A shadow crosses over Grey's eyes, as if they realize their misstep. She expects them to lie, but they finally say, "It's not hard to figure out."

"How many of the regents know what truly happened in Creed?" Lora asks.

"All of them. Well, perhaps not Qadira, unless Marisol told her before she stepped down."

All of them.

Lora can't stop her hands from shuddering now. She presses them behind her back so they can't see and shakes them to ease the pressure building beneath her skin. Just enough that she can think straight.

Her mother wasn't lying with her warning, though Yris certainly wasn't telling Lora the full truth. All the regents know what happened in Creed. They could have ousted Yris if they let that knowledge spread. They could have done... Well, Lora doesn't know exactly what they could have done, but they could have done *something*. There's only a thin difference between knowing and doing nothing and being an active participant. They are complicit in all of Yris's sins.

That doesn't surprise her for Amos or even Harlowe and Dedryk. But Briar, Busura, and especially Grey? They were supposed to be better than that. The betrayal stings, like a slap across her face.

Lora doesn't try to hide her fangs now. "And you've just gone along with it because... What? It made you all richer? Gave you cheaper labor? Saved our precious forest?"

Grey stands slowly, and when they take a step closer, the air grows even colder. "Don't act innocent, Lora. We all also know the role you played that day, too. Your hands are stained with that blood."

The words are a vice that reaches behind her sternum and yanks her heart out through solid bone. Her fingers spasm at the pain, tightening into fists so hard that her nails bite into her palm. Her canines elongate into points.

Ayc takes a step forward, half shielding her as he growls, "She was a child, you fucking asshole. A child none of you did a damn thing to protect." His eyes glow red in the darkness. Shadow weaves between his feet, twirls around his arms. Grey stumbles back a step before they gather their composure.

"She's still basically a child." They peer around Ayc at Lora. "Listen to us, Lora, before you do something you regret. You're young. You're naive. And—"

"I am getting very fucking sick of my youth being flung back in my face!" She flashes her canines, focusing on her rage. "If you truly find me so incapable, why did you support me for the Sovereignty Trials?"

They say nothing for so long, their silence becomes an answer.

"You didn't support me," Lora realizes.

When they still say nothing, she snarls.

"Did you?"

They lift their palms in a helpless gesture. "Don't get me wrong. I think you have the potential to be a tremendous Sovereign. Hellevi has raised you well. You've done good already, but I don't think you were ready for sovereignty yet. But if you heed the counsel of those who know better, I'm certain you'll achieve that potential still. But be careful, Lora. You get to decide what the story of your reign will be. You want to leave a legacy. You don't want to be made into a villain."

Villain. Villainess. The word that has been thrown her way since she was a child. The word she's tried so hard to escape because she wants so desperately to be out of the shadow of her mother's legacy, only to earn it the moment she drove that fossil into Marcellus's neck to spare her people from the fate of him as Sovereign. Now, they're using it as a weapon to keep her in line. She won't allow it.

She draws up her chin like she's wearing a crown. Because she fucking *is*. "If being remembered as a hero means being a simpering coward who never stood for anything, then I assure you, I'm quite content to be made a villain."

Grey sniffs, a disapproving noise that Lora barely hears. She's too busy basking in the smile Ayc beams upon her, like it's sunlight, and she's a rose in bloom, drinking it in.

"Well," Grey says, "I can see your emotions are getting the best of you. We should discuss it tomorrow."

It's so close to her own line—*no need to get so emotional*—that Lora wants to show him what it looks like when she *does* let her emotions get the best of her. She's barely clinging to control.

"You're awfully condescending for a sack of shit," Ayc says.

Grey cuts him a look. "Perhaps, you should learn to keep your mouth shut."

"I'd rather choke on my own dick. But thanks." Ayc's smile twists into something frightening as his eyes, once more, tint with red. The shadows creep away from his feet, toward Grey. "Now, tell your Sovereign good night, before my shadows come to play."

The look of fear is unmistakable as it flashes across Grey's face. They swiftly sweep a bow. "Good night, my lady."

They disappear back into the woods, back in the direction of the party. Lora stands, numb, listening to the soft bubble of the creek beside her, to the whisper of the wind in the trees. There's an eruption—the one she buried when Grey interrupted her— brewing deep within herself, but she hasn't yet felt it. It's only a matter of time. It's building stronger than before, rumbling her very foundations.

Ayc faces her, worry written in the tightness of his jaw. "Are you all right?"

The words crack her open. The volcano erupts. The overstimulation, the exhaustion, the fury at all the injustices of the world, the feelings of inadequacy, and this realization: Grey is not on her side. None of the regents will be on her side. The path to helping Aluina, the citizens of Lux Aester, is closing off. There are thousands—millions—who need her help, and she isn't sure how to help them.

This fucking world is full of one injustice after another. She feels them all like wounds in her soul. As Sovereign, she's supposed to be able to fix this. And she doesn't know how to fix it. Without a broken treaty, she has no army, and she can't break the treaty without the regents, and none of them are on her side.

She's going to fail them.

"Lora?"

She shakes her head. If he says one more kind word, she's going to break. And she can't break. Not here. Someone will see her. Someone will use it against her.

"I'm fine," she lies. She turns on her heel and rushes for the bridge, walking, but only just barely. Ayc follows her, and she wishes he wouldn't, but if she stops to fight him, she'll fall apart.

She crosses the bridge and darts toward the white billowing shapes of their tents. She sweeps into her tent, even more grateful that Bronwen put up that spell for silence.

Because she is going to explode.

This fucking dress is suffocating her. She yanks at it, needing it off her skin. Some of the applique leaves come off in her fists as she rips it overhead and flings it away from her. It leaves only the thin skin-toned slip behind. She thinks of pulling that off, too, but Ayc throws the flap of the tent open. He pauses there, his long shadow falling over the ground at her feet, casting strange and odd angles due to the single lantern hanging from the tent frame.

"What do you need?" he asks once more.

"You can go. I'm fine." Her voice is steady, which is not what she can say about herself. Her insides are quaking. She wants to pound her fists into the earth and scream until her voice shatters.

"You're not fine."

She whirls on him and adds a bite to her tone. "I want you to go!"

He doesn't even flinch. "I'm not leaving you," he says firmly. There's a tenderness in his gaze still. No, not tenderness exactly. Something deeper, stronger. An adoration she certainly doesn't deserve in this moment.

"You impertinent ass," she snaps, even though she doesn't know why. Even though she hates herself for it. "Always the noble fucking cinnamon roll! Can't you just listen to me for once in your fucking life?"

That intense emotion in his gaze never wavers. He even dares to fucking smile. "It won't work, my lady. I like it a little too much when you're mean to me. It won't make me leave you."

She stabs a finger toward the door. "Go! I cannot afford for anyone to see me as weak."

"You're not weak. Everyone falls apart—"

"*I* cannot fall apart. I am Sovereign! And I can't—" An invisible hand clamps around her throat, and she tries to speak around it. "I can't..." It clamps down harder, and she tries to pull in a breath, but her lungs are flattened. They refuse to expand. The breath turns into a gasp. "I can't fucking breathe."

Ayc surges across the space between them. Her vision is tinting with black, and she can scarcely see. But she can feel him. His tender, gentle hands on her bare biceps, the back of her shoulder, pressing her forward. And then she's against something solid, soft yet strong at once, like being wrapped tightly in a favorite blanket. It grounds her, and finally, oxygen pours into her lungs. Only then does her mind clear enough to realize that she's in Ayc's arms, against his chest. She knows just as quickly that she should pull away, but she doesn't fucking want to. She has wanted to be held by him for nearly as long as she can remember, a strange, inexplicable desire she could never quite fathom. But now that she's here, it makes complete sense. It feels safe, it feels good, it feels right—like a piece of her soul she didn't know existed is snapping into place.

So instead of pulling away, she presses her face deeper into his chest and clings to him. Her fingers tangle in his corset strings, locking him in place. She holds on to him like he's the piece of driftwood she was once left on in the middle of the ocean, the only safety against all her fears. Her shoulders tremble, and his arms tighten further around her.

"I'm here," he whispers into her hair. "I have you."

"I'm not weak," she mutters against his chest, not even sure why.

"Look at me, Lora." He leans back, and his arms lift from her back. She doesn't have time to mourn their absence before his fingers brush along her cheeks, wiping away the trails of tears she did not realize even fell. His hands frame her face, the metal of the rings he wears cool against her skin. He gently tilts her head back until she's looking into his eyes, that eternal shade of blue that her own eyes have started to reflect, the ring of blue in the midst of her own deep brown. His eyes do not burn with red, and yet, there's a fire there. And it burns for her.

"I *have* you," he breathes. "If you need to scream, scream at me. If you need to cry, cry in my arms. If you want to fall apart, I will put you back together. And I promise you, I *swear* to you. I will never—not for a single second—doubt that you are anything less than the strongest, most fearsome, most glorious creation that has ever lived on this earth."

Her breath comes in little agonies. She forces oxygen down her throat, but she still feels winded. She's aware of every part of her body, agonizingly aware of every particle of skin that he's touching, and more than that, every inch of skin that he *isn't* touching. That he's never touched. That she desperately wants him to touch.

And the only thought that occurs to her is:

What the fuck am I doing?

Because with him looking at her like that, like she is a goddess whose feet he would worship at, she can't remember why she has been fighting him for so long. She can't look at his lips and remember why she shouldn't be kissing him. Can't look at his body and not wonder why the fuck he's still wearing clothes. There isn't a part of her that isn't aching, that isn't homesick for his touch like a sailor longing for a cottage by the sea. And his hands are the only thing to stop the hurting.

Love is vulnerability, she reminds herself. And it's true. But it doesn't feel right. It doesn't feel like the whole story, the way that a single word rarely makes a complete sentence.

Here, in this moment, she does not feel vulnerable. She feels strong. Just like that night on Harlowe's boat when Calliope's pain was ripping through her, Ayc steadies her, holds her together, makes her believe she can withstand the whole world if he is by her side.

Ayc makes her feel *strong*. And for a moment, she is not afraid. Not of him. Not anymore.

So she does the only thing that makes any sense in this divine-forsaken world.

She kisses him.

FORTY-TWO

AYC

No matter how many times he's kissed her, the brush of her lips on his is a reckoning. It shakes him to his very soul. A growl rises within him, and he very nearly loses himself to it. Only at the last moment does he remember himself enough to lean back.

"Stop."

Her eyes widen in surprise, and her mouth parts. And he's just as surprised. With her face still framed in his hands and that damn slip that mirrors her skin, making her look utterly bare, she's so beautiful, his chest aches. He must be a total fool to pull away from her.

"Fuck," he curses. "I can't believe I'm saying this, but we should stop. If you still want me in the morning, then you can have me. But we shouldn't do this. Not if you're not thinking clearly. I don't think I can live through you telling me kissing me is a mistake again. Twice is enough."

She drags her bottom lip into her mouth, and the sight of her teeth against her full bottom lip is a jolt straight to his cock. Fuck. He's dying for her.

"If you want me to think straight," she whispers, "you have to stop touching me. I can't think straight when you touch me."

Ayc greedily sweeps his thumbs across the roundness of her cheeks once more, soaking in the velvet smoothness of her skin, before he pries his hands away and drops them to his sides.

He searches her over. The vibrations of panic he sensed coming off her skin have eased. She wraps her arms over her chest and runs them up and down her bare biceps, like she's cold. He turns to grasp a knit blanket draped over the back of the fainting sofa. It's soft as butter as he tucks it around Lora's shoulders.

"Thank you," she whispers.

"Do you still want me to go?" Ayc asks.

She shakes her head. "It seems selfish to ask you to stay, but—"

"I'll stay," Ayc says without hesitation. It's perhaps a terrible idea. It'll be a special kind of torment being here with her, with close proximity to a large bed that he can think of so many good uses for. And that's not even mentioning the fainting couch. With just a glance, he can imagine her sprawled out, her legs draped over either side of it so she's spread wide open for him.

Get it the fuck together, Ayc, he snarls at himself, shaking away the internal image. She is looking for comfort. Friendship. She doesn't need him salivating over her. But that damn slip is making it quite difficult.

"Your guards will be suspicious if I stay," he says, lowering his voice. He gestures outside to where they can see the silhouette of Shae's form, cast there by the lanterns in the camp. "I can leave and sneak back in if you like."

"Do you think it necessary?" she asks.

No. But she is the one who the gaze of everyone in Everadyn is upon. If he has to slip into the shadows and steal into her bedroom like some dark fairytale creature, he'll do so. "I'll do whatever makes you comfortable."

"You don't have to whisper. Bronwen spelled the tent for silence to grant me privacy."

He wishes he didn't know that information. Perhaps then he wouldn't be imagining how loudly he could make her scream.

Fuck!

He pivots on his heel. "I'll be back."

Perhaps, after he jumps into the river to freeze some sense back into his heated skin.

"Is she all right?" Shae asks, when he exits.

Ayc nods. "I believe so."

Shae opens her mouth like she might say more before snapping it closed again and resuming her guarding position.

"Good night, Shae," Ayc says before moving into the night.

He forces himself to walk back to his tent. His is nearly as big as Lora's, for practical reasons, given that Muffin is inside it. He lets the shield he's been building between him and Muffin fade. The party grounds are close enough Ayc could be in contact with him if he wanted, but nearly as soon as they arrived in camp, Muffin fell into a deep sleep, and sometimes, their dreams are a bit...something.

As soon as Ayc lowers the shield to check, a mental image of a sheep crosses his mind, peacefully frolicking through a pasture. And then it screams when talons sink into its ribs, and it's devoured in a spray of blood and gore. Ayc throws the shield back up before he wretches.

Davos stands outside Ayc's tent, pacing a line in the leaves, his feet somehow not making a sound. He nods as Ayc approaches, and Ayc knows he will depart as soon as Ayc enters the tent. But he also knows that the camp is surrounded by Silvae's city guards. They would hear if anything went wrong.

So as soon as Ayc slips in the front of his tent, he wills himself into shadow. He waits until he's certain it's been long enough for Davos to leave before he slips back out again. He goes around the camp the long way so he can approach the backside of Lora's tent, keeping far enough away that Shae won't hear his footsteps if he missteps. Once there, he slips beneath the tent.

Lora is sitting on the bed, her knees folded beneath her, the blanket still wrapped around her shoulders. She's turned off the lantern, letting night descend upon the tent as though the light was too much. At the movement of the tent, she leaps to her feet. She kicks up her foot and drags her knife from her boot.

"Easy, villainess," he says with a chuckle, reappearing. "It's just me."

She relaxes. Instead of returning the knife to its sheath, she sets it on a small table beside the bed, next to where she's placed her crown. She resumes her previous position and pulls the blanket more tightly around her. He stands where he is, uncertain what he should do next.

"For fuck's sake, sit down," she says, slapping a hand down on the bed beside her.

Every fiery nerve in his body tells him sitting in that bed with her is dangerous, but he forces himself to calm. Still, he flops down as close to the opposite edge of the bed as possible, and though he stretches his legs out as though this is casual and comfortable, he's mentally calculating the expanse of bed between him and her. The answer is too little... and too much. Inches and miles all at once.

"Do you want to talk?" Ayc asks.

She looks like she might be a million miles away, and Ayc almost thinks she didn't hear him until finally, she says, "I don't know."

"Well, how about this?" Ayc props his hands behind his head. "Have you heard the one abou—"

She snaps her head in his direction. "No."

His lips twist in a smile. "Well, I figured one of us should talk."

She huffs out a breath. "You're an ass."

"I know."

The silence lingers between them. Bronwen's enchantment must not disguise the sound outside because he can hear people returning to camp—Irving and Peregrin's voices rising and falling, Saga's bark, Tavish's laugh.

"I don't understand what is happening," Lora says at last, shifting to face him more. Irritation plays in her tone as she explains. "I've never liked parties, but I could tolerate them. Now,

I feel like it's all too much. The noise and the people staring and the idle, meaningless conversations. I feel it like a thousand little touches over and over again until I want to scream. It doesn't make sense."

"I think it makes perfect sense," Ayc says. "Before, you didn't have the responsibility of a whole country upon your back. The whole damn world, if you truly think about it. I think the fact you're coping with that all the time might also make it difficult to deal with things you normally cope with well. Your energy is elsewhere." He hesitates, mulling over the wisdom of his next statement, but he cares more about helping her than he fears making her upset. "I know Xylie struggles harder with speaking when she's stressed about other things."

She flinches, staring not at Ayc but somewhere beyond his shoulder, at the headboard he rests against. "Do you think I'm like Xylie?"

"Do *you* think you're like Xylie?"

She narrows her eyes. "I asked you first."

"Yes, but what I think doesn't really matter."

She says nothing for a long moment. She stares at the place on the wall behind him. Finally, she whispers, like a small protest. "We're quite different."

"Yes," Ayc agrees. "Your needs are different, but in some ways, you're quite the same. You don't like parties or loud places. You flutter your hands when you're upset, but then clench them into fists, so no one sees. I think you're choosing, consciously or not, to mask it. Because you never had the choice to do anything other than hide it. Your mother never gave you the option. But you don't have to hide it, Lora. Not with me. Not with any of your Five. You know that, right? Your job is to be strong for the world; ours is to be strong for you."

He desperately wants her to understand. In these last few weeks since confessing his pain, he's found that being honest about his struggles has offered a newfound freedom. Scarcely anything has changed. Peregrin slips him gryphon feathers, and Lora had an actual mattress put into the wagon where he's been staying with Muffin, easier on his back than a cot, but other than the accommodations, they have treated him no differently. Neither like he's made of glass nor like he's made of steel. They treat him like he's a living being, with his own unique needs, as they always have treated one another. Even Xylie handled the truth with a grace that told him she's known all along and was simply waiting for him to be ready.

The love of his friends has offered a buffer between Ayc and what the true problem has always been: his own self-doubt. His own internalized prejudices that, as Reselda has said, he applies to no one but himself. There's still a voice deep that whispers that he'll never be strong enough, good enough, that he's unworthy of the gifts he's been given because his body has limitations that others do not. But he's getting better at crushing that voice beneath his heel, at chasing it back into the shadows. When his doubts attempt to coil like choking vines around his mind, Muffin has begun to snarl back:

"Tell that voice—the one that says you're not good enough—to shut up. You are not weak. *You are a dragon."*

He wants that freedom for Lora, too. He wants her to know that she doesn't have to be afraid to be seen, that she doesn't have to carry the world alone. Things are less heavy when you let people really love you.

She shifts a little closer to him until their knees almost brush. His skin buzzes at her proximity.

"I just feel so angry," she admits, with a weight that makes him understand exactly how difficult the confession is. "I feel all these injustices all the time. They live beneath my skin. They rule every thought in my head. I can't shut it off. If I can't convince the regents to break the treaty, I don't know how to help Aluina. I've failed them."

The line between her eyebrows deepens, and this time, Ayc can't resist the desire to reach over and smooth it with a thumb. Her mouth parts with surprise, but she doesn't pull away.

"You have not failed them," Ayc says. "We will figure out a

way. Together. Even if it's not the neat path we wanted. Even if we have to become villains."

He wishes he could tell her, not for the first time, about the three coins he still holds in his pocket. About how she's already helping with the rebellion by working with Calliope. But he can't. He has to find the leader first. If only he could just decipher what Calliope said to him, what part of what she said was a clue. He's been going over it for weeks with no luck.

Lora sighs, drawing him from his thoughts. "I never wanted to be a villain. I wanted to be someone my people loved, not feared. Not detested."

"People are fools." Ayc lets his hand fall, the memory of her skin still vibrating on his. "Sometimes, they fail to recognize what is best for them."

Lora groans and drops her face into her hands. "Fuck. It doesn't feel like enough. Nothing will ever feel like enough."

Ayc's chest aches, like he's feeling her agony deep beneath his own ribcage. He wants to ease it because she doesn't deserve to suffer, not when it's her goodness, her powerful sense of justice, that is causing her such heartache. He glances around the room as though he might spy something. And he does.

"Sometimes, when Xylie and I have moments when the world feels like too much, music helps." He slides off the bed. "Does it help you?"

She lifts her head. "Sometimes."

He strides across the tent to a small table beside the lounge, where a small wooden statue of a winged horse sits. But its mouth is open—the only thing that makes him recognize it for the recorder it is. "Is this yours?"

"Yes. My grandmother must have sent it for me."

"Want to listen to it?" He waits, his fingers poised over it, knowing it'll be activated by a single touch. He doesn't want to do anything that will make her overstimulation worse. She stares at him for a long moment, then nods.

He taps the horse's wing, and a burst of music feels the tent.

Fast, uptempo, and with a unique rhythm he recognizes immediately.

"I fucking love this song!" Ayc cheers and slides back to the bed. He thrusts out his hand. "Dance with me!"

His heart hammers to the rhythm of the song as he awaits Lora's response. He expects her to say no, to deny him, but she doesn't. She lets the blanket fall off her shoulder, revealing her powerful arms and the soft folds of her stomach and hips. She stands up. She takes his hand. She *fucking* smiles.

As he pulls her toward him, his grin is wider than he thinks it ever has been before. He lifts his arm, and she spins beneath it. They break apart to dance on their own, and she's still, objectively, a terrible dancer. But he loves it. Loves the way her hips sway out of time to the music, the way the slip moves over the valleys and mountains of her flesh. Gods, she's so fucking beautiful that it's difficult to remember that he, too, should be dancing because he wants to sit and watch her.

He begins to belt the lyrics, and she clamps her hand over his mouth. "Oh, divine, you're a terrible singer."

"I know!" he laughs.

And then they are both singing, dancing in a way that doesn't match the beat. There's a magic in this moment, a completely ordinary one. He feels it in his chest like he's swallowed sunlight, and it's made brighter by the smile on her face. The fact that she's trusting him with this side of her, the one that she shows so few, feels like the best gift he's been given. And when her laughter joins his, his heart nearly bursts with the joy of hearing it. He wants to drink in this moment, savor it in his soul, memorize every detail so he can survive on it in his darkest days.

Everything disappears beneath the magic of this moment, beneath the spell of laughter and music and *her*. The song ends only for Lora to start it again and again and again until Ayc's back can take it no more. He collapses on the bed, still laughing, the pain little more than a distant, nagging reminder to take a break.

"Are you all right?" Lora says, collapsing beside him, her chest rising and falling quickly.

"I'm wonderful," he says. He studies the way her taut curls spread over the blanket and how sweat glistens against the rich brown of her skin, like morning dew in a rich spring garden. He wants to lick it up, wants to inhale her laughter down into his lungs. It's scarcely fair, the way she works herself deeper into his soul with each passing day.

He loved her when he thought her wicked, and he loves her even more now when he's heard the music of the laughter and the way she looks lit up in joy. She is everything, every sweet contradiction, rolled into one, and he will never get enough of her.

"Every time I think it's not possible for me to adore you more, you prove me wrong," Ayc huffs, pushing the long, damp strands of hair out of his face. "It's *quite* annoying."

Her breaths cut off. A heavy silence falls.

Fuck. He can never keep his mouth shut.

"I'm sorry."

"Do *not* be sorry." Her words snap in the air.

He rolls to his side. The movement causes the bed to dip, and she slides closer, just enough that their bodies nearly press together, and he's looking down upon her. She doesn't pull away, only locks her jaw like she's determined. Of what, he isn't certain until her hand rises to his chest where his shirt and corset vest dip down. She keeps her gaze locked with his as she slowly, purposefully pushes the collar aside and runs a single finger across his collarbone.

It would be the most innocent of touch if not for the way she bites down on her bottom lip, if not for the way it seems to draw a line straight to his cock. It rises in response to the smallest of her touches, already hard and aching for her.

He says her name like a warning. "Lora."

She says his name like a dare. "Ayc."

"*Lora*," he growls.

Not until morning, he promised, but that was before. Before a tint of silver rose to surround her dilating pupils. She coils her hand into the collar of his vest, holding him in place.

"Aye." This time, she says it with a smile that has the power to ruin him just before she yanks him downward.

Their mouths meet with a clash. Her mouth parts for him, and he dives in, sweeping his tongue over hers. He moans at her taste. It's divine, like the sharpness of fae wine and the sweetness of chocolate pudding and like the eternity of paradise, all as one. All rational thought is quickly erased from his head. He can't decide if he *should*, only knows that he *must*.

She drags his lower lip between her teeth, and he fucking loves it, the ferocity of her. He pulls back to survey her body beneath him, the heave of her chest, her full breasts nearly spilling from the slip. The silk of the slip teases his palm as he traces over her curves. He fists his hand where the fabric bunches at her hip, grasping a hold of one last shred of restraint. He has to be sure.

"Tell me to stop," he says between his teeth, like he's pleading, because he is. Like it pains him because it does. "Tell me you don't want me."

She shakes her head.

He gathers more fabric into his fist. The silk falls from her bent knees and rakes down her thighs.

"Tell me this is a mistake." He teases his fingers down the inside of her thigh, not too low, but enough. Enough that she gasps, and the breaths that follow are little more than shallow pants.

"Tell me I'm not under your skin," he breathes against the hollow of her neck, so when she swallows, he feels it against his lips. Her hand falls onto the back of his neck, but not to push him away, to press him closer. He adjusts so he hovers over her body, placing his elbow beside her head to support his weight. He slips his knee between her legs. So close. So fucking close.

She's the one who shifts, just enough that the softness of her center presses against the firmness of his thigh. And fuck! *Fuck!* She is so wet. He can feel it through her underwear, seeping into his pants. He drags his tongue across her collarbone to taste the sweat there and gives her one more chance.

"Tell me more of your lies."

She whimpers, her hips giving the smallest of rocks, seeking friction. He doesn't offer it. Only remains completely still.

"Words, Lora," he demands. "If you want me, I need words."

She rocks again, her soaking pussy gliding against his thigh. Her words are breathy, almost a moan. "Do you remember what I told you before we last kissed?"

He lifts his head to study her face. "You said I would be your ruin."

Her eyes blaze completely silver. "Ayc?"

"Yes?"

"*Ruin me.*"

FORTY-THREE

LORA

His eyes are twin fires in the darkness, blazing just above her. She sees them through her world of silver, and something deep within clenches. She moans and rocks harder. The firmness of his thigh rubbing over her sensitive flesh is exquisite, but it isn't nearly enough.

"You want me to ruin you, Lora?" Despite the way his voice sounds barely restrained, his hands are utterly slow and intentional as two of his fingers hook into the left strap of her slip. "Do you want me to show you exactly what you deserve? Exactly how much pleasure you can handle?" He works the strap down her shoulder, then repeats the process with the other. "Do you want me to make you come, over and over again, until I've ruined any chance you'll ever settle for anything less than *my* hands upon you?"

Goddamn that fucking mouth of his. She hates it, and she loves it. She wants to find whoever taught him to speak like that and write them a thank-you letter. Or perhaps punch them in the face because she would very much like him to shut up and fuck her now. But oh, she loves the way his breath torments her skin, the way the silk teases her nipples as he pulls down the front of her slip ever-so-slowly.

"Is that what you want, my lady?"

"Yes." She works her hips even harder, and he shifts back his knee, taking away the pressure she desperately needs. A little growl works up her throat. The ache is alive. It pulsates in the very core of her, demanding attention, threatening her with its intensity. She has been in agony for what feels like forever, and she needs it to end.

His thumb grazes over the hill of her breast, over the peak of her nipple through the slip. She hisses at the jolt it sends through her, her toes curling.

"Are you certain?" he asks, and his voice is more serious now. "If morning comes, and you regret this—"

"I won't regret this." She cuts him off because she can't handle the way uncertainty creeps into his eyes. Not when it's her own damn fault, the way she's pushed him away every time they've been this close, led him to believe it was ever about him, when it never was. She works her fingers into his hair and trails her words like kisses against the stubble of his jaw. "I won't regret *you*. I've wanted you far too much—for far too long—and I'm not sorry for it. You're right. I was afraid, but I'm not afraid anymore. The rest of the world can be damned. But—" A small breath of reality returns to her chaotic mind, and she adds, "No one can know."

He tenses. She drags her tongue across the column of his throat. He groans. The shadows around her seem to darken, his affinity making them come alive. A thrill weaves through her. She loves the power she has over him. The way he doesn't try to hide it.

"I want this to just be you and me," she whispers, dragging her heel up his leg. "No one else. The rest of Everadyn doesn't get to have their opinion on this. Nor the rest of the Five. Not yet." When her foot reaches his hip, she presses against him, drawing him closer until his hips seal with hers. "Deal?"

A frown teases the corner of his lips. "We can trust—" She

rocks her hips once more, but in this position, her center doesn't glide on his thigh. It glides against the hard bulge of his cock. She bites her lip to hold back a moan, but he doesn't have the same restraint. He whimpers. It's the only sound to describe it. He fucking whimpers for her. "You know what? Fuck it. Deal."

Her smile of victory is cut off by the assault of his lips. The kiss is brutal, teeth and tongues, a pattern that continues when he breaks from her mouth and forges a path down her throat. She clutches him closer and shifts her angle so every glide of her hips rubs her clit against his hard cock. Even through the fabric, she's so coiled up she could come just like this.

But then he shifts away once more.

"Bastard," she snarls.

"Now, now, you don't get to come until my hand is on you."

"Then hurry the fuck up!"

He chuckles. And she thinks she's wrong. She fucking hates him. "Patience. I've waited far too long to touch you not to savor every part of your body now."

He fists her slip at her ribcage and pulls down. The straps pull taut on her upper arms and strain against the seams, but they give enough that her right breast springs free. The sound he makes deep in his throat is nearly feral. He lowers his head and sweeps a tongue in a languid circle around her nipple. Her fingers clamp down on the strings of his vest as her back arches off the bed.

"Gods, you are fucking perfect." He covers her breast with his entire mouth, sucking it in, granting it a pull that tugs all the way to her clit.

She can't stop the gasp, "Fuck." Her hips buck, seeking friction. Relief. He sucks harder, the red in his eyes burning slowly brighter. She can feel his shadows now, stroking against the skin of her arms, weaving gently through her hair, cool but gentle. She doesn't think he's doing it on purpose. She's making him lose control.

"Ayc." She tries to put a command into her voice, but with every play of his tongue against her sensitive flesh, he draws a whimper that cuts off her words. "Fuck." He catches the other side of the slip with three fingers and frees her other breast. He administers the same torturous treatment to it. "I need— *Fuuuuck.*"

He smiles around her breast, his eyes twinkling with that same damn mischief that almost always plays there when he's teasing her. She wants to bite him, and she wants to take a mental image of it and store it in her memory so she'll never forget the way he looks wrapped around her body.

"What is it?" His breath teases her already tortured nipple. "What do you need?"

But his hand reaches back to tease her knee. Because he already knows.

"I need you to stop fucking with me and start *fucking* me."

"Fucking you with what?" His tongue darts out to flick the tip of her nipple. His fingers strum on the inside of her thigh, inching just a little closer. She marvels at the sight of his painted nails gliding against that intimate stretch of skin, the gold of his rings contrasting against the brown. "There's so many options."

She bares her teeth. It only makes his smile widen. "Have I ever told you that you're an impertinent ass?"

"Yes, many times." This time, it's his teeth that pluck at her nipple. He's so careful it doesn't hurt, but the hint of sharpness against her tortured flesh makes her writhe.

It is so good. It's unfair how good this is. She would let him torture her forever if the ache in her pussy wasn't screaming with need. "Ayc," she demands.

"First, my hand," he says. "Then my mouth. Then my cock. Deal?"

"Yes, deal," she pants. "Get *on* with it, then."

"So impatient."

She loves this—this push and pull between them. The way they tease each other and challenge each other. The way they wrangle for control, surrendering it back and forth, without either one feeling like they've lost it. It's always been that way between them, and she can't see why it would be different now.

He adjusts his weight onto his elbow and removes his hands from her. She growls, and he grins as he slowly works his brass rings from his right hand. Her breath catches at the sight. Something so simple as him removing his rings should not feel so erotic, but as each one falls onto her mattress, it feels like a promise of the pleasure to come. A tremor works through her, her vision painted with silver.

"Look at you," he coos. "Trembling for me. Don't worry. I won't make you wait much longer."

Divine's sake. His fucking mouth.

She latches her fingers into his hair and pulls him down to her mouth. He controls the pace, timing each sweep of his tongue as he returns his hand to her thigh and slowly works his fingers toward her center. She bites down on his lip as his fingers brush against the edge of the thin fabric that separates her from his touch.

"Gods, you're so wet for me. Such a good girl."

"I am not a good girl," she seethes against his skin, grazing her teeth down his throat. "But you can be such a good boy for me."

Any of her previous lovers might have recoiled at that. Taken it as an insult. Refused to give up control. But his eyes flare red, and he moans.

"Touch me, Ayc. Right now."

He kisses her once more. He thrusts his tongue deep into her mouth as he brushes the thin underwear aside. She's shaking, trembling, nearly unhinged with anticipation. And then, with one more stroke of his tongue against hers, he slides his finger up her center.

"Fuck!" he growls into her mouth.

She might have done the same if she wasn't rendered unable to speak as his fingers glide from her entrance to her clit, sweeping a lazy circle around the sensitive bud. The pleasure sends sparks shooting through her, spreading to the ends of her fingers, down to the tips of her toes.

He is an artist, and perhaps she's his painting. That is how she feels as his fingers explore her pussy. Slowly. Leisurely. He studies her face, and when her eyes flare brighter with silver, he lingers, his own eyes burning red.

"More," she demands, pulling at his hair. She thinks it might be hard enough that it hurts, but he hisses like he likes it.

"Yes, my lady." He lowers his head back to her breast. He nips gently, even as he slides his fingers inside of her. Her back arches off the bed, and she bites down so hard on her lip to keep from crying out that she tastes blood.

Yes. Oh fuck yes.

She's needed this, needed him for so fucking long. But nothing could prepare her for how good it is. The way he so quickly adjusts to her response, how soon he finds that place within her that has his every stroke feeling fucking divine, the way he keeps his thumb circling her clit at the same time.

She drags her nails down his back, his shoulders, aiming for purchase, even as his mouth chases across her body. One moment, it's on her breast, the next on her neck, and then back to her mouth. He times each languid sweep of his tongue with a deep thrust of his fingers.

And she is so close. So fucking close.

"You feel so fucking good," he groans, his mouth worshiping at the altar of her shoulder.

"Imagine how I'd feel on your cock."

The words have the desired effect. He adds a third finger and pounds into her, the heel of his hand striking her clit with every thrust. She rocks her hips to the rhythm of his hand, and the entire world succumbs to rapidly building pleasure.

"Ayc," she means it to come out as another demand, but it's more akin to the mew of a cat. His response is another growl and to press his thumb directly on her clit. Pleasure erupts through the base of her spine, the start of an orgasm that feels almost overwhelming with its power. "Ayc."

"That's it, my lady," he coaxes, driving her ever closer. Closer. Closer. "Say my name as you come. Let me hear you scream it."

The orgasm slams through her. Her spine bends, her hips

buck, and stars erupt before her eyes. He rides her through her pleasure, never relenting his touch, whispering sweet praises into her ear that she drowns out with a scream. Perhaps it's his name. She's too lost to tell.

When she returns to herself, every muscle in her body sags limp with relief deep into the mattress. She gasps for breath. He hovers over her, his eyes still blazing as he watches her chest rise and fall. He raises his hand, glistening in her, to his lips. He licks his fingers clean and moans. "Fuck, Lora. You're the sweetest thing I've ever savored. I want more."

"Good," she breathes. Because so the fuck does she.

He slides off the bed and kneels on the ground between her legs. He wraps his hands around her thighs and yanks her toward the edge of the bed. She rakes her nails through his scalp, and he practically purrs in delight. His breath teases her swollen bundle of nerves.

Motion catches her eye. She jerks her head toward the tent flap that ruffles like someone is about to peek in. "Ayc," she warns as she yanks on her slip to hide her exposed breasts.

Ayc flings her skirt downward and disappears into the shadows. She sits upright seconds before Veni slips into the tent.

Veni freezes at the tent entrance. "Oh, sorry. I thought I heard something. Wanted to check in."

Fuck. Heat flushes to her cheeks. Had she been so loud that she managed to overwhelm the spell Bronwen placed on the tent?

"Everything is fine," she says, though her words are still a bit breathless. Her body still thrums with the pleasure of Ayc's touch.

Veni cocks his head. "Are you well? You look a little..." He hesitates, and she cuts him off, not wanting to hear whatever word he's going to come up with.

"I'm *fine*. I was almost asleep before you barged in here. Get out."

He holds up his hands, backs out of the tent, and secures the flap back into place.

"Ayc," Lora calls. She searches the shadows, halfway

expecting him to leap out and startle her. "Ayc!" she calls again, but there isn't an answer.

He's gone.

AYC

Muffin had better be dying. They better be fucking dying because that is the only justified reason for the screaming that is happening in Ayc's head. As soon as he disappeared into shadow, he felt Muffin hammering against the shield Ayc placed between them while his fingers were deep inside Lora. Ayc absolutely did not want Muffin to overhear the arcane thoughts in his head as Lora screamed his name, so he kept it locked in place until he sensed Muffin trying to get through. When he let it drop, Muffin was crying:

"Ayc, where are you? Ayc, come! I need you!"

Lora was still talking with Veni, so Ayc had no choice but to dart beneath the tent the way he came.

"I'm coming, Muffin. Stay in the tent."

He races toward the tent, still hidden in the shadow. Muffin's head pokes through the tent flap. They shake it, agitated, before retreating within. Ayc follows after and allows himself to reappear. Muffin paces in the little room the tent offers. Their tail whips, threatening to knock the tent posts down.

Ayc's irritation dies, replaced with a sinking feeling in his gut. *"What is it, Muffin?"*

"Can you feel it?"

"Feel what?"

"Something is wrong. Something is coming."

A shiver works down his spine. He's never seen Muffin this upset, and Ayc has no idea what they're sensing, but they trust them. And if something is coming—

"Lora!" Muffin's voice roars in time with his own thought. *"We have to protect Lora."*

Ayc spins around and races back out of the tent, Muffin following behind. A crack of wings sounds above as Tempest dives from the sky above and lands in the center of camp so hard, the ground shakes. Dirt and leaves spray upward in a cloud. Irving bolts out of the tent next to Ayc's, doing up his belt. Peregrin follows soon after, their short hair ruffled, their shirt untucked, but the look on their face is deadly serious.

"All guards awake and to the Sovereign," Irving's voice booms through the camp.

"Tempest senses something," Peregrin explains.

"Muffin senses something, too," Ayc replies. The dragon paces behind him, growling lowly, but no more coherent words flow across their connection, just waves of fear and rage. Tempest's feathers ruffle, and her beak cracks. Off-duty guards swiftly stumble out of the tents, swords already in hand. Searching around the camp as they stumble toward Lora's tent, but nothing seems amiss. The forest around the camp is still. Calm.

"Does Tempest know—" Ayc begins, but he's cut off by a noise, one that starts as a flutter and ends in a storm. It takes him a moment to recognize the sound. Wings. They pound against the air as birds lift from their perches in the trees and soar overhead. Fleeing.

Fear clamps around Ayc's sternum, his heart freezing in his chest.

What is happening that nature itself is spooked?

Irving watches the cloud of birds go. "Fuck. That's not good."

Bronwen flings herself over the bridge from the direction of the party, her hair flying behind her. She holds out her hand, and her staff flies from her tent. "No," she murmurs, "no, no, no."

Ayc takes a step toward her, but his attention is seized by Lora leaving her own tent only to find a wall of guards. She's well protected. Still, it's not a choice. His feet instinctively change course and vault him toward her. She locks eyes with him between two guards, and she hopes she sees in his face that he's sorry. That he didn't want to leave her. That—

"Ayc!" Muffin calls.

Ayc freezes. Static buzzes in the air, the same static Ayc has felt coming off Bronwen's skin. Magic. But this magic makes the air grow cold. His breath becomes visible before his lips. He's felt like this before—when they encountered the wraiths in Somnia Ignis.

A flash of blue light blinds him like lightning has exploded in the center of the camp. And when it fades, it's not a wraith who stands in the middle. It's a woman. A woman with a beauty that feels as unnatural as she feels cold. She wears a black sorcerer's cloak and a black lace gown so thin and sheer, she might as well be wearing nothing at all. Her red hair tumbles over her shoulders, but it isn't a color of red that occurs in nature. Not a scarlet or even an orangey-blond. It's the color of blood, cut straight from an artery, too bright for her porcelain skin. And Ayc knows, instinctively, whoever this woman is, he should be deeply, deeply afraid of her.

Behind her are three cloaked figures. Their sorcerer cloaks are all in different colors—greens and blues and purple—but the hoods are all drawn up, hiding their faces.

"Fuck," Bronwen breathes.

The woman's eyes turn to Bronwen. One glows silver, and the other glows green. They do not fade, even when she smiles. "Bronwen. So nice to see you again."

Bronwen swallows, not quite able to disguise the fear in her face. "Greetings, my lady Supreme."

FORTY-FOUR

AYC

Muffin lets out a low growl.

"Easy, Muffin. She's not our enemy."

It's not supposed to be a lie, but it feels like one. Nothing about the Supreme sorcerer feels safe. Tempest snaps her beak and digs her claws deep into the dirt. The guards don't put away their weapons, not even Peregrin, even though the Five know of the letter Lora sent. Even Bronwen, who—as Lora predicted—wasn't happy about the decision.

Seeing the Supreme, Ayc understands explicitly why Bronwen is so wary of her. Even creatures inherently fear her. Goosebumps prickle Ayc's skin. He freezes entirely when she turns those still-glowing, unmatched eyes upon him and Muffin.

"I heard Everadyn had a dragon rider, but I didn't know whether to believe it," she says, a wide smile parting her lips to reveal teeth that are unnaturally white, so bright they gleam in the lantern light. "Your dragon is quite beautiful."

Ayc's mouth is utterly dry. He can't swallow. "Thank you."

"Lady Serene," Lora greets as she slips through her wall of guards. She's pulled her cape over her slip, clasped it in front, and returned her crown to her head, but her curls stay slightly askew.

She looks as though she's just woken from sleep. No one knows except him that she's been put astray by how her head thrust into the mattress while she came around his fingers. He wants to go back to that moment, feeling the warmth of her core contract around him, seeing her face contort in that exquisite way that fucking shattered him—instead of watching her walk so calmly toward a dangerous and powerful being.

Veni and Irving keep close to her shoulders as she approaches the Supreme, and Ayc grinds his feet into the earth to resist the urge to join them. Muffin creeps forward, their head low to the ground like a lion about to pounce. The fear and rage still come across their connection, but the scale is tipping further to rage. Ayc holds a hand before them to halt their approach.

"She's wrong," they protest. *"She's unnatural."*

Ayc doesn't deny it because he feels it, too, like some innate part of his being recognizes the threat. *"She's not going to harm us,"* he reassures, though it's as much for himself as it is for Muffin.

Lora stops when she's still a few feet away. Still far too close. She tips her chin in a subtle nod of respect. "What do I owe the honor of your visit?"

Serene doesn't offer any demonstration of respect in return. "You did invite me, did you not?"

"I invited you to Wyntra at a date of your choosing. I had not yet received a response."

"Well, consider this your response."

Ayc clamps his jaw to silence whatever retort leaps to the tip of his tongue. It seems that everyone wants to play games with Lora, to test her, to attempt to catch her off guard. But perhaps Lora knows it because she gives a gracious smile. Like Lora is the only one in this camp who isn't intimidated by her.

"Fantastic," she says. "No time like the present. Would you like to come in and have a seat?"

"I would," Serene replies. "Thank you."

Lora turns and leads Serene back toward the tent. "Bronwen and Peregrin, please join us," she calls over her shoulder. "Ayc, you too. Bring your bracelets."

When she disappears within, shadows trail into the glow of the lantern above her tent like they're trying to follow. The twinge in Ayc's temple tells him that he's the one doing that. Ayc grinds his teeth harder and clamps down on his power to regain control. The shadows retreat. Veni, Irving, and Davos duck in after Lora before Serene can enter, but it doesn't ease the riot in Ayc's vein. He can't see her, can't protect her.

The three people who arrived with Serene move as one, like shadows following the Supreme. As they turn, Ayc catches a glimpse beneath their hoods. He recoils. Golden masks cover their eyes, gleaming momentarily in the moonlight, leaving only slits for vision. Beneath the mask, the lower half of their faces lay in various degrees of decay. Skin has turned necrotic and gray. Rows of teeth show through holes where skin has rotted away entirely.

Wraiths, his mind cries, remembering the ones in the dragon cave all those weeks ago. But they're too alive. They're something else entirely.

Peregrin starts toward the tent, but when Bronwen takes a step, Ayc catches her arm.

"Bronwen, who are those people?" Ayc whispers.

Bronwen shivers and rubs her hands up and down her arm. "They're her Siphons."

"Her what?"

"They're sorcerers. The masks they wear allow Serene to pull from their energy instead of her own, so they pay the cost."

Ayc recoils in horror. "They take the pain upon themselves."

She nods. "And it makes her more powerful than any single sorcerer should be able to be on their own."

"Who would willingly do that?"

"I don't know, but they *are* willing volunteers—or so she says. And they keep coming. She burns through them in a few years' time." Bronwen tugs on his sleeve to pull him toward the tent. "We need to get in there."

"I have to get my bracelets from my tent."

She releases him and marches forward. "I'll meet you in there."

"Keep her safe," Ayc says.

Bronwen freezes and whirls back around. Magic buzzes off her skin, and though Ayc very much doesn't like that it's directed at him, he likes that this Bronwen is back instead of the petrified one she was moments ago.

"This is the Supreme," she hisses, stepping back toward him so she can snarl the words in his face. "The strongest magical being that has ever walked the face of this earth. She is ancient and powerful. A legion could not bring her down. If she decided to kill Lora and everyone else in this camp, there's not a damn thing that I or anyone could do to stop her. And Lora invited her here to look at your fucking bracelets."

Muffin growls low behind Ayc. No words, only a general warning. Ayc holds up a hand to settle them.

Ayc can't argue her point. He's let Lora put herself in danger to help figure out his past, and yes, he's a fucking idiot for that. But what they did can't be undone, and he can't stand a second more being out here with Lora in that tent.

"I will be there in two minutes," Ayc says.

He rushes to his tent, and Muffin trots after him.

"Ayc, don't go near that woman. She's wrong. I've felt that feeling before, when I was an egg. My mother would chase it away, but it always tried to return."

The wraiths. It's odd that Muffin, too, senses the similarity. It only makes Ayc go faster. He goes to the small box he left on his bed. He found it in a shop in Audori, one spelled only to open for his hand. It's the only thing he's trusted leaving the bracelets in since he hasn't been wearing them. He pulls them from the box.

At the very touch of the leather, his power recoils. He never noticed the sensation before, the way something within him shrinks back at the contact, until he began going extended periods without them. He tucks them into his pocket.

"Stay here."

Muffin shifts in front of him, blocking his exit. *"Don't go."*

"Lora is there with her. I have to go." His heart is pounding with every second she is out of his sight.

"Then I'm coming with," Muffin says.

"No!"

"Yes."

"No."

"Yes." Muffin snaps their jaw. *"I'll take a chunk out of her ass if she tries anything. It'll taste foul, but that's a sacrifice I'm willing to make."*

"I don't have time to argue with you. There's nothing you can do against the Supreme." Ayc sidles around the dragon, and Muffin allows him to go. But as his fingers brush the tent flap, Muffin lets out a long sigh.

"The last time I let you out of my sight, I thought you were not coming back."

Ayc's chest aches. *"I am coming back. But for now, I can't focus on protecting both you and Lora. I promise I'll call for you if anything goes wrong. And then you can take a chunk out of her ass."*

Muffin hesitates, sweeping their tail uneasily. Then they nod. *"Go. Protect Lora. She is ours."*

Ayc has no idea what Muffin means by that, and he doesn't have the time to sort it out. He shoves out of the tent. All the other guards still stand outside the tent, tense, hands on the hilt of their weapons. He slips past him and into the now-illuminated queen's tent.

"It's quite a position you've secured yourself, Bronwen," the Supreme says, from where she sits cross-legged before the table, across from Lora. Bronwen sits on the narrow side while Peregrin perches on the edge of the nearby couch, balancing their cane between their legs. Ayc isn't sure where Tavish and Xylie are, but he hopes they stay far away.

Irving, Veni, and Davos stand only two feet behind Lora, far closer than they would normally linger. Serene's three siphons stand at the edge of the tent, utterly motionless, like discarded dolls.

And just behind all of them is the bed. It takes all of Ayc's will not to lose himself in the memory of how her ample breasts looked over her slip, how they felt on his tongue, how every fucking, bountiful curve of her was one he intended to praise and hadn't yet gotten to. He needs to focus, which would be so much easier if Lora didn't look up at him at that moment. She draws her bottom lip into her mouth. It's still swollen from his attentions. He wonders if his bottom lip still bears her bite marks. He almost hopes so.

"First of Everadyn at only twenty-three. Impressive. I never thought you were an ambitious one." Serene's voice snaps him back. She reaches toward a sprig of grapes on the table. Green and black bleed from the pointed tips of her fingers all the way to the knuckle. After seeing her Siphons' faces, he wonders if she, too, might be slowly rotting away. "But I'm pleasantly surprised to see I was wrong." She snags a grape and pops it between her unnaturally white teeth.

Bronwen tightens her hands together. "I simply have good taste in friends."

Ayc sits down on the opposite side of the table from Bronwen, meaning the Supreme is now only inches from his side. The cold of her presses past his skin and into his bones. He pulls his bracelets from his pocket and lays them on the corner of the table. The sooner she looks at them, the sooner Serene can leave.

"Are these the bracelets you wrote me about?" Serene plucks one up.

Ayc holds back a cringe at the sight of his oldest, most precious possession in her rotting fingertips.

"Yes," Lora says. "I was hoping that you could identify the enchantment that's on them and perhaps give us any insight into who might have spelled them?"

Serene arches an eyebrow. "Could you not work it out, Bronwen?"

Bronwen's fingers are so tight around nothing, all color has leeched from her knuckles. "The sorcerer took great pains to disguise the enchantment."

"Yes, I did."

Ayc jolts, knocking his knee on the table. "You?"

She drags her gaze over him in a way that makes his skin go

from cold to frozen. He's seen that look before, the interest, the curiosity, but there's something sinister when it's her. "Oh, you're her son, aren't you? The boy she wanted so desperately to protect. I don't know who your father was, but she wanted to make absolutely sure that they would *never* find you. Paid quite a price for it."

"What did she pay?" Ayc demands, his voice sharp.

"She was a baker," Lora adds, softer, sending Ayc a warning look. "Surely, she couldn't have afforded what this would cost."

Serene flicks her fingers. Red sparks flare into the air and then settle. "I rarely deal in gold. When you live as I have, you accumulate quite enough. But you're right. It did cost quite a bit."

"Of what?" Ayc asks.

Serene cocks her head, her blood-red hair tumbling over one shoulder. She looks amused, like she's waiting for him to figure it out on his own.

"Sacrifice holds power," Bronwen whispers, almost to herself. She said that once before, when she spelled their camp to ward against the Drakr. Blood, love, sacrifice. All of it could make magic stronger.

It's not Bronwen's words that make the terrible realization connect in his mind. Nor Peregrin's soft curse. No, it's the way Lora sneaks her hand beneath the table to rest it on his knee. The way she blinks rapidly a handful of times before she shifts her emotionless mask back into place.

No.

His chest feels hollow, filled not with heart or lungs but with that single word. *No.*

"How many years did you take from her life?" Bronwen grips the edge of the table. The blue glow that ebbs from her palms slowly warps the wood beneath.

"Thirty," Serene replies, as though she hasn't even noticed Bronwen's loss of control. She chuckles as she turns her attention back to Ayc. "Oh, don't look so stricken, handsome. Humans die young all the time." She plucks off another grape and rolls it between her fingers. "How old was she when she died?"

Twenty-eight. His mother was only five years older than he is now when she died, and that's because, somehow, Serene manipulated fate. Stole the thirty years his mother should have had with him. How different would his life have been if she had survived? He'd have never gone to Creed...or to Everadyn. He might still be in the sleepy forested village of Hearth. Maybe they would have run that bakery together. But bitch—this rancid, fucking bitch—took his mother away from him.

The shock has turned to rage. It solidifies within him, cold and fierce as a blizzard, not even calmed when Lora presses her palm more firmly on his knee.

"Go fuck yourself," Ayc snarls.

Serene throws her head back and laughs. "Oh, he's a bold one. It's been a long time since anyone has had the courage, or the foolishness, to speak to me like that. I like it. But perhaps you should put these bracelets on. You seem to be losing control of your magic." She gestures to the tent wall.

Shadow creeps up the walls of the tent in grasping hands of darkness. The burning ice in Ayc's chest isn't rage; it's his power. Or perhaps it's both. He's so enraged, he hasn't even registered the cost. It feels so distant, caught behind the mental wall he's learned to hide his chronic back pain behind. It almost feels like nothing.

"Let it go, Ayc," Bronwen warns. "It'll burn you out."

Ayc is certain it won't. He's used more before, against Calliope, and he's angry enough he wants to find out.

But Lora squeezes her fingers over his knee, a reminder that any loss of control might harm her, too. And he can hear Muffin, as though from a great distance, calling out his name. He takes a breath, and the shadow retreats, but not enough. The anger doesn't loosen its grasp on his sternum, so he picks up his bracelets, and despite the protest deep within, he puts the bracelets back on.

In a blink, the shadow disappears.

"Ayc," Muffin says. "*Are you all right? You feel like lightning before it strikes.*"

"I'm fine. I lost my temper. I'll be fine."

Muffin grumbles something unintelligible, but they remain where they are.

Lora strokes her thumb across Ayc's knee. This time, it gets through, soothing the ache like a balm against a wound. She keeps her attention focused on the Supreme.

"How did you do it?" she asks. "Manage to hide all of his Drakr powers, except for his ability to heal? Bronwen said that would be quite difficult."

"Oh, I didn't exempt his ability to heal. It should have blocked all his Drakr abilities. I warned his mother that she'd be taking a great risk. She didn't seem too concerned. Perhaps your mother had some distant fae blood."

If it's true, it's certainly not something that his mother ever told him. But he's beginning to suspect that his mother had a lot of secrets she didn't think were necessary to share. All along, he chalked his birth up to some horrific encounter, some great misfortune too traumatizing for his mother to speak of. But now Ayc feels certain of nothing. Not when his mother died to protect him from his father.

Serene tosses the grape aside. It rolls down the table and stops on the edge of a plate toward where Bronwen's hands have left impressions in the wood.

"You need to get ahold of yourself, Bronwen, darling," Serene says. "You're slipping."

Bronwen's lip curls, revealing that her teeth have sharpened.

Serene turns her focus back to Lora, a twisted smile working up her porcelain cheeks. "Speaking of slipping, where is your Second, Loraphne? I so looked forward to seeing her again."

Lora stiffens at the mention of Xylie. The same tension works down Ayc's spine, drawing the muscles taut and painful.

Fuck. If Serene took half of Ayc's mother's life, what deal did she require of Xylie?

It's Bronwen who demands it. "What did you take from her?"

"Has she not told you?" Serene clucks her tongue. "My, then who am I to reveal her secrets?"

"Whatever deal you made, it was my debt to pay," Ayc says. "Perhaps we can renegotiate."

"Ayc," Lora and Bronwen both warn together.

"I never renegotiate once a deal is made. I warned Xylie of that. But if you would like to make a different deal with me, I might have something in mind." She reaches a hand out to him, and it takes every last bit of his will not to recoil or to retch when her bruised fingertips make contact with his skin. It feels like cold grime brushing against the stubble on his chin. "Or perhaps you'd come willingly."

He'd rather choke on his own dick. But he has a feeling she doesn't handle rejection well, and if he says it so bluntly, he might spend the rest of eternity as a frog. Or maybe just chained unwillingly to her bed.

In his hesitation, metal scrapes against metal—Lora grasping a knife from a plate holding a loaf of bread. The briefest flash of silver warns Ayc that, if he doesn't do something quickly, Lora is going to remove the sorcerer's fingers. And though a little thrill goes through Ayc at that thought of her possessiveness, he imagines that will result in this entire camp and everyone inside being turned to ash.

Beneath the table, he clamps his finger over Lora's hand, where it still rests on his leg.

"You flatter me," Ayc lies smoothly, knowing better than to offend Serene. "But I fear I must decline."

Her fingers caress over his jaw once more, but this time, they use a little more of her nail. "Must you? And why is that?"

"Does *no* require an explanation, Lady Supreme?" Lora asks, an edge creeping into her tone as she adjusts her hold on the knife. "Can I interest you in some bread instead?"

Serene finally removes her hand, and Ayc swallows down the rancid taste of bile that worked up his throat.

"No, thank you." Serene stands. "I should be leaving."

Lora drops the knife and jumps to her feet. "Wait. What deal did Xylie make?"

Serene sweeps toward the entrance of the tent, her cloak

flowing behind her as though caught by an invisible wind. "You should ask *her* because I certainly won't tell you. But..." She pauses and grins back over her shoulder, her silver and green eyes gleaming even brighter. "Tell her I hope she does hurry up with her charade. She's certain to fail, and I do like four more than I like three. A nice even number."

Serene throws open the tent flap. Her three Siphons follow at her heel, and it's then, catching sight of their eerie masks, that Serene's words land like a punch in Ayc's throat.

Four. Not three.

No.

Fuck no.

Lora makes a sound like a choke and vaults over the table toward the tent entrance. But by the time she flings the flap aside, there's another flash of red. Serene and her Siphons are gone as quickly as they came.

FORTY-FIVE

LORA

Serene is gone, but the cold she brought with her remains. The warmth has completely leached from her bones. She stares at Ayc and sees reflected in his gaze the same horror that coils around her ribcage, piercing her lungs like a needle, threading them with panic.

Xylie can't have done this. She's too smart for this, too smart to take a gamble on a deal that might result in her being that woman's Siphon, to be used up and drained dry. But then, it wasn't a matter of being smart. It was a matter of how far she was willing to go to protect Ayc.

Ayc whirls toward Lora. "If she had magic affinity, we'd know. Wouldn't we?"

It's a foolish grab at denial, and his desperation is written all over his face. Bronwen clutches her arms to her chest, her pale cheeks flushed, a shiver working through her body. She doesn't say I told you so; she doesn't rage. Both would be fair. Because Bronwen tried to tell them. She tried, and they told her to shut up.

Lora spins to where Peregrin still sits on the lounger, leaning over their cane. "Xylie has affinity, doesn't she? And don't tell me to mind my own business. If I was at Wyntra, as Sovereign, I could look at those records myself."

Fuck. She should have done that already. As soon as Bronwen told her of her suspicions, as soon as Xylie said she didn't want to do her final testing.

Peregrin sighs. "When she did her very first testing, Xylie tested with a potential for magical affinity higher than I've ever seen. But a potential is just that. Potential. It doesn't truly indicate how strong they will actually be. But Serene desperately wanted her to train at Velphin."

"I bet she did," Bronwen mutters.

"But Xylie didn't want to go to Velphin," Peregrin continues. "Even at that age, she wanted to be an alchemist, and her parents didn't believe that the harsh practices at that school would be beneficial to her, given her nature. They feared her needs would go unmet."

They pause, and Lora swallows at the mention of Xioran and Cirys. Xioran may have been Yris's half-brother, but they couldn't have been more unalike. He was much more akin to her own father, who was a close friend. He was kind, happy, and had an unfaltering sense of justice. Losing Xioran and Cirys to the Drakr raid at the same time as Lora's father was exiled was a blow she can still feel the ache of. It bonded her and Xylie even closer despite the fact that Xylie couldn't utter a word.

Recalling that brings other memories.

"No one was sure how Xylie survived the Drakr attack," Lora says. "I heard that Cirys hid her in a cabinet with a spell, and that's how she survived."

Ayc nods like that's the story he heard, too.

"But I also overheard a gryphon rider say that the entire village was burned to the ground. So which was it?" Lora asks.

"From what I heard from gryphon riders who were there," Peregrin says, "Xylie was found in the ashes, surrounded by half a dozen dead Drakr, who had not a mark on them. I'm not sure what she did, but it was a surge of power that many magical wielders in Lycendi said they felt."

Ayc swears under his breath and casts his eyes upon the roof of the tent. Lora still glimpses the moisture that momentarily rims his eyes. She loves the way that he loves Xylie, the way he's always looked out for her, the way Lora's heart isn't the only one feeling raw at thinking of the trauma Xylie has undergone.

"Whatever she did, that amount of power should have killed her," Bronwen says, "as young as she was."

"And it didn't," Peregrin says. "Because she's that powerful."

"Why didn't Yris send her to Velphin?" Lora asks.

Peregrin sits up straighter and shrugs. "Your mother is patient. I think she wanted to send her when she was certain Xylie was over her trauma and would survive the school. She's never had a lot of faith that a physical hindrance isn't the same as a lack of strength, but she's not wasteful."

"So what exactly would have been the condition of Xylie's deal?" Ayc directs the question at Bronwen.

Bronwen flinches. "I don't know."

"But you've suspected something for a long time," Lora says, softening her voice. "And I should have listened to you long ago."

"Yes, you should have," Bronwen snaps. She presses her eyes closed, looking like she immediately regrets it, but Lora deserves that. "I'm sorry. I only suspected because I know Xylie imbues her potions with magic. Then she stopped, and strangely, that seemed to be right after she made the deal. I suspect that the condition of Serene's deal was that Xylie is to no longer use her magic. Because if Serene can't control that power, she would want it gone."

"And if Xylie slips and uses the power?" Ayc asks, his voice thick.

Bronwen shakes her head, tears rimming her eyes. "Then she becomes a Siphon."

"No!" Ayc roars. He presses his fists to his temple, his body buckling at the center as he shakes with his rage. Lora recognizes his rage is a thin veil for his pain. She feels it, too, like a serrated knife down the center of her soul. She wants to wrap her arms around him, but mostly, to be wrapped up in him. Because the person they both love is in danger.

"There has to be something we can do," Ayc snaps, straightening and pacing. Lora is grateful his bracelets are back in place, or she fears the shadows would be destroying everything in sight. "She never should have made that deal. She was a fool."

"Don't be angry with her," Lora says. "I'm the one who sent her."

"And she went for me." He stabs a finger to his chest. "She *never* should have gone."

"Shut up!"

The voice comes from the tent flap. Xylie stands at the door, her hands fisted at her sides. Tavish stands beside her, his cheeks puffed out in a way that tells Lora they've heard everything. The guards did not stop them or warn of their presence. Why would they? Lora has always made it clear that her Five are never to be impeded.

Xylie parts her lips again, but this time, no words come out. She shakes out her fists so that she can sign. *"Do not speak about me as though I am still a child. I am not. I knew what I was doing. I don't regret it. I would do it again."*

The last hope that they guessed wrong dies a bloody death in Lora's gut. Lora wants to yell, to scream, to grab Xylie by the shoulders and shake her. But she forces herself to draw a breath. Xylie is right. This was her choice to make. And Lora must be the one to remain calm because Ayc cannot.

Lora closes the distance between them. She lays her hands on Xylie's biceps, gently like an embrace. Right now, Lora doesn't want to be Sovereign speaking to her Second. She just wants to talk to her little cousin.

"I don't blame you, Xy," Lora says. "We are not angry. We are merely worried for you."

Ayc drags his hands over his face, dragging in a deep breath and releasing it. The thundercloud of anger dissipates, leaving only the thickness of fear in his throat. "I don't want to lose you. *Nothing* would be worth losing you."

"You won't lose me," Xylie says. *"I told you that what I sacrificed was something I parted with willingly. I never wanted to be a sorcerer."*

"What if you slip?" Bronwen asks.

"I won't slip."

"Holding back affinity is difficult," Ayc says. "It often feels like too much, at least to me. Are you certain?"

"Yes. Because the whole world always feels like too much. Since the moment I was born, I've had to learn how to block it out. Affinity is but one small part of that."

Lora swallows. She knows exactly what Xylie is describing. "And if you *do* fail, we will be there to protect you. We won't let you go without a fight."

Xylie attempts to protest, but Ayc cuts her off. "That isn't up for negotiation. She will not take you. Not so long as I breathe."

"Do not say that." Xylie's fingers tremble. *"I can't bear to lose you."*

"And I can't bear to lose you."

He closes the distance between them until his arm nearly brushes Lora's, and the three of them create a triangle. Lora's world narrows down to just the two of them as Ayc pulls Xylie into his arms. She goes, burying her head into his chest.

"You are my best friend," he whispers down upon her braids, and though the words are meant for just Xylie, they swell to fill the room. But he doesn't hesitate, doesn't care if he's showing himself vulnerable. "You've saved my life more times than I can count. Since the time you showed up as a scrawny, heartbroken thing, you've stood with me in all my worst moments. You've sat with me when I thought the darkness would claim, and I won't let you face this alone."

Lora presses her eyes closed against the swell of warmth in her eyes. The way Ayc loves is beautiful—fearlessly and unshamedly. He does not care if all the world sees. She wants to love a little more like that, if she can find the courage.

Ayc leans back, and Xylie lifts her head. He gently wipes away a tear that has made a track down her deep brown skin. "She cannot have you," he repeats. "She will have to go through me first."

"And me!" Tavish blurts. A bit of growl deepens his voice. Xylie jerks toward him in surprise.

"I've been wanting to kick her ass for a long time," Browen says with a delicate lift of a palm that glows faintly blue with her power.

"You're a fool to think any one of us would surrender you," Peregrin says. "Even Tempest wouldn't let harm befall you so long as she still has strength to stand. You are not alone."

Xylie sniffs as she presses her fingers to her hand and lets them fall in a simple sign that's somehow infused with gratitude. *"Thank you."*

A smile teases her lips, but a tear still slips down her other cheek. Lora catches it with her knuckle, and Ayc locks eyes with Lora. His jaw tightens. She understands, without words, what he's saying. Ours. Xylie is theirs to protect, and they *will* protect her. Together. Her heart expands so much her chest aches. She doesn't think her ribcage was meant to contain it when it's this full—of fear, and hope, and love.

Peregrin clears their throat. "We can make a backup plan in the morning. For now, we're all tired." They shuffle past the rest of them, toward the door. "I suggest we get sleep, so we are thinking more clearly."

Ayc throws Peregrin a snarky salute. "Whatever you say, Commander."

They swing their cane toward Ayc's head, slow enough he ducks easily. Bronwen glances at Lora, who nods before she shuffles to the door. Xylie and Tavish follow, but Xylie pauses to glance back at Ayc.

"Are you coming?" she signs.

"Oh." Ayc casts a glance at Lora, a question in his eyes.

Fuck. Lora doesn't want him to go. She would like nothing better than to forget about this terrible night and fulfill the promises he made her. First his hand, then his mouth, then his cock. She searches her mind for something, anything to say that would give him permission to sneak back into her tent. But she can think of nothing that wouldn't sound suspicious. Besides, her three guards still stand in the corner of the tent, and knowing Irving, they will all be on high alert. The little privacy she had before Serene showed up is gone.

The fucking bitch.

Lora sighs. "I'll see you in the morning, Ayc."

"See you in the morning, Lora."

When she goes to bed, she goes alone, cursing the divine for their cruelty.

FORTY-SIX

AYC

If Ayc was the sort of person who prayed, he might plead to some god or goddess to just have five minutes alone with Lora. But as the tour through Totus Omni progresses, fate only grows more and more unkind.

The Totus Omni all seem overjoyed when Lora's party rode into town. This is *their* queen, and they gladly open their doors for them to stay with them in their small but lovely homes. Which means their party is often split between many houses, and Lora almost never has a private room. She's always surrounded by someone—her guards, another of the Five, or one of her citizens vying for attention. It leaves no opportunity to think about sneaking back into her room or even being able to have a conversation with her about what happened.

His hands ache to be back upon her, but more than that, he wants to know if she regrets it, if she's going to tell him it was a mistake once again. Every so often, he catches her looking at him, and he thinks he recognizes the look in her eyes.

Longing.

But perhaps it's wishful thinking. Perhaps he only wishes to see what he's feeling in his heart reflected.

They end the tour through Totus Omni in Avia, Lora's home village. Ayc knows as soon as they enter the village because flower petals rain down on their heads from the guard platforms above, a rainfall that continues as they pass the homes built in the trees. People lean from upper windows to cast fistfuls of flowers down upon them.

Ayc leans out the window of the carriage and grins up at them. A glance behind him tells him Muffin is doing the same, their snake-like neck curling out of the covered wagon—a much larger one Lora upgraded to when Muffin outgrew the first. Those who catch a glimpse of the dragon react in various ways. Some point and gasp, others duck back inside.

In the center of the village, only a small crowd has gathered to meet them, and Ayc is grateful Lora will have a reprieve from the large crowds she hates. Hellevi is at the forefront of those gathered. She races forward and is beside Lora by the time Lora swings from her horse. Hellevi embraces her and lays a kiss on Lora's head. Xylie throws open the carriage door and rushes out, and Hellevi pulls her into her arms as well. She sweeps her hands over Xylie's face and says words that Ayc thinks are, "My sweet girl. How are you?"

Ayc steps from the carriage and stretches his arms above his head. He's ceased to care if anyone notices his stiffness and openly uses the stretches and exercises Reselda has taught him to relieve the long hours in the carriage.

Ayc starts toward the wagon. He's surprised when Veni rushes past him, breaking from the ranks to embrace a woman in the crowd who sits in a wheelchair. He thinks he recalls someone —perhaps Veni or Lora or even Xylie—mentioning Veni's mother in passing. Veni sends nearly all his money back to Avia for her care.

The wagon groans and shakes as Muffin jumps out of it. They land ungracefully, nearly tumbling on their face. The earth vibrates a bit at Muffin's thud. They've spent the last two days slumbering, and they've grown once more. They are still awkward, adjusting to their new body shape.

"Who is that person?" Muffin asks, curling their tail to gesture their horned spade toward Hellevi.

She's Lora's grandmother.

"Hm." Muffin stretches out their legs before themself like a cat. *"You should show her the rebel coins."*

"Why? Whatever clue Calliope gave me, it has nothing to do with Hellevi."

"No, but Lora's father was a part of the rebels, was he not? That's why he was exiled?"

"Yes, but how do you know that?"

"If I look deep enough into your mind, I can see your memories. I've been using them to learn about the world. Sometimes, I do it when you're sleeping, though that makes it difficult to distinguish between your memories and your dreams." They cock their head. *"Why does Lora make those sounds in your dreams? Are you harming her?"*

Ayc chokes.

"Are you all right?" Tavish asks, coming to stand beside him, hand wrapped in Saga's Kindred leash. "You look very flustered."

He swallows. "Fine. Really." Internally, he yells, *"Fucking damnit, Muffin! Some things are fucking private! No more looking into my past memories... or my dreams."*

Muffin flexes their wings, almost like a shrug. *"Do you want to know what else I learned?"*

Ayc massages a hand into the sore muscle of his shoulder. *"I'm scared to say yes".*

Muffin's lips spread apart, flashing teeth like a smile. *"Why did the dragon's tail get dirty?"*

Ayc blinks. *"Why?"*

"Because it was drag-on it on the ground."

The dragon chortles. It's the only way to describe the sound that comes from their mouth, their sides heaving. Ayc can only stare. His dragon looked into his memories... and learned how to tell fucking awful jokes. The noise is drawing attention from the crowd, who've been studying the dragon from afar.

"Are *they* all right?" Tavish asks.

"Yes," Ayc says. "And I suddenly understand now."

"What?"

"Why people want to do me bodily harm when I tell them jokes."

Muffin stops laughing abruptly. "*I don't understand. Is that not supposed to be a good joke?*"

"*They're never good. That's the whole point.*"

"*Then how did I fail?*"

Ayc can't argue with that logic, so he doesn't try.

"I don't know," Tavish says. "I quite like the jokes. Most of the time."

Lora beckons to Tavish and Ayc, and Ayc's stupid heart does a silly leap in his chest as her gaze lands upon him. His feet step toward her, but he hesitates, remembering.

"*Quick, Muffin, tell me why I should ask Hellevi?*"

"*She feels...wise. Do you think her son was involved in a rebel group she knew nothing about? Or do you think she was involved, too? Maybe she still is.*"

It makes a tremendous amount of sense. He doesn't know Hellevi well, but he knows Lora well enough to know that Hellevi is mostly responsible for everything he loves about her. No, that isn't quite right. There are parts of Lora—a viciousness, a ferocity, a sharp point on the bejeweled dagger she can be—that were honed there from Yris. He can't deny he loves those parts, too. But the justice Hellevi and her father, Josias, instilled within her is what directs that blade.

Still, it's a gamble. He's been warned about mentioning the rebel group to anyone not already involved. But with the regents steadfastly standing against any attempt for Lora to assist Aluina, she needs to know about the rebels in order to provide aid that way, which means he needs to collect five coins as swiftly as possible.

So, perhaps, it's a gamble he should take, if he gets the chance, and pray he doesn't get his tongue cut out.

"*No one will harm you, Ayc,*" Muffin reassures, clearly sensing his thoughts. "*I will tear open their chest and eat—*"

Muffin trips on their front feet and tumbles ass over horns

across the forest floor. Guards scramble out of the way to avoid being bowled over. Muffin lands on their wings, feet up in the sky. The crowd murmurs; a few dare to laugh.

Ayc swallows down his own laugh and fights to keep the sarcasm from his voice. "*That's very comforting. Thank you, Muffin.*"

"*Fuck you,*" Muffin replies, rolling to their feet and shaking off the dirt the way a dog shakes off water.

"Ayc, you and your dragon stop fooling around and hurry up now!" Hellevi calls.

Ayc starts toward Lora once more. Her bottom lip is caught between her teeth, like perhaps she, too, is trying to refrain from a smile or laugh. She keeps her eyes fixed on him, and he thinks he sees it again. The longing.

Xylie and Bronwen's backs are turned. He takes a chance. He signs, "*I miss you.*"

She releases her lip. Her mouth twists into a smile that is brief, but it's his and his alone. Her hands move subtly, keeping the signs small. But he knows their meaning all the same.

"*I miss you, too.*"

It isn't just the sign that makes his insides twist, but what he sees on her thumb. He's certain that it wasn't there before now, as though she's only dared wear it now that she's in Avia, her hometown.

She's wearing his ring.

One of the rings he dropped in her bed before he slid his fingers inside of her and then left there after. He thought he lost it, because it wasn't among the rest, which showed up in his pack the day after. But she kept it. Claimed it. Claimed him.

The feral thing deep within him purrs in pleasure. He'll take that as an answer.

It's nearly midnight. And Ayc is baking lemon drizzle cookies in Hellevi's kitchen. He feels all the hours of the long day in the dull ache in his lower back, but he almost doesn't mind it. It was a long day, but it was a good day, filled with good people and good food, and a town hall where those who attended left with eyes shining with hope.

He focuses on a bit of shadow beneath the kitchen table, willing it to climb up the cabinets. It took a second for the shadow to listen to him again, after he wore the bracelets, even for a small amount of time. But now the shadow reaches the rim of the bowl. He wills it to stir the spoon around the bowl, and it works. It rattles against the side of the bowl more than if he used his hand, but it's progress. It's little compared to what he did to Calliope a few weeks ago, but that was unintentional and could have killed him.

Ayc takes the spoon in hand and lets his shadows fall. He wants to remain as quiet as possible. Soft breaths come from the three guards who are asleep in Hellevi's living room. Xylie, Bronwen, and Lora are in the guestroom upstairs while Tavish and Peregrin are staying with the neighbors. Ayc, as usual, will be sleeping in the wagon with Muffin.

Right now, Muffin is hunting with Tempest, racing after squirrels and raccoons and whatever other poor beasts are too slow to escape Muffin's rumbling form. Ayc checks on them every now and again, but mostly keeps himself shielded so he can avoid the sounds of bloodshed, bone crunching, and little animals screeching.

He's layering the cookies on a baking tray when a squawk of a stair gives away movement. Hellevi treads carefully down the stairs and past the slumbering guards. Still, every single one of them wakes long enough to note who moves close to them before settling back to sleep.

"I do hope that's lemon drizzle cookies you're making," she teases in a whisper.

"Would I dare make anything other than your favorite?" Ayc replies, giving a cheeky grin that doesn't match the way his heartbeat quickens. The three coins press heavily in his pocket. He told himself that if he could find a way to get Hellevi alone, he would take a chance, as Muffin suggested. They aren't exactly alone. There are slumbering guards only a few feet away, but perhaps he doesn't need to use words. He caught her speaking with signs to Xylie earlier today. Veni is sleeping at his mother's house, and as far as Ayc is aware, none of the other guards know how to sign.

Hellevi slides back a chair at the kitchen table and sits. "Have you seen Lora?"

Ayc stills. "I thought she was upstairs."

"She told me she was going on a walk and went out the back steps. Don't look alarmed. Irving is with her. I simply wondered if by going on a walk she meant..." Hellevi cocks her head, letting the words hang.

"Meant what?" Ayc drops the last of the dough onto the tray and slips it into the oven. When he faces her, Hellevi only shakes her head.

"Nevermind. It isn't any of my business."

Ayc frowns, unsure what she means by that. He glances at the door, torn for a moment. If Lora's still out there, taking a walk, perhaps he can find her. Perhaps he'd have a chance to finally speak with her in semi-privacy. Irving is there, but if anything is going to unfold between them, Lora has to accept that her guards are going to know. There's no plausible way for her to keep anything hidden from them for long.

Or he can take a chance with Hellevi.

Ayc slips his hand into his pocket and rubs the riveted edge of a coin along his finger, undecided. Then, he slips it from his pocket and sets it before Hellevi. He signs, *"Do you recognize this?"*

She pinches the coin between two fingers and turns it over in her hand. Her face is as carefully guarded as Lora's so frequently is. He can't read any emotion that appears on her face. For a painful heartbeat, he fears he's made an error. Then she grasps his hand and places the coin back into his palm.

"Wait here," she signs.

She retraces her steps past the guards and up the stairs, this time avoiding that squeaky step. He works on the lemon glaze as he waits, and she's back before he finishes. He sets the bowl down swiftly as she steps before him. She grabs his hand again and presses another coin into it, already carved with his name.

"*Who sent you to me?*" she asks, making sure her back is turned to the guards.

"*No one. I guessed. Probably against the rules.*" He tucks the coin into his pocket, next to the other three, slightly afraid she might grab it back. He'll place them all back in that box later, the one he keeps his bracelets in.

Hellevi flicks her wrists. "*A willingness to break rules is sort of a prerequisite to being a good rebel. But how were you so certain I'm part of the group?*"

"*Because Josias was.*"

She blinks at the spelling of his name, and her lips mouth the name soundlessly. Ayc swallows. He hopes that one day, he'll get the chance to meet Josias. Surely, he's a wonderful man. A few months from now, Yris will tell Lora where he went, and she'll be able to pardon him.

"*And because my dragon thought it was worth taking the risk,*" Ayc adds.

"Ah," she says aloud, with a wisp of a smile creasing her round cheeks. "We should always trust the opinions of dragons."

Ayc slightly lowers his shield and hears the scream of some poor, unfortunate animal being shredded apart. He shudders and thrusts his shield back up. "Not always, but most of the time."

She falls silent again, allowing her hands to speak for her. "*Don't tell Lora. Not yet. Everything is too precarious. I should have told her long ago, but I feared what Yris would do if she had any proof I was involved, too. She wanted so desperately to keep Lora from me, to have total control over her.*"

Ayc nods. He knows Yris too well to think that wasn't the right choice.

"*We'll tell her. Soon as it's right to do so.*"

Ayc nods. Yes, they will. He's so close to having the last of the coins. "*Do I get a clue on who to look for next?*"

She shakes her head. "*You didn't get a clue that led to me. Follow whatever clue you were last given.*"

Ayc winces. Damn. He's hoped she would have given him something easier than Calliope's non-clue. *"She didn't really give me one. She said she did, but we were merely talking."*

"What did she say?"

He's replayed the conversation over in his head many times. *"Something about there only being one Drakr she trusted. And it isn't me."*

Hellevi taps her chin. "Hmm. Sounds like a clue to me."

Something returns to Ayc, a part of the conversation he forgot, banished no doubt by the fall he took right after. *Asbjorn could use another shadow wielder.*

Fuck. There's another Drakr within Asbjorn.

"How would I find the one other Drakr who is on your side?" he asks Hellevi. If he can't risk telling Lora about Asbjorn, then he can't bring it up to a random Drakr.

Hellevi lifts her palms. "I have faith you'll figure it out."

Ayc sighs. He doesn't have faith. It feels nearly impossible now, but he can't give up. Not when he's so close.

He slips on the oven mitts and slides the cookies from the oven. They are perfectly golden brown.

"I'm curious," Hellevi says. She's returned to the kitchen chair. "Does Lora know you bought her tapestry?"

Ayc sets the tray on top of the stove. "Not unless you told her."

"No, but you *should*. Perhaps now. I think you'll find Lora on the porch swing outside if you want to look. I'm certain she's there." There's a twinkle in her eyes, a look of mischief—a look one gets in their eye when they are definitely meddling in their granddaughter's affairs.

Ayc hesitates. If he goes, he fears he'll confess something. But then, perhaps it's something Hellevi figured out long ago, long before Ayc and Lora did. Something she figured out when he kept going back into the booth at the festivals to be among Lora's creations, when he paid an entire year's salary to take that tapestry home. After all, it was only a few weeks ago when Ayc lay on this floor and overheard Hellevi and Lora speak of him, talking about how Lora chose him because the Council of the People advised Lora to choose someone she hated.

And you chose poorly.

His reaction was to assume the worst, to assume that Hellevi did not think he was good enough to be on Lora's team. But now, he realizes what she was truly saying.

Lora didn't hate him. Perhaps, like Ayc, she never really has. It's all been just a silly game they've played because this thing between them is so big and so real, they've both been terrified by it.

Ayc smiles. "I thought you said it wasn't any of your business."

"I'm a grandmother." She shrugs. "I can't help but root for her happiness. And sometimes, with Lora, that means giving her a good, hard push in that direction." When he doesn't immediately move, she shoos him. "Do I need to give you a good, hard push as well?"

"I'm going," he says with a laugh.

He has to step over a guard to get to the front door. They squint an eye up at him, but he shushes them before slipping out the front door. The plants on Hellevi's front porch have blossomed even further. He tucks his hands into his pockets as he passes through so that when the buds of the flowers snap out, they don't inadvertently catch his fingertips. When he steps off the porch, he realizes that Hellevi, of course, was right. A porch swing hangs from the lowest branch of the mighty tree Hellevi's house is built into, and Lora sits upon it, her legs folded beneath her, wrapped in a knit blanket.

He pauses, taking her in, and he wishes for a moment that he was the type of artist who painted portraits instead of decorating cakes. Because he wants to capture her exactly as she is in this moment, swaying on that bench, eyes closed, looking utterly at peace. Irving, who stands a few feet away, clears his throat to alert Lora of Ayc's presence, and Ayc nearly curses at him for ruining the moment. Then, she opens her eyes, sees him, and smiles. She doesn't try to hide it. She lets the smile roam over her face until it shines in her eyes.

And fuck, that smile is for *him*. It makes him feel as though he holds the whole world in his hand.

"I was just enjoying the quiet," Lora explains.

"May I join you?" Ayc asks.

Lora shifts over on the porch swing to make room. The swing isn't built to hold two people. Their bodies press together, but she only leans closer, sealing their hips and ribs tight. She adjusts the blanket to fall over his lap as well. When she slips her hand into his beneath the blanket, his heart leaps in delight, and a thrill races through his skin. Fuck. He's had his hand inside her. He's heard the sound she makes when she comes. And yet this, their fingers laced together where no one can see, feels just as intimate. Especially when he can still feel his ring wrapped around her thumb.

Irving clears his throat. "I'm going to walk the perimeter. Shout if you need me. The guards and I will hear you."

Soft footfalls carry him away. Gods bless Irving. Ayc opens his mouth. There's so much he wants to say, and he fears he might only have moments before they're interrupted, but Lora squeezes his hand.

"Can you just sit with me for a minute?" Lora asks. She lays her head on his shoulder, her ringlets tickling his neck. And fuck it, talking can wait.

They sit in silence, soaking in the quiet, memorizing the weight of her on his shoulder. The wind sings softly as it passes through the leaves and stirs the wind chimes on the front porch. Ayc traces his thumb across the soft skin of Lora's knuckles, and they're so close, she can't hide how she shivers. He grins. She shifts a little, her thigh grazing against his pocket, grazing against the sharp lines of the box he still has tucked within.

"I have something for you," Ayc whispers.

"That was impressive," she says, her voice vibrating in amusement.

"What was?"

"I think you went a full five minutes without saying anything. Must be a record."

He pokes her rib with his free hand, and she jerks away. "Don't."

"Are you ticklish?" he asks.

"No. And I'll punch you in the throat if you try it."

He almost tries. It's not a healthy response because he absolutely believes he'll end up on the ground, unable to breathe. But he does love her ferocity. Instead, he adjusts and pulls a box from his pocket. She releases his hand, and his palm aches from the absence. He spreads it over her knee instead, and she doesn't pull away.

"What is it?" she asks.

"A box."

She rolls her eyes and slides it open. She blinks at the two pieces of curved metal that rest in a soft field of velvet, a delicate emerald stone secured on either side.

"They're enchanted ear cuffs, like Xylie's," Ayc explains. "The maker of them lives here in Avia. These are a little more subtle than the ones I got her. When you're wearing them, they'll look like you're only wearing an earring in your upper ear, but the maker swears they're just as effective."

She runs a finger over the curve of one but says nothing.

"I thought perhaps they would help you when the world is inconsiderately too loud. You can only wear one if you want. If you're worried about not being able to hear something important."

She closes the box and slips it into the pocket of the sweater she's wearing. When she looks up at him, her eyes are as bright as a sunlit day, a brilliant, endless shade of blue that reflects the color of his own.

"I'm such a fool," she murmurs.

His eyebrows pull together in confusion, but she silences any question he might formulate when she grabs his shirt collar. She yanks him toward her and presses her mouth to his. The kiss this time is different. Their last have been frantic with desire, guzzling water because they were dying of thirst. This is slower, a sip of fine wine, a savoring of sweetened ale that slowly builds. There's desire here, but something more, something he's only dreamed of. Something as bright as a full moon, as sweet as coming home after a long journey. He doesn't dare to name it, can't bring himself to believe it, only basks in her the way he would bask in the first warm day after a long winter chill.

"Lora," he breathes. There's a confession on his lips, one he'll not be able to take back, but he can scarcely keep it in. Those three words are the greatest thing he's ever held. They are bigger than the whole night sky, and he doesn't know how to keep them within anymore.

But her tongue presses against his lips, pressing the confession back down with a growing urgency. She swings her leg over his lap until she's astride him. The change of position makes his insides quake as her soft center seals over his cock through their pants. She nips at his mouth, and he slips his hand into her hair, careful not to pull at her curls. Her hands palm his shirt that hangs loose about his hips. Once it's removed from her path, she sweeps her fingers over the hard ridge between them, trailing over the lines of his cock. And he nearly leaps from his skin.

"Fuck." He grasps for his last shred of common sense. He keeps his voice low, still aware that Irving is somewhere out in the dark wood. That anyone could be out there. "Lora, I want you. I want you so badly I can't even think, but your grandmother is awake. She could look out a window and see us. Anyone could find us."

"There's no window that looks out on this swing," she assures. She drags her tongue from the hollow of his throat to behind his ear, even as she loosens the ties of his waistband and slips her hand inside. The tips of her fingers hesitate just before the aching flesh of his cock. He moans.

"Anyone could walk by," he scarcely manages the protest.

She pulls back, and the grin on her face is nothing short of wicked. Fuck. He can put that smile on the long list of things he never wants to forget.

"Tell me to stop, and I'll stop," she offers, but cruelly she chooses that moment to tease her fingers over the tip of his cock. His back arches so hard, he fears his soul might be ejected from his body. That tiniest little brush completely undoes him.

"You don't have to repay a gift," he says.

"Fuck that," she purrs, lowering her mouth to his ear. "I'm doing this because I *want* to do this. I let you touch me, and now, I want to touch *you*. Bite you. Choke you. Claim you as mine." She pulls at his earlobe with her teeth. "Would you like that, Ayc?"

He's gone. Any hopes that he could say no are gone with those words. "Fuck, yes. Yes, to all of that." He pulls her head back to him, sealing their lips together so that when she boldly wraps her fingers around him, her mouth muffles the sound he makes. She pumps her hands up and down, and he's so overwhelmed that it's her—his Lora—whose hand is upon him that he nearly loses it fast. He clamps down on the urge.

He doesn't want it to be like this. When he comes for her the first time, he wants to be buried deep inside of her. But Lora isn't giving him much choice. She's taken up a brutal rhythm as she glides her hand up and down his entire length, occasionally twirling her thumb at his tip. Her hips work over him as she does. The porch swing rocks and quakes. He palms her full, perfect ass. His fingers pluck desperately at her waistband, wanting to return the pleasure she's giving him, but his befuddled mind can't remember how gods damn clothes work. She's dragged his shirt open and is worrying at his collarbone with her teeth so fiercely, the small part of his brain that's still working thinks she might leave a bruise. *Hopes* she'll follow through with her words and leave a bruise. He wants her to dig in her nails, her teeth—he wants to be marked as hers and hers alone.

He is so pathetically, desperately, hopelessly in love with her.

"Lora, slow down," he begs, managing to choke out the words through the groans that are building in his throat. "I'm going to —" He can't finish the words, not when she slides her free hand upward to frame his throat. The pads of her fingers press against his hammering pulse, and his vision floods with red.

"Harder," he whisper, begs.

She tightens her grasp on her throat, sealing off just a bit of his air, even as she presses more firmly on the tip of his cock.

She growls in his ear. "Come for me like a good boy."

And he's gone. He can see nothing but red as pleasure erupts through him. He clings to Lora, unable to breathe past the hand on his throat, and somehow, that makes it even better, even more powerful. He swears the world itself quakes.

Someone is yelling his name when he comes back to himself, and unfortunately, it isn't Lora. It's distant. Faint.

He lowers his mental shield slightly. *"What, Muffin?"* Even in the mental link, his voice is weak. He gasps for air, faintly aware that Lora has loosened her hold on his throat.

"Ayc! Ayc! Are you all right? You sound like you're dying."

His every muscle is limp. Pleasure still ripples through his nerves. Ayc sags forward and buries his face into Lora's neck, laying a stream of kisses across the arch of it. *"I am well, Muffin. Very well. Put up your shield, too, please."*

Muffin begins to protest, but Ayc snaps the shield back into place between them. He can't help the laugh that works its way up his throat.

"What is it?" Lora asks, working her fingers through his hair, more gently this time. He melts beneath her touch.

"Muffin fears I'm dying. I think I might be." He drags in another deep breath and leans back to glance down at himself. He's going to have to sneak through the woods before anyone sees him and jump into the river to wash clean of the mess she's made of him. "I fear I'm the one you've left in ruins."

"Good." She smiles wickedly once more. "That was fun. No other man's let me take that much control before."

"You have been with very, very foolish men."

He runs his fingers along Lora's waistband, but Lora seizes his wrists and carefully climbs off his lap. She stands.

"We should stop. Go get cleaned before we're caught."

"Oh, I see how it is," he teases. "You're fine with people

catching us when I'm the one being embarrassingly debased but not yourself, yes?"

"That's exactly how this works, yes."

A crunch sounds in the forest, still far enough away that it's clear that Irving is headed back in their direction—and that he's purposefully trying to warn them. Ayc springs to his feet and wills himself to the shadow.

Lora blinks at the suddenness. "Ayc," she hisses.

He doesn't answer until he's behind her. He lowers his lips to her neck, and she trembles at the touch. "Yes, my lady?"

He slips his hands down to her hips, still within the shadow. She leans back into him and arches her neck so he can nip at her throat. Her breath is a little short when she says, "We'll be back in Wyntra in a few days."

"And?"

"And then I want you in my bed. *Every* night."

She can't see his smile, but he makes certain she can feel it, pressing it into her skin. "*Gladly*, my lady."

FORTY-SEVEN

LORA

Ayc's shadows linger on Lora's skin even after she's certain Ayc has slipped away. They tease at the bare skin of her fingertips and circle around her ankles, as real as a physical touch. She's not certain that Ayc intended to do that or if the shadows have been altered somehow by his desire for her, but she adores it—the icy cool touch of it. Her heart is still pounding, her palms delighting in the thrill of touching him.

"Is everything well?"

The shadows scatter as Irving calls from behind a nearby tree, one last warning to respect her privacy. Fuck. That was reckless, but she doesn't regret it. She knew the risk she was taking, even if Ayc had not so respectfully reminded her of it. Besides, they were quiet. Her hand around his throat ensured that.

Still, she can't be so careless again. It's clear that Irving might not know exactly what unfolded, but he knows enough that something *is* unfolding between Ayc and Lora. Otherwise, he wouldn't have left.

Irving steps out from behind the tree. He looks around. "Did Ayc leave?"

"Yes."

Irving shifts his weight from foot to foot, his lips parting and then closing again.

"Is there something you'd like to say?" Lora asks.

"If I might be forward, my lady."

Her body flushes with warmth. Ayc has ruined those two words for her. She's never going to hear 'my lady' again without thinking about how Ayc has breathed those words into her skin as he's made her come. He's filled those words with so much pleasure. Even now, his reply of *"Gladly, my lady"* rings in her ear, full of promise and pleasure.

"I don't want to overstep, but I want to make something abundantly clear," Irving says. "Guards are trained to see everything—and nothing at all."

"What does that mean?"

"It means we will be discreet. Nothing you do in your own private life will ever be spoken about by any of the guards. I trust all of them explicitly, and I would remove them from service if they ever failed. Whatever you do, if you do not wish people to know, no *one* would find out from a guard."

"Not even Peregrin?" Lora asks. It's not that she doesn't trust the rest of her Five. It's simply that if they know about her and Ayc, they get to formulate opinions about them. And Lora isn't ready for anyone else's opinion.

The dimple in Irving's cheek flashes briefly at the mention of Peregrin before disappearing. "I get the sense that Peregrin knows almost everything but also wishes they *didn't*. But they would not learn it from me."

Lora slips her hand into her pocket and traces the edges of the wooden box containing the ear cuffs that Ayc gave her. The kindness that made her realize just how foolish she's been, piling up all the excuses to keep him away. Not all her fears are unfounded, though.

"And if I were to have someone who I wanted…privacy with," Lora says, choosing her words delicately. "How much danger would he be in if people were to find out? As captain of my guard, do you think people might want to harm him?"

"Perhaps," Irving replies without hesitation. "They might want to, but they will fail. Because your guards will protect anyone you love, the way we protect you. And besides"—the dimple appears again—"Ayc is quite powerful. I would not have left you alone with him if I didn't think he's more than capable of protecting you. He proved that with Calliope; he protected you when no one else could even stand."

A bit of guilt tints the final sentence.

"You need to let that go," Lora says. "It's not your fault."

He ticks up his chin. "It's my job to protect you. And I failed. I won't do so again, not so long as I still breathe." He pauses, then adds, "My point is...please don't let fear steal your happiness."

Lora bites the inside of her lip. She doesn't know that the fear of losing Ayc, of feeling what she felt in that hospital when she saw him die, will ever fully fade. But it's overwhelmed by a spark of something new. Hope. A hope that she can have something for herself. She'll give everything else for Everadyn and Aluina. But not this.

She gets to have this for herself.

"Thank you, Irving. Good night."

Her guard trails after her as she reenters her grandmother's house. Ayc must have been baking because the room smells like cookies and the softest hint of lemon. She diverts momentarily to grab a cookie from the plate sitting on the table. It falls apart in her mouth, the taste mixing with the sweeter taste that still lingers on her tongue—the taste of the baker who made them.

She slips upstairs and into her old childhood room. Irving leans against the wall beside the door. She nods at him one last time before closing the door, holding the knob to keep the latch as quiet as possible. Bronwen is asleep on the pallet made up on the floor, her hair scattered over her pillow. Xylie sleeps on one side of Lora's large bed, her dozens of braids wrapped in silk, burying her face in the pillow to hide from the moonlight that comes in the window. Lora maneuvers around Bronwen carefully to the other side of the bed and freezes.

A roar builds up in Lora's head. Her hands shake. A dark sprig of flowers lies on her pillow, inches from her cousin's face.

Midnight.

She springs to the side of her bed, ensuring she kicks up her heel high enough that she can drag her knife from her boot. "Xylie, Bronwen, wake up!" she hisses, even as she grasps Xylie's arm and pulls her from the bed. Xylie lets out a startled cry and fumbles to get her legs under her. Bronwen bolts upright. Irving flings open the door.

Lora searches the darkness of the room, aware that whoever lay the midnight on the pillow might still be there. "Bronwen, light!"

Bronwen thrusts up her hand, and light bursts through the room, scattering the shadows. No one. There's absolutely no one here.

"What is it?" Irving demands. His hand rests on his sword. Feet pound on the creaking stairs, the other guards rushing upward at the sound of their voices.

Xylie's hands shake as Lora pulls her backwards, even as Irving's hand falls on her shoulder and stirs them toward the door. He's issuing commands, orders on how to keep her safe, but all Lora can see is that sprig of midnight on the pillow.

First, Wyntra, and now here, in Avia, in her grandmother's house—in the only place she's ever truly thought of as home. The guards surround her now, and she doesn't feel safe. Not for herself and not for her Five. She eyes the cloaks they wear around their necks, the ones that will render them invisible if needed. And she knows it deep in her gut.

Whoever put that midnight on her pillow is someone she trusts.

Which means she can't trust anyone at all.

Irving is already issuing orders, his voice distant in Lora's still rattling ears. He commands a guard to go wake the others. *All* of the others. He commands the other two to stay with Lora, and then he's running down the stairs two at a time. Lora barely catches his explanation. He's going to look outside the house.

Bronwen rushes after him, pressing two of her fingers into Lora's elbow before she goes.

The most logical thing is that the culprit came in through the window. But when? How? She and Irving have been outside for the last hour. Surely, they would have noticed someone creeping around in the dark.

She searches her memory, trying to think of anything, but she was too distracted with Ayc. But surely, Irving would have noticed—

A hand brushes her back. Lora jumps.

"It's me, sweet pea," Hellevi says softly. "What's going on?"

Lora explains as one of the guards directs them to go downstairs. Lora wraps her arm around Xylie's shoulders as they go, and together, the three sit on the floor on the blankets that the guards abandoned. Magdon is just behind her while Shae searches the house, filling the small home with clatters as she looks through closets and opens every cupboard in the kitchen like someone might have squeezed themselves inside.

Meanwhile, Lora holds fast to Xylie's hand. Her cousin stares into the fire. She doesn't seem afraid, uneasy by the fact that someone stood over her as she slept. It's a reminder of their message.

I can hurt you. I can hurt anyone you love.

Hellevi rubs small circles into Lora's spine with a slow, steady pressure like she did when Lora was a child. It never failed to put her to sleep. It soothes her nerves now, too.

The door slams open. Lora jumps to her feet, reaching again for the knife she tucked back into her boot. The guards whirl toward the door.

"Lora!"

Her heart leaps at Ayc's voice, the way fear and urgency are wrapped around the two syllables of her name. He vaults toward her, and she nearly runs to him. She's taken a few steps toward him before she remembers Xylie's and Hellevi's presence and plants her feet.

"I'm fine," Lora says.

When he closes the distance between them, his hands rise to her face, his palms cupping her cheeks with a gentle firmness. He searches over her face as though to be sure. She savors his warmth, not realizing how cool her face had become. But the touch is too intimate. In the corner of her vision, Lora can see Xylie tip her head curiously. Perhaps Ayc sees it, too, because he quickly drops his hands.

"I saw guards running out of their houses," he explains. "They're starting a search."

He's changed his shirt. The clean one clings to the damp skin from where he must have washed in the river. Little beads of water drip down his throat and disappear down his collar. His hair is pulled higher on his head than usual, so it wouldn't get wet, she assumes. He's still a mess for her, and she might rejoice at the sight of his ruin under different circumstances.

"They said you found midnight," Ayc adds.

Lora nods. "I found it on my pillow. They put it there while Xylie was sleeping next to it."

Ayc jerks his gaze to Xylie, the red flashing in his eyes.

"*I'm fine,*" she quickly signs. "*I was sound asleep. I didn't hear a thing.*"

"Did either of you touch it?" Ayc demands.

Lora shakes her head. Xylie echoes the motion.

"All right." He drags his gaze over Lora once more as though reassuring himself that she's, in fact, unharmed. Then he twists back toward the door. "I'm going to go help them find who did this. They can't be far."

Lora catches his hand. "Ayc, wait. I think that's a waste of time."

He turns back. "Why?"

Lora hesitates, glancing at Shae and Magdon. Surely, it can't be Shae. She's been trustworthy and loyal. She shows a fierceness in protecting Lora that's only outmatched by Irving. But she was also the one who stood outside Lora's door all night when Irving was taken. She could have so easily set that midnight on her pillow.

"Both of you step outside, please," Lora says. "You've searched the house, and no one is here. I'll yell for you if I need you."

"My lady," Shae begins to protest.

Lora adds lightning to her tone, a sudden crack. "Now."

Shae scowls, but she pivots toward the door. The other guard follows. Ayc tracks them as they go, the lines of worry about his eyes growing darker.

"Do you think it was one of your guards?" he asks.

"I think it's someone I *know*," Lora replies. "How else would they know my grandmother's house?"

"This village is small," Hellevi says. "They could have simply asked someone."

"But if they crawled in through the window, who would know which window leads to my room?"

"Why would any of your guards have motivation to harm you?" Ayc asks. "None of them are politically connected. They have nothing to gain with harm falling upon you and a lot to lose."

"Unless someone paid them well."

"*Why would they wait until now?*" Xylie asks. "*It's been weeks since the first one.*"

"I don't know. Clearly, I did something to piss someone off."

Ayc arcs an eyebrow at her and mouths one word: "Grey."

She spoke with Grey about her desire to break the treaty with the Drakr. With all the other regents, she's been more guarded, trying to assess their feelings regarding Aluina without actually declaring her intent. Does that mean Grey has threatened her? Or did they simply tell someone? Perhaps one of the other regents?

She doesn't know. She presses her thumb to her temple, her pulse suddenly pounding through it. Ayc's hand flinches, shifts forward, and then curls into a fist, like he's fighting the urge to touch her. Hellevi stands and walks into the kitchen, opening up a cupboard.

"We'll figure it out," Ayc reassures. "We'll talk to Peregrin and Irving."

At least she can be certain of Irving. His memories were wiped clean; he could not have faked that. Veni and the rest of the new guards are also unlikely. They didn't arrive in Wyntra until after the first sprig of midnight was found in her bed. Which leaves only a handful of others.

Perhaps she's wrong. But she feels it in her gut.

Someone she trusts has betrayed her.

Hellevi returns and presses a pain tonic into Lora's palm. She drinks it down without thinking. If she waits too long, the migraine will only get worse. A splotch of white catches Lora's eye, and she turns her head toward the window. There, framed in the glass, is Muffin, his red eyes blinking. "Ayc, I think your dragon is currently crushing my grandmother's flowers."

Ayc sighs. "I know. They are worried about you. They're becoming quite protective."

Lora blinks. "Of me? Why?"

Ayc shrugs. Muffin retreats from the window just before the door swings open once more.

Irving and Veni slide into the room, and they're quickly followed by the rest of the Five. Tavish still rubs sleep from his eyes, holding Saga's handle. Peregrin looks as though they might have been sleeping in their armor because they appear nearly as pristine as always. Muffin tries to sneak their head in the door, but Bronwen presses it closed in their face. A moment later, they return to the window.

The bodies make her grandmother's home feel smaller than it is, all of them clustering around each other. Lora uses the excuse to stand a little closer to Ayc, feeling his body heat, letting her pinky brush against the tips of his fingers.

"Veni found something," Irving says, his words taut.

That was quick. How much time has passed? Veni was given the night off and was staying with his mother, yet here he is in his guard's cloak already. He steps forward. A ripped piece of blue cloth is clutched in his hand. But not just any blue. The same brilliant blue of the bag that was found under her bed.

Lux Aester blue.

"I found it about halfway up the tree, beneath your window,

caught in on some bark," Veni explains. "It must have caught on their cloak on the way up."

"Fucking bastards," Ayc seethes beneath his breath.

It's such an obvious clue. Either the person they have hired to sneak into Lora's room is the most foolish person alive, or someone is purposefully planting clues to make her turn elsewhere.

"I'm going to turn Amos inside out," Bronwen adds.

"We don't know that it was Amos," Lora says.

Her Five look at her in surprise.

Veni fists the piece of fabric hard enough that his hand shakes. "Who else could it be? It matches the bag you found beneath your bed. It can't be just a coincidence."

Lora says, "It proves nothing. It could still be anyone. Nothing directly ties Amos to it. If I'm going to behead him, I'm going to be quite certain that I'm beheading the correct person."

"Then we need proof," Ayc says. "And soon."

Bronwen strides toward Veni. "Let me see it."

Veni passes her the cloth with a grunt of frustration. Bronwen paces away, turning the blue cloth over in her hand, muttering to herself.

"Tavish," Lora asks, "do you sense anything?"

"Yes," Tavish replies, "but I can't get a clear direction. If I think of who is responsible, it seems to come from too many directions at once, and I can't make sense of it." He sighs. "I'm sorry."

"Don't be," Lora says. "For now, I'll send a letter to Amos demanding he increase efforts to find whoever is doing this."

"Come on, Lora," Veni snaps. The look of frustration on his face isn't masked. In this moment, he's acting like her childhood friend. Not her guard. "If he's the one behind it, you can't trust him to be honest."

Irving holds up a hand, cutting a look toward Veni that makes him flatten his lips in a long line. He backs away, still shaking his head so that his turquoise curls toss.

"I'll send a few guards of my own to investigate within the territory as well," Irving says.

Lora swallows. What if he picks the guard who is the one sneaking things into her room? Perhaps she should suggest sending two different groups to ensure at least one is not—

"No," Ayc says, interrupting her thoughts. "Send me, and if there's evidence, I'll find it."

"Send you?" Irving repeats. "Like, as a spy?"

Ayc nods.

"Ayc," the protest comes unbidden to Lora's lips, but he cuts her off.

"I can go where others can't. We no longer have the luxury of not taking full advantage of my affinity. Not if you aren't safe."

It has never crossed Lora's mind to use him with those powers in such a way. She's never even thought to ask him. Yris would have. She would have abused the power of the Binding stone to make him do unspeakable things. Be her assassin. Her spy. Rule over her enemies with an iron fist. It's why Ayc lied to Yris, why he pretended to be incompetent with the sword when he isn't. Lora would never have asked him to do it, but he's offering it to her willingly.

A thousand excuses jump to the tip of her tongue. But all are petals growing on the same withered stem, excuses to hide the truth.

She fears losing him. Spying on regents is forbidden by law. If he's caught, the regents could demand he be punished or never trust her again. But she brushes the thought away. If he's caught, she'll refuse to harm him, whatever the consequences. If her being Sovereign can endanger him, it can also protect him.

If loving him makes her wicked, then she will be a wicked queen.

Love.

She loves him.

Of course she does. She realized it as soon as she saw what lay in the box he gave her on the porch, the gift that says that he sees her. Really sees her and accepts her in a way she's not sure anyone else does. And she sees him. Loves him.

She's been a fool to deny it for so long. She's loved him since he was a foolish boy, grinning as she held a blade to his throat. She's loved his relentless kindness and goodness in the face of all the ways the world has been unkind. She's even loved him telling those awful jokes that make her want to punch him in the face, though she will die before she ever admits it.

Loving him makes her vulnerable, yes. But it also makes her dangerous. She stormed into that Lux Aester Temple during the Sovereignty trials to save him, and, yes, she fell into a trap. But she also spilled a river of blood on the temple floor.

She'll do it again if she must.

"It may be the best way to get solid evidence of Amos's involvement," Peregrin says when Lora doesn't speak.

No one else offers an objection.

Ayc folds his arms over his chest. "I have to do something, Lora. I can't just wait while you're in danger. I can't bear it."

Of course he can't. Because neither could she.

"All right," Lora agrees. "But not yet. When we visit Lux Aester on tour. When we can all go and be there if something goes wrong."

"That is *week*s from now," he protests.

"Then we have time to plan carefully," Peregrin says. "The regents are aware of your power. If Amos has something to hide, he will undoubtedly be watching you closely. If you go missing, they'll increase guards for whatever they are hiding. We'll have to plan a distraction."

Ayc shakes his head. "And what if they decide not to simply send a message next time? What if next time they are coming to kill her?"

Blue turns to red once more in his eyes. A growl sounds through the window, loud enough that even Saga jumps, and Tavish has to shush the dog with a soothing hand. Both dragon and dragon rider are testy.

"I'll station a guard *in* her room if I must," Irving says.

Lora shudders at the thought. No, she doesn't intend to go to bed alone when she returns to Wyntra, but she doesn't want a guard staring at her as she sleeps either.

"We can put up a blood protection spell instead," Bronwen says. "It'll have to be reapplied every night, but I can do it. We should have been doing it already."

"Won't that eventually exhaust you, night after night?" Ayc says. "Blood magic makes it easier for isolated magic, but it can take a cumulative toll if done too frequently."

"Impressive." Bronwen gives him a teasing smile. "Someone has been studying the books on magic I recommended."

"Will it?" Lora asks.

Bronwen's smile falls. "Yes. But I'll manage."

"Can you use my blood?" Ayc asks. "Would it spare you the cost?"

"It's generally not advised that you use someone else's blood for your own magic. But, yes, if necessary, we could. I will let you know if I can't manage."

Lora doesn't like the idea of Bronwen spending so much energy to keep her safe, but if it's what they have to do to ensure no one attempts to slit her throat in her sleep, then that's what she has to do.

Irving rubs a hand over his chin, considering it. "Very well."

Lora nods at the cloth still held in Bronwen's hand. "Did you sense anything?"

"Nothing." Bronwen hands the cloth to Irving. He carefully tucks it into his pocket. "There's absolutely nothing to sense. It's almost like it's brand new and never had an owner."

Which is odd, but then, most of the guards have some degree of magical affinity. Perhaps they've cast some spell to hide their presence. Or perhaps it's someone else entirely. Her fatigue seeps into the marrow of her bones.

"Then maybe set the barrier," Lora says. "I would like to go to bed."

Veni makes a sound like he's trying to talk, but the words get stuck in his throat.

Lora cocks her head at him. "Yes, Veni? Is there anything else?"

Veni stares for a long moment. Then he shakes his head. "I'm going to search more. See if there's anything else I can find." He walks away, slamming the door a little too loudly behind him.

Bronwen heads for the stairs. She slips her hands into the slit of her nightgown and pulls out the dagger strapped to her thigh. Peregrin and Irving step toward the door, tipping their heads together, already whispering. Hellevi turns to put another log on the fire. Xylie stoops to scratch Saga's ears.

Lora's gaze shifts to Ayc to find him already looking. She feels the intensity of his blue eyes in the depths of her soul, a sea of emotion she could drown in. Her thighs clench, and she fights for a breath. Even in moments like these, he can undo her in one look.

If she had her own room, perhaps she would say fuck it. Fuck her desire for privacy, let the world know, and then she would take him to bed with her. She wonders how well she would sleep with him in her bed. It's debatable. Perhaps, she would sleep wonderfully curled into the warmth of his body, and perhaps, she would fuck him until the sun came up. Either way, at least she wouldn't have to think about the rest of the world for a few hours.

Soon.

For now, she takes advantage of the others' distraction and brushes her fingers against his. Their hands lock for just a second before she makes herself pull away. When she turns toward Xylie, a smile plays on her cheeks, as if someone wasn't just standing over her in her sleep.

FORTY-EIGHT

LORA

Yris is the unwelcome sight that greets Lora when their party arrives back in the courtyard of Wyntra. She stands near the doors to the castle, her arms crossed over her chest, the dark velvet of her dress whipping like a flag in the brutal wind. Dark clouds hang full and boggy in the sky, threatening rain at any moment.

Lora swings from the saddle. Her legs feel stiff from the days of riding from Avia, and fatigue has settled into her bones. Despite Bronwen's boundaries, she's slept little in the tents they've pitched along the way. She's been too busy listening to the movement of the guards, more of them awake at a time than ever. Lora fears that if she closes her eyes, she'll awake to find someone dead. It hasn't helped that all the Five began sleeping in the same tent, one of them awake at all times. Nor has it helped that she's noticed that Muffin and Tempest have started taking shift prowling or flying over the camp, their superior senses always watching.

Now, Lora doesn't want to deal with her mother. She wants to go to bed.

And she doesn't want to go alone.

Her head turns towards the carriage just as Ayc steps out of it, already doing a series of stretches that Reselda taught him to loosen the stiffness. He immediately looks toward her, grinning when he finds her looking. Fuck. She hates that smile of his, hates how it entangles her insides and strokes the fire within her.

He winks at her like he knows.

Fuck him, she thinks. Which is actually precisely what she wants to do.

Lora hands off her reins to a stable boy and approaches where her mother waits. "The castle still stands. Is there something you need from me?"

"I have a report that needs to be brought to your attention," Yris replies. "Immediately."

Lora is certain that Yris doesn't have the same definition of what needs attention immediately. "Oh. And what is that?"

"I received a report a few minutes ago that pirates have attacked another warship. Admirals are awaiting further orders."

Lora blinks. Well, Captain Morrow and his crew are, perhaps, working a little too hard. That, in fact, will need to have her attention. What type of Sovereign would she be if she didn't respond to the distress of her armies?

"It's on your desk." Yris turns on her heel and leads the way.

Lora follows but can't stop herself from glancing back to where Ayc is waiting for Muffin to jump from the wagon. Just the sight of his back coils the desire tauter.

Soon. Very soon.

It's not nearly as soon as Lora would like when she tucks away the report, sends letters to the admirals with further instructions, and kicks her mother from the office. Yris has already mobilized more aid and resources to hunt for the pirates, so there isn't much to be done. Lora leaves her office to take another letter to the aviary, sending her favorite bird to take a private message to Morrow, to warn of the increased patrols—and to encourage him to slow down their efforts. She's certain that, between Calliope's gifts, his abilities as a water elementist, and the sorcerer on board, they will avoid capture, but they will cast suspicion upon her if they continue at this rate.

The sky over the ocean has turned pink when Lora leaves the aviary and hurries through the halls. She forces herself to first go to her room and private bathing chambers to swiftly shower off the grime and sweat of the day. She leaves her crown on the nightstand, knowing it will be safe behind the barrier Bronwen has already created. Lora dresses in her favorite loose silver nightgown that stops at her thighs and pulls her long cardigan over it.

She's taken this path to Ayc's kitchen so many times. She used to sneak there in her teenage years all the time. This time somehow feels the same and utterly different, all at once. The longing, deep in her soul, certainly echoes what she felt then, though now she understands it far better. She never went to that kitchen wanting chocolate pudding. She went because she wanted him. She was never old enough, brave enough, free enough to admit it.

Until now.

She quickens her pace. Her heart hammers with every step that carries her back to him.

"In a hurry, my lady?" Veni teases as he follows next to her.

Lora huffs and says nothing. She's not in the mood for his games.

Shae also trails behind them, much further back. Lora spoke to Irving about her concerns that one of her guards might be responsible for putting midnight on her pillow, but he's ensured her that the locations of all the guards were verified through independent witnesses. Shae was asleep on the floor of her grandmother's house, and no guard ever saw her leave that spot. She could not have done it, and Lora dislikes that she even questioned her loyalty. She dislikes even more that the more answers they seem to get, the more confused she is about what happened.

Veni leans closer and drops his voice. "I'm happy you and Ayc are no longer avoiding this thing between you."

She glares at him. "Did Irving say something?"

"Of course not. Did you forget that when I arrived at Wyntra, I arrived to find you and Ayc in a very…interesting position? Besides, the tension between you two is so thick I could shoot a bolt at it from five hundred yards and still hit it."

"And yet you still flirted with him?".

"Only because I knew it made you jealous and thought, perhaps, if you realized you were jealous, you would stop being a fool and do something about it."

Lora pauses, her canine teeth vibrating. She suppresses their elongation. "You're lucky I'm in a hurry because it means I don't currently have the time to beat the shit out of you for that."

She begins walking once more, pretending that she doesn't hear Veni's chuckle.

"You deserve this, you know?" he says.

"Deserve what?"

"To be happy. You don't always have to punish yourself for your mother's mistakes."

She doesn't want to analyze that statement, not when it scrapes like sharp silver against her skin. They round the corner, and Lora catches sight of Ayc's door.

"Veni, how far will Irving allow you to be away from me?"

"I suppose it depends on the situation."

"Well, however far away you can be, be that far away."

Veni pauses at the end of the hall, a twisted smile curling onto his face. "Have fun," he calls after her.

She tosses him her middle finger over her shoulder, ignoring his laughter. She stops before his door and takes a breath. Somehow, despite the heat blazing beneath her skin, something on wings flutters about her stomach. Nervous. Fuck, why is she nervous? She's never been nervous before with other partners, and it scarcely makes sense now. She's already been laid bare before him. She's already had his cock wrapped in her fingers. But still, she's twisted up inside because everything about this feels different. It feels as though, if she knocks on this door, her world as she knows it might tip sideways, might quake apart and reshape into something entirely new.

This isn't anyone.

This is *Ayc*.

Her cinnamon roll boy, the one who's been under her skin since the moment she met him, buried deeper with every act of kindness, every daring smile, every terrible joke. There's no going back from this, but she doesn't want to go back. This precipice is one she's stood on too long, and she's ready to fall.

She lifts her hand and knocks.

No answer.

"Ayc?" she calls. "It's me. Lora."

Fuck, what is she doing? Anyone could see her here, hanging outside his door. Impatiently, she tries the doorknob and finds it unlocked. She slips inside.

"Ayc?"

The kitchen is empty, in its normal tidy state, broken only by a bowl of pudding that's been left on the counter. Almost like he knew she was coming. But there's no sign of Ayc and no sign of Muffin either. Muffin is most likely in the Sovereign's Garden or with Tempest. They are getting much too large to comfortably stay in Ayc's kitchen, and the garden gives them a safe place to roam where other people won't be. Perhaps Ayc is with them. He's certainly not here. He would have heard her. Unless he's asleep.

The door to his bedroom is ajar. She wanders over to peek inside. "Ayc?" she calls just a little louder. Still nothing. She hesitates before pushing the door open further.

No Ayc. It takes only a glance to know he's truly not there, but still, she remains fixated. She studies the room greedily, soaking in the little elements that make him up: the wardrobe with the bright corsets peeking out, the pots of nail polish and kohl on the stand by the door, an old guitar covered in dust she's certain he attempted to play twice and never touched again. Then she sees it, hanging on the wall over the bed, and her breath stills.

Right here, in the middle of all the things that speak of Ayc, is her.

Her tapestry.

It's one of her favorite creations. She weaved it, inspired by Avia, remembering a moment of her childhood when she and her father would lie on the forest floor and gaze up at the stars. Mostly, when she creates a piece, whether it be a tapestry or clothing, she always focuses on what she could have done better. She hyper-fixates on the imperfections until they are all she can see. Not this one. This one, she was oddly content with.

She almost kept it, except they needed the money to free more people from Lux Aester, and she knew it would sell. People wanted to own pieces created by the Sovereign's daughter. She knew some merchant with more money than sense would pay a hefty price for it, so she dared price it higher than most. It took a while to sell, and Hellevi reported she sold it at a hefty discount. But she never, not once, mentioned who she sold it to.

Lora's mind grapples with the information, putting the pieces together. Ayc bought her tapestry and hung it in his room. Not recently. Not since the Trials. But years ago. He was supposed to hate her for all she did to him, and yet, he bought this tapestry even though it must have cost... She does a quick calculation from what she remembers from the numbers Hellevi gave her and from the records of Ayc's meager salary. The amount of time he must have worked and saved in order to buy it refuses to connect in her brain.

He couldn't have. He just couldn't have. It means something that makes the earth feel like it's already reshaping, her insides already quaking. She presses her fingers to her lips, feeling like she might sob even though she doesn't quite understand why.

The door to the kitchen swings open. Ayc stumbles in, and he must have noticed the guards at the end of the hallway because he calls her name. He locks onto her, and his eyes drag over her frame, lingering longest on her exposed legs beneath the nightgown. He must have showered and changed, because he's now wearing a loose tunic and breeches, and the ends of his hair are damp as it hangs loose around his shoulders.

"Sorry," he says, "I was with Muffin in the garden." He shuts the door. Locks it. Strides toward her with a smile on his face so bright it could compete with the sun.

She shakes out her hands. There are too many thoughts in her head, too many emotions in her chest.

And he must see because he pauses a few steps away. His smile falters. "Are you all right?"

"Why?" It's the only word she can get to come out. "Why did you do it?"

"Why did I do what?" Ayc reaches out his hand, and Lora shakes her head. He can't touch her because it will overwhelm her with how good it feels, and she is overwhelmed enough. Even if it's good. And what is swelling up inside of her is good. But it is more powerful than she can bear.

He drops his hand. "Fuck, Lora, what did I do this time?"

"The..." She presses her eyes closed and drags a breath through her nose, seizing control of her emotions. It feels like trying to cram every happy thing she's ever felt into a box, but bits of light and color keep springing from it. "The tapestry."

"Oh," Ayc says, glancing past her into the room. He winces. "That."

"You bought it?"

He rubs the back of his neck. "Obviously."

"How did you afford it? I know what you made before. It must have cost you an entire...an entire..."

She can't bring herself to say it, but Ayc merely shrugs, like the amount was trivial. "An entire year's worth."

An entire year?

The goodness of it collides like a healing balm against a brush, pouring across memories of her mother mocking her tapestries. Of telling her they were a waste of time. Of commanding her to get up from weaving, go into the yard, and practice fighting. This action is pushing on the bruises she didn't know were there, and her voice is harsher than she means.

"That was money you were saving for a Severing stone, wasn't it? Why would you spend it on my tapestry?"

Ayc leans back on the edge of his counter and shrugs again. "I wanted it, so I bought it. It's as simple as that."

It isn't that simple. The amount of money makes it far from simple. For a rich man, it would have been nothing, but for him, it was everything.

"It wasn't worth what you paid for it."

"It was worth it to *me.*" His eyes briefly flare with red, a warning that she's angered him. "I wanted it because it's beautiful, and I loved it. Because it reminded me of my home in Aluina. And because it reminded me of *you.* I would have paid more if I had it."

"Why?"

He throws up his hands. "Fuck, Lora, have I not made it obvious? Do you not understand what you are to me? Clearly not, because if you did, you wouldn't keep asking me why?"

"And what am I to you?" she demands.

He shakes his head and locks his jaw, the lines of frustration engraved on his face. Why wouldn't he be frustrated? When he probably *has* made it obvious. With every word, with every action. She knows he has feelings for her, but she has been too busy running away from her own feelings to let herself truly feel the depth of *his.* But now she needs to know, needs to hear it.

She takes a breath and lowers her voice. "I'm sorry, Ayc. I really am. I haven't been listening. Not well enough. But I'm listening now. What am I to you?"

He runs his hands over his face. When he drops them, he lets out a breath—one-half sigh of defeat and half huff of determination.

"You're air," he breathes.

She blinks. "I'm what?"

"You're the air in my lungs, and the beat of my heart, and the only place that still feels like home. I can't breathe—cannot live—without you."

She can only stare at him. It sounds like something out of her romance books, one of the beautiful, infuriating things that men written by women like to say that reminds her of poetry but never quite makes logical *sense.* "What does that mean?"

He presses a fist into his temple and growls a note of frustration. "For fuck's sake, I'm in love with you."

AYC

The words hover in the air.

He can't take them back.

He doesn't *want* to take them back.

They've been trapped inside his chest for too long, shaking at his ribs, kicking at his sternum, demanding to be free. It's a relief to have confessed them to her.

"I love you, Lora," he says again.

She doesn't move. She scarcely even looks like she's breathing. Her mouth parts, and her eyes widen in disbelief. And suddenly, he understands it. Why she was so upset about the tapestry. When she said the tapestry wasn't worth it, what she really meant was *she* isn't worth it.

Rage roars up within him, hot and bright. He could strangle Yris or Wylder or whoever left her with this scar that makes her react in disbelief that someone could love her the way that he loves her.

It's an injustice too great to be left untouched. She has to understand the depths to which he adores her. He closes the distance between them and brings his hands up to cradle her face.

"I love you," he insists. "I have loved you since I saw you fall into that fucking river and realized that I can't breathe if you're not breathing. I have loved every part of you. Your ferocity and your mercilessness. Your kindness and unending goodness and relentless sense of justice. I love your smiles and your laugh and your fucking awful dance moves."

A breath of a laugh flows over her lips. Something bright is entering her eyes, like a rosebud unfolding. She curls her hand into the front of his shirt like she fears he might disappear. So he keeps going.

"Every day I've spent with you since you asked me to be your Fifth has only made me love you more. And I know I'm a ridiculous ass. A fool who has never dared dream you'd ever love me in return, but—"

"Shut up," she hisses. Her hands latch onto his neck, her fingers sliding into his loose hair, pulling him close so he can feel her words against his chin, his cheek, his ear. "Shut the *fuck* up. I haven't fought this—fought *you*—for so long because I felt too little for you, but because I feel too much. I stormed a temple for you. I willingly surrendered the Trials. And I would do it again. I would do anything for you. Give up my crown. Burn this world. All for *you*. Do you understand?"

Ayc releases a shuddering breath. The words are enough to nearly bring him to his knees. An entire rainbow of emotions floods into his chest, each brighter and more iridescent than the last. Relief and hope and love and the realization that sometimes, not often, but sometimes—the world can be that kind.

There is nothing more beautiful than this: the realization that you love and are loved in return.

She leans back. The intoxicating darkness of her eyes blends with streaks of bright blue, like a cloudless day. A blue, he realizes, that matches his own eyes perfectly, *because* she loves him.

He drags her face back to his, finds her mouth with his own. There's no distance between them now. Not miles or millimeters and no longer the game. They are finally done pretending.

Fucking finally.

"Why the fuck are you still wearing clothes?" she demands against his lips.

"That," he says, pushing her sweater from her shoulders; it falls to her feet, "is a *very* good question."

He worships kisses along the newly exposed flesh of her shoulder. He fists the fabric of the gown, the fucking silver gown that highlights her body. Her fingers yank at his shirt, slipping beneath and gliding up the bare skin of his chest. His cock instantly hardens, straining against the ties of his breeches, begging to be free. Begging to slide into her warmth.

He's thankful Muffin isn't here because Ayc intends to take his time to explore every inch of her body, taste her until everything sweet is ruined by the memory of her flavor. He intends to make her scream in pleasure until she's hoarse from it.

Muffin. Shit.

He remembers himself enough to quickly lower the shield between him and Muffin. He gets a surge of cursing that flutters down the path, and Ayc is certain that practicing flying maneuvers with Tempest isn't going well.

"Muffin!"

"Not now," Muffin snaps back.

"I'm going to have the link between us closed tonight. Close the link between us at your end, too."

A sense of horror ripples between them. *"Oh, dragon tails, are you and Lora—"*

"I'll talk to you in the morning, Muffin."

Ayc snaps the link closed once more, even as he tugs Lora's gown upward, pausing at her hips. One more matter of business, and then he'll get her naked. He won't be able to think straight after. "Monthly potion?"

"Yes. You?"

"Yes."

He yanks her night gown upward. She lifts her arms, and he tosses the fabric to the side. He takes three steps back and drinks her in. The red of his vision highlights her every curve. The heaviness of her breasts, the softness of her stomach, the width of her hips, the dagger still strapped to her thigh, the tuft of hair at the apex of her legs. She's more beautiful than any of her tapestries, more exquisite than the night sky, a better fantasy than any dream he could possibly conjure.

"Lora," he groans. "Fucking look at you." He can't make any more coherent sense, but she gives him a flash of that wicked grin. He's already weak, and that smile nearly makes him buckle, makes his knees hit the ground to worship her like the divine being she is.

"Well," she says, "if all you're going to do is stare, you might as well return the favor."

He's too busy staring at her for the meaning of the words to strike. She snaps her fingers to get his attention. "Clothes off. Now."

Fuck. He loves it when she commands him.

"Yes, my lady." He's grateful that he chose a loose tunic instead of his leather armor after he showered when he returned to Wyntra. He can undo buckles, or he can look at Lora's naked body—he can't possibly do both. He reaches behind him to grab his loose tunic and haul it over his head. She tracks his every movement, and when his hands fall to his belt, she drags her bottom lip between her teeth.

This differs from the woman who hid from him when she asked him to help her swim in the Ever River. But perhaps she hid her eyes not because she feared looking but because she very much wanted to look. He grins at the thrill of her eyes upon him and works his pants and underwear down his hips, never losing sight of her eyes. He revels in the silver that works from her wide pupils across her irises as she drags her gaze across his hard cock. It leaps at her focus, like her eyes are a physical touch. He soothes his fists over his shaft, trying to ease the ache, but it's nothing compared to the memory of her hand or the promise of her warm cunt.

Her eyes flash. "Don't make me jealous."

"Then come here."

She steps toward him until only a breath separates them. She drags her nails ever so gently down his chest, careful not to cut him, but sharp enough that it sends shivers chasing down his spine.

"Mine," she growls.

"Yours," he agrees.

He hauls her toward him. His hands dig into the abundant flesh of her ass. He moans as his cock presses against her abdomen, as her nipples brush against his chest. Finally, nothing separates their bodies.

"I am so fucking yours," he growls against her lips.

She pulls at his hair, sealing their mouths once more. As her tongue spars with his, her hands roam his body, scraping across his shoulders and down his spine, grasping urgently at his ass. He slides his hand between them, filling his aching palm with her breast. The flesh spills over, there's so much of her. He needs to feel the roll of her nipple on his tongue again, the sweet little bud. He needs to get her to a place where every part of her is within reach. He can scarcely think with how she kneads at him, so he goes to the closest horizontal surface: his counter.

He presses her backward until her hips meet his counter, then breaks away from her mouth to slide his hands down to the back of her thighs and lifts her onto the edge of the counter. He returns to her breast, lifting the hefty weight toward his mouth. She thrusts back her head, the most exquisite gasp fluttering past her lips. He swirls his tongue around the peak, even as he devotes attention to her other breast with his fingers. Her back arches, and she flings her hands backward to steady herself. One hand lands squarely in the bowl of pudding he made for her and then left foolishly on the counter after he chilled it.

She lifts her hand. Thick chocolate coats her fingertips.

He breaks away from her breast. "Fuck, I'm—"

The apology freezes on his lips as she drags the chocolate-coated hand down his neck and chest. A long handprint forms across his skin. Her mouth follows soon after, first her lips, and then her tongue, then her teeth. Her fangs are exposed, nicking against the delicate skin of his nipple.

"Fuck, Lora," he moans. He gathers her thick hair in his hand and pulls just enough to arch her head back. She hisses, but her eyes flash with silver. "Do you like that? Do you like it when I'm rough with you?"

"Yes," she seethes through her teeth, offering the consent that he needs to pull a little more. Her back arches further, thrusting up her chest. "I'll like anything you do to me. I want you so fucking much."

He chuckles, reveling in the control she's offering him, even though he knows that if she snapped her fingers, he would fall to his knees and obey her every command. Is this how it will be between them? The constant giving and taking of power and dominance. Fuck, he hopes so because he loves it. He wants to submit to her, and he wants to conquer and make her melt beneath his touch.

This is power and surrender, and he fucking wants it all.

"*Do* you want me?" He encircles her wrist, slides her chocolate-coated fingers into his mouth, and licks them clean. Her eyes gleam as she watches him, and he smirks as he removes her fingers from his mouth and guides her hand between her legs. "Show me how much you want me. Spread your legs. Let me see how wet you are for me."

A slow smile works up her round face as she slides her legs apart. She uses two fingers to slide apart the walls of her pussy. She's glistening and quivering and fucking perfect, and he watches her greedily as she slowly drags a third finger through her center. She swirls it around the peak of herself and lets out a whimper.

"Now who's making who jealous?" Ayc teases, giving her hair a gentle tug.

She lifts her fingers back into his mouth. Fuck. It's better than anything he's ever tasted. Sweet as cinnamon, sharp as the anise that her hair is scented with. She presses her fingers deeper into his mouth, gliding along his tongue, working toward his throat, nearly gagging him. Her eyes gleam wickedly, telling him she knows exactly what she's doing. He pulls away and uses the hand still wrapped in her hair to steer her to lie back, bracing her back with the arm wrapped around her shoulder.

She spreads out on his counter and drops her knees to the side. All of her is on display. It's all he can do to resist the urge to dive between her legs. After waiting so long, he wants to savor this moment like he's at a banquet.

"Gods, you're beautiful. Where should I begin? Should I kiss your breasts some more...or perhaps the back of your knees? What makes you squirm more, I wonder?"

"I've had enough of your teasing," she says, baring her teeth. "Shut the fuck up and eat this pussy like a good boy."

Good boy.

Those two words might as well be a stroke against his cock. On the porch swing, it was enough to make him come. Now, it unravels all his plans to take it slowly. Fuck it.

He'll have dessert for dinner then.

With a growl, he seizes her thighs and hauls her to the very edge of the counter even as his knees hit the floor. A deep moan rips through his chest as he drags his tongue through her center. The taste of her makes him feel like a starving man who just got his first taste of something real. He wants to devour her, wants to live off her and nothing else. Nothing will ever be this sweet. Except perhaps the cry that soars from her lips.

"Fuck me, Lora." He scatters kisses across her thigh. "One taste, and I'm already a ruined man. I'm never going to stop craving you."

She pushes up on her elbow and glares at him. "Shut up. Just shut up and fuck me with your tongue. I need—"

Whatever else she's going to say falls apart in a cry as he presses his tongue against her.

He explores her with his tongue, thrusting inside her, circling around her opening, swirling lazily around the apex, dragging long strokes up and down. He studies her reactions, noting when she gasps and when her back arches and when she falls silent.

"Tell me what you like," he implores between tastes. "I want this to be perfect for you.

"It's good," she gasps. "Divine, it's so fucking good."

But when he works his tongue over her swollen bundle of nerves once more, her hands seize his head, fingers tugging at the roots of his hair. "There. Right there."

He obliges eagerly, delivering fast and quick strokes to her clit. She writhes, her hips bucking against his face without rhythm. One day, he wants her to sit upon him and fuck his face just like that, but for now, he flattens his palm on her lower abdomen and holds her still. She tightens her hold on his hair and presses him closer, digging her heels into his shoulder so he works her faster.

He slides two fingers of his free hand inside her entrance, and she clenches around him, her muscles already quivering. Gods. She's so fucking beautiful like this, surrendering to her pleasure, coming undone under his mouth and his hand. She latches her free hand onto her breast, rolling a nipple between her fingertips. His cock jumps at the sight. He doesn't have nearly enough hands to touch her in all the way he likes. And perhaps his power knows it because his shadows are crawling onto the table, like fingers grasping toward her. He's uncertain what they might do, so he grasps hold of his control, shoving it down deep, a fight for control that becomes even more difficult when her whimpers become words.

"Oh, fuck, Ayc… I'm almost… Please… Ayc…"

He thrusts his fingers faster, harder, the way she liked it before, making sure to stroke that spot with every movement. "That's it, villainess," he coaxes, growling the words against her. "Let go for me."

The warm walls of her pussy flutter around his fingers, and he seals his mouth against her, sucking and licking and driving her closer to the edge. The walls clamp down upon him. Her hands twist in his hair as her back bends. Despite his restraining hand on her stomach, she bucks through her pleasure, writhing so hard she crawls away from him. He releases her stomach and grasps her thigh to haul her back to his mouth, riding her through the waves of pleasure. The sight of her face done up in pleasure makes heat surges to his cock. If he let himself, he could come just at the sight of her falling apart on his tongue. He drops a hand and clamps down upon himself to silence the urge.

Her body slumps back on the counter, and he uses it as his cue to slow down his pace, to change to long, languid sweeps of his tongue. Little shockwaves work through her, her legs trembling around his head. She's still making little noises, muttering words that sound like 'so good' and 'so fast.'

He stands, grabs the stool that he sits on to decorate cakes, and drags it closer. He's too lost in Lora to notice any discomfort now, but his knees and back won't be kind to him tomorrow if he's not careful. And he intends to do this tomorrow. And the next day. And the next.

He'll live between her thighs if she lets him.

He flops down onto the stool, grasps her leg, and drapes her ankle over his shoulder. He lays a kiss upon the inside of her calf, dragging his lips toward her knee.

"What are you doing?" she asks, and he adores the way her voice is a little hoarse, the way her curls fall over her face as she pushes up onto her elbows to look at him.

"Isn't it obvious?" He kisses the back of her knee, and her legs shudder involuntarily. He grins.

"But I've already come."

"Good. I want another."

She surges upward and seizes his hair, trying to drag him upward, even with her leg still wrapped around his head. "And I want your cock inside of me."

His cock twitches, but he catches Lora's hands and disentangles them. He holds her wrists loosely. She could break away, but she doesn't.

"Listen to me, my lady. Outside of our bed, you're *always* in charge, without question. But when it comes to this, we take turns, yes? And right now..." He pauses to grasp her chin in her hand and growl the next words against her lips. "It's my fucking turn. Now, lay your ass back down. I'm not done tasting you yet."

Her eyes flare with silver, and he isn't sure whether it's anger, desire, or both. Either way, he likes it, and she ultimately lays back down. He dips his hand into the chocolate pudding bowl.

"What are you doing?" she asks.

"I remember a certain scene in a book of yours. I think it went a little something like this." He sweeps the pudding down the inside of her thigh. She jumps involuntarily.

He laughs. "You *are* ticklish."

"I hate you," she snarls.

"Keep telling yourself that."

With his tongue, he traces the path of chocolate he's made from her knee all the way back to her pussy. The salt of her skin and the arousal that has dripped down her leg make the chocolate pudding sweeter. By the time his mouth has worked down the slope, her breath has quickened, and a quiver has returned to her legs. She presses her heels into his shoulders, urging him closer.

He goes slower this time, aware of how sensitive she must be. He glides gently through the length, from her entrance to her apex and back down again. He lets his hands slide up her body, grasp ahold of her breast, slide across the hills of her stomach, enchanted by the way his black-painted nails look on her body. When she's back to making the sweet little noises, he presses into her entrance. He fucks her with his tongue as her hips grind against his face, and his thumb slowly works her clit. It isn't long before she's slapping the table once more, her heels digging into his back, uttering half-screams, half-sobs of pleasure.

He takes her in. She's glorious in the ruin he's created. Sweat gleams over her throat and her brow, her curls cling to her cheeks. His chest clenches at the sight of her, and if he wasn't already utterly gone for her, he swears he would fall right then.

She moves like lightning, surging upward, sliding off the counter and onto his lap. The stool rocks, and he seizes the counter to keep it from tipping over. His hand spasms tighter as she seals her drenched core over his hard cock. A shudder works its way down his spine. She locks her fingers behind his head and yanks him to her lips. She sucks his tongue inside her mouth and groans.

"Fuck," she says. "I love tasting myself on your tongue. Proof that you're mine. Perhaps later, I'll taste myself on your cock and know that's mine, too."

He whimpers. There's no other word for the sound those words make him utter. It only grows louder when she rocks her hips, gliding over his hard shaft. She is slick and warm and so fucking perfect. He buries his face in her shoulder as he bites down on his own tongue, a sharp burst of pain to keep himself from erupting just on the contact.

"Fucking gods, Lora," he utters.

The power has flipped. She's now completely in control. Which is fine. More than fine. He can scarcely see through the red in his eyes, only the shape of her body and the dark coils of shadow curling up around them.

"First, your hand. Then your tongue," she reminds him, panting against his mouth. "Now your cock."

The shadow wraps around the stool, steadying it as she tightens her legs around him. She braces a hand on the counter behind her, enough to create space as she lifts off him. Her other hand sneaks between them, wrapping around his cock and directing it toward her entrance. She hovers there, swirling just the tip around her entrance but not pressing down upon him. She holds him there as his hands clutch her ass, the heat ripping through his body, his shadows rising and swirling, threatening to block out all their light.

And still, she doesn't move.

"Lora, for fuck's sake," he curses.

She chuckles and dips downward, just a few inches of glorious warmth, before retreating again.

He sputters nonsensical curses until he finds words. "You're a vicious, cruel thing. Do you want me to beg?"

She grins. "Perhaps."

"Lora, plea—*ffuuuckkkk.*"

She slides onto him, letting the tip of his cock fully into her entrance. The stool shudders and tips, and he can barely focus enough to lock the shadows around it to keep them from falling. He stares at the place where they've been connected, enchanted by the sight of how she takes him so fucking well. She grips his shoulders and lets her forehead fall onto his. She, too, fixates on their joining. She rocks up and down, slowly working more of him inside of her, and with every new inch, their sounds echo each other—sounds of both longing and relief. He tries to memorize everything: the silver in Lora's eyes, her pussy as it adjusts to every new inch of his cock, her breasts brushing against his chest with every movement. Until her ass meets his thighs again and she is buried to the hilt.

She fits around him so well, it's like she was made for him. A ridiculous thought, but it's how it feels as the unyielding pleasure works through his spine and coils at the base of his abdomen. He wants to forever stay in this moment, this first feel of their bodies connecting, but Lora whimpers, brushing her lips against his temple. "Ayc, I need more."

It sure as fuck is not going to happen on this stool.

"Counter or bed?" he demands.

"Bed."

He can't bear to part with her even for a second. He gathers his shadows around him and lets it take her weight as he stands. It works—she's weightless and locked in place around his cock as he moves toward the bedroom. She digs her heels into his lower back and leans back, trusting the shadows as she rocks, rising and falling on him, the glide of her almost making him stumble. He sputters more unintelligible curses as he pushes through the bedroom door.

When he reaches the bed, he lets himself fall backward, and the impact drives her deeper onto his cock. She hisses and slaps her hands down on his chest. She flings her head back, her eyes bright moons in the shadows that are rising around them. Her breasts bounce with each collision as she rises and falls. Every single inch of her is perfection. He digs into her hips, holding on.

Her mouth parts, but then she bites down on her lip, and that won't fucking do. He surges upward, wraps his arms around her, and flips them. He knows if she didn't want him to do so, she could have stopped it, but she grins as her back hits his bed and his weight falls upon her.

"Open your pretty mouth, Lora," he growls into her ear as he pulls back and slams into her. Again and again, punctuating each of his words. "Moan for me. Plead for me. Instruct me. Tell me every little fucking thing you like. If I'm not utterly convinced that what I'm doing pleases you, I stop. *Your* pleasure is *my* pleasure."

"Don't you dare," she hisses, wrapping her legs around him and rocking her hips to meet each thrust, cuing him to find a rhythm with her body. She's so responsive, so fucking clear about what she wants. All he has to do is listen. "Don't you dare fucking stop. It's too good. This is too fucking good."

And it is.

It has never, not once, felt like this. Sex has always been good, but it's never felt like perhaps he might be losing his soul entirely. His soul is hers now. She is the only thing in existence; he's so utterly wrapped up in her that he does not remember where she ends and he begins.

The world fades around them. Or perhaps that's just the wall of shadow that weaves around them, spinning like a cyclone. He barely feels it. Barely sees it. There's only Lora, the soft, pleading sounds she makes, the kisses she frantically leaves against his jaw and neck, the way she digs her nails into his back, barely avoiding breaking skin. And the pleasure—the earth-shattering pleasure that's building within him, the way it makes the world turn red, hued only by the silver in her eyes.

They drive into each other, meeting thrust for thrust, flipping across the bed. At times, she rises upon him, driving down upon him without mercy as he swirls his thumb around her clit. The next, he takes back the control, driving into her hard enough that he has to brace her head so it doesn't slam against the wall.

"Yes," she moans, "Harder."

He wants it to never end, but it's too fucking good to last. Only by some force beyond him has he lasted even this long. Only by the gryphon feather he swallowed an hour before has his body been able to keep up this pace. He slips his hand between their bodies and finds where they're joined, her soft bud that he works between his fingers. He can feel her tightening around him, strangling his cock.

"Come for me again, Lora," he growls. Or maybe he's begging—he's so close, he's not quite sure. "Come on my cock, and let me feel you as you lose yourself again."

"Ayc!" Her walls spasm around him, and he increases pressure until his name turns into a cry.

She bites him to silence the sound, her teeth sinking into his collarbone. He roars as the sharp burst of pain explodes pleasure through every muscle of his body. His movements become desperate, frantic, chaotic. He starts to pull out, to spill upon the bed, but she locks her heels around him and presses him closer.

"I want to feel you, too," she hisses against his ear.

And he's gone.

With one last thrust, he buries himself deep and finds release. Her name is a growl, perhaps a sob, and he loses himself completely to the pleasure.

He returns to himself in parts. First, he becomes aware of Lora's body still beneath him, then the ache of his fingers with how tightly he's grasped the blankets. He releases his grip. The lights have gone out, but with his Drakr vision, he can see Lora beneath him just fine.

"Are you dead?" Lora asks softly, nuzzling his neck with her nose.

"I think so," he says with a bit of a laugh.

She lays a kiss on the place where she bit, soothing what he's certain will become a bruise. He truly doesn't care. "Do you want to call off your shadows? They're quite cold."

He pushes himself up farther and glances around. It takes him a moment to realize that the lights have not gone out. They are completely covered in shadow. He waves his hand in a shooing motion, and the shadows dart back to where they belong. He blinks in the light of the lamp above them.

"Sorry. I'm not certain how that happened. I was a bit… distracted."

"Can't imagine why," she murmurs, lazily brushing her fingers down his chest.

Fuck, he needs to be careful, or perhaps he should consider wearing his bracelets when they fuck. He doesn't feel weakened by his shadows yet, but the last thing he needs is to burn himself out with his power. Though he can think of far worse ways to die. He lets out a little laugh at the thought.

"What?" she asks, with a breathy laugh of her own.

"Nothing," Ayc replies.

He gazes down upon Lora. She looks…happy. Beautifully happy, her eyes shining violet. And he's still buried within her. He claims her mouth in a quick kiss before he shifts backward. He groans at the loss of warmth.

"Stay right there." He returns to the kitchen, grabs a rag from a drawer, and wets it at the kitchen sink. When he gets back, she's still there, her knees spread apart. Something deep and carnal within him gives a satisfied growl at the sight of her dripping with him.

"Fuck," he says, but he bites his lip to silence himself. "May I?" he asks, lifting the cloth.

She nods, and he gently wipes up the mess he's made of her. She stares at him as he works.

"Ayc?" she says.

"Yes, my love."

Whatever she was going to say freezes on her parted mouth. It's only then that he realizes what he said. Not 'my lady,' as he meant. My love.

He crawls over her, still in his bed, the place he's dreamed of her countless times. He lays a kiss on her collarbone, then her neck, then her lips, whispering a new term of affection in each new place of skin. "My villainess. My lady. My love."

"Get dressed," she commands. "Come to my bed with me. That's where Bronwen put the protection spell." She pauses, then adds with her wicked smile. "Bring the pudding."

FIFTY

LORA

In the morning, Ayc serves her chocolate pudding and orgasms for breakfast.

Lora licks the chocolate from the spoon as Ayc hides beneath the blankets with his head buried between her thighs. She thinks that this is perhaps what everlasting paradise is like. If she's mistaken, then she simply doesn't want to go because anything less will be eternal torment.

He's certainly taken her seriously when she told him to ruin her. She's lost track of the number of orgasms he's coaxed from her body until her every muscle is limp with ecstasy. Now, he's even ruining chocolate pudding. She'll never be able to eat it again without thinking about it on his body, on her body, or the taste of it on her tongue as he makes her come.

Ayc does something new and *very* interesting with his tongue, and Lora nearly chucks the spoon across the room involuntarily. Her back arches off her bed, and he chooses that moment to do that thing he does with his fingers inside of her. She isn't even sure what it is, but it sends her spiraling every time. The orgasm rolls through her like a tidal wave that leaves her gasping for air.

"Fuck, Ayc," she murmurs, slumping onto the mattress once

more. She lets the spoon fall beside the bowl on the bed. Her eyelids drag closed, pulled down by the lack of sleep.

She drifted off twice last night, but she didn't think it was for long. The first time she woke up clutched in his arm, their legs tangled around each other, already aching for him to be back inside of her. As soon as she moved, he was awaking, offering words of praise and pleading as she moved down his body to wrap her mouth around his cock. To give his back rest, she eagerly climbed onto him and rode them both relentlessly toward a pleasure that was merciless in its power, perfectly content to do all the work if it meant seeing that look on his face as he broke apart. The second time they awoke, his mouth was between her legs in moments. He paused only to pass her the bowl of pudding.

She now feels like she could sleep for days in a blissful, satisfied sleep.

"What time is it?" she murmurs. There's light creeping between the cracks in the thick curtains, but she can't begin to guess how long it's been there.

He peeks his head out of the blanket. He's a mess, his hair twisted and tangled, his wide smile glistening with *her*. But divine, he's beautiful.

"I couldn't fucking care less," he says.

He crawls up her body, scattering kisses across her hips, her stomach, each of her breasts. He marries their hips together once more, his hard cock pressing against her sensitive flesh.

She shoves his shoulder. "Get off me, you insatiable ass. I need sleep."

He laughs and flops onto his side beside her. He curves a hand around her hip to pull her closer until her skin presses against his. She glances down to marvel at how well the palm of his hand fits around her, the way his painted thumb looks as he caresses across her hipbone. She lifts her fingers to trace across the weaving, pearly lines of the mark Muffin left on his arm, wandering all the way up to the little bruises on his collarbone, each in the shape of her teeth. They are already fading, and it's a pity because she quite likes the sight of her on his skin.

"Does it hurt?" she asks.

"No." His lips twist upward. "I enjoy being marked by you."

She shivers. She can't explain the feeling of possessiveness that rises up inside of her, one that's always been there but has only grown stronger through the night. She wants him marked with her teeth, her nails, the scent of her body. She wants the world to know that he is hers.

She captures his mouth with hers, her tongue gliding past his lips. The taste of him, mixed with the flavor of her, makes her groan. Her fingers claw down his chest, careful not to break skin. She needs to remove the poison fingernail polish as soon as possible so she can scratch him without fear of leaving a permanent scar like the little white pricks that dot his throat. She licks at those now like she might be able to ease them away.

"Now, who's insatiable?" he teases against her ear.

She drags herself away and flips to her opposite side. "Shut up."

His fingers skate across her hipbone, and his mouth worships at the back of her neck, a silent question, a testing of the waters. And damn it all, her heart's rhythm picks up. Heat rises through her pussy. Fuck. She is, in fact, insatiable. She slides her ass back, pressing it against him in a silent invitation.

"What are you doing?" He feigns a naïve tone. "I thought you wanted to sleep." But he lifts her leg to drape it over his own hip and shifts even closer.

"You're such an ass."

"I know." He reaches between them to align the head of his cock with her entrance. "But *you* love me, anyway."

She does. Fuck, of course she does, but she has no words as he joins their bodies once more, taking her slowly, inch by delicate inch. She's sore, in the best way. The sharpness lends depth to her pleasure. He slips his left arm beneath her to cradle her head and the other drapes around her ribs to hold her close, his palm pressing at the base of her stomach, his dragon's mark visible. He selects a pace that's lazy and diligent and fucking perfect: the way that every inch of his hard shaft slowly drags across her inner walls.

She arches against him, thrusting up her breasts. And he's so attentive that he notices the cue. The hand that cradles her head slips across her sternum to play with her needy nipples, interchanging soft strokes with skillful plucks of his fingers and firm embraces.

How is it this good? How is it possible that it's already this fucking good between them? She thought having a partner so in tune, so eager to listen to her body and her words, was a fairytale meant only for her dirty books. The only time she's come close are the nights she's spent with other women, but even that did not have the fire of her connection with Ayc. And here he is, carefully guiding her toward yet another powerful orgasm.

And then someone knocks on the door.

"Ignore it," Lora whispers, reaching a hand behind her to grasp his hair between her fingers and pull him closer. "They'll go away."

"My lady," Irving's voice booms through the door, "I'm sorry, but you're needed."

Lora bites back a groan—and not the good kind. Ayc doesn't still, nor does he hurry, rocking in and out of her at that exquisitely measured pace.

"What is it, Irving?" she calls. More quietly, she mutters, "Someone had better be dying."

Ayc chuckles and slips his right hand lower so that his middle finger glides through her slit and circles around her clit. She nearly swallows her tongue in an effort not to cry out.

"Damara will be here soon," Irving reminds her.

"I'm going to kill that bitch," Lora hisses.

"Did she come a day early again?" Ayc whispers, swirling his fingers a little faster while never changing the rhythm of his hips.

"No, this is the agreed upon day. I simply forgot. And you need to stop doing that, or I'm going to forget again."

He stills with his fingers pressed squarely at a place that

makes her squirm, his cock so far inside her she can feel him everywhere. Her hips rock involuntarily, craving the friction.

"Do you truly want me to stop?" he laughs against her neck.

"Bastard."

Another knock.

"And a messenger just arrived to report that the regents are at the front gate as well."

Every muscle in Lora's body stiffens. She feels Ayc do the same.

"Which ones?" she demands.

"*All* of them."

"Well, fuck," Ayc mutters, finally removing his hands from her. "That can't be good."

Lora scrambles from the bed, ignoring how something deep within her rebels at the loss of Ayc's body against hers. She doesn't know why all the regents have shown up to see her, but she knows it doesn't bode well in her favor. If they didn't want to ambush her, they would have sent a letter first. She rushes across the room and throws her wardrobe open, but Ayc appears at her side.

"You need to bathe first."

"I'm not sure there's time."

"Make time." He grasps her shoulders gently and steers her toward her private washroom. "Damara has the Drakr sense of smell. She will scent me on you." He makes a sound, a vibrating noise deep in his chest nothing short of animalistic, before he clears his throat. "And as much as some deep instinct loves the idea of that, we have to be careful until we're ready for people to know about us."

"Fuck, you're right."

He grunts and reaches around her to pull the door open. She glimpses a tightness in his jaw, and words slip to her lips before she can stop them.

"I'm not ashamed of you."

He jerks toward her in surprise, lines forming between his brows.

"I don't want to keep it hidden because I'm ashamed of people knowing. I just want to…" She isn't sure what the right words are. She just wants him to desperately understand.

"Protect me," he finishes for her with a roll of his eyes. "I know."

"To protect *us*," she corrects. "I have so little privacy, so little that the world doesn't get to know of and interest themselves in. I know we can't keep it hidden forever, but I just want it to be…just *ours*, for a while longer."

The line of his jaw softens. "It's always going to be just you and me. Fuck everyone else."

She swallows. He makes it sound so simple, and she wishes she could trust that it would be. Her worry must show in the lines of her face because he smooths his thumb across her brow.

"Hurry. I'll sneak back down to my room and change."

She nods. "Meet me in the Great Hall. I'll have the attendants put the regents there. Damara will have to be patient."

"Perhaps you shouldn't meet with them," Ayc says.

She arches an eyebrow. "What?"

"There's no emergency large enough that all seven of them should be here. We would know about it. Irving would have disturbed us sooner. They've come here to ambush you, Lora."

Her teeth vibrate, and she digs them together to keep them from growing points. "I know."

"Don't meet with them," Ayc says. His voice rumbles with a bit of rage, making it a growl that makes her thighs clench, a reminder of the way he talked to her last night. It doesn't help that she's still naked. "Tell them you're busy, and go meet with Damara as you planned. Tell them you'll meet with them at a later time, but they can't show up here and demand to see you. You are not at their beck and call. You do not bow to them. They bow to *you*."

He's right. Damn, of course he is. "And what do I do if they refuse to leave."

Ayc shrugs. "Then I'll feed them to my dragon. Muffin is curious at what human tastes like."

"That is a deeply unsettling statement," Lora says.

"Don't worry. As I've said, they're deeply protective of you."

"All right. I'll tell Irving to send a guard to Peregrin and let them know about the situation. They can meet the regents and ask them to come back later. Peregrin will have no problem with handling them." She pulls a robe she hardly ever wears from her wardrobe and wraps it around herself, so she'll at least be decent when she sticks her head into the hallway to speak with Irving.

Ayc grabs his clothes, scattered on her bedroom floor. She can't drag her gaze away from him as he swiftly dresses. He returns to brush a brief kiss to Lora's lips before backing away from her. Slowly, like he doesn't want to go. She understands the feeling.

"You should shower as well," she says. "Because *you* smell like *me*."

"Good."

The last sight she sees before he disappears into shadow is his mischievous grin. That one she hates because she loves it so fucking much.

When Lora opens the door to her bedroom, Bronwen is staring back at her.

"I know," Bronwen says.

Lora's heart leaps into her throat. She swallows it back down and keeps her voice calm. "Know about what?"

"About the regents. How they're at the gate."

"Oh." Lora fights not to let her relief show. "Are they still there?"

"As of five minutes ago when I looked outside, yes."

"That's unfortunate." Lora pushes a strand of hair, still wet from her shower, off her cheek. She doesn't have time to do the long routine she normally pampers her curls with after washing them, but she was afraid that Ayc's smell might linger in her hair. After all, his hands were all over her hair. "I sent a message with

Peregrin that they needed to make an appointment unless some tragedy befell their clans overnight that I haven't heard of. If Peregrin did not get them to leave, I fear they won't."

She looks over at Irving, who shakes his head. "I haven't heard back from Peregrin yet."

"Should we have them wait in the great hall?" Bronwen asks. "If they keep standing at the front gate, people are going to talk."

"No." Lora sidesteps around Bronwen and slips into the hallway. Bronwen falls into step beside her. Irving and her other guard wait a moment before following at a distance. "We're meeting with Damara, and then I'm going back to bed."

Lora desperately wants to finish what she started with Ayc and start other things. Lots of other things. There isn't a single thing that she needs to do today that can't wait until tomorrow.

Bronwen glances at her sharply. "Lora, the attendants said you've been in bed all day. It's past noon. Are you feeling well?"

"Just another migraine," Lora reassures.

Bronwen grasps her arm, stopping them both, and pulls Lora around to face her. "Are you certain? Why is your hair wet?"

"I forgot about Damara's visit. I was in the middle of washing it when I was told she was here."

It's the first lie that Lora can think of, and she thinks it's rather convincing and flows off her tongue smoothly. But the lines in Bronwen's furrowed brow deepen even further.

"Your normal wash day isn't until tomorrow," she points out.

Divine damn Lora's regimented and rigorous schedule for hair care. And damn Bronwen for being her roommate for four years. Of course, she would notice a change in Lora's very particular habit.

"So?" Lora shakes her off. "I felt grimy from the road and wanted to do it sooner." She narrows her eyes in a silent dare for Bronwen to press further, which she knows is a mistake. It's only going to make Bronwen more suspicious.

But she doesn't press further. "Would you like me to dry your hair for you?"

Normally, Lora avoids letting Bronwen style her hair through magic; its power ultimately damages her hair. But seeing as she's about to meet with a powerful enemy who already suspects she's fucking her Fifth, it might be best to allow it this time.

"That would be good, thank you."

Bronwen wiggles her fingers over Lora's head. Her scalp tingles with the heat of magic, but in moments, her hair is dry, coiled in its ringlets, though they are slightly frizzier than her normal care would allow. They walk the rest of the way to the courtyard in silence, Bronwen shooting Lora strange glances. Lora worries that perhaps something about her appearance will give her away. Is she wearing a glow to her cheeks that says, *'I just had the best sex of my life'*? She certainly hopes not.

The rest of the Five are already waiting in the courtyard near the center fountain. Ayc is already there, and he immediately turns. A grin spreads across his face at the sight of her, followed by a shadow that crosses his face as he sees what dress she's chosen. The heat in his eyes brings her immediate satisfaction. He's always liked the Noxumbra dress on her, and Lora's come to like it, the velvet against her skin, the way it allows her to freely move, the way her armor fits over it. While she toured Noxumbra, she had so many fantasies of Ayc removing it from her body, and she realized that today would be the perfect opportunity.

Ayc carefully tucks his head to hide his expression behind his damp hair. Lora's cheeks ache with the strength of the smile that involuntarily pulls upon her lips. She schools it quickly and sneaks a glimpse at Bronwen, concerned that she noticed. But Bronwen isn't looking at Lora. She's narrowed her eyes at Ayc, and Lora bites back a groan when she realizes what Bronwen is focused on.

His hair. His *wet* hair.

Fuck. She's been around Bronwen for five minutes, and already, Bronwen is suspicious.

A beat of wings draws Lora's eyes upward. Muffin flaps their wings hard, coming around the torrent of the castle. They're still far from graceful. They drop altitude before regaining it in jerking motions, but it's more progress than when they were last at

Wyntra. Tempest follows close behind, snapping at the dragon as though delivering instruction. Muffin drops lower as they near the courtyard, and Lora braces herself as they come in for a landing. They make contact with gravel and press their front legs in front of them and their rump downward. They slide a few feet before coming to a rest.

Ayc and Xylie clap.

"Much better progress, Muffin!" Ayc calls.

The dragon trots toward them. Their lips are curled backward, flashing teeth in a smile that makes the creature look absolutely ridiculous.

"You know they look like you when they smile like that," Lora says to Ayc as she comes to stand beside them all. "The resemblance is frankly uncanny."

"On the contrary," he says, not looking at her as though he doesn't trust himself. "I don't have scales."

Lora shrugs. "How would I know?"

Ayc snorts but hides it behind a cough. Xylie frowns at them. Tavish puffs out his cheeks the way he does when he's trying to hold back some emotion. Tempest circles above them, casting a shadow over the courtyard. She chatters her beak.

Peregrin swears beneath their breath. "Tempest says Damara isn't alone. The gryphons on watch are spreading the word to the others. There are three dragons."

The little bubble of joy Lora has been cradling since last night threatens to burst. Three dragons. Ayc's smile tumbles from his cheeks, and he finally looks at her. She sees how she feels reflected in the way his eyes widen.

Who has she brought with her this time? Brekken and Caius? Lahlis?

"What color of dragons?" Bronwen demands.

Peregrin pauses for a moment, listening through their link. "Orange and purple."

Caius and Brekken then. Fuck.

Lora's hair stands up as static rises in the air. She looks

sharply at Bronwen. Magic dances around her fingertips, but she swiftly draws in a breath, and the magic disappears.

"Are you all right?" Lora asks. "You need not go if you don't want to."

"I'm fine," she insists.

"Are you certain? I would like to avoid an international incident."

"I'm certain."

"Urbain is wanting to know orders," Irving says, gesturing to the agate in his ear. "Do you want them to sound the alarm?"

"No," Lora says. "We'll see if we can handle it peacefully. Tell him to have them escorted in and then remain available. No one walks off that beach before I speak with them."

Irving steps away to relay her message.

"Should I put my bracelets back on?" Ayc asks, his nose wrinkling at the idea.

"Surely they know you're Drakr by now," Lora replies. "So there's no point in hiding your scent. But..." She pauses. "Keep your shadow affinity under control. It's best they don't know about that yet." She does not want them to understand how powerful Ayc is. Not yet. Not if she can avoid it. She doesn't want them to see him as anymore of a threat.

Ayc nods. "I'll keep it under control."

Lora surveys the others. "Tavish, Xylie, are you coming or staying?"

"Going," Tavish says without hesitation.

Xylie nods and signs, *"I want to see the dragons."*

Lora doesn't ask Peregrin or Ayc. She knows their answer. Instead, she turns and marches toward the entrance to the barracks. Her Five and her guards—more than just the two now —follow behind her. Muffin makes a displeased growl. She arches an eyebrow in Ayc's direction in a silent question.

"They want to come, too," Ayc explains. "I insisted they stay."

"That's wise," Peregrin says. "I don't trust Caius's or Brekken's dragons not to attempt to eliminate Everadyn's only dragon."

"Just Caius's and Brekken's," Ayc asks. "What about Damara's dragon?"

"Best not trust hers either," Peregrin says.

"Peregrin, what happened with the regents?" Lora asks as they make their way through the street. She can see the three dragons now, breaking through the crowds. Gryphons, likely the ones on patrol, follow on either side at a distance, escorting them in.

"I told them you would not be seeing them today," Peregrin replies, "and they were welcome to make an appointment, but they said they would wait until you were no longer busy."

Lora snorts a breath through her nose. "They will be waiting all night then. I will not yield to their every whim. Whatever they've come to ambush me with, it'll have to wait."

"I applaud that choice," Peregrin says with a tick of a smile.

She knows that's a tremendous compliment, and it warms her heart.

The dragons have landed by the time they make it to the beach. A scattering of gryphon riders pace along the beach and on the cliffs above. Ayc falls into step beside Lora, his hand flexing beside his sword. She lets hers rest on her short swords on her hips. Damara turns away from her brothers, thrusting up a hand toward them to signal them to wait, and storms down the beach. They wait where they are next to the three dragons. Kivka is pacing again, every movement digging that vicious collar into her throat. Lora looks away.

Xylie utters a gasp behind her. It's the first time that Xylie has seen Kivka up close—the first time she's seen the vicious collar. When Lora glances over her shoulder, tears shine in Xylie's eyes. Tavish must sense it because he reaches for her hand with the one not holding his cane and squeezes it gently.

Lora swallows and turns back, allowing her irritation to rise. "I thought I told you to always come alone," Lora calls when Damara is still several feet away.

"I'm sorry," she blurts with a sincerity that catches Lora off guard. As she marches toward them, she swats hair out of her face. Lora has never seen her look anything but composed, but she looks frazzled now.

She stops before Lora and plants her hands on her hips. "My father believes I am not handling my job appropriately and sent Brekken along to ensure I'm doing a satisfactory job."

She cuts a look down the beach. Caius has ignored her command and saunters toward them. Brekken barks something at him that gets lost in the wind. When he ignores it, Brekken rushes after him.

Damara heaves a low growl of displeasure beneath her breath. "Unfortunately, Iolite does not go anywhere without Kivka, so Caius had to come along."

"Why not?" Bronwen asks.

"Because Iolite and Kivka are mated."

"Mated?" Lora repeats. "Like how wolves mate for life?"

"Yes and no," Damara says, and to Lora's surprise, she keeps going. "It's for life, yes, but it's more than that. It's an intense and instant bond that occurs from the moment they meet. Some say it's forged by a split-second choice while some say it's fate, and there's no choice at all. I'm inclined to think it's the latter. Otherwise, I'm certain Kivka and Iolite would have broken their bond long ago. How do you think Caius captured Kivka? She was a free dragon before she mated with Iolite and stuck around too often. Long enough Caius managed to get that collar around her neck."

Each word has felt like a hand slowly tightening around Lora's throat. Love is vulnerability, her mother always said, and for this poor dragon, it has been. It has put her in literal chains.

"That's fucking cruel," Ayc says, glaring down the beach at Kivka.

Xylie sniffs.

"Thank you," Caius says as he comes to a stop behind Damara. He still remains ten yards away, close enough that she can hear his voice but far enough that it would take a few strides to reach him and slit his throat. Static rises in the air once more, but it quickly fades as Bronwen gathers control. Lora can't blame her. The sight of his face so close is all it takes for her canines to elongate.

"Dom Vari take cruelty as a compliment," Caius says. "Kivka shouldn't have been so careless if she didn't want to be at the end of my chain. It's why I'm so careful who I fuck. Nothing would be worse than being mated."

Ayc stiffens. "Is that something else they say Drakr and dragon share?"

"Rarely," Damara says, shooting a glare at her brothers, her eyes briefly flashing red. "But some lore says that each Drakr has one true mate, just like dragons. Many have testified to experiencing that instant and unbreakable connection, forged at the time of meeting, a love fierce enough to consume them."

Lora can feel Ayc's tense with every single word. She grinds her teeth against the desire to tell Damara to shut up. She does not want to hear that the man she loves might have a true mate, especially not when he was inside her only an hour ago. Perhaps that's what Ayc is thinking. That there is someone else out there who is his mate, who he belongs with. The very idea of someone else touching his skin the way she has touched it makes Lora feel violent and dangerous.

It's just ridiculous lore, like their idea that fae descended from dragons and gryphons. It's not true.

Damara twists toward Lora once more. "According to lore, being loved by a dragon is as fierce and all-consuming as fire."

Lora fights not to look at Ayc. If she looks, Damara is going to see far too much.

Caius snorts. "Foolishness."

Lora whirls her focus toward him. Someone at which to aim the feelings welling up in her chest. "You are not welcome in my castle. You can stay on the beach."

"We've already discussed that," Damara assures. "He's agreed to stay if Brekken can come with."

"Very well," Lora agrees. She'll allow Brekken. He intervened when the battle broke out between Caius and Bronwen. She doesn't trust his motivation, but he protected Bronwen, and he's at least more level-headed than Caius. "Captain Irving, please send a message over the agate to Commander Urbain. I want gryphon riders to have their eyes on Caius at all times. If he tries to leave this beach, they can kill him. Something makes me think the dragons won't try to stop them."

Cauis scowls, making him look even more hideous than Lora already finds him.

She can hear Irving murmuring, passing on that command to Urbain.

"Let's go then," Lora says.

She begins to turn but pauses when Caius turns to Brekken and extends his hand. It looks like a handshake. Caius even offers a grin and a "Have fun, brother," but Lora catches it. Something passes hands. She doesn't know what. Brekken tucks it into his pocket too quickly.

They're up to something. She'll need to warn her guards and her Five not to eat or drink anything in case they intend to poison someone. She won't be able to let her guard down for a moment.

Something tells her she isn't going to return to bed anytime soon.

As they make their way back down the group, Irving slips past her Five and taps Lora's elbow. As they walk, he stoops his head low to speak into her ear.

"We have a problem," Irving whispers. "The regents broke through the front gate."

FIFTY-ONE

LORA

Lora considers, however, briefly, how bad it would be if she had all the regents cut down by her guards like she might do for any invading army. It might rid her of a few causes of her migraine, but it's just as likely to immediately cause a whole host of others. Their families, clans, and successors might all decide to come for her neck.

"What orders do you want me to give?" Irving asks. "Would you like me to have them arrested for trespassing?"

Another tempting idea, but one she can't see going well for her, especially not when she's about to be entertaining Drakr. She could threaten them with an arrest, but they might attempt to call her bluff. "No, put them in the great hall. Tell the guards to tell them I'm giving them exactly five minutes."

She glances behind her. Brekken and Damara study her carefully, noting the exchange. She's not certain they heard, but she certainly doesn't want them to hear whatever it is that the regents have come to ambush her with, and she doesn't trust that the regents won't show up to her meeting with the Drakr if she waits any longer to deal with them. She'll have to find a way to keep the Drakr preoccupied while she gets the regents out of her fucking castle.

"Everything all right?" Ayc whispers to her while they climb the narrow path upward, his breath teasing her neck. He's so close that she's tempted to stop suddenly, knowing his back would press completely against her back.

"The regents decided they weren't taking no for an answer," she says.

"What a bunch of shit-filled pies with bastard crusts."

Lora chokes down a laugh. "Will you tell them that to their faces?"

He winks. "If it pleases you, my lady."

Fuck. My lady. It makes her thighs clench, though she admittedly prefers 'my love.' Especially when he's whispering it against her thighs.

She shakes her head, stealing herself to think clearly. Right now, she needs to be Sovereign. Later, she can be his love.

When they reach the courtyard, Lora has a plan. Near the door of the keep, she turns to face Brekken and Damara. "Unfortunately, the captain of the guard has informed me that there's an urgent matter that needs my attention. It'll only take a few minutes. An hour, at most. Peregrin and Bronwen, can you see that our guests are made comfortable until then and have a place to freshen up? Afterward, we can have dinner."

"Hopefully, it's not as violent as last time," Damara says, and Lora doesn't like the way she glances at Brekken like the words are meant especially for him.

He's too busy studying Bronwen. The marked half of his face is hidden behind his brown hair, but his deep blue eyes sweep over Bronwen in a way that seems like he's memorizing the shape of her. Bronwen nods to Lora and turns to Brekken. He gives a smile and sweeps a bow, and there's something about that smile that makes Lora's chest clench. Fuck, Damara didn't lie when she said Ayc looks so much like them. That smile is uncanny.

"Follow me," Bronwen says, pushing the doors open. "I'll escort you to a room."

Brekken follows, but Damara looks to Peregrin. "I was hoping to visit the Archives. I do love books, and I hear Wyntra has quite the collection. Would you mind escorting me there?"

Bronwen glances over her shoulder. Lora doesn't like the idea of them splitting up, but she doesn't want to make Damara suspicious, so she only nods. Bronwen continues, and Peregrin leads Damara in the opposite direction.

Lora steadies herself with an inhale. "Tavish and Xylie, can you go speak with Zinnia and ask her to make sure there's enough food for our guests?"

"Are you sure you don't want us to go with you to face the regents?" Tavish asks.

"No. They're lucky they are getting me. I'm not letting them think all of my Five are going to drop what they're doing whenever they decide to throw a tantrum."

They nod and hurry off in the direction of the kitchens together. Lora looks to Ayc. Irving and her other guards are still close, but it's the most privacy they've had since they left her room.

"What do you need?" he asks, lifting a hand to brush a strand of her curls back from her face. He drops his hand quickly, but her skin hums where the tips of his fingers grazed.

"Come with me," she says. "Bring Muffin."

AYC

Ayc lets Muffin go first. The dragon buzzes with excitement to finally be a part of something. They rock back on their hind legs and then slam their front claws down on the double doors of the great hall. Ayc uses his hand to undo the latch of the door so they swing open. Muffin crushes back to the ground and bares their teeth, issuing a low growl that has a few gasps uttering from the room.

"Do I look fierce, Ayc?" they ask nervously across their link.

"The most ferocious thing on four legs," Ayc replies as he swings around the door to stride in next to Muffin.

All the regents are on their feet. Dedryk clutches a chair, half lifting it in the air like he plans to use it as a weapon. When he sees Ayc, he lowers it. Ayc pulls at his power, just enough to make the shadows in the corner of the room swirl. It's easy because he's fucking angry. Fucking angry that they would dare show up here like this, angry that they couldn't take no for an answer. So when Lora sent him before her, he was glad to have something to do. The anger only disrupts the shadows more when Ayc searches across the room once more and realizes there is one extra person in the room.

Seated next to his father at the table is Wylder.

Fucking gods, what game is Dedryk playing? To bring his son with him—Lora's previous friend and lover—as though he believes he can use whatever power Wylder might still have on her.

"Where is Loraphne?" Dedryk demands, tracking Ayc's every movement as he and Muffin make their way to the front of the great hall. Ayc sits on the steps to the dais in front of Lora's throne and Muffin stretches at the top of the platform, fixing their red eyes on the crowd.

"Your Sovereign is busy. She sent me." Ayc lets his vision flash red, fixing it on Grey, who is looking anywhere but at Ayc directly. It flares brighter when he catches sight of Amos, who has positioned himself behind a candelabra as though that might give him protection from Ayc's dragon. He remembers the blue cloth found with the midnight in Lora's bed, and he has to grab taut to his power, lest his shadows surge toward Amos.

Muffin swings their head toward Amos. *"Is that the one who means Lora harm?"*

"I think so."

Muffin growls. Puffs of smoke coil in the air before their nostrils. Amos retreats a few steps. Wylder bolts upward from his slumped position, but does not fully rise. Harlowe and Dedryk reach for weapons that are not around their hips. Busara presses their lips together, but Qadira smiles, wonder in her eyes.

"What the fuck do you want?" Ayc demands.

"We wish to speak to the Sovereign," Harlowe says, stepping toward him.

"So you've said. About what?"

"That's for us to discuss with the Sovereign. Not with her Fifth."

"You should have sent a letter then so she could have prepared for your visit. As it is, she's busy. She'll be here as soon as she can. If not today, we can set you up in rooms for the night and clear her schedule for tomorrow."

Briar mutters something beneath his breath. Qadira sighs, draping her wrists off her folded legs like she's so bored, her bones are starting to give way.

"This is unacceptable," Dedryk says. "If we had come here because we needed urgent aid—"

"If some disaster had befallen one of our lands, Dedryk," Busara says, her voice measured, "the Everadyn Sovereign would have heard of it by now."

Good to know there is at least one voice of reason in the room.

Ayc says, "If you would tell me more of what you are here for, I could deliver that message to my lady and perhaps get you all back home more quickly. Some of you have traveled a very long way."

Harlowe and Dedryk exchange a look, but it's Grey who finds a fragment of courage to speak buried down deep in his cowardly soul. "We wish to speak to her about Aluina. We all know she wants to break the treaty. We wish to bring the issue to a vote so that we can rest easily knowing our new Sovereign isn't about to throw us into war."

Ayc drags a breath in through his nose to steady his nerves, his power. The ache in his back is worsening the longer he keeps stirring his power, making the shadows writhe around the edges of the room. He was already sore this afternoon despite the tonics he took. He didn't truly mind; every tender pull of his muscles reminds him of how deeply he thrust into Lora's sweet cunt last night. He'll gladly pay the price for that. He's certain he'll mostly forget about it as soon as he's back in her bed. But for now, he has to be aware of his limits.

He'll have to let himself rest soon, but not now, not when his emotions shudder through him. If they've come, then Grey must know the votes do not lie in Aluina's favor. By triggering a vote, however, they can then vote on how long they must wait until the issue can be voted on again, from a minimum of one to ten years. Government, he's learned from the professors and from the books Xylie reads as they travel in the carriage together, is full of such tedious rules.

That's their intention. To ensure that they will not have another vote for ten years. Ten years while Ayc's people suffer.

The side door opens, and Lora sweeps inside. She's been waiting there for the right moment to enter. She wanted to make them sweat, to drill in the fact that she wouldn't simply be available to them no matter what ridiculousness they pull.

"You all have five minutes," she growls as she storms toward her throne.

Wylder stumbles to his feet at the same moment as Ayc rises from the stairs. He stares at Lora, following her every moment dressed in her glorious dress and armor. And Ayc knows that look —the one of longing. It raises something dark within him. Something vicious. Something that makes him want to remove Wylder's eyes from his skull for looking at *Ayc's* love. It's a possessiveness that is powerful and overwhelming.

Just like Damara described.

When she described the concept of mates, Ayc knew he's felt that feeling before, that instant spark of something. He felt it when Lora broke into his world and put a knife to his throat. He's felt it ever since, even when he thought he hated her, even when he tried to make his feelings stop. And after last night, he feels it in a way that penetrates his very soul.

She is his. Fucking *his*.

Perhaps what Damara said about Drakr is another ridiculous

piece of lore. Perhaps what Ayc is experiencing is nothing more than what everyone has when they love this deeply. Or perhaps it's something bigger than them both. Perhaps it's fate. It doesn't matter.

She is his. He is hers.

Lora doesn't even look his way when she perches on her throne. Ayc steps to her side, leaning his shoulder against the side of her throne. He draws his power to him, lets it swirl around his feet. He imagines the image he creates. Lora on her throne, her shadow wielder on one side, his devoted dragon at the other. Shadows swirling around them all. He sees Amos take another step toward the door.

"If a vote is what you've come for, I could have saved you time," Lora says. "I won't be calling for a vote. You can leave."

"You would dare deny us?" Dedryk hisses.

"Dare?" Lora scoffs. "As though I answer to any of you. Have you forgotten whose head wears a crown? I do not bow to you. I do not bow to anyone."

Her eyes burn silver, and fuck, Ayc would bow. He would bow to her and only her. He wants to fall to her knees, wants to worship her in that throne.

"This is a mistake," Amos dares to protest like he's more than chicken shit. "You will regret it."

"Is that a threat?" Ayc snarls. Shadows creep toward Amos's feet. Ayc's back spasms, but he can hold it just a little more.

"Stop it!" Amos cries.

Little chicken shit.

Lora holds up her hand. "Hold on, Ayc."

He lets the power fall completely. The shadow returns to the corners and beneath the table and behind the pillars. He lets them be still for now, so that he can rest.

Lora leans forward. "Out of curiosity, if I brought it to an official vote, would any of you say yes?"

Harlowe hits his fists against the table before him and glares around him at the other regents. Briar looks away. "We don't have to tell you how we would vote. Call an official vote or—"

"I would vote yes."

Ayc's eyes snap to Qadira. She sits up straight in her chair and adjusts her skirt over her crossed knees. She gives Lora a polite nod of her head. "I only agreed to come today because I want our Sovereign to know that she has one person on her side. Sal Maris and our sailors are no cowards, and my grandmother was a human from Aluina. We will sail with you."

Lora grants her a grateful smile.

"That makes two," says Busara, standing and smoothing down her robes. "Aluina and Everadyn have a friendship that stretches nearly to the beginning of our history. I believe it ought to be restored."

No one else speaks. The long silence stretches on. Briar shifts. Grey sighs. Amos, Harlowe, and Dedryk continue to turn various shades of red.

"That means I only need one more vote," Lora says, standing from her throne. "And if one of you don't change your mind, then I'll simply find a way to replace you."

Dedryk snorts. "You wouldn't dare!"

"Oh, but I would. If you mean to treat me as a villain, then I mean to be a good one. Amos and Dedryk, you both have reelections coming soon, do you not? I'll be looking for your replacements."

"No one will run against me," Dedryk snarls. "I've run unopposed for the last three elections."

"I'll run," Wylder says.

Lora's mask collapses for just a second, her mouth parting in obvious surprise. Wylder catches it in the corner of his eye, a smile that turns Ayc's stomach appears on his lips. If he's offering to go against his father, it can only be for one reason: to win back Lora's affections.

Jealousy creeps through him. Shadows threaten to awaken. Ayc clamps down upon his power as the pain rises.

"What?" Dedryk wheels on his son.

"The plan was always for me to proceed you," Wylder says. "Why not now?"

"The plan was for you to be *Sovereign*."

"And I am not. Lora is, as she deserves to be. And I will gladly serve her. I will win the election, and I will vote yes to break the treaty for no reason other than because I want to see Drakr burn for what they did to Ryker. You should want that, too, Father."

Dedryk's mouth hangs open, but only nonsense and random syllables pour forth.

Amos stabs a finger in Wylder's direction. "See! See the way she poisons the mind of your own son. We never should have let her wear that crown. The wicked queen. The bitch!"

Ayc reaches for his power, his rage so cold, it burns like ice, but before he grasps ahold of it, Muffin stands. They flare out their wings behind Lora's throne and roar, louder and more powerful than Ayc has ever felt it. The room shakes. The stained glass above them whines like it might shatter. The regents fling their hands over their ears and duck their heads as though expecting fire. The air before Muffin's mouth shimmers, sparking white in the light. A cold wind sweeps through the hall until they snap their jaws shut.

A laugh sounds from the corner of the room just as Damara steps from the shadows. She looks relaxed, as though perhaps she's been there this whole time.

As though she's heard everything.

"Oh, dear," she says. "Don't all of you know you should never anger a dragon?"

FIFTY-TWO

LORA

Fucked.

They are absolutely and completely fucked.

If Damara heard the conversation between Lora and the regents, then she would get on her dragon, ride back to Drakr, and inform Lord Lahlis and her queen that Lora does not wish to be allies. And they will be coming for Lora's head. They will try to burn this city to the ground.

Perhaps that's for the best. Perhaps it's a good thing they have been forced into war. She would have liked more time to prepare, but it is ultimately what they wanted. She just has to survive this moment.

"What's that you called her? A cheat?" Damara muses.

She moves slowly like a prowling tiger, effortlessly dragging shadow with her, as she moves toward the front of the great hall. Muffin shifts forward, planting their front feet in the steps before Lora's throne, angling their body before her. Irving and Shae break from where they've stayed by the side door, reappearing from beneath their cloaks and stationing themselves just behind Lora. Even Wylder shifts closer, though she certainly doesn't want his protection now. Ayc steps forward, so he begins to shield her other side, his hand falling to his sword. She resists the urge to grab his hand, fisting her fingers around the armrests of her throne instead, her heart picking up its pace with every step Damara takes.

But the Drakr doesn't head for Lora. She stops directly before Amos. She looks him up and down, her nose wrinkling in disgust.

Even from here, Lora can see the bob of Amos's throat as he swallows. His heel slips backward, then plants in place, as though he's fighting not to run. In any other situation, Lora would have found great satisfaction in seeing Amos cower before a powerful woman. But Lora feels the same slick, oily feeling of fear crawling down her back.

"You're the regent to Lux Aester, aren't you?" Damara sniffs a little, and the smile she gives him is sharp as a knife, even though her teeth remain perfectly flat. "Ah, yes, I can smell the hypocrisy on you. After all, it was *your* victor who was the cheat. My father told me he had at least a dozen people helping him other than his Five. It's how he finished those tasks so quickly. He had them all preparing, so all he had to do was show up and complete the final step. But that wasn't enough, was it? He had to make a deal with the Drakr just to be certain. Didn't all of you wonder why the Drakr suddenly showed up to kill two of your victors?"

"I didn't wonder," Busara says, drawing herself from her chair and positioning herself to face Damara squarely. She's devoid of even a tremor, and the look fixed upon her face states that she is too old to be bothered by Damara's theatrics. "I assumed the Drakr were once again meddling in things they should not."

"It's because Marcellus made a little deal, wise one," Damara says to her before shifting her focus back to Amos. "And I'm willing to bet *you* knew about all of it. I'm willing to bet you *helped* him. Before you go throwing around the word 'cheater,' look in the mirror because Lora was offered the same deal, and she had the courage and the honor to tell us no. She's the only one who finished all seven tasks with any kind of fairness. She and her Five earned their positions."

Lora doesn't understand why Damara is defending her

against Amos's accusation and spilling all his dirty secrets. Right now, Damara should be making the quickest exit. She should never have revealed herself at all. She could have stayed hidden and carried the knowledge of Lora's meeting—and fuck, of Ayc's shadow affinity—back to her lands. What exactly is she doing?

And, fuck, where is Peregrin? What did she do to them that she was able to escape from their sight?

Dedryk finally breaks from his stunned, frozen position. He forces on a charming smile as he steps closer. "We were just discussing... Whatever you heard, we don't mean to actually break the treaty."

Damara rolls her eyes toward him. "I don't need a man to tell me what I did or didn't hear with my own ears. Nor does your Sovereign need you to speak for her." Damara looks back at Amos. She stares at him, her eyes slowly turning a red that contrasts with the smile that builds on her lips. A quake has started in his shoulders. She raises an empty hand toward his face, and no one, not a single person, moves to defend Amos.

But she only taps a single finger against his nose. "*Boop!*"

Amos leaps a foot from the floor, and Damara throws back her head and laughs, before she twists around and saunters a few more feet toward Lora's throne. "Ugh. Men are the worst. I'm so grateful that I'm not attracted to them."

She is utterly unhinged. Lora might have liked it if they weren't sworn enemies.

"Are *you* planning to break the treaty?" Damara says as she stops at the foot of the dais.

Lora narrows her eyes because how is she supposed to answer that question? With a lie that won't be believed, or the truth that will start a war?

Damara winks. *Winks.* Lora isn't certain what she means by it or why Damara defended her. What the fuck should Lora even do now? Still, perhaps the smartest thing to do is keep the regents here, but they are unarmed. Briar has a bit of affinity, and Qadira is a wind elementist—both powers might be useful. But she can't trust that any of the regents will go to any significant risk to protect her. Besides, she's sick of looking at their faces.

"We can discuss it in private," Lora says at last. "All the rest of you...get out of my castle."

Amos turns on his heels and storms away. There's no surprise there. If Damara kills Lora, it'll be doing him a favor. The others at least have the decency to hesitate. They look at her, then at each other.

"Go!" Ayc snarls. "And if any of you shows up here uninvited again, I'm going to feed you to my dragon."

Muffin gives a low rumble of agreement, and they scatter. Only Wylder and Qadira remain.

"Will you be all right, my lady?" Qadira asks, cutting a glance to Damara.

"Yes, Qadira," Lora says, even though she's truly not certain what's going to happen when they walk out of this room, and she could use an air elementist at her side.

Qadira studies her for a moment. And Lora is grateful— grateful that today, she has found out that this woman is a true ally. "Still waters, my lady," she says at last, twisting around. "I will linger outside in case you need to summon me back. I'll see you soon."

Wylder, however, still hasn't budged. He glares at Damara's back like he can make his eyes into daggers to cut her down. Damara plants her hands on her hips and sighs wearily but does not look at him.

"Wylder, leave," Lora prompts.

"I will not leave you in danger."

Lora wants to laugh at the irony. The man who poisoned her. Who said nothing with the other victors conspired against her. She's grateful for his offer to run against his father. He's young, but everyone wanted him as Sovereign. Perhaps his clan will choose to accept him as regent. But if he made the offer because he thought it might undo everything he's done to betray her, he's wrong.

"I don't require your protection, Wylder," Lora says. "I never have."

He pulls his gaze away from Damara and plants it upon her. There it is, the longing, the fire that used to draw her back in, even when things between them cooled. She always flung herself back at him, hoping that this time, she might find what she was missing. She fucked so many people of every expression of gender, hoping she would find what she saw in her books. But she didn't because she didn't love them. Not the way she loves Ayc, and nothing will ever compare now.

"Lora," he protests.

Shadows flare in the corner and swirl outward, toward Wylder's feet. Lora glances first at Damara, but she shakes her head. When Lora turns to Ayc, his gaze is shimmering red. Wylder retreats from it, but it slowly stalks after him, a creeping river of shadows that nips toward his boots. Finally, he turns and saunters away. Before he closes the door, more guards shift into the great hall. The side door opens, and other guards step in as well. They stay at a distance, but their hands are already on their weapons. Damara notes them as casually as if she were window shopping.

"Where's Peregrin?" Ayc demands.

"Probably still standing outside the privy I told them I needed to use." She waves her hand. "Don't be angry with them. It's quite hard to keep tabs on a shadow wielder as old as I am. I disappeared into their shadow when they thought I went inside. Could have happened to anyone."

Well, at least, she hasn't harmed Peregrin. Irving mutters something quietly into his agate, something that sounds like an order to find Peregrin.

"So..." Lora begins. Her heart hammers unsteadily on her sternum, but she forces her shoulders to relax, to keep from letting the fear show. "You heard that."

Damara nods. She keeps her hands folded in front of her, away from that red blade of hers. "You are trying to convince the regents to break the treaty with the Drakr and go to war." It's not a question.

Lora stiffens, sliding her hand to the hilt of her sword. Ayc shifts another step forward, preparing to position himself directly in front of her if he must.

And then Damara smiles. "Good."

AYC

Ayc tries to weigh Damara's smile. Is it an act? Is it a clue? Either way, that deep, monstrous thing inside of him refuses to settle. He feels the same protectiveness rippling from Muffin, whose red eyes fix upon Damara. If Damara takes even a step closer, he isn't sure what will happen, whether he'll remove her head from her shoulders or Muffin will devour her. She's stronger than him, and Muffin is untrained, but surely she can't take them both—not to mention Lora and the rest of the guards in this room. The smartest thing would be to not let her leave this room alive.

But then, she's also not a fool. She knew that would be their thoughts before she even revealed herself. And instead, she's chosen to defend Lora. And now, she's smiling at them, like this turn of events pleases her greatly.

"Good?" Lora repeats. "What game are you playing, Damara?"

"I told you that you would much rather work with me than with my father. That's because you and I have a mutual interest."

"And what is that?"

"The liberation of Aluina."

Disbelief flutters through Ayc's fingertips. He tightens his hand over his sword.

Lora scoffs. "And we're just supposed to trust you? How do we know you won't run to Lahlis and tell them everything you've heard?"

"Unfortunately, you don't know," Damara says. "But if I wanted to do that, the most foolish thing I could have done is reveal that I've been hiding. I'm quite certain you've decided it isn't wise to let me leave this room. But I am being honest with you." She shifts her gaze toward Ayc. "Us bears have to stick together."

She hooks her fingers around her collar and pulls it down. There, stitched into the inner lining, is a bear. Like Ayc wears on his own collar. Like Lora wears on the inside of her cape. Almost exactly, except—

Ayc nearly stumbles down the stairs.

Damara covers it swiftly, but not before Ayc catches the difference. This bear is not just a silhouette of the mighty beast. This bear's mouth is open. Roaring. Like the coins he has in a spelled box in his room.

Asbjorn.

Calliope's words. She's only known one other Drakr she trusts.

Damara? Ayc's head spins. Damara is a rebel?

"You serve Lahlis and Queen Volkna," Lora says. "And you want me to believe that you are some hero in disguise and not my enemy?"

"Oh no," Damara says. "I would never profess to be a hero. For too long, I was content with the power that being a Drakr gave me, lost in the rhetoric my father spewed. I saw the injustice. Saw the way I've been sneered at because of my round ears, or Brekken has taken abuse because he comes from a lower class, but I chose to look away and bask in the privilege that being Dom Vari offered, no matter what my privilege cost others. And then Creed was massacred. Then, the last borders of protection fell from around Aluina. Before that, I was complicit. But after, I was forced to be an active participant in the oppression of my own people, and I could not stomach it."

"Yet, you remain at your father's side," Lora says. "You continue to put their blood on your hands."

"Because I understand the advantage my position gives me.

The knowledge of the inner workings of the Drakr movement. I have not wasted it."

If she is truly Asbjorn, if she's been a spy for the Aluina rebellion, then, of course, her position is valuable. A secret weapon.

She continues, her voice steady, "I've done very bad things to very good people in order to keep my father's trust. If I am ever talked about in history books, I will be remembered as a villain. If there is an eternal damnation, then my soul will be tortured for all of eternity, and it will be fair penance. But I have kept my position, played my father's sick games, and I have waited for an opportunity like this. For a queen with a love for Aluina to rise to the Everadyn throne."

Ayc can't swallow. He can scarcely breathe. He studies Lora from the corner of her eye. Her emotionless mask is firmly in place, but her chest does not rise or fall. Like she, too, is holding her breath.

"Why are you really here?" Lora asks. "Why did Lahlis truly insist you come so often? Why is Brekken here?"

Damara paces before the steps, her hands planted on her wide hips. "Did you know that Queen Volkna has a gift of dreams? I think that you would call her divina, but the Drakr do not believe in gods or the divine. Some people just have gifts. She has dreams that can be hard to interpret but have been known to accurately foreshadow the future."

Ayc's chest grows taut. How does one fight against an enemy who can foresee the fortune? Who might dream of you coming?

Lora shakes her head. "I didn't know."

"I didn't think so. Drakr have many secrets, but that is one we've kept close to our chests. They would kill me for telling you." Damara flicks her wrists as though that bothers her little. "Volkna reports her dreams only to Lahlis. According to him, she has had many dreams, but there is one she's had over and over and over for decades. For as long as Everadyn stood with Aluina, she dreamed of a bear wearing a crown, devouring a dragon. According to Lahlis, that dream stopped when Creed fell. She has not dreamed of anything but dragons ruling the skies for over ten years. And then, a few weeks ago, she had a new dream.”

Lora leans forward, her fingernails scraping against the metal of the throne. “What dream?”

Damara halts her pacing and faces the throne once more, but she’s no longer looking just at Lora. She’s focused on Ayc, too. “A crowned bear steps out of the shadows and sits down upon a throne while a dragon and gryphon bow at their feet. Do you know what day that was?”

A suspicion rises, but Damara only pauses for a beat before continuing. “The day you won the Trials. The day you drove a tooth through Marcellus’s neck. Something about your victory changed the future.”

“You upturned the hands of fate,” Ayc whispers, remembering the stone that turned on Lora’s Chronicler, the last quest that needed to be completed for Lora to win. Fate changed at that moment.

Lora reaches up to run her fingers across the broken leviathan tooth around her neck. She finally looks fully at Ayc, and he reads the same emotions in her eyes as float in his chest. Disbelief, fear, hope.

“Now, Queen Volkna dreams only of a victory for a bear. My father is nervous. Jittery. In a way that I have never seen him before. That fear has only grown as he’s heard that Everadyn has a dragon rider. One that is not only a Drakr, but also an Aluinic human and has the ear of the Everadyn queen.”

Ayc’s hands tighten on his side.

“I’m here because he wants me to keep an eye on *you*,” Damara says, pointing directly at Ayc. “He doesn’t like not knowing exactly who you are. The only thing that’s calmed him is my reassurances, telling him that I know for a fact that Ayc has no shadow power other than going invisible. A lie, I assure you, I plan to keep telling him. I think he’s suspicious I know more than I’m saying. Hence, why he’s sent Brekken and Caius.”

“Then I can’t trust Brekken?” Lora asks. “He’s not like you.”

“No.” Sadness crosses her eyes, and Damara blinks rapidly.

"No. There is goodness in Brekken. He is the one sibling I can say that I love. I practically raised him, ensured he survived the brutal trainings my father subjects all his children to. He despises our father for the same reasons I do. It's not possible to love a man that cruel unless the same cruelty runs inside you, the way it runs in Caius. I have seen Brekken willingly take punishment upon himself in order to show mercy. But I'm not certain that, if a moment comes to choose between his loyalty to me and his loyalty to our father, he will choose me. You can't trust him."

The side door opens, and Peregrin rushes in so quickly, they nearly stumble but catch themself on their cane. Red heats their normally gray skin as they narrow their gaze upon Damara. "There you are. Is everything all right, Lora?"

Lora rises from her throne. "Everything is fine, Peregrin."

"I apologize for letting her out of my sight." An unusual twist of guilt shows in their voice. "I did not mean to fail you."

"You did not fail me," Lora reassures. She takes one step downward. Muffin, who has been strangely silent through this entire exchange, shifts out of Lora's way. "Is there anything else you would like to tell me?"

"Not yet," Damara says.

"I don't like that answer," Ayc says. It means there's more that needs to be said, more that Damara is keeping hidden under her armor.

"I don't trust that my brother isn't getting restless," Damara says. "The last thing any of us needs is for him to show up and overhear or see that I'm conversing with you in private. That will seem suspicious. You have two choices right now. You can choose to trust that I'm on your side. Or you can kill me. I won't go down without a fight, but I certainly would understand if you don't want to take the chance."

Ayc knows what he would decide, but he has information Lora doesn't that has him convinced, information he still can't tell her. Her narrowed eyes look Damara up and down, and then she heaves a breath through her nose.

"I'm not going to kill you," she says.

From the corner of his eye, Ayc thinks he sees Peregrin smile, but when he looks, their expression is fixed back into annoyance.

Muffin shakes out their wings, drawing Ayc's focus. *"Can I meet her dragon now?"*

Ayc nearly barks a laugh. Of course that would be their concern. *"Next time she comes,"* Ayc promises, and he hopes there is a next time. He doubts between Brekken and Lora, he's going to get a chance to speak about Asbjorn with her in private. *"When Kivka and Iolite are not here. Iolite can't be trusted, and Kivka is too unpredictable."*

"Is that the one I hear crying in pain and begging to be free?"

Ayc grits his teeth, his chest creaking as he pictures the dragon with blood dripping down her scales. If he ever gets the chance, he's going to put that collar around Caius's neck and pull so he knows how it feels.

"Ayc," Damara says.

He turns toward her.

"Don't let Brekken grab a strand of your hair."

Before Ayc can ask what the fuck that's supposed to mean, she walks away. "Now, if you'll excuse me, I really *do* need to use the privy."

Ayc rushes down the two steps from the raised platform. Lora catches his wrist, making him hesitate enough that Damara is already out the side door. Peregrin follows closely after, a few guards falling in behind Peregrin.

Lora trails her thumb on the inside of his wrist, drawing his focus to her.

"What do you think Volkna's dreams mean?" Ayc asks. "A bear on a throne. Aluina has not had a king or queen since the Creeds fell."

"I don't know," Lora says. She glances around her, like she's ensuring no one but her guards are still in the room. The ones who entered step out once more, and Irving and Shae resume their places by the separate doors, granting them space.

"We can sort it out later," she says.

She slips her hands into his hair, which has now dried, and

draws his head down to her lips. It takes him by surprise since two of her guards are still here, but he's not about to complain. The warmth of her lips still feels like a shock to his soul, like it is brand new, and yet, it brings awareness to all the places her mouth has been. His chest, his neck, his thighs, his cock. Just like that, he's hard, straining against the leather armor until it aches.

He barely notices Muffin heaving themself to their feet and heading toward the door. *"I'm leaving. I don't want to be here in case you two start doing whatever you do that sounds like dying."*

Ayc snaps the link between them closed.

At the sound of the door letting Muffin out, she pulls back much too soon, and he groans. "What was that for?"

"Because I wanted to," she says, a little smile tugging on her lips even as she plays with the cord around her throat. The one that used to be his. "Because I missed your lips on mine."

The door shuts again. He glances around to verify it is still just her guards before turning back.

"Just on your lips?" he teases, keeping his voice low enough that neither of the guards can hear. He stoops his head to lay a kiss on the sensitive flesh beneath her ear.

She shivers even as she nips at his throat.

"Careful," he whispers in her ear. "If you keep teasing me, I'm going to bend you over your throne and fuck you on it."

Silver highlights the brown of her eyes. "Promise?"

Fuuuck.

A knock sounds on the side door. Lora steps away from him. Irving opens the door, and Zinnia enters, pushing a tray of food. A reminder that they have a dinner with two Drakr—one who appears to be on their side and one who has something up his sleeve. Something that involves Ayc's hair, apparently.

Still, he can't stop himself from whispering, "Promise."

FIFTY-THREE

AYC

I t's ten minutes into dinner, and Bronwen and Brekken have yet to join them. Damara sits on Lora's right, but the two chairs to her left are empty. Ayc has sat on the opposite side of the table, both to position himself far enough away to heed Damara's warning. And also because he'll have an easier time keeping his hands to himself if there's more space between him and Lora. Even if he's tracking her every movement as she brings her goblet to her lips.

"Should we send out a search party?" Tavish asks, faking a laugh.

"Maybe," Lora says, without any humor in her voice. She glances at Damara. But surely, if there were problems, if a battle broke out between a shadow wielder and a sorcerer, they would have heard it. The whole castle would have shuddered.

Lora is rising from her chair when the side door bangs open, and Bronwen rushes in. "Sorry," she says, as she nearly sprints to the table.

Brekken follows at a more relaxed pace, his face fixed in the same stony look of nonchalance. He takes the opposite way around the table, the side of the table that Ayc is on. Ayc swivels around to follow him as he goes. He passes far too near, watching Ayc from the corner of his eyes, but he doesn't reach out for him. Perhaps, if Ayc hadn't turned around to stare at him, he might have.

What the fuck does he need one of Ayc's hairs for?

Bronwen slides into his chair, and even from down the table, Ayc can see how deeply red her normally pale cheeks are.

Lora leans closer. "Are you well?" she whispers.

"Very," Bronwen says, flicking her wrist as though shooing away the concerns. "We lost track of time."

Ayc frowns.

Damara cuts a look toward his brother as he sits down beside Bronwen, a look that could slice through tungsten. "Doing what, dear brother?"

"Having a stimulating conversation," he answers without hesitation.

"Oh?"

"Yes, we were debating the benefits and disadvantages of shadow and magical affinities. She believes that magical affinity is stronger than shadow, and I fear she misunderstood what all we are capable of. I enlightened her."

Bronwen makes a sound nearly like a squeak but covers it up with a cough. She grabs her goblet and gulps it down. Lora locks eyes with Ayc down the table, arching an eyebrow in a way that clearly says, *"What the fuck?"*

Ayc lifts a palm because the fuck if he knows.

"What's for dinner?" Bronwen asks, though her plate before her is already laid out with meat pastries and thinly sliced, fried potatoes.

Lora flicks her fingers at her plate.

"Aw, yes, well," Bronwen says. "I'm sorry we made you wait. Let's eat."

An awkward silence falls over the table, filled with only the chewing of food and the scraping of plates. Ayc wonders if he should attempt to break the silence. He's just selecting the right joke to tell when Brekken, who was so silent last time, makes the decision for him.

"Did you cook these, Ayc?" He points his fork at the pastries.

"No, this was prepared by our excellent kitchen staff. I'm afraid my duties as Fifth have not allowed me much time to bake."

"So no more chocolate pudding?"

Ayc's tongue tingles with the memory of sweet chocolate mixed with Lora's sweeter arousal. He clears his throat, fighting not to look at Lora. "Only on special occasions."

"And how long have you been a baker in this castle?"

Ah, there it is again, digging back into Ayc's past. The curiosity makes a little more sense now that he knows about the Drakr queen's dreams. But they are foolish to think that it has anything to do with him. Even with Lora catching his eye and shaking her head, he's smart enough to be careful how he answers. "For several years now."

He sets down his fork and leans forward around the table. "How many exactly?"

The tension grows around the table. Peregrin sets down their fork and picks up their knife, hiding it in their lap. Lora's hands disappear beneath the table, likely to position them more closely to the knife she's surely wearing on her thigh. Bronwen stares wide-eyed at him, looking suddenly horrified.

"Brekken," Damara says. A warning.

He snaps his blue-eyed gaze upon her. "It's a simple question, sister, that should have a simple answer. Since you're unable to provide that answer, I was sent to do it." He returns his focus to Ayc. "Let me be less subtle. I want to know how long you've been in Everadyn."

Ayc forces a smile. "And I want to eat five pieces of cake without my stomach making me beg for merciful death, but we can't always have what we want, Brekken."

"Five years?" Brekken presses. "Ten?"

There's a weight to the second number. Ah, so they do

suspect, or perhaps, just fear, that Ayc is connected to Creed. And it's best they never know that Yris defied Lahlis to spare his life.

"Three hundred and ninety-eight," Ayc lies, picking up the glass before him and tipping it toward Brekken. "I look good for my age." He sips on the contents and finds that Lora has had the wine watered down, which is probably for the best.

Brekken's brow furrows. "Are you always this difficult?"

"Yes," Lora says. "Brekken, if there are politics you would like to discuss, we can discuss them, but let's leave my Fifth's past out of it. He has a right to his privacy."

Brekken keeps his eyes fixed on Ayc, a look so intense that Ayc feels like he's trying to gaze into his very soul. Ayc forces his smile to not waver. He even wiggles his eyebrows and crosses his eyes. That seems to break Brekken from his trance.

He looks away, a muscle in his jaw tightening. "Very well."

Silence again. This one thick enough it feels like a physical touch raking down Ayc's back. The hair on his arms stands up, lingering until Tavish breaks it by asking.

"So, what creative uses *do* you have for your shadow?"

Bronwen jerks, choking on a potato. A burst of magic explodes from her fingertips. The sparks collide with Lora's goblet and fling it in the direction of the dais and Lora's throne.

"Fuck, sorry," Bronwen says, shoving back her chair.

"Allow me, my lady." Brekken springs to his feet, even though Lora has already stood as well.

Brekken and Lora reach for the cup at the same time, and both wrap their hand around it. Ayc tenses as Brekken's hand covers Lora's fingers, a tension that remains when Brekken doesn't immediately move.

Brekken cocks his head, surveying Lora slowly. Ayc pushes his own chair away from the table. Lora jerks away from Brekken, bringing the goblet with her.

"Wait," Brekken says, "you have something here."

He reaches forward swiftly. She leaps away from him, but not before he plucks something from the shoulder pad of her armor.

Brekken stands too, something pinched within his fingers, something too small for Ayc to see at this distance.

"This isn't one of your hairs," Brekken muses. "It's far too straight...and light in color."

Ayc's teeth grind as he realizes what has happened. He plants his palms on the table. The icy chill of his power threatens to rise within him, but Damara cuts a sharp look toward him. She will keep his secret, but Brekken will not. He grabs hold of his control.

Brekken cocks his head at Lora once more. "Tell me, my lady. Do you often wear your Fifth's hair on your armor?"

Ayc feels eyes shift to him, but he doesn't look away from Lora, who refuses to cease glaring at Brekken. Ayc was a fool, nuzzling her too close.

"I fail to see what you're trying to suggest," Lora says coolly. She strikes out like a snake, attempting to grab the hair from his grasp, but he's too swift. He's retreated several steps in the blink of an eye.

"Give it to me," Lora snarls.

Brekken turns on his heel and storms toward the door. "Come on, Damara."

Lora draws her dagger. "Do not let him leave," she barks. Three guards appear from beneath their cloaks and shift before the door. Veni. Irving. Another guard whom Ayc doesn't know.

Brekken freezes. Shadow rises from his feet, swirling up his ankle—a reminder of what Breken is capable of. Ayc bursts to his feet. He's certain that Brekken isn't about to be stopped without putting up a fight. He has tremendous power; it'll be difficult to stop him. Perhaps Damara outmatches him, but she can't do so without giving away her true loyalties or harming her brother. Ayc isn't certain she's willing to do either.

Damara rushes to his side. "Brekken, we discussed this. We agreed. The best thing is to keep the peace between our two countries. Doing this will not keep peace."

"I agreed to nothing," Brekken says. "Father will not be kind if you keep disobeying him. I am trying to help you."

"I did not ask for your help," she snaps.

Everyone is on their feet now.

Xylie's hands move frantically in the air. *"Do not let him leave with the hair. He could do any number of things to Ayc with the right alchemy."*

Bronwen is already moving toward Brekken. "Sit back down," she says through her teeth, her canines already sharp, "or I will make you."

He twists halfway toward her, shaking his head as though he's disappointed. "Come now, *my lady*," he says, infusing the *my lady* with honey, thick and sweet and suggestive.

Bronwen's eyes flash. "Fuck you."

He clucks his tongue. "But darling, you already did."

Bronwen's power slams into his chest, an orb of blue so strong, the impact of it slides Ayc's feet backward and rattles the dinner dishes. Brekken collides with the ground near the door. He rolls several feet, swearing under his breath, and comes up on his knees, the hand that held the hair clutched into a fist. Damara—struck by the magical force, too—lands on her rear but quickly scrambles upward.

"Ayc!" Muffin calls across the link. *"I can sense your heart racing. What is wrong? Should I come?"*

"No," Ayc calls back. *"Go to the courtyard. Get Tempest. If Brekken makes it into the courtyard, stop him."*

Brekken rises, and shadows rise with him.

"Bastard," Bronwen seethes, a ball of blue energy forming in between her fingers as she marches toward him.

Someone will die today, Ayc realizes. All because of some fucking hair. If they fight, someone isn't going to come out alive. A guard or Bronwen or Lora... All because they are once again trying to protect him.

"Stop it!" Ayc yells. He races forward, sliding across the stone, until he stands between Brekken and Bronwen. He ignores Lora calling his name and places a smile on his lips. "Let's just calm down and talk about this."

Brekken looks him up and down. "You're either very foolish or very brave to come between a sorcerer and a shadow wielder."

"I'm a bit of both, to be honest. Just tell us what you want with my hair."

"You've already proved you don't want to talk."

"I'm suddenly feeling gabby. What do you want to know? Do you want to know when I came here?"

"Ayc," Lora says softly.

Without turning, he knows she's stepped closer. He can sense her as well as he can feel his own heartbeat. But no, he's not going to risk someone getting hurt just to protect him. If the Drakr want to know his past, want to know if he came from Creed, then perhaps it's time to stop hiding it. Truth always has a way of coming to light, and if that means they try to kill him, they can fight it out then. But if there's still a way to survive this without bloodshed, then he'll take it.

"For starters, yes," Brekken said.

"Ten years ago."

Peregrin sucks a breath through his teeth. Bronwen's static makes Ayc's hair stand on end.

A fire burns in Brekken's eyes. "As in when the Creed family met justice?"

"You mean when they were *massacred*," Bronwen snarls.

The red in his eyes sparks, overtaking the blue. "That family had that coming. They are every bit as cruel as the Dom Vari when it comes to their own offspring."

"What are you talking about?" Ayc asks. The crown prince, the king and queen's only child, was alive and well until Yris had them slaughtered.

Brekken draws in a breath through his nose, and the red fades. The color of water, just like Ayc's, returns. "Next you're going to tell us it's a coincidence that a human boy was brought to Wyntra at the same time Yris was ordered to kill every single person in Creed."

"What does it matter?" Lora says. "It's been a decade."

It's Damara who answers, her voice sounding tired. "There were rumors that reached all the way to Drakr that the crown prince had a bastard child who lived in Creed castle."

Ayc swivels his head toward her, his mouth dropping open as he finally understands. "That's what this is about? You think I might be the crown prince's son? You think I'm…what? The last drop of the Creed royal line?" He laughs. He can't help it. It's beyond absurd. The wildest thing he's heard.

Brekken glares at him.

"I'm afraid you're wasting your valuable time," Ayc says. "I'm the bastard son of a mother who was a baker and whatever Drakr asshole sired me. I am not a Creed."

"Let's find out for sure, shall we?" Brekken reaches into his pocket and pulls out an alchemy bottle. It's clear, revealing the liquid inside to be a bright shade of orange, like the sunset over the western sea.

Xylie gasps, drawing Ayc's attention. *"A lineage potion,"* she signs.

"A what?" Bronwen asks.

"A potion that can identify if someone's bloodline matches the ingredient it was made with," Lora explains.

"Damara retrieved a bone from Siobhan's grave," Brekken says. Siobhan, the Everadyn fae who was King Cypress's mother.

"If Ayc is who he says he is, the potion will remain orange. If the lineages align, it will turn pink."

"This is a bad idea," Peregrin says.

"Why?" Ayc says. "I'm not a Creed. Let's prove it."

"You don't know who you are, boy. Your mother went to great lengths to ensure that."

Ayc swallows hard at the reminder, but he lifts his chin and meets Brekken's eyes. "Do it."

Brekken undoes the lid of the alchemy vial and slides Ayc's hair within. Lora's hand lands on Ayc's coat, pulling him backward, signaling him to create distance between him and Brekken. He follows her lead even though he isn't afraid. This whole foolish matter will be done within a moment.

Brekken returns the stopper and shakes the bottle. The room seems to hold its breath, except for Ayc, whose lips twist in a confident smile.

"Ayc, is everything well?" Muffin asks.

"Yes, Muffin, everything is—"

Ayc cuts off. He blinks.

The potion is doing something. Swirling. Lightening. Changing.

Ayc's smile slips. The world beneath his feet seems to shift, never to be the same again.

Because the potion is pink.

FIFTY-FOUR

AYC

It's not possible.

It's not fucking possible.

Ayc isn't Creed. He isn't Aluina royalty.

He's a baker. Nothing more.

The room is eerily quiet, or perhaps he's gone deaf. There's certainly an impossible buzz in his ears. When Lora tugs on his coat again, he doesn't fight her; he only slides backward as Brekken looks up from the potion in his hand. "Well, I guess that—"

"Well, fuck!" Damara swears loudly, loud enough that Brekken jumps and turns to his sister like she might be unwell. She coolly steps before Brekken, placing her body before Ayc so all he can see is her brown hair. "Was I supposed to go to Siobhan's grave?"

Brekken recoils. "Did you not?"

"Did I go dig a bone out of a decades-old grave?" Damara sticks out her tongue, faking a gag. "Ew. No."

Oxygen finally enters Ayc's lungs. Of course, that's the only explanation. Damara manipulated it.

"Then what the fuck did you put in the potion?" Brekken demands.

She shrugs. "Just a strand of hair."

"Whose?" Lora snaps.

"Mine," Damara says. She glances over her shoulder and winks at Ayc. "I always love it when I'm right."

The truth slams in, the world shifting once more.

He is not Creed.

But he is Dom Vari.

He is Lord Lahlis's son.

It's not any better. To suspect it is one thing; to have it confirmed is another. Everything feels tainted with this new truth. The room, the air he draws into his lungs, Lora's hand pressing more firmly into the small of his back, and most importantly, the blood racing through his veins. The blood he shares with Damara, and Brekken, and Caius, and the fucking queen of Drakr.

"See," Damara says, turning to Brekken. "Father is paranoid. I have tried to reassure him that there isn't any way that Ayc is Creed. Look at him. He looks like us. Fuck, he could almost be identical to you before Iolite marked you."

Brekken cocks his head and studies him. Ayc wants Brekken to say she's wrong, say the potion messed up somehow, but instead, he sighs. He tips his head forward, his face disappearing behind his hair. "You're right. Another one of Father's bastards, just like me." He lifts his chin to look at Ayc again. "I'm sorry. I do not wish our father on anyone."

Our father.

Ayc wants to punch him. He wants to be sick on the floor. Instead, he bares his teeth, wishing for the first time that he had the ability to sharpen like the Drakr's can. "Are we done?"

"Yes," Damara says. "We're done." She takes a step toward Lora. "One day, I hope we can share a meal without one of my brothers being an opposite ass. Let's go, Brekken."

She starts toward the door. Lora lunges forward and seizes her arm.

"What will your father do when he learns the truth about Ayc?" Lora says. "That he survived Creed. That he's his son."

Ayc bites back a groan. It feels even worse to hear it on her lips.

"We won't say anything," Damara says. "We will tell him the test showed no link to Creed blood and nothing more. Right, Brekken?"

Brekken hesitates, his gaze shifting to Ayc's other side, where Bronwen stands, still holding her small orb of magic. "We'll say nothing," Brekken agrees.

Lora releases Damara with a nod. "Will I see you in two weeks?"

"I'll be here," Damara agrees before she turns and walks away.

Brekken glances at Bronwen once more. He sweeps a bow. "Until next time, my lady."

She lifts the middle finger of her free hand, and he smiles before sweeping a bow.

Ayc finally remembers what Brekken said. There was no time to think of it at the moment, the insinuation he made. *Darling, I already have.*

They fucked. That's why they were late for dinner, why Bronwen was flustered, what Brekken really meant about being creative with his shadows.

For fuck's sake...

Bronwen fucked his brother, and he was an absolute dick about it. And quite frankly, Ayc would rather not deal with that. The room already feels like it's spiraling, spinning away like it might take him with it.

Brekken turns on his heel and marches away. The guards do not move until Lora nods at them to signal them to open the doors. A few break away to stalk after them and escort them back to the beach.

"Are they coming?" Muffin asks. *"Should I attack them?"*

"No, Muffin. Let them go."

Muffin pauses for a beat, but a flicker of sympathy crosses the link between like a hand laid on Ayc's shoulder. *"Are you all right? You sound like you might be weeping?"*

Ayc grinds his teeth harder—hard enough that his jaw hurts. *"I am not weeping."*

"But—"

Ayc slams the link between them closed. He can't handle Muffin being in his head right now. *He* can't even handle being in his head right now. It feels dark and desolate in here. He doesn't recognize the place.

You have no idea who you are, boy, Peregrin said.

And they were right.

Everyone is staring at him, patiently, sympathetically, waiting to see how he will react. But Ayc doesn't know how he's supposed to react to this. He doesn't know what to think, to feel, only that he would very much like to feel nothing. Perhaps to simply cease to exist for a few moments so he doesn't have to deal with the impending reckoning.

Xylie is the first to speak, giving a simple sign, *"Are you all right?"*

"I'm fine," he says. He fumbles with a smile, but he can't make it stick on his face. Lora's hand tightens in his coat. She's touching him, not caring that everyone can see them, and that feels like too much. He steps away from her. "I'm fine," he repeats again, but he's already retreating to the door.

"Ayc."

He's not certain who has called his name. More than one voice, he thinks. He feels his eardrums shaking. His icy power is flaring. The shadows slither out of the corners like snakes. He thinks he might implode, and if he does, he's going to take everyone with him.

"I just want to be alone right now," he says.

"Are you certain?" Tavish asks.

"Yes," he says.

"Ayc." There's too much in Lora's voice. That one syllable gives too much away, like she stitched love into every letter before she let it come from her tongue. Her footsteps sound on the floor after him, and those, too, are laden with declarations. Like she would drop everything to follow him. It's all he dreamed about yesterday, but in this moment, it feels too good, too bright, like he's stood in the dark too long and is squinting directly at the sun.

He partially turns but keeps walking, keeps his eyes directed at anything but her. "I'm fine, Lora. I just need a moment on my own. Please."

He doesn't give her time to argue before he steps into the shadow and wills himself to disappear.

LORA

Lora watches the side door open, the shadows shifting so Ayc can remain hidden within. She rubs a hand over her sternum, but it doesn't help the ache that's there. It doesn't feel like her own. It feels like Ayc's. Like she feels how the truth is twisting him up and ripping him in two. There are so many things she wants to tell him, to reassure him, but she knows he's not ready to listen yet. Perhaps she should follow him anyway. After all he did for her, somehow sensing that she didn't need to be alone like she claimed.

I'm here, she wants to whisper. *I have you.*

But the door closes.

Peregrin drags in a loud breath and exhales it as a long curse. It's exactly how Lora feels.

"Should I go after him?" Lora asks. She glances at Xylie, at Bronwen. Bronwen is better at this than Lora is, and Xylie knows Ayc better than any of them. Both of them shake their head.

"It's quite a shock," Bronwen says. "Give him a second." Her fingers shake as she pulls at her braid, the one that has been messy since she came to dinner.

Because she was fucking Brekken.

Ayc's brother.

Fuck's sake.

Lora wants to ask how that happened, and she doesn't want to know at all. After all, during Adamant, both Bronwen and Lora fucked their share of people who were practically strangers, people she scarcely even liked. It was almost its own sport to take to bed people who might try to kill you the next day. Sometimes, Lora found it hot and fun, and sometimes, it left her feeling dissatisfied, depending on how good a partner it was. Lora will never shame Bronwen for it now or doubt Bronwen's loyalty because of it. Sometimes, sex is just fucking sex.

Besides, with the dick that Brekken was to her in the aftermath, Lora knows Bronwen will never give him the privilege of touching her again.

Perhaps it's best to just let that go.

"What should we do now?" Tavish asks.

There's the question.

"I have some work I need to do in my office," Lora says. She crosses back to the table and picks up one of the abandoned meat pies. It's one of her favorite dishes that the kitchen makes. "We can all discuss everything over breakfast after we've slept. Xylie, if you see Ayc, will you tell him I want to speak with him when he's feeling able?"

No one protests her departure. Veni opens the side door for her, and she slips out. She hears feet rush behind her and already knows that it's Bronwen. Her First falls into step beside her, and they remain silent for a long time as they trace a path to Lora's office, trailed by guards. Lora searches the shadow as though she might be able to find Ayc hidden within one, like she might know it's him, like a tug on her heart.

"Are you angry with me?" Bronwen asks at last.

"Why would I be?"

"Because Brekken and I... Fuck, I'm sorry, Lora. I promise you it was nothing more than a hate fuck." She tugs at her braid, clearly distraught. "I don't know what I was thinking. We were just debating, and he called me my lady, and his eyes went red, and he touched me with his shadow, and—"

Lora stops and holds up a hand. Bronwen's cheeks are flushed, and fuck it, Lora understands. She understands all of that. The banter, the sweet molasses of my lady, the way a pair of red eyes—evidence of how much she's wanted by someone so powerful—can turn her into a tangled bundle of want and need. And the shadows, the way their cool fingers brushed her skin, the way they carried her to Ayc's bed while he was locked inside of her. It's enough to make want churn low in her belly, enough to make her want to find Ayc and fuck away whatever doubt and self-loathing he's currently letting himself wallow in.

She draws in a steadying breath. "I'm not going to shame you for sating your desires, Bronwen. But it *is* messy. He's an enemy. We're going to end up on opposite sides of a war. Besides, if he hurts you, I'm going to have to kill him, which may or may not cause us to go to war sooner than we're ready. So maybe, fuck someone else?"

"It won't happen again," Bronwen reassures.

"Good. Then we don't need to speak of it again."

Bronwen cocks her head. "Is there something you would like to tell me? About you and Ayc?"

Of course Bronwen knows. Lora is certain that after tonight, most of her Five are going to suspect, are going to wonder how his hair ended up on her armor. But she's not ready to talk about it, not ready to share all her feelings. She wants to bury it like a treasure deep in the earth, make a map that only she knows how to read, not because she doesn't value it, but because it's the most important thing that has ever been *hers*.

And once people begin to know, there's no undoing it. It'll travel until, eventually, everyone knows. Eventually, Lora's mother, who still lives in this castle like a ghost ready to pop out at the least convenient moment, will know and get to sneer about it.

So she says, "Not tonight. That's a truth that's just ours for a little longer."

Lora continues walking. Bronwen doesn't follow her, but when Lora glances back, she's smiling. Not like she's shocked, but like Lora has just shared a secret that has made her very, very happy.

Lora waits for Ayc in her bedroom. She paces. She tries to read one of her books. She sits down at her loom and stares at the empty frame like she can will a project to begin itself. She tries to knit but only ends up making the ball of yarn as tangled as she feels. Plucking at knots that only pull tighter is her last straw. "Fuck this."

She tosses it aside and heads for the door.

"Has anyone seen Ayc?" she asks Shae.

"Let me ask." She adjusts the agate in her ear, murmuring low. She listens as Lora runs her hands up and down her biceps. She's still wearing the black dress, still dreaming that Ayc will find her and peel it from her body, but she's removed the armor. Summer is approaching fast, but the nights are still cool in the castle, and her arms prick with goosebumps.

"No one has seen him," Shae says.

Which means he's trying hard *not* to be seen. Otherwise, one of the guards who roam this castle would have seen him. She's in no mood to go searching for him. She just wants to know where he is. She knows she has two options to find him. She can talk to Tavish, or she can talk to Muffin. And since Tavish is terrible at keeping secrets, she finds herself in the Sovereign's Garden.

Muffin gleams like an opal beneath the light of the nearly full moon. They lift their head, and it now looms above her, the red eyes gleaming in the darkness.

"Is Ayc in here with you?"

They sway their head side to side. A no.

"Do you know where he is?"

They nod.

"Can you take me to him? I'll meet you in the courtyard and can let you in through there."

In response, Muffin stretches out their wings. The moonlight glistens off the rainbow that swirls through the membrane of their wings. They spring from the earth, the gust of wind tossing Lora's hair into her crown. For a moment, she doesn't think they will clear the wall, but at the last moment, they tilt upward toward the sky.

Just like their rider, they have learned a lot in a small amount of time, and it takes her breath away.

AYC

Ayc sits at the steps to the dais within the great hall. He's not quite sure how he wound up here. He's spent the last few hours wandering around in the shadow as though perhaps he would find a way to get lost in it. He took a swim in the ocean like he could wash away the feelings of disgust that penetrates down to the bone. And when that didn't work, he found himself here, staring at the place where he learned the truth of his birth as though if he stares long enough, he can convince himself that it didn't happen.

The door creaks open. Lora enters the great hall with Muffin beside her. She searches around the unlit room, her eyes narrowed. "Ayc, I know you're in here. Muffin must have sensed you because they led me here. Show yourself."

Ayc wills himself to reappear, and her eyes lock onto him. He's kept the link between Muffin mostly off, but he grew wary of Muffin slamming against it with their concern, so he lowered it enough that Muffin could sense him. But not enough that they could read his thoughts. Ayc isn't even sure what's going on in his own head. He doesn't need to subject Muffin to it.

Muffin nudges against it again now, and Ayc lowers it further.

"I dislike that you're making our Lora worry," Muffin says.

"Our Lora?" Ayc repeats. *"What do you mean our Lora?"*

They've been calling her that a lot, and Ayc has yet to get an answer.

Muffin only snorts, slowing their pace as Lora and they make their way toward Ayc. She's still wearing that dress, her thick thighs sliding from between the swaths of dark cloth. He watches her every move, his body growing hotter with every step she comes closer to him.

When she reaches the dais, she lowers herself on the step beside him, carefully settling the fabric of her dress around her knees. "I have you," she says softly, laying her hand over his, resting on the stone. "What do you need?"

His chest aches at those words, the ones he has said to her. Like she can see inside him, see the wound in his chest. It's not a new one, but before, it was scabbed over, and now it's been torn open, raw and bleeding.

Still, he lies. "I'm all right."

"Liar," Muffin huffs as they stretch out on the ground before the dais.

"If you were all right," Lora says, "we wouldn't be sitting on a cold stone floor right now. We would be in our bed, finding new ways to make each other scream."

Our bed.

Fuck. He's a fucking fool.

"You're right. We should definitely be doing that instead."

When he tries to stand, she grabs the back of his coat and tugs him back down. "Ayc," she says in a warning voice that only sends a thrill down his spine.

"I'm serious. I'm certain getting lost between your thighs will be the perfect cure for whatever ails me."

"And what is ailing you?" she asks. She picks up his hand and holds it in both of hers, holding his gaze like a new parent cradles an infant. With a tenderness that says they could do this forever. That Lora will wait for as long as she has to for him to talk.

It's in this moment, more than any other that has gone before, that Ayc is certain that this thing between them is real. That it transcends what is physical. That it is large and deep and endless as the sea, too big to be contained, too beautiful to truly comprehend.

He lets out a breath. "I don't know," he says honestly.

"Is it because Lahlis is your father?"

Ayc cringes. "No," he says. "I mean, yes, but also no." He scrubs his free hand over his face, knowing he's making no sense.

Lora patiently runs her thumb over his knuckles. "You're not your father. No more than I'm my mother."

"I know that. I do. I just feel…Uncertain. Like someone has ripped my foundation out from beneath my feet, and I don't recognize the way the world looks. It's what Peregrin said. I don't know who I am."

Lora sets her chin on his shoulder. "I know who you are."

Through the fanned darkness of her eyelashes, her eyes shine a bright blue, reflecting him back at himself. His heart aches in a glorious way.

"*As do I,*" Muffin says. "*I looked into your soul, and I knew you. And I chose you. I would choose you again.*"

Heat stings at the back of his eyes; his vision blurs. He blinks, swallows hard. "And who am I?"

She slides her hands onto his cheeks, locking him in place. "You're Ayc fucking Waylonder. The Fifth of Everadyn. You're a dragon rider. A shadow wielder. A baker extraordinaire. And a teller of jokes that are objectively awful."

"They're not all—"

She places a finger over his lips. "You're one of the strongest, kindest people I know. And most importantly"—she smiles, and she's the most beautiful thing that has ever existed—"you're the man I love."

The words knock the wind from his lungs. It shakes away the cobwebs that have woven through his blood and places a solid foundation back beneath his feet. Maybe being loved is to be seen—really seen—for who you are, even in the moments you can't see yourself.

He clears the emotion from his throat. "You forgot luckiest bastard alive."

"And pain in our ass," Muffin adds.

"Speak for yourself, little shit," Ayc says, a smile crawling onto his lips.

Muffin playfully smacks him on the back of his head with their tail. This time, they are better at controlling the force. It makes Ayc laugh.

Relief flutters through Lora's face. Her shoulders relax as she drops her hand, as though his laughter has undone her worry. "Do you think Lahlis ever sits around brooding, wondering if his Dom Vari blood makes him evil, or do you think he's too busy being evil?"

Ayc snorts. "All right, all right, I'm done brooding. You've made your point. I feel better now."

Mostly, at least. The thought of being Lahlis's son is still unsettling. The idea that he has at least three siblings he knew nothing about before a few weeks ago is strange. And he can't even begin to think about how his grandmother is a queen. It's all an unfamiliar ocean, but the reminder of her love has anchored him.

"Good." Her lips tug playfully, and she slips her hand down her thigh, into the slit of her dress. He follows the movement, wondering whether she's reaching for her dagger or something else. They are both very interesting possibilities. "Would you like to talk some more, or would you like to play?"

The teasing tug of her lips and the slight emphasis she places on play has Ayc certain that whatever she has in mind, he's going to like it very, very much. A pulse of anticipation thrums through his cock, awakening him.

"Muffin, find somewhere else to be," Ayc says, but the dragon is already on their feet, scrambling to the opposite side of the hall. Ayc calls upon his shadow affinity to open the doors. The dragon has barely escaped when Ayc pulls the door closed again. The boom settles, and Ayc offers his reply.

"What did you have in mind, my lady?"

There's a soft sigh of metal, and she pulls her dagger from the slit of her dress. It gleams in the moonlight as she holds it between her hands, spinning the tip around the pad of her finger, enough that the flesh gives but not enough that it breaks.

His cock jerks. Fuck.

"It involves my dagger," she says, with her wicked smile. "You told me you dreamed about it." She sets the flat of the blade against his arm, gliding it up slowly. His nerves sing beneath his coat sleeve. "Would you like to experience it for real?"

His jaw locks in anticipation. His voice falls to a growl. "Fuck, yes."

She continues the slow climb with the knife, turning the tip to trace along his shoulder, his collarbone. He can sense the sharpness, even beneath his armor, and every muscle coils not with fear but desire. "Tell me if I do something you don't like, and I'll stop," she whispers softly.

"I promise you, if you do it, I'll like it."

She lifts the tip of the knife to the bottom of his chin. The sharpness whispers against his flesh but doesn't break. Doesn't hurt, but promises danger. States that his life is in her hands. That she owns him completely. It brings back so many memories of him pinned against the wall when he tried to convince himself he hated her, even when he drank up the nearness of her.

She drags the dagger slowly through the stubble of his jaw, her eyes turning a silver that matches her blade. Fuck. He is fully hard now, his cock straining, begging to be free.

"Do you love me?" she asks.

His breath is becoming pants, so great is his hunger, but he manages. "Yes."

"Then get on your knees."

His smile is wide enough that it hurts as he slides from the step he sits on toward the floor of the great hall. She keeps the knife carefully trained beneath his chin as he lowers himself to his knees.

She turns the blade, flattening it against his chin, the tip against his throat. She stands, drawing his head with her so that he has no choice but to drink in her lithe movement, the expanse of her legs, the way her hair spills over her abundant breasts.

"Stay," she commands. "Don't say a word."

He presses his mouth closed as she removes the cool silver from his throat and backs slowly away from him, up the stairs, back toward her throne. She lowers herself on the edge of the throne, letting the skirt fall so that all of her legs are bare, an expanse of thick flesh and smooth skin he wants to devour. She lifts her chin, the crown on her head blinking in the moonlight. Her eyes tinge with silver as she looks down upon him.

He drops his hands between his knees and lowers his head, going deep into his bow. He is her devoted. Her supplicant. He will worship her forever.

His glorious, wicked queen.

She beckons him with the knife. "Crawl to me."

LORA

He doesn't just crawl. He prowls. His red eyes glow in the darkness, like a creature of the night, as he moves on his hands and knees up the stairs, trained upon her like she's his prey. The shadows swirl around him like they are made alive by his power. Like he is so lost in her, he can't control his affinity, and all she is doing is sitting here.

He's magnificent, and he's hers.

Fucking *hers*.

When he reaches her, he sits back on his heels, resuming the supplicant position at her feet. She gently caresses the knife over his chin. He doesn't flinch. Instead, he makes a sound—something between a growl and a groan. She feels the noise like a stroke to her cunt, the one that is already wet and needy for him. Fuck, she loves the control he's giving her.

"You look so pretty," she says. "On your knees for me."

She doesn't know what is coming over her. She's never been like this with anyone else, but the way his eyes flash when she dominates him makes her ache even more. With others, she felt she had to make herself feel small. But he doesn't just accept her powerful and ruthless side; he revels in it.

"Do you want to worship me?" she asks.

"Yes." He dares to rest his hands on her knees, pressing her legs further apart. His eyes drink in the skin of her thighs, where her underwear peaks out from the slits of the dress.

She slides her free hand into his hair and pulls his head back so he's looking into her eyes, pressing the knife against his skin, careful not to cut him. She knows it hurts, just a little, but he fucking grins.

"*Beg* me for it," she says through her teeth.

"Please." He can't move his head, but he slides his hands higher on her thighs, and she spreads for him. "Please, my queen. I beg you. I'll say anything. *Do* anything you want. Just let me worship you like the goddess you are. Let me taste you again. Let me make you come."

She's already throbbing, aching. How did she go so many years without his mouth upon her? Now, it's only been a handful of hours, and yet she craves him like she needs her next meal.

She releases his hair but glides the knife so the tip rests against the nape of his neck, allowing him freedom to move toward her. He grasps the front panel of her skirt and tosses it aside. His hands slip beneath her ass, palming handfuls of her thick flesh. She lifts her hips. He drags her underwear down her body and tosses them over his shoulder. She drapes her legs over the arms of the throne and tilts her pelvis upward, offering herself up to him like an altar. She pushes the knife against the back of his neck to guide him forward. He hisses, and for a moment, she fears she's cut him, but then his mouth is on her, and she thinks of nothing. Nothing but the warmth of his tongue as it glides through her center.

"Command me," he says, each word snuck between long, languid sweeps of his tongue.

She can barely talk, barely think, barely manage to keep her knife trained upon him without cutting him.

Then he pulls back, scattering kisses on her lower belly, ignoring her growl of frustration. "Tell me exactly what you want."

She seizes his hair and guides him back to her pussy, and grinds against his mouth. "Do not fucking stop."

He moans, his fingers digging into the flesh of her thighs. The tip of his tongue circles the area where she needs it most, and she hisses out a *Yeesss*. "Just like that. Swirl your tongue around my clit. Faster."

He obliges, working over her bundle of nerves with increased speed. Pleasure ripples through every muscle of her body, so intense she feels as though she's losing herself to it, until it's the only thing in existence. But she needs more.

"Suck me into your mouth. I want— *Fuuuckkk!*"

She arches backward and seizes the back of her throne as he obeys. The pressure is exquisite. She's floating through clouds of pleasure as he drives her closer to release, right here on this throne that was once her grandfather's and then her mother's. And now it's fucking hers. This throne has never felt fully hers. Until now, as he worships her upon it.

Fabric rustles and a buckle jingles. She opens her eyes, but she can see nothing more than his glowing red eyes as he locks around her pussy. But she knows he's wrestling with his armor to free himself. He doesn't slow his attentions. He can't. She's holding the knife so close to his neck he can't retreat. She might be suffocating him, might be drowning him, but he moans, the deep noise vibrating against her. She hears the glide of flesh against flesh as he takes himself in his hand like he's trying to find some relief.

She locks eyes with him. "Are you going to come too? Is that how much you like it when I fuck your face with my knife at your neck?"

He releases another groan and nips at her clit before swirling his tongue again. Faster, applying more pressure.

"Just like that," she groans. "Now put your fingers inside me. Fuck me hard."

Rings ping against the floor, a sound that will never not make her skin buzz with anticipation. She peers down to watch his painted fingertips crawl along her thigh before disappearing within her. He plunges in two fingers, immediately finding that spot deep within her.

"So fucking obedient," she says, her voice nearly a whine now. She rocks against him, finding a rhythm with the movement of his mouth that makes the pleasure climb even higher. "Divine, you're so fucking obedient."

He picks up an unforgiving pace, both with his mouth and with his hand. Her legs quiver. Her hands shake. She's about to lose control. She tosses the knife aside, no longer trusting herself not to injure him. It lands on stone and glides across it. She seizes his hair instead, using it to hold him steady as she chases her pleasure toward that pinnacle. Higher. Faster. He never relents. More words come from her mouth, nonsensical now, losing all command. *Yes.* And *please.* And *oh, divine.* And *good boy. My good fucking boy.*

The orgasm slams through her like a tidal wave. She nearly drowns in it, so strong she can't breathe, can't scream, can only cling to him and to the top of her throne to ground her to the earth.

He slows but continues to taste her. Her hips jerk at each pass over her clit, but he continues like he means to make her clean, to drink her up entirely. "Fuck," he growls. "I'm never going to get enough of you."

She tugs at his hair to pull him upward. He covers her body with his own, finds her mouth. The mix of her tang and the sweetness of him might just be her new favorite taste. His cock presses against her stomach, and she reaches between them and works her fingers over the soft skin of his hard shaft. She teases her fingers over the head, finding it already wet.

He swears again. "I thought I told you if you kept teasing me, I was going to fuck you over your throne."

"So you said," she says, giving him an inviting smile. "How disappointing that you are all talk and no act—"

Her words disappear into a shriek that swiftly turns into a laugh of delight as he grabs her wrist and yanks her to her feet. Just as quickly, he spins her around, crushing her back to his chest. His hand clamps down on her lips to silence her. Just like that, the power has switched control. Now, it's his turn.

He so easily surrenders to her that it takes her by surprise, the strength of him, the fierceness. It shouldn't. Submission is another form of strength, a sign of unshakable trust. Her body relaxes against his chest, ready to embrace this role as well. There's freedom in control, and there's freedom in surrender. With him, she finds she likes *both* just as well.

"Shh," he says, lifting his hands from her mouth. His chest rumbles against her spine, his breath tickling her neck with barely withheld laughter. "If you scream too loudly, your guards are going to think I'm harming you and come in here. Even though"—he closes his teeth around where her pulse still beats erratically, and she moans at the sharpness against her skin—"I do like making you scream."

"Ayc," Lora sighs, pushing her hips backward to grind against his cock, eliciting yet another curse. The fabric of her dress separates them, and she reaches upward to work the straps off her shoulders. He helps glide it down her hips. When it lands at her feet, she kicks it aside.

She's utterly bare in the great hall. She feels everything, and for once, she wants to. The texture of his leather armor against her spine, his hard shaft pressing against her ass, his hands squeezing both her breasts as she arches her head backward.

His palm releases her breath to cup the back of her neck. He bends her forward. Her hands slap the back of her throne. He rakes a hand down her spine, over the curve of her ass, dipping into the seam of her body. He stops to roll a thumb around the tight little hole, and she gasps. He's not touched her there yet.

"Has anyone fucked you here?" he asks.

Her skin, all the way to her scalp, pricks at the thought. She shakes her head. Once, a classmate played with the tight ring as she worked her tongue over Lora's clit. Once the initial pressure eased, the pleasure was different and interesting and good, but Lora struggled to shut off her head, her thoughts, her worries. So she gave up, pushed her classmate on her back, aligned their cunts, and fucked them both to completion.

She's been curious, but she's never tried again. A shocking number of men don't know how to warm up a pussy properly before wanting to sink their dick in. She didn't trust them to properly prepare her ass. And Wylder... It never felt right. But it feels right with Ayc. Everything feels right with Ayc. She trusts that he'll make it good for her. So fucking good.

When he asks, "Would you want that?" she nods.

"I fucking want that. Not today, but someday. I want everything with you."

"Fuck, I love how greedy you are for me." He groans as he reaches between them and aligns the head of his cock with her entrance, and slips inside. She drops her forehead onto her bicep as she stretches around him, biting her lip to hold back a whimper.

"I love how you fit around me so well," he praises. "I was made to fill you up."

As he takes control of their pleasure, he's an intoxicating mix of brutality and tenderness. He wraps his hand around her hair to hold her steady, never hard enough to damage her curls, and drives into her with a rhythm that leaves her panting and her toes curling with every thrust, her breasts swaying beneath her. His other hand caresses down her spine, digs into her hipbone to change the angle of her pelvis so his every movement glides against where she needs him. His shadows join in, and she's still certain he doesn't mean to, that they are driven by his intentions and desires. They tease up her body, swirling around her breasts like cool fingertips. Fuck, she can feel him everywhere.

Well, almost everywhere.

He murmurs sweet praises that rapidly take on a keening edge that tells her he won't last long, and even that makes her feel powerful.

He releases her hair and wraps his arm around her, pressing her back against his chest. The change in position offers a new angle within her, and she moans. He's built her up so fast; she's trembling, but she needs more. And as though he can sense it, he trails his hand upward, past her sternum, until his palm rests over the column of her neck. He doesn't squeeze, only embraces her throat. Waiting.

Fuck. She arches her head toward his shoulder. He deepens his thrusts, and she rises onto her toes with each one.

"Touch yourself," he commands against her ear. "Play with your needy clit."

She slips one hand between her legs and strokes, finding the same swirling motion he worked with his tongue. His shadows still work at her breast, giving her the stimulation she needs. Almost there. She's almost there.

She lays her free hand over his, the one that covers her throat. She presses in with her fingertips so his fingers clamp down on her pulse. He applies the pressure she cues him to give, no more, no less, and the surge of power—the feeling of being completely in control and completely out of control—flings her over the final edge. She sobs out her release, her knees nearly buckling. He holds onto her as her world explodes with stars.

She's too lost to know for sure what happens next. One moment, she's soaring in her pleasure. The next, she's seated on her throne once more, sprawled onto her back, her ass hanging off the edge as he thrusts within her once more. He's lost all rhythm, his hands clinging to the gryphon's wings that make up the back of the throne. She drinks in the cords that stand out in his neck and the shades of crimson that war in his eyes as he studies her beneath him. Their flesh grinds together, and he's keening, growling, swearing, whimpering, a series of nonsense that ends with the roar of her name as he slams deep within her one final time.

"Lora!"

He sags against the throne, gasping for breath. She disentangles from him and stands long enough to push him gently into her throne before crawling back into his lap, her feet tucked between him and the arm of her chair. He holds her tightly, sprinkles reverent kisses on her knuckles as he folds their hands together.

"I need to get something to clean you up," he says.

"In a minute." She nuzzles into his neck, breathing in the smell of him, reveling in the unsteadiness of his breath. A strange feeling flutters in her heart. A lightness, an ease. It's reminiscent of a day when she was a child, running with Veni through the streets of Avia in the middle of a perfect summer, when his mother wasn't sick and her father was still there to yell at them to not go too far.

It's a beautiful feeling, here in Ayc's arms.

She thinks it's called peace.

FIFTY-SIX

AYC

The Stella Rune mountains hold a beauty that Ayc has previously thought only belonged to the towering trees of the Forest of Elodie. He's seen the mountains from a distance—flying in airships, from his time in Noxumbra, from a building in Totus Omni territory where a space in the trees allows for just a glimpse of the peaks. They've looked like tall, majestic guardians, hovering over the earth like they mean to protect it. But those views have paled in comparison to being in the mountains, staring above at the alpine forests that give way to cottony clouds and occasionally glimpses of snow-capped peaks.

The Lycendi people who live in villages built on the mountainside are hardy people, born and living in air that has Ayc gasping for breath with the least exertion. They are welcoming and intelligent and kind. But the time he spends in their village still does not adequately prepare him when he visits Splendor.

The university is suspended on an island of earth that hovers over a lake that stretches so far he can't quite see the other side when standing on its edge. Splendor's twisted turrets, made of black granite, reach toward the peaks that surround them on almost all sides.

Lora and her Five are led on a tour of the school and the famous museum. It takes hours to traverse through all the displays: history, science, strange artifacts. A large fossil of the dragon is suspended on the ceiling, and Ayc is grateful that Muffin and Tempest went off soaring together to find dinner. It's not the only bones on display. There's a small adult fae who was discovered in a bog pit, nearly perfectly preserved, and an entire skeleton of a giant. Ayc doesn't look at either for long. He doesn't know why, but the sight of it makes him sad.

He mainly spends half the time watching Xylie's eyes light up as she explores and half the time pretending he isn't looking at Lora. Pretending he doesn't ache for her so greatly, he feels like he might come out of his skin. He hasn't gotten more than a few fleeting moments with her since they left Wyntra. He's surviving off longing looks and the brush of her pinky finger against his knuckles as she walks by him.

He's certain that the Five, at least, know about him and Lora. Bronwen certainly does. And Xylie's side glances and Tavish's smiles suggest they know, too. But no one has asked, and Lora hasn't wanted to tell. He certainly understands why she wants to keep things professional as they visit and travel. He could scream for the world to hear that he's the luckiest bastard alive to get the honor of touching her, but also, it's ultimately no one's fucking business.

What they've carved out for each other in those few days at Wyntra has been sacred, holy. It's as fun as it is sexy, as tender as it is rough. In those hours after their duties are done, they belong only to each other. They laugh and they banter and they fuck. And it's so fucking good. It's worth being protected.

So he's been good. He has behaved. He doesn't pull her behind a tapestry just so he can taste her lips for even a heartbeat, like a dying man licking the dew from a flower because he's so thirsty. They will be back to Wyntra in a few days.

But first, they are going to see the dwarves, which means tomorrow, they are venturing *under* the mountain.

The thought makes a shiver run down his spine, or perhaps

that's just the skeleton of the giant, who, from this angle, looks like they might be a little sad, too.

The carriage bumps along the narrow mountain pass that weaves deep into the heart of the Stella Rune mountains. Ayc feels every rock in his aching back, despite the feather Tempest gave him and the pain tonic Reselda—who sits beside him—slipped him an hour ago. It feels like someone is shaking his body, and he tightens with every jostle. Even Tavish and Xylie look uncomfortable. Tavish cringes, and Xylie has set the book she was reading aloud—a book on dwarven culture—aside. Luckily, she was nearly finished, and Ayc has somehow gotten his brain to listen to most of what it said, so he feels prepared.

There are many entrances to the passages and caves deep within the Stella Rune mountains that house the dwarven kingdom, but the dwarves keep them secret, so they are headed for the main entrance, Heimat. As Ayc arches his back to stretch the muscles, trying to find relief, he hopes they get there soon.

Xylie rubs her hands up and down her legs. Ayc might have thought it simply to ease the ache from how long she's been sitting. His own ass is numb. But he recognizes it as one of her stims.

"You all right, Xy?" Ayc asks.

Xylie signs, *"I wish we weren't going. The stories about lies in the depths of Heimat…"* She stops. Shivers.

The chapter in the book that explored the religion of the dwarves stated that they were mostly atheists. But their lore went deep. They believed that something evil lived in the depths of their mountains. Once, children went missing at night. Screams could be heard echoing in the bottomless abyss. Supposedly, decades ago, many great dwarves gave their lives to trap the evil behind a gate infused with magic. The book states they keep a guard upon that gate even to this day. Ayc isn't sure why they would bother to guard a gate for centuries if there wasn't some truth, some residual fear.

"I fear what lies in the dark down there," she says.

"The shadows and I are friends," Ayc says. To prove his point, he swirls a finger, and a bit of the shadow at Saga's front paws rises to dance around his fingertip. It's getting easier to control. He barely feels the cost of this intentional display. And the unintentional displays, the creative ways magic has come into play when he's lost inside Lora's body, are things he hardly notices in the moment. They leave him exhausted but don't harm him. Nothing an hour or two of blissed-out sleep can't fix.

Xylie only rolls her eyes.

"It's just two days," Tavish reassures. "It'll be all right."

She sinks more heavily into her seat with a sigh. Her fear makes him uneasy, but he forces himself to shake his head. Everything will be fine…as soon as they get out of this damn carriage.

The carriage driver commands the horses to stop, and the carriage stills. Reselda lets out a breath. "Thank the divine."

Ayc slides the window back. The great wall of a mountain rises above them, and a door is carved into it, so large that the cluster of people who wait before it seems small in comparison.

"Here," he says with a grin.

Anxiety gives way to excitement. Someplace few Everadyn have ventured to go. Xylie exhales through her nose. Saga's tail thumps on the floor of the carriage while Ayc slides out. In the scattering of attendants and guards rushing to position, he instinctively searches for Lora. She's sliding off her horse gracefully, handing off her reins, and she turns her head, searching too. She finds him looking. Smiles. Not a smile she gives others, feigned and practiced. A smile that shows in her glistening eyes more than her lips. A smile that is all his.

His chest aches. Fuck. Just four more days. If he were better at math, he might count the hours, too.

Wings snap against the air above them a moment before

Muffin lands with a spray of rocks and a trembling of the earth. They nearly tip forward onto their face but right themself with a flare of their wings. The poor horses shy and neigh, still unable to get used to the creature, to turn off their natural instincts that they are prey.

Tempest lands beside Muffin much more gracefully and snaps her beak in a reprimand. Muffin has come so far in such a short amount of time, able to keep up with them in the air instead of having to rely on the wagon—tremendous progress from even a week ago. But they've undergone another growth spurt, taller than Tempest now when they extend their neck, and it's brought another bout of clumsiness.

The journey to Drakr is rapidly approaching, and Muffin wants to go. They're determined to be able to make the long flight. Ayc hasn't decided whether or not to let them, unsure whether taking them into the midst of an untold number of dragons is a good idea.

"Do you think anyone saw that?" Muffin asks, glancing around.

"No," Ayc says, though, by the way the dwarves are pointing, they definitely did. *"They're too busy looking at how pretty I am."*

Muffin snorts. The breath coils before his nose, but Ayc can feel how cold it is, even from this distance. *"You're such a fucking liar."*

"That they're not looking or that I'm pretty?"

"Both."

Ayc shakes his head as he walks away to join where Lora and the other Five have gathered. As soon as he's there, Lora turns on her heel, purposefully not looking at him again, and starts toward where the welcoming party is waiting.

The dwarves are all short in height but broad. They wear plain tunics with short sleeves that show arms decorated in ink. Each one of them holds at least one, decorating their skin that ranges from the paleness of marble to the depth of onyx. There are images of mountains, colorful galaxies, and spiraling white patterns. They are beautiful and unique, the way they've turned themselves into works of art.

A masculine-appearing dwarf walks forward. He wears his black beard all the way to the bottom of his sternum and laugh lines around his eyes. Both of his arms are so covered in black ink, only artful peeks of peach show through to give the patterns depth. Ayc can't quite make out what all the pictures are, but the result is striking.

"Welcome!" he booms. "I'm Orn, the minister of the Stella Rune dwarves. Such an honor to have you."

"He tells no lies," says another dwarf, stepping forward, a smile on his face.

Ayc recognizes him immediately.

"Ah, yes." Orn slaps a hand down on Candor's shoulder. "I've heard you've already met my brother."

LORA

"Does your brother know about your...hobbies?" Lora asks as she walks with Candor down one of the streets of Heimat. The city is carved out of the mountains, the shops on either side made from the very stone the way the Totus Omni houses are carved from the trees. Through some feat of alchemy or engineering, they've strung lights along the tunnel, and as the day has progressed, the lights have dimmed to mimic the fading of the sun, so now there are only lanterns and the soft orange glow from a few shop windows.

"Yes," Candor says with a soft chuckle. "He's never understood why I prefer the sea to being in the earth, but he understands why I do it. Justice and equity are values that run deep in any true dwarf's heart."

Lora has never known a dwarf well enough. She regrets that now. Fennix—her mother's First—is the closest she has ever come to one. He boasted about his dwarf blood, but it was distant. And he could not be more different than the dwarves she has met today.

Lora looks around her, studying the artwork painted on the tunnel wall, hearing the laughter that drifts from the shops. "It's beautiful here."

And not just the architecture. All day, she's gone through the shops, taking the same tour she's been given by most of the clans, but her gold has been nearly useless here. Instead, they trade. Loaves of sourdough for books, spools of yarn for eggs, trinkets for time volunteered. Totus Omni exchange things at times, but this is an entire system made entirely without money holding so much power. Everyone does what they can for the community—attending to the greenhouses, caring for their herds of mountain goats on the slopes just outside, and looking after the children as they gather them all together, from babes to teenagers.

It's a beautiful, simple life. She can't help but feel the choice to keep dwarves distant, for Everadyn to be allies on good terms but never close, was intentional from the previous Sovereigns. After all, if someone could see the way they lived, they might question how their own country does things. It matches nothing of what she's been told, of the jokes about dwarves that passed around her classmates. If not for the books she has read, the education she has received, she would not have known.

"Thank you." Candor's eyes crinkle when he smiles. "It's a quiet life here under the mountains, but it's a good one." He wiggles his eyebrows. "So long as the thing in the deep stays locked away."

"Enough of that now," Orn says, coming from a cross-section of tunnel. His voice echoes. He only has one volume, and that is loud.

Lora is grateful for the ear cuffs Ayc gave her. She feared they would harm her awareness, her need to be on guard, but it hasn't rid her of all noise. It's filtered them, lowering the loudest and turning off the everyday noises that she was always too aware of —the way that lights buzz or clothes rustle. She's felt far less frazzled during the tours and the crowds and the parties. It's amazing what a difference it makes to allow herself the freedom of attending to her own needs and to accept accommodations. It makes the world a friendlier place.

Orn slaps a hand on Candor's shoulder. "I leave you alone with our guest for ten minutes, and already, you're trying to frighten her with our lore."

"Is there truth to it then?" Lora asks, recalling the books she read in preparation for the visit. "Is there evil locked away in the deep?"

"Oh, it's true," Candor replies. "There's a gate at the lowest level where we still station some of our best warriors. No one alive truly recalls what is in there."

"But you're certain it still lives?"

"Sometimes, guards hear the darkness calling their name."

Lora shivers and quickly changes the subject. "Where did Ayc and Bronwen run off to?"

Xylie, who has been jittery during the visit, wanted to go to the quarters not long after the arrival. Tavish volunteered to go with her. Peregrin accompanied Tempest and Muffin outside on their hunt—something they could have been trusted to do on their own, but Lora thinks Peregrin might be a bit claustrophobic. It left her, Bronwen, and Ayc to explore the streets on their own, accompanied by Shae and Veni, who kept to her shoulder, as well as a scattering of other guards. At some point, they separated, Orn leading Bronwen and Ayc to something that he swore they would like while Lora was still browsing books. Logically, she knew she didn't have time to read them, but she wanted to buy them all. She forced herself to choose only two from dwarven authors she's never heard of. Candor haggled for her and agreed he would help repair a bookshelf before he left back to sea.

"They ventured into Fjola's shop," Orn says. "I think they both mean to get a tattoo."

"Oh, no," Lora says.

"Fjola is a wonderful tattoo artist," Candor reassures.

"I'm certain. I have no fear of the artist's talents. Only of my Fifth's tastes."

If Ayc tattoos her name on his ass or something ridiculous, she's going to strangle him. Except he *likes* that. Fuck. She needs to come up with new threats.

Even at the thought, her lips tick upward in a smile that she swiftly suppresses. Her smiles have seemed easier lately, her heart lighter. And Ayc is absolutely to blame.

"I wouldn't worry too much," Orn says. "Every scar and tattoo tells a story. At least tattoos are a story you choose to tell. Even if it's a funny story."

"Speak for yourself," Candor says. "You're the one with a billy goat on your rump."

"Show some damn respect, you ass. You know full well that his name was Surehoof, and I fucking loved that goat."

"Rest in peace, Surehoof," Lora murmurs.

The brothers throw their heads back and laugh.

Fifteen minutes later, Lora is seated in the minister's office. It's a room built at the very end of the main tunnel, with plush couches and armchairs set facing each other and a roaring fireplace to banish the chill. There's a sign in the window that reads:

Come the fuck in.
Everyone is always welcome.

When they first walk in, Orn flips the sign around to the other side, which reads:

Even the wicked must rest sometimes.
Be glad to hear from you tomorrow.

"Do you smoke a pipe?" Orn asks as Lora settles into one of the sofas.

Lora can't lie, not with Candor in the room, but she finds she doesn't want to. Orn is already headed for the fireplace, taking down a box and pulling a pipe from it.

She nods. "Sometimes. I get migraines."

"Ah. Do you have one now?"

She shakes her head.

"We can pretend," says Candor, flopping down in an armchair.

Lora gestures for Veni and Shae to have a seat. They hesitate.

"You can protect me just as easily sitting as you can standing."

Veni and Shae finally sit, but they perch at the edge of the couch. Orn presses a pipe into Lora's hands, and she fits it between her lips. She would never have considered smoking in front of any of the other regents, but Orn has put her more at ease within a few hours than any of the regents have with years of knowing. Besides, she's forging a friendship, and there's nothing that bonds people better than sharing a pipe.

Orn discusses his latest project—the development of further housing to address overcrowding. Candor speaks of his crew and how they are faring. There's no talk of weather or idle conversation, just what they are passionate about. Lora finds that conversation much easier, and as the smoke makes her body relax and her mind less active, she finds herself talking, too. About her frustrations with the regents, about their unwillingness to break the treaty, about how she wished Everadyn was more like the dwarven society.

"Change is hard," Orn says. "And it takes time. We are a much smaller kingdom than yours, and our history is full of the blood we spilled to get here. Sometimes, it takes time...and the heads of a few greedy people on pikes."

Lora snorts. "Don't tempt me."

"Know this." Orn leans forward in his chair. "You are the first Sovereign in Everadyn who has taken the time, the effort to see the dwarves of Stella Rune. That will not be forgotten. When the time comes for you to take up sword and axe for Aluina, I will be at your side, and I will ask for volunteers to do the same."

A swell of emotions rises up. She came here prepared to bargain, to draw up new treaties, to pass aid for aid. But Orn has offered it freely. She swallows, ensuring her voice is steady before she speaks again. "Thank you. I know it is not your battle."

"On the contrary," Candor disagrees. "I think if there is a wound in the world, it's everyone's responsibility to heal it. If left alone, it festers. The infection spreads until no place in the world is immune to it. No one is free until everyone is free."

When Lora leaves the office, she leaves richer, not from any monetary gain but from the knowledge that she has allies. True allies. The fuzziness of the pipe lingers in her head as she ascends the stairs up to the visitor's room they have been given, a round cavern built with a series of rooms—though regrettably not enough for Lora to have her own.

A small fire glows in the center. Tavish sits by it, switching between strumming on his lute and throwing a ball for Saga. The tune he plays is happy, a romantic ballad. A smile dances upon his lips. Candor slipped a letter from Calliope to him earlier. Lora makes a note to herself to find a way for Tavish to meet up with her again. She knows all too well how it feels to miss someone you love.

Bronwen sits cross-legged on a wooden chair near the flames, looking down at her arm.

"Did you get your tattoo?" Lora asks.

Bronwen extends her arm. Several blue tiger lilies wind around her arm, connected by swirls of blue that remind Lora of Bronwen's magic. It's very Bronwen, but also, perhaps, it's a tribute to Ryker. He always surprised Bronwen with a lily before a difficult day—a test or challenge or just when her sadness crept up on her. No one ever knew where he got them because the weather in Adamant was not temperate enough for the lilies to grow there. Somehow, he found a way.

"I love it," Lora says.

"Me too," Bronwen says.

Lora waits in case Bronwen wants to say more, in case she wants to tell the story behind her choosing this particular permanent scar. She doesn't. So Lora asks, "What did Ayc get?"

"He got 'villainess' written on his ass."

"He didn't!" Lora exclaims much too loudly. She slaps a hand over her lips.

Bronwen laughs, and Tavish breaks off playing, pressing his knuckles to his lips to hold in his own laugh. Fuck. Tavish definitely knows.

"No, he didn't," Bronwen says. "But you should see the look on your face."

"Bitch," Lora hisses as she marches toward her room.

Bronwen playfully flips her off, and Lora tosses the same signal back.

Lora opens the door to her room, perhaps a bit too loudly because Xylie is sleeping in one of the three beds. Her back rolls toward Lora, her breaths rising and falling steadily. Lora closes the door, Shae and Veni stationing themselves outside. She crosses to her bed and sits down on a quilt that looks like a dwarf who really loves yellow made it. Something crinkles. She stands, rolls back the covers, and picks up the blanket. On the bed is a scrap of parchment. She brings it closer to read the scrolled words.

I miss you.
Meet me here?

Ayc

Below his signature is a scrawled map—a series of tunnels, and there is an X marked on the spot. A smile grows on her lips. He's found a place for privacy. And just like that, she couldn't sleep if she tried.

She reverses course, back out the door. She flashes Veni and Shae the letter, and just to be certain, she bends to whisper in Bronwen's ear that she'll be back in a bit and not to wait up. Bronwen catches sight of the note and doesn't bother hiding her smile.

As she follows the map's path, she can hear Shae softly cursing. "We should have told Irving where we're going. These damn agates don't work well underground. I don't know if it's the stone or all the magic that makes this place work."

Lora isn't concerned. Hopefully, Irving is resting before he takes his next shift, and there's no reason to wake him up only to tell him she's sneaking to some private corner like a reckless teenager. Between Ayc, Shae, Veni, and herself, there is little that could threaten them.

Still, she grows a little uneasy as the map carries her past the public areas and deeper, beneath the mountain, past the greenhouses and caverns that have been turned into warehouses. The areas have grown quiet, closed for the night, and still, the map leads her down, into undeveloped tunnels. The air grows cooler with each step, the darkness pressing down upon them. Shae calls up an orb of light and commands it to light her path.

Shivers work down Lora's spine. Something feels...wrong down here. She feels like oil is dripping down her spine, thick and sticky and leaving behind a residual sensation she wishes she could get rid of.

"Something doesn't feel right," Veni says, giving voice to Lora's thoughts. "I don't think Ayc would lead you all the way down here just for a chance to be alone."

She glances around at the empty walls and the impenetrable darkness just ahead. "You're right. It's foolish. Let's just find him so we can go."

And then someone screams further down the tunnel. A scream so shrill and panicked, it makes her blood drain from her body. She might never feel warm again because the voice is screaming her name.

"Lora!"

"Ayc!" she yells back. There's no conscious thought, only sheer panic driving her toward Ayc's screaming voice. Her booted feet pound against the stone, drowning out Veni and Shae as they yell at her to wait. She can't wait. Each note of his scream tears at her chest, threatening to tear it asunder.

He screams her name again, and she rounds a bend in the tunnel. A gate of ancient iron twisted together looms ahead of her. Signs cover every inch of the metal, offering warnings in every language.

BEWARE! EVIL LIES BEYOND THIS GATE.

Certainly, this can't be the gate which lore speaks of? If so, where are the guards?

Why the fuck is it open?

And why are Ayc's screams coming from the other side?

"LORA!"

Lora's feet move in response before she can think, aiming for the gate.

"Lora, wait!" Veni seizes her arm and hauls her away from the gate. "You can't go in there."

She tries to whip away from him, but he holds her fast. Shae positions herself between Lora and the gate, her two-handed sword already drawn.

"I can't leave him!"

The screams cut off as suddenly as they've begun. Lora tries to slide around Shae, but Veni holds her fast. When she tries to look, all she can see is a thick wall of shadow at the end. All she can feel is cold that leaves her body shaking.

"Ayc!" she cries.

And then he runs from the darkness. He's limping, clearly hurt, but he's running as though someone—or something—is chasing him.

"Hurry!" Veni yells, still fixing Lora in place.

"Move your ass, Ayc!" Shae demands.

Lora's heart stands still as he closes the distance toward her. Almost there. Almost.

And then a giant hand made of long, sharpened bones for fingers, reaches from the darkness, wraps around Ayc, and rips him back into the shadow.

FIFTY-SEVEN

AYC

"**C**ould you crunch any louder?" Ayc asks Muffin as they take the long walk from the entrance of Heimat to the visitors' cavern where they are staying.

In response, Muffin snaps down harder on the femur of whatever creature has become their meal tonight. There's still blood on their teeth, even though the bones have been picked dry.

Ayc cringes, shoving up his shields to block out their ornery laughter floating over his mind. He pulls back his sleeve to peek at his new tattoo. The silhouette of a bear strides across his wrist. He knew as soon as Bronwen asked if he wanted to get a tattoo, he'd get a bear. He lived most of his life wearing those bracelets with a bear—his people—on his wrists. It seemed only right to put them back now that he no longer wears the bracelets.

The skin is still a little red and itchy, but it's healing fast. Fjola must use a special ink to ensure the tattoo remains permanent, despite the fae and dwarf healing abilities, but Ayc loves the way it looks on his skin.

He feels a tapping against the barrier in his mind, Muffin requesting consent to speak to him. They're no longer chewing, so Ayc does.

"Is getting permanent pictures on the skin a coping mechanism I'm unaware of?" Muffin asks.

"Coping mechanism?"

"Yes. Bronwen did it to remember her friend who died."

Ayc's hand flexes at his side, recalling how tightly Bronwen held it when she got her tattoo. Not because of the physical pain, but because of the tears. There seemed to be some catharsis there, because she smiled, too, and told him funny stories that involved Ryker, Lora, and her and a few unfortunate chickens, that had them both laughing hard enough that Fjola had to pause her work.

"And you," Muffin continues, *"did it because you're refusing to face the truth."*

"The truth. About what?"

"About your father. You're pretending it doesn't bother you, but I see it creeping in the corner of your head, behind the walls where you usually put your pain."

Ayc's jaw tightens. *"I'm not pretending. I'm fine."*

Muffin snorts, and Ayc snaps their link closed. He doesn't want to think about it. He's doing just fine not thinking about his bloodline and has no desire to start now. He has so many other things he would rather be thinking about—like if he might be able to find a way to sneak into Lora's bed tonight.

When they arrive back at the cavern, Bronwen looks up from the book she's reading by the fire. She frowns and then bursts to her feet.

"Where's Lora?" she demands.

Concern flushes the warmth from his face. Muffin's own worry slams against the closed link between them.

"I haven't seen her since before our tattoos," Ayc says. "Last I saw, she was with Candor."

Bronwen's eyes widen. "She left here ten minutes ago. She said she got a note that you were meeting her."

Cold. Ayc's entire body grows cold, like the blood has drained from his body. His own shadow shifts and grows longer as fear and anger intertwine and pull on his power. Muffin lets out a growl like they feel it, too.

"What note, Bronwen?" Ayc demands.

"The one you wrote her," she says.

"*I* didn't write her a note."

Bronwen's pupils dilate with the same fear Ayc can feel in his soul. "Then who did?"

LORA

"Stay there!" Shae yells as she races through the open gate. "Veni, do not let her come through that gate!"

Veni's hold tightens, and Lora swings her elbow back into his gut. He releases her with a gasp of pain, but she makes it only a step before she slams into his magical shield. She didn't even know he had mastered that spell already. It's something taught to every guard, but it takes them years to master, given how little affinity most guards have. Yet, the transparent turquoise forms around her, locking her in place. She swings around to face him. Blood drips from his nose down onto his uniform even as he fiddles with the agate in his ear, trying to call for additional aid and cursing. Clearly, he isn't getting through.

"Let it go, Veni!" she says. "It's too much for you."

"It is," he agrees, his face screwing up in pain. "But I'll die before I let you enter that gate."

The screams change their tune from one of terror to one of a sob. "Help me, Lora! Help me!"

She wants to sob with it. Shae rushes into the deep darkness, but Lora wishes she wouldn't go. At least, not alone. She's certain she'll soon hear two people screaming. However skilled a warrior Shae is, whatever monster grabbed Ayc will require more than one person.

Lora kicks her foot against the shield. It wobbles but doesn't give. "Please, Veni. They are going to die. If we don't help them, they're both going to die."

"Better them than you."

"My life is not more important than—" Lora cuts off. The glow of Veni's magic shines off the sign on the gate. All air surges from her lungs as she catches sight of the sprig of midnight on the sign. It's a larger sprig than all the others. Impossible to miss. She was meant to find it, to understand the message. She ignored the warnings, she continued to push, and this is her consequence.

"Shae, stop!" Lora calls. "It's a trap!"

But the guard—the one who has protected her since she was a child—keeps running toward the sound of Ayc's screams. It's not him. She's certain of it now. Ayc, like Veni, would die before begging her to come help him if it meant putting her in danger. He would be telling Shae and Veni to get Lora the fuck out of there.

"No," Veni growls between his teeth, his fangs sharpening as he sees the midnight, too.

His shield dissolves, but Lora doesn't run forward. Instead, she sucks in a breath and exhales it in a scream. The loudest, most shrill scream she can manage. Shae flings herself around to look.

"Run!" Lora shrieks again, her throat raw from it. "It's not him. We have to shut the gate!"

The screaming mimicking Ayc's voice stops. It only makes Lora's heart pound harder. Whatever creature, whatever dark magic has been imprisoned here knows its game is over. Shae races back toward the gate. Lora searches the darkness behind her, expecting the giant hand to come out at any moment.

Veni rushes around Lora, grabbing hold of one side of the iron gate. He heaves on it, grunting with the effort, but it doesn't move. Lora surges forward to help him. A shock of cold, like plunging into icy water, rips through her as she passes the threshold of the gate, but she locks her teeth and grabs ahold of the gate. Even with their combined strength, the iron gate refuses to move.

Shae reaches them and grabs hold. Finally, the gate begins to move. It scrapes against the stone, the sound of iron against granite echoing through the tunnel. Much too slowly. Lora searches the thick darkness, her muscles coiled, her stomach clenched, expecting a monster to appear at any moment. It doesn't come, and they slam the gate closed. Shae throws down the latch.

"Do you think closing it restored the magic to keep it closed?" Lora asks, gasping for a breath.

A wheezy sound rises in the air, so contorted and echoing that it takes her a moment to realize what she's hearing. The hair on her arms stands on end. It's laughter. Not coming from behind the gate but from behind all three of them.

The three spin around as one. Lora draws her sword. Veni hauls his crossbow off his back.

A human-like face as large as Lora is tall looms out of the shadows at the end of the tunnel. Thin skin pulls across bones that are too long, angled too sharply toward a pointed jaw. Only slits in the skin sit where the nose should be, and no lips cover the teeth, leaving the long, decayed points fitted in a permanent smile. The too-round eyes bear no pupil, no iris, only a milky white that is still, undoubtedly, looking straight at them.

It creeps forward, its massive body on all fours. It walks on its wrist bones, the skeleton hands bent backward. Its knees are drawn up as it perches on its back toes. Its body is hollowed out, only bone in some places, thin skin dangling loose in others. Lora's breath grows colder with each of its steps. She feels like a child, terrified of the dark, an inexplicable terror she could not shake. But she was right to fear the dark if these are the things that sometimes lurk in it.

It's an evil she's never seen before, and it has been unleashed on the dwarves because someone wants her dead.

It laughs again, teeth parting to let out the sound.

"Lora," it says, and it's Ayc's voice it mocks her with.

"Fuckfuckfuckfuckfuck," Veni mutters.

He pulls the crossbow's trigger. The bolt slams into its forehead and embeds. It roars, but not in pain. In rage. Its breath reeks of decay, and a tattooed arm, still full of flesh, is stuck between its back molars. So that is what became of the guards.

What will become of this city if she does not stop it?

It reaches out with its skeletal hand, grabbing at Lora with fingers as sharp as a bone sword. Shae launches herself in front of Lora and brings her sword down upon its fingertips. The sword severs the first two fingers.

And the beast only laughs as they swiftly grow back.

Shae strikes again, and Veni loads another bolt, but Lora sheathes her swords and spins to the gate. She unlatches it and thrusts her entire weight upon it. It gives more easily this way, pushing through the grooves they created in the stone. Still, it's slow.

Veni's crossbow twangs again. Shae's sword slashes in the air. It doesn't matter. Like the wraiths who could be blown apart and still live, Lora is certain this thing can't be killed. If it could be, the dwarves would have done so centuries ago.

"Help me, Veni!" Lora calls. "We have to trap it. It's our only hope."

Veni leans his back against the iron as he loads another bolt. His weight makes it swing more quickly, and soon, it's back to where it was when the creature escaped.

Shae shrieks in pain. Lora turns back to find blood streaming from her shoulder. One of the beast's fingers has punctured through. Her sword drops from her hand, the severed arm too weak to hold it. The beast laughs as it drags her forward. She grabs a knife off her belt and stabs at the hand, but she's not strong enough to free herself.

"Stay back!" Veni orders Lora. He drops his crossbow, grabs his sword, and flings himself forward. He's nearly there when the beast flicks its wrist and sends Shae flying.

Lora screams as Shae's body impacts the stone wall.

Veni roars in rage as he severs the beast's wrist. This time, its cry sounds like pain. It doesn't bleed but swings the arm bone at Veni. Veni parries it like he might a sword as Lora stoops to pick up his abandoned crossbow. The crossbow has never been her strength, but she's grateful that Adamant forced herself to train with every weapon. She pulls one of the bolts from where it's strapped to the handle and begins to load it, glancing up at Veni. The beast's hand is slowly growing back, but Veni slices through its fingers as they grow. Shae lies on the ground, not moving.

The beast rears back on its knees and seizes Veni with its other hand, pinning his arms to his side. He lifts him toward his face, toward his teeth. Lora raises the crossbow and fires. It misses the eye she aimed for and slams into the slit of his nose instead. It snarls in agony.

"Drop him, bitch!" Lora calls. "I'm the one you want."

"Lora!" Veni growls, but the beast drops him like a ragdoll. His knees buckle beneath him as he hits the ground. He shrieks in pain. The beast looks down upon him as though sensing he's wounded, reconsidering who its next meal should be, like it's a predator and he's found helpless prey.

Lora knows you never run from predators. It triggers their animalistic instincts. And so, she drops the crossbow, yells "Hey!" at the top of her lungs, and runs in the other direction. The earth shudders as it picks up the chase, just as Lora predicted.

She draws her blades as she runs down the tunnel. She needs to buy time. She won't be able to close the gate again on her own. She can only hope that someone is on their way. That one of Veni's messages did get through. That the gate is equipped with alarms that have alerted the dwarves. Hope that someone will arrive soon.

She runs faster. The darkness is so thick, she can't see her own feet as they slap against the stone. Can't see the body of the fallen guard until she's tripping over it. She slams to the ground, one of her swords sliding from her grasp. She crawls forward, attempting to get over the body of the poor fallen dwarf so she can stand. The monster's hands latch around her legs like vices, the grip so hard it hurts. She can't kick, can't turn. She glances over her shoulder, and all she can see is its milky eyes and bare grin.

This is how she dies. And it makes her angry. She wants more time. More time to help her people. More time to help Aluina. And selfishly, more time with Ayc. She isn't done loving him yet.

She bellows in rage and slices blindly behind her back. She impacts bone, but not with enough force to cause the invincible creature to release her. It pulls her backward, and she scrambles for purchase on stone. Her fingernails break, but she can't hold on as it lifts her legs from the earth.

A roar shakes the tunnel, not from the creature, but a sound she's come to recognize. A dragon.

She throws her head back just as a streak of white flies through the air and slams into the creature's back.

Muffin!

Muffin's impact catapults the monster sideways, bearing Lora with it. She throws her arms to protect her face as she slams back into the ground.

The creature shrieks. Wings flap. Muffin snarls. She moves her hands to see Muffin clawing across the creature's torso, digging their talons in and shredding skin from bone as they go. Muffin reaches the arm holding Lora and sinks their teeth in. The fingers release Lora's legs, and she scrambles upward. Her legs hurt from the monster's grip, threatening to buckle beneath her, but she grits her teeth.

The monster shakes its arm, but Muffin holds on, snarling, ripping through flesh, digging into the bone. The creature draws back its other arm, ready to swing at Muffin. Lora raises her sword, preparing to lunge forward, but a ball of shadow slams into the hand and pins it against the tunnel wall.

Lora turns to the sound of feet. A crowd of people are rushing toward her—dwarves and Irving and Bronwen. But Ayc—her Ayc—runs faster than the rest, his hand outstretched to control his shadow.

"Not my dragon and not my woman, you ugly motherfucker!"

FIFTY-EIGHT

LORA

Ayc steps in between Lora and the creature. A cry of relief jumps to Lora's lips, but they are not safe yet.

"Lora, run for the gate!" Ayc commands.

She shakes her head. She won't leave him.

"Lora, move your ass! I'm not going to ar—"

He cuts off as bone cracks. Muffin tosses the severed arm aside, and the shrieking creature swings with what is left of its arm. It collides with Muffin's chest, and they slide down the tunnel on their side. Their wing bends beneath them, and their talons scrape against the stone. Bodies rush around Lora, separating her from Ayc. Someone grabs her arm—Irving, she realizes—and tugs her. But her legs refuse to obey.

She can see Ayc's arms shake as he sends more shadows to hammer the monster. He'll burn himself out again; he'll do it for her because that is how much he loves her.

Muffin, too, will get hurt. The dragon is already shoving to their feet. They've never seen battle before, never trained for this, and yet, their mouth parts. They roar. Something glows in their mouth.

"Fuck, they're going to breathe fire!" Ayc yells. "Get down."

Irving yanks Lora downward, tucking her body beneath his. A shield domes over all their heads, glowing a blue that tells her it's Bronwen providing them protection. A jet pours from Muffin's mouth, but it isn't fire. It's white, with shades of the lightest blue, glistening with its own light. Even through Bronwen's shield, Lora can feel it, burning against her skin, not with heat, but with cold—like she stuck her hand into snow. It strikes the monster's face and body and solidifies, forming around it in jagged spikes.

It takes Lora a moment to recognize what it is.

Ice.

The monster is encased in it, frozen in place, the ice wrapping from its face down to its feet, where it is latched to the stone. She doubts the ice has killed it, but surely, it would have killed any normal creature.

"Go, go, go," a voice yells. Perhaps it's Irving. Perhaps it's Peregrin. She isn't certain. "We have to close the gate!"

Hands drag her upright, shoving her forward, and this time, she goes. Her legs still ache, but she pushes past it. She glances back. Ayc and Muffin and Bronwen make up the back of the party, never fully turning from the beast.

Lora stumbles through the gate, and the others pile behind her. Irving, Davos, Orn, Candor, Peregrin, and a few dwarves she doesn't know. She holds her breath as Bronwen and Ayc make it closer. The monster begins to stir, curling one of its skeleton fingers, then another. Suddenly, it gives a shake. The ice breaks apart. Shards fly through the air, forcing Ayc and Bronwen to duck.

Muffin bursts another blast of ice, but it's weaker this time. Not enough to freeze the monster in place, just enough to make it fling up its hands, but even that fades.

"Run!" Lora calls. They have enough distance. They can make it.

This time, they listen. They turn and run, Muffin following. The evil creature trembles as though cold, and its arm hasn't fully regenerated. It limps forward. Ayc and Bronwen fling themselves through the gate. Muffin slides through it after them, nearly bowling two people over with their wings. Lora lunges for the gate and finds four other people already there. Orn and Candor, Irving and Peregrin, and Lora all tug on the metal, and the gate slides closed as the monster comes to a halt. Their face looms. They wrap a hand around the gate and pull. The latch creaks. Lora tightens her hold.

"The magic has been broken," Orn says, drawing an ax from his belt. "Bronwen, can you restore it? Use my blood. It has to be dwarven blood."

He drags the axe against his palm, opening it up. Bronwen grabs his fist and begins muttering. Static rises in the air. The iron beneath Lora's hand grows warm and vibrates. Lora clings harder as the monster yanks again. A wall of shadow rises before the gate, and the monster releases, hissing in frustration.

"Kill," it shrieks. "I will kill."

The gate shakes so hard, Lora fears it might tumble. And then it stills.

"There!" Bronwen says, sounding winded, like she's run five miles in under thirty minutes.

The shadow drops down, and the monster reappears. It swipes against the gate but screams with fury as though it hurts. Still, it presses its face close, its foggy eyeballs within inches of Lora.

"You would have tasted so pretty, my sweet."

Then it turns and slowly retreats back into the shadows it came from.

Lora gasps for breath. Her sternum aches from the way her heart has bounded against it, and she doesn't think it will beat a normal rhythm for a long, long time. She searches around her. Muffin ruffles their wings but looks utterly unharmed. The dwarves give them a wide berth, murmuring something under their breaths, a word in dwarvish she doesn't recognize. Veni sits against the stone wall, all color drained from his face, his teeth bared in pain, his leg crooked. Reselda kneels beside him, and though Lora can't find Shae through the cluster of people, that is a relief. If Shae was badly injured, Reselda would be with her, not tending to Veni's legs.

Lora finally lets herself turn to Ayc. He wipes blood from his nose with his sleeve, but he's fine, already drinking her in. His other hand fists like he's struggling to hold himself back.

Fuck it.

She flings herself toward him, throwing her arms around his neck. Her mouth finds his, and she doesn't care—doesn't fucking care—if the whole world sees. If the whole world knows. His kiss is brief, but fierce in its response, a reassurance to each other. He's alive, and somehow, so is she.

He pushes the hair away from her face, searching her over. "Are you all right?"

She nods. "I'm fine. Someone lured me down here. The gate was already open."

Orn swears. "It would have taken powerful magic and someone of dwarven blood to break through that magic. Someone powerful must want..."

He says more words. Lora can hear them, but they grow distant until they are nothing more than a murmur. Muffin has moved further down the tunnel, allowing Lora to see past them to where Shae still lays where she fell. Irving kneels over her. He picks up her sword, lays it over her chest, and folds her hands over it.

Like you do when a warrior falls in battle.

"No!" The word is half a cry, half a groan. She thrusts herself out of Ayc's arms and rushes forward. They have to do something to save Shae. Surely, she can't be...

She can't be.

But as she comes closer, Lora can see the place where her head contacted the wall, the way it has caved in, and the contents have spilled out. She can see how Shae's eyes stare without seeing, everything that made her who she was extinguished like a candle blown out by a merciless wind.

I'll follow you into the dragon's fire, she once said.

And she had.

She gave everything. And it's all Lora's fault.

"I'm sorry," Lora tells Irving. "I'm so, so sorry."

He stands and wraps an arm around her shoulders. For that moment in time, he is not the captain of her guard. He's the man who has always looked after her. It's who she needs because right now, she doesn't feel like a Sovereign. She feels like a girl who just lost her friend.

"Let's get you out of here," he whispers.

AYC

"It's my fault," Lora whispers like she doesn't mean for anyone else to hear her. Maybe he wouldn't have if her back wasn't pressed against his chest as they sit near the fire. He curls his arms around her, holding her close, slowly inhaling the smell of anise through his nose. He allows her presence to slowly soothe away the terror that raged in his heart like a violent storm as he ran to where Tavish said he could sense her, unsure if he would make it in time.

But she's here. She's safe in his arms, where she belongs. The rest of the Five have settled around the fire, too, despite the late hour. Ayc and Lora are in plain sight, the truth of what's between them no longer hidden.

It has been a chaotic few hours since they were able to seal the gate. Orn, along with a handful of dwarven investigators, searched the area, trying to find the answer to who broke the magic and unleashed the monster. They spoke with Veni, who managed to give a detailed report even as Reselda set his leg. He's now in one of the guest quarters, sleeping off the sedative that Reselda gave him.

Lora also gave her testimony. Ayc has never seen fear like that in her eyes. That creature—whatever it was—is going to haunt both of their dreams.

It doesn't make sense. How someone managed to impressively fake his signature and then sneak into the depths of Heimat, incapacitate the guards, and unleash the beast. The why is as clear as the midnight left on the sign. It was an attempt to kill Lora, and they didn't care who else the beast murdered after that. Who knows how many would have been killed if Lora hadn't immediately lured the beast back into the gate or if Muffin hadn't been there?

All of which is why Ayc can't bear the words Lora has just uttered, that she's holding herself responsible for Shae's death.

"It's not your fault," he says, talking low into her ear. "Shae's duty was to keep you safe."

Lora shakes her head. "If I had not been so determined to keep us a secret, I would not have gone."

Bronwen shifts a little closer. "Lora, we *knew*. Surely, you know that we've known."

Lora stiffens. "Yes. Even more reason I should not have gone."

"Stop that," Peregrin snaps from the other side of the fire. "You went because you trust Ayc, and that note looked just like his handwriting. If Irving left that note for me, I would have gone, too. There's not a single person who does not know what he means to me, and yet I would have taken any opportunity to have a bit of privacy with the person dearest to me. Someone exploited your trust and your affection, and that is not your fault."

Lora sucks in a breath and releases it unsteadily. The tension in her shoulders releases slightly, but Ayc thinks it's going to take many more reminders for her to release the guilt. She has a habit of believing the world rests upon her shoulders, and mostly, she's not wrong. But he'll make damn sure she won't carry it alone.

"Even if you had seen through the deception," he says, "the gate was still opened. If you had not gone, many more people would have died. You, Shae, and Veni saved this city."

"That was mostly Muffin," Lora says, gesturing to where the dragon has curled up nearby. They raise their head, their lips tugging backward. A feeling of pure delight sweeps through their link, a preening at her compliment.

"Don't say such things," Ayc teases. "All this praise is going to go to their head."

Even if Ayc himself has praised Muffin many times since they breathed that ice. It was one of the most extraordinary things he's ever seen. The dwarves who have filed in and out, checking in on the group, have all whispered in awe, repeating a word that sounds like "Murrenigh". Ayc has no idea what it means, but he knows it's said in the utmost respect.

"They've earned it," Xylie signs from Ayc's other side. *"I wish I could have seen it."*

"Tell her I'll demonstrate it sometime," Muffin says. *"I think it might be a while before I can do it, though. I have felt it building for quite some time...but now I feel...empty."*

"It'll come back, I'm sure," Ayc replies.

He passes on the message to Xylie and then studies her. It never felt right to hide his relationship with Lora from her, and he would have told her as soon as Lora was ready. She doesn't appear angry, but still, he signs, *"I'm sorry I didn't tell you about me and Lora."*

Xylie rolls her eyes. *"Please. I knew you were in love with her before you did."*

Ayc chuckles. He's certain she did. *"You might have told me."*

"Would you have listened?"

"Not to a single word."

Lora has watched the exchange carefully. "So, then you're all not mad that we were keeping secrets?"

"We talked about it," Tavish says with a shrug. Saga's ears perk up, but he doesn't open his eyes from where he's been sleeping with his head in Tavish's lap. "We all knew something was happening between you two, and we figured you would tell us when you were ready."

"Mostly, we're just happy for you," Bronwen says.

"And relieved," Peregrin adds. "It was about fucking time you two stubborn asses figured it out."

Ayc laughs, and Lora tucks her head closer to his chest to hide her smile behind her hair even as she locks her fingers through his. It's further evidence of what Ayc has always secretly known. That they have always been inevitable, that fate has pulled them together since Lora stormed into his life.

"*Our Lora,*" Muffin agrees, resting their head back down on the stone.

"*Why do you keep calling her that?*" Ayc asks.

"*I am bonded with you, and she is a part of you, so she is ours.*"

"*She's a part of me?*"

They heave a breath like it should be obvious. "*Did I not tell you that I looked into your soul?*"

"*Yes. And?*"

"*I looked into your soul, and I saw her there. I knew her from the first time I saw her because I knew you.*"

Muffin's voice is too calm for words that hammer into Ayc like he's an anvil. She's in his very soul. It's the way it's always felt.

Soulmate.

Of course, he already suspected. Already knew, really, deep down. But hearing it confirmed by someone who can see into his soul shakes Ayc ot his core.

"*But you've not always called her that,*" Ayc says.

"*Your bond has only grown more fierce since you two have grown more...intimate. The bond I feel to her is different, but the protectiveness I feel for you extends to her. If anyone harms her, I will end them.*"

Ayc smiles at that. "*Thank you, friend. You saved her life. You saved me, too.*"

The only response is a contented noise, like the purr of a cat. Lora caresses a thumb over Ayc's shoulder. "What did Muffin say?"

"I'll tell you later," Ayc promises. Some truths should still just be between them, and this feels like one of those.

Candor, Irving, and Orn enter the cavern together. Peregrin uses their cane to push to their feet and turns toward them. Lora stands as well, Ayc reluctantly letting her go. As Orn passes by Muffin, he bows his head and murmurs the same word. "Murrenigh."

"What is it the dwarves keep calling me?" Muffin asks.

"What does that mean?" Ayc asks Orn. "Forgive me, I don't speak dwarvish."

Orn pauses. "It's a combination of dwarven words, actually. Best translated to your tongue, it means 'ice that burns like fire.'

"Murrenigh." Muffin turns it over in their head, like they are tasting it. *"Murrenigh. I like it."*

"Anything new?" Lora asks the dwarves.

Candor and Orn both shake their heads.

"I want to speak with Veni again in the morning, when he's more recovered," Candor says. "I get a sense that he was…not lying, I would know that, but like he knew something more than he was saying."

Lora frowns. "Veni is one of my oldest friends. I trust him completely."

"Perhaps it was just the pain," Tavish suggests. "He did not look well."

When Ayc last saw Veni, he was helping Reselda get him from the tunnels and into bed as he hopped on his good leg. He kept murmuring, *I'm sorry, I'm sorry,* as Ayc assured him he did well and pretended not to see the tears trailing down his cheeks. Ayc could only imagine the pain. Broken bones take a long while to heal, even for the fae, and if they don't heal right, they can cause lasting pain. Luckily, by the time he was in bed, he seemed calmer, more able to answer the dwarves' questions.

Candor nods. "I'll speak with him in the morning."

"We can speak now," says Veni from the open doorway to the room he's been put in. He shuffles forward on crutches, not bearing weight on his leg. "There's something more I need to tell you."

Reselda rushes out of the room after him. "Whatever it is, it should wait. I've given you a pain tonic and a sedative. You're not thinking straight."

"No, I should have said something weeks ago."

Ayc shoves to his feet. His muscles coil, a wariness settling in. There's something about the glossy fear in Veni's eyes that he doesn't like. Muffin and the rest of the Five also stand as though they sense something, too.

Lora steps forward, and Ayc holds up a hand like she's walking toward a threat instead of a friend and guard. She steps past him.

"Veni, you should go back to bed," she says softly.

He shakes his head. "I need you to know that I had nothing to do with tonight. I didn't know anything was going to happen. I would never have let you go down there if I did."

"Truth," Candor says, crossing his burly arms over his chest. "But I suspect not all of it."

Ice rises in Ayc's veins as a suspicion sinks in deep. Lora doesn't know, doesn't suspect. He can see it in her face.

"Veni—" she begins.

Veni holds up a hand to cut her off. "But the other times... That was me."

"You aren't making sense. What other times?"

But Ayc knows. He sees it clearly through his eyes as they tint with red. He senses what Veni is about to confess.

And Ayc is going to fucking kill him.

Veni swallows, like he knows the next words will be his last. "I'm the one who put midnight in your bed."

FIFTY-NINE

LORA

Lora hears the words, but she can't comprehend them. She feels like she's dropped a stitch as she's knitting and trying desperately, hopelessly, to fix it, to turn back the project before she made the critical error. Perhaps then, she will not have to rip up all her hard work and start again. Perhaps now, she won't have to lose her oldest friend.

"What?" Lora says.

Veni breathes fast, like he's run three miles on that broken leg. "The night of your coronation, I put midnight on your pillow. And again in Avia."

No. *No*. This is a prank, like when he snuck a snake into her bed. Any moment, he will say he's just kidding, and it will all be over. But he doesn't. He only stares at her, his eyes swimming with guilt.

Her hands shake. She wants to flap them before her face to cool the heat that is rising. But she fists them at her side.

Shadow rushes past Lora's feet. It doesn't hurt her, but as it barrels toward Veni, she knows it will hurt *him*. Lora is too frozen to intervene, but Reselda flings herself before Veni.

"Stop it!"

The shadows halt at her feet.

"Get out of the way."

Lora almost doesn't recognize Ayc's voice. It's deep, dangerous. His eyes burn with a red more complete than she's seen before.

"I know you are angry," Reselda says, "but I will not permit you to harm an injured patient."

The shadows don't retreat.

"Ayc, please," Lora says, her voice weak.

The shadows disappear entirely. The redness in his eyes fades. He takes a step toward her, but she shakes her head. If he's kind to her in this moment, she'll have to feel it, and she's not ready to feel this yet. She has to deal with it logically. Not with emotion. She has to pretend Veni is just an enemy, not her friend who has betrayed her.

Irving marches forward, silver glinting in his eyes. "Your injury is the only reason I'm not throwing you in shackles right now. Speak! Explain. Everything you know. Right now!"

Reselda steps aside, and Veni leans heavily on his crutches as he rushes to get the words out. "I came to your coronation, Lora. I know you don't know I was there because I never got the chance to say hello with everything that happened, but I was there. I stayed at the Roaring Gryphon that night, and there, someone approached me."

"Who?" Peregrin barks.

"I don't know. Not for sure at least."

"Don't fucking lie," Bronwen snarls. Strands of blue weave up her arms, crackling like a fire.

"He's not," says Candor.

Veni nods gratefully at the dwarf. "They kept their hood on the entire time. I didn't recognize their voice, but their cloak was blue. Lux Aester blue. That's why I left the bag beneath your bed —and the cloth in the tree. I thought for certain it would tip you off to who it truly is. I still think it was Amos or someone Amos sent."

"Why?" Irving presses.

"Because I don't know anyone else in Lux Aester who could have afforded the amount of money they paid me."

"You betrayed me for *money*?" Lora spits. A spark of anger rises, and she clings to it, letting her canines grow long.

Veni closes his eyes against it. "My mother's dying, Lora. She gets sicker every day. I thought with that amount of money, I could afford to enter her name into the lottery for the golden root enough times that she would be picked. Only to find out, much later, that they weren't doing that this harvest."

Lora swallows. Most of the golden root lottery is equal and fair, with everyone getting equal chances for the plant. But one or two of the cures are drawn from a pool of names where the same name can be entered multiple times, each additional one requiring a donation to the university. The practice can fund Splendor for an entire decade. A necessary evil, to allow inequality, the powerful cure undoubtedly going to the richest. But Splendor used that money to train new healers and do the research to produce more cures. It saved so many additional lives by allowing that practice. But this year, with the limited harvest, Lora and Busara agreed to keep it all equal. They would find another way to fund the university.

Veni's betrayal does not feel any better just because he had a justified reason.

"You could have told me about your mother," she snarls. "I would have helped you."

"How, Lora? I know you. You would not have broken the rules to hand me golden root, and that's her only chance. The treatments are no longer working, and she will not survive until the next harvest."

Lora looks to Reselda. Prior to her change in jobs, she cared for Marrya for years. Reselda doesn't give an answer to her silent question—she would never betray her patient's privacy—but there's a sadness in her eyes that she can't hide.

"The person who met me assured me they meant you no harm," Veni goes on. "They only wanted to send a message. I knew it wasn't good, but I justified it by saying it was no different from when I was pulling pranks on you when we were kids. They said they would make sure no one was outside of your room, but they promised me no one would be hurt. They swore it. I didn't know they were going to hurt Irving."

Lora remembers the look on Veni's face when he saw her in the courtyard, when she told him what happened to her captain. She thought the color draining from his face was just sympathy.

It was guilt.

"And what about Totus Omni?" Irving says, through his own pointed teeth. "You were her guard then. You took an oath to protect her, not scare her."

"I got a message when we were in Silvae that asked me to leave more midnight. The same person found me again while I was taking a piss."

It lands like a slap. In Silvae, right after she spoke to Grey. Had Grey been able to get a message to someone who took the word poorly? Or was there someone following her? Was the blue cloak an invisibility cloak, like the one Marcellus once wore? Did she have someone watching her at all times?

And then she remembers that night in Silvae. Veni stepped into her tent, interrupting Ayc. Veni told her he thought he heard something. A lie because the spell should have prevented all sound. He wasn't checking in on her. He was creeping in to leave a message.

She feels sick. She presses her fingers to her lips, afraid she might actually vomit.

"I told them no at first," Veni says. "They offered more money, but I told them to fuck off. Then they threatened to find someone else to do it, someone who might be a little messier than I was and...I don't know. I got angry. I thought if I left another clue, you would finally have enough to stop Amos. I should have just had the courage to confess."

"You fucking coward," Ayc snarls.

Muffin releases a deep growl. Veni flinches, but Muffin doesn't creep forward, doesn't take a bite from Veni like Lora gets the sense the dragon might want.

Irving has a stranglehold on his sword. "If you had the courage to tell us, tonight might never have happened. Shae might not be fucking dead."

Veni's throat works. "I know." He looks like he might cry, and Lora tells her foolish heart that she shouldn't care that he hurts. But she doesn't know how to turn it off, to just stop caring about him. Instead, her chest feels like it is bleeding.

"You are stripped of your duties as royal guard," Irving says.

Veni nods like they already knew that was coming.

Irving turns toward Lora. "My lady, what do you want me to do?"

Lora is not prepared for that question. She reaches for the swords on her hips to have something to hold on to. Her hand closes around only one. Her other, the sword she's owned since she was young, was left behind the gate downstairs. She knows the law. She knows what she would do if this were any other person. But this is not any other person. This is Veni.

Her heart wants to grant him mercy. It understands that he did what he did because he loves his mother. But if the world thinks that anyone can threaten her without consequence, they will never stop threatening her.

Bronwen presses two fingers into her elbow. Ayc hovers at her side. Xylie sniffs. Veni was her friend, too.

Veni dares to meet Lora's eyes. "I'm sorry," he says. "I'm really *fucking* sorry."

She believes him. She wishes that it could change anything at all.

But it doesn't.

"Reselda, put your patient back to bed. Don't let him leave that room. If you need a rest, you let a guard stand outside the door. He's officially a prisoner of the crown."

"What crime does he stand accused of?" Peregrin asks, their voice shockingly gentle, sympathetic, as they remind her of protocol she's forgotten.

"Treason," Lora says.

Veni gasps. There are only two punishments if he's found

guilty before the court, a punishment *she'll* have to decide, so great is the crime.

Death or banishment.

"Lora, please!" he begs.

"It's *my lady*," she snarls back. Her eyes flash with silver, and she isn't sure if it's tears or rage. Perhaps because it's both. "Only my friends call me Lora."

She turns around and marches away, ignoring all his protests. She marches to one of the doors, not absolutely certain that it's hers but fully certain she doesn't care. It must be hers because she feels the pulse of Bronwen's protection spell as she passes through. And there's the little box where she left her ear cuffs sitting on her mattress, before she went to find Ayc.

Someone touches her arm, and she knows it's Ayc by the shape of his hand, the gentle brush against her spine that almost spells *I love you* completely on its own. But more file in with him. Peregrin and Bronwen. Even Tavish, Xylie, and Saga linger at the door. It's too much. Her skin feels like it's peeling from her bones.

"We should write Amos and demand he come provide answers," Peregrin says.

Lora nods. "Yes," she manages, though she's not certain there is air in her lungs. Whatever is there grinds in with every breath like ground glass.

"Maybe it's time for torture," Bronwen suggests.

"Everyone shut up," Ayc snaps.

Peregrin's and Bronwen's eyes widen as they turn to him.

"We can talk about this in the morning. We've *all* had a fucking wretched night, and we should sleep."

Lora knows he's doing it for her, sensing that she needs a moment to be alone. They must get the hint because they all retreat. Even Ayc turns to go.

He pauses with his hand on the doorknob. "I'm here if you need anything."

She grasps his wrist. "I need *you*."

He steps back, shuts the door, and pulls her toward him. His arms knot behind her back, and his forehead presses into hers.

The weight of it steadies her, makes it feel like there is oxygen inside her lungs instead of glass.

"Scream, cry, or fall apart?" he asks, his breath warm on her cheeks.

"I don't know," she whispers. She's feeling too many things, too big and all at once. She doesn't know what to do with them.

He nods and steers her toward the bed. She's not certain fucking is the solution to this, but she might be willing to try if only to forget everything else for the moment. He pulls them down on the bed, but instead of going for her clothes, he yanks the blanket up over both of their heads. It suffocates the remaining light. She can only see the shape of his head, feel his breath on her ear.

"What are you doing?" she asks.

"I used to do this when I was younger. I would pull the covers over my head and pretend the rest of the world didn't exist. So that's what we're doing. Pretending the rest of the world doesn't exist."

She inhales a breath because she loves the thought of it. Just her and him, the only two things in the universe. But it doesn't ease the way her sternum feels like it's cracking open.

"It still hurts," she says, a tear slipping down her cheek.

He releases a deep sigh and presses her closer to his chest. "I know, my love. I know."

The tears come, and she lets them.

She does not fear falling apart anymore. She thinks she knows now that there is strength in letting yourself feel. One can only shatter if they've let something in deep enough that it can fracture them when it's lost. And caring and loving are the epitome of strength.

She knows she is strong enough to put herself together. And more importantly, she knows there will be someone to help her do it. More than one. She's always had someone at her side. She knows that now. There's always been Peregrin and Xylie and Bronwen and Tavish...and Ayc. Her Ayc, who kisses her tears and holds her until she falls asleep.

It has always been all right to fall apart.

But this is the first time she's let herself believe it.

When Lora returns to Wyntra, one of her guards is wrapped in mourning cloth and covered in sweet oil. Another is in shackles.

When Irving placed them on Veni's wrists in Heimat, Veni promised they were unnecessary. He swore he wouldn't run, but Irving told him if he didn't shut up, he'd gag him, too. He hasn't said a word the entire way home, not as they carted him through the mountains, into an airship, and back to the wagon for the day's ride to Wyntra. All that time, and Lora hasn't asked for the shackles to be removed. Her days of trusting him are long over.

She doesn't even glance in his direction as she leaves the courtyard and heads into Wyntra. She has a funeral to prepare so Shae can be laid to rest on the sweeping fields outside Wyntra. She has Amos's visit to prepare for, as well.

He's already been summoned, and they expect him to arrive the day after tomorrow. Not to mention, the invitation to meet the Drakr queen looms only a month away, and she has to either prepare for a small army to cross the ocean between their lands or her entire army to go to war. She isn't quite sure which one, and Damara hasn't sent her usual letter to set up another visit, so she's certainly not about to help.

Someone falls into step behind Lora. Her hand instinctively goes to the dagger at her hip, but her old swords are no longer there. Instead, two are strapped to her back. They were gifts from the dwarves before she departed. Orn knew of the loss of her blades down in the depths and gifted her with the pair before she left. The blades are exquisite, their craftsmanship exceeding even some of the best of Audori blades. The moonlight-colored blades are blended with metals that make them lethal to every race of fae, and the black hilts feel like they were made for her hand. They are longer than her previous blades, making it impossible to wear them on her hips. She'll have to practice with their new weight and length, but she already bears an affection for them that she rarely feels toward non-living objects. Except, perhaps, for her books.

"Reaching for your blade, Lora?" Ayc whispers as he falls in beside her as they enter the great hall. "Should I be afraid or excited?"

Lora releases her dagger and at marvels how her lips still tug upward despite everything on her mind, coaxed into a smile just by the sound of Ayc's voice. She pauses in the hallway. The door has closed behind them, shutting out the rest of the party. Only Irving now stands with them, and he turns his back, his ear shifted toward her but giving them as much privacy as he dares. Good. She's certain that it won't be long before the entire castle knows that she and her Fifth are fucking, and she's come to terms with that, but that doesn't mean she wants their entire relationship on display.

"Neither," she replies. "I fear I need to work."

A smirk crawls upon his face. He drops his voice into a low, low whisper, so even Irving can't hear. "You can work. I can *assist*." He wiggles his eyebrows.

"I fear your idea of assisting will ensure that I don't get any work done."

"Oh, I'll be most helpful."

"I regrettably must pass."

"Pity," he says good-naturedly.

It truly is a pity. She longs for him to make her forget everything that has transpired or is about to transpire. Fuck, she hopes she doesn't remember her own name by the time he's through with her.

"Tonight?" she asks.

"Always making me wait," he teases, then shrugs. "Oh, well. I've waited years for you before. I suppose a few hours is nothing."

He grins at her in a way that's so adorable, it nearly makes her angry. She's unsure whether she wants to kiss him or bite him. Perhaps both.

In her indecision, he takes her hand carefully, his fingers

gliding over the sensitive skin on her inner wrist. He brings her hand to his lips and whispers a sweet kiss across her knuckles. Somehow, he marries a promise into that touch that ties something within her into a taut bow. It tugs when he draws his thumb over where he just kissed.

"Until tonight," he says, weaving more promises into the words.

Irving clears his throat, and Ayc takes a step back swiftly. Irving nods down the hallway to where Lora's mother stands at the end. Her eyes spark with silver as they fix upon Ayc.

She knows.

Fuck.

Yris finding out about their relationship was inevitable, but Lora foolishly hoped for a few weeks of peace before Yris attempted to assert her opinion into it.

Yris's feet fall without making a sound as she walks toward them. Ayc stiffens more with every step, but he doesn't turn to look at her, nor does he leave. Embers stir in his eyes. Lora will never blame him for how deeply he hates her.

Yris draws herself to a halt and lifts her chin like she still wears a crown. She opens her mouth.

Lora thrusts up a finger in her face. "Not a damn word."

"I was not—"

"Not. A. Damn. Word," Lora repeats slowly, emphasizing each word. "Unless you have something important for me to know, the only thing you should be saying to me is farewell as you walk to your chambers and hide there as you always do when I return to Wyntra."

Yris's eyes narrow, and Ayc looks away to hide his gloating smile. Lora braces herself for the fight of wills, but Yris only says, "Very well. You have a visitor in the great hall."

"Who?" Lora asks.

"Not you," Yris says. She nods toward Ayc. "The baker."

"Me?" Ayc arches an eyebrow. "Who is here to visit me?"

"I did not ask. They just arrived, all the way from Lux Aester. Lora, your grandmother is with them."

Hellevi is here?

Ayc casts her a glance, but Lora is already moving, sliding past her mother in the direction of the side entrance to the great hall. Ayc falls in beside her again. He reaches before her to pull open the door and then enters right after her.

Her grandmother sits at the table dressed in her favorite purple trousers and tunic. The smile she gives Lora is as familiar and comforting as taking a large breath of air. The girl seated beside her is familiar, too, but it takes Lora a moment to place her, particularly with how she hides halfway behind her veil of hair. But as soon as she catches a glimpse of her face, Lora remembers. The Lux Aester girl who risked everything so Xylie could sneak out a hospital window and save Ayc.

Avabeth.

SIXTY

AYC

Avabeth.

She's scrunched in her chair, curved over herself loosely, like a mouse folding upon itself to avoid being seen by a cat. But the cat is the world, and shrinking in upon herself is a conditioned response to everything. She looks like she's scared of the very air. But she's here, sitting next to Hellevi, a very long way from home. Which means she must have done something incredibly brave.

Ayc remembers the letter he received a few weeks ago. Between Muffin, his newfound power, the Tour, and Lora, he's scarcely had time to think about it since. It was coded, subtle, but Ayc knew there was only one reason a married woman of Lux Aester might write to him. He immediately took action, getting in contact with the new leadership of the organization that Lora and Bronwen set up. Even as he did, he wasn't certain she would have the courage to flee from her husband. And it must have worked because Avabeth is no longer in Lux Aester.

"You did it!" Ayc exclaims with a laugh and a clap of his hands.

Avabeth jumps in the chair. Hellevi slips a hand onto her shoulder, and she settles.

"Welcome, Avabeth," Lora says in a much more even tone. "To what do you owe the honor of your visit?" She punctuates the question by arching an eyebrow at Ayc. Questions scrawl into the angle.

As though given permission to exist, Avabeth scrambles to her feet and dips low into a curtsey. "My-my lady, I...uh..." She stumbles as she straightens, catching herself on the table.

It's too painful to watch her flounder, so Ayc explains about Avabeth's letter. About how she requested that he follow through with the offer he made in the hospital—that he would help her be free.

"I was surprised," Ayc says, glancing at Avabeth. "And very happy."

A blush warms her cheek, and she dips her head once more to hide her face. "Thank you for helping me. I-I came because..." She gulps a breath. "I have important information."

"What information?" Lora asks.

Avabeth shifts her gaze between them. "I...I, uh, meant to tell only Ayc. I am not important enough to take the Sovereign's time."

Lora rolls her eyes. "Nonsense."

She makes her way to the table, and Ayc follows her. She doesn't sit at the head of the table, where she's sat for almost every meal and meeting. Instead, she sits at the one directly across from where Avabeth stands. Ayc sits next to her.

"*No one* is unimportant," Lora says gently. "Especially not you. Please have a seat, Avabeth."

Avabeth lowers herself stiffly in the chair. She clutches the edge of the table like she might blow away in a slight breeze if she does not.

Hellevi rests a hand on her shoulder. "Go on, dear."

"F-first, I would like to make a...a request."

Ayc glances at Hellevi, whose eyebrow has crept up minutely. Apparently, she is not aware of a request.

"In ex-exchange for the information, I would like..." She gasps a breath. "I would like something in return."

Lora sighs. "I don't enjoy something being offered only to have it held over my head."

Red erupts in Avabeth's freckled cheeks. "No! I'm sorry. I don't mean... It's just... It's the only thing I have, and I need help. The Lux Aester courts don't allow for divorce. Well, they do, but only under severe grievances, and I can't file one because I won't win. And I would be punished even if I tried. But you're Sovereign. *You* could grant me a divorce. I thought, perhaps, you might help me, in exchange for the information, but you're right. I'm sorry. I'll just tell—"

Lora holds up her hand. Avabeth cuts up with something like a squeak.

"You want a divorce?" Lora asks gently.

Tears well in Avabeth's eyes as she nods. She reaches down to her side and brings up a small brown bag. She flips it open and shoves aside a few pieces of clothing—what Ayc suspects is all she managed to bring with her when she fled—before grabbing for a file of papers at the bottom. "I've written out and collected evidence of a list of grievances, but I wish it to be clear that this is my fault. My husband isn't a cruel man, and I don't wish to sully his name. I—" She cuts herself off, dropping the cluster of papers and swiping at the tears working down her cheeks. "I am not strong enough to be what the divine wants."

Hellevi soothes a hand over Avabeth's back. Ayc's chest aches. She may have fled Lux Aester, but he fears it'll be a long time before Lux Aester loosens its hold. Before she's able to dig up the weeds and roots they planted in her head.

He leans across the table towards her and lowers his voice. "Avabeth," he says softly, "you were seventeen years old, barely old enough to consent. He—"

"I did, though," she insists, still sweeping furiously at her cheeks. "I married him willingly."

"There's a difference between whole-hearted consent and

obligation," Lora says. "Of doing something not because you want to but because you feel you have no other choice. Everyone worth even a fraction of the grace you're extending understands that difference. Your *husband*"—venom enters her words—"knows that you were not willing. He did not care."

"No, no. It's my fault. All my sisters, my friends—they were married just like I was. And they wear their duty beautifully. Like a pearl necklace." Avabeth touches her throat, then makes a choking sound. "I don't know why it suffocates me. Why I feel as though I can't breathe."

"Because it's a leash, Avabeth, not a necklace," Ayc says, because fuck, he knows that feeling. "It's a chain that has been wrapped around your neck all your life, and we don't feel those chains until we tug against them. Your friends might be content with the life they've been given, and that's all right. But it's not meant for you. You can be free if you want to be. Let us help you."

It's as though Ayc has taken a hammer to a dam within her. A sob quakes through Avabeth's body, the only warning before her defenses utterly collapse. She folds inward, stooped by great sobs. Ayc wants to go around the table, wrap his arms around her, but he's quite certain a man touching her is not what she needs.

As though she knows it, too, Lora reaches across the table and takes Avabeth's hand with both of her own. Avabeth's sobs stutter for a moment, then continue. She grasps onto Lora with her other hand, clinging tight.

The gentleness in Lora's voice reminds Ayc of all the reasons he loves her and adds a few more. "Avabeth, do you want a divorce? Yes or no?"

"Yes."

"Then you're divorced."

Avabeth's eyes widen. "I have not given my reasons."

"I do not need a reason. You want to be free, so you are free."

"My husband will—"

"He is *not* your husband anymore." Lora adds a bit of force to her words.

Avabeth shakes her head, her hair waving before her reddened cheeks. "You don't understand. He'll try to come for me."

"Then he will go through me," Lora snarls. "You are no one's property. You belong to no one but yourself. Do you understand?"

Fuck, Ayc thinks. How he loves this woman.

Avabeth nods. She runs the back of her hands under her eyes and nose, streaking moisture across her cheeks. She releases a few more sobs as Lora holds her hand and Hellevi rubs her back. Ayc sits in silence, cursing men who wish to possess and thanking the universe that women such as Hellevi and Lora exist.

When her tears slow, Ayc takes the opportunity. "Hey, Avabeth."

"Ayc," Lora warns beneath her breath.

He ignores her. Some things will never change between them. "What do you call a pile of cats?"

Avabeth sniffs. "I don't know."

"A *meow*-tain."

As the cat's sound leaves his lips, Avabeth's eyes widen, her tears halting in her surprise. Lora sends him a look that says she's going to hurt him later, and fuck, he hopes so.

"Get it?" Ayc grins proudly. "*Meow*-tain."

Avabeth gives a watery laugh, brushing away the last of her tears with a knuckle. Hellevi rolls her eyes but smiles.

Lora says, "Forgive my Fifth. He thinks he's funny."

"I am funny," Ayc says. "If I were a mountain, I'd be *hill*-arious."

Lora releases Avabeth and slaps him with the back of her hand. He only laughs.

"*If our Lora murders you,*" Muffin says, confirming that they have been eavesdropping the entire time, "*I will be on* her *side.*"

"*I would expect nothing less.*"

"Where will I go?" Avabeth asks.

Lora releases her hand and leans back in the chair. "You have quite a talent for healing. Have you thought of attending Splendor's school for healers?"

"Oh, no, I couldn't," Avabeth says swiftly. "Perhaps I can work in your kitchens. I'm a hard worker."

"I'm certain you are. We can discuss it later. For now, I would like to know what information you have."

Avabeth clears her throat, then again, and again. Lora folds her legs beneath her and settles into the chair like she has all day—though she does not. Ayc mimics her casualness, crossing his arms over the table and leaning closer. Perhaps it helps, or perhaps it's Hellevi tapping a finger between her shoulder blades because Avabeth begins.

"Did you know that Marcellus was my uncle?"

"No," Ayc says, though he supposes it makes sense that they are related since Marcellus brought her to Yris's Sovereign Day. Marcellus called her Sister Avabeth, but then, he called every Lux Aester woman *Sister*, regardless of relation. He was a fucking weird shitbag.

"By marriage," Avabeth says. "His wife—well, widow, now. Tabytha. She's my father's sister. I was there when she received word that he was killed. We were rapidly sewing her a new dress before she went to join him in Wyntra, but then Amos's letter arrived with the news of his death. She was distraught, though I'm not sure if she grieved the loss of her husband or the loss of the throne more, and she dropped the letter. I don't think she even read all of it before she did." Avabeth rifles through her bag on the table. She pulls out a paper, folded and bearing the sun pressed into bright blue wax. "I don't know why I took it, but once I saw it, I knew you needed to see it." She holds it out to Lora. "I was very happy you won."

Lora takes it from her hands carefully, and Ayc leans closer to read it over her shoulder. The news of Marcellus's death is delivered bluntly. The angry words Amos uses to address Lora make Ayc's power tug at the leash he keeps it on, but it's the last paragraph that steals Ayc's breath.

Ayc struggles to untangle the feelings of both fear and rage. He searches Lora's face. It's unreadable as she wordlessly holds the letter out to Irving, who has stood quietly behind her this entire time.

He scans it quickly, his eyes gleaming with silver as he gets to the end. "Let me arrest him," Irving says through his teeth as he looks up. There's something almost pleading about the request, like he's begging Lora to let him protect her. "It's enough. It bears his signature, and we have Avabeth's testimony."

Lora glances at Ayc, who nods.

"Take the letter and Veni to a high court judge," Lora says. "If they issue a warrant based on that and Veni's testimony, then go. That way, none of the other regents can ever say I used bias."

Irving nods. "Done." He walks a few paces away, reaching his hand to the agate in his ear. Davos slips into the great hall, and only then does Irving slide out.

Ayc is certain the high court judge will agree to issue the warrant. There's enough evidence to bring Amos in on suspicion. Lora reaches for Ayc's hand under the table, and he holds on to her even as something dark smiles within him.

Ayc can't wait to see what that fucker looks like without a head.

LORA

The dungeon of Wyntra is clean and well-lit, but she hates it. It's full of too many memories of long nights spent curled onto cold stone when she once again failed to meet one of Yris's ridiculous expectations. But seeing Amos behind bars might be healing something within her, making her like it just a little more.

Amos perches on the very edge of the stone bench, his body stiff and his arms drawn in like he's trying to touch as little as possible. He shoves to his feet as soon as she passes the threshold of the dungeon and comes into his view.

"Are you comfortable?" she asks.

Irving and Ayc follow close behind her. Irving, for obvious reasons, and Ayc because when she received a knock on her bedroom door to inform her that the gryphon riders charged with arresting Amos had returned, he was tied with silk scarves to her headboard. And she was sitting on his face.

"Make him wait," Ayc grumbled, his voice barely audible. "It'll be good for him to sweat."

"I thought I told you to shut up," she hissed back, sinking her weight back down until the only noise he could make was a moan as he devoured her. Her fingertips are still buzzing from an orgasm so intense, she left tooth marks in her headboard.

She's determined not to let Amos ruin that glow for her, though she's certain he'll try. For the same reason, she doesn't look toward the other cell, where Veni leans against the bars. She has avoided speaking to him, though she has ensured that his mother received an anonymous list of the best solicitors in Everadyn who can represent him in court. She is not her mother. She will ensure that he has a fair trial, one that takes into account how helpful his testimony has been in bringing Amos to justice.

"You have the wrong man," Amos says, marching toward the bars of his cell. Lora stops before him, far enough that he can't reach through and grab her. He would have to be a fool to try. Irving would cut off his arm without hesitation, and Ayc might strangle him with his shadows.

"The courts will decide that," Lora says, crossing her arms

over the simple tunic she chose from her wardrobe, paired with breeches. She realizes that she's covering where the leviathan tooth hangs on her neck and lets her arms drop so Amos can see it.

"The courts will decide whatever their Sovereign wants them to decide," Amos says.

"I have instructed them to rule based on evidence. I believe it can speak for itself."

Amos scoffs. "The evidence you have contrived in your feeble mind? I'm certain they will. Throw in a bat of your eyelashes, and maybe they'll take my head, too."

"Perhaps we can make a deal," Lora says. "When you're found guilty, I'll recommend exile over beheading. You can live your life…just far from Everadyn."

He curls his lip. "And what do you want in return for this *generous* offer?"

"I want to know who you hired to do your dirty work for you. You didn't approach Veni in that bar. You didn't steal Irving's memory. Who helped you?"

It's imperative that she know. Even if Amos is found guilty and executed, if they don't know his accomplice in the crime, she will never sleep easily. Whoever he hired has been all too familiar with her every movement, has known things that haven't made sense. Amos couldn't have done any of that. And if they find this person, there is a chance they can restore Irving's memory.

Amos rolls his eyes. "You're so close to the point that if it were a poisonous snake, it would have done us all a service." He grasps the bars and leans closer to them. "That's how I know it wasn't me. If it was me, I would have left a snake in your bed, not some silly flower."

The shadows shift in the corner of Amos's cell. His eyes widen as he whirls toward them, but the shadows quiet quickly. Ayc takes a deep breath, the sigh through his nose heavy as he regains control. Lora made him promise that if he came, he wouldn't harm Amos, no matter what he said. Lora won't stoop to torture. Not only because it is unethical, but also because it's untrustworthy and ineffective. People will confess to absolute nonsense to get the pain to stop.

"I'm only offering this one chance, Amos," Lora says firmly. "Tell us who you hired."

Amos turns back around. "Oh, I wish I *had* hired someone. Perhaps if I hadn't hesitated to go through with my plan, I wouldn't be here right now." His eyes glow silver, but then he shrugs, and it fades. "Instead, I let the fool queen live, and you arrested the wrong person. And now we're both going to end up dead because of it. I hope I at least live long enough to see you lose your throne."

Ayc surges toward the cell, but Lora catches his wrist. He halts. "You know something, don't you?" His voice is a roar. His arms are trembling, and she thinks it's the effort to hold back his power. She can feel it coming from him like a winter wind.

Amos walks backward, though not in retreat. He is measured, with the calmness of a man who has embraced his fate as he walks to the gallows. "I do. But I'll never tell."

"You will," Ayc warns, his eyes flaring red.

"What will you do?" Amos says. "Torture me? I've known Lora since she was born. I know all of Yris's disappointments. She doesn't have the stomach for torture. And even if she did, I'm far more afraid of them than I'll ever be of you."

"Them?" Irving demands. "Who are you speaking of?"

Amos only smiles, and he is so unlike the man Lora last saw, cowering before Damara, that Lora shivers. Not with fear but with doubt. She shakes the feeling away like cobwebs lingering on her skin. It's Amos. All the signs point to Amos, and now that she has him, he's going to say whatever he can to try to keep his neck in one piece. He's pointing the finger elsewhere. That's all.

So then why does he have the calmness of an innocent man who thinks he'll soon be free?

"Come on." It's Veni's voice that rises softly, gently, like a soothing tide. He's come to the wall of bars that connect the two cells. "If it's someone else, if you have proof, then provide it. You can go back to your family. It could save your life."

Amos paces away from the cell door and perches back on the bench. "I think I'm prepared to meet the divine."

He locks eyes with Lora; Ayc wraps his hand around her elbow and tugs her toward the door as though wanting to keep her from hearing the next words. She hears them anyway.

"Are *you* ready, Loraphne?"

SIXTY-ONE

AYC

"He's lying," Peregrin says from where they stand at the corner of Lora's desk, their arms crossed over their chest.

Peregrin met Irving, Lora, and Ayc here to discuss what to do with Amos. Bronwen and Tavish are in Lux Aester, searching for any further clues and information that might be gathered within Amos's homes. They rode with the gryphon riders who went to Lux Aester and have not returned. Xylie sits in a chair with her legs folded beneath her, mimicking her cousin's position, where Lora sits behind her desk. Ayc leans against a bookshelf, feeling like shadows live in his chest, so dark is his anger and unease.

Before he walked into that dungeon, he was gleeful. He thought Amos would buckle, that he would jump at a chance to spare his own life. He wasn't expecting that calm, unyielding man they met, willing to die before telling the truth that might spare him.

"He said he's more scared of them," Irving says. "Who could that possibly be?"

"Who knows?" Peregrin says. "And from what you've said, he's determined not to tell."

Ayc fingers curl at his side. He wants to wrangle Amos's neck. The impulse is so strong, he fears it. He's never been a violent person, but he's relearning what he's capable of when the woman he loves is in danger.

Even now, Lora works the cord of the leviathan tooth between her fingers. Her face is guarded, and yet Ayc can glimpse something deep in her eyes. The tiniest seed of fear. "Perhaps he's lying. Perhaps he just means to scare me."

"We could petition a judge to use truth weed," Peregrin suggests. "It'll take a while because I'm sure whoever represents him in court will fight against it. As is their right."

"It's worth taking a chance," Irving says. "He could simply refuse to speak to us if we make him take truth weed, but we might be able to get some answers. The judges are likely to grant it, given the weight of his crime and the potential safety risk to our Sovereign."

"Perhaps I could convince him to talk," Muffin suggests across the link.

"No. As tempting as it is, Lora said no torture."

"Not torture. Only ice."

"No, Muffin."

"Just his great toe."

Now they're just being ridiculous. Ayc closes the mental link between him and Muffin. They know full well that the two times they've breathed ice since being beneath the Stella Runes mountains, it was unpredictable and poorly aimed. They would kill Amos, and then his successor would cut off trade. He only hasn't because of Lora's wise decision to allow the high court to issue the warrant.

Xylie snaps her fingers to draw their attention. *"There's something I keep wondering."*

"What's that?" Peregrin asks, forming the signs as they speak. They've come a long way since they first requested Ayc teach them a few weeks ago.

"Does Amos know how close Irving is to Lora and Ayc? Does he know that Veni and Lora were friends?"

When Xylie's hands fall back into her lap, Peregrin glances at Irving. Ayc mulls it over. All along, this has been so much more than the midnight that's a threat. They've wanted to send Lora a message: She's alone. There is no one she can depend on. People she loves can get hurt. People she loves can forget her. Her closest friends can betray her. And that means that either Amos or the person he hired has intimate knowledge of her relationships.

Would Amos possess that knowledge?

Ayc grinds his teeth. Nothing makes fucking sense.

Lora plucks at her cord once more. "Request the truth weed from the judge. And keep talking to him. Maybe after he sits in his cell and the reality of his own headless corpse sinks in, we will be able to convince him. Hopefully, Bronwen and Tavish will be able to find something."

Peregrin and Irving nod to her and step out of the room. Davos remains at the door of Lora's office, his broad back briefly visible before the door closes. Ayc studies Lora, who stares at her desk, her brow furrowed like she's trying to solve an invisible puzzle engraved on the wood.

He opens his mouth, unsure whether he's going to ask her something or tell her a ridiculous joke—anything to distract her —when she lifts her head. She wears a smile, but he's seen enough of her real ones to know this is simply theatre.

"It'll be all right," she says. "This whole thing is about to be over."

He doesn't believe her. Not then, and not hours later, when he lies beside Lora in her large bed. Every other night here, he's slept deeply, pressed close to Lora's body, breathing in the sweet anise smell in her hair. Now, his heartbeat sounds loud in his ears, each thud reminding him that a threat is in the dungeon below. Peregrin and Irving spent multiple hours interrogating Amos, but he's apparently grown a backbone and is keeping his mouth shut.

Lora grunts in her sleep and rolls away from him, untangling their legs as she rolls to her other side. She, too, has been restless tonight, cuddling close and then shifting away. And with every grunt, with every bead of sweat that pops up on her forehead, Ayc fears more and more that he might be about to do something foolish.

Ayc reaches across the mental link, but Muffin is in a deep, dreamless sleep. Ayc slips out of bed slowly, so as not to wake Lora, and grabs his pants and shirt from the floor.

"Where are you going?" Lora murmurs. She peeks through her curls at him.

He curses himself. She's such a warrior. The jingle of his belt buckle must have woken her.

"I can't sleep. I'm going to go bake."

She lifts her head. "Cinnamon rolls? We haven't had them in so long."

The hope in her voice is so adorable, it's enough to make him change his mind. He should absolutely go to his kitchen and stay far away from the dungeon.

"Of course," he agrees, returning to the bedside. He lays a kiss on her head. "Go back to sleep, my love. I'll bring you one warm in the morning."

She tucks her face back into the pillow. He dresses, pulls on his boots, and steps outside. Bronwen isn't here to put up the barrier, so there are three guards in the hallway. Since he's no longer sleeping next to her, Ayc leaves the door slightly cracked as he steps out and catches Magdon's eye. "Keep an ear out."

Magdon nods xir head.

Ayc means to go to his kitchen and bake. He knows it's what he should do, but as he passes the staircase that spirals into the dungeon below, he hesitates. Something pulls him in the direction. He battles against the tug, clinging to his own commonsense.

But perhaps Ayc might be able to get through Amos's thick skull. Amos knows that Irving and Peregrin, under Lora's orders, will not succumb to harming him. He doesn't know that Ayc will not give in to the temptation. Ayc doesn't know what he's fully capable of when Lora is at risk, but he doesn't have to hurt Amos. He only has to scare him.

"Fuck," he swears, before he sweeps toward the staircase. The guards who stand at the top, placed there after Veni took up residence, study him but do not stop Ayc. He is Fifth. He can go where he wants in this castle.

The guards at the bottom, before the locked door of the dungeons, don't immediately open the door.

"Is there something you need, Sir Ayc?" one asks.

"I just want to talk to him."

They hesitate once more before one heaves a sigh and reaches for a key on their belt. They unlock it, and the heavy door swings open. Ayc steps inside and freezes.

It feels like he's stepped inside a blizzard. The cold pierces straight to his bone, the type of cold he felt in the caves when the wraiths appeared, when he faced the monster below Heimat, and when the Supreme sorcerer appeared among them in Totus Omni. His breath is visible in the air as it passes his lips.

In the first cell, Veni lies sleeping on a cot. But in Amos's cell, a figure looms over the stone bench. A blue cloak gathers around them—a Lux Aester blue. The light outside the cell glints over metal as the stranger lifts a knife above their head, already covered in blood.

"Stop!" Ayc roars.

He flings himself toward the cell, reaching for his shadows. The person turns their head, and he nearly falters. A silver and a green eye gleam from beneath the hood, before he shifts his hand in a sweeping gesture. A wall of shadow rises from the floor and slams into the intruder. They tumble off their feet and slam into the stone, still holding their knife. They throw back their head and laugh. Then, the air crackles like lightning, and they are simply gone.

Ayc slams against the bars and yanks on the door. It's still locked. One of the guards appears beside him, fiddling with his belt. An alarm is sounding—here in the dungeon and at a distance—echoing through the stone like the shrill screech of a teakettle. Veni vaults upward from the bench in the cell next door, but Amos is motionless on the stone bench, an arm dangling downward. Blood drips down the side and pools on the floor.

Fuck, fuck, fuck.

Finally, the guard swings the cell door open, and Ayc rushes in. He knows as soon as he lays eyes upon Amos from above that it's too late. A gaping slash parts Amos's neck. He doesn't breathe. Doesn't flinch. His eyes are closed, like he never even woke when the sorcerer appeared in his cell. He was dead in moments.

Dead.

Their best chance at finding out who helped him, now dead by their coconspirators' hand.

"Fuck!" Ayc snarls, backing away from the growling pool of blood.

"*Ayc!*" Muffin yells. "*What is that terrible noise?*"

"*In a minute!*" Ayc says back. He's too busy thinking, trying to figure out what the fuck he's supposed to do next.

"Is he dead?" Veni asks, nearly screaming to be heard over the alarm.

"Did you see anything?" Ayc demands in return.

Veni shakes his head. "The cold woke me. I couldn't figure out why I was so cold. I heard something—perhaps the knife being drawn—right before the door opened and you came in. That's how swiftly it happened."

Then she appeared, right there in the cell. She disappeared and could be anywhere right now.

Lora.

He spins toward the guard. "Does someone have eyes on the Sovereign?"

"Yes," calls the other guard who stands in the doorway, cupping his hand over his ear as though to help him hear his agate better. He says something more, but Ayc can't hear him. Ayc hurries closer. It isn't necessary, as the alarm finally silences. "Her royal guards see her. She's being secured in her chambers."

"Bet she's furious about that," Ayc mutters to himself even as he sidles around the guard to step into the staircase. He nearly collides with the two guards who were once at the top of the stairs.

"Should we call the healer?" a guard asks.

"Yes," Ayc says, "but tell her it's just to tend a body. He's already dead."

"Is our Lora safe?" Muffin demands.

"Yes. On my way to her now."

The burst of affinity he used in the dungeon has made his muscles ache, but he pushes the discomfort aside and forces himself into a sprint back to Lora's chambers. More guards have gathered around the doorway, but it's Magdon who slides into Ayc's path. The door behind xem is still cracked, just as Ayc left it.

"No one gets near Lora's chambers before they confirm their identity," xe says.

"Magdon, it's me."

Ayc hears footsteps inside, the slap of bare feet against the stone, hurrying toward the door.

"I know it looks like you," Magdon says. "But there's alarms going off, so you're going to have to prove it."

He appreciates the protectiveness and the protocol, but how the fuck is he supposed to prove he isn't a sorcerer in disguise? Lora appears in the crack in the doorway, but she hesitates there.

"Hey, Looorrrraaa," Ayc practically sings in the way he always does. "I really liked what you did with those black scarves yesterday." The ones she tied his wrists up with and then secured to her headboard before she rode his face. She'd shoved another in his mouth before she wiggled down his body and seated herself on his cock. "Perhaps next time, you should—"

Lora shoves the door open further. "It's him. Let him in." Her hair is tossed, and she's hastily thrown on a heavy robe that drapes to her ankles. It's a recent purchase, much more modest than the one she had before. Practical, considering how often Ayc has her naked now.

Magdon steps aside, and Lora shuts the door behind Ayc. "What the fuck is happening?"

"Amos is dead," Ayc says.

"What?"

He explains every detail he can remember. The feeling of cold, the blue cloak, Amos's gaping throat.

"What were you even doing there?" Lora asks.

Ayc shrugs. "I just wanted to talk to him."

She arches an eyebrow and opens her mouth, but Irving shoves into the room without knocking. Peregrin isn't far behind. They were both clearly woken from slumber, their shirts untucked, their sword and knife belts thrown over one arm. Ayc starts to explain again, but cuts off when the door opens once more, and Xylie slips in. They are all here. Safe and alive.

"Again," Lora says.

When Ayc finishes, Irving demands, "Did you recognize them?"

"Their hood was up the entire time, but..." Ayc hesitates. He doesn't want to admit his suspicion because he fears it will make it true.

"But what?" Peregrin presses.

"But whoever they are, they reminded me of Serene." His heart feels like it leaps into his throat. He swallows hard to speak around it. "The cold. The silver and green eyes. The disappearing so suddenly. Everything about it reminded me of Serene."

"Why would Serene work with Amos?" Lora asks.

Xylie's fingers tremble slightly as she signs, *"Perhaps he made a deal. And now she wants to ensure his silence."*

"Teleporting is a rare gift," Peregrin says. "From my understanding, it takes a tremendous amount of power, and few are capable of it. Onanna is not even capable of it."

"*Serene* is capable of it," Irving says.

Ayc resists the urge to shiver and instead steps closer to Lora's side. He doesn't touch her, like he wants, nor does she touch him, but she shifts closer until he can feel the warmth of her body. He doesn't like knowing that the most powerful sorcerer in existence conspired to threaten Lora.

"It doesn't make sense," Peregrin says. "I don't understand why Amos would be willing to pay the price Serene would demand just to leave midnight in Lora's bed. Or what Serene's motivation in killing him would be?"

"To ensure he keeps his mouth shut?" Ayc suggests. "So no one learns of the part she played."

"And what if he didn't?" Lora says. "What if he blabbed the moment he was caught? What would I have done to Serene? She's so powerful it would take a legion of men to bring her down."

"Then perhaps we should send a legion." A harsh edge lines Ayc's voice. Somewhere in his head, he knows he's being unreasonable. But he can't help it. The anger is rising within him, and it's all he can do to remain calm so his shadows don't rise with it. He wants this to be over. He wants Lora to rest knowing that those who threatened her are no longer breathing, and their best chance of that happening is dead. Murdered by someone who could teleport into this room right now if she wanted to. And there's nothing he could do.

"They will not harm our Lora," Muffin growls across their link. *"Not while we yet breathe."*

Lora threads her fingers through Ayc and leans against him. The feeling of her weight anchors him. He releases a breath.

Xylie catches his eye and signs, *"She's all right. She's safe."*

Which is meant to be comforting. It would be, except it's a lie.

"Going after Serene is tempting," Peregrin says. "But we need every soldier we have with all that lies before us. Let's not make a sacrifice unless we are sure it's absolutely necessary."

"I wish Bronwen was here," Lora says. "To investigate further. Surely, if it's the Supreme, she left behind some energy that can be traced."

Peregrin says, "There are sorcerers in the gryphon army. They can have a look."

It's at least something. A direction. A possibility that might lead them to something more. Ayc doesn't let the hope grow too big. After all, the sorcerer purposefully left no trace when they took Irving and messed with his head. But it—or perhaps the way Lora still holds his hand—allows him to take a breath.

"I'm having guards search the castle as we speak," Irving says. "I'll get in communication with Commander Urbain. I'm sure he's heard the alarms and is increasing patrols. I suspect the intruder is long gone, but if not—"

A knock sounds on the door.

"What?" Irving barks, marching toward the door. It swings open to reveal Magdon.

"My lady, your mother is here and wishes to see you," xe says.

Lora tenses, and Ayc bites back a groan. Neither of them has seen Yris since they accidentally ran into her in the hall, but Ayc should have known the reprieve could not last.

"Unless she has something vitally important to tell me, tell her I'm busy," Lora says.

Yris calls from the highway, her voice grating down Ayc's spine. "I only wish to lay eyes upon my daughter to ensure she's safe!"

Lora rolls her eyes, but she releases Ayc and marches toward the door. Magdon stands frozen, xir eyes wide in the room's dimness, uncertain of what xe is meant to do. Lora positions herself in front of Magdon, glaring over xir shoulder where the top of Yris's head is visible.

"There, you can see me," Lora says. "I'm perfectly well."

Yris releases a breath, a deep one that sounds profoundly like relief. Ayc will never understand Yris. How she can show a fragment of care and concern in one moment but absolute disregard in another. He's uncertain he ever wants children, but if he ever did have a child, he knows he would tear down the very fabric of the earth to protect them and ensure their happiness.

Lora grabs the door to push it closed, but Yris calls, "Allow me to call Onanna. If there's an intruder, she'll be able to locate them. And she can place protection spells over the castle. I know your sorcerer isn't here at the moment, and besides, Onanna is far stronger."

Lora cocks her head as though considering it. "Onanna can look, so long as Irving and Peregrin go with her. So she can immediately report to them anything she finds."

"Agreed," Yris says quickly.

Ayc doesn't like it. He hates Onanna. With her own eyes that glow silver, and her strange voice, she's almost as terrifying as Serene. But something has to be done to investigate and ensure that Lora is protected.

"Irving will be there in a minute. Wait outside." Lora shuts the door and glances at Peregrin. "Is that all right?"

Peregrin dips their head. "I'll watch her closely."

When Peregrin and Irving leave, Lora and Ayc stand in silence. Xylie stands, her fingers strumming against her thigh, rocking from heel to heel. "I can't shake the feeling that we're wrong."

"What do you mean?" Lora asks.

"Perhaps we asked Amos the wrong question. We asked him who he hired because we assumed he was the mastermind."

"And?" Ayc presses.

She lifts her palms. "What if Amos wasn't the puppeteer? What if he was just the puppet?"

CHAPTER
SIXTY-TWO

LORA

"I never thought I would be happy to see your face," Lora admits reluctantly as Damara saunters down the beach toward her and her Five. When Damara last left, Lora wasn't certain she would see Damara again or if—now that Lahlis knew Ayc wasn't some secret Creed love child—they would drop the illusion of diplomacy.

Damara grins as she comes to stand before them. "Nice to know I've grown on you." She shifts to look at Ayc, standing on Lora's side. Her smile pulls wider. "Hello, brother."

Ayc tenses. Lora really wishes that Damara did not have to bring up their connection. Ayc hasn't spoken of it much, but Lora knows the connection still chafes, like fleece against her skin.

"Hello, Damara," he says flatly.

The wind stirs, blowing Damara's tangled brown hair away from her face. She sniffs. "Are you two aware that you reek of each other?"

Ayc grins like he's proud.

"We're aware," Lora says. She twists back to the path she took. "Dinner?"

"Unfortunately, I can't stay too long, but I will walk with you and grab something for the road. I don't wish to have another journey back with an empty stomach."

She joins their midst, a party that is no less guarded than when last Damara was here on her own. Gryphons still fly over the dragon she left down the beach and pace on the cliffs above. Royal guards and gryphon riders surround Lora in her Five. But Lora is now certain that Damara isn't going to slam a knife into her spinal cord.

At least, fairly certain.

Damara steps to Lora's other side as they make their way back up the beach. "I wish to discuss your visit to Drakr."

The permanent knot within Lora's stomach pulls tauter. In a few days, they'll go to Sal Maris for a little over a week. After that, they will have a brief stint at Wyntra before heading to Drakr lands. They have been preparing for weeks already to ensure that they have a small army to go with them—and some of Everadyn's best sorcerers—enough of a force that the Drakr will hesitate to mess with them. But it's enough of a risk that neither Lora nor her Five have completely decided if it's wise for them to go.

Lora grasps Damara's arms and pulls her to a halt. "If anything you told me last time was true, then tell me. Is it safe for me to go to Drakr?"

"Oh fuck no," Damara responds.

The rest of her Five dig their feet into the sand and whirl toward Damara. Irving and Davos step closer while the gryphon and their riders on the beach linger at a distance.

"You're walking into enemy territory," Damara adds. "That will never be safe. My father has repeatedly reassured me he means you no harm and instructed the dragon riders of Morkt Hemma that no harm should befall the new Sovereign. But I am not so foolish as to think that nothing is up his sleeve. If you come, bring a small army with you and cast every protection spell you can think of. And I do hope you'll come. There's something I need your help with. Something critical for the safety of both our nations."

"And what is that?" Lora demands.

Damara looks around, noting all the eyes upon her. She lowers her voice. "Can we go somewhere private? Just you, your Five, and the captain of your guard."

Lora glances at Peregrin. They nod. Their lack of hesitation is reassuring. All the Five know of what Damara told them last she was here, and they've all agreed that they are cautious but optimistic that she might be on their side. Especially with the way she protected Ayc.

Twenty minutes later, they are all settled in Lora's office, the privacy spell firmly in place. Lora perches in her chair while Bronwen sits on the edge of the desk between her and where Damara settles into one of the visitors' chairs. Lora is grateful that Bronwen and Tavish have returned from Lux Aester. They found little… except that Amos happened to be growing midnight in his greenhouse, without having a legal license to do so. Damning evidence, but nothing that either confirms or denies a connection with the Supreme.

As Xylie pointed out, they are uncertain of the role that Amos specifically played, but a judge of the high court ruled that there was significant evidence that he conspired against the Sovereign. At least, that has kept Amos's replacement from doing anything drastic. They are preparing for an election, and Lora's organization has put forth their own candidate. Lora doubts they will be successful and get elected, but she will be sending as many funds as she can get away with to ensure they have every opportunity to reach as many ears as possible.

As for the sorcerer who killed Amos, Onanna searched for clues that night and found only that the imprint of magic that was left behind was some of the most powerful she had felt. When Ayc asked her about the Supreme, Lora didn't like her response. *I'll double up the protection spells.*

Even now, Lora can feel the buzz of the protection spell that Onanna put over the castle days before. Everyone has remained on edge—especially Ayc and Irving—as though expecting the castle to come under siege at any moment. She's certain it does not help Ayc that she sleeps fitfully and sometimes wakes up gasping for air so loudly, it startles him awake. She lets him hold her after, but it does not ease the stickiness that the dreams of being soaked in her own blood have placed on her skin.

The lines on Damara's forehead are doing nothing to assist in the feeling of tension. It fills the air like an oncoming lightning storm, making Lora's hair stand on end.

"What is it you need?" Lora asks.

"A distraction," Damara says. "Long enough for me to search Morkt Hemma."

"And what exactly are you looking for?" Bronwen asks.

"Not what. *Who*."

"You certainly love your dramatics and building the suspense, don't you?" Ayc says, from where he leans on the bookshelf, his arms crossed over his chest. Xylie and Tavish stand next to him while Irving and Peregrin loom behind Lora's shoulders.

"When you've lived as long as I have," Damara replies, "you'll take whatever chance you can to amuse yourself."

Lora sighs. "Then *who* are you looking for?"

"Queen Volkna."

Lora blinks. "I don't understand. Am I not meeting with Queen Volkna?"

"I doubt it. No one other than my father has seen Queen Volkna in *over* ten years."

Lora's hands tighten around the desk as a tornado of emotions weaves through her. Confusion. Disbelief. Annoyance. The same emotions flicker through the expressions of the others.

"How does someone lose a queen exactly?" Tavish asks, gently, still clinging to some degree of politeness.

"Excellent question," Damara replies, giving a strained smile. "I don't know. It took me forever to even notice she was gone. She's hidden herself away in that castle with her dragon for decades, ever since her mate was killed trying to ransack a wild dragon's nest. She's always used Lahlis as a mouthpiece and never appeared in public, so it seemed no different at first. But eventually, I started hearing rumors among the Dom Eldi staff, and I started asking subtle questions and figured out that no one other than my father has seen her since before the Creed massacre. Not even the staff."

"Did Queen Volkna not give the order to attack Creed?" Ayc asks.

"It was Lahlis who orchestrated that deal with your mother," Damara replies, nodding to Lora. "And Lahlis who gave her the command to destroy the Creeds. He said it was Volkna's wishes, but it seemed peculiar to me, even at the time. She never wanted to take a chance of harming the Creeds, not when she dreamed so regularly of a bear devouring a dragon. Twelve years before, she sent Lahlis to negotiate a peace treaty with the royal family at Creed. It didn't go well, but still, Volkna never wanted to completely ruin the peace between them, at least, not until her dreams changed. My father was so frustrated by it. And then, Volkna's policy suddenly changed. But I don't think it was her who changed it. I think it was Lahlis. I suspect he did something to Queen Volkna to imprison her and has her hidden away, perhaps under some spell that allows him to use her gift of dreams without her being a threat. And so long as she lives, he also avoids the bloodbath of his few remaining siblings—not to mention his and their offspring—challenging him for the throne. With the situation as it is, he can effectively be king of Drakr without ever earning the throne."

Lora's chest tightens as Damara states every new detail. She wishes Candor was here to confirm what Damara is saying, but her gut—if she can trust it—tells her that Damara isn't lying.

"My father got wind of the questions I was asking the staff," Damara continues. "And since then, anytime I'm at Morkt Hemma, he has me watched. Either by himself, one of his inner circle, Caius, or sometimes even Brekken."

Bronwen issues a little growl at the name.

Damara arches an eyebrow. "Goodness. He certainly got under your skin, didn't he?"

Bronwen lifts her chin proudly. "On the contrary, I loathe him."

"I did not say you didn't. Hate can burn just as passionately as love."

A bit of color stains Bronwen's cheeks. A few broken sounds leave her lips, but Peregrin shifts forward to stand at the other side of the desk.

"And what do you want us to do?" they ask.

"I require nothing other than your presence. While you are there, all eyes will be focused on you. I will have a rare opportunity to search Morkt Hemma. Perhaps your Fourth might be of some assistance."

"I can't sense anything about your queen," Tavish says, tightening his hand on Saga's leash. "I tried to think in that direction and immediately felt like my head was being split open until I looked away." He presses a thumb into the center of his forehead.

"There is much magic over Mórka Hemma. We do have our own sorcerers, though magical affinity is more rare among the Drakr. Once within the walls, you should not meet as much resistance. If I can find her, perhaps I can free her from whatever way Lahlis has kept her captive, and she can reclaim command of Drakr lands."

Lora fists her hand around the leviathan tooth at her neck. "And why should we help you? How does it benefit Everadyn or Aluina if Queen Volkna leads instead of Lahlis? After all, she, too, wanted the lands of Aluina to herself. Her warmongering mother went to war against Everadyn to try to claim our lands, too. Why is she a better enemy?"

"As I said, Volkna has always had different policies when it came to Aluina. Did she long after their resources? Yes. Did she believe it was worth the risk to claim them? No."

"But now that the Drakr have them, would she willingly let them go?" Ayc asks.

"I don't know," Damara admits. She shifts toward the edge of her chair and leans toward the desk. "But I know my grandmother. She is powerful. She's held her throne for so long despite many who have tried to take it from her. Lahlis must have tricked her if he's gotten her under his control. If I can free her, she will be furious. She will rain fury down upon him and everyone who helped him. Many of those people play a key role in Aluina's continual oppression, and having them dead is very good for Aluina. It will ease much of their suffering and give the people a chance to fight back."

Lora weighs all the information, trying to ensure she has it organized in her head. "So you are asking me to walk into what is potentially a trap, so you have a chance to free an enemy—hoping she will do us a favor and destroy our other enemies?"

Damara purses her ruby-red lips. "That does sum it up, yes."

"I don't like it," Ayc says. "Not if we're putting Lora in active danger."

A dark cloud has hovered over Ayc these last few days. Lora is coming to terms with being Sovereign meaning she'll never be completely safe. Ayc seems to have realized the same, but it's made him on edge.

Damara leans back, giving him a sympathetic smile. She parts her mouth, and Lora doesn't want to hear her commentary on his feelings, so she presses on, "And what are the consequences if I say no? If I fail to show up? Does Lahlis mean his threat to come to war?"

"Yes," Damara says. "He will secure your allegiance, or he will come for Everadyn lands. We have been preparing for the transition in power for quite some time, knowing Yris would step down at fifty years. I promise you that whatever preparation you have done since you assumed the throne, it will not be enough. You need more time."

Lora scrubs a hand over her face. Her options seem like varying degrees of *fucked*, and not in the pleasurable sense. **But** Damara makes tremendous sense. If she's right, it could mean immediate relief to Aluina's suffering. It could mean an end to Lahlis. Neither choice is the right one. It's simply a matter of which messy, violent path they wish to take.

"Damara, can you allow me to speak to my Five alone?" Lora asks.

Damara nods and rises. She picks up the plate of sandwiches that they brought with them to the office and steps into the hallway, already crunching down on one.

Lora looks over her Five, studying their solemn expressions. "What do you think?"

"I don't like it," Tavish says. "Either option gives me a stomachache."

"What do *you* want to do, Lora?" Ayc asks. The shadows still war in his eyes, but his voice is gentle, an open implore that tells her he would yield to her choice, even if it's different than his own.

But now she must decide.

If Lora goes, the person she is risking is herself, her Five, and her small curated army. If she stays, she is risking everyone in Everadyn. She's seen Drakr wrath, the villages that burned. Thousands of innocent people will die, not soldiers who volunteered, knowing the risk. She does not trust what Lahlis has planned, but someone else will pay the price if she doesn't risk it.

"Wyntra will burn if we don't go," Lora says.

Peregrin glances at Irving, and she knows what they are thinking. Zinnia and Ember. And there are so many more. Avabeth in the kitchens. Lovelace, her accountant who has loyally handled all her nefarious activities. The staff who have served her so faithfully. The Archives and all their knowledge. The little public library in the corner of Wyntra where she read almost the entire children's section when she was younger. Much of her aerial army.

She releases a breath, deciding.

"I am in favor of going. But I'm asking for a vote. If most of you believe we should stay, then we stay."

Bronwen looks at Peregrin, and Xylie glances at Ayc, and Tavish lets out a deep, deep sigh. But one by one, they all press a hand over their chests, like they did in the Trials.

"I go where you go," Ayc says.

And fuck, she loves him so damn much. She loves them all so much.

"Then we will go," Irving says. "Urbain and I have been preparing, but given the new information, I will ask for even more riders to go with us. Perhaps I'll write the commander of the navy and ask for a couple of battleships as well."

Lora nods. "Xylie, will you open the door and let Damara back in?"

Xylie, who is closest, opens the door. Damara stands on the other side, licking her fingers, half the plate of sandwiches consumed. Perhaps she's learned that in Wyntra, if she doesn't eat quickly, she's likely not to get to eat at all.

She reenters, pushing the door closed with her foot.

"We will go," Lora says.

"Excellent!" Damara exclaims. Then, more solemnly, she adds, "I swear, Stjarna and I will do everything I can to protect you."

"I appreciate that," Lora says.

"I fear I must go. But first…" Damara looks to Ayc. "Would your dragon like to meet mine?"

AYC

Ayc still isn't certain that this is a good idea, but the excitement that is buzzing across Muffin and his shared link makes him smile. At the very least, leading Muffin down to the beach to meet with both Damara and her dragon will give him the opportunity he needs to get her alone. Lora wanted to send a guard with them, but Ayc asked her not to. There would still be gryphon riders on the cliffs, and they will have to eventually trust her.

Muffin walks with Ayc through the barrack streets, their tail nearly taking out a cart as they swing it with excitement. "*Do you think he will like me?*"

"*What's not to like?*" Ayc asks and cringes as, this time, Muffin strikes a cart of newspapers, scattering them through the street.

He'll send the printing press some money. Muffin seems to be where most of his money is going, anyway. Kids are so expensive.

"Wait," they say when they reach the cliffs, where Muffin will have to fly to the beach below. They are far too big to make it down the path. *"I've been thinking, and I think I've finally decided."*

"On?"

"My name."

"Oh." Ayc turns completely to Muffin, wanting to give this moment the respect and attention it deserves. *"What have you decided?"*

They flutter their wings, and the sunlight that pours through the thin membranes scatters rainbows on the grass. *"My name is Murrenigh."*

Ice that burns like fire.

Ayc smiles. *"It's perfect, Murrenigh."*

"I like it." Their lips pull back into a smile. *"Though I still like to be called Muffin, just only by my friends."*

Ayc smiles in return. *"So I can still call you Muffin?"*

"Bold of you to assume we're friends," Murrenigh says, before they launch themself into the air, rocketing toward the sky without warning. The laughter that floats down the bond tells Ayc that Murrenigh is only teasing, but still they call, *"Of course you can."*

They are already high in the sky. The powerful burst of wind and the suddenness of their flight demonstrate how far they have come in the last few weeks. They'll be ready to make the crossing to Drakr, but Ayc still fears taking them. What if the Drakr rider's dragons attack them? They would not survive it.

Ayc lets out a breath. So many that he loves are in danger, but he can't make them stay. He won't hinder their freedom.

A rumble sounds on the beach below, loud enough that the cliff beneath Ayc's feet tremors. Stjarna launches into the air, their cobalt scales contrasting against the gray sky. Ayc holds his breath as the beast soars toward where Muffin circles. Stjarna is three times larger than Murrenigh. If Stjarna decides to attack, there's little Ayc can do from such a distance.

"Muffin!" Ayc calls. *"Shit, I mean, Murrenigh!"*

Laughter soars back through their link. Stjarna reaches Muffin and banks before colliding, turning to the right in a graceful maneuver. Muffin copies the movement, though not quite as gracefully.

"I'm fine!" Murrenigh called back. *"He's my friend! He wants to teach me battle maneuvers dragons use. Not gryphons. Dragons."*

Ayc smiles as Stjarna leads the much smaller dragon in a spiral. Glee pours down the link, so thick it tastes like guzzling champagne: sweet and bubbly. No matter how much Murrenigh grumbles, Ayc knows they've struck up a friendship with Tempest. Still, Ayc suspects there is something comforting that comes from being amongst someone so like yourself, a community that comes from deeply shared experiences.

"Dragons aren't meant to fly alone," Damara says as she steps up from the beach path to where he's standing. His sister stops beside him.

Sister.

Shit. He's thought it many times today, and yet, it always clangs like he's standing inside a bell—loud and jarring. He can't quite make himself believe it, can't make it fit in his head, like a puzzle piece that belongs to a different puzzle entirely. It's best he go back to completely avoiding it, the way he has been. So he locks the information back in his head, back behind his walls, where he keeps painful things.

Murrenigh was right.

But he doesn't have time to sort out feelings now. If Ayc is going to ask about Asbjorn, he must do so now, or he might never have another opportunity.

He cocks his head in a gesture toward the cliff that juts out over the beach, the one that Ayc and Lora stood on when Lahlis's red dragon, Sarck, landed before them. He wants to create distance from the gryphon riders on the cliff. Damara nods and follows. They walk side by side until they reach the end, watching their dragons dart above the crashing waves.

Ayc pulls a coin from his pocket and holds it up for her to see. "Does this look familiar?"

A grin splits across his face. "Sure does." She reaches into her own pocket and tosses him something so quickly he nearly doesn't catch it. It's a coin. It already has his name. "I was hoping you would sort it out."

Well, damn. That was easier than he thought.

"The bear on your collar gave it away." Ayc retrieves the rest of the coins and holds them in his palm before showing her. "Five coins. You're the last one I needed."

She arches an eyebrow. "Well done. It took me a couple of years before I managed that."

"How did you become connected to Asbjorn?" Ayc asks. He can't imagine who took a chance on Lord Lahlis's daughter.

"That is a long story. And perhaps one day I'll share it. But not today."

Ayc isn't at all surprised by the avoidance. He shrugs. "How do I find the leader? Do you give me another clue?"

She hums beneath her breath, a faint smile teasing her ruby-painted lips. "I think you've probably already gotten enough clues. I'm surprised you haven't figured it out already."

Ayc rolls his eyes. "Come on, Damara. Give me something. A riddle even."

She clucks her tongue. "Who taught you manners? You didn't even say please."

"*Please,*" Ayc presses.

"Much better," she says with a nod. "And yet, the answer is still no."

His voice takes on an edge. "Damara—"

"No." Her shoulders shake as though withholding a laugh. "If you ask me again, I'll shove you off this cliff. Give you the Dom Vari sibling treatment you missed out on."

Ayc winces.

"The news of your bloodline isn't sitting well with you, is it?" Damara asks. "I don't blame you. Being Lahlis's child doesn't sit well with me either, and I've been aware all my life."

Ayc has to swallow multiple times before he can make his tongue work. All that comes out is avoidance. He truly does not wish to speak of their connection. "Speaking of Lahlis, do you truly trust that Lahlis means Lora no harm? So long as she can convince him she wants to uphold the treaty?"

"I think we'd be foolish to trust Lahlis."

"Then you'll be willing to lead Lora into a trap on the off chance of finding your queen." The words are laden with fire as they leave his mouth, but Damara doesn't shy away from the burn. She only smiles at him sympathetically.

"Have you told her? That she's your mate?"

Ayc locks his jaw and says nothing. No, he still hasn't told Lora what Murrenigh revealed to him, how deep their connection goes. This thing between them is still new, and the last thing he wants is to scare her by telling her they are connected by fate. He wants to tell her when it feels right to do so, and between Veni and Amos and the looming visit to Drakr, it has not felt right.

"That mating bond chafes, doesn't it?" Damara asks.

"Do you speak from personal experience?" he replies.

She turns away, searching over the sea. Her shoulders shift downward, and her shadow stirs unnaturally at her feet, like it's swaying in the wind. "Yes. But alas, that's ancient history."

"What happened?" Ayc asks, then swiftly says, "I'm sorry. You don't have to tell me."

"I think it would be nice to tell someone." She draws in a breath. "Her name was Juniper. June. And my, she was as beautiful as summer, and what we had in a few short months was paradise. But I was not worthy of her, and she saw that in time. I think fate picked the right person, but time got it wrong. She was not meant to be with the person I was then. I was so brainwashed by my father's nonsense that I couldn't even see the way it harmed the person I loved most. Couldn't see or didn't care enough to see it. Perhaps the person I am now could have been worthy of her, but not who I was then."

Ayc swallows hard. He can't imagine how much he would

loathe himself if he lost Lora due to his own foolishness. "We have fae blood. Perhaps it's not too late for a second chance."

Her shadow grows even longer. "It is," Damara says. "She died in Aluina years ago. She was human. She married for money and safety, had children, and died at an elderly age fifteen years ago. And yet I miss her every day. And I do not wish you to ever experience what I experienced. I *will* protect Lora."

Tears glisten in her blue eyes, and for the first time, Ayc feels something. A connection, perhaps. That she could, in fact, be family, not just in blood but in some way that matters. He's too scared to trust it—not yet, at least. But for the first time, he dares to hope.

"Do you promise?" Ayc asks.

She smiles. "I promise, brother."

SIXTY-THREE

AYC

The ship sways through the waters of the Bellum, the spray of the icy water parting before the *Vanguard's* hull several stories below. Ayc stands at the rail on the ship's stern, watching the skies as Murrenigh struggles to keep up with the ship. Tempest remains faithfully at their side. They've had to land at night, sleeping on the deck of the warship. The rest of the fleet of gryphon riders who are escorting Lora to Drakr have flown ahead and landed in Drakr, making the flight in far less time than the ship.

It's been hard to keep track of Murrenigh in the continuous gray skies above the Bellum sea. Their white color hides amongst cloudy sky so perfectly. It's an ability that will one day be an advantage, but now Ayc's stomach is constantly in knots. Twice since leaving Wyntra two days ago, Ayc has lost sight of Murrenigh for so long he feared he lost his dragon to the ocean. The little shit wouldn't even respond as Ayc hollered down the link to them and he rushed around the deck, searching the skies. Every time he thought he saw them, it was merely a glint of light. Both times, they reappeared a few minutes later, cackling at the prank.

Ayc regrets that Murrenigh didn't stay behind, but in the end, it wasn't his decision. Murrenigh refused to be separated from Ayc and Lora. So now Ayc just has to find a way to survive in the Drakr homeland and get his dragon and his soulmate and his dearest friends out alive.

Ayc lets out a long sigh, leaning against the railing.

"That sigh sounds like it came from the depths of your soul," Peregrin says as they step up beside him. "How is your pain?"

"I'm fine."

"Well, in case you're not." Peregrin holds out a small white feather pinched between two fingers. One of Tempest's small feathers. "Tempest told me before she returned to flight this morning that you need to start asking for them when you need them. Or she's going to take a chunk out of your ass."

Ayc smiles as he takes it. He wasn't lying. The pain isn't bad. His lower back is still tight from the bed he and Lora are sharing onboard. It's much too small, not meant for two, but he's grown used to sleeping next to her body. Even in Sal Maris, where they Toured for a week, Ayc often snuck into whatever room she stayed in. He's unsure if he'll ever be able to sleep again if her body isn't close to his.

Tempest's call carries across the sky as she nudges Murrenigh's tail with her wing, correcting the angle that was slowly directing them toward the waves. Ever the devoted teacher.

"She's so good," Ayc says.

"The best," Peregrin agrees. "Is there anything else you need?"

Ayc thinks about the coins that he still keeps in his pocket, though he's not sure why he's brought them with him. It's a risk, but he couldn't bring himself to leave them. What if he figures out who the leader is? What if they're close by? What if Damara changes her mind and simply tells him who the leader is?

"No," Ayc says with yet another heave of a sigh. "I'm going to go make some tea." Or perhaps something stronger. They are still a full day out from the southern Drakr coast.

He makes his way downstairs, passing the dozens of sailors

who are forever moving around. They busy themselves like honeybees in a hive and whisper about pirate queens who can take out an entire crew without even touching them. They're all afraid of what will happen if they see a black flag on the horizon, and Lora can't exactly reassure them that she and all her Five and a few of her guards now have bracelets tucked in their pockets to protect from such a thing.

He stops by the galley to get a cup of tea to drink down the gryphon feather. When he leaves, he nearly runs into Tavish and Xylie in the hallway, headed toward deck with their arms hooked together. It's strange to see the two without Saga. Tavish made the painful decision to leave Saga behind. Saga bravely went into a dragon's den on Somnia Ignis and would loyally follow Tavish anywhere. But somehow, this felt scarier. The dog is being tended to by Zinnia and Ember. When Tavish left him there, he joked that Saga will have gained a stone from all the treats that Ember will give him, but he also cried when he said it. Ayc doesn't doubt that Tavish's connection to his dog is every bit as close as Ayc's is to Murrenigh. A completely ordinary magic.

Still sipping his tea, Ayc follows the memorized path down into the heart of his ship to where Lora's quarters are. She's spent most of the time here, trying to pretend that she's not in the ocean. He knocks on the door once before he slips in.

Lora reclines against the headboard of a bed secured to the ceiling so it sways gently with the ship's movements. Her eyes dart up momentarily before she looks back at the page. Ayc leans on the door and sips his tea as he watches her consume the words like they are air. He knows better than to interrupt her, but he doesn't have to wait long before she snaps the book close and tosses it to the end of the bed with a growl of frustration.

He whistles lowly. "Damn. Do your books always make you so aggravated?"

"Frequently, yes," she says. "I just want them to fuck already."

"Who?" He wiggles his eyebrows. "Because I might have some suggestions."

She glares. "I'm talking about the characters in the book."

"Ah." He drinks down the last of the tea, the last fibers of the gryphon feather that have collected at the bottom of the cup making him shudder. "So annoying when fictional people won't do what we want them to do."

"It is," she agrees emphatically. "It's this dwarven author I picked up in Heimat. And the main character just can't decide between her chess rival and her best friend since childhood. And it's like—" She throws up her hands. "Just fuck them both!"

He grins. Fuck, he loves her like this, so worked up over a book. He wishes things were always this simple, that nothing else in the world existed that could make her this impassioned, other than the low stakes of a good romance book.

He moves toward the bed. "Just fuck them both, huh?"

Her mouth opens for a moment before she says. "Well, I mean…" She yanks at the collar of the loose tunic she's wearing like it's suddenly a little warm.

He revels in it. There's so little that gets her flustered, and he likes it. He drops his voice low, the one he uses only when it's just them. "Is that something you would like, Lora? Fucking two people at once?"

He swirls his finger, and a bit of shadow rises from behind her to caress against the side of her throat. His skills have grown considerably, especially when it comes to playing like this with her. Perhaps it's easier when he has the right motivation.

She shivers, and Ayc isn't sure if it's from the cool touch of his shadow or the fantasy. He's not even sure how *he* feels about the fantasy. He's fucked two people before, a couple at a festival who invited him into their bed. It was fun, and so now he finds himself equal parts intrigued and afraid he might cause bodily harm to anyone who touches Lora.

"It's an interesting thought," she says. "Perhaps, some things are just for books. I'm not entirely sure I'll ever be willing to share you."

"If you're certain. You are more than enough for me, although I'm pretty sure I'd do anything to make you happy." He wills the shadow to tease her hair, and her breath quickens, just the way he likes it. "In fact, I've been practicing some things."

She arches an eyebrow. "Oh, like what?"

There's a soft click as Ayc wills his shadow to lock the door. "Do you want to see?"

She pulls her bottom lip between her teeth and nods.

He glides his fingers through hers and guides her to her feet. He undresses her slowly, leaving kisses on the insides of her wrists and the hollow of her collarbone, working his tongue over the bud of each of her nipples, dragging his teeth across her hipbones. All the while, he wills his shadows to tease across her skin, spiraling her breast and brushing down her thighs until she's moaning for him. This might be the last privacy they get. After they land in Drakr, who knows when next they will be alone and safe enough to relax like this? He means to make the most of this moment.

He lingers on her mouth the longest, drinking in her taste. "Do you trust me?" he asks.

They've had long conversations about what they like, what they might be open to trying, what they absolutely don't like, and the words to use if things are too much. So even though he asks, he's certain she'll like what he has planned.

Still, she nods.

"Then put your wrists together."

Her eyes gleam in interest, their color a magnificent brown, as she obeys. A coil of shadow raises and wraps around both her wrists. She tugs experimentally, but he doesn't let the shadow loosen.

She smiles. "You're getting stronger."

There's pride in her voice and love in her eyes. He pinches her chin between his fingers and tilts her chin so he can see the gleam there better. "You've not seen anything yet. I'm going to make you beg before I'm through with you."

"Promise, Ayc?" she nearly whines.

"Promise." He brings her mouth to his, and she meets it with a violence, a kiss that's more teeth than lips. She drags her bound wrists down his chest, creating friction that has him straining against his trousers for freedom. When her hands somehow find his belt, her finger slipping into the loop, he protests, "Lora, behave."

She drops to her knees, and his heart goes utterly still. Fuck. He can't inhale looking at her : his shadows wrapped around her wrists, coiling around her body, as she looks up at him with silver eyes and a wicked grin. The powerful woman who won't bow... except to him.

"Do I *ever* behave?" she asks. "I thought I warned you that I'm *not* a good girl. Now, undo your belt and let me taste you."

This isn't how he planned for this to go. Her pleasure is his pleasure. Her pleasure comes first almost every single time. But fuck, he can't say no to her. She's the one bound, but she's reminding him that's she's still the one in control. That he's the one who is clay in her masterful fingers.

He tosses his shirt aside before following her command and ridding himself of his pants as well. His cock stands hard against his lower stomach. She leans forward and drags her nose along his shaft. Her tongue follows. His hips jump, and his hands fly forward to grab something. There's nothing but her head. He gathers her curls carefully in his hands and tugs—enough she tips her head backward, away from him.

She whines. A delightful noise. He wants to hear it again.

The shadows are so responsive to his will. He wants to touch her sweet pussy, but he can't reach, and so it does it for him. It swirls between her parted legs, working across her center. She's told him his shadows often feel like fingertips, but cooler and lighter. He wills them to work like his own fingers might, touching her in that way he now has memorized. She rewards him with a moan even as her bound fingers rise defiantly to tease against his balls.

He removes one of his hands from her hair and wraps it around his cock. "Is this what you want?"

"Please."

That word on her lips flares his eyes with red. "Fuck." He lines the head of his cock up with her lips, brushing across their velvety fullness. "You like to wreck me, don't you?"

She nods and parts her lips for him. The first embrace of her warm mouth ruins every hope he has of appearing dominant. A groan rumbles deep in his throat as he glides across her tongue. She works him in inch by inch. He nearly loses focus on his shadow, and it's a feat of strength to will it to continue to brush against her pussy.

It's not the first time she's taken him into her mouth. He's lost track of the number of times she's made him absolutely fall apart this way, but he's still, nearly immediately, a pathetic, whimpering mess. She works him toward the back of her throat, swirls her tongue around him, groans deep in her chest like this gives her as much pleasure as tasting her gives him. He holds tightly to her hair, careful not to tug, and restrains himself from thrusting any deeper. He lets her control the movement, but it's a fight he might lose at any moment. Especially as she glides her fingers backward, across the expanse of sensitive skin behind his cock. She doesn't stop, and he nearly comes out of his skin when he feels the pressure of her thumb at his taut opening.

He thrusts involuntarily. She chokes, and he quickly pulls back, even though she follows the noise with a deep, satisfied hum. She frees her mouth for a moment, his wet cock slapping back onto his stomach. She swirls her thumb again.

"Do you like that?" she asks, even though she knows. She knows he does, even though she's never touched him there. Still, she's asking consent, and he gives it as a strained "Fuck" and "Yesss" through his teeth.

She applies more pressure. She doesn't push past the tight ring, but teases it. Still, the effect spirals pleasure deep at the base of his spine."You know, I found a supplier who makes these toys. Ones that I could wear and I could use to fuck you here. Would you like that?"

Ayc has died. He's died and gone to paradise because it's the only explanation for that series of words coming out of her mouth. Of all the things they've talked about, they haven't talked about this because it never crossed his mind to ask. She's enough. Whatever way she lets him give her pleasure is an honor. Whatever way she gives it back it a blessing. But yes, he would like that.

Fuck, he would *really* like that.

"Would *you* like that?" he asks back, through his teeth.

"Would I like to see you whimper for me as I fuck you?" Her eyes flash silver. "Yes."

"Fuck." Now, he knows he'll definitely survive the Drakr homeland because he refuses to die before he experiences that. He drags his fingers across her jawline. "Why are you so fucking good to me?"

Her smile twists into something more genuine. "Because you deserve it, Ayc," she says before she using her bound hands to guide his cock back into her mouth. "You deserve all of it."

And for once, he believes it.

As she stares up at him with those wide, adoring eyes, she works him, groaning all the while. The pleasure is too great. He can no longer keep control of his shadows, other than the ones still wrapped around her wrists. They glide over her body in gentle but unfocused ways as he mutters words of praise mixed with delirious curses. He's already close when she pulls back so only his tip is still in her mouth and lets saliva drip over her fingers. She returns her joined hands up back to that point of pleasure. As she picks up her pace of fucking him with her mouth, she uses the moisture to press in. She only manages a fingertip, but it's all it takes. The burst of pressure and pleasure flings him over the edge. He spills down her throat, and she drinks him down with a smile.

"Thank you," he praises, gasping for breath. He pulls away and drags a thumb over her mouth, dabbing up one last remaining drop. "I'm going to repay you for that."

And then he vanishes into the shadows.

Lora searches for Ayc in the shadows, even though she knows she won't find him. Her heart thuds in anticipation. She's not sure what he has in mind, but she knows that it means pure pleasure.

"Get on the bed." His voice booms from across the room, threaded with a growl that makes her clench deep in her stomach.

Her hands are still bound. She presses her feet beneath her, and though she could manage on her own, she feels a warm hand on her elbow guiding her to her feet. It's gone just as quickly. She lays upon the bed utterly bare. She knows he's watching her somewhere, so she gives a wicked grin and sneaks her bound hands toward her center. She's already soaked for him. The way he teased her with his shadows and the sounds he made while he came making her hot and needy. But his voice barks out.

"Hands above your head."

When she doesn't budge, the shadows tug, yanking her hands against the pillows. She lets out a breath of surprise. His powers have grown so fast—even Bronwen is amazed by it. The Dom Vari blood mixed with his ability to withstand pain have made him formidable in a small amount of time. The more creative uses are a very nice product of that.

She tests the bondage, pulling at the shadow. It only wraps around her more, not hurting, but limiting her movement and pinning her in place. The lantern above them goes out, and she gasps as she plunges completely into darkness. Dark curtains hang over the portholes, blocking out every sight of the ocean outside so she can pretend she's on solid land. Her eyes swiftly adjust, but still, she can see only shapes. She hears a distant cough of a guard, the creaking of the ship, feet on the floors above.

Then, fingertips trail across her thigh.

They are there and gone in an instant. Moments stretch on as her skin pricks in anticipation. She waits so long she almost snarls at him, but then his fingers pluck at a nipple. He repeats the process again and again. She can't see him, can't hear him move. His touches come out of nowhere, finding her breasts, her thighs, her hipbones, the back of her ankle. Fuck, it works. She's panting in anticipation, her pussy throbbing, screaming to be touched.

"Ayc!" she demands.

"Spread your legs for me, my love."

When she resists obeying, a shadow wraps gently around each ankle and yanks. It's fast, but it doesn't hurt. He's always the perfect mixture of rough and tender, and he's using the shadows the same way.

She pulls back, but the shadow once again won't let her move. She's spread open for him. Vulnerable. Needy. Desperately hungry for his touch. It does not come.

"Ayc!" This time, it's pleading.

A finger drags up her pussy, and she arches off the bed. Or she tries to. The bonds hold her tight, keeping her in place. Her heels dig into the bed.

"Ayc, touch me. Please."

His shadows respond to her pleading. They sweep over her skin like cool fingertips. They find her breast and her thigh at the same time, swirling around her nipple, gliding toward her center. *Yes.* Wet and warmth glides across her other breasts: Ayc's mouth, sucking her in. The contrast between the heat of his tongue and the cold of his shadows is exquisite. She writhes, trying to get more of herself into his mouth, but he pulls away too quickly.

She whines. His shadow answers her need as it finally— fucking finally—makes contact with her center, sweeping up and down like it did when she was on her knees. It feels like Ayc's hand but softer, lacking his warmth. It speeds up, its movements becoming quicker and quicker, until it's nearly vibrating against her.

"Fuck, yes," she moans.

He's tortured her so sweetly that she's going to come already.

And then the shadows stop. All the shadows but the ones keeping her bond retreat.

"You bastard!" she snarls.

Ayc's laugh is so close, she jumps. "You know what words to

use if you want me to stop," he reminds. "Bastard only makes me want to do it more."

The words *stop* or *no* will get this to end immediately. She knows it. But she spits again, "Bastard."

The shadows descend upon her once more, sweeping over her skin like a million tiny fingertips. Ayc's hands are among them, his palms flat as they chase across her belly. His mouth finds her shoulder, and his teeth find her nipple just as the shadow presses against her entrance.

Oh. *Oh*. He's never fucked her with his shadow before.

He hesitates.

"Words, Lora," he requests.

"Yes," she agrees. And the shadow plunges inside of her. It's harder than the shadow has been before, reminding her more of a cock than a finger. She writhes against it as it thrusts in and out of her. Still invisible, Ayc continues his play of teasing fingertips and sudden kisses. The shadow moves so quickly, so deeply, that she's quaking again. She bites her lip to hold back her cry, the sign she's about to break apart, but he knows because he withdraws again.

She sputters nonsensical threats, tears stinging at her eyes, but none of them are the words needed to make this stop. This is torture, and she wants to come, but she also never wants this to end.

"More," she demands.

He descends upon her once more. More shadow. More touching. This time his shadow works her clit gently while it plunges into her again and again. Ayc's hands caress every inch of her body, and she wishes it was his mouth, but she's determined not to beg. Not when every sensitive place is being attended to. Or so she thinks until a piece of shadow breaks off to swirl around her asshole. They still haven't gone there. Not yet. Not until now. But now she's certain. She bucks against it, desiring more pressure.

More. She needs more.

"Words," he demands again.

"I want it," she pants. "Yes, I want it."

There's a shush of a drawer being opened and shut, the pop of a bottle being opened. Ayc palms her ass, and his fingers replace his shadow, working over the taut opening with something slick. Lube. Fuck, she wishes she knew they had that earlier. She might have been able to push her finger deeper, without fearing she would hurt him. Next time.

His shadows continue to work her clit but pauses at her entrance as he works a finger around her hole. She still can't see him, can barely see anything, as he adds a little more pressure.

"Relax for me, my lady," he coaxes.

She forces herself to sag deeper into the mattress. The continued attention on her clit helps, but it's still so much. So much pleasure that it almost hurts. Tears sting at her eyes as he pushes inward, making his way past the first taut ring. He's so in tune that when she tenses, he stops and makes his shadows work faster. Only when she relaxes again does he press onward.

Then his finger is inside her, and her body relaxes, giving way from pain to pleasure. He works the finger in and out, and it goes smoothly. It coils pleasure that is deeper and fuller than what she's experienced before.

"Fuck, you're so perfect, Lora," Ayc says. "You're doing so well."

"Please," she begs, and she's not quite sure what she's begging for. She's standing on a ledge that she needs to fall over, but she can't get there. "Please."

"Of course, my love."

He plunges his finger in and out, then adds a second. She bows off the bed, but it's still not enough. Then his mouth is on her clit, lapping at her like he means to clean up the absolute mess he's made of her. He continues to fuck her ass with his fingers. His shadow returns to her breasts, plucking and teasing, and then slams once more into her pussy—picking up the pace.

Fuck, she's so full. She can feel him fucking everywhere.

The orgasm surges through her with a force she's unprepared for. She strains against the bonds, but she can't get away from him, and so it builds and builds. She falls over and over. She cries, and screams, and begs, and curses. And he. Does. Not. Stop.

She comes down, only for him to build her back up again. Still invisible, he crawls up her body and fits his cock inside of her pussy. She almost whines that it's not her ass before his shadow takes the place of his fingers, filling her with a new width and breadth. Ayc holds onto where her hands are bound as his shadow and his cock find a rhythm. As Ayc slides in, the shadow retreats, and as the shadow pounds deep into her, Ayc shows some mercy.

She can feel his weight pressing her deeper into the mattress, can feel his hips striking hers, can feel his cock so deeply inside her that her stomach aches with it. But it's still not enough.

"Let me go. Release my wrists. Let me touch you."

He relents, and she seizes ahold of him, touching his hair, his back, clinging to him as she once again feels like she's about to fall. The shadow finds its way to her clit, swirling over the aching bud. And just like that, she tumbles, reeling and lost in the pleasure. She barely hears him roaring in her ear as he falls with her, his shadows scattering, his body becoming visible once more.

In the aftermath, he cleans her up with warm water and lays kisses like prayers onto her wrists and ankles where he bound her. He murmurs sweet nothings against her skin until she tugs him down to the bed beside her. She curls against his chest. More. She wants more of this. Years more. Decades more. Whatever war she has to face, whatever fury she must survive, she'll face it if she can come back to him.

"I love you," she whispers into his skin.

He makes a sound, almost like a purr. "I never tire of you saying that."

She turns her head to brush it against his skin, just above his breastbone. "I love you," she breathes. Strange, how those words once made her feel so scared and now they make her feel powerful, especially when he makes that sound again. The purr. She chases after it by pressing another kiss to his throat. "I fucking love you."

"Mmm," he murmurs. "I fucking love you, too."

His long hair falls into his face, and she reaches to brush it aside. The blue in his eyes are hazy with a contentedness she understands completely, because she feels it within herself. She hates a little that she has to ruin it, but the ship is carrying them ever closer to the Drakr shore and she's waited long enough.

"Should we talk about it?" she asks.

"Talk about what?"

"How you're going to see your father?"

His smile disappears. "No."

She sighs and lets her head drop back down on her shoulder. "I think we've avoided this conversation long enough." He's quite gifted at it. All the times she's tried to bring it up in the past, she's started strong and then somehow forgotten all about it. His head between her legs tends to make her forget most things. "You can't run from your feelings forever."

"Xylie," he whispers.

She frowns. "What?"

"Bronwen. Tavish, Peregrin." He counts them off against her skin, his fingers drumming against her spine. "Zinna, Irving, Ember. Hellevi." He pauses to brush his nose against hers. "*You*."

"Ayc—"

"Those are the names of my family," he says. "Not Lahlis. Not my blood siblings." He drops his forehead to hers and his smile is so bright it could rival the sun. "The only family I need—the only family I want—is the one I've found in you."

SIXTY-FOUR

AYC

orkt Hemma appears every bit as beautiful and terrifying as Somnia Ignis. Its massive walls are built on the edge of Niend Drieg, a canyon that stretches as far as the eye can see. The castle's towers look like a dozen swords jutting toward the sky, threatening to impale any of those who approach from the sky, like the two dozen Everadyn gryphons who have ridden with Lora to the city. Ayc and his party have been able to see the gleam of its silver for miles as they made the days-long journey from the coast of Drakr lands within the shadows of the Untamed Mountains. Even at night, the city seems to glow in the moonlight.

Ayc stands at the front of Lora's small army, having gotten out of the wagon to join where she stands near the canyon's edge. He keeps himself still a few feet from the edge, not wanting to come any closer. Damara, who has traveled with them since they landed in Drakr, explained that the name of the canyon meant the Never-Ending Death, and Ayc hates that it feels accurate. He can feel the heat from there, smoke spiraling upward, releasing a foul smell of rotten eggs. Sulfur. Xylie told him the canyon is part of the lava flows from Brinfall, a volcano deep in the Untamed

Mountains, whose glacier peak Ayc has occasionally caught glimpses of, towering over all the others. It stretches west as far as the eye can see. The only way across its gaping mouth is the stone bridge that stretches across and leads to the towering front, spiked gate of Morkt Hemma.

Somewhere from behind the walls of the castle, a dragon roars, loud even from this distance. Lora sways a little closer to Ayc, her arm brushing his.

"I can hear the other dragons," Murrenigh tells Ayc from where they stand beside Stjarna and Tempest, a hundred yards to Ayc's right. The other gryphons keep back dozens of yards. *"They are angry the gryphons are here and angrier that their riders have given the order that they're not allowed to kill them."*

Ayc shudders. *How many are there?*

"Many," Murrenigh replies. They shake their head. *"I can't tell a number. Stjarna is telling them to be calm. That we aren't enemies. The one called Iolite is saying the same. Kivka says that she hopes the Everadyn queen kills them all, which only riles them up once more."*

"Damn." Ayc's anxiety lurches upward, and he resists the urge to take Lora's hand in his.

He glances behind him at the fleet that has come with them. The entirety of Lora's personal guard, the best and brightest of the gryphon fighters. A few sorcerers are among them. Even Captain Urbain is here, aboard his massive gryphon. Agates equip Urbain's ear, connected to Irving's and the rest of the guards. If anything goes wrong, they can communicate—hopefully, if the spells on Morkt Hemma do not prevent it. If anything, Peregrin could send a message through Tempest. They've thought through plan after plan. Damara has helped, talking through escape routes and showing them detailed maps of the inside of the castle. They're well equipped in case anything goes wrong, and yet, unease has settled into Ayc's gut like he swallowed broken glass. He doesn't want to walk across that bridge, but he will.

He goes where Lora goes. Where the rest of the Five go. Where his *family* goes.

"Ready?" Damara asks, walking over to where Ayc stands. She

is dressed in dark armor that, even on this cloudy day, gleams red wherever the faintest light touches.

Lora glances at the rest of her Five, who have gathered nearby. "Are we ready?"

One by one, they press their hands to their chest. Ayc feels the pound of his heart against it, but they are ready, and they will face it together.

Lora, her guards, and the rest of the Five make their way toward the bridge, but Ayc swings toward Murrenigh. A general feeling of dread passes over their link, and it's so entangled with his own emotions, he's not sure who is feeling it. Himself or his dragon.

"*Keep our Lora safe,*" Murrenigh says.

"*Always,*" Ayc promises. Still, his feet do not budge. He hates leaving Murrenigh here.

"Stjarna will watch over him," Damara says, with a sympathetic bend of her lips.

Tempest steps forward and cracks her beak as though to say, *Me, too.* She's already looked after Peregrin and Ayc, ensuring that each of them had a fresh feather to drink down as they drew close to Morkt Hemma.

Ayc reaches out to her, and she leans closer so he can run a hand down the feathers on her neck. She makes a sound almost like purring.

"Ayc!" Peregrin calls from where they've paused halfway to the bridge. "Stop petting my gryphon like a damn dog and get over here."

Ayc chuckles. "I'll look after them too," he tells Tempest, who bobs her head in a nod.

"They're always so cranky," Damara rolls her eyes in the direction of the gryphon rider.

"Not really," Ayc says. "You just haven't known them quite long enough."

She barks a little laugh and walks in the direction of the bridge.

Ayc steps up to Murrenigh and strokes a hand across the smooth scales of their neck. "*See you soon, friend.*"

Ayc joins their party, where they await him on the bridge. Irving and Davos already stand on the bridge, ready to walk ahead of Lora and shield her. The other guards part to let Ayc join the Five and Damara in the center. Together, they start across the bridge. Ayc takes Xylie's arm, and they step forward together. Her bag bumps between their hips, her alchemy bottle jingling between them. She's armed to the teeth.

"You all right?" he asks.

She nods. She feels steady, a deep inhale passing her lips. It feels like she's grown up so much in the last few weeks. She has always been enough, just as she is. But watching her step into her role of Second, finding strategies to cope with her struggles with more grace than many could, has been as great an honor as watching Lora do the same. He's so proud of her.

Ayc makes the mistake of glancing past the shoulder-high wall that lines the edge of the bridge. Hundreds of feet down, through the tendrils of steam, he catches sight of a river of lava that cuts through the center of the rocky base. He swiftly looks away.

As they near the gate, Lora glances back over her shoulder, her brow furrowed. He crosses his eyes and sticks out his tongue. She rolls her eyes and turns back around.

The massive gates swing open into a courtyard. Xylie's hand bites down on Ayc's bicep. At least a dozen massive red eyes swing to face them. Dragons line either side of the path that leads through a courtyard. They stand between towering pillars, an array of nearly every color and pattern: jewel tones and earthy tones; stripes that dip down their ribs like claw marks and spots that ripple down their spines. Some dragons are free and relaxed, while others wear collars like Kivka. The ends of the chains are fastened to metal hooks in the stone. The ground beneath the dragons is saturated with ever-deepening shades of red until it's nearly black—like the stone has been soaked time and time again for decades by the dragon's blood.

But every single red eye of the massive creatures is turned upon them.

Ayc swallows and reaches forward to Lora's elbow, whose hands coil into fists. The guards reach for their weapons. Bronwen's energy buzzes around Lora's forearm, blending with the blue of her new tattoo. Tremors wrack through Xylie's body.

"What is it?" Tavish asks as though sensing the increase in tension.

"Dragons," Ayc replies. "A lot of dragons."

The path leads past them to another set of doors into the castle itself. They will have to walk by all the dragons to reach it, where one breath will boil them in fire. Or acid. Or whatever else can come out of these dragons' mouths.

"They won't hurt you," Brekken says as he appears in the middle of the path that stretches before them. He saunters toward them, dressed just like Damara, a dark cloak sweeping behind him. "They've been given strict instructions to obey."

He stops before them, and Damara greets him with, "Hello, brother. Is everything well?"

"Yes, Father seems in good spirits," he says, but his eyes have drifted to where Bronwen stands beside Lora. He drinks her in, making Ayc wonder. The sex was meaningless to Bronwen. Was it to him?

"I like your tattoo," Brekken says.

"Do you?" Bronwen asks. "Well, I *dis*like that you're still breathing."

"Huh." The sound is adjacent to a laugh, his lips twisting in amusement. Bronwen only looks pointedly away.

Xylie flaps her hands, the flutter drawing eyes upon her, including Brekken's.

He cocks his head. "As I said, there's no reason to be afraid."

Xylie narrows her eyes, and her hands snap in the air. If Brekken can't understand what she's saying, surely her emotion is clear. In case it isn't, Lora translates.

"She is not afraid," Lora says. "She's angry." Lora inclines her head toward the dragons. "It's cruel."

Any trace of amusement disappears from Brekken's face. "Yes," Brekken says. "It is." He turns on his heel. "This way."

Ayc tightens his hold on Xylie's arm as they set through the threshold of Morkt Hemma and in front of the first dragon—a dragon whose earth-colored scales shimmer with undertones of green, reminding him of a mossy forest. Each of the dragons track Lora, her Five, and her guards as they make their way down the cobblestone. They aren't the only ones. Ayc occasionally sees the shadows move or a cloaked figure in dark armor moving in the darkness cast by the mighty dragon. Ayc tries to move steadily, to hide his fear, even if his anxiety makes it difficult to take every step.

They are halfway through the path when a dragon makes a sound—a great grumbling noise of discontent that comes immediately to Ayc's right. Xylie freezes. Ayc tries to tug her on, but she doesn't move and turns to stare at the dragon, who's only a dozen feet away.

Kivka looms over them, her head wearing a crown of several horns bent toward the center. Blood drips down her chest. She makes the sound again, but lower this time. Ayc doesn't like the way Kivka stares at Xylie, like perhaps she's found her next meal. But no, that's not right. Ayc doesn't trust the dragon, but there's something in its eyes that almost seems sad. She makes the sound again, but deeper this time. Almost like a groan.

Ayc's heart hammers against his sternum. "Come on, Xy."

Her fingers shake as she signs, *"I feel like she wants me to help her."*

Ayc glances around. He doesn't see Cauis anywhere, but surely, he's somewhere close. But dragon riders in their dark cloaks appear on the path behind them, noticing that they've stopped. Magdon has stopped behind Ayc, staying with them, but the rest of the party is moving onward.

"Ayc," Murrenigh warns, *"Whatever you are doing, the other dragons and their riders don't like it."*

"We have to go." This time, when Ayc tugs Xylie, she comes

with him, though she glances over her shoulder at Kivka. Ayc can feel the eyes of the dragon the entire way to the door.

Lora stares over her shoulder at them, arching her eyebrow in question.

"We're fine," Ayc mouths.

The group comes to a halt before the massive doors. They open inward. Bronwen helps Tavish up the stone staircase that leads to them, the stone a color that makes Ayc wonder if it came from the volcano itself. As Ayc passes through the door, he notes the cloaked figures who stand at each of the doors like dark, silhouetted statues, their heads bowed. More dragon riders? More servants? Ayc isn't certain, but something about them coils his stomach into another knot.

The inside of the castle reflects the Drakr's preference for black and red. Deep black stone forms spiraling arches over their head as Brekken leads them down the hallway, but the windows are made of various shades of red-stained glass. A crimson glow casts over everything. Ayc memorizes the turns Brekken takes, comparing them to what he memorized of the maps Damara showed him. He sends a quick prayer to the divine that they do not need that knowledge. He still doesn't believe in higher beings, but he figures it can't hurt.

Brekken turns one last corner. The hallway ends in a large, round door. A dragon is carved into the wall around it, its front claws holding the door, its tail draping toward the floor. Its open mouth centers above the door, the teeth sharpened to dozens of deadly points. Two rubies make up its eyes, and Ayc feels like it's truly watching him, peering down into his soul, wanting to devour. He restrains a shiver.

The doors open to reveal Caius. At the sight of his face, Ayc longs to grab hold of his power and slam the shadow into his face. It's such a punchable face. He's not wearing his bracelets, and it would be so easy and satisfying. But Damara has still not revealed to Lahlis about Ayc's power, so he has to keep it under control. When Lora and her Five discussed his power, they all agreed it was best they keep it hidden for as long as possible, but it was also best he not place a barrier between himself and his power. Wearing the bracelets feels like an illness he has to recover from, and he wants to be at his strongest if he needs that power. Still, he tucked his bracelets into the pocket of his coat. Something that has the ability to suppress Drakr power is not something they should be without.

"Greetings," Caius says.

Only Bronwen lifts her hand in greeting. Her lips pull into a taut smile as she wiggles her fingers. Her magic sparks from her fingernails. She drops her hand quickly, but not before flashing only the middle finger of her hand.

Caius pretends not to notice, focusing on Lora instead. "So glad you all decided to show up. I wasn't certain you had the nerve."

Lora tilts her chin higher. She's dressed in her black and gold armor, and her onyx crown gleams in the red light. "Why would we fear coming to the home of our allies, Caius?"

He opens his mouth, but a voice booms from within. "Enough of your dramatics, Caius. Let in our guests."

Damara and Brekken snap upward, their spines going rigid, before they visibly force their shoulders to relax. Even Caius's arrogant smile falters. Ayc's muscles tighten enough that it reminds him of their ache. Perhaps this tension is simply the impact that Lahlis has on his children.

Children. Including him.

Fuck.

The truth breaks as though from a dam he's been carefully hiding it behind. It floods through him, draining warmth from his skin. Muffin was right. Lora was right. He should have faced his feelings long before now because it feels like he's drowning in the reminder that this man is his father. The wickedness and monstrosity that runs in his veins also runs in Ayc's.

"There's no part of your soul that resembles that man," Murrenigh tells him, and it's a relief that even this deep into Morkt Hemma, they are still connected. Peregrin, then, can still communicate

with Tempest, who can send a warning to all the other gryphons if needed.

"You do not know him," Ayc says.

"Stjarna does, and he's my friend. We have compared notes. We both agree that our riders are more bear than bastard."

Xylie brushes her arm against Ayc's, but no one else looks at him, not daring to draw attention to him. He draws strength from the contact, from Muffin's words, and steels himself. He will have to face this pain later. He can't deal with it now.

Caius walks into the room, allowing them to enter. Ayc is unsure if he should be relieved or wary that they have not asked them to remove their weapons before entering their hall. Irving and Davos exchange a look before they enter first. Lora and Bronwen enter right after, Bronwen's staff cracking with each step. Peregrin and Tavish enter third, their canes tapping against the marble floor. Then it's Ayc's and Xylie's turn, followed by the three other guards.

The room reminds Ayc of the great hall, all pillars and a towering dome ceiling. But there's little light here. Despite the red windows that line the sides and form an artistic pattern at the back of the room, it's dim in here. Shadows coil into geometric shapes like decorative statues throughout the room. Lahlis's power, showing off how effortlessly he can wield it as he reclines in a chair at the head of the large table.

No, not a chair. A throne.

It's the only word for the grand thing, made of silver whose back bears spikes just like the castle and whose arms are carved into dragon talons. Dressed in armor and a red cape, Lahlis drapes himself upon the throne like he belongs there. All he's missing is a crown.

Ayc's father, the wanna be king.

There are similarities between Ayc and Lahlis. Now that Ayc allows himself to look, he can see it clearly. Their height and the coloring of the hair and eyes mimic one another, but Ayc notes the staunch differences, too. There's something hard and unflinching in Lahlis's face. If Lahlis is cut from stone, then Ayc is shaped from clay. Softer. Gentler. More like his mother.

Lahlis doesn't bother standing as Lora comes to a stop at the other side of the table, and so she offers no inclined head, no note of respect.

"Lord Lahlis," she greets.

"Queen Loraphne," he replies with that toothy, vicious smile. He sweeps a hand toward the chair. "Please have a seat."

Brekken pulls out the chair for Lora, and she nods at him before taking a seat. Soon, they're all situated, Lora's Five clustered at one end, while Lahlis's children join him on the other side of the table. Damara sits next to Tavish, separating him from Caius, while Peregrin positions themself between Brekken and Xylie, leaving Bronwen and Ayc at the chairs closest to Lora.

A meal has already been set on the table, a roasted pig with an apple shoved into its mouth, surrounded by cooked vegetables and fruits. Lahlis reaches forward to grasp the knife tucked onto the plate. Ayc tenses, but he stabs it into the flesh of the pig.

"Let's eat," he says. "I'm sure you're hungry from your long days of travel."

"Where is Queen Volkna?" Lora asks. "Is she not joining us?"

Lahlis doesn't flinch, doesn't falter, doesn't hesitate. "I fear she's not feeling well."

"I've come a long way to meet with her," Lora says, no suspicion in her tone. Only a carefully measured pinch of annoyance.

"That you have," Lahlis agrees. "But I'm afraid it won't be possible. You'll have to settle for me."

If Ayc didn't already trust Damara, this would be a confirmation of her tale. Queen Volkna is either dead or stashed somewhere, with Lahlis playing king in her absence. Magdon shifts in the line of guards that have formed behind Lora, but no one else gives way that they know anything more.

"Very well," Lora says.

Silence blankets the table as each of the Drakr serves up their own plate before Damara pushes the pig on its platter and the knife further down, so they can all serve themselves. Lahlis plucks up a carrot from his place and plops it behind his teeth, chewing as he studies Lora in a way that makes Ayc want to stab a knife through his eye socket. Damn, Lora's violence has rubbed off on him.

Lahlis waits until there's food on every plate before he fills the silence. "I feared that we would not make it here, but I'm hopeful that you and I will leave here as, well…" He twirls his fork in the air.

"Friends?" Lora suggests.

"I think that is too strong a word. Friends do not want to slit their friends' throats, as I'm certain you would do to me if you thought you could get away with it."

"On the contrary, Lahlis, it's my greatest wish we get through this visit without a single drop of blood split." She keeps her tone blithe, even as she severs the meat on her plate into careful, bite-sized pieces. "Does that mean that you would like to kill me?"

"My hope has always been to avoid that. As I said before, you're a pretty—"

"Do not finish that sentence." The words growl out of Ayc's mouth before he can stop them. He can control his power, which surges within him like an avalanche, or he can control his mouth. He can't do both.

Lora's hand clamps down on his leg beneath the table. Lahlis's eyes flicker with embers. Irving steps a little closer.

"Your human never ceases to annoy me, does he?" Lahlis stabs his fork into the slab of meat and sniffs, his nose wrinkling. "Or I suppose I should say Drakr since he's no longer hiding. Do you know that you reek of him, Loraphne?"

Lora lifts her chin and smiles like she's proud. "I'm aware."

"Pay him no mind, Father," Damara says, with a little flick of her fingers in Ayc's direction, like she's batting away a fly. "You know how protective Drakr males can be of their mates."

Ayc's heart lurches into his throat. What the fuck is she doing?

Lahlis cocks his head. "Ah." He says the syllable as though it explains everything. The red fades from his eyes, so perhaps Damara knew what she was doing. Still, Ayc would rather Lahlis not know. Particularly because he hasn't yet shared that truth with Lora. "Is it true? Is he mated to you?"

Lora's hand tightens on Ayc's knee, glancing at him from the corner of his eye. "Is that not just lore, like Everadyn fae descending from gryphons?"

"Perhaps." Lahlis crushes a potato beneath the tines of his fork. Disgust cuts into his tone. "I've seen it ruin too many people for me to doubt that it does exist. It turns so many strong, levelheaded people into whimpering fools who think the sun only rises for their mate and would sacrifice anything for them."

"I think what you've just described is love," Bronwen says, an edge to her voice.

Caius snorts. "A useless emotion."

"I find that love is more powerful than magic," Bronwen snaps back. "Not that I would expect the likes of you to know that."

Caius's lips curl back, revealing pointed teeth. "Why don't you shut your bitch mouth?"

"Watch it," Brekken snarls, flashing his own sharpened teeth.

Caius turns the vicious, knife-like smile upon him. "Have something you want to share, brother?"

"Let's maybe calm down," Damara says, her voice a coo, like she's trying to soothe an irritated dragon.

"That would be wise," Peregrin agrees.

Brekken barks back in the Drakr tongue. Caius and Damara speak at once, in their foreign language. Bronwen murmurs something beneath her breath. Lora hisses for everyone to shut up, but Caius shouts something over her.

Ayc's power thrums in his veins, crystallizing it for his cold. He hears Murrenigh calling from a distance. He grasps Lora's hand, still on his knee, and reaches for Xylie's elbow. Tension is rising so swiftly that it all feels like it's going to explode, and he's preparing to have to fling them both to safety.

And then Tavish blurts: "Well, fuck! This is going splendidly!"

Silence falls for the stretch of two aching heartbeats. Then Lahlis throws back his head and laughs. The sound makes Ayc clamp down on his power, but it makes him feel no less cold.

"Ah, this feels just like every family dinner I've ever attended," Lahlis says.

Lora's chuckle hides her nervousness, but it's far from genuine. "How did you avoid anyone getting stabbed?"

"We didn't," Lahlis says. "Such is the Dom Vari way. But rest assured, I don't intend to kill you, Loraphne, or any one of your Five. And my children will do as I tell them, no matter what mouth Caius has on him. You are here, and Damara tells me you do not intend to break the treaty. So long as I find no evidence otherwise, I hope our alliance stays strong through the next century."

Lora picks up her goblet and lifts it in a salute. "To a hundred years, Lahlis." Ayc thinks the smile she gives Lahlis is her best theatre yet. She even makes the sip she takes of the goblet look convincing, though Ayc knows she doesn't let the liquid touch her lips. Beneath the table, she tightens her hold on his knee, a reminder that whatever game they play today, Ayc and Lora and the promises they have made between them are not theatre. They are what is real.

Lahlis lifts his cup, too.

"Did anyone get stabbed?" Murrenigh asks.

"Not yet," Ayc replies.

"That is not reassuring," Murrenigh grumbles.

Tavish releases a nervous laugh. "Well, uh, that's a relief. But I'm afraid I'm going to piss myself. Is there a privy nearby?"

It's the excuse they thought of to get Tavish away from the table. Simple but effective. Just as planned, Damara pushes herself up from the table with a roll of her eyes. "Come on," she says, as though aggravated, "let's go."

Tavish gets up from the table, and Damara takes his arm. They need only to distract Lahlis and his sons long enough to give

Damara and Tavish time to search for the lost queen. If all else fails, starting another argument might be effective.

Everything is going exactly as planned.

The door swings open before they reach it, and a cloaked figure walks in, their head bowed. Damara freezes, pulling Tavish to a halt. The figure strides to Lahlis, hands him a large ream of paper, and then lingers at his side. Lahlis turns over the packet in his hand. A cavernous frown forms on his face as he unrolls it. Two papers unfurl. One, a simple sheet of paper scrawled with dark ink. The second paper is much thicker, like leather. The words are engraved into it instead of written upon it, reminding Ayc of the kind of parchment that Tavish reads.

"What is it, Father?" Damara says, releasing Tavish and striding back toward the table.

Lahlis holds up a finger as pointed as a knife, a cue for her to be silent. She presses her red lips into a flat line, but continues to slowly approach the throne. Lahlis lifts the thinner paper to read it. Brekken leans closer, and the color slowly drains from his face.

"Father?" Damara presses.

Lahlis lets out a tremendously long sigh. "Fuck."

"Is something wrong?" Lora asks. Her hand leaves Ayc's knee for the first time, reaching instead to the dagger at her belt.

Lahlis clucks his tongue and shakes his head. "I'll admit. You had me fooled. You've played this game well, Loraphne. But I'm afraid it's over now."

The air shifts. A cold hand of fear sweeps down Ayc's back. Clothes rustle as everyone shifts—reaching for weapons, no doubt. Ayc clamps a hand on his sword, even as he teases his power, keeping it in his grasp.

Something is wrong, Ayc warns Murrenigh. *Be ready.*

A growl comes across the link.

"What do you mean?" Lora demands. "Who is that from?"

Instead, Lahlis looks at the messenger who still stands beside him. "Let her in."

The figure returns to the door, slips out, and closes it once more.

"Let who in?" Damara demands.

Lahlis only smiles, and this time, every one of his teeth are pointed.

The door opens once more, and Yris walks in.

CHAPTER

SIXTY-FIVE

"**M**other?" Lora shoves to her feet and swings upon her. "What the fuck are you doing here?"

"Do you think I wish to be here?" Yris asks as she strides past Lora, past her Five, and walks to the table where Lahlis sits. "Do you think I wanted to have Onanna teleport me here? It feels like my divine damned skin is being ripped from its bones every time."

Onanna can teleport? That new fact nags at Lora's mind, but she doesn't have time to consider why right now. Not when Lahlis makes a shooing motion at Caius. Caius swiftly stands. Yris takes his chair and sits at Lahlis's right side. He smiles at her like they are old friends. And they are.

Silver tinges Lora's eyes. Her suspicion is painting a picture that just isn't fully complete, but she grasps enough that the rage is already rising, making her insides rumble like she's once again a volcano about to explode. If that thick piece of parchment is what she thinks it is, then this game is, in fact, up. From the opposite end of the table, Lora can only make out the engraved letters and the name Tavish. It's from Calliope. A love letter, maybe, but a love letter that bears secrets no one but Lora and her

733

Five should know. Calli would have sent the letter with a secure bird, but no one would have been there to receive it. No one but Lora's mother.

In that letter is proof of what Lora has done. She's conspired with a Tenebra prince and a pirate queen. And Yris just teleported it here to hand it to Lahlis. All the proof he needs to start a war. To kill her. To kill them all.

"What the fuck game are you playing?" Lora snarls, her teeth already sharp. Ayc rises to his feet on one side, Bronwen on the other, clutching her staff. Her guards step closer.

"I am doing what I said I would do," Yris says. "Protecting Everadyn. Ensuring the country I love continues to prosper."

Lora clutches the leviathan tooth she wears around her neck, feeling the broken edge dig into her palm. Using it to cling to her last hope that she has not lost this game already. "Then why are you betraying me?"

"It didn't have to be this way," Yris says. "I've never lied to you. I have always wanted to see you on the throne, but you wouldn't listen to me. Even when I sent that fool childhood friend of yours to leave midnight in your bed or had Onanna rip apart your favorite guard's head, you still wouldn't listen."

Lora is going to ignite. That's how it feels when the truth snaps into place. Her head is so on fire, she can barely think, can barely see.

"It was you?" Peregrin demands. They plant their hands on the table and shove to their feet, the chair screeching as it scrapes against the floor. "I questioned Onanna myself. She could not have been the one who harmed Irving. She was seen elsewhere."

Yris rolls her eyes. "Do you think we would not cover our tracks well? Make sure we had multiple witnesses who claimed to see Onanna? Give us some credit, Peregrin."

Lora feels like she might vomit, but she swallows down the taste of bile. Of course, it was Yris and Onanna. Of course. They were fools to not think it. Onanna was powerful, but utterly careful to not let anyone see just how powerful. Lora should have guessed she could teleport. Should have known she could have fucked with Irving's memories. And Orn said that opening the gate Heimat would have required dwarven blood. Fennix has dwarven blood. Onanna and Fennix could have easily done it together under Yris's command.

It was but another one of Yris's sick games to teach Lora a lesson. To isolate her, to show her that her friends could be hurt or that they would hurt her. To make her feel like she needed to make herself smaller and fall into line in order to succeed.

"What about Amos?" Bronwen demands.

"A scapegoat that you fell for," Yris explains. "Tiresome fool he was, but he did prove useful in the end. I feared he would squeal, so I had Onanna kill him. It was her idea to spell one of her eyes temporarily green. It kept you looking in all the wrong places."

Ayc lets out a huff of a breath, and it's visible in the air. The air coming from him is cold as the depths of the deepest winter. It was Onanna he caught a glimpse of in that cell, but Onanna tricked him. They didn't look at her; they let her investigate because she so clearly convinced them that Serene was involved in their plot.

Yris has played them all.

Yris looks back at Lora. "I've given you ample chances to yield. To prove that you can be the Sovereign that Everadyn has needed. But you have been too stubborn."

"Yris did try," Lahlis admits. The way he still slouches on that throne is far too casual for the heightening tension, betraying the utter confidence he feels that they aren't in the middle of a game; he's already won and is just waiting for them to catch on. "Up until now, I did believe we would be working together. But I fear you partnering with pirates to circumvent the treaty is the last fucking straw."

"Father," Damara says, holding out her hands as she takes a few steps closer, "let's discuss this rationally."

Brekken sits still, glaring hard at the table. Caius grins another gleeful smile of teeth sharp as knives.

"What is there to discuss?" Lahlis asks. "Loraphne has proven to be a wicked queen and has no interest in keeping our relationship mutually beneficial. We were fools to require Yris to step down at fifty years when the relationship has benefited me so. It only makes sense to give the crown back to her."

The crown presses down upon Lora's head. She's more aware of it now than ever. It's always been a heavy weight, but it is hers. It's fucking hers. She earned it, and she is not giving it up. Not until she's ready. Not until she's seen healed what must be healed.

"You can't have it," Lora snaps. She hears rustling and murmuring behind her, Irving muttering into his agate. She hopes Peregrin is speaking with Tempest and Ayc with Murrenigh. They and the army they brought with them are going to have to fight. The path where every single person comes out alive is closed. Yris hammered that one shut herself.

Yris stretches out her hand. "For the sake of your Five, take off your crown and give it to me. No one has to be hurt." She glances at Lahlis, who inclines his head as though considering, and then shrugs in a blasé agreement.

Yris continues, "You can come with me and explain that you couldn't handle the pressure. There will be a new Sovereignty Trials in time, which I will compete and win and reign for another hundred years."

Every word is a blow. Every word makes Lora angrier. She feels the crackle of Bronwen's magic and the icy chill as shadows creep around her feet. She's certain those are Ayc's. She knows their touch intimately, even as she knows that today they will not be as gentle as she knows they can be.

"I'll have to banish the Five, of course," Yris says. She glares down the table at all of them. Peregrin grabs Xylie's arm, pulls her to her feet, and steers her further away from Yris and the table. "We can't risk them causing problems, and knowing all of you, you would cause problems. You're all stubborn, self-righteous fools. You can go to Aluina or Tenebra. I do not care, so long as you never set foot in Everadyn again."

"We'll have to capture the dragon, of course," Caius says with a laugh. "It'll be much better under Drakr control."

"No!" Ayc roars. Shadows rise, coiling over his arms.

Brekken's mouth falls open. Lahlis shoves to his feet. "I thought you said he had no power."

"Did I?" Damara says. She laughs. It's light and airy, but somehow it still sounds like she's coming apart at the seams. Like someone upset the gameboard that she was moments from winning, and she must laugh, or she'll cry. "Oh, I've lied about a lot of things."

Lahlis's eyes burn red, but he wheels on Yris. To her credit, she doesn't even flinch. "*You* did not tell me, Yris."

She calmly gets to her feet, shrugging her shoulders. "If Lora was to reign, it benefited us to keep it secret. You understand how these things are. It's irrelevant. He is not that powerful. At least, not yet." She slowly approaches Lora, her hand outstretched. "Come on, Loraphne." Yris sounds tired. Exasperated. "Enough with the theater. The choice is an obvious one. If you say no, your Five die here. Now. Do not make it harder than it needs to be."

Lora looks to her Five, the ones who are the most extraordinary people in all the world. It's their lives that are at stake. If Lora fights back, she will survive. Yris has never cared what her daughter wants, but she does want to keep owning Lora the way she always has—like she's a possession. Like she's something to be owned, but not loved. But if she fights, her Five will die. It's a well-placed threat. Yris knows her well.

Lora shifts her gaze beside her to Ayc. He's already looking at her, and his love for her is written all over his face. She loves him so much that she knows she could do it for him. She could surrender her crown for him and face whatever her mother has planned, if only to ensure he lives.

But he shakes his head. He lays his heart over his sternum. One by one, the others do the same. Even Tavish, who can't see them, must know because his hand rises and rests on his chest.

Tears burn, and for once, Lora lets them burn. Even as she flares her eyes with silver and whirls back on her mother. "No!"

The word bellows from the very recesses of her soul, as deep and piercing as a gryphon's cry. "We do not bow!"

Yris blows out a long breath. Lahlis's eyes blaze red. He sweeps his gaze around, taking in his children, issuing them commands. "Leave Lora alive, but make her surrender. Break her legs if you must. Kill the rest."

Caius reaches for his sword. Brekken presses slowly to his feet. Lora's guards all surge forward. A hand grabs her arm and shoves her backward. Other guards are grabbing her Five and pushing them behind as well, until her guards form a wall of bodies. The shadow statues on the side of the wall buckle and form a wave that surges toward them. Ayc grunts, his cheeks flushing, like he's trying to hold them back. They slow, but they are still coming. Bronwen summons a blue orb that surrounds Lora and her Five, a shield. Lora opens her mouth to scream to include her guards—to include Irving—but there isn't time. The shadow rises up on either side of them, only a foot away, about to crash over them like a tsunami.

Then it stops, frozen in the air.

"Damara!" Peregrin yells.

She's thrust up both her hands, holding both sides of the shadow at bay. Her arms shake as Lahlis flexes her fingers. Caius, too, lifts his arms, and her arms shake more. She turns. She looks at Lora. No, not at Lora.

At Ayc.

Her brother.

A drop of blood already drips from her nose. She won't be able to hold it long. And now her father knows exactly whose side she is on.

"Run," she says.

And they fucking run.

SIXTY-SIX

AYC

It feels like ripping out a piece of his soul to get his feet to move away from where Damara holds the tides of shadow —cast by both Caius and Lahlis. Ayc tried only moments ago to stop the surge, but it felt as though an axe blade impaled into his skull. Perhaps that's how Damara feels as her arms shake. Still, she lifts her arms above her head, pulling the shadow up until it forms a wall that separates Lora, her Five, and her guards from Yris and the Drakr.

It's going to kill her.

But Lora's arm wraps around Ayc's elbow, and she's tugging him toward the door. Out. He has to get Lora out. He has to get them all out. Perhaps if it was just him, he would stay with Damara, but he has to go.

He searches around him, even as he starts to move. Lora has Xylie's arm, and Peregrin yanks Tavish along. Bronwen moves in the center, keeping a shield around them, while the guards form a second shield of flesh around it.

"Move, move, move!" Irving yells.

They've only made it a few feet when a roar shakes the walls of the castles. Not one roar. Many, like every dragon in the courtyard is bellowing.

"Murrenigh, what's happening?" Ayc shouts down their link. He already sent one message, the moment he saw Yris, and warned Murrenigh that they weren't going to get out without a fight. Peregrin surely sent the same message because Murrenigh confirmed that the gryphons knew, too, that they were preparing to fly.

"The gryphons are taking to the sky," Murrenigh calls in return. *"But so are the dragon and their riders. They're going to fight."*

"Fuck!" Ayc swears. *"Stay away from the fighting, Murrenigh. Just like you promised."*

Murrenigh doesn't respond.

"Murrenigh!"

Murrenigh can't fight. Not against the mammoth dragons that have been trained in battles for decades. They've only just learned to fly, only just learned to breathe their ice. They will stand no chance.

"Muffin!"

Still, no answer.

Davos flings the door to the hall open. A cloaked figure stands on the other side. There's a flash of silver; Davos flings up his sword, but it's too late. A spray of blood coats Bronwen's shield as Davos crumples. Irving embeds his own blade deep into the person's hood. They, too, crumple.

Lora alters course and flings herself toward the edge of the shield, toward Davos's body.

Ayc seizes her around the waist. "He's already gone," he says, swallowing down his own bile. "We have to leave him."

"Fuck!" she roars as Ayc shoves her forward, past Davos's body and into the hallway.

More cloaked figures appear. The guards surge forward to engage them with bursts of blue and green light. It's hard to track the movement, as they never slow as they run through the hallway.

Irving gasps for breath as he impacts with a Drakr and is

driven into the wall. A wall of green protects his throat from the red blade, but the grit of Irving's teeth, his sharp canines flashing, showing the effort he's using to hold it. Peregrin flings a knife. It slams into the Drakr's back, but he doesn't fall. Ayc flexes his fingers, focusing all his intent on the shadow that Irving casts. It rises up and wraps around the Drakr's neck. Ignoring the pain pulsing through his jaw, Ayc twists his wrist. A crack sounds over the din of clashing swords. The Drakr falls.

Ayc releases the power before a wave of dizziness fully overtakes him. He just snapped someone's neck with his power. He didn't know he could do that.

Irving nods at Ayc, and then they're running again. Most of the Drakr they meet do not have shadow powers. They fall quickly beneath the guard's magic and blades. Peregrin's knives fly out of their hand. Xylie clutches an alchemy bottle in her hand but doesn't throw it; within these close quarters, it's too great a risk. Lora holds her dwarven-made twin blades in her hands and strikes out whenever a Drakr gets too close to the shield. Ayc snaps another neck with his shadows, nearly buckling to his own knees with the effort. But he clings to the remnants of his strength.

He calls out to Murrenigh again and doesn't get a reply, and he tries not to let the panic consume him. He would feel it if Murrenigh was hurt...or worse, dead. He's certain that entwined as their souls are, he'd feel it.

They reach the entrance of the castle. The doors are wide open. The bellow of dragons and the shriek of gryphons can be heard coming from the sky above, but Ayc can't see from this angle. Only Iolite and Kivka remain in the courtyard. Kivka yanks at her chain, shaking her head, only causing more blood to spurt on her chest. Acid drips from her teeth onto the chain on the ground, but by some magic, it remains intact. Iolite nudges Kivka's ribs gently with her nose, but Kivka does not soothe.

They don't turn to go that way. Irving leads them straight onward. They discussed this, the various options they could use to escape based on the maps that Damara drew for them. Irving is leading them to the safest route, he thinks. But they turn the corner and meet with a solid wall of Drakr, at least a dozen, perhaps more.

Fuck, fuck, fuck.

Irving spins around. Blood splatters his face, staining the places where his dimples normally reside.

"Turn around. Back the way we came. Guards, hold the line."

The three guards who have run behind them surge to the front. Magdon and two whose names Ayc can't recall in this moment. He regrets not learning them. They are not hesitating to do their duty now, and it will surely be their last act of bravery. They are far too outnumbered. All they can hope for is to buy the Sovereign time, a price only their blood will pay.

"No," Lora hisses.

Once more, she surges forward. Once more, Ayc grabs ahold of her and turns her around, keeping her within the boundary of Bronwen's shield.

"I don't want them to die for me," she seethes through her teeth.

"I know, my love," Ayc says, "but I'll throw you over my shoulder if I must."

She growls her frustration, but she turns and they run back down the hallway. She may hate him for this, but he doesn't care. Because they are not *her*. Perhaps something good in him has died. Perhaps he is a wicked villain because he will mourn the guard's deaths, but he will not regret them. He would lose a hundred before he loses Lora.

"Tavish, find us a way out!" Irving yells.

They're nearly back to the front now, the open front door. Tavish stabs a finger straight ahead of him just as Caius and Yris walk around the corner of the hall. Shadow broils at Caius's feet, rolling with him with every step. He grins daggers, even as his eyes gleam red.

"Do not hurt Lora," Yris warns. "I don't care what you do with the others, but do not hurt my daughter."

Lora seizes the dagger at her hip and heaves it down the

hallway, straight for her mother's face. Shadow catches it when it's inches from her nose and tosses it aside. Caius thrusts his hands forward, and a ball of shadow flings down the hall toward them. Bronwen snarls, and blue light surges from her palm. The shield ripples and thins as her energy is used elsewhere. The dark ball collides with her energy several feet from them. The dark and light tangle together, Bronwen grunting, Caius spewing foul insults until the tangle disappears.

More shadow creeps along the floor, only a dozen feet away now. The shield reappears, Bronwen gasping for breath. So Ayc focuses on the shadow, even as pain ripples across his skull like it's splitting apart. Caius is strong; shoving against his power feels like shoving a brick wall. Ayc grits his teeth and puts more effort, and slowly, the wall budges. The shadow slows to a crawl. Caius flashes a smile and pushes back. The ache of Ayc's resistance spread across his back and down his legs. He shoves it aside, places it behind that wall, and summons all his strength. He reaches for his rage—rage at Yris for all she has done, rage at Caius for being so proud of his own cruelty. With that burning anger, his eyes flood red, and the shadow turns backwards. It becomes his. Caius's smile falls.

It speeds up and slams against Yris and Caius's legs. Their backs collide with the ground.

"It's not possible," Yris gasps. "It's not possible that you're that powerful already."

"You taught me how to withstand pain," Ayc replies.

They're back on their feet in a moment.

"Tavish?" Irving demands, looking behind him. There are Drakr rounding the corner behind them.

"We should go that way," Tavish says, pointing at the open courtyard door. "I'm sensing something."

Kivka and Iolite are still there, but they have little other choice. Bronwen's shield should protect them. Ayc hopes.

"Let Irving in," Lora commands.

Bronwen lets the shield open a crack. Peregrin seizes Irving and yanks him inside before Bronwen snaps it shut again. They bolt down the front steps. The roaring and screeching of gryphons and dragons is even louder now, making Ayc's eardrums rattle. He can't bring himself to look up, not when two dragons are right before him. Kivka and Iolite whirl their heads in their direction. Even Iolite seems anxious now. She chops her jaw and shakes out her amethyst wings. Smoke coils from her nostrils.

Something pelts their scales from above. Rain is Ayc's first thought; it's what it sounds like as it drums against the stone of the courtyard, but the rhythm is too inconsistent. A large drop lands on Bronwen's shield above their head and drags a red line down its slope.

Blood, Ayc realizes. It's raining blood.

Finally, Ayc flings his head back. In the skies above them, gryphon riders and dragons are meeting. They soar through the sky before colliding, weaving through the spiked turrets, breaking apart before slamming back together. Gryphons work together to surround one dragon. Magic and shadow meet hundreds of yards up in collisions of light and dark. And though none are falling, it's only a matter of time because more than one is hurt. Enough are hurting that it's raining blood.

"*Murrenigh!*" Ayc yells, searching the skies for a little spot of white and not finding it. "*Where are you?*"

"*Not dead yet,*" Murrenigh retorts.

"*What the fuck do you mean yet? Are you somewhere safe?*"

Xylie darts out of the shield and directly toward Kivka, and Ayc drowns out whatever Murrenigh says with his cry of "Xylie!"

Lora echoes it and lunges, but Irving catches her.

"Keep going! I have her!" Ayc calls, racing after her. He catches her in a few bounds, only two yards from Kivka. The dragon and their mate snarl, and Ayc knows that at any moment, these dragons can disintegrate every bone in their bodies. He isn't sure why they haven't yet.

He seizes Xylie's shoulders. "The fuck are you doing?"

"I have to help her!" Her voice is loud and clear. It startles Ayc that she's found it in so stressful a situation. Her eyes burn a silver that Ayc has never seen this brightly in her eyes. Blood still rains from the sky, dripping on her cheeks, his cheeks.

Fuck. Ayc glances to where the rest of the party are running, but more slowly, back at the door to the castle, where Drakr will come at any moment. Then he looks back at his best friend, a firm resolution building in his spine.

"All right, but quickly," he says. "Any ideas?"

Xylie holds out her hand and approaches the dragon slowly.

Iolite bares her teeth.

"We're just trying to help!" Ayc calls, still glancing at the door. "*Murrenigh, tell Kivka and Iolite we're just trying to help.*"

"*I'm a little busy!*"

"*Doing what?!*"

There's a beat of a pause. "*They say they won't eat you.*"

"*But not that they won't burn me to a crisp?*"

There's no answer, and Ayc doesn't have time to wait for another one.

He sighs. "*Reassuring. Thank you.*"

Kivka drops their neck, and Xylie sprints the remaining steps to seize the collar. Ayc joins her. The dragon moans and shudders as they pull on the collar, but it doesn't budge. At the front, its edges appeared to meet, but there's a keyhole, like it's a shackle.

"Fuck, it needs a key," Ayc says.

He's about to haul Xylie away, kicking and screaming if he must, when a voice shrieks from the door of the caste.

"Get away from my dragon!"

Caius strides down the steps, rage rippling over his face. His shadows stampede forward once more, and Ayc isn't sure he'll have the strength to fight it again. But he reaches for his power— and his sword—anyway.

"She is not yours!" Xylie yells, her eyes glowing silver once more. "She will never be yours!"

A surge of power rents the air. It isn't energy. It isn't lightning. It's an explosion like a volcano erupting. The courtyard, perhaps the world, quakes. It slams into Ayc's chest and flings him through the air. He slams into a stone pillar. His back roars in fury.

The world spins and dips. Murrenigh and Lora both scream his name.

He shoves to his knees, trying to gather his bearings. Caius, too, has been thrown against the stone, as have Yris and the Drakr at the entrance of the castle. But he's already sitting up, shaking off whatever force Xylie hit them with.

Xylie. Fuck.

Xylie lies crumpled on the stone near Kivka's talons. The great beast sniffs at her and coils back her lips in a growl. She swivels her head toward the castle. Caius's eyes go wide in horror.

Because Kivka's collar lies shattered on the ground, little more than dust and a few scrapes of metal.

Kivka utters a roar that quakes the entire courtyard. She carefully, so very carefully, steps over Xylie's body, eyes still trained upon Caius. He scrambles backward on his hands and knees. Yris retreats into the castle, as do the Drakr. Kivka and Iolite both stalk forward. Caius utters a scream as he leaps to his feet and runs. Acid blasts from Kivka's mouth, and Ayc looks away, not wanting to see if it finds its mark. All he hears is more screaming.

Ayc scrambles across the stone to Xylie, his lungs moving but not drawing in air. She's sprawled on her back, her cheeks ashen. His fingers skate over the skin of Xylie's neck until he finds a pulse. It's steady. He lets out a breath.

"Ayc, is she all right?"

Lora's voice is closer than it should be, right behind him. The group has returned, still within Bronwen's shield. Their enemies are preoccupied by Iolite and Kivka, who are both wreaking havoc. They've collapsed the front doors and have now taken to the air, clawing and spitting acid and breathing fire upon the turrets. They only ignore the one where a massive golden dragon has been speared upon one of the towers.

"Alive," Ayc says through his teeth. Because he's angry. He doesn't understand why the fuck she would do this. Serene will come for her.

She'll *try* to come for her, he amends. He'll rip Serene apart when she does.

He gathers Xylie in his arms, cradling her to her chest. His back feels as though it's ripping apart as he lifts her, more from his impact with the stone than her weight. He grits his teeth and gathers his shadows around him to help support her weight, then steps back into Bronwen's shield as she allows an opening for him.

They exit the courtyard to find that the bridge no longer stands. It has been ripped apart, sections of twenty feet gaping between solid stone. Acrid smoke rises between them and the next solid stone. Even if they could pass the gap, the field beyond, where they left their army, is nothing but flames. Their soldiers are in the sky, or they are dead.

Ayc glances into the afternoon sky, trying once more to find a streak of white amongst them. Stjarna—riderless—colliding with a green dragon and ripping open their belly with their back claws. The green dragon shrieks in pain. But Murrenigh is nowhere to be seen.

"To the left!" Tavish calls, pointing a trembling hand to the side.

Between the castle wall and the canyon, there's a narrow ledge, barely wider than Ayc is. He swallows. Irving eyes it and then around him as though searching for options, before quickly realizing that they have none.

"Go!" Irving demands. He pushes Peregrin first, then Lora, then Tavish. "Keep your left hip on the wall, Tavish. Don't step to the right."

Ayc clutches Xylie closer to his chest, fitting her face into the crook of his neck. The weight of her makes it more difficult to balance in the thin space. He can feel Bronwen close to his back, so Irving must be taking up the rear. He can't smell the sulfur, so Bronwen's shield must be protecting them from it, but the haze is growing thicker, as though they are slowly descending into it.

"I think there's a path up ahead," Tavish calls. "That leads down into the canyon."

"Is that wise?" Bronwen asks.

"It's better than staying up here," Peregrin says. "Damara said it was a viable option."

Did Damara say the canyon was a decent escape route? Ayc can't remember that part of the conversation when they discussed ways to escape.

A beat of wings sound, cracking against the sky. But it doesn't come from above. It comes from below. A great red form rises from the canyon. Sarck. Lahlis's dragon opens his mouth and fires. Bronwen throws up her other hand, groaning with the effort of the shield. The fire bowls around them until the shield is completely coated with the red and orange flame.

The heat rises and rises, sweat beading on Ayc's skin. Bronwen's groans turn into a scream as she fights to hold the shield against the force of the flame. And still, the fire comes.

"*Ayc!*" Murrenigh calls.

The fire cuts off. Bronwen presses a finger to her temples. Ayc and Lora take a step toward her.

Sarck cranes their neck back, flames building in the back of their mouth.

"Run," Bronwen pants. "I can't hold the shield much longer."

But running is not an option. They will fall. On that ledge, they are stranded. They can go back to the castle, but where from there?

Ayc clutches Xylie to him, prepared to shield her with his body if he must. His armor is fire-resistant. Perhaps she'll survive it.

A glint of light catches his eyes. That's all it is. A glint. And then Murrenigh appears from nothing—as suddenly as Ayc stepping from the shadows.

They bellow, their ice leaving their mouth at the same moment as Sarck's fire. The streams meet, and the fire turns to steam in the air. Sarck snarls and snaps toward Murrenigh.

Ayc screams across their link in warning.

"Murrenigh, fly!" Lora yells.

Murrenigh's wings break hard against the sky as they pivot back the way they came. Sarck lunges after them, every single beat of their massive wings taking up three of Murrenigh's own. Sarck will catch them. It's only a matter of time. And Ayc's heart screams as he grabs hold of his power, drawing shadow from the depths of the abyss before them, but his body aches and his arms shake from holding Xylie, and he will not save Murrenigh in time.

A gryphon's call rips through the sky a moment before a black streak surges from the other side of the canyon and slams into the solid red of Sarck's side.

"Tempest!" Peregrin calls.

Sarck bats at the gryphon. She stays close to their body, her claws embedded in their ribcage, slicing through scales because that is what her claws were designed to do. Murrenigh turns and slams into the other side, biting down on Sarck's spine. Then the three are tangled in the sky, half falling, half flying, breaking apart and slamming back together. All Ayc can hear across the link is, "*Ayc. Lora. Xylie. Tempest. Protect them. All of them.*"

Bronwen shoves Ayc forward. "Go! They are buying us time."

Ayc can't. He can't leave them. He could sooner leave his soul on the ledge than leave Murrenigh, his dragon, and Tempest, the gryphon who has looked after him since he was a boy.

"*Go!*" Murrenigh roars. "*Go! Get Lora and Xylie out of here, or I swear, I'll eat you myself!*"

Xylie. He's still carrying Xylie. It's enough of a reminder to get Ayc going again. Ahead of them, Peregrin nearly stumbles off where the cliffside has broken. Lora seizes them and then points down. There's a ledge even smaller than this one that leads down at a slope.

"Tavish, do we go down?" Lora asks.

"Yes."

Murrenigh, Sarck, and Tempest remain entangled as their group starts the descent. Ayc can scarcely look at them, too busy trying to see where he can put his feet. All he can hear is the continued cry of "*protect, protect, protect*".

Then pain shrieks through Ayc's head, but not his own. It's accompanied by a bellow of "*NO!*" drowned out only by Tempest's screech of agony. Ayc throws his head back to see

Sarck's jaws clamped down on her spine. He shakes her like a dog. Ayc can hear bones crunch even a dozen feet below. There's blood. Too much blood. And Ayc can't tell whose it is.

Peregrin screams. It sounds as though their very soul is rending apart. Ayc feels it echoing in his own chest.

Murrenigh pulls back. Their movements seem weak, dazed, but they roar, sending ice directly at Sarck's wing. They flap their wings, the frozen one scarcely moving, and immediately begin to fall. They release Tempest. Ayc expects her to fall, but she beats her wing, once, twice, and slices their claws through Sarck's other wing. And then she tumbles from the sky, but Sarck falls with her.

And so does Murrenigh.

Sarck's front talons are wrapped around their tail. Murrenigh fights against the tug, beating their wings hard, but still, they are being dragged from the sky. All three of them fall—straight toward where Ayc stands.

Ayc and his family fling themselves against the wall of the canyon, but there's nowhere to brace as Sarck's body slams into the cliff just below them. Rocks break. The ledge beneath them disintegrates. And they fall into darkness.

This is it.

After everything, this is how Ayc dies.

He has enough time as he falls to clutch Xylie to his chest and look to his right for Lora. His Lora. His soulmate. And as she reaches a hand out toward him, too far to touch, he's grateful for the time he's had with her. It isn't enough.

Forever wouldn't have been enough.

SIXTY-SEVEN

LORA

When Lora opens her eyes, she's certain she's in eternal damnation. The world is smoke and heat. Ash feels like it's clogging her lungs, and every bone in her body feels as though it's broken, shattered. She hears moaning near her. And then she hears her name.

"Lora!"

Ayc. She knows his voice from the way something deep within her immediately awakens. At least, if they're in eternal damnation, they are here together.

He calls her name again, and she shoves herself upright despite how her back screams at her. Her eyes water, and her nose burns from the smell of sulfur, but slowly, she adjusts. She takes in the sheer rock cliff to her left and the bubbling stream of lava to her right. They've fallen hundreds of feet into the canyon. How is she still alive?

It comes back to her. The blue that surrounded her—that surrounded all of them. It slowed her fall like she was slipping through thick mud instead of free air. Bronwen, slowing their fall. She screamed as she did it, the pain of the magic that was saving them ripping her apart. It wasn't enough to stop them completely, and Lora remembers nothing from when she impacted the ground until now.

She catches sight of forms lying around her. Tavish is closest but still a dozen yards away. Ayc and Xylie lay side by side, dangerously close to the lava. She spies Peregrin near the cliff and Bronwen a dozen feet from Ayc. She doesn't see Irving, or Tempest, or Murrenigh. Sarck is at least nowhere to be seen, but her chest aches as Ayc calls for her again. This time, it sounds nearly like a sob.

"I'm here!" she yells back. "I'm alive. Are you?"

He groans. "Just barely."

"X-Xylie?" she fights to ask.

"Fine! I cushioned her fall. How are the others?"

She forces herself to her feet. The world dips and spins. Her head doesn't feel right. It feels like someone has shoved a feather pillow into her head instead of a brain, but she stumbles to Tavish's side. He's breathing, not bleeding anywhere, and his pulse is strong.

"Alive," Tavish croaks, "though I'm unsure if that's the preferable option."

Peregrin is unconscious, and so is Bronwen, blood streaked down her face. But neither have visible wounds, and both moan when she shakes them.

She still can't see Irving or their dragon and gryphon, but she tries not to think of it too much. She refuses to consider whether they fell into the lava. She finally lowers herself to the ground next to Ayc.

"You're all right?" he asks, grunting the words.

She nods, but that makes her head spin. "I'll live. Can you move?"

"I just need a minute," he says through his teeth in a way that tells her he's in much more pain than she is. She hears a wheeze with each breath, and she's worried that he's broken some ribs. He winces with every breath. "Murrenigh... Do you see Murrenigh?"

She shakes her head. "Can you hear them?"

"No, but I—" He grunts again, more color draining from his face. "I can sense them. They're dreaming of only darkness."

"Perhaps they're just unconscious," Lora says. She sets a hand on his sternum, reassuring herself that his heart still beats steadily. "We'll find them. We'll find Murrenigh and Tempest."

She prays to the divine that they're both still alive, though she knows that at least one of them will not be. So she says a different prayer. She prays that Peregrin wakes up. That the grief does not rip them both away.

Ayc releases a shuddering breath. It ends in a cough. Her own lungs are burning, too. Eventually, they'll suffocate down here. "What do we do?" he asks.

She looks to Xylie, to the bag with her alchemy bottles. Liquids of every color seep onto the stone. She reaches for it when she hears the sound of boots on rocks. Multiple boots, drawing closer.

She snaps her head toward the wall as her mother steps out of the smoke. She is not alone. Onanna stands on her right side, her dark cloak pulled up past her forehead, her silver eyes glowing from within. Fennix stands on her other side.

"It's a good thing I told Onanna to put that tracer in the leviathan tooth," Yris says when she stops a few feet away. "Otherwise, we would never have been able to find you."

Lora reaches back to draw her sword, but a spear of Onanna's black magic flies past her in warning, and she drops her hand.

"I wouldn't do that, Lora," Yris says. "We don't want to hurt you, but we will if we must."

"You fucking bitch!" Ayc snarls, trying to shove himself upward. He cries out in pain and falls backward.

If he can't stand, the pain must be horrible. He knows how to withstand pain. A shadow rises at Yris's feet and then falls as Ayc moans.

Yris looks around. "Well, they're all half dead, anyway. We could probably just leave them, but better safe than sorry. Kill them."

Fennix draws their knife without hesitation.

"Stop!" Lora roars with such a force that it ends with a cough at the sting of the smoke.

Fennix stills.

Yris sighs. "Are we still playing games? Or are you ready to surrender?"

Lora weighs her options. They are all shit. Her captain, dragon, and gryphon are lost. Her army is preoccupied. Her guard is dead. Her Five are unconscious and wounded. She's concussed. Yris and Fennix are the most skilled fighters of their generation. Onanna is powerful, perhaps as powerful as the Supreme.

They've lost. That fact is clear.

Lora chose to fight for what she believed was good—for the freedom of all people, not just the wealthy few. She was made out to be wicked for it, and she was fine with being the villain. It was worth it if they won in the end. But if her mother kills Ayc and the rest of her Five, Lora will have lost everything. Perhaps it's a fool's hope, but she still believes this fight is one worth going to war for. Perhaps it'll take decades, centuries, but so long as they live, they have not lost entirely.

But they have to live past today.

Lora slides backward, toward the lava flow. The heat of it nips at her calves, and she grinds her teeth.

"Lora, what do you think you're doing?" Yris snarls.

"I think that I'm going to throw myself into this lava if you dare touch a single one of them." Lora lifts her chin to remind herself that this crown on her head is hers. No matter what happens, it's *hers*. "I will jump, and your crown and your daughter will be gone. Is that what you want?"

"Stop being ridiculous."

"Let them live," Lora says through her teeth, "and I'll come with you willingly."

"Lora!" Ayc gasps. He tries to get upright again, but this time, he only makes it to his elbows.

She looks away from him, her eyes burning from more than just sulfur. She fears that if she looks at him, she won't be able to go through with this.

"I offered you that deal," Yris says. "You said no."

She stalks forward a step, and Lora slides her other foot backward. She's teetering on the edge now. Yris freezes. Ayc grasps for her foot but can't quite reach it. If Onanna tries to use force, it could risk knocking her back into the lava, so the sorcerer does not move.

"I changed my mind," Lora says. "I'm saying yes."

Yris cocks her head, considering. Fennix's knife relaxes at his side.

"The boy has become too powerful," Onanna protests. "With the shadow power and the dragon—"

"His dragon is dead," Lora says, ensuring that her voice is adequately thick to sell the lie. At least, she hopes it's a lie. "And as for his powers..." She thinks swiftly. "Ayc, do you still have your bracelets in your pocket?"

She must know what he's thinking because he bares his teeth. "No. Fuck, no."

"He does," Lora says confidently. "They suppress his power. Put them on him. Onanna can spell them so no one can take them off. He'll be powerless. You won't have to worry about him."

"No!" he growls.

She swallows and does not look at him. She knows what she's doing to him, the prison she's placing him back in by her own suggestion. She hates herself for it, but there's no other way to save his life.

"Look at them, Loraphne," Yris says coldly. "None of them are going to make it out of this canyon alive. They'll suffocate here before they even wake up enough to walk out. And even if they do, they'll never make it out of Drakr alive. All of them will be hunted."

Lora *is* looking at them. They are unconscious and hurt and defeated, and they are still the strongest people she knows. They have survived things other people can't imagine, and they will survive today. And then they will come for her. "Then you have nothing to lose."

Yris growls through her teeth. "Fine, Onanna, do it."

"No, Lora, no!" Ayc says.

She wants to go to him, wants to kiss every inch of his face, wants to promise everything will be all right—it's just going to be bad for a bit. But if she does, she'll surrender her position. If she does, she'll have to deal with the thought that she may not see him again. Not for a long time. Perhaps not ever.

And that she can't bear.

"No," he says again as Onnana stoops beside him and finds the bracelets in his pockets. "I go where you go," he says, and it's both a promise and a plea.

"Not this time," Lora says, a tear sliding down her cheek.

Onnana grabs his arm, and he jerks back. "No! Without my power, I won't be strong enough to save you."

"Yes, you *will*," she snarls, annoyed that he still can't see it. That he doesn't know how extraordinary he is. "You've always been the strongest person I know, even before your power. You'll find me, and you'll save me. But you have to live."

"For fuck's sake," Yris growls. "Either hold still, human, or Onanna will slit your throat."

Ayc freezes, his eyes still locked on Lora's. But he offers Onanna both his hands. She mutters words beneath her breath as she hooks each of the bracelets onto his wrists with bruised fingertips. Just like Serene. Like she's rotting from the inside out.

"Walk back to Yris," Lora orders when the sorcerer is done.

She hisses at the command but slinks away.

Lora dares to take a chance, to steal just one more moment. She kneels at Ayc's side and presses a kiss to his mouth. Hard and gentle, sweet as cinnamon, sharp as anise all at once. Just like they have always been. He clings to her, his fingers sliding into his hair, like he might be able to hold onto her tight enough to get her to stay.

"You are my mate," he growls against her lips, and her heart flutters. "Wherever she takes you, it will not be far enough. I will not rest until I have you back. If they want me to be a villain, then they have one. I will tear this world apart to find you again. No one will be safe until you're in my arms again."

She bites back a sob, pressing a reverent kiss against his wrist, against the bear cuff he wears once more. "I love you," she breathes. "Let me go."

"Never," he growls.

And though his hands release her, though she stands and walks toward the three who await her, Lora knows he means it. They will both live another day, and they will fight until there is no more air left in their lungs. And they will be together again one day. She will fight fate itself if she must.

As Onanna seizes her arm and teleports all four of them away, she feels as though all of her is shattering. Like every cell in her body is being ripped apart. She knows that when she comes back together again, she will not be the same.

And the world should fear who she will become.

SIXTY-EIGHT

AYC

R AGE.

Hotter and brighter than the lava that rolls beside him.

That is what Ayc feels as he's forced to watch Lora walk away from him. Each step she takes makes him feel like an endless darkness, so deep and great it could consume the world. He quakes with it.

His body has failed him. He couldn't pull upon his power because the little he tried, he felt as though he was dying. And now he can't even feel that. Devoid of his power, his soul feels hollow, an echo chamber for his internal scream.

When Onanna grabs Lora's arm and teleports them all away, Ayc bellows out his rage loud enough that his throat feels hoarse. He slams his fist into the rocky earth again and again.

"It's all right, Ayc," Tavish says softly. "We'll get her back." He coughs, a racking sound. "But we have to get out of here. It's getting hard to breathe."

It is. The sulfur makes Ayc's nose feel raw and his lungs thin, like paper being slowly shredded apart. The reminder makes reality break through the river of heat and grief and rage. It snaps something in place within him: a purpose, a mission, so he doesn't get swept away.

Lora is gone. Everadyn will likely soon think that all her Five are dead, and Yris will instill herself back on the throne, just like she always intended. But that is Lora's throne, and that is Lora's crown. She is the only one worthy of it, and Ayc will get it back for her.

But first, they have to get out of this canyon. Ayc needs to wake up his family. He needs to find his dragon. Ayc has been calling for them, but they haven't responded. But they are not dead. Ayc knows it. They feel their presence in their mind still, though no words or images come across their link. Unconscious, perhaps. But alive. Ayc refuses to believe anything else.

He rolls to his side and reaches for the bag at Xylie's side. He's slightly concerned that if he moves it, the material, which has thankfully not exploded, will ignite. But he reaches inside nonetheless, careful of the broken glass. He finds pain tonics, five of them. Not enough for the journey that he senses before them, but they will have to do. He also finds a bottle labeled Reviving Drops. Xylie, always planning for the worst.

He forces himself to drink only half of a pain tonic, tucking the others in his coat pocket. It'll take a while to kick in, but he doesn't have time to wait. He uncorks the Reviving Drops, pinching Xylie's jaw, and drips a drop on her tongue. He counts to five before he adds another.

Xylie's eyes fling open. They no longer burn silver, but Ayc feels like they're different somehow. Wiser, more powerful, like her magic that has been so carefully held at bay has been called to the surface. Does the Supreme already know? Did she feel Xylie's power somehow?

"What happened?" Xylie signs.

"We fell into the canyon." It's the short answer, but he doesn't have time to explain everything. "Are you very hurt?"

She shakes her head.

Good. It seems that his body truly did cushion her fall, which might explain why his chest cavity feels like it's buckled.

He presses the half-empty pain tonic into her hand. "Can you drink, or do you need help?"

She pushes herself into a sitting position, blinking around her, but she lifts the tonic to her lips.

He still can't make himself stand, so he approaches Bronwen on hands and knees. The loose rock grinds into his palm, even through his gloves. He's certain he has broken something because every movement hurts; every inhale feels like he's being stabbed.

It takes three drops to revive Bronwen. She doesn't open her eyes, only groans. "Are we dead?"

"Not yet, but we need to get out of here. Drink."

He gives her all the pain tonic. If they're going to make it through miles of canyon, they need her to be strong enough, recovered enough, to shield them once more. She drinks it down greedily and peeks her eyes open.

"Is everyone all right?"

The question is a slam into his gut.

"Irving! Tempest!"

Ayc jumps at the sudden scream. Peregrin is now on their feet. They turn a slow circle, stumbling with each step. Their cane lies in shattered pieces on the stone behind them. Each one of their cries is a little more desperate, and Ayc's chest feels even more like it might turn to dust. He's never seen his mentor like this. Like they are clinging to their last shred of hope.

"Tempest! Irving!"

"Here!" Irving stumbles from the smoke, coughing and waving the air around his face. He limps, and there's a bleeding gash on his head, but he's alive.

One small breath of relief is all Ayc can manage before Peregrin flings themself toward him. They fall to their knees before Irving races to reach them and haul them back to their feet. Peregrin clutches Irving's cloak, a noise coming from their throat that can only be described as wailing.

"I can't hear her! Irving, I can't hear Tempest. I can't *feel* her."

A sob works up Ayc's throat. He knows what it means. Even

now, he can still feel Murrenigh, the same way he can feel his skin on his body. If Peregrin cannot, then...

Then...

FUCK!

Ayc imagines Tempest begging for treats outside of his window when he was a boy, hiding him behind her wings as he slept in the gryphon pasture, bearing Lora and Ayc through the air on a rescue mission. Something within Ayc shatters, a feat that seems impossible, because he already thought he was irrevocably broken. For now, he swallows down that pain, buries it deep. Later. He can feel it later.

"It's okay, love," Irving says, clutching Peregrin tightly. "Perhaps she's too far away. Perhaps she escaped to someplace safer."

"No," Peregrin says. "I felt her go silent. I cannot hear her."

Bronwen clutches Ayc's shoulder, for comfort or perhaps just to pull herself upright. Tears stream down her dusty, bloody cheeks. She glances around. Her fingers tighten.

"Wait. Where is Lora?"

Irving jerks backward, holding Peregrin by their shoulders so they don't fall. He looks around. "Where the fuck is Lora?"

Ayc opens his mouth, but the words get stuck in his throat. The noise he makes instead sounds dangerously like a sob.

"She's gone," Tavish says. Xylie has made it to his side, and they are helping each other stand. "Yris took her. She traded herself so they wouldn't kill us all."

The aftermath of the words lingers in the air. Sadness and rage are as tangible as the acrid smell of sulfur.

"We'll get her back," Ayc says through his teeth. "But we have to get the fuck out of this canyon before we suffocate."

"I can cast another spell," Bronwen gasps through sobs that shake her body. "I just need a minute."

He rubs his hand over her back before finally shoving to his feet. His knees want to buckle, but the pain tonic has taken off enough of an edge that he doesn't collapse. A sound fills his head, soft at first and then rapidly growing. Crying, but this time, it's coming from the link.

Murrenigh is awake.

"Murrenigh!" Ayc calls down the link. *"Where are you?"*

No answer. Only more sobbing.

"Tempest," Peregrin murmurs, "we need to find her. We can't leave her."

Ayc swallows. *"Murrenigh?"* he calls again.

"H-here, Ayc. We... we are both here."

"This way," he says, even as Tavish points a finger in the direction he stumbles.

There's no sunlight this deep, no ability to tell the difference between east and west. He can't even hear the echoes of the battle that was waging above, and he doesn't know if that's because he can't hear it or because it has been called off.

Everyone is on their feet, stumbling. Xylie and Tavish—and Peregrin and Irving—hold on to each other, while Bronwen—still sobbing softly—manages on her own. Murrenigh is not far, though Ayc can't see them in the dimness until they are nearly upon them. Murrenigh is in the center of stones that have fallen from above, and they are not alone. They are beside Tempest, who lays still in a pool of feathers and blood.

Peregrin utters another cry and falls to their knees. Irving tries to help them, but they scramble across the stone and blood on their hands and knees. "I'm sorry. I'm so sorry," they moan when they reach her. They fling themself on her neck, burying their face in her feathers.

Murrenigh draws themself to their feet. Ayc blinks through his own tears to focus and rushes as fast as he can to them. He throws his arms around the dragon's neck.

"I could not leave her," Murrenigh says, their words coated with what sounds like soft sobs.

"Of course not. She's your friend. Are you well?" Ayc pulls away and searches Murrenigh over. A few scratches tear across their scales, but none of them are deep from what Ayc can see. *"Are you wounded?"*

"Yes, yes, I am wounded. Not physically, I do not think. But something deep within me hurts like I am dying. What is the name of this?"

Ayc scrubs a hand over his face, smearing his tears and soot. *"Grief. This is called grief."*

Thanks to Tempest's feathers, Tavish's gift, and Bronwen's shield, they make it out of the canyon.

It didn't feel quite right, plucking feathers from Tempest's still body. But as Irving reasoned, Peregrin would need them. The magic of the feathers has been the only thing keeping the poison in Peregrin's veins at bay, keeping them alive. And Tempest's soul would never rest if they didn't do what was necessary to keep her rider alive. So as Peregrin sobbed into Irving's chest, Ayc, Bronwen, and Xylie stuffed their pockets full. Every one of them swallowed one down their blazing throats, and the magic sustained them as Tavish led them down a side canyon that had a ledge and pathway out. Every step of the climb hurt, but they finally made it to the top, miles from Morkt Hemma.

The castle is in ruins from what they can see from this distance. Many of the turrets that stood against the horizon yesterday are gone. The skies are mostly quiet above them, but ever so often, a dragon roars. Ayc can see it now, where they've made camp in the shadows of the Untamed Mountains, behind a massive boulder they hope hides them from any searchers. He stares at it, like perhaps if he stares long enough, he will see Damara aboard Stjarna, flying toward them.

Is she dead? Did she die for them? Did she escape somehow?

Ayc doesn't know. He asked Murrenigh if they could hear Stjarna, but they could not. Her fate is unknown. It's illogical, probably, but he clings to the hope that she made it out. That she survived.

That is all he has now.

Hope.

Ayc draws his coat closer to him. The night is cool, and their fire is dwindling, offering little warmth. They lit it out of desperation, to cook meat from the deer that Murrenigh hunted and brought back to them. They cooked strips of meat at the end of a knife and let Murrenigh consume the rest. The dragon will need their strength, will need to grow.

Ayc is still astonished that they survived the battle with Sarck. He studies where Murrenigh lies, their head and tail curled toward their body like a cat. Ayc thinks back to the moment before they appeared, the way they were nothing but a glint of light until a second before they slammed into Sarck's side.

"Are you awake?" Ayc asks Murrenigh. Most of the others are asleep, passed out from exhaustion. Ayc volunteered to take the first guard, but Peregrin is awake as well, leaning against the stone, twisting a feather in their fingers. Bronwen's staff sits next to them in place of their cane.

Murrenigh lifts their head. *"Yes. I cannot sleep. When I do, I dream of Tempest's screams."*

Ayc cringes. But he understands because he fears dreaming too, for much the same reason. He both longs for and dreads finding Lora there. It'll be a comfort to see her, but the agony will be worse when he wakes to find her gone once more.

"Did you turn invisible?" Ayc asks. *"Or did I imagine that?"*

Murrenigh nods their head. *"I hid in the sunlight. The way you hide in the shadow."*

"Is that what you were doing when we were on the ship?"

"Yes." The smallest hint of a smile plays on their lips. *"I did it once when I was younger, when I escaped from the kitchen and Lora found me. When I breathed ice, the power came back. I've been practicing."*

"Little shit. You might have told me."

"Yes, but teasing you was more fun." They chuckle, but the sound dies quickly with a grunt.

Ayc remembers Damara telling him about how black dragons could hide in the shadow. Perhaps this is an ability unique to white dragons. Ayc rubs his chest. The ache there worsens when he thinks of Damara. He remembers those last moments, when she placed her body between them and Lahlis's shadow. He remembers Peregrin crying out.

There was something strange about it—that Peregrin was the one who called out to her. It wasn't a benign cry. It was one calling to a friend they feared losing. Yes, they've all spent the better part of a week traveling together across the lands of Drakr, but this felt different. Deeper.

Something scratches at his brain. Ayc has been missing something. He feels it now, like he's glimpsed something out of the corner of his eye without realizing. When he told Damara she didn't know Peregrin well enough, she laughed. And when he asked for a clue about the leader, she acted surprised he hadn't figured it out already. Like perhaps it has been before his face this entire time.

He presses his hand into the inside pocket of his coat. His coins are still there. All five of them. What did all of the people he met in Asbjorn have in common, a link he's missed until now?

Oh, gods...how could he have missed it?

He looks at Murrenigh, feeling the realization connect within their mind as well. "*Of course,*" they say. "*Who else would it be?*"

Ayc's head whirls with confusion, with disbelief, and then settles on anger as the truth firmly roots into place. He shoves to his feet, ignoring the cry of his ribs at the sudden movement. He storms to the other side of the camp.

"*Ayc...*" Murrenigh warns softly, but Ayc ignores them.

Peregrin stands as Ayc approaches, still leaning against the boulder. They look ill, green with distress, and it should give Ayc pause. But it doesn't. He's too fucking angry.

"I have something for you," Ayc says, keeping his voice low.

And as though they know, Peregrin holds out their hand.

Ayc drops the Asbjorn coins one by one onto their palm. "It's you, isn't it?" he hisses. "You're the leader of Asbjorn."

Peregrin closes their fist around the coins and sighs. "It took you long enough, boy."

SIXTY-NINE

LORA

The room that has been her sanctuary these last few months is now her cage. Yris told her she should be grateful that she's not in the dungeon, that instead, she's in her bedroom with her books and her baskets of yarn and the smell of Ayc still lingering in her sheets.

But Lora refuses to be grateful for the scraps that her abuser gives her.

It's only been a day since Onanna teleported them away, and already, Lora has paced this room enough that her legs ache. Every weapon has been stripped from the room, from her leviathan necklace to her lamps, anything of weight. They've left her loom and some crochet hooks, but none of the knitting needles. Even some of her thicker books have disappeared from her shelves, and she swears she'll take Fennix's grubby little fingers for that alone. Some of those were special editions with stenciled edges.

Lora knows everything that is missing because she's searched everything over, trying to find any possible route of escape. But whatever spell Onanna has placed on the room makes Lora feel like a thousand insects are biting her skin whenever she approaches the window or door. She's screamed herself hoarse, and no one has heard her.

Yris and Onanna have been nothing but thorough. But Lora is determined to stay vigilant. If they let their guard down for even a moment, she will escape this place.

The door opens without a knock, and Yris slips in. Lora glares at her, baring her sharpened canines as her lip curls back. It's a peculiar sight. She's never seen her mother carrying a tray before.

"I've brought you dinner," Yris says.

When Lora doesn't move to take the tray, she sighs, storms past Lora, and slams it on her vanity.

Lora arches an eyebrow. That seems a bit irritable, even for her mother. "Is something the matter?"

Yris turns toward her, lifting her chin even though her head is noticeably still devoid of a crown. "It seems something is wrong with the crown."

Lora tries to hide her amusement. "Is there?"

"It will not change shape back to my golden circlet. It won't change at all. We have laid it upon the ceremonial pillar, and it still will not revert back to me."

Lora smiles.

"We will need you to participate in a crowning ceremony, like we had at your coronation, to see if that will trick the magic."

"How will I do that, Mother?" she asks. "As you've told all of Everadyn—and the world—I and Five are dead. If that's true, shouldn't the crown revert back to you?"

Yris glares at her. "You can relinquish your poor attitude at any moment. I am demanding your assistance."

"No." The word tastes good on Lora's tongue. She may be in this cage, but Yris, Onanna, and Fennix are far away from her Five. More than that, they're convinced that her Five are dead. They've always underestimated people like them. It will be their undoing. But so long as they think that, the power they had over her is gone.

"No?" Yris repeats in a snarl.

"No." Lora smiles. "Whatever magic is in that crown still

recognizes *me* as Sovereign, and I will do nothing to help you trick it. I will not surrender. I will not bow."

"You will never leave this room until you do."

"We'll see about that."

"Do you still think your lover is going to come save you? I told you, they would never have made it out of there alive."

Lora's smile only widens. She has learned something her mother can never understand. Love is powerful. It is the most dangerous force on earth.

And Ayc will come for her.

Or she'll escape on her own, whichever comes first. Whatever the case, so long as she survives, so long as she resists, she has not lost this war between them.

"The plan isn't to keep you here forever," Yris assures. "In a couple years' time, you can rejoin society. We'll make up some excuse of lost memory or that you realized you were too young and disappeared. Then, you can join an Elite army. You can take part in the Fledging ceremony and see if a gryphon bonds with you like you've always wanted."

Lora's smile wavers at the reminder, at the thought of Tempest. The thought of it makes her want to scream. Or perhaps go at her mother with her teeth. She pushes it away so she can keep her wits about her.

"The timeline will speed up if you cooperate," Yris says. When Lora remains silent, Yris growls. "It doesn't ultimately matter. The regents will accept me stepping back into my old role until a new Sovereignty Trials can be arranged. And then, I will win those Trials and rules for another one hundred years. Perhaps after a century, you'll prove that you can be the right Sovereign. You will at last choose to obey and conform to the way things have always been."

Lora steps closer, letting her smile grow more and more wicked with every step, remembering words that Ayc once uttered. They are perfect for this moment, so she says them slowly, emphasizing every one.

"I would rather choke on my own dick."

Yris's eyes flare silver. She spins toward the dresser and picks up the tray. "Very well. We'll see how stubborn you can be when you don't eat."

She storms away and slams the door closed behind her.

AYC

Of course it is Peregrin.

Ayc doesn't understand how it has taken him so long to see it. Except that he trusted Peregrin. He would never have thought Peregrin would keep a secret like this from him. From all of them. From Lora.

But Peregrin is the only one who makes sense. Wren and Peregrin had history. They spoke of it vaguely on the ship in the Trials. Peregrin said that they knew Vidar, though Ayc doubts it has anything to do with Zinnia's history. And when Calliope stepped foot on that ship, Peregrin demanded she leave, like they were a commander yelling at an insolent troop. They didn't fire a knife into her heart like they could have done—*should* have done. And Peregrin spoke about Josias like he was their friend.

And then there's Damara. Peregrin never fought back against her, remaining silent at times that didn't make sense. They acted horrified when they found out about the truth weed. They offered to be alone with her and allowed Damara out of their sight so she could eavesdrop on the regents and gain Lora's trust. All of it felt out of character because it was a carefully orchestrated game.

This has all been a fucking game.

"It's you," Ayc repeats. "It's been you this whole fucking time."

His voice is loud enough that Irving startles awake. He sits up. "Is everything all right?"

"Everything is fine," Peregrin replies.

"The fuck it is," Ayc snarls.

"*Ayc,*" Murrenigh says gently. "*Perhaps now is not the time.*"

Ayc drags a breath through his teeth. No, it isn't the right time. The day Lora was crowned would have been the right time for Peregrin to tell the truth. Now, it's too late. And Ayc should be sensitive to the way his mentor's heart has been completely shattered today, but he feels too hurt. Too betrayed.

"Why didn't you just tell me?" Ayc demands. "Years ago?"

Irving rises to his feet. "If this is about what I think this is about, perhaps we should discuss it another time?"

Ayc whirls toward him. "So you've been keeping it secret, too?" Of course he was. Peregrin doesn't keep secrets from their partners, and with Irving positioned as a royal guard and Zinnia as a maid in Wyntra, there was little that went on in those walls they didn't know about. How perfect for a rebel organization. Irving even said that he remembered things about Peregrin that Onanna missed when she pulled memories from his head. Perhaps this is what he meant. He remembers Peregrin as the leader of Asbjorn because he ensured Onanna did not find those memories. He sacrificed everything else to keep that a secret.

It made sense, but everything should have changed the day that Lora won the throne.

Ayc shakes his head. "Did it not occur to either of you that you could have just told Lora? You had me running around solving riddles and playing games."

Peregrin draws a long breath through their nose. "I had my reasons. I wanted everyone in Asbjorn to trust you the way I trust you. I wanted to be fair and not play favorites."

"And what about before?" Ayc snaps.

"Before you were a boy, imprisoned by the Sovereign."

Ayc's sides ache. He clamps a hand down on his hips to provide support as he grits his teeth. They have a point, and he can't argue that. "But what about Lora?"

"I thought that the best way to succeed was if Lora won the regents over and broke the treaty. Asbjorn does not have the resources to take on Drakr alone. We needed a Sovereign on our side."

"That does not answer why you didn't just tell her. Perhaps if you said something, we wouldn't fucking be here. She wouldn't be—"

He cuts off, unable to say the word gone without choking on it.

Irving stares down at their feet, the guilt clear in his eyes.

"The rebels in Aluina do not trust her yet," Peregrin explains. "The leader there is testy, and I wanted Lora to show, through her own actions, that she was worthy to be trusted."

Ayc wants to yell more, wants to tell Peregrin how little those excuses actually make sense, but he clamps his hands into fists. He breathes. There is not a single reason Peregrin can give that Ayc will accept now. He will not forgive Peregrin for that choice. Instead, he grabs holds of the small amount of information.

"Where is the leader of Aluina?" he demands.

Peregrin hesitates, glancing at Irving, who nods. "Last I knew, he was somewhere in the Northeast province of Aluina."

A plan is quickly forming in Ayc's head. The Northeast province is on the other side of the mountains. It'll be a hard journey to cross, dangerous if anyone finds them on the border. They have no supplies, no food, nothing but their clothes, their weapons, and his dragon.

And the dream of holding Lora in his arms again.

"Then we're going there," Ayc says. "We're finding the rebels. And then I'm getting the woman I love back."

Peregrin glances to where the shadows of the mountains can barely be seen in the moonlight. "Murrenigh is still too small to ride. They won't be able to bear a rider for months. And without Tempest..."

They cut off. The grief paints impenetrable shadows in their eyes, and no matter how angry Ayc feels, it twists something within him.

"I'm sorry," Ayc says. "We can talk about it more in the morning. Grieve. Scream, cry, fall apart if you must, but don't you dare fucking give up on me."

"Never," Peregrin swears. "Tempest would haunt me for all of eternity."

"She was the best," Ayc says, his own voice thick.

"Yes," Peregrin agrees. "She was." They pause a beat, and then add, "We will get Lora back, Ayc. I promise you. Today, we mourn. Tomorrow, we fight."

Ayc nods and walks away before Peregrin sees the tears in his eyes. Murrenigh rises to stand at his side. Ayc keeps his gaze fixed on the distant silhouette of the mountains and clings to the new direction, the purpose.

It feels impossible, and not just the physical path before him. Everything feels impossible. The dreams that Lora and he share seem further away than ever. Dreams for a simple, beautiful life together. Dreams for a better world, for a liberated Aluina, for the ability of all people to be free to live and love as they choose.

And yet, there is courage in daring to dream when everything feels impossible.

And so...he dreams.

A FINAL WORD FROM THE AUTHOR

Last November, I almost gave up. I almost put down my pen, closed my laptop, and said goodbye to my dream of being an author. If you're from my community, you know why. I know you know why.

I told the editor of this book I didn't know if there would be a second book. And they reminded me that we needed stories like mine more than ever. So I sat in the darkness of my own mind for a few days. And then I got fucking angry.

And then I decided to be a bitch who would not bow.

If anything in this book seems like a critique of what is currently unfolding in the world, you're right. I know it might have been hard to read, just like at times it was hard for me to write—to take all my anger and frustration and fold it into these pages that still, hopefully, inspired hope. I know the ending is hard and bleak, just like the world right now is bleak and hard. But I hope you remember, as Ayc did, that it takes courage to dream when everything feels impossible.

So dream, dear readers.

Dream of a better world, a freer world, a more just world.

If fantasy has taught me anything, it's that tyrants always fall and the most unlikely heroes can change the course of the world. I hope the characters in this book show you the power you have.

Do not let them take it from you. Do not let them take your joy, either, because joy is resistance. Build community and support the ones around you. Fight when you can; rest when you need to. If the world wants to make you a villain for standing up for what's right, then let them do it.

And remember...

WE DO NOT BOW!

In love and villainy,

ACKNOWLEDGMENTS

When I sat down to write book one, I had a dream: to write a romantasy book that made people like me feel seen and to one day build a community where those same people can feel safe to be themselves. What I wanted was a community, but what I found is a family. I took a leap of faith and sent a book into the world, and I have gotten so much back. So much love and support and goodness, that I'm not sure how I'm going to say thank you to all the people who need thanks in any cohesive manner. But I'm going to give it my best shot, knowing I am the luckiest star in the night sky, and I'll never forget that fact.

Hey, Rob, my dearest spouse. You've been by my side for ten years, and life has certainly thrown us some curveballs, huh? And I wouldn't have wanted to face them with anyone else. Thanks for all the solo parenting, the pep talks, the willingness to breathe life into this silly little dream of mine. These books would not exist without you.

Hey, Em, thanks for dragging me out of all my doubt spirals and stopping me from yeeting this book out a window. I'm really sorry I made you cry in my living room. Multiple times. That really wasn't cool of me. You are the bestest friend a person could ever hope to have.

Hey, Rizing, your opinions and insights are so critical to what this story is. But mostly, thank you for how fiercely you fight for your community. You are as fearsome as a leviathan and as glorious too.

Hey, Megan, my wifey, thanks for being one of the first to read and finish, and for your unending friendship. I'm glad you liked the butt stuff!

Hey, Poppy, I will forever be grateful for your stunning and precious friendship. Thank you for the way you bring my story and my characters to life in your glorious artwork. I'm so glad I chose you. It had to be you; it could only be you.

Hey, Holly, thanks for always fighting in all my battles and for proofreading and blurb help. Now be a good girl and drink your smut water.

Hey, Renee, thank you always being in my corner. No, you may not sell my legs.

Hey, Andrea, thanks for dragon eggs and t-shirts and your dedication to support indie authors and businesses. Never bow.

Hey, beta readers. Your time is a gift, and I appreciate it greatly. Thank you from the bottom of my heart. But especially thanks to: Patty, thanks for always making me laugh with all your 'Fuck you, Campbell'. Kimber, sorry about the onions. And Kate, thank you for giving me feedback that will help shape book 3.

And also to Amanda, Micca, Stephanie, Jenna—all of you had the hand in this book, even if it was just the support that you give me constantly.

To Moss, my sensitivity editor, thank you for always helping me learn and grow and for assisting me to keep the book as sensitive as possible.

To my editor, Charlie Knight, for believing in this book, understanding my vision, and always pushing me to make it better. Thank you for calming me down about deadlines and for being available to bounce ideas. Thank you for advocating for my story.

To the owners of indie bookstores, not only here in Washington, but across the United States, who have given my book a place on their shelves, who have invited me to signings, and hyped me up to readers. You have made my dreams come true.

And most importantly, to every single reader who I've come in contact along the way—who has met me at events, who has slid into my DMs to tell me they loved my book, who have told me that my book has made me feel seen. You all are my dreams come true. You make me laugh and cry in joy and keep me writing on all the hard days. You make me dare to dream on the days that I'm scared. You give me courage and hope that a brighter world awaits us all—if we're willing to fight for it. Thank you. Please, never stop dreaming or finding yourself as you get lost in the pages of books. I'm also really sorry about that ending. No, you can't send me your therapy bills.

And last but not least, to myself. I'm not always kind to myself, but I'm going to be now. I'm gong to speak to me the way those who love me speak to me.

Hey, Campbell—sunshine, midnight, love—all this love is yours because you deserve it. All this community is here because you created it and nurtured it. All the support made the road easier, but you still had to walk it. You had a lot of reasons you could have given up, but here you are, writing the acknowledgements of your fifth book, professing your love for a community you created. Yes, *you*! Congratulations, you badass, motherfucking dragon!

Now, onward. Book three awaits us all.

ABOUT THE AUTHOR

Campbell (they/any) writes fantasy romance with breathtaking adventure, diverse found families, and of course, toe-curling spice. They hail from the PNW where they can be found hiking with their family, seeking inspiration for their next novel within alpine forests and beneath waterfalls.

https://linktr.ee/cacampbellwriter

www.ingramcontent.com/pod-product-compliance
Lightning Source LLC
Chambersburg PA
CBHW031227310726

48971CB00004B/912